FUTURE PERFECT

Chris Evans is an award-winning author whose books are available on the SF Gateway.

Roy Kettle co-wrote several novels with John Brosnan, two of which were made into movies.

PRAISE FOR *FUTURE PERFECT*:

"Future Perfect is a sharp, witty, ingenious conspiracy thriller set in the worlds of science fiction geekery, political chicanery and crackpot cultery that skewers real-life analogues with merciless precision while advancing unsettling notions of the way our lives have been shaped by fifty years of true believers. Roy Kettle and Chris Evans know this world from the inside, and yet open it up to the uninitiated. I enjoyed this book immensely and the alien waves penetrating my tinfoil hat convince me that you will too."

Kim Newman

"A dogged amateur sleuth, a trail of clues through the jungle of mid-twentieth-century pulp fiction, and a startling conspiracy theory. The revelations keep you hooked and the detail sparkles. Unmissable."

Stephen Baxter

Books by Chris Evans:

Omega

Mortal Remains

Aztec Century

Chimeras

In Limbo

The Insider

Capella's Golden Eyes

Books by Roy Kettle (written with John Brosnan):

Slimer

The Fungus

Tendrils

Bedlam

FUTURE PERFECT

Chris Evans and Roy Kettle

Pitchblende Books

Cover art

Published by Pitchblende Books

www.pitchblendebooks.com

An original publication

ISBN: 9780992879006

Chris Evans and Roy Kettle assert the moral right to be identified as authors of this work.

This is a work of fiction. Unless permission was granted in advance (thanks DRL), any similarities to actual persons or events or organisations are either coincidental or unintended consequences of artistic licence.

With much love to our families:

Fiona, Ceri, Gwen

Kathleen, Jennifer, Nathan

ACKNOWLEDGEMENTS

Special thanks to John Jarrold, Colin Murray, Carole Simpson, Jonathan Eeds, John D. Berry, Stuart Brenton and Kathleen Mitchell for their help and suggestions.

A number of other people gave invaluable advice and practical assistance. You know who you are. We are very grateful. Any subsequent errors are our own.

Future Perfect

Prospect Park, Brooklyn, July 1972

The young man in the dark suit walked purposefully through the park, doing nothing to attract attention to himself. He checked the crowded playgrounds, but they contained no one of interest to him. Music was playing from a radio nearby: Jimi Hendrix singing "Stone Free", a jarring anthem to the anarchy of the times, its churning rhythms agitating his mind.

He hurried on, taking a path past the ball fields. Lately he had become highly sensitive to sounds. With forewarning he could block them out, but a police car siren was lacerating, the abrupt ringing of a telephone like a jolt of electricity. His colleagues at work had noticed. They were worried about him, he knew.

It was a hot day, and he lay down for a moment in the middle of the meadow. The sky was that vast featureless blue that made you feel you could fall into it and be lost forever.

At the zoo, children were clustered around the wire-mesh fences where the goats and sheep were housed, attentive parents at their sides. He veered away, satisfied that none of the adults was the man he had come to think of as the Shaper. Weeks of observation had shown that the Shaper favoured more tranquil destinations, often spending the entire afternoon basking in the sun. Sometimes the Woman and Child were with him. A keen eye was all that was needed; a keen eye and the courage to take action when the moment came.

All around him there were families and individuals dotted around on the green expanses. Ordinary people at their leisure, ignorant of how so much of life could be determined by someone like the Shaper. For all he knew there were others, secret Makers of the World who dictated everything. But he could only take action against the one he knew. The one who had shattered his own life.

The carousel. Children clung to the golden poles, riding horses, a giraffe, a lion. They whirled past, though with a curious staccato sensation, like a motion picture with missing frames. He walked on, dodging a teenager on a home-made skateboard, thinking of his lost Minna, a woman of grace and tenderness whose life had been extinguished by the Shaper. And no one knew. No one except he knew.

He had been forced to use the resources of the agency to track down the Shaper's home address and had been almost disappointed to find him an ordinary-looking man living in an anonymous brownstone. He even had a mundane day job at the Methodist Hospital on Park Slope. His role as the Shaper was secret, known only to a few.

"Hey!"

He had collided with a fat man in a windowpane shirt and plaid shorts, almost knocking him over.

The man stepped back with a surly look. He bulged out of his clothes as if he had been inflated inside them.

"Not enough room on this path for two?" he said with sour aggression. And getting no reply: "What's so funny, pal?"

His own laughter felt distant, remote from himself. He walked on.

And abruptly there he was.

The Woman and Child were with him, sitting in a grassy space just along from the carousel. The blonde-haired Child was perched at the Woman's lap, in a white romper suit, both of them wearing sun hats, the Woman in a sleeveless lemon dress, her arms and legs sun-browned.

The Shaper lay on his belly in faded jeans and a white cheesecloth shirt, reading a paperback book, his spectacled eyes shaded under a Yankees cap.

Keeping the bushes between himself and them, he circled, surreptitiously drawing closer. For a moment he felt the self-control seeping out of him. He steeled himself, crouching as he crept forward.

The Child spotted him first, pointing as he approached. The Woman's mouth opened in alarm as he drew his Smith and Wesson. He heard her shout, saw the Shaper roll over and start to get up, still holding the paperback, a science-fiction novel with an egg-headed alien on the cover.

He straightened his gun arm, pointing the pistol straight at the Shaper's face. Again there was a softening inside him, a flicker of uncertainty. It was unfortunate that the Woman and Child were present. But no. They were his companions. They must know what he was capable of.

"You can't control me," he told the Shaper. "You've no idea what I can do."

The Shaper looked as if he didn't know who he was. He looked terrified.

The Woman lunged at him. He flung her to the ground, heard the Child start to bawl. The Shaper had raised the book to his face, as if it could somehow offer protection from a .38 Special. The bullet penetrated it effortlessly, blood bursting in all directions, the Yankees cap flying off. It was the first time he had fired it in the field.

The Shaper toppled, the book falling away. He fell on his back, his face a mangled bloody mess.

The Woman was screaming. She grabbed the Child. Both of them were covered with blood splatter.

He stepped over the Shaper, wanting to be certain he was dead before he made his escape. He shouted at the corpse:

"Didn't predict that, did you?"

ONE

The headline in the free newspaper was: DOOMSDAY CLOCK MOVES NEARER TO MIDNIGHT. What was it this time? Another rogue state claiming to have tested nuclear weapons while its citizens lived in peasant splendour? The latest neocon initiative to impose Republican notions of freedom on some ancient civilisation? Or even, as my business partner Ashad liked to suggest, a secret weapons programme financed by all those missing Iraqi oil dollars?

But it was none of these. A list of extreme weather events was followed by a report of renegade survivors in the Chernobyl exclusion zone who had apparently withstood lethal doses of radiation and were now preying on local inhabitants. Stronger and fiercer than ordinary humans, were they a worrying prelude to a sinister new turn in human evolution?

Evidently the newspaper thought so; but this wasn't all. A hitherto unknown star had winked on in the northern constellation of Draco. Its relative closeness meant that scientists were suggesting it be monitored carefully. More significantly, the newspaper's astrologer was concerned that both the location and the timing of the new star were full of ominous portents. Like buggering up his star charts perhaps.

I stuffed the paper into a recycling bin and walked into the hotel. It was ultra modern, undulating with tubes and bulges that had no doubt given some architectural awards committee a rush. A young woman wearing pale makeup and a frosty expression was seated at a reception desk.

"Name?" she asked.

"Randall. Nick Randall."

She tapped keys on her laptop. I spelled out my surname.

"Freelance, trade or fan?"

"Trade."

She scrolled, studying the screen. Her name-tag read KIRSTY. She was about half my age, maybe early twenties, her nails painted oyster pink. On the wall behind her was a big poster with a swirly galactic motif carrying the words: VISIONARIES, A CELEBRATION OF FANTASTIC FILM.

"I don't have you listed," she announced.

"That might be because I haven't registered."

A flash of annoyance. "It's twenty pounds for the day."

And the day was already half gone. She pushed the credit card processor at me, but a £20 note was easier. She took it like I had offered her a used tissue. It *had* probably been up a few noses.

"What did you say your name was?"

"Nick," I said patiently. "Nick Randall."

She typed it in. "Company?"

"Xponential Productions. Starts with an X."

She started to enter this, then stopped and looked up.

"You made *The Artificial I*."

Our in-depth fly-on-the wall series about the world of reality TV programming. It had been broadcast on an obscure digital channel and got one respectable review—which was pretty good since it had only got one review at all.

"Not me personally, I told her. "But, yes, we produced it."

"I thought it was brilliant."

This was better. "And *DisOrg*?"

"Oh, yes, that's us, too."

DisOrg was a knockabout animated feature about a bunch of disabled secret agents, mostly incapacitated in the cause of duty, still capable of righting wrongs, albeit unconventionally. "A refreshingly un-PC satire," the *Telegraph* had called it. "*Mission Impossible* meets jet-propelled wheelchairs." It never made it beyond the independents, though DVD sales were still healthy.

"Is there going to be a sequel?"

"If we could get the funding. And that's looking pretty unlikely at the moment."

She finished entering my details and rummaged in her little strongbox, producing a £10 note which she offered to me.

"Actually, you only have to pay half after one o'clock." She looked decently shame-faced. "You caught me at a bad moment. I've been sat here all morning with nothing but lukewarm coffee and a stale biscuit."

"Right," I said, snatching the note from her and flourishing it. "Tea or coffee?"

She looked at me as if I was joking. "I could murder a decent cup of tea. Just milk."

I started making my way down the sinuous corridor.

"I haven't done your badge," she called after me.

"If I'm arrested you can vouch for me. Are you vegetarian?"

"Only if they eat pork pies."

I went straight along to the womb-like main hall. On the stage a panel discussion was taking place, four figures hunched over microphones and laptops while a scattered audience of professionals, passers-by and film buffs listened.

At this point my new mobile rang, or rather made a chortling noise. It was Ashad.

"Any luck?" he asked immediately.

"I've only just got here."

"I checked again. There's over a dozen names on the website. Our man could be any of them."

"Or woman."

"I can't understand why they didn't give us a name." His Brummie accent was echoey. "It's a bit bloody suspicious—"

"Ash," I interrupted, aware of his tendency to see hidden plots everywhere, "let's not get overheated about this. It was just an email."

"OK. But it might be a wind-up. A waste of our time."

"We've been over this already. It's worth checking out. We should be showing our faces here anyway. Let me get on with it."

"Well, be careful, know what I mean? And even if you're offered something, don't make any big promises, especially in writing. Ring me if there's any development."

"I deliberately came without a pen. Aren't you supposed to be in a script conference or something?"

"I'm on a comfort break."

"You're in the loo, aren't you?"

"Where else could I talk freely?"

"I'm going now," I said, and cut the call.

The hotel restaurant was just along the corridor, quiet in the post-lunch period. I loaded a tray with tea, a frilly tuna salad and a couple of Danish pastries.

"Wow," Kirsty said when I delivered it. "You shouldn't have."

She had made up my badge, name and especially the company capitalized in neat bold letters. I clipped it on my shirt pocket.

"I had an ulterior motive," I told her. "I'm supposed to be meeting someone, but I don't know who. Someone from the Filmscope Foundation. Ring any bells?"

"Sounds familiar," she said, turning back to her laptop. Her fingernails tap-danced over the keyboard. "Of course. Cyrus."

"Cyrus?"

"Cyrus Hammond. He's head of their UK operations."

"Where would I find him?"

Another pink flurry on the keys. "He's doing a panel on the future of film right now."

"In the main hall?"

She nodded. "You can't miss him. American, lots of white hair, fit-looking for his age."

I headed down a twisty corridor, feeling like I was inside a giant alimentary canal. Plasma screens were showing trailers for upcoming blockbusters. I felt a pang of envy. Something like a blockbuster was just what Xponential needed if we weren't to go under.

The panel discussion was winding down. A video link to Los Angeles had the action star Ryan Carmichael saying goodbye in an intense self-congratulatory way. California tanned and handsome, Carmichael had shiny eyes that were as blue and empty as the sky. Eccentric and self-absorbed, he was also hot property, having starred in several recent hits.

Cyrus Hammond was instantly recognisable, an older leonine man in a loose-fitting pale suit. I loitered as he came down from the stage and offered my hand.

"Nick Randall, Xponential Productions. You asked me to attend."

He shook but didn't show any sign of recognition. I had anticipated that my name, or at least the company's name, would be familiar to him.

"We advertised recently and got an email response from your Foundation," I said. "We're looking for intellectual property—" I stopped myself, aware that I was in danger of slipping into corporate-speak. Hammond was probably badgered all the time by people hoping for a hand-out from his Foundation. According to their website they had helped with the funding of several interesting movies in recent years.

"We're looking for the next Philip K. Dick," I said. "Or at least someone whose work is just as inventive but not currently under option."

"And you got a reply from us?"

"Well, it wasn't signed but it came from the Foundation's address. Suggested that we make contact here at the festival."

Hammond led me into a bar, asked me if I wanted a drink.

"Let me," I said. "I'm the one who approached you."

He gave an insouciant shrug. "Perrier, ice and lemon."

I ordered two. We took them over to a corner table and sat down.

"So," he said, "Xponential does—what?"

"We're a production company based here in London. We make stuff that interests us. Documentaries, contemporary drama, zany satire—you name it, we've probably done our own twist on it. Half our output is for television, mostly cable and satellite, the rest for cinema release. Next year's our tenth anniversary."

I listed some of our recent productions. He rolled his ice in his drink, not saying anything. I could tell he recognized some of them; if he ran a movie foundation, it was his business to know what was out there.

At length, when I was done, he said, "Another Philip K. Dick?"

"Something along those lines."

"That's a pretty tall order given that he was a one-off."

"Well, we're not looking for a clone. But someone whose work might have similar fascination and potential. In cinematic terms."

He contemplated his glass. "Did you know Dick barely made a living from his writing? That he existed on dog food for a while? And that by the time *Blade Runner* was released in 1982 he was already dead?"

I knew the story. Dick's estate must have been doing very nicely ever since, given the success of movies like *Total Recall* and *Minority Report*.

"Now every corporation between here and Hollywood is ransacking his back-list for material. That your idea, son?"

His tone was just short of patronizing, a southern gentleman slapping down an upstart Limey. I didn't let it ruffle me. "We're hoping to find something we can turn into a commercial movie. A story or proposal or script that's out there somewhere but hasn't been picked up. Anything that challenges the conventional way of looking at things, that has great visual potential and hopefully audience appeal. Check us out if you don't know us already. You'll find that we're no cheap and nasty outfit. We believe in what we do and we do it well."

Hammond was watching me from behind his glass. Watching and waiting.

"We've also got a looming cash crisis," I confessed. "Some of our backers are demanding a more commercial project before they'll stump up any more money. Without it we won't be able to finance all the other worthy stuff that's never going to make us rich."

Two women and a man came over and began chatting to him. They were young and professional looking, obviously in the business, asking him questions about the British Film Institute. He was friendly enough, but his body language and the fact that he didn't get up made it plain to them that he was in the middle of something else. They took the hint and drifted away.

He had a certain magnetism, there was no doubt about that. But then people who held the purse-strings generally did.

"The obvious properties have all been snapped up by the majors," he remarked.

"Don't we know it."

"You might have to dig a little deeper if you want to find some gold."

I liked the idea of that. "That's why we've been sending out feelers everywhere."

Hammond abruptly got to his feet. "Come with me," he said.

He took me to the room hosting the art show. The tables were cluttered with models of vampires, cyborgs and extraterrestrials with more tails and tentacles than a Borough Road fishmonger's. One wall was devoted to whimsical portraits of favourite movie characters: Chewbacca eating a burger, the Alien sipping a cocktail, that sort of thing. Another held meticulously realistic landscapes of imaginary planets with multiple suns, ringed gas giants and thrusting spaceships out of a host of Freudian wet dreams.

It wasn't the kind of art that appealed to me. But in one corner was a display of what looked like a page from a graphic novel, a series of bold, dramatic scenes showing a man whose hands were sinking into a warped console while his brain opened up like an exotic flower under the impact of the bizarre images flooding through it.

Each fragmented panel had been sketched with marker pens, the outlines executed swiftly and assuredly, the colours hatched in without fuss. The strip had an air of confidence and brashness quite in contrast to the rest of the reverential stuff on display.

"Ever heard of Leo Parrish?" Hammond asked me.

"Who?"

"I thought not. Aren't too many that have."

He was looking at the same strip as me. I had the impression that he approved of the fact I had been attracted to it.

"He was a writer," he told me. "So far down the pecking order he was practically invisible. Hard to find his stuff these days. I do believe these are scenes from one of his stories."

"Really?" If the artwork accurately reflected the writer's imagination, maybe I was in business. The display had a NOT FOR SALE sign on it. The artist's name was Claire Whitney.

"Would you like to meet her?"

"Does she know this Leo Parrish?" I asked.

"You remember *Nightscapes*?"

"The TV show?"

"Do you recall the episode about the blind man who's given artificial eyes that let him see the secret creatures which really keep the world of humans running?"

I did. *Nightscapes* was an American anthology of weird tales, broadcast in the graveyard slot on Channel 4 about five years ago. A mixed bag of psychological horror and dark techno-fantasy, it had been patchy in quality and never made a second series.

"His wife died," I said, with reference to the tale. "The creatures reanimated her, but he didn't exactly welcome the results."

Hammond was already walking out. I followed.

"It was based on one of Leo Parrish's stories," he told me.

"The special effects were pretty ropey."

"But you remembered it."

"Sure. It was unsettling enough despite that."

"Claire Whitney brought the original story to the company's attention. I believe she acted as the agent when they optioned it. That's about as much as I know. But if you want to find out more about Leo Parrish, she might be a good place to start. Then, if you can get something together, we can talk money."

Hammond led me into another room. This one was filled with children playing tame-looking computer games, with a fenced off corner where toddlers were rolling around with inflatable Minions from the *Despicable Me* movies. Central tables had been set aside for more hands-on activities like modelling and artwork.

Three adults were present, a thin young man with spiky hair, an elderly woman in a white smock who was asleep on a chair beside the toddler pen, and a woman in her late thirties who was overseeing the kids sketching and painting.

Now with a sudden briskness, Hammond took me straight over to the younger woman.

"Miss Whitney," he said to her, "this is Mr Nicholas Randall. He'd like to have a word with you."

I offered my hand. "I'm usually known as Nick."

She shook it, her hazel eyes giving me a quick once-over. She was good-looking, wearing jeans and a black T-shirt that accentuated the lean muscularity of her body. Her hair was drawn back in a loose ponytail.

"Mr Randall was impressed by your contribution to the art show," Hammond said. "I told you I'm not the only one with good taste."

"Really?" she said sceptically, still eyeing me.

"Really."

"It's there under false pretences. There's no connection with any film or TV show."

"Interesting you should say that," I responded. "I thought it had the air of a particularly good storyboard. Do you draw for a living?"

"After a fashion," she replied, tucking an errant strand of hair behind one ear. She had a smear of green paint on one cheek.

She didn't elaborate but asked me what I did.

Hammond had already melted away. "I'm in film production," I told her. "Small company but we punch above our weight. A big minnow in a sea of sharks."

"Is that so?"

"Can I buy you a drink? I'd like to pick your brains. It can be somewhere really public so you can escape if you decide I'm a nutter or a bore."

She glanced at the artwork table, where four adolescents were busily working away on their compositions, and at the old woman, who was still fast asleep.

"Daniel," she said to the skinny guy, "can you keep an eye on things for ten minutes?"

Daniel, was thrashing a soggy lump of modelling clay as if auditioning for the Richard Dreyfuss role in *Close Encounters*. "No problem, mum," he said.

The bar was more crowded than earlier but we managed to find a couple of stools. She didn't want a drink.

"Are you here on business?" I asked.

"Not really. I got an invitation out of the blue, along with a request to contribute something to the art show. I don't get many opportunities to display my work. We're just here for the day, got free registration in exchange for a couple of hours' supervising the kids' room. So you produce movies?"

"Features of all kinds. I'm the co-owner of the company."

"Really? What have you produced?"

I gave her a varied shortlist. She focused on a recent TV documentary investigating the continued existence of possible new "black sites" where political prisoners were being held by the US government on foreign territory.

"That was mainly my business partner's doing," I confessed. "He's got strongly developed anti-authoritarian tendencies. Loves a good conspiracy theory."

"Is that all you think it was?" she said.

"Not at all. We wouldn't have made it if we didn't think there was something in it. There's more in the pipeline. I just didn't want you to think we only do deep and earnest. We like to make our share of fun stuff too."

"Have you got children?" she asked.

"No," I replied, a little startled at the abrupt change in conversational direction. "My ex-wife and I spent too many years dithering about whether we should or not. Is your husband here with you?"

There was no wedding ring on her finger.

"We divorced years ago," she told me. "He was a serial womanizer."

"He must have been off his rocker."

I said this without thinking, without consciously intending to flatter her. She gave me a penetrating stare.

"It was just an observation," I said. "How old is your son?"

"Why do you want to talk to me, Mr Randall?"

"I'd much prefer it if you call me Nick. I'm really not trying to pick you up, if that's what you're thinking."

I couldn't tell whether she was looking at me with scepticism or a kind of amused tolerance. Probably a combination of both.

"The artwork you did. I thought it was pretty imaginative. I'm told it was based on a tale by someone else."

"You're right, I was story-boarding it. Just for fun."

"Looked intriguing. Might make an interesting movie."

She didn't bite on this, so I prompted: "Who wrote it?"

"You won't have heard of him."

"Try me."

Now she was starting to look—not exactly cornered, but uncertain of me again.

"Is this my big break?" she asked with more than a hint of sarcasm. "Are you going to tell me you want to send it to Hollywood or something?"

"Hardly. I'm just interested.

What was going on here? Why the reticence? The suspicion?

I fumbled in my jacket, produced a company card and laid it on the bar. It carried my name and Ashad's.

"See?" I said. "I'm on the level."

"Leo Parrish."

She said it like someone reluctantly divulging a secret.

"Do you know him?" I asked.

"No."

"I gather—Cyrus Hammond told me you once sold a story of his. To a TV company?"

"Why were you asking him about that?"

All her wariness was back in full force.

"I wasn't," I assured her. "He volunteered the information."

She didn't look mollified.

"Is there something I should know?" I asked. "I'm just interested because our company is looking for movie material."

She relented. "Sorry. Force of habit."

I was about to ask her what she meant by this but her mobile started ringing. She extracted it and took the call. As she listened, her expression slowly changed from quizzical to concerned.

"You'll have to excuse me for a few minutes," she told me.

And then she was up and off.

Ten minutes later she still hadn't returned. In the play room a man and woman I hadn't seen before were trying to stop one toddler from pounding another into submission with a big fluffy mallet.

"Claire Whitney?" I said to the man.

He wrestled the bludgeon out of the toddler's hand, looking distinctly harassed. "She had to go."

"Any idea where?"

He shook his head.

I tried the other rooms, the hall. There was no sign of her. Cyrus Hammond was back on stage in the hall doing a variation of a pub quiz, the raucous audience firing movie-themed questions at him and three others. For some reason he was now wearing sunglasses and a cream fedora.

I made my way back to Kirsty on the reception desk. “I don’t suppose you’ve seen the woman who was running the kids’ room. Claire Whitney?”

“She left a few minutes ago.”

“As in ‘left the building’?”

“I assume so.”

All my instincts told me she wasn’t coming back. “We were in the middle of a business meeting. She left before we could exchange addresses. You wouldn’t happen to have any contact details, would you?”

She hesitated, and then worked her keyboard before shrugging. “Normally we’re not supposed to give out that information, and I won’t have to battle with my conscience this time, either.”

She swivelled the laptop to show me.

The box said only: CLAIRE WHITNEY FREELANCE

There was a blue underlined ampersand next to her name. “What’s does the symbol mean?”

“Oh, that’s just a hyperlink between people attending who have some important connection like working for the same employer. Makes the admin much easier.”

Someone else came up to the desk. While Kirsty was distracted I clicked on the ampersand.

The page that filled the screen gave the details of anyone who had a key association with Claire. But there was just one name.

Mine.

TWO

There was an unfamiliar floral smell in our office corridor. I wasn't expecting to see a new female receptionist smiling at me as I entered.

"Can I help you?" she asked brightly.

"Well, you could start by telling me who you are and what you're doing here."

"Ah," she said, quickly recalibrating. "Are you Mr Randall?"

"I am. And you are...?"

"Jamilla. I'm Uncle Ashad's niece."

I could see the familial resemblance. I knew that Ashad, though a Midlander himself, had family in south London. In recent months he'd become concerned with what he called "our security" and we had both agreed that our current hopeless receptionist would have to go. In typical fashion he had made a pre-emptive strike.

Jamilla looked perky and keen. I knew from previous experience that this wasn't necessarily a good sign.

Then I looked around me. For once the place was properly welcoming, magazines stacked neatly on the coffee table, a potted palm standing sentinel beside the door. The desk was tidy. The furniture had been subtly rearranged to create a better sense of space. And it shone. The floral smell was polish.

I caught her trying to hide a vindicated grin.

"Nice," I said, po-faced so as not to encourage her unduly. "Any calls?"

She handed me a list. Jotted down in a neat hand were names, companies, contact numbers. A column for each. None of them was urgent or earth-shatteringly important, but I was impressed.

As if on cue, the phone rang with a brisker tone than the last receptionist had ever managed to coax from it.

"Good afternoon," Jamilla said in a businesslike office accent. "Xponential Productions. How may I help you?"

For an instant I imagined that the call might be from the elusive Claire Whitney, but it turned out to be someone wanting to know if we were interested in a film script he'd written about a newsreader with Tourette's Syndrome.

While he was pitching his idea to me, with expletives unfortunately not deleted, my mind started to wander. Back at the hotel I had made quite an effort to find out more about Claire Whitney and why my name was linked with hers. Kirsty's database gave no information apart from what was listed. I had persuaded her to page the guy at the festival who'd actually set up the system, but when he turned [illegible] he had barely glanced at the screen before muttering that he was only responsible for the software, not for how people used it.

Meanwhile there was no sign of Claire Whitney herself. It was frustrating but also the kind of thing you get used to in this business, where promising avenues have a habit of turning into blind alleys. I had left one of my business cards in the playroom just in case, scrawling a note on the back asking her to make contact when she returned. *If* she returned. I left another card at the reception desk for Cyrus Hammond. By then I couldn't afford to hang around any longer; Ashad had gone to west London, and one of us needed to get back to the office.

I phoned him *en route* with the news of my meetings. Clearly distracted and traffic-buffeted, he was on the Chiswick roundabout with a cameraman and the redoubtable Valerie Patterson, our office manager. They were looking into an idea for a documentary based about a travelling circus that planned to tour the entire length of the North and South Circular Roads around London.

I told him that I had a promising lead that was well worth following up. For once he didn't badger me for details, claiming that he and Val were having "creative differences" over the Roads project. It was only now that I understood the other reason for his reticence: he knew I was going back to the office and would find out about Jamilla. Well, it was pretty low-key nepotism, and if Jamilla proved half as competent as she appeared I wasn't going to complain.

Our workplace is a cluster of split-level rooms over a parade of shops in the lower end of Charing Cross Road. You climb the concrete stairwell, sticky with old carpet tape, passing the main office on the floor below us where Val rules and most of the actual nuts-and-bolts stuff gets done, until you reach the giddy heights of the top floor. It used to belong to Vir-2-ality, an internet graphics company that vanished up its own avatar during the dot-com crash. If their web designs were anything like their office décor, it's no wonder they went bust. The walls were painted in swirly shades of vibrant cerise with ceilings of textured biscuit-brown. When I first visited the place I felt like I was trapped inside a gigantic rhubarb crumble.

The first thing Ashad and I did was whitewash everything and cover the walls with vintage movie posters. On the very uppermost level we've got a viewing theatre and editing suite, while in the main area below there's a little galley kitchen, a shower room and enough space for a couple of roll-up mattresses—useful when we have to do an all-nighter. We crammed office furniture and wide-screen TVs and stacks of electronics into every available alcove. We're short of shelving, and our desks are piled with paperwork, promotional materials, and DVDs from a host of different sources. Everywhere you go you have to negotiate trailing cables from various pieces of kit. On the floor there are heaps of scripts, books, comics, videos and 35mm film reels, all strategically placed to deter health and safety inspectors.

Ashad and I like it that way, though we knew we needed to do something about getting the stairwell cleaned and re-carpeted—which would involve a conversation with Nigel, our weird landlord whose bank account is greatly enhanced by our rent. It's not exactly Movie Central, but anyone visiting can tell that we mean business. Messiness equals creativity, right? Well, in our case I like to think it does exactly that.

I sat in my own cluttered work space trying to squeeze creativity out of it. My PC was relatively new and pretty zippy, so when it failed to track down anything useful about Claire Whitney or Leo Parrish it did so very quickly. I found a couple of references to Claire Whitney, but both were associated with the film festival. She had no website and didn't appear on any list of artists active in any media. Did she work under a different name, or was the artwork I had just seen a one-off, something she had done for the fun of it?

I had even less luck with Leo Parrish. I tried various search engines and consulted everything from Wikipedia to on-line databases of science fiction and fantasy writers. There were plenty of links to the artist Maxfield Parrish and a few listings for other Leo Parrishes who clearly weren't the man in question. On the Internet Movie Database I found a mention of Leo Parrish as the author of the *Nightscapes* episode based on an original story entitled "The Cosmic Controllers", but nothing further, not even when and where the story had originally appeared.

While it was clear that a writer by the name of Leo Parrish had existed, details were infuriatingly elusive. Website addresses linked to his name were awaiting redevelopment or unavailable. I kept getting irritating "There is an issue with security on this website" messages. What was that supposed to mean? I was only researching a writer. If I had had Ashad's disposition I would have been convinced that out there in cyberspace were hordes of programmers and hackers gleefully writing code with my name on it to thwart me. Was it relevant that both Cyrus Hammond and Claire Whitney had initially been reluctant to tell me about Parrish, or that I found myself mysteriously linked to her?

Jamilla appeared and handed me a coffee.

By our usual standards it was absolutely delicious. She had obviously got hold of something better than the powdered sheep droppings Ashad bought. Real milk, too.

"A woman just phoned with a message for you," she told me. "She wouldn't give her name. She said you'd know who she was."

I felt a little burst of expectation. "Did she say she'd seen me earlier today?"

Jamilla shook her head.

So much for Claire Whitney. I tried to think. "Was it a brisk, no-nonsense woman with a Yorkshire accent?"

I was referring to Val, but again Jamilla shook her head. "She said she didn't need to speak to you, just wanted you to be reminded about tonight. American. Quite posh."

Theresa. My ex-wife.

*

When Ashad bowled in half an hour later, I was staring at the screen with a combination of bewilderment and disbelief.

"You've got to speak to her," Ashad said immediately. "She wants to do it as a *drama*. It'd be a glorified soap opera."

I was used to Ashad lurching into a conversation about whatever happened to be preoccupying him. He had to be talking about Valerie and their disagreements over the Travelling Circus project.

Ashad is a burly, boisterous man who is never short of an opinion or two. But the small and wiry Valerie was more than his match. I wasn't inclined to be referee in their latest dispute.

"You want my honest opinion?" I said. "I think it's a daft idea because you'll never get permission for it to go ahead. In any case we have more pressing issues."

I told him how long I had spent trying to track down some information on Leo Parrish. I explained all the frustrations I'd experienced. I stabbed a furious finger at the computer screen.

Shortly before his arrival I had found a website called *Occam's Eraser*. It was devoted to exposés of conspiracy theories—the Moon landings being faked, government lies about the Roswell spaceship crash, Princess Diana murdered by the royal family, that sort of thing. It had a text-only entry on Leo Parrish:

Leo Parrish is a fictional science fiction writer, purportedly active in the late 1950s in small-press genre magazines. It is believed that Parrish was invented as an elaborate in-joke by a group of fans, partly for their own amusement and partly in order to expose shortcomings in critical commentary within the field. Excerpts from alleged stories were briefly circulated before the joke ran its course. The Leo Parrish name was subsequently appropriated by in-house screenwriters in sci-fi related media.

Ashad stared at the screen, his fingers rasping the dark stubble on his chin. Today he was wearing a typical outfit of a purple paisley shirt with baggy cargo pants.

"Bollocks," he said at last.

"It doesn't make sense," I insisted. "Hammond and Whitney didn't strike me as the types that would be taken in by a con trick or a joke."

"Maybe they're the ones behind it."

"No."

"How do you know? You've only just met them."

"You'd have to have been there, Ash. They were on the level. Anyway, Claire Whitney's illustrated a Parrish story. There was an episode of *Nightscapes* based on one of them."

"Says who?"

"Cyrus Hammond."

"Well, that's a good argument, using information from one suspicious character to support another. Look, the website says other writers used the name so there might actually be some worthwhile stories out there. Maybe this Hammond chappie simply didn't know Parrish was a house-name."

"No," I said again. "They both believed in Parrish as a real person. And why would anyone want to con us?"

Ashad gave an incredulous snort. "Get real. Look at what we do. We've made our careers out of being flies in other people's ointment. We've got plenty of enemies out there."

I wasn't buying it. "It would be much too elaborate. There are easier ways of getting to us. What would be the point?"

V-shaped folds appeared between Ashad's bushy eyebrows. His paranoid frown.

"They wanted to be sure we were both out of the office," he said, as if he had just received a revelation. "Jamilla!"

She promptly appeared, wearing yellow household gloves.

"Any callers today?" Ashad asked her.

"Only the postman."

"What time did you get here?"

"Nine o'clock, like you said."

"Did you use the keys I gave you?"

She nodded.

"No sign of forced entry?"

"It was all locked up."

"Only the postman?"

She let out a sigh.

"I opened the post earlier," I said. "The microphones hidden in the jiffy bags clogged up the shredder."

"I'm not joking. There's people out there who don't like what we're doing. Just as well we've got Jamilla in to keep an eye on things, eh?"

It was his way of checking that I was OK with her. His instinctive concern for others was what saved him from total surrender to his persecution complex. Not that it was entirely unjustified. Ashad had been a radical as a young man, joining the Socialist Workers Party and relishing a good demonstration to show his solidarity with the working classes in their relentless battle with the oppressive forces of the capitalist state. Since then he had moderated his opinions only slightly, and being a man of Asian Muslim extraction didn't help nowadays. It was almost certain that there were files on him somewhere.

"She's a vast improvement on the last one," I admitted. "And the rubber gloves are very fetching."

Jamilla poked her tongue at me quite sweetly. There was a click from the DVD recorder and she said to Ashad, "The six o'clock news is just coming on."

It turned out that he had asked her to keep an eye on the day's news broadcasts as they were likely to be relevant to a current project. She had obviously set the recorder too in case we weren't around. We switched on the big plasma screen just in time to see Zhuyldz Muvart's beefy face fill the screen.

With his shaven head, thick neck and a nose that looked as if it had lost an argument with more than one fist, Muvart could have easily been taken for a professional wrestler rather than his

Supreme Excellency, the President of the Republic of Khanistan. He was wearing an indigo tunic embellished with several metres of silver braid and enough gold medals to front a hip-hop video.

"Is that a navy uniform?" Jamilla asked.

"Admiral's," I told her.

She looked bewildered. "I thought—"

"Don't ask." Khanistan was a landlocked central Asian country, with few rivers and even fewer lakes.

Muvart was shown giving a typically bombastic speech, his stubby forefinger jabbing the air as he ranted at a packed audience of obsequious subordinates. Despite appearances, it was generally felt that he was a shrewd operator who liked to stir things up internationally as a way of quelling domestic unrest.

The voice-over was more sober in tone, informing us that he had once more denounced Western imperialism and was threatening radical action to counter the continued threats against his country's territorial integrity. Having already suspended shipments of the uranium ore which were his country's prime asset, he was now talking of active measures to counter foreign intervention in his country's affairs. The exact nature of these measures wasn't specified.

The BBC had commissioned a documentary from us which was intended to compare Muvart with other recent dictators and discern whether he represented a real threat and what the international response might be

"Well, that was scary," Ashad said when it was over. "I want to read what he actually said and see if we can incorporate it into what we already have. Jamilla, can you get us an English-language transcript. The contact number's on our list. As soon as possible, please." He turned to me. "That chappie you know who was Muvart's intelligence chief. Can you arrange an on-camera interview?"

I had met the man a few weeks previously. He was a cousin of Muvart who was currently working as an English language tutor to Khanistani émigrés, having fled his homeland when his public criticisms of the president made it suicidal to stay.

I located a sticky note with his name and mobile number. "Give him a call and see what you can arrange."

"I thought you wanted to do it," Ashad said.

"No, it's OK. I need to follow this up."

I indicated the Parrish stuff that was still on-screen. Ashad opened his mouth and then closed it again. Jamilla was still hovering.

"What sort of fee do you reckon he'll want?" he asked.

"I'm sure he'd take anything reasonable. We'd need to guarantee his anonymity."

"Jamilla," Ashad said jovially, "this could be your chance to learn how to make secret payments in used banknotes. Give the man a call for me, will you?"

"Anything else?" she said, glancing at her watch.

"That's all. Your boyfriend can wait a few minutes longer."

Jamilla gave him a mortified look and went off. As soon as she was gone, Ashad leaned across my desk.

"What's up?" he said to me.

"Listen, Ash," I said candidly, "I know the Muvart documentary is important. But so is this. We've got to prioritize finding an original commercial project. Something tells me this could be it."

Ashad scrutinized me. "So why have you got a face like a wet weekend?"

"It's frustration. Something's not right here. Why can't I find out anything about this Parrish guy? Why are some people claiming he doesn't exist?"

*

"Let me get this right. There's a non-existent science fiction writer whose non-existent stories you might want to make into movies, if only you could get to read them. Of the two people who've heard of him, the woman has vanished and there's something not quite genuine about the man, despite the fact that he introduced you to the vanished woman in the first place."

Theresa gave me a self-satisfied smile and took a sip of her white wine, lounging comfortably on the cream leather sofa we had both once owned but fortunately I had never liked. She was wearing a designer business suit with a white silk blouse. She had been late home from a meeting, she claimed, and hadn't had time to change before I arrived. I knew better. These days she always power-dressed when we met up. I think she wanted to expunge all my domestic memories of baggy T-shirts and lounge pants.

I had gone for something more robust and manly than her Pinot Gris, opening a bottle of Shiraz. It wasn't a competition of course, but it wasn't far off. We hadn't parted on bad terms, but the bickering that had underscored our last years together had never quite gone away.

"Parrish is—was—real," I insisted. "I don't know what's going on with Cyrus Hammond and Claire Whitney but I'm convinced they weren't lying about him. I just can't find out anything at all apart from that odd reference to him *not* existing."

"Nicholas. Nicholas. You just don't know the first thing about the internet, do you?"

She was in one of her superior moods, the use of my full name being the signifier. Boston-born, Theresa could trace her family back to the Pilgrims, and although she wasn't a snob she had an air of New England aristocracy about her which sometimes manifested itself as a weary disdain.

I didn't respond. She took another hearty mouthful of Pinot. She was interested, I could tell.

"Am I to assume you're asking for my help?"

"Can we cut the crap, Theresa? Of course I'm bloody asking for your help. Who better than you?"

Theresa was an IT consultant to one of the big banks, working out of Canary Wharf—or Thatcher's Phallus, as Ashad always called it. Don't ask me who exactly consulted her, or about what precisely. My inability to take a geeky interest in her work had been one of many marital irritations.

She rose and took off her jacket. "OK, let's see what we can find."

Her dinky netbook was open on her desk in a corner of the huge living room. She had bought a Shoreditch flat with half the proceeds from the sale of our house. Most of my share had gone into Xponential.

I stood behind her, hoping I'd be able to pick up some tips. She did a few cursory searches for Parrish, linking his name with various other key words. Then she went into a long list of bookmarked search engines arranged in a way which grouped together those with particular search functionalities rather than limiting herself to those dedicated to writing.

To begin with she had no more luck than me, finding even more blocked and inaccessible sites. However, she persevered in the face of 700,000 hits for "Leo + Parrish", let alone nearly 6 million for Parrish alone. But there was nothing of any use.

"All right," she said with a determined air, "Let's try some common misspellings and typos."

"Misspellings?"

"Like Parish with one R."

There was indeed a reference to a Leo Parish on *Oracula*, a general Q&A and information site run by science fiction and fantasy fans. Someone with the web-name Q~reass had posted a query about Parish, with one R, and another writer called Rhodri Davies had briefly responded that his work was well worth tracking down but very hard to find, even if you knew how to spell. Davies went on, evidently with a certain irony, that his name was spoken of in hushed reverential tones by Those in the Know, usually when the uninitiated weren't in earshot.

This was tantalizing, even if it was intended as a joke. Theresa followed up the link and found that Davies ran an on-line news bulletin called *Homeopape*. It was well past its hundredth edition, but there were no references to Parrish, no matter how many variations on his name she tried. Still, I now had a couple of email addresses which Theresa cut and pasted into an email that she sent to my work PC. It was too late to make direct contact tonight.

Theresa drained her glass and requested a refill.

"Now let's take at look at this website you found," she said.

I noticed that the top button of her blouse was now undone. The equivalent of a man rolling up his sleeves, I told myself, though not especially convincingly.

On *Occam's Eraser* she read the paragraph about Parrish, then scrolled back and forth and flicked between pages.

"This seems to be written by someone who didn't do the other material on the site. The style is different and so is the layout."

She highlighted a few words then moved to another page. After she had repeated the exercise a few times, I could see what she meant. Different margin settings and line spacing.

"Maybe the website allows postings by other people," I said.

Theresa looked dubious. "Let me poke around a bit and see what happens."

I did my best not to slip into a coma as Theresa wrote line after line of what I took to be computer code. I topped up her glass and my own. As she worked she gave me a mini-lecture about biases in search-engine algorithms and how obscure sites are harder to find because they appear low down in page-rankings. I nodded enthusiastically and made affirmative noises.

Eventually, she ran the cursor along a line of code.

"That's the http vector for whoever added this paragraph."

"Right."

"You haven't got a clue what that means, have you?"

"Nope."

"You can go to a website—" she clicked the mouse to open another window "—where there are listings for the vectors."

"Ah. The vectors. They've got a new album out, haven't they?"

She was studying the list. "It's a site called Opanon."

She looked up at me for the first time in what felt like hours.

"Opanon," I said dubiously. "It sounds like some sort of medication."

"Well, actually it is. But it's also short for Online Posting Anonymous. It's a kind of electronic clearing house for people who want to cover their tracks. Whoever made the insertions was careful to ensure they couldn't be tracked back to source."

Her eyes were a little glazed, which was just how my brain felt.

"So have I learned something helpful or not?"

She stood up and stretched. She looked at her empty glass and tapped it meaningfully. I poured her more Pinot.

"You've got the two websites that appear to suggest your man Parrish actually exists, plus you also know that someone is adding bits to one of them and doesn't want anyone to know who they are. The rest is up to you. I've drunk so much that my fingers are beginning to find the gaps between the keys. Anyway, if I told you any more trade secrets, I'd have to bill you."

"Thanks a lot," I said. "I owe you one."

She gave me a long intense stare. Then she wobbled and I caught her by the arms to prevent her from spilling her wine over the plush cream carpet. I lifted the glass from her hand and set it down on the desk.

"Whoa," she said. "Stop the world, I want to get off."

An alcoholic flush had spread from her neck to her high-boned cheeks. It occurred to me that she probably got as tense as I did prior to one of our meetings. She had lapsed from a state of high focus to drunkenness.

I managed to manoeuvre her back on to the sofa. Her arms were around my neck, and she clung on.

"You know what I miss, Nick?" she said, looking up at me with eyes that were now distinctly bleary.

I had a feeling I did.

"The sex. Just the sex. The regularity of it."

I had always imagined she would have plenty of suitors once I was off the scene, but maybe it wasn't that simple.

My phone made a warbling noise. I disentangled myself from her and stepped away.

It was a text, the very one Theresa had sent me several minutes earlier, a delayed response from our sluggish office forwarding system.

When I turned back, Theresa was softly snoring. She never looked more attractive than when in repose.

I eased off her high heels, fetched a blanket from the bedroom and draped it over her.

As I was leaving, my phone warbled again. Another text.

I had to read it through several times before I worked out that it was from Claire Whitney.

THREE

South Harrow was unknown territory to me, and I expected to find it awash with public school toffs; but emerging from the tube station I saw a mix of down-at-heel shops and shabby office blocks. I trudged up the road. Soon drab commercial outlets gave way to huge playing fields, too big and flat to be up on the Hill itself alongside the School. I could imagine Ashad fulminating that the government should move in, bulldoze the cricket pavilions and build homes for first-time buyers. He hated anything that smacked of privilege. Green spaces were only worth preserving when everyone had a decent roof over their heads.

The houses were more stately on the lower margins of the Hill. The one I wanted turned out to be a solitary Victorian heap with crumbling red bricks and flaking pediments. The road itself was busy: lots of traffic but few pedestrians. I wondered if she had driven here.

A paved driveway led past an assortment of overfilled wheelie bins. No cars were parked there but the drive also went round the side of the house. As I climbed the stone steps to the front door I saw net curtains twitch in a ground floor window. I wondered if this was my collector.

Claire Whitney had put me onto him. The text I had received at Theresa's said:

> *Hi Nick Sry 4 sudden awol cldnt b hlpd. Meet ½r Townsend scifi LP collector 2moro 10am. F2b Tygoria Hse Bessborough Rd Harrow. C4n C x*

It wasn't the sheer poetry that had fixed the message in my mind. Maybe it was the unexpectedness of it. Maybe it was having to work at the translation. Maybe it was the little *x* at the end.

I had emailed back *Thnx. CU there. N.* It took me longer than writing it in full. While en route I had actually phoned Jamilla for help in deciphering the whole of the text. Apparently C4n was shorthand for "Ciao for now". Naturally Jamilla had wanted to know why I was asking, so I told her it was a message from my accountant. I had resisted the temptation to add a little *x* after my name in my reply.

There was a squawk box by the main door and I pressed the second button, noting there was no tenant listed alongside it. Or in any of the other slots, for that matter.

"Who's there?" came an electronically shrill voice.

"Nick Randall," I said. "From Xponential Productions. Am I speaking to Arthur Townsend?"

"Yes."

"Sorry I'm late."

"*Grggleswk*. Do you have some identification?"

I wasn't expecting this. "Well, I have a business card and my driving licence."

"Hold them up to the camera. *Swweenneep*."

I spotted a cheap webcam untidily taped to the side of the porch. I waved cheerily and held up the card and licence, following his instructions for them to be held closer or further away until the low quality lens could focus.

"What do you want?"

The voice was peevish but I told myself it was just the ropey loudspeaker.

"Claire Whitney arranged for us meet here," I said.

"Who?"

"Claire Whitney. The artist. I believe she contacted you."

"I've never heard of her."

I frowned. "Is that Arthur Townsend? The science fiction collector?"

There was a raucous burst of static in which I managed to detect an affirmative noise.

"Look, Mr Townsend, it's quite difficult holding a conversation like this. Let me in and I'll explain."

"Oh, I don't think so. *Zzzvbnk*."

The background humming of the entry phone stopped abruptly.

I pressed the doorbell again and said quickly, "My company is making a science fiction movie and I've heard you're an expert on sci fi."

"SF," he said.

"Of course. We're looking to employ a consultant. For money."

No immediate response to this. Could I hear him breathing? Or was it just the oceanic hiss of white noise?

"The author I'm interested in is Leo Parrish." I figured that being specific might convince him of my credentials.

A long silence followed, and I wondered whether he had gone off to fetch a can of Mace or a ray gun. Then the door lock made a noise like it had mad bee disease and I leaped forward before he changed his mind.

Inside, there was a tiled hallway with stairs going up the middle and doors on either side. It had an air of spent grandeur, the paintwork grimy, the walls papered with woodchip, which usually covered a multitude of sins. A pile of unopened post lay neglected on a little side table, most of it junk mail and final demands from utility companies.

I headed towards the side door where I had seen the curtains twitching. Even as I knocked I heard a scratching noise from within. I guessed I was under some scrutiny through the door's peep hole. I tried to look reassuring. The succession of keys being turned, bolts slid and chains unhooked made me think I was about to be admitted to the dungeons of Mordor. Arthur Townsend wasn't practised at it though, judging by his muttering and swearing.

Arthur proved to be a tall thin man in late middle-age with a pale face, a dark jaw and grey hair long overdue for a trim. He wore cargo pants and a T-shirt emblazoned with the head of an astronaut in a fishbowl helmet against which a raspberry ripple cone was splattering. The logo underneath said, *In Space No-one Can Eat Ice Cream*.

He looked past my shoulder as if expecting a SWAT team to be bringing up the rear. His eyes never stopped moving.

"You'd better come in," he said reluctantly.

I eased my way past him. He closed the door and immediately proceeded to re-bolt, re-latch and re-chain everything. While he was doing this, a woman appeared from the little galley kitchen beyond.

"Good morning," she said brightly. "I'm Molly."

"Nick Randall," I said with equal cheer, shaking her hand. She was Townsend's age, trim with bobbed chestnut hair and smartly dressed in a grey skirt and coral-pink blouse with matching earrings and necklace.

"Would you like some tea?" she asked.

"That would be brilliant," I enthused. I had overslept that morning and rushed off without eating or drinking anything. I was still feeling distinctly fuzzy from overdoing the wine at Theresa's.

Arthur hadn't quite finished with one of the deadlocks.

"Do you get much street crime around here?" I enquired politely of Molly.

She just rolled her eyes and went back to the kitchen.

Arthur led me into the front room and indicated an armchair beside the fireplace. His pasty face and shambling gait suggested that he wasn't exactly the outdoors type.

I sat myself down, taking in everything. The room was large and high-ceilinged. Two walls of it were stacked with multicoloured books and magazines that stretched from floor to ceiling. On the shelves in front of the books were customized models of Daleks, *Star Wars* storm troopers, Robbie the Robot from *Forbidden Planet* and a host of other alien, mechanical and bizarre biological figures including one that Xponential had had a part in creating.

Against the un-shelved wall a PC sat on a desk, its big monitor showing the house's front door steps. The desk was strewn with papers, magazines and used mugs. Next to it stood an impressive electronics stack that wouldn't have been out of place in our office. A sign taped to the desktop box said, "You don't have to be mad to work here, but I am."

"Seen enough?" Arthur Townsend said to me, slumping into another armchair opposite.

I leaned forward and offered my hand. "Nick Randall," I said again, in case he had forgotten.

He stared at it as if he was being introduced to Typhoid Mary. With no great enthusiasm, he put a palm in mine and we shook. I noticed that his forehead was misted with perspiration. It wasn't particularly warm in the room, but our Arthur was definitely in a sweat about something.

Molly entered and set down a tray on a coffee table between us. It held genteel rose-patterned cups and saucers with a matching teapot and sugar bowl. On a large plate was an assortment of biscuits.

"Would you like me to pour?" she asked.

"Yes, please." I wasn't feeling too fragile but I didn't trust myself to manipulate her best crockery.

She poured one for me and one for Arthur.

"Do help yourself to the biscuits," she told me. "And don't let Mr Grumpy Pants there put you off." She gave Arthur his cup. He evidently took his tea black. "Now you behave yourself and try to be pleasant. I'm sure Mr Randall's not from MI5 or the gas board."

I had rather hoped that she would sit down with us but she went off again with a busy air. I added milk to my cup and selected a custard cream from the plate.

"Sorry about the confusion earlier," I said to Arthur. "I was told by Claire Whitney that she'd arranged for the three of us to meet."

Still no visible reaction to the name. And where exactly *was* she? Had she been caught in traffic on the M1 or North Circular or wherever it was she was coming from?

"I really don't know what you're talking about," he said.

"Maybe she sent a message and you didn't pick it up?"

"I *always* check all my mail very carefully," he insisted.

I could imagine that he did. He would be very diligent about it. I took a bite of a biscuit and considered the possibilities. Perhaps Claire Whitney had actually forgotten to send the text. Perhaps it just hadn't got through. Perhaps—and this suddenly seemed a more likely scenario—Arthur had for some reason got cold feet about the meeting and was lying to me. He might have sent her packing earlier, long before I arrived.

In which case, why hadn't she been in touch to let me know? My phone was nestling in the breast pocket of my shirt where I could feel any quiet mode vibrations.

Then it dawned on me. Her original text had said *Meet ½r Townsend* and I had naturally assumed that this meant both of us. But what if she had meant me alone? She might have arranged it without reference to herself. A disappointing possibility, and one which still wouldn't explain why Arthur didn't appear to have been expecting me either.

It was all rather perplexing, but at least I had reached the inner sanctum.

"My email *and* my snail mail are being interfered with," Arthur announced.

"Oh."

"I've been subject to malicious viruses and spam."

I had this image of burly Food Police force-feeding him rotting pink slabs of meat.

"That's probably why you didn't know I was coming," I said, improvising madly. "Anyway, now that I'm here I'd like to explain my proposal. Claire's been helping me identify source material for a major movie that Xponential want to do. She felt that Leo Parrish's work would be just right. And she also strongly recommended you for your expertise in the science fiction field."

I usually try to avoid exaggeration, but sometimes the wheels need oiling.

"The only trouble is that we can't trace complete texts of any of his stories. Xponential would be willing to pay you for any material you could provide as well as an on-going consultancy fee during the pre-production phase of any movie."

I swallowed some tea and started on a second biscuit. Needless to say I hadn't discussed any of this with Ashad, but I didn't envisage problems if I made progress. Anyway, Arthur and Ashad had things in common: a fondness for disconcerting shirts, a tendency to five o'clock shadow and an almost religious belief in personal persecution.

Arthur still didn't look as if he was going to budge. On instinct I said, "You have heard of Leo Parrish, haven't you?"

He gave me a look of withering scorn. "Eighteen stories between 1957 and 1960. All of them in Shock and Awe."

"Shock and Awe?"

"*Shocking Stories* and *Awesome Adventures*. He never wrote—well, never published—anything else."

"And you have copies of these stories?"

He shook his head and my spirits sank.

"Only seven."

I perked up. "Seven's good."

"*Shock* and *Awe* were somewhere between a fanzine and a prozine."

I translated this as magazines written by sci-fi fans and magazines written by professionals. Not such great news. I didn't like the idea of Parrish writing only for the 1950s' equivalent of some semi-literate blog. Maybe he wasn't the undiscovered rough diamond I'd hoped for. But this was no time to be daunted.

"So," I said keenly, "tell me a bit about Parrish."

Townsend stared at me for a minute, then stood up and went to his desk. He grabbed a camera and photographed me. I was so surprised I just sat there.

"That's good," he said.

"Is it?" I wasn't quite sure how to continue. "Do you always take snaps of your visitors?"

"Things have been happening here. Not just my mail but attempted intrusions."

"Really?"

"Someone tried to force his way in, pretending that he wanted to read the electricity meter. My bicycle was stolen and dumped on the cricket ground and when I returned after retrieving it I saw two figures running away. They'd been trying to prise the window open. My employer has been asking questions about my private life, and I've heard people rummaging around in the back garden at night."

Blimey, I thought. You and Ashad should definitely get together.

"Only last week, my registration for the Worldcon was mysteriously cancelled."

Under my prompting he explained that the Worldcon was the World Science Fiction Convention, which this year was taking place in Miami.

"I've managed to reinstate that but I had to pay again. My doctor's signed me off work with stress."

I nodded furiously, still trying to accommodate the notion of Arthur holding down anything that I might consider to be a job. "And why do you think they're doing this?"

"I think they want access to my library."

I had the impression he meant more than just the books I could see around me.

"But why? Do you have many valuable books?"

"They're *all* valuable to me."

He took a crumpled handkerchief from his pocket and swabbed his face. I could smell his distress. There was nothing funny about it, whether or not his fears were rational.

"Have you been to the police?" I asked.

"Of course I have. They're useless. Don't think I don't know what impression this place makes on outsiders. They come here and look at me as if I'm mental. One of them had the temerity to ask me if I'm a Trekkie or a Whooie. I mean, these are policemen we're talking about! Another asked me how I could be sure that anything was missing. I could hear them sniggering on the steps after they left."

I finished off my tea, feeling a little guilty for my own preconceptions. "And the photograph?"

"Oh, I got the idea from the Logical Paranoia website. Criminals and spooks react badly. Obvious really."

"I see. And did I pass the test?"

"You didn't fail it."

He still wasn't entirely persuaded of my sincerity, so I played my last card.

"I sympathize," I said. "I really do. You won't believe the number of nuisance calls and messages we've had since we made *Absolute Hero*."

A light went on in his eyes. *Absolute Hero* was another one of our oddball animated features about a super-powered crime fighter whose main challenge was not the villains he fought but his inability to find a secure secret identity.

Arthur jumped up and snatched a figure from one of the shelves, which he showed delightedly to me.

It was the lead character himself, granite-jawed and muscle-bound in his lime and aubergine leotard and a skimpy black mask which conspicuously failed to hide any of his *über*-masculine facial features. I'd spotted it earlier and remembered how *DisOrg* had worked for Kirsty. The majority of the fan-base for the serial was teen to early twenties, though there were plenty of jokes for grown-ups too. Unfortunately we had lost the rights before it became *really* popular when the creators found a way of squirming out of their original contract.

"I'm hoping we can turn something by Leo Parrish into a successful enterprise too," I said.

Suddenly I had become his friend. I quite liked that, even if it was the equivalent of being someone who wasn't going to ransack his archives in the middle of the night. He drained his tea in one. I celebrated with another custard cream.

"Leo Parrish," he said. "An interesting choice. He was a much underrated writer but he had a very low profile. Like I said, he wasn't published in the major magazines like *Astounding*, *Galaxy* and *F&SF*."

I nodded sagely, though I had never heard of any of them.

"He had terrific ideas though, sometimes really bizarre, but always interesting. I believe that he was a great influence on a lot of more successful writers who came later like—do you know anything about SF?"

"Layman's stuff," I exaggerated. "I've heard it said that he was a poor man's Philip K. Dick."

Arthur shook his head vehemently. "He was his own man. Poor in a financial sense, perhaps. All but the best-known SF writers were in those days. Many of them had to churn out stories and write in other fields too—westerns, detectives, romance. Not Parrish, though, as far as I know."

"He was just a science-fiction man?"

Arthur nodded. "No wonder he gave up. *Shock* and *Awe* didn't have much clout, and he probably got bottom dollar for his stories, if that. I should think he finally decided to pack it in and get a real job. He was a loss to the field."

Arthur plainly didn't know anything about Parrish's subsequent life.

"So do you think any of his stories could form the basis for a movie?" I asked. "Can I look at some?"

"Did you ever see that series—"

"*Nightscapes*," I interrupted, keen to show some knowledge. "An episode based on his story 'The Cosmic Controllers'."

I could see he liked the way I said it, the precision of it. This meant more to him than mere money.

"A lot of his stuff is pretty wide screen, high concept. You'd need good SFX. Plenty of CGI."

Now we were talking professional shorthand. It was a bonding thing.

"That's doable relatively easily these days," I assured him.

"To be honest, I'm hazy on the details. I haven't looked at any for years. They were great when I first came across them but sometimes, you know, you can't recover that sense of wonder you experienced first time around."

"Well, we won't know till we try. Could I see some?"

He screwed up his face. This was a difficult decision for him, despite his enthusiasm. I understood that while he was eager to demonstrate his knowledge, the idea of me actually handling the raw material was a different matter. Did he think I was going to tear pages out or leave greasy fingerprints all over them? Then it occurred to me that the copies might be rather flimsy after half a century.

"I imagine they're somewhat delicate," I said.

Arthur nodded gravely. "They were printed on poor quality paper which has a tendency to yellow and crumble. And the poor binding means the glue has long dried up inside the spine."

"Rusty staples?" I empathized.

"Sometimes."

"I've handled old film stock," I told him. "I know how important it is to treat these things with respect."

He took a deep breath, a man on the brink of a momentous decision.

"Please wait here," he told me, and left the room.

I heard him exchange a few words with Molly in the kitchen. And then silence. After a short pause, I followed him out.

Molly, in pinafore and oven gloves, was putting something into the cooker.

"Hello again," I said, my gaze straying down the corridor to what could only have been a rear bedroom. It was also walled with books. Somewhere inside, out of sight, Arthur was rummaging around.

"Thanks for the tea," I said to Molly.

She hung the oven gloves on a hook. "Has he been behaving himself?"

We shared a smile. "I think I managed to get on to his wavelength," I said.

The kitchen window was open and there was just enough space to see out.

About twenty feet below us was a substantial walled garden with apple trees, lawns and flowerbeds. It stretched to the playing fields beyond and looked to be in much better condition than the building itself. Molly told me that she was one of the people who kept it in order. There were six flats in the building, and they had a rota system, though not everyone did their share.

A zigzag wooden flight of steps led up to the rear bedroom from ground level. A wheelie bin had been parked at the bottom, and another at the top on the little balcony outside the French windows. They stood like sentinels, bulwarks against the chaos and disorder of the hostile world outside.

"What's he doing now?" Molly asked me as she removed her pinafore and folded it into quarters.

"Looking for some magazines to show me."

"Well, I really must be going. I've got my own shopping to do."

I didn't hide my surprise. "I thought ..."

She slipped the pinafore into a drawer. "You thought I was his wife."

"Well, yes."

"And so I am. But we separated years ago. Let's just say our interests diverged."

I understood what she meant. She had the air of a competent, practical, down-to-earth woman. Her opinion of this place wasn't likely to be too different from that of the Harrow constabulary.

"I live in the flat opposite," she told me. "Pop in regularly to keep an eye on him. It's easier that way."

"I see."

"Well, no, I doubt you do," she said, not unkindly. "How could you? But it's better for both of us."

She gathered up a smart cream gabardine coat and went into the back room. I trailed in her wake.

Arthur was up on a small stepladder, inspecting the topmost shelf. Apart from the single bed parked against the chimney breast, the entire room was given over to books and magazines, on shelving, in boxes and crates, on the brimming pair of bedside tables. The French doors had a similar arrangement of locks and bolts to the front door, and Arthur had double-glazed the windows with great slabs of wired glass.

"I'm going now, dear," Molly said.

Arthur jerked around, almost toppling off the steps.

"The shepherd's pie is in the oven and you're to take it out by twelve o'clock."

He managed to nod.

"Twelve o'clock, don't forget. I'll call in later."

Arthur didn't move or say anything. He was looking at me as if I was a Visigoth who had just burst into the temple of Athena.

"You're going to have to let me out," Molly said.

Reluctantly he got down from the steps.

"Please don't touch anything," he told me as he went past.

Molly stole a moment to take me aside.

"Don't take advantage of him, will you? He's very vulnerable."

As soon as I was alone I took the opportunity to inspect the shelves. The books were in alphabetical order by author. I found my way to a stretch of Philip K. Dicks. It was much longer than I had expected, even allowing for copies of different editions of the same book and some oddities like short novels being printed with another author's stuck on the back upside down. How were you supposed to put those in order? And who'd sit on a tube train risking being sectioned because they looked like they were reading a book the wrong way up?

I had to admit, though, that there was something deliriously evocative about titles such as *The Game-Players of Titan, Our Friends from Frolix-8, Do Androids Dream of Electric Sheep?* They promised adventure and exoticism, an escape from the mundane realities of domestic life, the lure of worlds far more colourful and dramatic than our own.

Arthur returned and went to a corner of the room where he crouched over a box, hiding my view with the bulk of his body. When he straightened and turned to face me he was holding three magazines in clear plastic sleeves. They were *Readers' Digest* sized but not as thick.

Arthur insisted I go and wash my hands in the bathroom. Black nylon socks and Y-fronts were drying on a rack. I didn't linger. In the front room Arthur had cleared a space on his desk and spread the three magazines out for me to inspect.

As I had anticipated, they looked dog-eared and sorry for themselves. The page edges were tea-coloured and they gave off a smell of pepper and must. Two had "invisible" tape along the spine. Under Arthur's eagle eye, I was almost afraid to pick them up.

All three were editions of *Awesome Adventures*, with cover art that varied between the thoughtful and the lurid. The first showed a lost-looking robot family—mother, daughter and father—crossing a desolate landscape carrying a make-up bag, a teddy bear and a dinner service. On the second a silver art deco spaceship was crash-landing on top of a vast centipede and its green-skinned rider as others reeled back in alarm. The featured story here was "Mistake on Mars"—the mistake presumably being of that of the green-skins who were stupid enough to take their mounts out for a wriggle just as their planet was being invaded. The best thing you could say about the artwork was that it was serviceable, though the actual composition was vivid enough. If you were being really generous you might decide it had a certain retro kitsch value. Anyone without a well-developed sense of the absurd was unlikely to appreciate it.

I had the May, July and September 1957 issues. It was published bi-monthly at 25 cents. Parrish's name wasn't on the cover of the first two, though there were stories by him, "Atomic Avengers" and "Figure it Out", in both. By the September issue his story "The Copyist" was the main feature. I wondered what, if anything, it had to do with the cover showing a reptilian alien creeping into the boudoir of a female astronaut as she's divesting herself of her gold-lamé bodysuit.

"This is great," I said to Arthur. "Could I borrow these? I promise I'll take care of them."

He shook his head emphatically. "I'll copy them for you. What did you say about payment?"

I saw that he had a desktop printer with copying and scanning features but it would be a lengthy process. I had a feeling there was no alternative.

"I'd need to have them today," I said, thinking rapidly. "Shall we say a hundred pounds per story?"

He considered. "That might do, to begin with. I could print out the invoices as well."

I had hoped to get back to the office for a late lunch. I doubted that Arthur would want to share his shepherd's pie and I wasn't enthralled with the idea of a takeaway curry and can of warm lager while I waited under darkening skies for Arthur to laboriously copy Parrish's stories, page by fragile page.

Something thumped against the bay window.

Arthur swivelled. An aluminium ladder had appeared outside, propped against the frame. Seconds later a young man with scrubbing-brush hair came into view, scaling it rapidly, a bucket in one hand, various cloths handing from his belt. The front door buzzer sounded.

Arthur's gaze darted from the window to his monitor. The screen showed a girl in her late teens lounging outside the front door, blonde and pony-tailed, chewing a big wodge of gum, a notebook in her hand.

Arthur darted towards the window and swept back one of the nets. "Who are you?" he demanded to know of the young man beyond. "What are you doing here?"

The young man merely grinned at him before slapping a fat wet sponge against the pane and beginning to swab.

The doorbell buzzed again.

Arthur, caught in a quandary, was vibrating like a lump of iron between two poles of a magnet. Then he rushed to his front door.

While Arthur attempted to unleash himself from his own security, I decided that the best thing to do in this situation was nothing. Outside, the crew-cut man on the ladder swabbed and squeegeed the window panes. A trailing microphone lead from an MP3 player to his ears explained why he had failed to respond to Arthur's questions. When he seemed to be looking in my direction I gave a little wave. He failed to react, and I realized he couldn't see me through the nets.

I turned my attention back to the magazines. They were edited by someone called Ed Ridge, but the rest of the contributors to *Awesome Adventures* had names as exotic as their story titles: Nat Nietzold, Oskar V. Prego, Dirk Vanderzanders. I suspected that at least some were pen names. The paper was so coarse the black print had bled into it, but fortunately all the text was still legible. Only in the sheltering hands of a collector like Arthur Townsend could these magazines have lasted half a century.

Arthur had finally burst out of his self-imposed shackles and was confronting the girl on the doorstep. I moved nearer the door to listen.

"—in the rota," the girl was saying lethargically, pointing a pen at her notebook. "Flat 2b, Tiberia House."

"Ty*g*oria House!" Arthur almost screamed at her.

"I didn't order any window cleaners."

"It's down here," the girl insisted, sticking her tongue through her gum and tapping the notebook. "We wouldn't have come otherwise."

"Well, you can go away right now. I didn't ask for you."

"We've already started."

"Nobody asked you to!"

She gave a shrug of utter indifference. "You'll need to pay."

Arthur's reply was muffled by a thump from the rear of the flat. Crew-Cut was still working on the bay window at the front. I rose from the desk and hurried through into the back bedroom—and promptly tripped over one of Arthur's book boxes.

Fortunately I went sprawling straight onto his bed.

Now I couldn't be certain about this, but I thought I caught a flash of movement outside the French windows. By the time I had picked myself up there was certainly no one there. It was difficult to see out through the wired glass, but it looked to me as if the wheelie bin outside had been moved.

I hurried into the kitchen and thrust my head out of the window there. No one was in sight in the garden, but the bin at the top of the stairs was turned at an angle, and the one at the bottom had been moved aside.

OK, I told myself, they'd probably sent someone around the back to do the windows there. Someone who'd been startled by my flying leap onto Arthur's divan and had fled in fright. It was a logical explanation. But somehow I didn't buy it.

I went outside and found a distraught Arthur still protesting furiously as a white van reversed in the driveway. Pony-tail was at the wheel, Crew-Cut sitting beside her. I couldn't see anyone else. They must have moved quickly because the ladder was gone from the window and had presumably been stashed in the back of the van.

Arthur was quivering with rage and frustration.

"What do they want?" he asked, looking at but not really seeing me. It was a question directed at the Gods of the Universe, or whoever it was that directed human affairs. "They just won't leave me alone. What do they want?"

As the van disappeared out of one end of the driveway, Molly appeared in the other. She couldn't have had time to do any proper shopping, but perhaps some instinct born of long association had told her that Arthur was in peril and she had returned to come to his aid.

He almost collapsed into her arms. His heated description of what had happened was punctuated with whimpering noises. Molly took his arm and led him inside while I hovered, now feeling rather surplus to requirements, like an intruder myself on the weird intimacy of their partnership.

"I'll put the kettle on," was all that I could think of to say.

"That's all right," she told me, settling Arthur in an armchair. "We can manage from here."

I understood that it was time for me to go. Automatically I picked up the three magazines on the desk. Arthur didn't even notice. He was trembling, staring into the empty fireplace.

"All right if I borrow these?" I half whispered to Molly.

She nodded, gently propelling me towards the door. On the threshold I said to her, "I think there may have been someone around the back."

She wasn't really listening; she wanted to get back to Arthur.

"He might be right," I persisted. "Someone could be trying to burgle the place."

Another distracted nod. "I guarantee you I'll be asking to see the police. And this time I'll make sure *I* speak to them."

I turfed out one of my cards and forced her to take it. "Tell Arthur I'll look after them. He can contact me any time on that number."

For an instant she brightened, her nose simultaneously wrinkling at the ancient odour of the magazines. "Perhaps next time you'd like to bring a lorry and take the rest of them."

FOUR

"Wait till you see this!" Ashad said, taking me by the arm the moment I walked into the office and leading me straight towards the plasma screen. He was wearing a cream cowboy shirt with leather patches that looked as if he had dried it by wearing it in bed. The profusion of stud buttons and chocolate-coloured frills had obviously made the matter of ironing it out of the question.

"What have you been eating?" I asked him, detecting more than a whiff of garlic on his breath.

"Hummus," he told me with surprising approval. "And something with chickpeas, feta and—what are those grains? Cous cous. Jamilla got them in. Not bad for veggie food."

Normally Ashad's idea of lunch was a burger or pepperoni pizza with something tooth-rottingly fizzy to drink. Against all his anti-corporation instincts, he had a huge fondness for Coca Cola. He crouched by the stack and switched on the DVD. "Where have you been, anyway? I was expecting you an hour ago."

"Uh ... I was delayed. The alarm clock melted."

It was our shorthand for any kind of transport problems since it had actually happened to Ashad when he bought a cheap and nasty one. I didn't specify, and Ashad didn't ask. In fact, I had got back from Harrow in good time and had spent the past hour sitting in a nearby pub, eating a sandwich and reading through one of Leo Parrish's stories.

"Jamilla picked this up from the web," Ashad said, activating a grainy video news item from an American TV network.

Emerging from the entrance of a club house was Bennett Irwin, the US Secretary of State for Defense. Casually dressed, he had evidently been about to start a round of golf when confronted by a female reporter, who asked for his reaction to the latest speech from President Muvart of Khanistan.

"Inflammatory," Irwin said bluntly, trying to push his way past, his severe-looking face unsuited to the niceties of smiles.

"What credence is being given to the possibility that he'll carry out his threats?" the reporter asked.

Irwin's jaw went hard. He looked conspicuously annoyed, though whether at the reporter's intrusion or the thrust of her question, it was impossible to know. His gold-rimmed spectacles glinted as someone off-view took a photograph. He strode towards the first tee.

The reporter and her camera operator kept pace with him.

"What action is the administration considering against the threats?"

"I'll be meeting the president later today."

"And advising him?"

"You don't give in to bullies. You face up to them, eyeball to eyeball. You don't blink."

"Are President Muvart's accusations true?"

Irwin stopped and turned. "Exactly what accusations are you referring to?"

"That the CIA has been undertaking covert operations in Khanistan, against the wishes of the government there?"

"No."

"The Khanistani government claim to have documentary evidence—"

"Hold it right there," Irwin interrupted testily. "There is no government in the sense that we would recognize it in the United States," He walked off again. "Their foreign policy is dictated by one man, who can make any accusations he pleases, secure in the knowledge that no dissenting voices are allowed. Concerned nations should be considering what actions they can best undertake to encourage internal pressure for democratic reform. We hope to be working with those governments who share our values of freedom and human rights to make representations to that effect."

The reporter thrust her microphone closer. "So you'd favour a change in government there?"

"I'd favour dialogue, where it's possible. Should President Muvart decide to moderate his tone there is every opportunity for constructive talks between our two nations."

"Really?" The reporter was sceptical. "What can you tell us about the likelihood of the administration providing direct support for dissident elements within Khanistan?"

Again Irwin paused, as if he needed time to consider his words.

"No options have been ruled out at this stage."

"Would that include material support for armed guerrilla movements?"

He started to say something but stopped himself by muttering an aside to his caddy.

"Dr Irwin?" the reporter prompted.

Irwin was adjusting the strap on his leather glove. "As you very well know I don't discuss matters of strategic policy with reporters before I've consulted the President. Any announcements will come from him. Now you'll excuse me, I have a game of golf to play."

He walked off again, and when the reporter tried to pursue him a burly security man loomed in the field of vision and the camera viewpoint swerved, showing sky, then grass to the accompaniment of muffled noises as though someone was grappling with the microphone. The clip ended.

Ashad was grinning at me.

"What's so funny?" I asked. "Irwin wasn't exactly reassuring on the idea of using diplomacy rather than military muscle."

"Exactly! Did you see how he was busting a gut trying not to tell the reporter what he *really* thought?"

"Well, he was pretty blunt in his opinion of Muvart's style of leadership."

"Yeah, but what about all the other stuff he wanted to say? He was practically biting his lip."

"Are you going to edit it in?"

"You bet I am. But I'm hoping we might get more. Face to face, even. My sources tell me that he's coming to Europe to talk to security heads."

"Your sources," I said sarcastically. "Do you mean that dodgy bloke in the Foreign Office?"

Ashad wagged a finger at me. "He's been very reliable up to now. Word is, Irwin's due to visit London first. If we could get wind of his itinerary we might be able to ambush him ourselves, toss a few awkward questions of our own his way."

I liked the idea of that. "We could quiz him about the black sites."

"We'll ask him directly if the US government is keeping foreign nationals imprisoned anywhere within the EU. And whether the so-called Enhanced Interrogation Protocols are just a fancy name for torture."

I smiled. "So you won't be wanting to provoke him, then."

"That's the whole point. Keep on at him until he gets angry and says something indiscreet. I know his type, all that righteous fury bubbling under. I'll take Zoran and Milos along."

Zoran and Milos were émigré Serbian brothers who worked as a mobile camera team. We often employed them for potentially tricky assignments. As well as being extremely good at their job they were also undaunted by stroppy politicians and their bodyguards, having survived strafing and sniper fire in their native country during the civil war. Not that there should be any difficulty in gaining access to Irwin, given that it was a co-production with the BBC.

"You could also ask him when he's expecting The Rapture," I remarked.

"What?"

"Irwin's a member of a right-wing Christian group that believes they are going to be physically raised up on Judgement Day. They call it The Rapture."

Ashad looked like a child who had just been gifted quadruple the usual pocket money. "No kidding?"

"There are websites listing well-known believers—politicians, sports personalities, movie stars. You're not the only one who's been doing some background research."

"Bloody hell," Ashad said contemplatively. "So he's even more of a nutter than we thought."

"Muvart's not exactly Mr Rational either," I pointed out. "How did you get on with his cousin?"

"He called to say he couldn't make the morning meeting. We rescheduled for two o'clock. What time is it?"

Ashad never wore a watch. Maybe he was afraid it would melt.

"Half one," I told him. "Where are you meeting him?"

He had already leapt to his feet. "Outside the Tate Modern. I'd better get my skates on."

"Where's Jamilla?"

"I sent her to pick up some documentary footage on the Afghan-Khanistan border wars. She should be back soon."

"The border wars? That was thirty years ago, Ash."

"So? There's always a chance we might find something relevant to today. Anyway, it's got sound bites from Irwin's role model."

I had to puzzle that one out. "Henry Kissinger?"

Ashad grinned and nodded. "You know I just can't resist those graveyard tones."

He disappeared down the stairs towards the washroom, pulling off his shirt as he went.

"Anything else I need to know about?" I called after him.

If he made any reply, I never heard it as he closed the washroom door.

Presently I heard running water in the pipes. Ashad hadn't asked me anything about my meeting with Arthur Townsend. In a way I was glad. There would be plenty of opportunity to tell him about it later. After I had had time to ponder it all myself.

I extracted the three issues of *Awesome Adventures* from my backpack and took them into the alcove where we housed our photocopier. I had spent the train journey reading the first two.

Very carefully I opened the first magazine and laid the pages as flat as I could on the glass without cracking the spine. "Atomic Avengers" was about a team of scientists trapped in a contaminated zone when a "nuclear pile" goes critical. Buried alive under a "null-rad dome" put in place by those outside, they emerge decades later to wreak havoc on the world that abandoned them.

At only twelve pages, the story swept the reader along at breakneck speed and proved mercifully easy to copy. "Figure It

Out" told of an apparently deaf boy who wins prizes on radio shows by demonstrating a remarkable gift for swiftly answering complex numerical questions. The "hearing aid" the boy wears proves to be a radio receiver linked to a "mini-numerator" devised by his ailing father, whose invention was spurned by business interests and is subsequently buried by them after his death.

Both stories were very readable and intriguing. Not necessarily movie material, but with enough energy and invention to keep me turning the pages as the tube train trundled its way towards central London. They were also more sophisticated than I had anticipated, both in theme and writing style, though I had actually read them in a slightly distracted state. I was distracted because I had begun to wonder if I was being followed.

It had started soon after leaving Arthur's. At first I was fine. I had texted Claire Whitney with the message: *Made it to Arthur's. Very interesting meeting. Like to talk it through with you*. I wasn't expecting an immediate reply, and I didn't get one.

As I crossed the road to South Harrow tube station, a white van cruised by and pulled over close by. It sat there with its engine idling and its left indicator winking. No one got out. It looked like the van Pony Tail had been driving, but I couldn't be certain. Why would Pony Tail and co. want to follow me? It was ridiculous. I had just spent over an hour in the company of one of the most mentally besieged men I had ever met, so it was hardly surprising that I was feeling twitchy. I did contemplate walking past the van and just looking in to be sure, but the idea made me even more uneasy. Instead I scuttled into the station.

Negotiating the ticket barrier with fumbling haste, I headed speedily for the platform. Not exactly the actions of a go-getting hero, I'll readily admit, but after my time with Arthur I wasn't looking for any further aggravation or indeed any sort of confirmation that his worst fears were justified. All I wanted was to nestle down with the Parrish stories as soon as I could.

While I waited for the train, I kept looking around, checking out anyone who came after me. I saw no one suspicious. The train came rolling in.

The carriage was less than a quarter full. I found a solitary seat at one end, settled down with relief. A man in jeans and a slate bomber jacket got on just before the doors closed. He walked to the other end of the carriage, slumped into a seat. I did a last scan, spotted no one who looked especially furtive or inquisitive. I took the earliest issue of *Awesome Adventures* and made myself comfortable.

I read the first two stories in a feverish state of curiosity and anticipation. At regular intervals I glanced up, checking the faces. Twice I caught the eye of the man in the bomber jacket, who sat with his hands in his pockets and his knees going up and down. He was a lean and wiry Caucasian in his thirties, hair cut short with prominent wedge-shaped sideboards. His slightly battered-looking face gave him the air of a retired flyweight boxer, though he might have been a Zen-practising vegan for all I knew. He was still making pedalling motions and on both occasions he appeared to be looking directly at me, though I got no visible reaction when I returned his stare. Probably he wasn't doing any such thing, and it was just a trick of the long perspective down the carriage. Even so, I remained conscious of him, willing him to get off at the next, and the next, stop, my mind only ninety per cent focused on Leo Parrish's stories.

Despite this I knew that Parrish had something, not least the ability to grab the reader's interest and propel him through the story. Though written in a no-frills prose style with a minimum of psychological depth, the stories were so much better than their context promised. I glanced at a few by other writers in the magazines and found them pretty crude knockabout pieces in comparison. Parrish was aiming to do more than just spin an adventure: he wanted his stories to be thought-provoking as well as fun.

There are eighteen stops on the Piccadilly Line between South Harrow station and Leicester Square. The guy with the sideboards sat there through all of them, now chewing mightily instead of air pedalling but otherwise not occupying himself in the slightest. Most passengers on London trains had strategies for shutting out the oppressive proximity of other people: they made phone calls, listened to music, texted, lost themselves in books, magazines, newspapers. Once I saw a woman knitting a multi-coloured scarf that looked as if it might eventually stretch the entire length of the Northern Line. Not our man. His jaw was working hard, but nothing else was moving. Not even his eyes. They still seemed aimed in my direction. Was this the third person I may or may not have glimpsed at the back of Arthur's flat? Was he tailing me?

I contemplated getting off at South Kensington, where I could just cross the platform and pick up a Circle or District Line to Embankment. If Sideboards followed, he would be plainly visible on the platform and I could try to lose him by moving about on the train or by taking a circuitous route up to the office when I got off. I had this image of myself striding purposefully along various back streets and alleyways, darting in and out of WH Smiths and Next and Boots like someone in a chase movie, background music pulsating as I immersed myself in the hordes of tourists around Trafalgar Square. But frankly, I couldn't be arsed. With each stop the carriage was now becoming increasingly crowded, and by the time we reached Green Park I couldn't see Sideboards at all.

Even so, when I got off I paused on the platform and went through an elaborate routine of untying and re-tying the laces of my shoes. I felt like a complete ham, but I took enough time over it for the train to have departed and most of the platform to have cleared. Then I straightened and looked up and down. No sign of Sideboards anywhere.

Close to the office was a pub where there was an upstairs room with leather sofas and pumps dispensing a variety of decent ales. I settled myself in a quiet corner with comfortable chair

Leo Parrish's "The Copyist" took up half of the third issue of *Awesome Adventures*. It had nothing to do with the prurient cover image and instead concerned a man claiming to have been abducted by "angels" who later furiously began writing down a series of instructions in an indecipherable script. He also drew bizarre images of his abduction with great clarity. When the "brain tumour" which the doctors had diagnosed was removed, it proved to be an organized ball of cells that defied human biology. Was the man's story true? Were his writings and drawings messages from other worldly beings? The patient had no memory of his visions after the operation and the ball of cells mysteriously disappeared along with his journal so that the truth would never be known.

This was the story Claire Whitney had storyboarded. Its ambiguity felt quite modern, a precursor of movies such as *K-Pax*. I was impressed, even though it wasn't exactly what we were looking for. But I felt a renewed confidence that if I kept searching I might find something of Parrish's that we really might be able to turn into a movie.

When I finally looked up from the magazine I saw Sideboards standing at the bar. He wasn't staring at me, and was in fact in the middle of ordering a drink.

I didn't hesitate. I picked up my stuff and walked straight out.

Halfway down the stairs I wondered what the hell I was doing. Taking a few deep breaths, I retraced my steps, intending to confront him, to ask him outright if he was following me. Then I actually saw him cross the narrow landing and head up a further flight of stairs towards the loo. He was wearing a brick-red top, wasn't the man I had seen on the train at all.

Wanting to be sure, I returned to the bar and waited. When the guy finally emerged from the Gents I was able to see clearly that it wasn't Sideboards. I had spooked myself.

I walked out and wandered around a bit, dodging leaflet thrusters, inhaling the fragrant central London air to clear my head before going into the office. I didn't want to have to explain any of this to Ashad.

Here he was now, emerging from the washroom, freshly shaven, his tousled hair inexpertly slicked down with water. He must have sloshed it on because the shoulder patches of his shirt looked soggy.

"Don't forget we've got the Scorsese premiere tonight," he reminded me. "Seven sharp."

It was on at the Odeon Leicester Square. We had wangled invitations through a friend who worked for the production company. Always good to hobnob a little with the really famous, even if most of them don't have a clue who you are.

"Is that Lynx I can smell on you?" I asked, just out of mischief.

"Bugger off."

"Are you going to wear that shirt?"

"Why?" He looked totally surprised and starting tucking it into the waist of his cargo pants. "What's wrong with it?"

"Nothing," I said, deadpan. "It's perfect. Muvart's cousin's a big Roy Rogers fan. You'll go down a storm. You ought to wear one of those string ties and a Stetson for the full effect."

"Up yours."

*

After Ashad left, I photocopied the rest of the stories. I was pretty sure that Arthur would soon be phoning me, demanding the return of the magazines. Though none of the stories was movie material, "The Copyist" might make a decent one-hour drama, especially if we kept the period setting. That, though, could go into the Long-Term file. The main effect of the story was to encourage me that Leo Parrish might well have written other stuff with real cinematic merit. All I had to do was find it.

I joined Valerie downstairs for a brainstorming session on a sitcom idea that we both concluded didn't really have legs. She and Ash had also decided to abandon the Travelling Circus project and concentrate on finishing the Muvart documentary.

An hour later I was back upstairs. I did a search for *Homeopape* and found that the site had been named after a device from a Philip K. Dick novel that produced tailored newspapers. Rhodri Davies was a well-known figure in the science-fiction world and had won numerous awards for the quality and wit of his reportage and non-fiction.

The phone rang several times and I took the calls. There was still no word from Claire Whitney. I texted her a slightly more urgent *Where are you? Can we talk?* message. I was less puzzled by her not having shown as the fact that she hadn't bothered to contact me, if only to confirm that I had got my wires crossed about the meeting.

In the kitchen the work-top looked as if a baguette had exploded over a variety of dips and salad pots. Tubs of Greek yoghurt sat beside curried beans and lemon-scented quinoa, ravaged naans and pittas lay next to a very English cheese platter. Ashad had attacked it as if he had been in the grip of a feeding frenzy. Come the revolution, he was one of those socialists who would never be able to get by without a decent housekeeper.

I packed everything away into the fridge, swabbed the work surface and swept the crumbs from the floor. I didn't want Jamilla to think that her efforts to reduce our cholesterol levels would go unappreciated. I was also a little restless, for reasons I couldn't quite pin down. Yes, it had something to do with the whole sequence of odd events at Arthur's place. But that wasn't all of it. I had the kind of fretful sensation you get when you know you should be making connections but you don't even know where the ends are.

I went into the reception area to check Jamilla's message pad in case I had missed anything. On her desk was a new potted plant like a psychedelic cucumber with tiny scarlet dots down its ribbed sides. It sat next to a copy of the *Evening Standard*, which was open on a feature about the new star. Its magnitude was still increasing and it was now just visible with the naked eye. Opinion was apparently divided on whether the star had only recently burst to life or was actually a once-faint object now undergoing some kind of stellar upheaval. In either event, they had christened it Draco Nova.

Because I didn't want her to think I was badgering her, I had deferred actually phoning Claire Whitney on the mobile number she had texted me from. But now it was time. I imagined that she would have her phone close at hand, but it just rang and rang before finally clicking on to the automated voice message service.

"Hello," I said after the beep, already feeling foolish. "It's Nick Randall. I think maybe we were supposed to meet this morning at Arthur Townsend's. The collector? Or maybe not. Anyway, I had a very interesting discussion with him and he's provided me with some of Leo Parrish's stories. I really enjoyed them and think they could be the sort of thing I'm looking for. Could you give me a call so that we can have a chat about it? Yeah. Thanks. That's it, really. It was good to meet you the other day and I hope we can get together soon."

I cut the call, feeling more stupid than ever. Seconds after I replaced the receiver on its cradle the phone started ringing. I snatched it up.

"Nick Randall."

"He never showed."

This was Ashad, thoroughly cheesed off. He was obviously referring to Muvart's cousin.

"I've been waiting here for over a bloody hour. No sign of him."

"Did you try him on the number I gave you?"

"Of course I bloody did! Half a dozen times. I kept getting the message service."

"I know the feeling."

"What?"

"Nothing."

"I thought maybe he'd got the time wrong, so I gave him the benefit of the hour, but still no show. Was he on the level about this, Nick, or were we trying to deal with a flake?"

The frustration in Ashad's voice was close to anger: he hated having his time wasted.

"The guy was head of Khanistani security for five years," I pointed out. "He didn't give me the impression he wanted to mess us around."

Off microphone I heard Ashad hailing a taxi, then swearing when it evidently failed to stop. I knew I had given him the correct mobile number: we had double-checked it.

"Sod it," Ashad said to me, "I'm going home. I'll see you later. If he rings the office, tell him I think he's a prat."

"Yeah, right," I said dourly. "That's really going to make him want to talk to us."

"Is Jamilla back yet?"

"No, not yet."

"Tell her it's best bib-and-tucker tonight."

"She's coming? I didn't know."

"I told them she was our PA. She's eager to mingle with some real Hollywood icons."

He rang off.

An empty office can be a very silent place. I thought I heard a noise on the stairs outside, a slow, sticky, measured tread that I knew wasn't Jamilla or Ashad or anyone from the downstairs office, who all had their own methods for avoiding the carpet tape. It grew louder, somehow ever more ponderous and determined. Then it stopped. Right outside on the landing.

I went to the door and waited a few seconds before wrenching it open. When I saw who it was, I exhaled with a weird mixture of relief and apprehension.

I've always thought that of all British first names, Nigel is the most quintessentially English, though Theresa, who delights in challenging any generalisations that aren't her own, once scolded me that Nigel has Irish and Norman origins. She had made a point of researching it. But in my experience you don't tend to encounter many Irish or Normans or even Americans or Australians called Nigel. To me it speaks of middle England in all its multiplicity from croquet and Pimms to fag-ends and dodgy motors. And yet the Nigel who is our landlord fitted none of these stereotypes.

Tall and lean and usually dressed in leather, he was a pale looking man with intense eyes and weird mannerisms. As I lurched out on to the landing with a cheery "Afternoon!" he didn't so much as turn his head as swivel his eyeballs in my direction like a man wearing a neck brace.

"Nicholas," he stated in a manner that suggested there was some doubt about the statement.

"How are you keeping?" I said as blithely as possible. "Are you here for the rent? It's on standing order, isn't it?"

I was just blathering to avoid the long creepy stares that make you wonder what he's thinking and whether what he's thinking involves violence of any sort. Because although Nigel had a habit of materializing as if from another planet, there was about him a very down-to-earth air of menace.

"Health and safety," he told me without expression. "I need to do an inspection. For insurance purposes."

He didn't have much of an accent, though he was definitely foreign. Ashad and I had never been able to establish exactly what his original country or region of origin was, only that it's one of the many that sprung up after the USSR ceased to be a meaningful political entity. I mean who in the UK had ever heard of places like Chechnya, Ingushetia and South Ossetia before then? Finding out his real name might have been a pointer, but there was a certain pantomime comicality to his choice of Nigel, a comicality that it was always useful to keep in mind when you were actually around him to minimize the fear factor. He owned several properties in our neck of the West End and I don't think he financed them by winning prizes for good citizenship or devotedly nursing a rich grannie through her final days.

I led him through the office and showed him the fire door, against which we had managed not to shove any of our clutter. He pulled the bar down and swung the door open with a strength belied by his slender frame. I invariably noticed the long fingers of his large hands. I always tried to tell myself that they were the kind of fingers that would be perfect for dancing effortlessly over the keys of a grand piano rather than wrapped vice-like around a soft and yielding neck.

Nigel stuck his head out over the fire escape, looking down into the bleak back yard. He swivelled slowly as if he was a human radar scanner, but nothing living stirred below. Fortunately we had kept everything outside free of any obstructions too.

"OK," he said finally, pulling the door shut with such briskness and force I had to recoil. "Keep it so, yes?"

"Of course," I assured him, marvelling that I still had all my toes.

He turned and looked around at the interior of the place. He hadn't been inside since we first moved in, and I had the impression he was contemplating all our kit and wondering how much he could get for it if he decided to turf us out on some random pretext.

"Good, yes?" he said to me.

This query could have meant anything, and it was accompanied by something that might have been an attempt at a smile or just a showing of how well he had flossed that morning.

"Very good," I replied, heading slowly towards the door and hoping he would follow.

"I like movies," he announced. "Chuck Norris. Rocky. Lock, Stock and Smoking Aces. You make good movies?"

"We try to," I said pathetically, wondering if he was actually as clueless about our business as he seemed. I suspected not.

"So," he said when we reached the doorway, "all is well."

He was now peering intently at me as if he had asked a question to which he already had the answer.

"Well," I said, looking away towards the stairs, deciding to be bold. "There is one thing."

He didn't respond to this, just waited, still giving me the mad-gleam stare.

"We could do with a new carpet out here," I said.

"Tell me about it!" he retorted with feeling, lifting one of his feet and showing me his two-tone piebald brogues.

I couldn't actually see anything on them, but he was indicating that they had been soiled by his passage up the sticky stairs.

"This will be done," he told me earnestly. "We will all be satisfied by how it is done."

And then he strode off, going down the stairs at a brisker pace than he had ascended, ostentatiously flexing the fingers of both hands as if he was itching to get at the person responsible for the absent stair carpet so that he could massage his larynx while berating him for his dereliction of duty.

Or, just as likely, he'd forget about it the instant he walked out the door and we wouldn't hear from him for another six months.

As he went out, someone else entered. Jamilla came up the stairs, hefting a bulky carrier bag that I guessed was stuffed with the Border Wars footage Ashad had asked for. I beamed at the sight of her.

"Who was that?" she said to me, looking just a little alarmed.

"Don't ask," I told her.

I said it lightly, but I was bothered. Thwarted phone calls and abortive meetings, and then Nigel showing up unexpectedly didn't make for a tranquil state of mind. I couldn't escape the queasy feeling that things were going on in the background that weren't at all under my control.

FIVE

I jostled my way out of the packed Underground train and let myself be carried along the platform by the tide of commuters. My brain felt fuzzy from too much post-premiere fizz and too little sleep. Admittedly, the memory of Ash being mistaken for a cowboy strip-o-gram was a bright spot in my mental fog, but I was wishing I had opted for a duvet day.

I scarfed down a bacon sandwich and orange juice from the station shop before riding the escalator to the surface, waiting for the Tylenol tablets to kick in. I get my supply from Theresa, who stocks up on heavy-duty painkillers whenever she visits the USA.

Our building with its second-hand bookshop at street level is just a stroll from Leicester Square tube. Dodging traffic, I darted across the road, passing smokers huddled in doorways. Along the final stretch I always study the pavement or mutter loud nonsense to myself as I pass one of the recruitment centres of the Church of the Ascendancy. This is to deter any smiling cultists who might want to invite me inside to ENACT, which apparently means to Embrace Knowledge And Clarity of Thought. Can't anyone spell these days? They're mostly young and very presentable, kitted out in Marks & Spencer's casuals. You engage them in eye contact at your peril. I always feel like a heretic finding sanctuary when I reach the door beside the bookshop with its little anodized sign advertising our company's name.

Unusually the door was slightly ajar. Most of our staff don't arrive until after nine-thirty to avoid the worst of the rush hour, and because I had leapt out of bed in a hung-over panic I was actually half an hour earlier than normal and hadn't expected to find anyone there. Maybe Jamilla had got in ahead of me and was already busy with the spray polish. More likely it was the endearingly dozy Ross Buchanan, one of the first-floor gophers who hailed from a friendly village in Fife and had a habit of forgetting that he wasn't still living there.

The Tylenol was finally starting to soothe my synapses and I took the stairs two at a time. The main office was still locked, and when I opened it up there was no one inside. The place hadn't been cleaned that morning. I re-locked the door and continued up the stairs. Our office door was ajar and the lights were on. I pushed it and was about to call Jamilla's name when I saw papers scattered across the floor.

I went very still. Holding my breath, I tried to listen, aware that my heart had started to race. There was no noise from beyond the reception area but any intruder might have heard me coming up the stairs, so I didn't go charging in.

Jamilla's desk had been tipped over and her laptop lay entangled in the cabling of her telephone. Filing cabinet drawers hung open like huge mechanical jaws. Files, magazines, letter trays, pens and stationery were scattered all over the floor. I just avoided stepping on a framed photograph of Jamilla's family. Her desk drawers had been upturned, spilling their cargo. Everything was covered with a dusting of potted plant compost and rainbow paperclips.

I stopped and listened again, my heart doing triple time. There was nothing to indicate that whoever had broken into the place was still around. But I wasn't about to take any chances. Trying not to make any noise, I bent to grope for something long and club-like that I could see out of the corner of my eye. One muffled "Fuck me!" later I realized it was Jamilla's pet cactus. Every red dot held a minuscule spine and my palm was covered with tiny hairs. I dropped it and grabbed a narrow-necked vase that had somehow survived the trashing. I winced again and transferred it to my left hand. My right hand was already itching maddeningly.

The vase felt satisfyingly heavy, like a real weapon. Dried poppy pods spilled out of it and crunched beneath my feet, undermining my attempts at stealth. I crept into the main open-plan area, treading carefully to avoid the worst of the mess on the floor, scanning the alcoves intently, the fuzziness of my hangover entirely gone and replaced with a brittle alertness. After every step I listened again, but there was nothing to be heard apart from the slow hiss of air through my nostrils.

The place was in a right mess. Every surface that wasn't supporting a sizeable piece of kit had been swept clean, desk drawers and filing cabinets wrenched open, their contents dumped on the floor, our shelves of videos and DVDs, box files and old film stock chucked down with them. If I had thought it was untidy before I didn't have a word for it now.

I had to fight to suppress my anger and remain as alert as possible. Theresa and I had been burgled several years before, and I did my best not to touch anything that might have been handled by whoever had got in. We stored expensive portable kit like digital cameras in steel security cabinets. There were no signs that anyone had tried to force them.

The door to the fire escape was firmly shut. As far as I could see it looked as if none of our equipment was actually missing. The stacks were bolted to the frameworks that supported them but things like PCs and printers were readily nickable. Had I disturbed them in the act? Somehow I didn't think so. The place had an air of abandonment and I couldn't see any gratuitous vandalism or the kind of bodily deposits that some intruders leave.

I thought I heard a muted noise from the viewing theatre. Holding the vase tighter, I climbed the short flight of steps.

The theatre door was open a crack and someone was talking inside. I could tell from the way they were speaking that it was movie dialogue.

With an atavistic yell I hurled myself into the room, vase held high, looking frenziedly for a target. Someone was sitting in the front row. The film was *Some Like It Hot*. Tony Curtis was saying to Marilyn Monroe: "The ship is in ship-shape shape".

"Who the hell are you?" I shouted, barely keeping the wobble out of my voice.

The figure turned and then calmly rose, muting the soundtrack with the key pad in the arm of the seat. I could see it was a woman from the silhouette against the screen.

"Good morning, sir," she said to me.

I immediately figured that she was a policewoman. I flicked on the lights.

"I take it you're Mr Randall?" she said in a half-querying tone that was both sympathetic and fatalistic, the kind you might use when you're about to give a crime victim some bad news. "I'd rather you put down the vase, if you don't mind."

She looked somewhat amused at the sight of me. I set the vase down on one of the seats. She sidled light-footedly down the narrow aisle. She was in her thirties, in a stylish pinstripe trouser suit. Italianate-looking, with striking dark eyebrows that looked as if they had been put on with a black marker pen.

"This is obviously a shock," she said to me, "but I really do need you to tell me who you are."

"Ditto," I replied. "Given that this is my office."

She flashed a warrant card, said, "Detective Inspector Paula Merrick."

I made a point of taking a good look at it, remembering Ashad's first law of paranoia: they're never who they say they are. But the card looked authentic. Ashad's second law—the official identification will be fake in any event—really wasn't worth pursuing. She was a Metropolitan Police officer and her first name was actually given as Pauletta, though she spoke with a Home Counties accent that belied her Mediterranean looks.

"I may be wrong," she said, "but I'm guessing you're Nicholas Randall since you don't look like an Ashad Husseyin."

"It's Nick," I told her, still angry, staring at the mute banter of Tony Curtis and Jack Lemmon on the screen. "We normally charge for private viewings."

"It was running when I arrived," she responded. "But I admit, I couldn't resist watching."

"Bloody cheek!" I said vehemently, then, seeing her arch an eyebrow: "Not you. The bastards that did this, having the nerve to put a sodding movie on as well!"

Merrick gave a dry laugh. "Well, at least it was a good one."

"I'd have liked to have given them a good one."

She didn't respond to this bravado. "You'd be surprised at what intruders get up to. Like deciding to flush a toilet in the middle of a burglary while the residents are actually in the house. Your average villain isn't exactly a member of Mensa."

I could tell she was trying to take the sting out of the situation, but it didn't help. We went down to the main area of devastation.

"When did it happen?" I asked.

"We got a call from your cleaner around seven o'clock," she said. "He'd seen your front door open and shouted up, but there was no reply. I came over about an hour ago. I've had a good look around but there's not much in the way of obvious clues. We've already had prints taken from a few places but don't hold your breath. Even casual burglars have learned to wear latex gloves these days."

"They got in through the front door?"

She nodded. "We might need to get prints from you and Mr Husseyin for elimination purposes."

I eyed her. "How do you know our names?"

She indicated the mess on the floor. There were sheets of our letter-headed notepaper scattered everywhere. "What we couldn't find was your home numbers so we could break the news gently."

"Didn't the cleaner have them?"

"Apparently not."

That would have been Nigel's doing: he hired all the upkeep and repairs staff. Unlikely that he would have given his contact details to them.

"I take it Mr Husseyin is your business partner," Merrick said.

"Yes."

"It might be a good idea to phone—"

There was a noise from outside. Merrick slipped past me but I followed quickly, grabbing the plastic Oscar paperweight upturned in Ashad's waste bin. I really wanted to thump someone with it. Merrick wrenched the door open.

Jamilla stood there, her key raised as if she had been about to put it into the lock.

"Oh," she said, seeing the mess inside and the upturned statuette in my tingling hand. "Have I come at a bad time?"

I lowered the statue and stated the obvious: "We've been burgled."

She edged her way inside, clutching the strap of her shoulder bag as if it was a lifeline.

"This is DI Merrick," I told her.

"And you are?" Merrick enquired casually.

"Jamilla Ali," she replied, taking in everything, eyes wide open. "I'm Mr Randall's secretary."

Merrick glanced at her watch. The clock behind her said 8.55.

"Is this your usual starting time?" she asked Jamilla.

"It's only my first week. But I've been getting in about now."

Merrick let her past so that she could see the wider mess. To me she said, "And you locked up last night at what time?"

"About six," I told her, realizing that they could have got in at any time after.

"Just the three of you working here?"

"On this floor. Valerie Patterson, our office manager, has a key as well. Plus a few others."

The "others" included Nigel. Was this a follow-up to yesterday's visit?

"We might need to get statements from everyone. When are you expecting Mr Husseyin?"

Ash had still been hobnobbing with Hollywood luminaries when I'd left the post-premiere party to catch the last train home. Though he wasn't a boozer, he was a night bird and seldom got into the office before ten o'clock.

I exchanged a meaningful glance with Jamilla.

"Shall I ring him and see how soon he can get here?" she suggested.

"Good idea," I replied, at which point Merrick's mobile rang. She walked outside to take the call on the landing.

Jamilla pulled out her own mobile and started punching in Ash's number from memory. She looked calm, and I had to admire her aplomb. Last night she'd been cornered at the party by a numbskull financier who was convinced that she was an actor from *ER*, despite her obvious youth. I had been standing at her shoulder and we'd gone along with it for a little while, just for a laugh. Now I was worried that she might decide that working for Xponential entailed too much aggravation.

"Listen," I said softly to her, "things aren't usually this weird."

She gave a little shrug. "Do they know who did it?"

I shook my head, looking around again, unable to see anything that was actually broken. My fury had subsided to an angry puzzlement. It was a mess, but it could have been far worse.

I said as much to Jamilla while she waited for Ashad to pick up. When he didn't she left a brisk message: "Uncle Ashad, it's Jamilla. I'm in the office, about nine o'clock. We need you to come in urgently. There's been a bit of bother here."

A bit of bother. A very British way of putting it. Ash didn't need to know all the gory details until he phoned back or actually showed up.

Merrick came back in and handed me a card. "Here's my mobile number. Something's cropped up that I have to attend to. Let me know when your partner gets here and I'll pop back."

"Really?"

She smiled at my scepticism. "It's a promise. There may be more to this than meets the eye."

I wasn't about to let this go. "In what way? Is it a professional job?"

"Well, not in execution, no. But it doesn't look to me like the usual smash and grab either. Any idea of what they might have been looking for?"

She had a very candid gaze. Was there provocation in her question? Did she think I was withholding information? I shook my head helplessly.

"Have a think about it," she said as she left.

I followed her out on to the landing, frantically trying to think of any other pertinent questions as she went nimbly down the stairs

"What we should do in the meantime?" was all I could come up with.

"Changing the lock is usually a good start," she advised me, looking back up the stairs while swinging the outer door open. "Five-lever mortise is the minimum. The one you've got here isn't fit for a garden gate." She paused, eyeing me with what appeared to be genuine concern. "If you want some advice on improving your overall security I can get someone along to give your premises the once-over. Or there are a lot of private firms around if you watch out for the cowboys."

I considered before saying, "I'll discuss it with Ash—my partner."

"In the meantime I'd be grateful if you'd make a list of anything that's missing. If nothing's gone it might be because they were interrupted. You'll need a checklist in any case for insurance purposes, though you may be liable if your locks aren't up to scratch. You *are* insured, aren't you?"

"Nah," I said with a lightness I didn't really feel. "We got all our kit off the back of a lorry."

Jamilla had joined me at the top of the stairs.

"Any chance you'll catch them?" she asked Merrick with blatant doubt.

"Do you want the usual police bull or the honest odds?"

She had paused at the foot of the stairs, framed by the open doorway. When neither of us replied, she said, "It's extremely unlikely, unless we turn up prints we can reference or they've stolen something distinctive that comes to light if they try to fence it."

Again I had the feeling that she was directly addressing me, trying to prompt me into suggesting what they might have been after. I was still too stunned and angry to think of anything.

"Is it all right if we start clearing up?" Jamilla asked.

"Of course. I'll see you later."

And then she was gone.

Jamilla and I went back inside. She took off her jacket and set her bag down just inside the door.

"We'll sort out your area first," I told her. "You're the presentable face of the business."

This was sincere but also another less-than-subtle attempt to ensure that she remained sweet on the idea of working for us. She gave me a knowing look.

"My granddad has a corner shop in Brockley," she announced. "Just before Christmas someone delivered a present. Chucked it in through the door after it got dark. A Johnny Walker bottle filled with petrol and stuffed with a lighted rag. He's slow on his feet these days, my granddad, and I only just got him out of there before the place filled up with smoke. It had landed on a bag of sawdust. You know, for rabbits. There were boxes of firelighters on the shelf above."

"Bloody hell, Jamilla."

"I put it out by pouring bottles of Tizer over it," she went on, laughing.

"Do you know who did it?"

"Oh yes, a bloke that lives just up the road. He claims my granddad overcharged him for a loaf of bread. It took us all night to clear up and it still smells of smoke."

"Did you press charges?"

"It would have been more trouble than it was worth. Why are you scratching your hand?"

She hadn't been looking directly at me, but she had noticed.

"I grabbed your cactus. I thought I could use it as a weapon."

She took hold of my wrist and inspected my inflamed palm. Several tiny spines were still embedded in it.

"Stay right where you are," she instructed me, reaching for her bag.

*

Jamilla had just tweezered out of the last of the spines and was swabbing my palm with witch hazel when we heard footsteps outside.

"Hell's bells!" said a familiar voice in accented English. "What upon earth has been going down here, Nicholas?"

Nigel stood in the doorway. Beside him was a squat man who could easily have been a reincarnation of Doberman from *The Phil Silvers Show*. He looked as if he was being flattened by the huge roll of carpet he had just hauled up the stairs. Nigel barked something at him in what might have been Ossetian and he shrank from sight.

Nigel picked his way into the office, taking everything in with a series of rapid glances. He was wearing the same slate-blue coveralls as the Doberman clone, though it was hard to picture him crouching on the stairs, actually helping to lay the carpet.

"They got in some time before seven this morning," I told him. "The police have already been and gone. It doesn't look like anything was actually stolen."

Nigel absorbed this but his eyes were still active and I had a feeling that his ears were also pricked. He waggled friendly fingers in Jamilla's direction. She had gone over to her desk and was already hauling it upright. She gave him a strained smile.

Nigel briefly inspected the cylinder lock on our internal door. There was no sign of damage. He then went into the open-plan area and did a painstaking tour, ignoring any debris under his feet. I could tell that he was thinking furiously though his face didn't show it. Eventually he worked his way back to me just as his henchman appeared in the doorway again. There was another exchange in animated Slavic, Nigel plainly irritated, before the man retreated out of sight again.

"Do you have enemies, Nicholas?" Nigel asked me.

"What?"

"They messed this place up good an' proper but that was only show."

"What do you mean?"

"They came up the stairs."

It took a moment before I realized that this was a query rather than a statement. I nodded. "The lock on the outside door made it an easy option. Nice if you could get us a new one. Something decent, if you can manage it."

Nigel didn't so much as blink. "The locks were not forced. Slipped."

He'd obviously had his man check. "Maybe they used a credit card. If we could find it, we could use it to buy new ones."

I couldn't help the sarcasm. Even though I knew it wasn't in my interest to antagonize Nigel, I needed someone to blame for the mess.

Nigel suddenly started nodding, as if a hinge had gone in his neck. Behind me Jamilla whispered a satisfied "Yes!" as her laptop screen successfully lit up.

"You want I ask around?" Nigel said.

I considered this proposition. It was entirely possible that Nigel had strong links with the local criminal fraternity. It was entirely possible he *was* the local criminal fraternity.

"We don't want any trouble," I told him. "I've promised the police my full cooperation."

I hadn't actually done anything of the sort, of course, but I wanted to deter him from taking out any summary justice on our behalf.

He grinned, tapping a finger against the side of his nose in a knowing "We're-all-men-of-the-world" way. "I see what I can do."

"And the lock? We need a five-lever."

"I will sort it. I look after all my tenants."

Before I knew it, he was gone, pulling the door shut behind him.

The telephone was ringing. I told Jamilla not to answer unless it was Ashad. It wasn't, so I rang him myself. When he didn't pick up, I left a curt message telling him to come in as soon as possible.

I spent the next fifteen minutes helping Jamilla sort out her office, then went to fetch the asthmatic vacuum cleaner from the little cupboard on the landing. Nigel and his handyman were already gone, the carpet roll left lying down one side of the stairs. Doubtless the possibility of the police returning had hastened them on their way.

*

By the time Ashad arrived, Jamilla and I had restored most of the office to its former glory; or rather, in Jamilla's case, done plenty of actual de-cluttering and repositioning of equipment into more practical arrangements, tucking away cabling and stacking stuff on shelves that should never have been left on the floor in the first place. I had told her to leave my work space for me to sort out later on the basis that I would never be able to find anything if it wasn't in its usual unruly arrangement.

Ashad had phoned before he set off and I had told him the worst. He came through the door breathing hard, his cargoes half hidden by a baggy khaki T-shirt with a cluster of dingy-looking pink clouds in the middle of it. On seeing the relative calm and tidiness that now prevailed he came to an abrupt halt.

"Everything's fine," I told him. "We're on top of the situation."

This was some distance from the truth, but I didn't want him launching into one of his tirades about exploitative landlords or the fact that the police were too busy harassing innocent youths in hoodies to crack down on the real criminals.

"They don't seem to have taken anything," I told him. "And nothing's been damaged apart from some videos and box files that got trodden on. We were lucky."

Ashad let his breathing subside.

"Go through it again for me," he said with an eerie calm.

I gave him an even more detailed account of events than I'd managed on the phone, mentioning everything from Merrick watching *Some Like It Hot* in the viewing theatre to Nigel showing up unexpectedly with the carpet roll. Ashad took it all in but didn't say anything. I didn't like it when he was like this. I could almost see the thunderclouds massing behind his eyes.

The one thing I deliberately didn't tell him was that I had also rung Merrick to let her know Ash was coming in. Sooner or later he was going to have to speak to the police, but she wasn't likely to find him at his most amenable.

"So someone was probably searching for something," he said finally.

"Well, we can't be sure. But it doesn't look as if they were after our hardware."

"We both know the projects they'd have been interested in, Nick. Have you checked any of the files?"

"They?" I said.

"The spooks. And we'll need to get the office swept for bugs."

I sighed. It was predictable. While I was prepared to concede that we might not be dealing with a run-of-the-mill burglary, I didn't believe it was exactly Watergate either.

I said, "If they were government agents, then I'd like to think they'd be professional enough not to chuck our stuff all over the floor."

"You should have seen it, Uncle Ashad," Jamilla chipped in. "It was a right mess."

"They would if they were in a hurry," Ashad insisted. "Or wanted us to think it was someone else."

"We're just film makers, Ash," I reminded him. "We're not the local branch of Anarchists R Us."

Ashad swept a hand through his unruly hair. "You don't get it, do you?" Now he was angry, and his anger was directed at me. "We make stuff all the time that questions what the authorities are up to. Look what we're working on at the moment, the Muvart stuff—"

"The BBC's OK with it," I pointed out.

He wasn't listening. "Look at our iconoclastic approach to it all. Add to that the fact that I'm a British Asian with a track record in left-wing agitation."

I had heard these arguments before. It wasn't so much that I couldn't accept that there might be a branch of the security services keeping a weather eye on us: it was more that I couldn't see any reason for them to destructively interfere in our affairs.

The outside doorbell buzzed. Jamilla went to answer it.

"You may be right," I said to Ash, "but I think there are more plausible explanations than MI5 wanting to put some bugs in our telephones because we're doing a few programmes they don't like the idea of."

"Answer me this, then. Why send a Detective Inspector to a burglary scene? It isn't worth their time. She was here looking for something herself or planting something."

It was true I hadn't considered the notion that Merrick was too senior to attend a burglary scene, but she had struck me as a straightforward copper and had in any case hinted that it was of more than routine interest. Still, maybe Ash had a point. Only I wasn't buying into the spooks and bugs idea.

"Get real, Nick," he urged me. "You can't trust any of them."

Footsteps on the stairs. Jamilla saying hello in a mildly guarded way.

"You'll be able to judge for yourself," I told Ashad. "I think she's just come back to see us."

*

Seated in one of our high-backed chairs, Merrick crossed her bell-bottomed legs, flashing a pair of black Doc Martens.

"So," she said to Ashad, "if nothing appears to be missing, why do you think you were raided, sir?"

Up to now Ashad had been on his best behaviour. He was too agitated to sit down but was perched on the corner of his desk.

"You tell me," he said. "They're your people."

"My people?" Merrick gave a puzzled smile. "What exactly do you mean by that, Mr Husseyin?"

"Forget it."

"No, really, I'd be interested to know. In my experience when people use phrases like 'your people' they're usually making some sort of sweeping statement about a particular group, wouldn't you agree?"

Ashad opened and closed his mouth. He did have as much reason as anyone to agree with her. He glanced at me, and I gave him a warning glare. The blobs on his T-shirt weren't clouds. They were brains. There appeared to be small objects embedded in them.

"If nothing was nicked," he muttered, "they obviously had another reason for coming here."

"Indeed," Merrick agreed. "The question is, have you any idea what?"

She was addressing both of us. I shook my head, said, "Maybe it's a rival company eager to discover the secrets of our amazing success."

Merrick didn't dignify this nonsense with a comment.

"Come on, Inspector," Ashad urged her, "tell us what *you* think."

She was unruffled by his surly tone. "Let's assume, just for now, that it wasn't a random act, that whoever broke in threw everything around the place because they were frantically looking for something."

"I don't think so," Ashad said.

"No? Do you have a better theory?"

Her Home Counties accent was of the more attractive variety. The tones rolled over you, swaddling you in their rounded vowels and crisp consonants. I could imagine her reading the Shipping

Forecast, enunciating the familiar litany with reassuring aural authority.

"You know why they were here," Ashad said.

Merrick's frown conveyed polite incredulity. "Do you have information about the perpetrators?"

"Not exactly. But I know they have information about me."

Oh, oh, I thought. Here we go.

"I'm still not following you," said Merrick.

Her calmness and what I can only describe as her ease of presence was clearly having an unsettling effect on Ashad. He seemed unable to work himself up into his usual pitch of outrage.

At this point Jamilla appeared with a tray with fresh coffees for the three of us.

"Do you need me?" she asked Merrick. "I've got loads to do."

Merrick accepted a coffee. "No, that's fine. Thanks."

Ashad took his mug and gulped down a mouthful. As soon as Jamilla was out of earshot, he said to Merrick: "Why are you here? Two visits from a DI for a burglary? Not exactly routine, is it? Let's not play games, Inspector. Maybe it wasn't your people—"

"There you go again. By 'my people', do you mean the police? Are you saying your office was turned over by us?"

Ashad made to say something, then shrugged. "There are plenty of other people who will have been taking an interest in what this company does."

"Other people?"

"Authorities. Covert governmental agencies. Whatever."

"I see. And what exactly is it your company does? Nothing illegal, I trust."

"There's the thing, Inspector. Nothing that's illegal according to the statute book. But the kind of programmes and features we make don't exactly take a charitable view of how the ruling elite behaves."

"Really? Might be the sort of thing I'd enjoy myself. You can't have a properly free society unless you've got people around who are prepared to lift up stones and see what's wriggling underneath."

Ashad went very still.

"And there's nothing illegal about that either, as far as I'm aware."

Ashad shook his head. Or it might have been a sideways nod. "There are organisations working for the state that make their own decisions about what is or isn't acceptable according to their view of things. We're subversives if we do something they don't like, never mind that it isn't technically a crime."

"And our citizens are under more CCTV surveillance than any other nation in the world."

Again Ashad was taken aback. "That's true," he agreed.

"Even if it is, it doesn't follow that I'm out to get you, Mr Husseyin."

She sipped her coffee, set it aside, her gaze on Ashad all the while. "I'm assuming you've had run-ins with other authorities in the past."

"You could say that."

"I'm not interested in any of that. I'm particularly not interested in playing up to any preconceptions you might have about how police officers go about their business, however well-founded they might be. Now don't get me wrong. I know there have been problems with the Met in the past. And we're still not free of prejudice and short-sightedness. I know how difficult it can be dealing with authority when you're a person of an Asian background."

"And you're not like that."

"That's for you to judge. But I haven't come here to snoop, Mr Husseyin, or to interfere with your work. Tell me what you're doing that you think might be attracting unwanted attention and I'll make some discreet inquiries."

Ashad was clearly torn between suspicion and the hope that she might actually be sincere. But he couldn't permit himself to give her the benefit of the doubt.

"All right," Merrick said. "Perhaps you have good reason to be cautious. I'm going to tell you why I'm really here and what I think might have actually happened. All I ask in exchange is that you don't let it go any further."

Neither of us had been expecting this. Ashad showed no obvious reaction. He was still more subdued than I had anticipated. As if he was slightly in awe of her.

"OK?" Merrick prompted.

"OK," I said for both of us.

My adrenalin rush was long gone, and I could feel my headache returning. It could have been due to the motif on Ashad's T-shirt. The pinkish-grey brains had funny-looking purple screws and bilious orange hoop-ended arrows sticking out of them. They were not a pleasing sight to a man in my condition.

"Right," Merrick said, leaning forward in her seat. "There's a man who was once a senior figure in the US administration. He remains influential in Washington, with a Congressman son who's being touted as a possible future presidential candidate. When he was young in the 1950s he apparently made a living for a while writing sensational stories. Sleazy crime and horror stories, that sort of thing." Her tone suggested that she herself didn't consider this particularly disreputable. "He did it under pen-names before giving it up for a career in politics. Nothing ever emerged about his past when he was in the public eye, but now, with his son gaining prominence, someone has got word of these old skeletons in his closet. He's worried that it could undermine his son's career."

"Who are we talking about here?" Ashad immediately wanted to know.

"That I can't tell you."

"Can't or won't?"

"Won't," Merrick said bluntly. "Given the kind of programmes you tell me you like to make, it would be stupid of me, wouldn't it? As it is, I'll tell you honestly that I've changed some of the facts to throw you off the scent."

"So you're lying," Ash said bluntly.

She shook her head. "The gist of it is what's important. I'm told there were a few gossipy references to his writing past on the internet, and he was concerned that something more might get out. Maybe he wrote something graphic and offensive, I genuinely don't know. Apparently, though, it was enough for him to do a

'Who will rid me of this turbulent priest?' bit and somebody took him at his word."

Merrick paused to gauge our reaction so far.

"So what has this got to do with us being burgled?" asked Ashad.

"Apparently someone else—we don't know who—began looking for physical evidence, perhaps in the hope of preference or a favour or maybe even blackmail. There's been a series of break-ins, here and in America, aimed at people and institutions that might have had copies of the stories. Specialist book stores and libraries, literary archives, collectors and the like."

Merrick was now looking at me. I began to have a bad feeling.

"It might be why you were raided, given that there's no more obvious reason for the break-in. We liaise with the US authorities on this sort of thing. They've been monitoring the situation."

I strenuously refrained from looking at Ashad. He said, "Monitoring?"

"Checking internet traffic around certain keywords, that sort of thing. I doubt that you've even heard of any of the magazines this writer appeared in."

She unfolded a sheet of paper from her pocket and handed it over to us. There was a list of implausibly alliterative titles, most of which hinted at fairly downmarket contents. *Awesome Adventures* was among them.

I thought I'd been prepared but I hadn't *really* been expecting it.

"Or maybe I'm wrong," said Merrick, still giving me the eye. "Do any of these ring a bell with you?"

For some reason I wasn't quite ready to make what seemed a very innocuous admission. The background information fitted in with what had happened at Arthur Townsend's flat: all the hallmarks of an attempted burglary. But Claire Whitney and Cyrus Hammond had both left me with the impression that there was no interest in Parrish's stories, and this had largely been backed up by Arthur. And Merrick herself had admitted she'd changed a few facts to muddy the waters. Also, there would be plenty of other authors in all these magazines, authors who probably used various pen names in different publications. Merrick's man could be any of them.

I shook my head as casually as I could. "Sorry, Inspector, I'm not a fan of pulp fiction. Except the movie, of course."

Merrick didn't look convinced. "Are you sure that you don't recognize any of them?"

I pretended to study the list again, hoping that the self-consciousness I felt wasn't showing on my face.

"What name was this writer using?" Ashad asked.

Merrick smiled. "Maybe he wasn't a writer. Maybe he was an editor. Or an artist. Or someone selling dodgy merchandise through the adverts. I've honestly told you I haven't been entirely honest about the details. But believe this: someone wants to get hold of these magazines." She effortlessly lifted the piece of paper out of my hands. "And they're pretty ruthless in trying to acquire them." She folded the paper into quarters and pocketed it before standing up. "If you do think of anything, I'd be really grateful if you'd give me a call."

"You're going?" Ashad said.

"Can't sit around chatting all morning," she replied. "Though frankly I'd much rather be here than dealing with the mountain of paperwork that's on my desk. Excellent band, by the way."

She was indicating the design on Ashad's T-shirt. He just gaped at her. "You've heard of them?"

"Boltzmann's Brains? I saw them playing the other night at the Electric Ballroom."

"You're kidding."

"Naturally I was under cover. Looking to arrest anyone whose haircut I didn't like. Do let me know if you come up with anything missing, won't you?"

And she swept out of the room and down the stairs before either I or the dumbfounded Ashad could say anything further.

*

"Boltzmann's Brains?" I said to Ashad when I heard the downstairs door shut.

"They're a band."

"I gathered that." I could see now that the objects sticking out of the brains were bolts and male symbols. A not-so-subtle visual pun. Ashad was something of an aficionado of what he called cutting-edge music and often spent mid-week evenings watching obscure bands in venues all over London.

"She's quite a character," he remarked.

Was that admiration I could hear in his tone? Something made me hesitate to tease him about it.

"So," I said instead, "what do you think?"

He took a deep breath. "She seemed pretty down-to-earth. Though you never can tell."

"You believed her?" I was in the odd position of feeling more suspicious than him.

"Not the details. She told us she was faking bits, didn't she? But something's obviously going on that they want to keep a lid on."

"Don't you think it's a coincidence that I acquired those old magazines only yesterday? They're from the 1950s."

"No. Exactly the opposite. You've been trawling the internet looking up this guy Parrish and his magazines, and that sort of thing is easy to trace if you're monitoring a situation and looking for keywords. Or maybe the collector you saw mentioned your interest to someone, or any of those people you met at the film festival. The man in question's got to be Parrish, hasn't he?"

He was already over at his PC and working the keyboard.

I went to my own desk. The central drawer hung open, empty. Jamilla had piled everything that had ended up on the floor on it. I frantically searched the piles. Then went through them again. I called Jamilla, asking her if she had put everything back on the desk. Now wearing garden gloves, she was in the middle of re-potting her cactus. She assured me she had.

I checked the surrounding shelves, my filing cabinet, the desk drawer cavities and all other nooks and crannies. Nothing.

"There's no one in the US Congress or Senate by the name of Parrish," Ashad announced. He closed the window on his screen and got up. "I'm going out."

"Out?" I managed to say. "Where?"

"I need to pick up something from Ozzie."

Ozzie Hogg was a friend of ours who ran an electrical store on Tottenham Court Road.

"Pick up what?" I asked distractedly.

"Something that might be useful around here." He eyed me. "What is it?"

"Nothing," I said.

"Your face says otherwise."

I shook my head. "It's been a pretty fraught morning, that's all."

I didn't want to discuss it with him. I needed time to think.

Both the photocopies of the Parrish stories and the magazines themselves were gone.

SIX

"So what's his name?" I asked Ashad as the bus wove its twisty way through Knightsbridge and South Kensington.

"Who?"

"The guy at the Foreign Office. Your informant."

"Wally."

"Wally?"

"That's what I call him, anyway."

"Are you telling me that you don't know his real name?" I said. "Is it his *code name*?"

"Don't be bloody daft."

"Have you actually met him before? Or is he just the voice of the oracle down a phone line?"

Ashad sighed. "Give it a rest, Nick. He's a decent bloke."

We were sitting on the upstairs front seat of the double decker. It had been Ashad's idea to take the bus, just for a change. I had to admit I was rather enjoying the elevated view as we trundled unimpeded past congested Sunday afternoon traffic. I was trying to find small consolations in things after the burglary and the loss of Leo Parrish's stories.

Arthur was going to be furious with me. Three days had passed since the burglary, and I still hadn't phoned to tell him the bad news. Instead I had tried ringing Claire Whitney again, but this time hadn't even got the answer service, just a dead line. So I had dug out Cyrus Hammond's number and called Filmscope. It was answered by a prissy male secretary who announced that Mr Hammond wasn't currently available but that he would be happy to take my number and have him ring me back at his earliest convenience. Which might easily mean never.

I also hadn't confessed to Ashad that the stories were gone. We were busy with day-to-day stuff, not least ensuring that all our other projects remained on track. Ashad and Valerie were focusing on the Muvart documentary, and I had been working with a team of computer animators on the pilot of *Hail, Mary*, a comedy about a TV weather forecaster who discovers that she can actually control the weather. I welcomed the distraction, but in the meantime I was trying to make sense of all the secretiveness that hung like mist around Leo Parrish.

The idea that Parrish might actually now be a venerable power broker in Washington DC was hard to square with the vigour and invention of his stories. The Parrish of the magazines had a pretty wild imagination: not a quality you associate with the political world. What if he had actually once been not a Senator or Congressman but the director of some outré secret agency? Or even the U.S. equivalent of Q in the James Bond movies, in charge of a wacky inventions department where he could give his creativity free rein? In other words, a maverick working within the system, rather than some grey Capitol Hill eminence. By admitting that she hadn't told us the whole truth, DI Merrick had made the possibilities so numerous that it was really futile to speculate. But if Parrish *was* some high-ranking politico who didn't want anyone getting access to his old stories, then Xponential was never going to acquire the film rights to any of his stuff, no matter how cinematic. Which wasn't an outcome I was ready to concede. What I needed was more information about Parrish the writer. And more examples of his work.

At each stop the bus steadily filled up. Normally we tried not to do any business on weekends but Ashad had persuaded me that I should accompany him to the meeting with his contact at the Foreign Office in the hope of finding out more about the current situation in Khanistan and the elusiveness of Muvart's cousin.

I didn't have anything else on that weekend. The fitful relationship I'd recently rekindled with an old university girlfriend had finally spluttered out over the phone the previous evening when both of us admitted that our hearts weren't really in it. Never go back. Or at least don't go back and expect to find the furniture still in the same place. It was a relief to both of us finally to call it quits, but at the moment I was feeling as if both my professional and personal life had stalled.

"This guy Wally," I said to Ashad, "how do you know him?"

"We play squash together sometimes."

"Squash? You play squash?" I would never have imagined it, having always thought of Ashad as the quintessential couch potato. The only sport for which he'd ever expressed enthusiasm was cricket.

"There's a few of us who get together once a month for a knock around. I don't know him that well."

I felt as if I was seeing him afresh. "Are you any good?"

"I'm all right."

"You never told me."

"You never asked."

He said this without rancour. Like me, he was in a slightly morose mood, preoccupied with the burglary and unsettled by Merrick's revelations. Though he had plainly been impressed by her personal qualities, he wasn't so enamoured when she'd mentioned "liaising with the US authorities". Still, I preferred him sullen rather than launching into a rant about American foreign policy and the moral bankruptcy of successive administrations on both sides of the Atlantic.

The bus was now full, mostly with young men in blue jeans and white football shirts.

"So what's in it for him?" I asked. Wally would have signed the Official Secrets Act and was probably already in breach of it.

Ashad thought about this. "You'll have to ask him yourself. It's probably a simple sense of right and wrong." He lurched up from his seat as the bell pinged. "This is our stop."

We were at Putney Bridge station. Everyone on board piled out alongside us.

The name Wally had conjured in my mind a disgruntled middle-aged guy who had been passed over for promotion and now serviced his grievance by dishing dirt to troublemakers like Ashad and me. As a result I was surprised when Ashad led me over to a trim Asian man in his thirties, wearing grey trousers and a mustard-coloured jacket.

"Nick," Ashad said to me, "this is Walid."

Automatically I offered my hand. Walid took it, though not without a fractional hesitation, as if he would have preferred to get the measure of me before we made actual physical contact.

At that instant my phone ding-donged like a doorbell. What was going on with the ring tone? Ashad laughed. I moved away, leaving him and Walid to exchange greetings.

"Mr Randall," said a voice at the other end of the line.

It was a second or two before I recognized Cyrus Hammond's drawl.

"I understand you were wanting to speak to me."

There was a slightly guarded tone in his voice, as when we had first spoken in the flesh; though perhaps it was his usual manner.

"Thanks for calling back," I said, as Ashad and Walid marched off down the road, beckoning to me to follow.

"My apologies for ringing on a Sunday," he said, "but you weren't exactly high on my priority list. What is it I can do for you?"

This wasn't particularly promising.

"I was hoping you might be able to put me in touch with Claire Whitney."

I had to hurry along to avoid losing sight of Ashad and Walid among the crowd going in the same direction as us.

"Didn't you exchange contact details when you met?" Hammond was asking me.

"We did. Or at least she got in touch with me later. We arranged to meet up at the house of a person who had copies of Leo Parrish's stories. You remember telling me about Parrish?"

"I remember."

There was still that note of reserve in his voice. "For some reason," I said, "she didn't show and I couldn't contact her on the telephone number she gave me."

There was a pause, which I used to dart across the road after Ashad.

"I wouldn't bother her if it wasn't a bit of an emergency," I told him. "The thing is, I managed to get my hands on copies of some magazines containing Parrish's stories. I really liked them. You're right, he deserves to be better known. I'm still hoping that I can find something of his that's really filmable."

"You didn't see anything in the ones you've already got?"

I took a deep breath and made an instant decision to come clean with him.

"That's my problem. I haven't got them anymore. Last night our office was burgled. They were stolen."

There was a long silence at the other end. We were heading through a leafy park with the rest of the crowd. Fortunately Walid's mustard jacket coupled with Ashad's height made both of them easy to spot.

"That's rather unfortunate," Hammond was saying in a dubious tone.

"It's the honest truth," I assured him. "We've got no idea who did it. They took the original magazines and the photocopies I made. I borrowed them from a collector and he's not likely to want anything more to do with me when he finds out they're gone. I was hoping that Claire might be able to put me in touch with someone else who has copies of Parrish's work."

There was another protracted silence. I resisted the urge to say anything further, to apologize or explain myself in any more detail. I had a feeling it wouldn't wash with Hammond. He was either going to help me, or I could forget it.

"Have you got a pen?" he said at last.

I hastily fumbled one out of my inside pocket.

"I can give you her office address. She did some design work for the Foundation a while back."

"Great," I said, tucking the phone between my cheek and hunched-up shoulder, praying that no one would bump into me.

"Total Graffix," Hammond announced. "That's two words."

He spelled out the second of them. I scribbled it down on the back of my hand.

"They're in Mortimer Street."

"Central London?"

"Of course."

"Is there a phone number?"

"It's in the Yellow Pages. Good luck."

And he rang off.

I didn't have time to do anything further because Ashad was beckoning me on. Eventually we reached Craven Cottage, home of Fulham football club. The crowd was converging on the turnstiles.

It turned out that Walid was a season-ticket holder. Not only that, but he had tickets for his two teenage cousins, whom he regularly brought to matches but who were presently visiting relatives in Pakistan. Ashad and I offered money. Walid wouldn't have any of it.

It was some years since I had last been to a football match. I was surprised to see that Ashad looked positively cheery, given that he normally disdained football and could deliver a twenty-minute diatribe on the iniquities of financially bloated clubs with inflated ticket prices who constantly changed their strips and flogged grossly overpriced merchandise to minors.

We climbed halfway up one of the stands. The stadium was packed: it was the second game of the season, the visitors none other than the mighty Manchester United, whose fans were already chanting in the packed stand opposite us. On the pitch two paunchy men in white shirts were kicking giant-size footballs around a line of toothsome young women in skimpy outfits.

We took our seats. Walid sat primly, his palms flat on his knees, a squat black umbrella on his lap. Although he wasn't unfriendly, there was something very proper and self-contained about him. Ashad sat between us, as sprawling as Walid was demure.

"The object of the game," I said to him, "is to kick the ball through those sticks with nets on them."

"Ho ho," he replied. "One day I'll grill you about the lbw rule." He leaned closer. "Muvart's cousin's missing."

"What?"

"He didn't show because he's vanished. They think he might have been kidnapped. Or worse."

"Worse?" It was obvious what he meant. "They?"

"Presumably the spooks here have been keeping an eye on him, but Muvart probably has his own men in London, too. He doesn't like defectors, especially when they're relatives."

"They snatched him?"

"That's one possibility."

I thought about this. I wondered if we were in some way to blame.

"Did they know he was going to talk to us?"

"Walid doesn't seem to think so. That part of it is probably just a coincidence."

"Do the police or the intelligence services have any leads?"

Ashad gave a humourless laugh. "They may have done it. That's the other possibility."

I eyed him. "This is Walid's theory? Not yours?"

Ashad nodded. "It's fifty-fifty either way. He thinks it's unlikely he'll show up. Anywhere, ever again."

I didn't get this at all. "But why? Why would MI6 or whoever take him?"

"We haven't got to that part yet."

The stadium was homely and intimate in its way, the stands modest in size and affording glimpses of the Thames. The teams had no sooner trotted out than Ashad excused himself to search for something to eat. Walid turned to me for the first time and said, "Are you a football fan, Nick?"

I was very much an armchair supporter with no particular loyalties, but Walid didn't seem to mind. Soon we were exchanging views on the recent performances of the England football team, always a fruitful source of interminable debate. I did my usual trick of pretending to have informed opinions by spouting a mishmash of TV punditry and newspaper analysis. Which is what most men do when they talk football.

Not that Walid seemed to mind. I suspected he had a deep and subtle appreciation of the game and was happy to talk it through with lesser mortals like myself.

The game had already kicked off before Ashad returned with a hot dog so slathered with ketchup and mustard it looked as if a suppurating pustule had burst over it. Listening in, he interrupted us by stating that the Indian subcontinent had never produced decent football teams because its peoples preferred sports that involved hand-eye coordination: cricket, hockey, badminton, that sort of thing. Walid disputed this, and the two of them fell into a good-natured but quite impassioned argument which I decided it would be prudent to keep out of.

Ten minutes in, United scored. The home crowd reacted with mute resignation, as if it had been inevitable. While the game progressed I did my best to keep track of Ashad and Walid's conversation. Ashad had produced a notebook and was jotting things down.

According to Walid, western governments, and in particular the US and UK, had been taking the threats from President Muvart very seriously indeed for many months, to the extent that some Khanistani citizens in the west with suspected links to Muvart's regime had already been plucked covertly from their homes or off the street by US agents and deposited in various secret locations throughout Europe. At least one of these black sites was definitely in the UK, Walid asserted in a tone of righteous disgust.

"I gather you think Muvart's cousin might have been taken by the security services," I interjected.

Walid looked uncomfortable at having to discuss the matter directly with me.

"It's not a possibility that can be discounted," he said. "There's a suggestion that British and American intelligence agencies are especially keen to get their hands on close relatives of President Muvart."

"A suggestion?"

"Strong indications from people who have regular contact with these agencies or are in fact attached to them in some capacity. I have no information on their identities."

How much of this was hearsay? How much had documentary support? When I asked, Walid replied that very little, if anything, was likely to have been written down. It was up to us to do the digging that would uncover the evidence.

"I thought they'd already interviewed Muvart's cousin at length when he first arrived in the UK," I said.

Walid conceded this. "We believe that it's not further intelligence they require from him."

"We?"

"Those of us who are alarmed by our government's policies."

He worked for the government, and yet he was talking as if he wasn't a part of it. I suppose that technically, as a civil servant, he wasn't, but somehow I expected more loyalty from Foreign Office officials. A more diplomatic take on things.

"Then what *do* they want from him?" I asked.

This time Walid checked to ensure that no one around us was listening.

"Have you ever heard of Halstow Island?" he asked.

Neither of us had.

"Look it up. I believe it's a muddy lump of land in the Thames estuary, or at least it was until they built the Containment Centre. Unofficially, that is. Nothing has ever been made public. It was supposed to be a holding place for illegal immigrants. We believe it's actually become a joint CIA-MI5 base for what they term SPDs. Special Protocols Detainees."

Here we were, firmly in the land of Newspeak. Modern governments were masters of it: extraordinary rendition, collateral damage, friendly fire. Antiseptic verbiage that masked a toxic reality.

"Political prisoners?" Ashad asked, scrawling everything down in his own unique version of shorthand. He claimed he had developed it as a student to take notes during activist meetings but I suspected it was simply fast scribble that only he could decipher—and then not always.

"Possibly," Walid replied. "But more than that. The suggestion is that it's to do with experimental interrogation procedures of some sort. But that wouldn't explain the hints we've been receiving that the majority of detainees are ethnic Khanistanis."

The continual use of "we" made me wonder if Walid belonged to a secret group himself, an enclave within an enclave.

I decided it was time for a toilet break before the half-time rush. On my way I used my phone to locate the number for Total Graffix. I called it. True, it was late on a Sunday afternoon, but you never knew. Unsurprisingly, the phone rang and rang before clicking to the answer service. I didn't bother leaving a message. There was always tomorrow.

As I stood at the stall, I became conscious that someone was at my shoulder. And a little too close for comfort, especially since he didn't actually appear to be relieving himself. Was I being cottaged? Without looking directly at him, I was able to make out that he was wearing an off-white overcoat and a floppy black hat. Not the typical attire of your average football fan, though possibly an attempt to blend in by aping the Fulham colours. Was he going to open his overcoat and show me something I definitely had no desire to see?

Just as I was steeling myself to look at him face-on, from the other side a familiar voice said, "What do you think?"

It was Ashad, who began copiously relieving himself beside me. The other man sidled away and went out.

"I think," I started, then made a swift decision not to say anything to Ashad about my brief and ambiguous encounter. "I think you didn't manage to get all the hot dog into your mouth."

He zipped up and glanced at himself in the mirror before quickly splashing water on his face to get rid of the ketchup and mustard.

"We have to follow this up," he insisted.

I thought about it. "Can you trust him? I don't mean that he's lying to us. But I can't quite see what his agenda is."

"Transparent government," Ashad said bluntly. "We elect them, so they're accountable to us. There's also a moral dimension. Wally's a religious man. He just thinks a lot of this is wrong."

By religious, I assumed Ashad meant he was a practising Muslim. Why had he told me this? Was it relevant?

"You two ever argue at all?" I asked. "About his beliefs? You know, opium of the masses and all that."

"We've agreed to differ," Ashad said. "As my grannie used to say, the measure of a man is what he does, not what he thinks."

"You never had a grannie. Your parents made you out of spit and sawdust."

"And a dash of vinegar." He dried his hands. "This is meaty stuff, Nick."

"We still need better evidence than hearsay."

He flashed a little black USB stick which he had clipped to the pendant chain around his neck. A gift from Walid. It contained encrypted files which Walid claimed contained all sorts of hints and suggestions that Special Protocols Detainees were being held at a coastal or island site and that the bulk of them were of Khanistani origin.

Ashad looked highly satisfied. He loved it when his worst suspicions about the authorities were given credence.

Walid spent most of half-time on his phone telling one of his cousins about the state of play, presumably using a package awash with free international minutes.

About ten minutes into the second half there was a corner kick and Fulham equalized. Walid leapt up, shaking his umbrella emphatically but not actually whooping with delight. Here was a man who was used to containing his emotions.

Ashad and I were both thirsty, and I volunteered to get some soft drinks. There was a queue at the bar and I took my place in line.

I carry my rucksack around on my back when it's not fully loaded without thinking about it. I must have been more alert than usual because as I moved forward I felt a little tug on it. I thought I had caught it on something, but as I reached around to free it I grabbed a hand leaving one of the pockets. Pivoting, I saw that it was the guy in the chalky overcoat and black droopy hat. A pick-pocket, not a gay predator.

I yelled out as he wrenched his hand free. He was my age, with a wedge-shaped jaw and beady eyes. I made to grab him, but he pushed me hard and scampered past the queue, going down the nearest stairway. I was about to surge after him when someone grabbed me.

It was Ashad.

"What the hell was that about?" he asked me as some of the men in the queue offered me encouragement by imitating police car sirens and the theme from *Jaws*.

"Bastard was trying to pick my pocket."

I was still eager to hunt him down, but Ashad held me back.

"You'd never find him in this crowd."

"He's probably the only guy in a white coat and black hat."

"If he's a professional he'll whip them off as soon as he can and blend in."

I could see his point, though I was still fuming.

"Anything missing?"

I checked all my pockets, just in case, but my wallet and mobile were inside my jacket, and there was only an empty water bottle and newspaper in the rucksack. Neither had been taken.

"How come you got here so fast?" I asked him.

"Wally saw someone going down the stairs after you and thought it was the same guy he'd clocked before. So we decided we'd come after you, just in case."

"He noticed?"

"He's learned to be careful and keep his eyes peeled. Haven't you, Walid?"

He looked around, but there was no sign of Walid.

Ashad grinned. "He's probably hot-footed it back to his seat. Not really the physical type, our Wally."

"This isn't funny, Ash."

"No," he agreed. "But at least he didn't get anything. We could report it, if you want."

Both of us knew it would be a waste of time. Some of the younger men in the queue were now keen to advise me on what I should have done, their suggestions ranging from head-butting to a swift knee between the legs and accompanied by vigorous pantomime demonstrations. I let Ashad lead me away and we climbed the steps back to our seats.

Walid's was empty.

We sat down and waited. When he didn't return after five minutes, Ashad phoned him. No answer. Ashad then scouted the bars and toilets while I sat warily alone, wondering if the pickpocket still had me in his sights. I kept telling myself that he had been thoroughly scared off but I was rattled nevertheless.

There was no sign of Walid anywhere. We left the game a quarter of an hour before the end, deftly managing to miss an eventful climax in which United scored, missed a penalty, and conceded an equalizing goal to Fulham in the very last minute.

*

On our way back to central London, Walid finally phoned. He had been worried about the fight in case the police got involved because he didn't want to be linked to Ash and me in an official report. That's why he had taken off. No, he had no idea who the guy was but had simply noticed that he was unusually dressed and furtive. He was apologetic about abandoning us but adamant that he couldn't do any more to help. We were welcome to use his information but he stressed that we couldn't credit it even to anonymous sources. His name was not to be mentioned in any capacity and he couldn't be a part of any subsequent investigation on our part. He had his family to think of. Two young daughters, an elder brother who worked in the diplomatic service. All very delicate. It was up to us now.

"We need to watch our backs," said Ash with a certain amount of relish after relaying the conversation to me. "Not just to protect Walid. This could be big. We don't want us to end up vanishing like Muvart's cousin, do we?"

"At least it would make it difficult for our creditors to find us."

He detected the gloominess in my tone and waited for me to explain.

Ashad was so prone to persecution mania I had deliberately delayed telling him until now. "Walid was right. The same guy did follow me earlier. He was standing next to me in the toilet before you came in. Loitering with intent, I suppose."

"I remember," Ashad said as if he had only just recalled it. "The chap in the hat."

"We're not talking about an ordinary pickpocket, are we? They're opportunistic. This guy had been sizing me up."

"I knew it!" Ashad said. "You think we're being followed?"

"Who knows? He might have been just a thug, but I'm increasingly getting the feeling that we're wading through shark-infested waters. Up to our gonads in it."

There was no one else on the bus when we got off at our stop, and no indication that any vehicle had been tailing us.

Ashad announced that he was going to pick up an extra part for the piece of kit that Ozzie Hogg had made for him. Ozzie lived on the premises and was almost certain to be in.

"Are you going to tell me what is it?" I asked. Yesterday he had returned from Ozzie's with something heavy in a cardboard box that he wouldn't show me.

"You can see for yourself soon enough."

I told him I would meet him at the office. We had both decided it might be prudent to go in and check that everything was all right.

When I got there, the outer door was open. It turned out to be Nigel, supervising two of his henchmen, who were laying carpet on the stairs. A chunky-looking new lock had already been fitted to the entrance door. Nigel, for whom Sunday was just another day of the week, thrust a bunch of keys at me and told me to pass them on to "the necessary workers".

"Good, yes?" he said with reference to the carpet, a bottle-green paisley affair that looked as if it had been nicked from a posh hotel. They had cut it down the middle and had loads to spare.

The air was heady with the reek of carpet adhesive. Doberman and another equally squat guy were gluing down the edges while a cassette player blared out demonstrative Slavic folk songs. Both men were singing along, probably delirious with solvent fumes. It looked as if they had almost finished.

Nigel, who was obviously in a good mood, put an arm around my shoulder and propelled me outside to a big dark van emphatically parked on the double-yellow lines. Two teenage girls were sitting in the front, both wearing short skirts and skimpy tops. They looked out at me like exhibits framed behind glass.

"That is Olga and Valentina," he told me. "They are sisters."

I gave them a wave but neither reacted. Sisters. I doubted it.

"I have been making queries," Nigel told me, opening the back doors to reveal an Aladdin's cave of domestic and commercial accoutrements, everything from washbasins and mirrors to industrial-sized tubs of coleslaw and liquid detergent.

"No one knows anything," he told me.

"About the break-in?"

"No one knows anything," he repeated, his head oscillating in the usual radar-scanner way, presumably to check for traffic wardens.

"This is bad news," he told me. "Either it is some stupid fuckers who don't know any better, or it comes from higher up."

"Higher up? What do you mean?"

"Old Bill. Or security services. You need to watch your back."

He reached into the van, rummaged behind a length of black marble work surface and produced a bulky Jiffy bag sealed with silver duct tape.

"For you," he said, thrusting it into my hands.

I could tell immediately what was inside: a hard, heavy, vaguely L-shaped metal object with lots of knobbly bits.

He must have seen my astonished expression.

"Don't worry," he said, laughing. "It is a replica. Only a replica. SR-1, used by FSB and FSO. Very good for putting the frighteners on, yes?"

I had no idea what to say. I had a feeling it wouldn't be prudent to refuse the gift.

"Away," Nigel said. "Put it away before some nosey parker sees."

I unzipped my rucksack and stuffed the package into it.

*

Nigel and his men were gone before Ashad got back. I let him in and gave him one of the new keys. He was carrying something in a small shoebox.

"Nice carpet," he remarked as we climbed the stairs. "Maybe we should change the name of this place to Charing Cross Mansions."

"They've not long finished," I told him. "So what's in the box?"

Ashad went straight to one of the shelves and lifted down the bigger box. He laid it on one of the tables and took out a rectangular metal unit that looked like a cross between an old-fashioned radio and a fan heater. It had two rows of retro lights and gauges and even a little grille that might have come from a scale model of a 1950s' American car. Exposed wires and blobs of solder gave it a very hand-made appearance.

I had a feeling I knew what it was, or what it was supposed to be. From the smaller box Ashad removed something that resembled the heating element of a kettle attached to a flex. He jacked this into the back of the unit.

"You've got to be kidding," I said.

"Ozzie calls it the Bug Buster," Ashad replied. He flourished the heating element bit. "This is the wand."

"Does it do magic?" I asked, laughing at my own joke. I was feeling a little heady myself with the vapours still drifting in from the stairwell. Earlier Doberman and his mate had practically waltzed out of there when they were finished.

Abruptly there was a high-pitched whine, loud enough to make my ear wax tingle. Ashad hastily adjusted the volume, but the noise didn't diminish much.

He looked at me. Swung the wand in my direction. The whine went up in volume again. Red lights were whirling around on a little clock-like display that reminded me of a school Geiger counter.

Ashad couldn't keep the "I told you so" look off his face. He hefted the box and carried it around our office space, sweeping the wand over everything. The further away he got from me, the quieter the noise became. As he approached me again it turned into a frantic screech. The red lights were twirling with mad abandon.

Ashad turned a dial, and the thing fell silent.

He jabbed a finger at me and mouthed: "You've been bugged," without actually saying the words. Then he put a finger to his lips and motioned to me not to say anything.

He fiddled with the dials and turned it on again. This time the noise had been reduced to a tolerable mosquito whine that increased in frequency as he swept the wand over me. He turned off the audio again.

I stood up, took a step away from my chair. My rucksack was draped over the back of it. As Ashad brought the wand close to it, the dial lights were no longer flashing but were constantly lit.

I was convinced it would be the package that Nigel had given me, but when Ashad turfed it out and held the wand against it, the continuous display actually faltered a little.

"What the hell is this?" he asked.

"Nigel just gave it me. For protection. I'm going to dump it."

Ashad set the package aside without comment. We kept ferreting around in the various pockets of the rucksack, lifting out the newspaper, bottle of water and keys I had been carrying.

In the end, it turned out there was something attached to the inside lining of one of the pockets. I heard a Velcro-like ripping as Ashad tore it free. He held it up to show me.

It was a small black patch not much bigger than a postage stamp. Beneath the glossy upper layer was a printed circuit with a couple of flat black beads on it.

"Bloody hell," I said. "The guy at Craven Cottage."

Ash put a finger to his lips again. Placing the patch on the table, he dragged me downstairs and into our little shower room. He turned on the basin tap full pelt. I had seen those movies too, but I wasn't about to scorn it.

"Do you think it's definitely a bug?" I asked in a quiet voice, knowing that he was no more of an expert than me but not quite able to believe it.

"Has to be. The guy had a hand inside it, didn't he?"

"I assumed he was after my wallet."

"You didn't recognize him?"

I shook my head.

"It must be spooks," Ashad said emphatically. "Beyond that, your guess is as good as mine. But whoever they are, they're worried about us. I don't know why they didn't bug *me* though. I'm the one they know about."

It would have been a badge of honour for him. I still hadn't told him about the missing magazines. And it wasn't the right time now.

"Do you think we should warn Walid?"

Ash mulled it over. "No. He'd just panic unnecessarily. Let's hope him being there was simply a coincidence. I think this is about the generality of what we're looking into about Muvart, not the specific stuff with Walid. We'd better not mention his name though, and be careful what we say around here in future."

"They might have heard his name when you answered his call. And when you gave me the gist of it."

Ashad's expression grew dark, then brightened a bit. "Wally, Walid. Not obvious, is it? We've just got to hope they don't figure out who he is." He thumped his fist against the cubicle wall. "The bastards. Is this a free country or not?"

"We should get Ozzie to check that it is actually a security services bug."

Ashad nodded. "We need to stop it working first. Ozzie told me what to do if we found anything."

He disappeared for a few moments and returned with a length of aluminium foil from the kitchen. He wrapped it round the bug, pressing it firmly into every crevice.

We tried the Bug Buster again. This time it stayed silent. No lights came on.

We did a further sweep of the whole place just to check, probing the wand into every nook and cranny we could think of. Then we took it downstairs and spent even longer checking the main office. The place looked like a war zone, but only in the usual sense of desks and work spaces having been abruptly abandoned at five o'clock the evening before. We had a pretty creative team but none of us was remotely tidy apart from Valerie, who as usual had left her work station looking immaculate.

We found nothing further, so Ashad decided it was time to check Walid's USB stick.

Walid had given Ash a password that allowed us to decrypt the files without difficulty. There were over two dozen of them, mostly snippets from police arrest reports, prison referrals, security service briefings and inter-departmental Home Office correspondence. With that peculiarly British jollity that often masks unpleasant facts, the holding site was variously referred to as Butlins-On-Sea or Muckrake Mansions, neither of which contradicted Walid's description of a muddy island, though there was no hint of its location. More formal references to an HSDC probably signified a High Security Detention Centre, though the acronym with its high-street bank connotations engendered flippant references to "making deposits" and "moving collateral".

This was schoolboy stuff, but the banter only enhanced the whiff of disrepute. The Special Protocols Detainees were termed "full-boarders" and references to "suitable clientele" were in keeping with the suggestion that a particular category of persons was being targeted. The arrest reports indicated that mostly it was straightforward criminal behaviour that had brought about the initial prison sentences but that "transfer mandates" to the HSDC had occurred as a result of anything from inmates' sheer bloody-mindedness to "adverse ideological leanings". The earliest of these transfers was dated six months previously, so maybe the HSDC had only become operational then. Crucially, on the few occasions where names were given, they were distinctly Khanistani. One reference to "our cousins-in-law" was suggestive of US involvement in the scheme, while the documents as a whole plainly showed a network of collusion between the police, prison and intelligence services under the remit of the Home Office.

The entire patchwork assemblage, with its repugnant blend of glib and facetious verbiage, was thoroughly dispiriting. It made you feel at once furious and grubby and ashamed for your country. Even Ashad was shocked, despite his habit of assuming the worst.

It was getting late, and neither of us had any appetite to linger. Ashad was off to Brixton that evening to watch a piece of "radical performance art" by a friend of his. For nearly a decade he had been renting a loft conversion in Plaistow from one of his uncles. To save time he decided to come back to my place in Clapham for a wash and brush up before he went out.

Ashad hadn't made any comment when I stuffed Nigel's package back into my rucksack, and we didn't talk about it on the journey to my place. It was only when we were walking up the shady path to my front door that he asked to have a look at it.

Though we were screened from immediate observation, I double-checked that there was no one on the street nearby or peeking from any windows before I pulled out the package. I tore the duct tape free and we both peered inside.

The handgun was a dark blur under its bubble wrap.

"Bloody hell," Ashad said in his best Birmingham.

We unpackaged it without actually touching what was inside. It looked just like the real thing, very solid and menacing.

I wrapped it up again and stuffed it into the depths of the rampant privet hedge. Neither of us said a word.

While Ashad took a shower I ordered a couple of stir fries from the local Chinese takeaway. Then we started up my computer and did a search for information on Halstow Island.

The picture on Google Earth showed that it existed as a dark blob in the Thames estuary, with pale buildings like a scattering of ivory dominoes. However, according to the linked information they were all part of a “Meat Processing Plant”. Was this gallows humour on the part of some anonymous secret service bureaucrat? There was no mention anywhere of government involvement, but then it wasn’t likely to be advertised as such if it was a containment facility. Other searches provided only the same bland information, though on the local council website there was a reference to a “rendering facility”. If this was another example of black humour it was distinctly chilling.

SEVEN

Total Graffix occupied a neat modern building between a beauty salon and a big office block in the boarded-up throes of renovation. I swung the glass door open and walked through a reception area decorated in primrose and cream. There were arty photos and lithographs of the company's work on the walls. According to their website, they were a commercial design outfit with an ethical bent, producing visuals for the likes of charities, trade unions and cooperatives. But not exclusively. One of the pictures showed the camera-eye corporate logo of the Filmscope Foundation.

A fidgety man was sitting behind a canary-yellow reception desk.

"Good morning," I said. "Claire Whitney?"

I made it sound as if I had an appointment, as if I expected him to know I was coming. Rather than phoning ahead I had decided just to show up and talk to her face-to-face.

"I'm so sorry," he said. "You've just missed her. Was she expecting you?"

"I spoke to her over the weekend," I lied. "We arranged a one o'clock meeting."

Repeatedly clicking a ballpoint pen, he scanned a clipboard list. "She didn't let the desk know."

"Well," I said casually, "it was a last-minute thing. I hope you're not going to tell me that my journey's been wasted?"

"She went out earlier," he said, a trifle irritated rather than perplexed. "It's her lunch. On Mondays she usually goes to one of her *gatherings*."

His tone was laced with scorn. He was in his late thirties, wearing a black slim-fit shirt whose strained buttons advertised a paunch-in-waiting.

"Gatherings?" I said.

"The upwardly mobile?"

He was waiting for me to share the joke.

"You've got the better of me," I told him.

"The Church," he said. "The Sunrise crowd."

I didn't have a clue what he was talking about.

"You know," he said, "the Ascendancy. To infinity and beyond!"

He was mimicking Buzz Lightyear.

"Really?" I said with genuine surprise. "She's a follower?"

An emphatic nod. "She's religious about it."

He plainly considered this a *bon mot*. As receptionists went, he was as discreet as a dose of measles.

"Do you know what time she might be back?" I asked.

"One-thirty," he told me firmly. "She goes to their little *temple* in Covent Garden. Would you like to wait?"

"No thanks," I replied, already striding towards the door.

"Can I take a name?" he called after me. "Is there any message?"

"Tell her that her secrets aren't safe with you."

*

Nursing a cappuccino, I sat in a café just across the road from the temple. There was a newer and bigger one that had recently opened on the Embankment close to Charing Cross station but this had been the first in London. On a side street in Covent Garden, it nestled inside the grey walls of a Gothic Revival church. You had to look twice to spot the golden sunrise emblem above the door.

I had hotfooted it there by the most direct route. I was working on the assumption that Claire was still ensconced in whatever services or ceremonies the Ascendants conducted. I had to admit I was deflated to learn that she was a follower. I didn't have her pegged as a cultist. Not that she would regard herself as such, of course. The Ascendants preferred to be known as members of a church and wouldn't hesitate to sue any person or organisation who suggested otherwise. They claimed it was a full-blown religion and hence entitled to significant tax benefits.

I didn't really know that much about them, apart from the fact that they had emerged in the USA in the 1960s and believed that we all had innate mental powers which could be unlocked and "enhanced" by following certain rituals. To outsiders it appeared that some people had more potential than others, notably the Church hierarchy and high-profile followers prepared to hand over an appreciable tithe of their income. Everyone in the cult was an Ascendant who could progress through a series of mental gymnastics to eventually become one of the Elect. Attaining this elevated status enabled them to conquer everything from depression to drug addiction, as well as nullifying evil, conflict and pain. Nice work if you could get it. The fact that they attracted some high profile celebrities as members didn't make most people think them any less barmy.

Those followers who had managed to buttonhole me outside their meeting house near our office had left me uneasy with their full-frontal smiles and bright-eyed certitude. Did I want to understand the true nature of the world and the answer to life's problems? Did I want to take the first steps on the path to maximizing my mental and physical potential? Jolly enticing prospects, but actually I had a client who was giving me grief about some missing footage and I really needed to get back to the office.

Perhaps it was Claire's beliefs that had made her cautious in her dealings with me. She wouldn't want to advertise her affiliation with a church that most people considered to be high up the wacko scale. I needed to reappraise my approach to her if I was going to have any chance of finding out more about Leo Parrish.

I hefted the padded envelope out of my rucksack. Jamilla had thrust it at me when I had arrived at work that morning. On opening it I had immediately told her I wasn't taking any calls that morning and had ensconced myself in the viewing theatre for a couple of hours with a DO NOT DISTURB sign on the door.

The package was from Molly, Arthur's wife. It came with a note that said:

Dear Mr Randall,

I thought these might be of interest. Please consider our business now concluded. Neither Arthur nor I will be able to help you further.

Sincere regards

Molly Townsend

Inside the package were four more magazines, each protected by a thick transparent plastic sleeve and all mentioning Leo Parrish on the front. I almost yelped with delight. Three of them were issues of *Awesome Adventures*. The fourth was a similar looking production called *Shocking Stories*. Its brooding cover looked as if it had come from an earlier era, with a villainous-looking dictator-type glaring out of the page. Advertised as the "Electrifying First Issue", the magazine had EXALTATION emblazoned prominently across it, with Leo Parrish's name underneath. There could be no doubt that it was intended as the main attraction.

I looked again at Molly's note. It wasn't exactly cheering. Were she and Arthur being threatened? Had someone nobbled them?

I spent the first half hour just leafing through the magazines, deferring the actual reading of Parrish's stories like an excited child who was afraid of being disappointed. The three stories in *Awesome Adventures* had been published in consecutive bimonthly issues, suggesting that Parrish had by this stage become a stalwart of the magazine. *Shocking Stories*—a hubristic title if ever there was one, even by the overblown standards of such magazines—had been published later, in 1960. It carried a long editorial under the byline Ed Ridge, enthusing about the launch of the magazine, which was described as "a sister publication to *Awesome Adventures*, specializing in full-length works of IF on controversial scientific issues that will challenge and enthral open-minded readers for whom scientific speculation has no limits."

By IF I gleaned that the editor meant "imaginative fiction", a gloss on the more familiar SF. Unfortunately Parrish's story, which according to the contents page took up a third of the issue, was missing. The pages had been neatly cut out close to the magazine's spine. Clinical excisions, the work of a careful hand.

As far as I could judge, it was the only one of the magazines with missing pages. I was pretty sure Molly hadn't known. She had probably slipped the whole lot into the padded bag without looking inside them. And Arthur? Had he bought the magazine as part of a bundle at some auction, only to find later that the bulk of it wasn't there? How galling that must have been for him. And how mysterious and frustrating. Though perhaps he hadn't known because he was the sort of person who would have mentioned it. Did collectors actually read all the stuff they collected, or did it a lot of it stay permanently under wraps?

Like most magazines of that era, *Shocking Stories* was liberally laced with black-and-white advertisements for muscle-building pills, X-ray specs and correspondence courses. There were short stories by authors whose names read like wonky anagrams, a science-based article on the latent powers of the human brain and a long column in which other implausibly-named writers had been invited to give their predictions for the next fifty years of human progress. Atom-powered houses, anti-ageing elixirs and a World Government were among the favourites. Parrish's story was the meat of the issue—or would have been if I had had the complete magazine.

I had to restrain myself from phoning Arthur to ask how he had acquired it. I knew there was no point. No doubt Molly had been thorough in sending me everything by Parrish that was in Arthur's collection, but her note had been pretty explicit about not wanting any further contact. Perhaps Arthur was scared. He probably had good reason to be, given the dodgy characters in the white van. Something nasty was going on and it had to be connected with the theft of the magazines and the planting of the bug.

I scrawled a note on the back of Molly's letter, thanking her and saying that she and Arthur should be even more vigilant as there really were some unpleasant characters around. Jamilla could post it later. It was time I explored other avenues.

Already determined to go to Claire Whitney's workplace, I had managed to skim-read the three *Awesome Adventures* stories before I left. "The Weather Warriors" was set on an Earth beleaguered by an unstable climate and featured a crack team of scientists and adventurers who could calm storms and disperse locust swarms with "negentropy beams" and "bio-molecular insecticides". "Transmission" was a satire in which audiences literally became absorbed into hyper-real TV landscapes, enacting dramas viewed by a rapidly diminishing audience until the hero of the story managed to pull the plug. "Know Your Enemy" had Manhattan invaded by beings from another dimension whose exact mimicry of the human form meant that human resistance fighters were unable to distinguish them from true humans—as, in the twist to the tale, were the beings themselves, forgetting their origins and becoming so completely naturalized that normal life re-established itself by default.

All three stories struck me as stimulating and fun. "The Weather Warriors" would have had blockbuster potential in its own right, if only Roland Emmerich hadn't already made *The Day after Tomorrow.* "Transmission" might have worked well as a TV drama, but *The Truman Show* had stolen its thunder. "Know Your Enemy" still had potential, but more as a TV psycho-drama with modern-day resonances than the movie spectacular we were looking for.

I was leafing through the magazines when Claire Whitney emerged from the Ascendancy temple and walked briskly away. She was wearing a raincoat with the collar turned up, huddling into it like a celebrity seeking anonymity.

I slid the magazines back into the envelope, left some coins on the table and hastily exited.

My main priority was not to make my pursuit of her so blatant that I would scare her off before I opened my mouth. I moved quickly along the opposite side of the road, dodging pedestrians, keeping her in sight, quickening my stride until I was ahead. I managed to cross at a green light, whereas she was held up as the traffic started flowing again. I scurried along to a bookshop, loitering in the doorway and peering out until I saw her approaching.

Then, as if I had just emerged from the shop, I lurched on to the pavement and gently collided with her.

"Sorry," I began, and then with feigned surprise: "Good grief, it's you!"

She looked me up and down with instant recognition.

"Mr Randall," was all she said.

"This is strange," I blustered. "I was just thinking about you."

"Really?"

"I tried to ring you a few times," I told her. "I left a couple of messages."

"Is that so?" She was sceptical. "I don't recall them."

"Arthur Townsend's?" I prompted. "I thought you were coming too."

She took a little step back from me. As before, her hair was tied up in a loose pony-tail.

"I thought that we were meeting at his place," I said. "A few days ago. I showed up and got to talk to him, but I never heard back from you."

She looked around her. "Is this some kind of set-up?"

"What?"

"I haven't got the faintest idea what you're talking about."

I wasn't expecting this. "You arranged a meeting," I said.

"I did?"

"With Arthur Townsend. The collector?"

"I know who Arthur Townsend is."

"You texted me. I showed up at the time and place you suggested. I got to talk to him. Acquired some magazines with Leo Parrish's stories."

She looked blank. I began to feel that I was making some kind of awful *faux pas*. If we hadn't been standing in a very public place I think she would have already bolted.

Slowly she shook her head. "I'm sorry, but you must be mistaken. I haven't had any texts from you."

All the conversational strategies I had envisaged beforehand now shrivelled and died. What was this? Either she was pretending, in which case it was a mealy-mouthed way of saying that she wanted nothing further to do with me; or she was genuinely perplexed. Unless, of course, she was one of those people who are emotionally and intellectually fickle, whose moods and rationalisations shift like the wind.

No, I didn't think so. She was standing her ground, looking at me with a kind of bewildered incredulity. But an Ascendant, I reminded myself, a true believer in stuff that set most rational people's alarm bells ringing. Who knew what mind games she might be capable of playing or what delusions she herself entertained?

I got out my phone, found her number, showed it to her.

She shook her head. "It isn't mine."

Was she lying? In front of her, I called the number.

Nothing went off in her raincoat or the slim shoulder bag she was carrying. But then, how could it? The line was completely dead.

"See?" she said to me.

It didn't prove anything. Her phone might be switched off, or it might have been a spare one she only used at home.

I reached into my rucksack, withdrew the envelope and then the magazines. I showed her the covers, mentioned the Leo Parrish stories they contained.

"Molly sent them me," I told her. I flourished the accompanying note. "She's Arthur's ex-wife. I'd never have got them if you hadn't arranged the meeting."

She took the note, read it through.

"I didn't arrange any meeting," she insisted. "I haven't been in touch with you since we met at the festival. I lost your card."

Her gaze was calm and direct. It didn't waver.

"But you sent me a text," I insisted. "Giving me the time and place."

"It wasn't me."

"Then how come I knew where Arthur lives? How come I got these?"

I flourished the magazines again. She took the envelope from me and examined the postmark.

"You were lucky to get them," she told me. "There was a fire at Arthur's place on Friday night. He got out safely but his collection was destroyed."

*

She walked at a brisk pace while I recapitulated the story of my visit to Arthur's. I didn't get the impression that she wanted to be rid of me but was simply keen to get back to work on time.

When I described the text message to her, she just laughed.

"Do you really think I'd write something like that?" she said. "What do you think I am—a thirteen year old?"

She said it matter-of-factly, and of course she was right. Abbreviated messages full of that kind of shorthand were an adolescent thing. Grown-ups preferred to spell things out in good old-fashioned words. And not add kisses when addressing people they had only just met.

Someone else must have sent it. But for what purpose? While she wasn't unfriendly I didn't get the impression she was especially delighted to see me or inclined to help in my pursuit of Leo Parrish's work, so it actually made no sense for her to have contacted me in that way. When I asked again about her role in placing the *Nightscapes* Parrish story she shrugged it off, saying that she had just being doing a favour for a friend.

"So what about these?" I said with reference to the magazines. "Are there more of them I should know about?"

"I wouldn't flash those around, if I were you. You never know who might be watching."

She said it with a deadpan face. She might have been joking, but I wasn't going to make light of it.

"I know what you mean," I told her. "Someone was interested enough to plant a bug on me."

This stopped her. I had gambled on the shock value. I recounted the story, also telling her about the burglary and the loss of the first batch of stories. I knew that if she was reluctant to get involved with me then this could have the effect of scaring her off completely. But I felt it was important she understood that I was prepared to be candid with her.

"Arthur was scared too," I went on. "He thought people were after him. Looks like he was right. This is all connected with Leo Parrish, isn't it?"

She didn't reply.

"Who is he?" I asked. "Have you got him hidden away somewhere?"

"He's dead. He died years ago."

This one I hadn't been expecting. Did she really believe it? Was it true?

She walked off again. I followed.

"So why is there all this mystery and intrigue surrounding him? I heard he morphed into someone famous."

"I told you. He died years ago."

"Honestly?"

"Why would I lie about it?"

Why indeed? "So what's your connection with him?"

"There isn't really one. Cyrus was interested in getting some of his work on TV. I happened to be friends with someone in the production company. That's how it happened."

I didn't believe this for a moment. "But you're a fan of Parrish's work."

"So? That doesn't mean I have secret knowledge about him."

"Do you have copies of other stuff that I could have a look at?" I showed where the pages were missing from *Shocking Stories*. "I'm especially keen to get my hands on what should have been here."

She inspected the magazine, frowning. "Why would someone do that?"

"A good question. You don't happen to have this magazine, do you?"

She shook her head. "I'm not a collector. I don't have any. The pictures you saw were drawn from memory."

She wasn't giving me anything. We walked on in silence for a while. I thought about what to say next.

"Why did you take off so suddenly when we met?"

"Domestic emergency. It couldn't be helped."

She didn't elaborate.

"Have you been threatened yourself?"

"What do you mean?"

"I mean that people associated with Parrish seem spooked. Including you."

A hollow laugh. "Maybe somebody's trying to tell you something. Like, give it up."

There was a kind of stubbornness in her tone that was at odds with her words. She wasn't being frank with me, I knew that, but I had a feeling that she might be prepared to take me onside if only I could prove that I was genuine.

"I don't take kindly to threats and intrusions," I told her. "They only make me more stubborn. The more I've read of Parrish's stuff, the more I believe it should be brought to a wider audience."

She had stopped again. We were outside the Total Graffix building.

"Did you know," I said, "that your name was linked to our company on the database at the film festival?"

She gave me a suspicious look. "What do you mean—linked?"

"Just that. The electronic registration for Xponential had a hyperlink that showed your name."

I could tell from her face that this was as much of a surprise to her as it had been to me.

"Any idea why?" I asked.

She just shook her head. "I'd never heard of your company before that day."

Either she was an expert liar or someone unknown to either of us had been responsible.

"Who told you about the fire at Arthur's?" I asked.

"Cyrus phoned. He and Arthur are friends from way back."

I didn't bother asking why he should feel the need to ring her with the news. The link was obvious: Leo Parrish.

"Have you been following me, Mr Randall?" she asked bluntly.

"No. Well, not exactly. I came here today to find you, to talk to you about Leo Parrish. They told me you'd gone to a meeting. So I waited until you came out."

"Ah."

"I really don't want you to think I'm stalking you. I'm just trying to get my hands on as much of Parrish's work as I can. I don't understand why it's causing everyone so much grief."

She looked at me for a long time. It was a nice feeling. Those intense honey-brown eyes. The laughter lines around her eyes and the corners of her mouth.

Then she shook her head.

"I'm sorry. I really can't help you."

I exhaled long and slow. Put as much regret into it as I could.

"I'm disappointed to hear that. Why not?"

"I haven't got what you're after."

"I thought we might be able to bring you on board as a consultant."

"Nice bribe," she replied. "It's nothing personal, I assure you. I'm just not who you think I am."

"And who is that exactly?"

"Someone who can solve your company's movie problems." She stretched out her hand. "Goodbye, Mr Randall."

I took it and shook.

"Please," I said, extracting my wallet and removing another business card. "Take one. Just in case your change your mind."

She accepted it gracefully.

"Don't lose it this time," I told her."Is there a number where I can contact you?"

"You know where I work."

I nodded. She wasn't going to let me any further in.

"This temple stuff," I asked. "Do you go regularly?"

"Goodbye, Mr Randall."

"It's Nick."

"Goodbye, Nick."

She climbed the steps and pushed through the plate glass doors.

*

On the way back to the office I phoned Cyrus Hammond. This time he rather than his secretary picked up. I gave him the gist of my conversation with Claire Whitney, stressing that it had been a friendly but frustrating meeting. I told him about the package from Molly, and the missing pages in the copy of *Shocking Stories*. I commiserated about the fire at Arthur's.

He was eating something; I had obviously caught him at his lunch. But he seemed quite happy to talk to me.

"How do you know Arthur?" he asked.

"An interested party put me in touch. We met up a few days ago."

"Bad business," he said. "By all accounts the entire building nearly went up."

"Do they know what caused it?"

"Too soon to say. My guess would be faulty electrics in that old house coupled with all the books and magazines he had."

"Is he injured?"

"According to his blog, he was with his wife in her flat when they smelt the smoke. Nearly killed himself trying to get in there and haul his stuff out. He's in hospital. Smoke inhalation and nervous exhaustion."

It was all too easy to imagine Arthur frantically grappling with his own security system in an ultimately vain effort to rescue the many items that were of such value to him. Precious relics that he might never be able to replace.

I said, "He was scared people were after him, you know."

Hammond made an affirmative noise. "Well, he always was a twitchy type. Got het up pretty easily."

"You don't think he had any justification?"

"Who knows? Genuine guy, but high maintenance. Not many friends."

"Everything was destroyed?"

"Well, I haven't seen it, but I would imagine it's either burnt or reduced to pap by the fire fighters."

I wondered if the police had any leads. I wondered how far the people who were doing this were prepared to go. And why. *Why* remained the central issue.

"Do you have any idea what all this is about?" I asked.

He swallowed some food. "What exactly?"

I wasn't going to tell him about the bug and the burglary at my end, but I didn't have to be specific. "There's seems to be a lot of trouble around anything to do with Leo Parrish."

I heard him pour something. "You'll have to explain."

"It's just a feeling I have. Why would anyone want to cut a complete story of his out of a magazine?"

"Perhaps they didn't want to buy the whole thing. Those old magazines are very collectible. You pay premium. There are a lot of obsessives out there."

"This looks more like a literary version of extraordinary rendition."

He gave a belly laugh. "That's a good one."

"Any idea where I might get my hands on another copy?"

I heard someone come in and speak to him. Possibly his secretary. Off phone, Hammond said, "I'll get on to it," and then to me: "You could do worse than try Walt Suthersen."

Even I had heard of Walter Suthersen. He was a genuine Big Name in science fiction. His best-selling novel *Zeta Prime* had recently been made into a movie by Paramount, with an A grade cast and a budget to match.

"He knew Parrish back in the old days. Always claimed that he was a big influence."

"Claire Whitney says Parrish is dead."

Hammond took a swig of something.

"What's the accepted story on him?" I asked.

"He dropped out of sight more than fifty years ago. Rumour has it that he's still out there somewhere but I don't credit it. Neither does anyone who actually knew him."

"That doesn't include you?"

"No."

"Maybe he changed career."

Hammond wasn't buying this. "People die, you know? They get old, have accidents, fall sick. It happens. Lots of people think that John Lennon and Elvis are out there in hiding. Makes life more interesting. Doesn't make it true."

I could hear him shuffling papers and sensed that he needed to get on with other stuff.

"So how would I contact Walter Suthersen?"

"You're in luck," he told me. "As it happens, he's over in England on a publicity tour. Last I heard he was in Newcastle. I know there's a London date in there somewhere. Want me to find out when it is?"

"That would be great."

There was a brief silence.

"Anything else I can do for you?" Hammond asked.

I thought about asking him what connection Claire Whitney had with Leo Parrish. And whether he, Hammond, knew that she was an Ascendant. Not a good idea. They were friends, or at least had regular contact. For all I knew, Hammond himself might also be a cultist. I would have to avoid being rude about the cult if I was asking its members for help. The list of people I wasn't sure I could trust was getting longer every day.

*

Back at the office, I found Valerie with Ashad at his desk, sitting together in front of the plasma screen.

"Have you seen this?" Ashad said irritably the moment I sidled in.

On the screen President Muvart, resplendent in full regalia on a flag-draped balcony, was ranting into a microphone while below him a big crowd waved enthusiastically at what was evidently another state-sponsored rally in a Khanistani square.

I pulled my desk chair up beside them.

Muvart's words were muted, but the voice-over was in the unmistakable nasal twang of Alec Furneaux, a former colleague of ours who now fronted a brash current affairs programme called *Talking Points* for one of the cable channels. Its magazine-style format generally leant heavily on sports features and scurrilous celebrity gossip, but he did run the occasional more heavyweight item.

The screen flashed from Muvart to a picture of a terrified-looking man with half his face eaten away. Underneath it in lurid red lettering was the tag: NECROTIZING FASCIITIS: THE FLESH-EATING DISEASE

"That's just library footage," Ashad said dismissively as Valerie and I grimaced.

Dramatically Furneaux was saying: "Could this be the fate that the dangerously unstable Muvart intends to unleash on the British population? Has he already begun his attack on us?"

The clip switched to the sharp-featured Furneaux staring intently at the camera before he lapsed into his trademark air of amused disdain at the world's follies.

"Meanwhile," he said, "is the ghost of Michael Jackson haunting this recording studio—"

Valerie froze the picture with the remote. At my request she backtracked to the beginning so that I could have the full benefit of it.

"This is going out tonight," she told me. "I got wind of it from a mole at the company."

Valerie had contacts everywhere, and it was she who had actually cut Furneaux off our payroll when we discovered that some documentary footage he had supplied us had, to put it mildly, been artificially enhanced with the use of extras and a script that was fifty per cent fiction.

The current feature, only a few minutes long, made the startling claim that certain inmates of prisons in the UK were falling victim to a mysterious disease that caused their flesh to rot. Without any supporting evidence, Furneaux asserted that the disease was in all likelihood a type of necrotizing fasciitis and that it had deliberately been introduced there by Muvart's agents as a prelude to a full-scale germ warfare attack on the UK.

"It's bollocks," Ashad asserted vehemently. "A load of complete garbage."

I could tell that he was bothered. Bothered that Furneaux might have stumbled on something.

"I don't know," Valerie said. "Furneaux's cavalier with the truth, but he doesn't usually make it up completely."

"The whole thing is just a pile of wild assertions," Ashad insisted. "He talks about 'our sources' and 'information passed secretly to us', but there's no hard evidence." He flashed the black USB stick at his neck. "What we've got suggests something different and state-sponsored."

Valerie smiled indulgently; she had seen the files on the stick. “Are you sure you’re not just pissed off because he’s stolen a march on us?”

Ashad made to say something, but instead turned to me. “What do you think?”

I looked away from the frozen image of the victim. He was wide-eyed, the flesh peeling from his face. If Furneaux’s story was true, it would make our Muvart project yesterday’s news.

EIGHT

The tabloids were full of Furneaux's story the following morning. I had a small pile of them on my lap as I took the slow train to Woking. One paper claimed that the mystery disease was actually an enhanced form of leprosy, concocted in a secret bio-warfare lab hidden in the Khanistani mountains. Another was certain that Muvart supporters were deliberately getting themselves arrested so that their associates could sneak the infective agents into prisons where they could be spread through the food or water supply. A third had a double-page full-colour map of central London peppered with bile green explosions showing likely locations for bio-terrorist attacks. All of them had a hysterical tone.

Meanwhile the British government had issued sober denials that anything unusual was going on in Her Majesty's jails. On the breakfast TV news an unflappable spokeswoman had calmly announced that there was no evidence of any flesh-eating disease being deliberately spread through UK prisons; no evidence that ethnic Khanistanis were involved in any sort of plot to disseminate infective biological agents; no evidence that President Muvart was doing anything other than making strident accusations about the activities of foreign governments that had no basis in fact. The British government was, as always, fully committed to the agreed protocols for detainees and to upholding the human rights of everyone, both within its borders and beyond them.

It was the word "protocols" that got me, making me think of Walid's Special Protocols Detainees. Something wasn't smelling right here, and no amount of governmental air freshener could get rid of the whiff.

As the train pulled into Woking station, I stuffed the newspapers into my rucksack alongside the magazines with the Parrish stories that I had originally intended to re-read on the journey. They would have to wait. Whether or not Muvart was actually planning to unleash some form of germ warfare, this was a story that urgently needed clarification.

*

Biope Industries had a big gilded sign beside the road with the company name etched in black around a stylized daisy. Closer inspection showed that the flower was actually made up of organic molecules with linking strings and chains of atoms. From a distance, though, it looked suitably naturalistic, and the spanking new company headquarters advertised its ecological credentials with swathes of blond wood, solar panels and an undulating roof covered with grass and patches of wildflowers. A pair of wind turbines were whirring atop ventilation ducts.

To reach the entrance, though, you had first to get through the fence that ringed the entire site. It was tall and made of sprouting steel spears with three-pointed tips. You could have probably got over it with a long ladder and plenty of luck, but one slip and you were in big trouble.

I spoke into the intercom and was buzzed through, the gate inching open, leaving me feeling exposed and watched as I walked up the cinder driveway. A CCTV camera followed my every move. The entrance doors sat under a concrete Gothic arch, suggesting that you were entering a modern cathedral, though one devoted to scientific rather than spiritual enlightenment. Smoky grey glass windows implied openness while at the same time making it impossible to see what lay within.

As I approached the doors folded open. I walked into the building and went through a set of barriers similar to those in airports, immediately setting off a whooping alarm. This must have been a pretty common occurrence because the alarm's volume was turned down low and the rumpled-looking security guard beside the reception desk came forward with a weary "Here we go again" look.

Naturally he made me empty my rucksack and looked curiously at all the newspapers inside. Then he spotted the magazines, with their lurid covers of death rays, homicidal bug-eyed monsters and a bikini-clad woman fleeing from a tornado in whose maelstrom were whirling cows, cars and an entire mobile home.

"Research," I told him brazenly. "I'm a journalist."

He gave me a withering look but handed them back to me without a word. When we had finally established that it was my sinister-looking silver ballpoint pen that had triggered the alarm, he allowed me to retrieve my jeans belt and loose change and continue in a rather undignified fashion to the desk.

"Dr Gerry Broughton," I said to the receptionist, who didn't look up. "I'm Nick Randall. He should be expecting me."

She glanced at a screen, its bluish glow suffusing her features as she tapped a few keys. She wore a crisp white blouse with a dark skirt and jacket, looked every inch the acceptable public face of the company. Frowning at first, she finally took a plastic card from a pile.

"Please look at the camera," she said to me, still without making eye contact.

There was one mounted above the desk. Even as I looked up it flashed.

I blinked away the spots in front of my eyes. There was the whirr of a printer, and soon afterwards the receptionist handed me a photo-pass card with VISITOR stamped in large letters over a picture of me looking as if someone had just stuck a finger up my bum.

The receptionist switched on a smile like sunlight.

"Please go through into the foyer. He'll be with you shortly."

I clipped the card to my lapel and wandered through, wondering if there was a difference between a reception area and a foyer. Or a lobby, for that matter. A short corridor led into a large alcove where I sat down on a tubular sofa whose looping contours made it more an architectural statement than a practical piece of furniture.

A wall screen was showing a promotional video for the company. Apparently they were well on the way to solving world water shortages, creating cheap low-emission petrochemical substitutes, greening deserts with vast plains of GM foods, and producing minuscule batteries for storing power from spare generating capacity. Odd that with such wonders in their portfolio I had never heard of them before.

Everything in the place looked newly minted, unsullied by the ravages of time. Modern prints adorned the walls, exotic lilies blossomed from well-tended containers. Plenty of the money swilling around in the biosciences research trough had evidently ended up here. I wondered whether it had actually come from Biope's profits or was debt. Or had it been raised by private equity firms using those wonderful tools of modern consumer societies: asset-stripping, outsourcing to third world countries and downsizing of workforces? How long would the company be given to deliver its rewards? A few years, or a matter of months? These days people were impatient for fast returns on their investments. Maybe it was time we did our own warts-and-all feature on modern venture capitalism.

I filed the thought as someone came down the corridor. It was only when he beamed and bellowed, "Nick, you old bugger!" that I was certain that this was indeed my mate Gerry.

He shook my hand and gave me a big hug. We'd been close friends at university but hadn't seen one another for a while. In that time he had slimmed down and shaved off his beard, as well as replacing his ancient horn-rimmed glasses with contact lenses. It was as if he had been scrubbed and freshly re-made to fit in with his surroundings.

"You're looking good," I said to him, thinking that I actually preferred the old shaggy beer-belly look.

"You look as scruffy as ever," he retorted. "I saw that thing you lot did on reality TV shows. Excellent stuff."

He was nattily dressed in a slick aluminium-grey suit that shimmered under the recessed lighting. Quite a change from baggy corduroys and lumberjack shirts.

"What about you?" I said. "Mr Neat and Polished. You must be prospering."

I caught an instant's hesitation, almost a brief pained look, before his usual bonhomie reasserted itself. "It's company policy," he said, leading me towards the door. "Tell you all about it when we get to my lab."

"Your lab? Blimey, I'm impressed. The last time we met you were brewing up slurries in a Portakabin in Dunstable."

He laughed at this. "Well, it's not actually all my own. I share it with someone else. But it's a cracking working environment. State of the art stuff."

"I can see that," I told him, though this wasn't actually true because all the windowed rooms we passed on either side of the corridor had their blinds drawn. You would have had to go into them to find out what was going on. Mounted beside every closed door were security pass readers and keypads.

"How long's it been since I saw you?" he asked me. I could tell from his tone that he was testing me and would know precisely.

"A couple of years," I said without confidence.

"Three and a half," he informed me.

"You're joking." But I knew he was right. We had both been busy with our own careers and time had just slipped by.

"I've got two more kids," he told me. "Winifred and Wilhelmina."

It was an on-going joke between us. Gerry was never likely to have any children because he was gay.

"Listen," I said, "I'm sorry I haven't been in touch—"

He waved the apology aside. "So tell me what you've been up to. No patterings of tiny feet yet?"

I shook my head. "Theresa and I split up."

"Ah."

"It's amicable. There was no one else. Still isn't."

He put an arm around my shoulder. It felt strange not to feel his usual bulk, as if he was a stripped-down version of himself. Typically hospitable, Gerry made sure we stopped off at the cafeteria, where there were a dozen varieties of coffee and tea. I opted for a Guatemalan and resisted a delectable-looking pastry. As cafeterias went, this was definitely high end.

Gerry's lab was just around the corner. A white-coated woman in her late twenties was taking a folder from a filing cabinet as we entered.

"Nick," Gerry said, "this is Liz. Or rather Dr Elizabeth Martindale, C Biol M.Inst.Biol, to use her full and impressive title. Liz, this is my mate Mr Nicholas Randall—Old Nick as he used to be known to us when we were in our cups."

Despite Gerry's jollity she didn't crack a smile.

"Liz is a synthetic biologist," Gerry went on. "Her ambition's to make an amino acid that nature hasn't thought of yet. I'll lay you good odds that she'll succeed, too."

This was plainly meant to be flattering but nothing changed in her expression.

"Don't you have a meeting?" he asked her.

"Soon," she replied. "I'm just getting all the paperwork together."

She went off into the main part of the lab while Gerry rolled up an extra chair and settled me down at his desk. He plainly hoped that we'd be left alone so that we could chat. As did I.

I looked around the place with a mixture of curiosity and bewilderment. Forget test tubes, Bunsen burners and flasks of coloured liquids bubbling away. The lab was filled with heavy-duty kit that looked more like bulky photocopiers and things on articulated arms that might have come from a fiendish dental surgery. There was plenty of electronic hardware, too, including a computer on whose screen a complex multi-coloured molecule was doing a balletic twirl.

"This is nice," I said vaguely. "You must be pleased you got out of Dunstable."

He stiffened. "I didn't change jobs to get a new lab or more money."

Gerry had spent the best part of a decade working in Dunstable at a facility that was reputed to be an outlier of the Ministry of Defence's Microbiological Research Establishment at Porton Down. Naturally Gerry had never confirmed or denied this. I had always assumed he was happy there, a career civil servant content to indulge his fascination with minute wriggly things without the kind of corporate interference you get in the private sector. Then the facility had been sold to an outside agency, and soon afterwards Gerry had moved on.

I pulled *The Guardian* out of my rucksack and pointed to the front-page story entitled "UK Bio-terror Threat".

"What do you make of all this stuff about Muvart?" I asked him. "You know, planning a germ warfare attack and all that."

When I had phoned to arrange our meeting I had told him I wanted to pick his brains about the necrotizing fasciitis story.

"Bloody lunacy," he responded with patent disbelief. "Even if he had the expertise, Muvart doesn't have the facilities. You're talking billions of dollars to get a programme like that up and running from scratch."

"Well, he's not short of a bob or two, is he?"

"Most of his best people fled the country after the last round of purges. Half of them ended up in the UK. Working for the MoD, as it happens."

"So you don't give any credence to this story about inmates being infected with flesh-rotting bugs?"

This time he was slow to respond. His colleague had returned to her desk and was rummaging through her in-tray. She extracted a couple of sheets of paper and added them to the pile she was carrying. Our silence must have been obvious, but she didn't react to it.

I leaned closer to Gerry and said, "I'm hearing rumours that people are being detained by the government at a secret site. A lot of them are Khanistanis."

Gerry blinked behind his contacts, looking more than a little uncomfortable: he plainly wanted Dr Martindale to leave.

"Halstow Island?" I prompted.

No sign that he recognized this. Yet he looked bothered.

"What's your angle on this?" he asked me.

He was being uncharacteristically cautious. While working at Dunstable as a government employee he had never said anything to compromise his position, at least as far as I was aware, but he had leftish political leanings and had always shown a healthy disrespect for politicians. We had first met at a demonstration against plans to reduce subsidized student housing and had soon found that we had plenty in common: Ridley Scott movies, stand-up comedians, real ale. Gerry had always been popular, the cheery spirit at the heart of any party. It was as if the soul had been sucked out of him.

"I haven't got an angle," I told him. "I'm just trying to find out what's going on."

Dr Martindale was still loitering at her desk, to no obvious purpose. I swallowed some coffee, wondering if Gerry was pissed off that I had come to see him on what was essentially a business matter rather than just to catch up. But I had made it clear when I phoned him that I needed his expert opinion, so it couldn't be that.

"Liz," Gerry said abruptly, "be an absolute brick and leave me and Nick to have a chinwag, would you? I don't want to say anything that might pollute your ears."

He said it cheerily, but the good doctor looked offended by the suggestion. Casting me a rather stern glance, she picked up her bundle of papers and stalked out.

I looked at Gerry. "'Be an absolute brick'," I quoted. "Where did you learn to talk like that?"

"She went to Roedean," he told me. "I was just talking her language."

I couldn't tell whether he was joking. "Is she always that stand-offish?"

"She probably doesn't approve of your combat jacket. And didn't you have that backpack at uni?"

I had stuffed the rucksack between my feet. I had to admit it looked well travelled.

"Are we all right to talk here?" I asked.

"Of course," he replied.

"Only you seem a bit—well, not your usual self."

He gave me a long and steady look before sighing.

"Dunstable was all right," he said at last. "At least it was for the first few years. We had to make do and mend a lot, but it was a good cause. I wasn't doing anything *offensive*, you know?"

I didn't know, and I was aware he couldn't tell me exactly.

"Vaccines," he said. "I know what the rumours about the place were, but we were working on ways of countering disease, not causing it."

"We?"

"Our team. The department I worked for. We'd socialize with others in the recreation room and sometimes down the local, but at Dunstable we worked in tight teams and rarely talked shop outside. That was the unspoken agreement. But we all felt that we were doing something socially useful, in the early years, at least. When the labs were privatized, everything started to change. Increasingly there were rumours."

At that moment the printer on Dr Martindale's desk whirred and rolled out a sheet. It was as if she had invisibly returned to the room or was communicating with us, spirit-fashion. I was tempted to jump up and see what was on it. But I stayed put.

"What sort of rumours?" I asked.

"Rumours of dubious research programmes. At first I assumed it was something to do with GM foods. We had a lab working on them like we do here, but it wasn't anything sinister, just looking at ways of improving crop yields, increasing disease resistance, drought tolerance, that sort of stuff."

He paused. There was obviously some inner struggle going on. Best to wait and give him time to let him speak his mind.

"A lot of staff started leaving and were replaced by others. Paradys liked the thrusting, ambitious types who just got on with what they were supposed to do and didn't have much in the way of scruples. About anything."

"Paradys?"

"Paradys Biosciences. The company who took the labs over. You need a slick corporate name these days, something dynamic and aspirational. Then you can get on with whatever dirty business you fancy."

"They were doing illegal stuff?"

"Well, not on the surface. Nothing you could put your finger on. These people knew all the PR angles, how to accentuate the positive. They wore suits rather than lab coats—"

He stopped, looked down at himself and gave a flat laugh.

"Compromises," he said. "We all make them, eh? Maybe that's why I decided to get out of there. Before I got contaminated. Ethically speaking."

It was obviously still a source of some distress to him. Gerry had always been a very moral man in his own way.

"So what was going on?" I prompted. "Did you find out any more?"

"Oh, yes," he said softly. "It turned out that one of the labs there—one of the labs that was pretty much off-limits to most of us—was working on a project aimed at genetically engineering what were called Stealth Viruses. The idea is that SVs are modified pathogenic viruses that have had their DNA altered using plasmids. Not only don't they cause the disease any more, but they're actually more vigorous than the original—"

"I'd like to pretend I know what a plasmid is," I interrupted, "but I'd be lying. Basic layman's terms, please."

He laughed. "Say someone's got a cold. Their body's awash with the virus that causes it. So you give them the stealth version of the virus, by nasal spray, for example. The SV gets to work, multiplying rapidly inside them and stifling the original bug. They recover quite quickly, in a matter of days."

"That's brilliant," I said. "A cold cure that actually works."

He wagged his finger in a cautionary way. "I was just using that as an example. I think the team at Dunstable were using a polio or measles viruses. No one's really sure. But the thing is with this kind of research, there are always unintended consequences. In this case it turned out that the particular changes made to the SVs caused side-effects. These varied in degree, depending on people's particular genetic markers." He paused. "Which of course relates to their geographical or ethnic background."

"Really?"

"Really. We're all of us more or less prone to different conditions depending on our biological inheritance. There was talk of persistent skin rashes, lymph node swellings, prolonged fever and nausea. In some cases it was rumoured that the SVs ruptured body cells and caused massive internal bleeding. So people recovered from the original illness, only to swiftly fall victim to something just as horrible."

"Bloody hell."

"Bloody hell is exactly what the some of the original volunteers suffered. Now you'd have thought that would have spelled the end of the programme. But far from it. The rumour-mill had it that the research was continuing, that the SVs were now seen as a promising avenue for the development of GSBAs. Genotype Specific Biological Agents that could in theory be used on particular populations."

Here we were once more in the world of pernicious acronyms. SVs, GSBAs: they sounded like executive vehicles rather than sinister designer microbes.

"Everything was gossip and hearsay," Gerry went on, "but we all knew that it must have some basis in fact. So I started applying for jobs. And when the offer came from Biope, I got out of there as fast as I could."

I was thinking furiously. "So this latest story about a mystery illness among prisoners. It set you thinking?"

"Not to begin with. Then something crossed my mind."

He wasn't looking at me. "What exactly?"

"Well, it's pretty hard to credit."

He looked cowed. There was a time when he had considered governments capable of anything if they thought they could get away with it.

"So if this disease exists," I said, "it has nothing to do with Muvart."

"Fuck all," he agreed vehemently, as if he had been personally betrayed.

"Then it could have come from Dunstable."

"Maybe. Maybe it was an accident, like when the foot and mouth virus escaped from the Pirbright labs. Or it might be something completely different. Nothing to do with Dunstable."

He wasn't at all convinced of this. The Pirbright case had been all over the news and it had never been established with any certainty just how the virus had got out into the surrounding area. A leaky pipe was officially blamed, though I had once interviewed a senior employee who had assured me that the pipe in question was full of cobwebs. Somehow I didn't think that was the case here.

"You know what bothers me, Nick?" Gerry said abruptly. "I should have spoken up. Gone public with my my concerns. Ten years ago I would have done just that, phoned the press or something. But I didn't want to rock the boat. I didn't want to risk losing my job."

"Well," I commiserated, "it wasn't as if you were personally responsible for manufacturing the stuff, was it?"

"People have a right to know. For better or worse. The science would have been great if it had worked and actually cured illnesses. Instead it's got perverted. I'm glad you're rooting around about this, mate. Keep at it."

The printer was chuntering again, though this time nothing came out.

"So can I use any of this?" I asked.

Again he looked uncomfortable. "Well, you can't attribute any of it directly to me. I'm sorry. It might compromise my position here."

"Biope has connections with—who was it?—Paradys?"

He shook his head. "Nothing to do with them. But it's the same industry. And people don't like whistle-blowers."

I didn't like to see him squirming like this.

"Where's the company toilet?" I asked. "I'm expecting state of the art waterless urinals and bog rolls made from reconstituted sawdust."

"At the end of the corridor," he said. "But they're not just for this part of the building, so you'll need a pass to get out and in again. It's the same everywhere."

I pointed to my lapel pass. "This one won't do?"

He shook his head. "That's just to make sure you're not shot on sight. You need this sort of swipe pass." He held up the one on the chain round his neck. "I'll have to come with you."

The door at the end of the corridor had a key pad and a swipe-lock the size of a blockbuster novel. Gerry slid his card through the slot and keyed in his code. "My old student union number," he told me. "I often use it. Funny what sticks with you."

I had long forgotten mine.

Gerry waited outside while I relieved myself. There was a rank of gleaming deodorized urinals and air-blade hand driers. The place felt hermetically sealed, a bright windowless chamber with big mirrors on both walls that made me wonder whether they were one-way affairs, with security people sitting beyond, watching you while you took a leak to ensure you weren't using the facilities to pass on secret messages or hide dodgy packages behind the cistern. I could never have worked here: it was a corporate prison.

Back in the lab Dr Martindale had returned and was doing something on one of the computers. I smiled at her and she gave me the curtest of nods. Not exactly Miss Congeniality.

Gerry had told me that he was only able to give me an hour of his time: on a personal level our meeting was intended as a catch-up and a precursor to a proper night out sometime soon. He couldn't resist hefting my bulky rucksack from under the desk, holding it up as if it was an archaeological find from days of yore.

"What in God's name have you got in here?"

Then I remembered he had been an avid reader of science fiction as an undergraduate. I extracted the three issues of *Awesome Adventures*, mentioning that I was looking into the work of Leo Parrish. Gerry had never heard of him, but he spread the magazines out on his desk with a certain glee.

"Bloody hell," he said. "I haven't read any of this stuff in years. Look at that artwork!"

He was referring to the cover advertising Parrish's "Weather Warriors". The one with the voracious tornado, the flying cows and the frantic bathing beauty.

"Salvador Dali's probably rolling in his grave," I said.

"Sense of wonder, mate! Sense of bloody wonder! Where the hell did you get these from?"

It was good to see that he had recovered some of his usual verve.

"That's a story in itself," I said. "I'll tell you about it some other time."

Briefly I explained that I was interested in Parrish's work as potential movie material. I reminded him of how much we'd both enjoyed *Blade Runner* and said I was hoping to find a similarly screen-worthy story by Parrish, a writer with a coterie of admirers that was almost a secret society.

Then I told him about the break-in and how the magazines and photocopies had been stolen.

"Christ Almighty, Nick. You must be on to something."

Liz Martindale suddenly appeared from the further reaches of the lab.

"What sort of copier have you got?" she asked.

I was more than a little surprised by her sudden interest.

"A Kenwood Chef Superdooper Mark 2," I said, somewhat disconcerted and having no idea. I left all the technical stuff to Ash and Valerie.

"Is it new and reasonably well configured?"

"Well, yes, I suppose so. It does colour, back-to-back, reduce and enlarge. Though next time I want one that makes cheese sandwiches as well."

Not a glimmer of a smile. "Most modern office copiers would have a chip with digital records of the jobs they've been used for. The default is probably quite an extensive number of megabytes, so unless you do a huge amount of copying, you've probably still got the stories saved in the copier's memory. It would be a simple matter to run them off again."

I wanted to kiss her. Metaphorically speaking, that is. Her lips would probably be as cold as the iced water in the toilet fountain. As swiftly as she had appeared, she retreated back to her work.

Gerry was grinning at me, as if to say: She may be the Ice Queen, but she's clever and enterprising.

He returned his attention to the magazines. "So what sort of thing does he write?"

I thought about it. "He's pretty much his own man, as far as I can tell."

Gerry was already perusing the Parrish story, speed-reading bits of it, no doubt. In our student days he could race through a five-hundred page novel in a matter of hours.

I sat in silence for a short while. It was better to let the story speak for itself.

Finally he looked up. "This is really intriguing," he said. "If I didn't know better I'd say he was writing about a couple of actual cutting-edge high-tech ideas for tackling climate change. Can I borrow these?"

I was reluctant to stifle his enthusiasm. "That's a bit of a problem," I confessed. "I can't let these magazines out of my sight after what's happened."

"Ah."

"We could photocopy them."

This was the droid-like doctor again; she had apparently been listening in.

"We could do it here," she told me, pointing to the machine that not only resembled a photocopier but evidently *was* one.

I stood sentinel at her shoulder as she placed the magazines on the glass. She did it with due decorum, being careful not to split the spines and turning the pages with the lightest of touches. The photocopier rumbled and swished, its repeated flashes creating the impression that all three of us were engaged in some obscure technological ceremony of enlightenment and that Dr Martindale was our High Priestess.

As soon as it was all done I put the magazines back in my rucksack and zipped it up securely.

"Warm from the oven," Gerry said as he gathered up the copies.

It was time for me to be going. I said farewell to the enigmatic doctor, and Gerry walked me back to reception. Then, almost on a whim, said he would accompany me outside.

We walked down the cinder driveway towards the gates.

"There was a microbiologist at Dunstable called Sam Oliphant," he said quietly. "He was working on the SV project, and that's where I got most of my information from. He was troubled by what was going on. Very troubled."

Gerry had paused. His eyes were brimming.

"Your partner?"

He nodded. "We used to play pool together. That's where I found him, in the pool room. Hanging from the rafters with his own belt around his neck."

"Shit, Gerry. Did someone kill him?"

He shook his head and started walking again, furiously blinking away the tears. "Perhaps something good can come of it."

He produced a security card. It had a picture of a smiling grey-haired man in his fifties and PARADYS BIOSCIENCES stamped above it.

"We swapped cards so we could swipe each other's," he told me. "A little gesture against authority, but something personal too. I had to take mine back, of course, but I just didn't want to leave his on his body. I meant to drop it somewhere for a guard to find but never did. It was obviously a suicide and maybe they assumed he'd destroyed it as a final act of defiance. In any event, we were never asked about it." He shrugged. "Did you know they closed most of the place down a few months ago?"

I didn't.

"They've transferred the project to more modern facilities, with only a skeleton staff left while they decommission. Are you determined to pursue this?"

It wasn't the Muvart story I had been hoping for. Perhaps it was something even more important.

He was offering me the card.

"Are you sure?"

"I've got other photos. Ones with better memories attached."

Aware of the CCTV cameras, I slipped the card from his hand and hastily pocketed it.

"They've probably cleared everything out by now," he said. "But you never know."

"No reason not to look into it."

"Right. It works as a swipe card. You don't have to key in a number."

"That's useful to know."

"Sam Oliphant worked in the Lister block. It's still standing as far as I know."

At the gates we hugged one another again and I had a renewed sense that he was slowly withering away.

"Keep the faith," I said to him. "You haven't done anything wrong."

He still looked anguished. "Sometimes, Nick, not doing anything isn't good enough."

NINE

On my way to the station I phoned the office. Ashad had gone out, though Jamilla had no idea where. I explained about the photocopier's memory, and she accepted the task of trying to recover the Parrish stories from it with her usual aplomb. I told her that I expected to be back at the office soon after lunch.

I had originally intended to get something to eat en route, but the train was a fast one, and it conveniently stopped at Clapham Junction. On a whim I decided to get off and take lunch close to home in a new outlet that had recently opened up near the Common. It was called Dishful Thinking, a name so awful I just couldn't resist it.

In spite, or perhaps because, of the name, there was a queue at the patio entrance, mostly yuppie parents with infants belted into strollers with wheels big enough for a motorbike. Instead, I bought a sandwich pack from Tesco and strolled home, thinking that I had at least one cold beer in the fridge. It wasn't until I actually reached my front door that I realized something was wrong.

The side entrance door, though shut, was not on the lock. Someone had opened it and put it on the latch.

My heart gave a little lurch. I stepped back and considered my options. The young couple who lived downstairs were both High Achievers somewhere in the City who worked six-day weeks and were never at home during daylight hours. The neighbours on either side comprised a reclusive Asian family and an old couple who barricaded themselves inside their house and seldom emerged. I was on my own, with no one likely to appear to help me.

After all that had happened recently, I knew that this wasn't going to be an ordinary burglary involving a couple of spotty teenagers stuffing my music deck into a holdall. No, what was going on here was probably connected with all the sinister stuff that had preceded it, not least the burglary at the office.

I retreated back down the path, got out my mobile and DI Merrick's card. With twitchy fingers I tapped in her number and pressed the call button.

It rang for some time before I heard the service message. After the beep I hastily whispered: "It's Nick Randall. I've just come home and I think someone's broken in. They may still be inside. Can you call me as soon as you get this message?"

And then I most definitely didn't do the sensible thing, which was to skedaddle and loiter at a safe distance until the cavalry showed up or the intruders left. Instead, a combination of outrage and steely determination overtook me. Not even my still-tender hand was a deterrent. I stuffed my sandwiches in my rucksack, went back down the path and rummaged in the privet hedge. Though I knew I was doing a very stupid thing, I couldn't stop myself. Burgled, bugged, and now burgled again. I had had enough.

I pulled the pistol out of its wrapping. It looked exactly like the real thing, solid metal, with a wedge-shaped barrel. There was a little lever that might have been a safety catch. I didn't touch it. I closed my hand around the grip and gingerly fingered the trigger, already trembling a little. But I was determined to go through with it.

Slowly I pushed the door open and laid my rucksack down just inside. As I climbed the stairs I pretended to be calling the police on my mobile. Perhaps this wasn't very wise, but I wanted the intruders to know that I was coming rather than give them a last-minute fright that might provoke some extreme act of retaliation. I was also hoping that my fake but loud conversation would help disguise the fact that I was scared shitless. Nothing but insane bloody-mindedness was propelling me on.

Visions of being barged or simply hurled back down the stairs evaporated when no one rushed out on to the landing. But that only prolonged the suspense. Clearing my throat noisily, I strode into my living room, brandishing the gun.

A man of my age in a dark suit, white shirt and tie was standing casually by my desk in the alcove beside the TV. Both drawers of the little filing cabinet under the desk were open and he was holding a sheaf of CDs in his hand. The computer was on, a list of files displayed on the screen.

I did a double-take before I knew for certain that this was the guy I had wrestled with on the terraces at Craven Cottage. The same chiselled jaw and intense dark eyes. Only now he looked more like a malevolent undertaker than a pervy pickpocket. The bug planter.

"What the fuck are you doing here?" I said, thrusting the gun in his general direction with what I hoped was an air of menace.

He didn't move but stared warily at me.

"I asked you a question," I said with a bit more venom. "What are you doing in my house?"

"Isn't it an apartment rather than a house?" he said in an American accent. "Or a *flat*, as you people call it."

You people? If I hadn't cared much for him beforehand, my loathing now went off the Richter scale. But I knew it would be stupid to do anything precipitate: he looked like a tough customer and plainly wasn't fazed by my arrival.

"I've already called the police," I told him. "They're on their way."

"Is that so?" He sounded as if he couldn't care less. "And what are you proposing to do with the pistol? Shoot me?"

"At this moment that's an extremely attractive idea."

I felt so angry I was half-tempted to whack him over the head with it. I had expected him to be unnerved to be caught in the act but he wasn't even belligerently defensive. He was acting as if he had every right to be there.

"First you need to put your finger on the trigger," he said.

He had noticed. I was so terrified the gun might be real and go off accidentally that my trigger finger was wrapped around the guard.

"What is this?" I said. "Who the hell are you? First you plant a bug on me, then you break into my home—"

"I work for the security services, Mr Randall."

So he knew my name. It would have been odd if he didn't. Ashad's too, no doubt. How long had they been watching us?

"Security services?" I said scornfully. "What does that mean? I know night watchmen who say they're in the security services."

"We're very worried about you, Mr Randall. You and your company. You're up to your neck in some very hot water."

I took a cautious step forward, wondering if his confidence meant that he hadn't come alone and was waiting for an associate to spring a surprise on me.

There was no one in the kitchen and I couldn't see anyone moving around through the open door of the bedroom. It was hard to be sure, though, because I hadn't opened the curtains in there that morning and the room was dim.

"The pistol's a fake," he said boldly to me. "I can see that from here."

Was he bluffing? I forced a smile. "Nice try. Better not risk it, had you?"

"It's also illegal to carry firearms in the UK without a special licence."

"And breaking and entering isn't?"

"Put it away, Mr Randall. We need to talk."

Was he carrying a gun himself? Most likely, and it was probably just as well I hadn't got into a full-scale tussle with him on the Craven Cottage terraces.

"Let's get started then," I said. "Maybe you can begin by explaining what the hell gives you the right to break in here and start going through my stuff?"

He tossed the CDs down on my desk like a bad hand of cards. I kept my distance, still holding out the gun, steeled in case he made a sudden move on me. He didn't give any such indication. Instead he looked faintly irritated, as if I was some tedious subordinate distracting him from his work.

"I'm not telling you anything until you put the pistol away."

I waited. He just looked back at me with those tiny dark eyes of his.

"You've got a bloody nerve," I said. "Show me some identification. I'm sure the police will want to see it as well."

He reached into his inside pocket and withdrew a leather wallet which he flipped open. He held it out at arm's length. I moved a little nearer and saw what looked like a large credit card. It had a colour passport-style photograph and a silvery hologrammed badge, a shield with a rampant eagle above a vertical stars-and-stripes field. The word DEFCOS was imprinted in black down the leading edge of the card, and below the photograph I could just make out a name: Noah Byrnes.

Was I actually in the presence of a real-life government agent? I did everything in my power to look unimpressed.

"What's DEFCOS?" I said. "Department for Salad Vegetables?"

"Defense Coordination Service."

"I've never heard of it."

"We don't go around advertising ourselves. We're not Wal-Mart."

He wasn't bothered whether I believed him or not. Which irritatingly made him more authentic in my eyes. But I didn't intend to roll over that easily.

"You could be anyone," I insisted, praying for the noise of a police siren. It wasn't uncommon to hear them around here, and I hoped it might persuade Byrnes that I really was waiting for the local bobbies to show.

He tut-tutted like a schoolteacher to a tiresome pupil.

"That could be a made-up badge," I said. "You might have bought it on e-Bay."

He didn't rise to this but just put the wallet away. Swiftly and one-handedly, as if he was practised at doing it.

"Even if it's real, then that's a United States service ID. This is the UK, in case you hadn't noticed. You haven't any jurisdiction here."

"That's where you're wrong, Mr Randall. What do you think the word *co-ordination* means? We work trans-nationally with law enforcement agencies in many countries. Otherwise I wouldn't be here."

"So you'll have a search warrant, then?"

I saw a flash of anger at this.

Two things occurred to me: first, he had obviously hoped to have got out of there before I returned. And second, he had probably known I hadn't planned to be at home but had been wrong-footed by my last-minute change of plan. Which meant that our office phone was being tapped.

I walked to the bedroom door, keeping the pistol trained on him. He didn't try any funny moves, though I had the distinct impression he was more than ready to defend himself if necessary. Maybe he wasn't certain the gun was a fake, or that I had the nerve to use it.

I pushed the door open and looked inside. A few drawers hung half-open as I had left them and there was the usual tangle of sheets on my unmade bed. I couldn't see anything untoward. Possibly he had searched the room earlier and put my stuff back as he had found it. Or I had got home before he could check it out.

"If you haven't got a warrant," I said, "then this search is illegal."

He just stood there, his face set hard. It was almost as if I was the intruder, he now more furious with me than vice versa.

I took a gamble, stuffing the gun into my jacket pocket. He would either try to jump me or just walk out of there. But he did neither: he just held his ground.

"I'm waiting for an explanation," I insisted.

"Your interest in a certain personage has brought you to our attention."

"Personage?" I said witheringly. "What sort of word is that?" Although I was pretty sure I knew who he meant, I pretended to take a guess: "Do you mean that naughty President Muvart?"

"No. I mean a certain now-deceased personage. An author."

"An author," I said, determinedly playing dumb. "Now who could that be? Agatha Christie? William Shakespeare? Dr Seuss?"

With each silly suggestion I saw him grow more furious. But he was still keeping it under control.

"You know who I mean, Mr Randall. Leo Parrish."

*

In the kitchen I levered the top off a bottle of Becks and peeled open my sandwich pack. Byrnes loitered in the doorway.

"We know you're interested in him, Mr Randall," he said. "Perhaps I should elucidate why we are, too."

I didn't really feel like eating, but I wanted to convey as carefree an attitude as I could. I had shown puzzlement when he mentioned Leo Parrish's name and announced that I was going to eat my lunch while I waited for the police to arrive. But Byrnes wasn't fooled, though this sudden note of reasonableness in his tone was new.

"Not too many people know about Mr Parrish's work," he went on. "As you might be aware, he had negative visibility as a writer, but a small number of dedicated followers. You might even call some of them *fanatical*."

The emphasis on the last word made me look at him despite myself while cramming the sandwich into my mouth and trying to stop dollops of tuna and mayonnaise from squirting out.

"We don't really know why, but our intelligence sources have established that a certain terrorist group appears to be using codes based on key words in Parrish's stories to coordinate their activities."

"Wha—" I started to say, but my mouth was too full.

"That may seem unlikely, but some elements will go any lengths to conceal their intentions."

"What terrorist group?" I managed to say.

"In the interests of national and international security I can't possibly reveal that. But I can guarantee you that they pose a real and immediate threat. Which is why we've been name-checking all internet traffic associated with Parrish. And which in turn is how we know of your interest."

I took a swig of beer. Byrnes had relaxed a little, as if he had decided that I was now likely to be better disposed towards him given that he was sharing confidences.

"It's likely that the main reason they're using Parrish texts is their very obscurity," he told me. "We believe the main cell is located somewhere in the United Kingdom, but the security services have only fragmentary Parrish data. DEFCOS has been tasked with tracking down extant copies of his works with the aim of establishing a comprehensive database which we can share with other agencies. Do you see where I'm coming from, Mr Randall?"

At that very moment something in my pocket started playing *The Sugar Plum Fairy*.

It was my phone, still on the ring-tone shuffle whose novelty was starting to wear thin. The caller was Cyrus Hammond.

"Is it the police?" Byrnes asked sarcastically.

I didn't say anything.

"Aren't you going to answer it?"

I had this sudden conviction that he would lunge forward and wrench it out of my hand. He knew that my gun was a fake, that I presented no real opposition to him. But he just waited.

I cut the call and pushed the phone back into my pocket.

"Not an emergency then," he said pointedly.

"It can wait. But *I* can't. I still don't know why you're here."

"Of course you do, Mr Randall. Let's get right down to the bottom line, shall we? It's come to our attention that you've recently acquired original copies of Leo Parrish's work. We would be extremely grateful if you would surrender these to us."

"Surrender?"

"We need to take them away for scanning and dissemination to the appropriate agencies. The originals would be returned to you in due course."

"Really?" I said. "But rather than just asking me you decided to sneak in here and steal them instead?"

"We didn't wish to involve you unnecessarily in sensitive security issues. Can you blame us, given your chequered background?"

"Chequered?" I challenged. "What exactly does that mean?"

"Would you classify yourself as a *pat*riot, Mr Randall?"

The arch insistence on the British form of pronunciation did nothing to endear him to me.

"Being critical of your government's less savoury activities doesn't make you a scoundrel. Or a threat to the state. Guess what? In democracies it's allowed."

Byrnes actually growled, but then remembered that he was supposed to be persuading rather than antagonizing me.

"We'd greatly appreciate your cooperation. We urgently need the stories in your possession."

"I still don't see why you couldn't just have phoned and asked. It would have been easy to run off a few photocopies and post them to you. DEFCOS has an address in the UK, does it?"

I could see him simmering up with anger again. He did everything he could to suppress it.

"We require the originals, Mr Randall, not copies. We need to retain them until the current emergency has passed."

"Emergency?"

"We're close to neutralizing this terrorist cell, to extinguishing its threat completely. Once that's accomplished, Parrish's texts will no longer have the same, let us say, *resonance*. It wouldn't matter that they were in the public domain."

None of this made very much sense to me. "So I wouldn't be getting any originals back by return of post?"

He was doing his best not to react to my sarcasm. "Not in the short term, no."

"Or copies?"

I could see he was finding my queries tiresome. "The whole point of their usefulness to this group is their extreme rarity. Were multiple copies to suddenly start proliferating, it would muddy the waters and make our task of cutting clean through to the target well nigh impossible."

He certainly had an interesting way with words. No doubt he had been checking my computer and CDs for electronic copies of the stories, but I hadn't made any yet. The only ones I had were in my rucksack at the bottom of the stairs.

I had to stay calm, not do anything rash. Byrnes's story might be true but he had made no attempt to enlist my cooperation before breaking in. I had little doubt that he was an agent of some sort, but nothing he had done or said made me think I could trust him. His story also didn't mesh with what DI Merrick had told us. I was far more inclined to believe her.

"It's true I did get my hands on some stories," I confessed. "But if you've been monitoring my activities you'll also know that our office was recently burgled. All the stories were stolen."

I sensed a welter of emotions vying for supremacy under his chiselled exterior, none of them nice. In the end he just said quietly, "It would be a big mistake not to cooperate fully with us, Mr Randall."

"Well, I'd really appreciate any assistance your agency can give us in tracking down who might be behind it. Do you have a help line I could ring?"

He did a slow blink. "You have no copies of Leo Parrish's stories currently in your possession?"

"No." Strictly speaking, this was true, if you took a liberal interpretation of "in your possession" to mean not actually on my body.

"I find that difficult to credit."

"Guess what?" I countered. "I'm finding it hard to swallow that you planted a listening device on me and then broke in here rather than just asking."

My warbling phone told me I had a text. I didn't move. Neither did Byrnes. At length it went silent.

"Come outside for a moment, Mr Randall."

Without waiting for me, he went down the stairs. Praying he wouldn't notice my rucksack in the corner, I hastily followed. Fortunately he went past it without a glance, going down the path and out on to the pavement.

He walked a short distance along and pointed at the dowdy white Fiat Bravo parked on the speed bump. "Is that your car?"

"Why, yes," I said with mock astonishment. "However did you guess?"

"Please open the trunk."

"Over here we call it the boot."

"Please open it."

What was this about? Did he think I might have a stash of Parrish's stories hidden there? Hard to believe he hadn't already checked. Or was there some other agenda going on here? Would I open it up and find a dead body, or some object planted there to incriminate me?

I seldom use the car on weekdays and there was nothing in there apart from a few used supermarket carrier bags, an emergency toolkit, and a small holdall containing running kit for those rare occasions when I decide to exercise on the Common and dutifully drive there so that I can aerobically inhale the traffic fumes.

"What's in the bag?" Byrnes demanded to know, while at the same instant I thought I spotted another man in a dark suit coming out of the alleyway from the house. I must have been leaning slightly forward, because when Byrnes abruptly swung the lid down on me, my upper half went headlong into the boot.

The lock mechanism on the underside of the lid was digging into my back. Byrnes held it there for a few seconds before lifting the lid and dragging me up by the scruff of my collar.

He stuck his face right into mine, and this time I could see all the hatred in his nut-brown eyes. Before I knew it he stuffed a carrier bag over my head and tugged on the handles. His hand went into my pocket and wrenched the pistol out.

"Don't ever pull a weapon on me—" he started, but I brought my knee up between his legs. He staggered back with a gasp while I scrambled the bag off my head, old receipts and papery bits of onion skin fluttering around me.

And then a police car appeared at the far end of the road, two men inside. I started waving my arms madly, trying to attract their attention.

The car had halted. It started to reverse into a U-turn. I stood in the middle of the road, gesturing frantically. The car drove away and disappeared from sight.

Steeling myself to face up to Byrnes again, I turned back.

There was no sign of him or anyone else.

Not a curtain moved in the houses around me, and the pavements were deserted. Whoever might have come out of the flat after us was also gone. Had the entire bizarre pantomime passed off without a single witness?

I waited awhile before walking back to the house. The moment I was inside and had latched the security chain, a wobbly mush of feelings rose up and I had to hang on to the door handle until they passed.

*

The text was from Cyrus Hammond, informing me that Walter Suthersen was doing a signing at the *Worlds Beyond* bookshop on Oxford Street in two days' time. Hammond had contacted Suthersen and explained my professional interest in Leo Parrish. Suthersen would be happy to talk to me. I just had to show up and introduce myself.

After checking to see if anything was missing—and nothing seemed to be—I spent the next fifteen minutes at my front window, peering down at the street, looking for any sign that Byrnes and his accomplice might still be lurking. Only when I was satisfied that they had really gone did I go downstairs and unlock the door. I went around to the back garden, an untended haven for rampant brambles and bindweed. Worming my way into a tangled corner so that I was suitably screened from the outside world, I got out my mobile and called Jamilla.

"Xponential Productions," came her bright and businesslike voice at length.

"It's me. Take your mobile, go outside and use it to call me back on this number ASAP."

"Mr Randall—?"

"Now, Jamilla. Outside. Do it now."

Part of me felt absurdly theatrical, but I was also in utter earnest. About ninety seconds later, she called back.

"Are you on your mobile?" I asked.

"I'm standing on the pavement."

"Good. Did you manage to get those stories from the photocopier?"

"Of course."

"You've got hard copies of them? All of them?"

"Three, yes?"

"Yes. Where are they now?"

"On your desk upstairs."

I took a deep breath. "OK. Is Ashad back?"

"No."

"Valerie in downstairs?"

"I think so."

"I want you to go upstairs, put them in a big sturdy envelope, take them down to her and tell her to lock them in her safe. She's not to give them to anyone but me."

"Righty-o," she said sweetly.

"As soon as possible, please."

"Do you want an address label on it?"

"Just my name. And clear the copier memory."

"OK."

"You don't want to know what this is about?"

"Are you going to tell me?"

"If anyone calls in asking about them, you deny all knowledge. Especially if it's an American guy called Byrnes who claims to be working for the United States government. Or anyone sounding at all American, for that matter. Whatever he says, fob him off, don't let him intimidate you."

She didn't say anything to this.

"He may be aware of my earlier conversation with you about the stories. It's possible our office phone is tapped."

I heard her give a little sigh. "Anything else I need to know?"

"I think you're wonderful. Professionally speaking, of course."

As soon as she rang off, I phoned Theresa on her mobile. I had expected to get her answering service and I was surprised when I heard her say, "Yeah, Nick. This had better be important."

Her voice was thick and slurred. Was she drunk, or was it just a bad line?

"I need some help," I told her.

"Great," she said without enthusiasm. "Any chance I could get some, too?"

"Are you at work?"

"I'm at home. It feels like the 'flu."

*

It took me an hour to get over to Theresa's. On the way I stopped off at a local chemist to stock up with cold remedies. I was half-tempted to ask the pharmacist to take a quick look at my back because it now felt as if I had been branded there, but she was a genteel-looking woman and I didn't want to alarm her.

Theresa came to the door in her nightgown, looking completely washed out. I made her a medicated drink and started up the percolator for myself while she staggered back to the sofa and subsided under a duvet. The central heating was on and the place was stifling, that sweaty, sickly heat you get when someone's ill. In the background someone on the radio was talking about the US President's "inner cabinet", a right-wing group of key advisors who were said to be exerting an undue influence on American foreign policy.

"Maybe there's going to be a coup in the White House," Theresa said to me as I passed her the drink. "The lunatics will finally take over the asylum."

"I thought you liked this President. Or at least didn't consider him a dangerous maniac."

"His heart's in the right place. It's his head I'm worried about. Because he's got liberal tendencies he's felt obliged to surround himself with more hawkish characters full of righteous indignation."

"Like Bennett Irwin?"

She managed to look impressed. "He's the one that worries me most."

But she wasn't in any state for extended political ruminations. Having sipped her drink she slumped back on her pillow, using a remote to switch off the radio.

"Have you eaten?" I asked. "Do you want me to rustle up something for you?"

"Scrambled egg on toast. I think I could just about manage that."

While I was preparing it in the kitchen, she came teetering in, clinging to the doorjamb for support.

"So what did you want to talk to me about?"

"Go and lie down. I'll bring this through in a few minutes."

"Come on," she insisted. "Spit it out, Nick."

I stirred the eggs in the pan. "Ever heard of the Defence Coordination Service? DEFCOS?"

She leaned her head against the wall, looking like she was about to pass out. "Doesn't ring any bells."

"Apparently they're a US government agency that works across international borders, hunting down terrorist cells. I was visited by one of their agents today."

"How nice for you."

"He'd broken in and was going through my stuff when I got there. Remember I was interested in Leo Parrish? The writer? He told me I had to hand over any stories I had. It was a matter of international security."

Maybe it was her illness, but Theresa didn't actually look shocked by this. "Wow," she said without emphasis. "And did you?"

"No way."

The toast pinged.

"His name was Noah Byrnes," I told her as I buttered it. "He claims some terrorist group are using code words from Parrish's stories to organize their attacks. I think he was spinning me a line. But for whatever reason, he wants all of Parrish's stuff out of circulation. Dire warnings about reprisals if I fail to cooperate."

Theresa had closed her eyes; she was obviously having difficulty staying focused. I led her back to the sofa, plumped up her pillows and set the scrambled egg down on the coffee table in front of her.

She made a valiant attempt to eat it. I drank my coffee and took her plate away when she finally admitted defeat. She looked like she was ready for a nap.

"OK," she said, "now tell me what you want."

"Well," I said, "this obviously isn't a good time, but I was wondering if you could find out, or show me how to find out, if DEFCOS really exists and, if they do, why they're so interested in Leo Parrish. He's at the centre of all this, or at least his stories are."

"No," she said, heaving herself upright. "I don't believe I can."

"What?"

"There's something you should know. A couple of days ago I had a phone call from someone claiming to be from the US Embassy. He said they'd been reviewing my residence status here in the UK. It had come to their attention that some of my recent on-line activities weren't considered appropriate for a foreign national on British soil."

"You're kidding."

"Like what, I asked. He told me it was to do with an internet search I'd been making about—I quote—'sensitive security issues of concern to the British and American governments'. I wanted to know exactly what he meant. He mentioned Parrish's name but wouldn't go any further."

She started coughing and had to lie back again.

"You know me, Nick," she said at last. "I'm not inclined to let anyone steamroller me. But somehow I knew this guy was the real deal. He made it clear that they wouldn't hesitate to have me extradited if I persisted." She took a deep, laboured breath. "I can't afford that. My work's here. I've made this place my home. I'm not prepared to jeopardize it over something that's really none of my business."

She looked genuinely sorry and uncharacteristically defeated. Perhaps that was simply because she was ill. But someone out there was turning every screw they could to close things down.

"I'm sorry," I said. "I had no idea this business would create such grief, especially for you."

She waved this off, her eyes closed again. She looked feverish, ready to sleep.

I took her plate into the kitchen and washed up. When I came back out again, she stirred from her doze.

"I'd better be on my way," I said. "Unless there's anything else I can do."

"Well," she said, "under other circumstances I might suggest a quick bout of mindless sex. But I'm really not up for it."

Something occurred to me. "Even if you were, how could you be certain that it wouldn't be monitored by those who say they're concerned about your activities?"

I saw a flash of adamantine outrage at the thought. Theresa was always hard-line about invasions of privacy.

I gathered up my trusty rucksack. She motioned to me to come close.

"The thing is," she whispered hotly right into my ear, "Parrish intrigued me so I *had* been doing a bit more rooting around."

"Really?"

She took my hand in hers.

In her other hand she was holding a ballpoint pen. She turned mine over and on my palm wrote in bold capitals:

BABEL PHISHING

TEN

Arriving back in central London, I went straight to see Ozzie. He was a ferocious-looking Geordie, short and barrel-chested with a halo of black hair and a luxuriant beard. A long-time anarchist, he shared Ashad's distrust of governments and was entirely sympathetic when I told him of my need for a secure computer terminal where I could do a bit of net-surfing without any electronic eavesdropping.

He didn't have useful news on the bug that had been planted in my rucksack. It was a standard type, widely used by criminals, the police and intelligence agencies. No distinguishing characteristics, could have come from anywhere.

He led me down to the basement and set me up with a laptop that had wires coming out of it in all directions. I barely listened to his chatter about filters, firewalls and virus definitions as I typed "Babel Phishing" into the search engine and hit the return key.

To my astonishment, the site came up instantaneously, a star-speckled black backdrop behind a face-on view of a goggle-eyed and gaping silver fish.

"There you go," Ozzie drawled with a complete lack of surprise. "Knock yourself out."

With that, he strutted back up the stairs to the shop.

It turned out that the site was a forum for critical discussions on science fiction writers, most of whom were unknown to me. I couldn't find any listing for Leo Parrish, but there was one under the unlikely name of *Dai O'Seas*. The fact that the absurd name was italicized, unlike the others, alerted me. The fact that it had an ecclesiastical ring, like 'Parrish', gave me a fluttery feeling of excitement as I clicked on the link.

Within seconds I knew for certain that *Dai O'Seas* was definitely Leo Parrish. The site editor's introduction began by describing him as: "A name to conjure with, and preferably not to drop" and went on to say that: "D O'S was active in the late 1950s, producing stories for short-lived semi-prozines with titles likely to stir in readers feelings of Shock & Awe. He Whose Name Cannot Be Spoken For Fear Of Malign Retribution is regarded by many as a true original. In the space of only three years he produced a raft of stories that demonstrated great versatility and invention. Owing to the limited circulation of the magazines and his subsequent disappearance from the scene, his name is relatively unknown in the field and his reputation has always been higher than his readership. A cult writer par excellence."

Though cleverly designed to avoid any mention of Parrish's name, this kind of obliqueness would have been wearying if it had been carried on at length. Fortunately the rest of the site was given over to readers' comments and queries, with brief editorial responses. There were only half a dozen of them, but it was quite clear that in most cases they were from existing fans of Parrish's work who were complicit in the game of not actually mentioning him by name, presumably so that the likes of Noah Byrnes would not be able to locate the site and either shut it down or interfere with it in some other way, most likely by harassing the contributors.

The site's editor was Daffyd Rhodes, a name I suspected was also a pseudonym. Obviously enjoying the challenge of providing a disguised forum for a writer he plainly admired, Rhodes joked with one participant, who had referred to Parrish as "The Pope", that the writer had been well and truly excommunicated. To another, who actually mentioned Walter Suthersen and suggested that he and other well-known writers owed more to the neglected author than they admitted, Rhodes slyly agreed that the stories had never been of merely parochial interest. In response to a query about the author's only novel, which they referred to as *Larks*, he said that it was virtually unobtainable and the stuff of legend in more than one sense. And finally, to a query that said: "Who really is Dai O'Seas? Is this a joke?", he tersely replied: "Not from where I'm sitting".

I must have been studying the site for ten minutes or so when the laptop started bleeping like a heart monitor. The frequency increased, whereupon Ozzie reappeared.

"What's going on?" I asked him.

"You've got about thirty seconds," he told me. "Someone we probably don't like is trying to get a fix on the machine."

I'd already clicked on the site's Inbox. Quickly I typed in:

Seriously need your advice concerning D O'S. Genuine query, a matter of professional interest. Recent brush with a MIB has piqued curiosity. Please call.

"Wrap it up," Ozzie said bluntly, looming at my shoulder.

I inserted my mobile number and signed the message *Nick Randall, Xponential Productions* before clicking on SUBMIT.

The bleeping was now alarmingly rapid. Ozzie reached across me and shut the site down with a couple of key strokes.

*

It was six o'clock by the time I got to the office. Valerie had already locked up the main office and left, but Jamilla had hung on until I arrived. She was chewing a wodge of pink bubblegum while watching an archive clip of one of the space shuttles.

"What's that about?" I asked.

"NASA is bringing Atlantis and Endeavour out of retirement," she told me. "They're going up with instruments to take a closer look at that new star."

Apparently the star was now emitting higher-than-expected levels of X-rays and gamma rays, though the agency was stressing that they were still within the normal range.

"Ashad?" I asked. His mobile had been off when I tried to ring him en route.

"He hasn't been in all day. He phoned to say he's gone to the seaside."

I didn't have a clue what this meant. "Did anyone else call?"

"Just the usual," she told me, handing me a list. "No police or spies or dodgy foreign nationals. You look terrible."

"Tough day," I told her. "Did you get the stories to Valerie?"

She nodded. "All right if I go home now?"

I squinted at her. "Are you OK with all this?"

"All what?"

"This cloak and dagger stuff. I don't really know what's going on myself."

She shrugged, hefted her jacket and shoulder-bag. Then she made me jump by blowing a bubble and bursting it noisily as she went out the door.

I decided I wasn't going to go home that night. I would set up the camp-bed, get in a takeaway, maybe even go and see a movie in the West End like any normal punter. There was still no word back from DI Merrick. Maybe I should try Ashad again and tell him about Byrnes. No, it could wait. It had been a busy day and my back felt bruised where Byrnes had impaled it. Where was someone to slather on soothing ointment when you needed them?

I had sent the message to "Daffydd Rhodes" more in hope than expectation. I was gambling that he would pick up on the Man In Black bit and take a risk on me, having previously been able to confirm that both Xponential and I actually did exist. But only if he was so minded. If he was as suspicious as everyone else associated with Parrish, it was more likely he would assume it to be some plot by spooks and simply not bother.

In the end I passed on a movie and had pie and chips down the street at my local, easing it down with a couple of pints. The little bar was filled with a gaggle of Italian tourists, but the noise of their chatter didn't stop me from hearing a ding-donging from my phone.

The number wasn't familiar. I said my name and waited.

There was that silence you get when you're cold-called at home by someone on the other side of the world who's going to ask if you're the householder and could you spare a few minutes to discuss your home insurance or the latest phone package that will give you free calls forever anywhere in the universe.

"Hello?" I said.

"Xponential Productions?" said a male voice.

"Well, actually it's the pub at the moment. After hours, you know? What can I do for you?"

"You left me a message."

The voice was hushed yet breathless, as if it didn't quite know what to expect.

"Rhodes?" I said on a guess. "Daffydd Rhodes?"

There was a funny little laugh at the other end. It was over quickly.

"It's Rhodri. Rhodri Davies."

The beers I'd swallowed weren't exactly making me razor sharp. But the name was familiar.

"You run the *Babel Phishing* site?"

"Guilty, boss. And you ...?"

"Independent production company," I told him. "We make feature films, when we can afford them. Also documentaries and animations—"

"*DisOrg*!" he said with real enthusiasm. "*Absolute Hero*!"

"You've got it." I decided to get straight to the point. "I thought your website was fascinating. I'm very interested in Leo Parrish."

"Quite a few people are. Including plenty that I don't particularly want to be talking to."

I wasn't entirely surprised by this, but I didn't want to get sidetracked.

"I'm searching for movie material," I said. "Science fiction. Something challenging, like Philip K. Dick. I managed to get my hands on some of Parrish's stories. Fascinating. I'd like to find out more about him."

There was a silence. I had the weird sense that Davies was holding his breath at the other end of the line.

"Earlier today I got home to find someone going through my stuff," I told him. "He wanted me to hand over anything I had on Parrish. Claimed to be working for a US government agency. We've also had our offices burgled."

I was certain I heard him suppress another nervous laugh.

"The curse of Parrish strikes again," he said gleefully.

"This is funny?"

"Well," he said hastily, "not exactly. But it's pretty daft."

"Really? Why?"

"He's a writer. They act like he's Beelzebub."

"They?"

"Are you really who you say you are?"

I wondered what to say. "Do you know Arthur Townsend?"

"Art-To?"

I guessed that this was some kind of nickname. "I originally got the stories from him. Or rather his wife sent them to me. Just before there was a fire at his place."

There was a further silence that I felt was somehow contemplative. This time I didn't try to fill it.

"He reckons it was deliberate," Davies said at last.

"I bet he does. There were some dodgy goings-on when I visited him. Maybe his paranoia is justified."

"Did Arthur put you on to me?"

"No. My ex-wife tracked your site down. She's good at that sort of thing. Your discussions about Parrish are pretty well hidden."

"Needs must," he said blithely.

"Listen," I told him, "I'm rapidly reaching the point where I don't trust telephone conversations. Can we meet? I'd really like to find out more about Parrish. I don't know much about—SF."

He laughed again. I guessed that he was in his thirties and presumably Welsh, though he didn't have a discernable accent.

"You're based in London, yes?" he said.

"Charing Cross Road. I can give you the address."

"Have you heard of Walter Suthersen?"

Suddenly I knew what he was going to say. "The book signing?" I said. "At *Worlds Beyond*?"

"I'll meet you there."

*

Voices woke me. I had fallen asleep in the viewing theatre while watching *Grosse Pointe Blank* after returning from the pub. The hit-man theme felt appropriate, as did its absurdist style. But the movie had long run its course, the screen still bright but featureless. The voices were coming from outside.

Shaking the sleep from my head, I killed the screen with the remote. Slowly I levered myself out of my seat, my heart beginning to pick up pace as I contemplated the possibilities. I was pretty sure I had locked the office doors behind me, in which case it was highly likely that someone had just broken in. It was a man and woman, and judging by the way they were talking loudly and even laughing they didn't expect to find anyone here. They had even put the lights on.

I eased the theatre door open and poked my head out.

Ashad and DI Merrick were standing in the middle of the room.

Both of them were in party clothes, Ashad dressed quite smartly by his standards in a candy-striped shirt and skinny black jeans that really didn't suit his chunky legs. DI Merrick was wearing sheer black leggings that really *did* suit her, and a cropped soft leather jacket which she promptly took off to reveal a strapped flower-print top. Her hair was piled up in a kind of free-form top-knot and she had been liberal with her make-up, accentuating her dark eyes and her general sultriness. Never had anyone looked less like a plod.

They sat down together at one of the circular tables we sometimes used for conferences. As I listened to them talking I realized that they had been out for dinner together, followed by a visit to a club in Soho to watch a band I had never heard of. It was now past two in the morning. Though neither was drunk, they had both plainly had a little alcohol so that the usual inhibitions had softened. Ashad kept touching her arm as they talked about the band while Merrick smiled back at him even as she began to insist that she really had to get a night bus home. Ashad asserted that this was a bad idea and suggested that the two of them bed down in the office. He was gentlemanly enough to point out that there were separate sleeping bags, but I got the distinct impression that he would have been more than happy to crawl into hers.

I was torn between natural deep curiosity and the urge not to be a shifty voyeur. I didn't want to reveal myself because that might entail explaining to Merrick why I was skulking around the office in the middle of the night. I had no desire to get into that. Still, it would have been nice to have heard her explain why she hadn't replied to my phone message. Had she been with Ashad all day? On an extended date, perhaps, with her phone switched off?

I could scarcely credit how flirtatious Ashad was being with her. Though I knew he had had girlfriends in the past, in recent years he had never shown any inclination toward romance, or even the occasional fling. Too busy trying to put the world to rights. Yet here he was, telling her anecdotes about the various bands he had seen over the years, listening to her own accounts with the kind of rapt attentiveness he seldom showed to others. They steered clear of any discussion of politics or work, keeping it determinedly light and fluffy. It had all the hallmarks of a successful first date, two people who plainly enjoyed one another's company so much that they were reluctant to call it a night. And in Ashad's case at least, more than ready to take it further given the slightest encouragement.

I hadn't actually got around to making up a bed for myself earlier, so Ashad would have no reason to suspect I was here if he managed to persuade Merrick to stay over. I was ready to crawl back into the theatre the moment they started snogging, but Merrick finally rose and announced that she really had to get home. Nothing Ashad could say would persuade her otherwise. She had to be up early the following morning, she told him, and needed a few hours' decent sleep.

Ashad insisted on phoning for a taxi rather than leaving her to the mercy of the night buses, policewoman or not. From what I could gather she lived somewhere out Shepherd's Bush way.

The cab company he contacted was local, run by someone we knew, and it was only a matter of minutes before he got a call back to say a car was waiting outside. I imagined Ashad would bid her farewell at this point, but he announced that he would take her home and then have the cab drop him at his own place. As they went out I heard Merrick insisting that she was going to pay her half of the fare.

And then finally they were gone, the doors locked behind them, the entire place falling into a silence that felt deeper than usual. Stiff and exhausted and still nursing an ache between my shoulder blades, I crawled downstairs and dragged out one of the sleeping bags, feeling as if I had done something faintly disreputable but too tired to care.

*

In the morning I managed to wake before Jamilla got in. I showered, shaved and put on a change of clothes from my emergency stash. Then, about a quarter of an hour before she was due to arrive, I did a rather mean thing: I phoned Ashad at home.

Partly it was to find out if he was actually there or whether he had managed to inveigle himself into Merrick's bed that night. The other part of it was probably plain and simple jealousy that he had had a good night out with an attractive woman whereas I had ended up eating pie and chips in the pub on my own.

I had it sixty/forty in my mind that Merrick had resisted his advances, and I felt gratified when I suddenly heard his mumbled voice at the other end of the line.

"Whaaa ..." was the extent of it.

"Morning," I said brightly. "Did I wake you up?"

A muffled sense of movement and a muted groan. Then his bleary voice asking, "What time is it?"

"Just before nine. I thought I'd get in early today."

There was a kind of drowned thud, as if he had dropped the phone, or rolled over on it. Then: "You're at the office?"

He was obviously having difficulty processing information this morning.

"Yep," I said cheerily. "What happened to you yesterday?"

I had the sense that he was heaving himself up into a sitting position in the bed. A sudden thought occurred to me: Merrick might have gone to his place instead, might even now be lying right there beside him. I had no evidence for this, but I felt a renewed sense that I might be intruding on something private.

Before he could answer my question I said, "Don't tell me now. I think our phones might be tapped."

"What?"

I wanted whoever might be listening to know I was on to them.

"Long story," I said. "Talk about it when you get in."

More shifting around at the other end. "Is there some emergency?" he asked, obviously striving to get his brain into gear.

"No, no," I assured him. "Everything's fine here. Just thought I'd check in. Late night last night?"

There was a pause before he said, "You could say that."

"Not disturbing you, am I? Are you with someone?"

This was hardly fair, but I was enjoying myself too much.

"Of course I'm bloody not," Ashad said grumpily. "I'll see you later."

And he put the phone down on me.

When Jamilla walked in about five minutes later she took one look at me and said, "You spent the night here."

She had spotted my change of clothing, recognized the jeans and white shirt that I kept in the bottom drawer of my desk. It was the sort of thing women always noticed, whereas I would have needed to be wearing top hat and tails to register on the average man.

My mobile played the guitar riff from "Seven-Nation Army". I never knew what it was going to burst out with. The phone had been a birthday present from everyone in our offices, but it was Ash who had organized it. I was pretty sure by now that he must have got someone to nobble it for a laugh, most likely Ozzie. Assuming it wasn't a symptom of something more sinister.

DI Merrick was on the other end of the line.

"I've only just picked up your message," she told me, to the backdrop of a whooping police car siren. "Are you all right?"

Was she was in transit? I walked out of Jamilla's earshot.

"I'm fine," I said. "Only my dignity was bruised."

"So what happened?"

"Someone broke in. I caught him in the act going through my stuff. An American called Noah Byrnes. He claimed to be working for one of the US secret services. DEFCOS?"

I could hear the squawky voices of a police car intercom in the background.

"I've heard of them," she said. "They sometimes liaise with us."

"Really? And did they liaise with you on this burglary?"

She said, "Left here" to whoever was in the car with her, then: "What did he want?"

"He seems to think I've been stockpiling Leo Parrish stories and demanded I hand them over to save the world from terrorism."

Another pause while she said something to the driver.

"Are you on an emergency?" I asked.

"We're just taking a short cut. And have you?"

"Have I what?"

"Been stockpiling stories?"

"Of course not," I said, a little too quickly. "His angle on Parrish was totally different from yours."

The car intercom squawked again, and then abruptly went silent. So did the siren.

"They do have some jurisdiction over here, you know," she said.

"So he told me. But he broke in and treated me like I was a criminal. I've got every right to resent that."

I decided against telling her that Byrnes had assaulted me and that I had assaulted him back. Or that I had been waving a fake gun around. I had no idea how much I could trust her, given that she had already admitted that she wasn't able to tell us the full story about Parrish.

"So *is* there some terrorist connection?" I asked.

"I wouldn't go that far."

"How far *would* you go?"

More instructions to her driver, a brief whoop of the siren again.

"You'd better give me the details of exactly what happened."

"I'd rather speak to you face to face. Did you know our phones here are being tapped?"

I was fishing, since I wasn't sure myself.

"I think that's highly unlikely."

"Could you check? I'd like to know. I'm beginning to feel like a terrorist suspect myself."

"That's no joking matter, Mr Randall."

"What makes you think I'm joking?"

She didn't say anything to this. I had the impression that her car had now stopped. A door clunked shut.

"If you're prepared to leave it with me," she said, "I'll see what I can find out."

"Fine." I certainly didn't plan to go chasing down Byrnes myself or make some kind of formal complaint. I had a feeling it would have been like poking a stick in a beehive.

"Any news on the burglary?" I asked.

I could hear footsteps, presumably hers. "Nothing as yet," she answered. "Though your landlord is quite an interesting character."

"You think he did it?"

"I'm not saying that at all. Just that he's on our radar. Do you think he would have any motive?"

I had mulled this over myself. "He came round the other day and fitted a new stair carpet. I can't see why he'd first trash the place, then do that."

"To deflect attention from himself, perhaps?"

"I'm getting the impression you *do* suspect him."

"Not necessarily. We're pursuing more than one line of enquiry and ruling nothing out at this stage."

A rote 'fob them off' line, I was sure. I didn't say anything.

"I'm really sorry I didn't pick up your message until this morning. It was my day off yesterday, and I only use this phone for work messages. I didn't switch it on till this morning."

"I see."

"As it happens, I spent a very pleasant evening socializing with your colleague."

Well, what do you know, she was being more candid than Ashad. I played dumb. "Who?"

"Mr Husseyin. He didn't mention it?"

"I haven't seen him this morning," I told her, wondering if it was possible that Ashad had phoned her immediately after talking to me. Or *had* she been lying there next to him and had hotfooted it out of there to a waiting car immediately afterwards to belatedly return my call?

"Was it a date?" I asked.

She laughed. "I suppose it was. We had dinner and went to a club. He's good company."

"You should feel honoured. The last time he went out with someone from the police they had handcuffs on him."

She laughed again. I had no reason to suspect that it was anything other than spontaneous and genuine.

"I'm joking," I said. "He hasn't been arrested in years."

"Say hello to him from me," she said. "I'll be in touch later."

*

I was downstairs in an editorial meeting with Valerie when Ashad finally got in. He looked quite chipper. Slung over his shoulder was a video camera case.

As soon as we were alone together upstairs I said, "DI Merrick phoned earlier."

Incapable of guile, he looked at me like a guilty child.

"She sends her regards," I told him.

"I went out with her last night," he blurted.

"So I gather."

"There was this band. I thought she might be interested. So I phoned her."

I was slightly relieved to hear that it was he who had taken the initiative.

"Have a nice time, did you?" Then I stuck my hand up before he could start speaking. "No. Don't tell me. It really isn't any of my business."

"I like her, Nick," he insisted on saying. "She's—"

"Honestly," I interrupted forcefully. "I really don't want to know. Just be careful, will you? We've got a lot going on here, and she's a policewoman."

"We didn't talk business or sleep together or anything."

"Ash, I don't want to know!"

"I trust her. I think she's on the level."

I sighed. "Is that your head speaking, or is it coming from somewhere lower down?"

I knew it was unfair of me to be badgering him in this way, but he wasn't aware of what I had been through the day before with

Byrnes. I proceeded to tell him, and he was suitably outraged, wanting to lodge all manner of official complaints right there and then.

"No," I said. "I've told the detective inspector. She's promised to look into it. If you trust her, let her get on with it. The best thing we can do is carry on with our usual business."

"Oh yeah," he said dubiously. "What about the phone taps?"

"She said she'd look into that, too."

"Nothing showed up on the Bug Buster," he pointed out.

"Yeah, well, that doesn't exactly inspire confidence. In any case, do phone taps need bugs? I don't think so. And the ring tone on my mobile is all over the place."

Ash actually smirked.

"I had a feeling it might be you. I can't seem to re-set it. Any ideas? "

"None whatsoever, " he said with patent dishonesty.

I wasn't going to give him the satisfaction of pleading. Instead I told him about Gerry's revelations concerning the work at Dunstable and Paradys Biosciences. And the possibility that Alec Furneaux's over-the-top report might have some basis in fact. He started looking at me with a vindicated gleam in his eyes.

"You know where I was most of yesterday?" he said to me.

"Jamilla told me you'd gone to the seaside."

"I made a few new acquaintances at the West Halstow Yachting Club."

*

"It was choppy," Ashad told me as we stared at the video footage on the screen. "But they managed to get one or two interesting shots."

Ashad had been to North Kent, to the yachting club at the nearest place on the coast to Halstow Island. He had been granted an interview with club members, in particular those who were especially outraged by what was going on at the island. Apparently the waters in the vicinity had always been open to sailors until six months ago, and the new restrictions had annoyed the locals mightily. To such an extent that soon after they were imposed a husband and wife team had taken their boat out and sailed directly towards it.

The woman had shot intermittent video footage, and I could see the warning buoys with their flashing red lights around the island. There was plenty of spray, and the images were speckled and blurred, the blocky white buildings on the muck-black island constantly wobbling and shifting their contours with the swell and the beading of the lens.

At first not much was very visible apart from indications of a tall wire-mesh fence around the site. As the two senior sailors—a plucky couple, according to Ashad, despite being dyed-in-the-wool Tories—closed on the island, a Coastguard vessel appeared and made a beeline for them, cutting a big foaming chevron through the water. The yacht bucked and dipped, and just as it crested a wave, the woman had managed to hold the camera steady and zoom on the island.

There was a glimpse, no more than a second or two, of a little group of figures in olive-green overalls, walking in a line outside one of the buildings.

"See it?" Ashad cried.

It was quickly gone as the yacht dipped again.

Ashad backtracked the video and froze on the image. It was like looking through a veil of water, but there was every suggestion that the men were all black-haired and Asiatic.

"What do you think?" Ashad asked me.

Though the overalls were a different colour, comparisons with images of the inmates at Guantanamo Bay were irresistible.

"They might be just factory workers," I said. In the background were two figures in dark uniforms. "Are those guards?"

"You tell me."

The couple hadn't managed to get any further shots of the men before the Coastguard vessel veered across the yacht's bow and one of its crew pointed a megaphone directly at the camera.

"Let me guess," I said in the absence of a soundtrack. "He's inviting them to go on board for a shot of rum."

"Basically he warned them that if they didn't piss off right there and then, they'd be sunk."

"They didn't seize the camera?"

"I don't think they realized we'd been filming. It was one of those tiny digitals."

Both of us knew that this was potentially explosive stuff. Blurred and fleeting though the footage was, it suggested that people were being incarcerated on Halstow Island. Not conclusive, but why have an exclusion zone around an island if there was only a meat processing plant on it? And was there any link with the hints I had got from Gerry of dodgy goings-on in secret corners of the biosciences world?

I started thinking about the dead Sam Oliphant, whose security pass was in my pocket, perhaps all that remained of him now. We owed it to him to pursue this story as far as we could take it.

ELEVEN

I scouted the web for information on DEFCOS. There wasn't much, and some of it was contradictory. Set up in the aftermath of 9/11, it was described by one site as a field-operative offshoot of the National Security Agency, by another as a self-contained branch of the Department of Homeland Security, and by a third as the US equivalent of the UK's Counter Terrorism Command, active both in the US and overseas and tasked with gathering intelligence on international terrorism and working with other agencies on preventative measures. None of the sites listed agency executives but rather gave the impression that it was a protean organisation of relatively recent vintage whose structure and remit was still a work in progress. Which wasn't something I found particularly cheering. If DEFCOS agents felt that their spheres of influence weren't strictly demarcated, they might consider themselves free to take any action they considered necessary. Like bugging, burglary and stuffing carrier bags over the heads of people who annoyed them.

Needing some light relief, I switched my investigative attention to Walter Suthersen. By complete contrast, there was plenty of online information about him. A winner of many awards over the past thirty years, he was respected in the field as well as being popular and generous with his time at everything from small-audience readings to conventions where hundreds, sometimes thousands, of SF fans regularly gathered to celebrate their enthusiasms.

As a young man in 1960 Suthersen had briefly edited a professional magazine called *Vantage SF* before his own career as a writer of short stories and novels took off. However, what most intrigued me was a passing reference to him also acting as an adviser to a US Senate Committee on the Influence of Science Fiction Satire on National Morale. This had been a somewhat paranoid time in the US, which had also produced a Senate Report on Comic Books and Juvenile Delinquency. Apparently the formation of the committee had been stimulated by stories appearing in popular SF magazines of the day that were critical of business and advertising practices. Had some McCarthyite senator or congressman become concerned that the criticism was Commie-inspired and a threat to the pursuit of the American Dream?

I clicked on a link to the Committee's report and there it was in front of me. In a floating window I read that the Library of Congress had forwarded a complete archive of the Senate hearings to the British Library of Political and Economic Science, which had got a grant to put them onto its website. Apparently not even the Library of Congress itself did that.

I closed the window, and did a search of the report for Leo Parrish. There was no reference to him. Nor to Suthersen. Which was no surprise: if this was a document that *could* be automatically searched, any mention of Parrish would have come to light during Theresa's earlier trawls for the name.

By contrast there was a pretty exhaustive list of unfamiliar names of committee members, including that of the typist. He had either bashed out the report on a dodgy typewriter or been too hasty or inept because the report was littered with typos such as "presend-day" and "Scence Fiction". It ended by offering the Committee's gratitude to SFU and WXS.

A search for writers with these initials produced mixed results. There was none initialled SFU. I found one called Steven Utley, but he had been born little more than a decade before the hearing took place and hadn't started publishing until the 1970s. I had better luck with WXS. This referred to Walter Suthersen. He was actually a rare American without a middle name but according to his Wikipedia entry had in the past occasionally used X in the by-line of some of his earliest published work.

I scanned through the report. There were heavy-handed summaries of various stories designed to illustrate the appalling nightmares science-fiction writers were conjuring. A novel called

The Space Merchants by Frederik Pohl and C.M. Kornbluth was described as follows:

"*The Space Merchants* (aka *Gravy Planet*!) Businesses, portrayed as ruthless and rapacious, have taken over from Governments. Advertising, apparently the worst of these corporations, is shown to mislead the world into using unnecessary products and persuading them to colonize another planet for underhand reasons. A vicious and cynical story which seeks to undermine the whole basis of a civilized society. The book even suggests that the future might hold food shortages which could be solved by growing artificial meat."

Another novel, *The Stars My Destination* by Alfred Bester, was said to be "a scathing depiction of business as evil and over-powerful run by a decadent elite which is itself decadent and immoral as well as violent". A second C.M. Kornbluth title, *The Syndic*, was summarized as: "America run by organized crime which has taken over from the US Government and, disgracefully, this is supposed to have led to a good life for the American people. The US Government is based in Iceland!"

There was much more of this and frequent references to *Galaxy* magazine as being one of the worst offenders by publishing such tales. Whoever had written the reports appeared clunkingly literal-minded and blind to satire and irony. But it very much reflected the feverish climate of the day. The United States had been going through one of its periodic spasms of home-grown indignation, imagining enemies lurking in every nook and cranny of the Republic.

I skimmed the other summaries and eventually came to this:

Some stories demonstrate contempt for the actions of the United States Government and many aspects of ordinary American life, including daily commerce, television and religious observance. A diverse assortment of such stories from a range of publications was drawn to the committee's attention. Exhibits were introduced at the New York hearings where certain authors also appeared before the committee.

There was a long list of story titles with the authors' names alongside. Among them were "Transmission" and "Exaltation", credited to L.Oarrish by the cack-handed typist. "Transmission" was a satire on the dangers of watching too much television, and presumably the committee had also found "Exaltation" subversive, though nothing was specified in this part of the report.

Near the bottom I found a list of publishers and distributors of science fiction magazines. Against the name and address of Ridge Publications appeared "Awesome Adventures—21" and "Shocking Stories—2". Did the numbers refer to the particular issues they had actually looked at, or the total number of issues published? Whichever it was, the senators had evidently got their hands on the second part of Parrish's serial, by now as rare as a cuckoo's nest. Had Parrish himself actually appeared before the Committee? A question I could ask Walter Suthersen when I met him.

*

"For Heaven's sake," bristled the beanpole matriarch with the silvery hair. "How many more times? Keep the line straight, don't push and make sure you've bought at least one book in this store."

High heels clacking, she strutted up and down the ragged line in her snug cream knit dress, an elderly but well-maintained woman who plainly wasn't happy. Everyone in the queue looked a little bewildered at her agitation.

The queue itself comprised a motley bunch ranging from smartly-attired women to pear-shaped men in unflattering T-shirts and trousers belted above their navels: but everyone was patient and good-natured, even the guy holding a carrier bag bulging with enough books to stock a small library. No one was being obnoxious apart from Ms High Heels.

Meanwhile, the man we were all waiting to see had just sat down behind a table at the far end of the room, framed by displays of his books and posters for the forthcoming movie of *Zeta Prime*. Now in his seventies, Walter Suthersen looked older than the photograph on his website but he was instantly recognisable, a lean sun-browned man who looked as if he had spent plenty of his life outdoors.

Though I had passed *Worlds Beyond* many times I had never actually ventured inside the store until now. From the front it looked like a dingy specialist outlet, its narrow shop window plastered with movie posters that obscured the interior. I had envisaged it as a cramped rabbit's warren of geeky merchandise pored over by a furtive troglodytic clientele, prejudices that were confounded by the large brightly-lit megastore that opened up around me as soon as I crossed the threshold.

There were three levels. I didn't explore the basement, which was where the comics and graphic novels were displayed. The ground floor was devoted to computer games, film and TV merchandise, with rank upon rank of DVDs on fantastical themes. I was vain enough to check out whether any of Xponential's output was on show. We were represented by *DisOrg* and *Absolute Hero*, both carrying enthusiastic Staff Recommendations.

Upstairs in the Books department a sizeable advance queue had already formed in front of the signing table. Plenty of other punters were browsing the alcoves where books were organized into a bewildering array of categories: Dark Fantasy, Steampunk, Crossover, Hard SF. I could see what Gerry meant when he talked about a sense of wonder. It was on display practically everywhere you looked, sometimes a little too emphatically, but often with a knowing sense of its own absurdity.

I decided to buy one of Suthersen's books for signing. There was a whole section devoted to his work. During the 1960s he had written the "Far Frontiers" sequence of novels, which had apparently introduced a rich variety of alien species with inventive means of getting around his sprawling universe. Subsequently he had produced books about colliding universes, sentient stars and a series set in an alternative history where the Earth had an idyllic sister planet orbiting in counterpoint around the Sun. It was a heady mix, though according to the blurbs Suthersen's writing was notable for its complex characters and a fluent style with a trademark dry wit.

In the end I settled for the movie paperback tie-in edition of *Zeta Prime*. The cover featured a photograph of Ryan Carmichael, bulgingly enhanced and sleek-skinned, subduing a trio of mottled aliens with cumbersome foreheads and goats' eyes. Not exactly an advert for complex characters, and even less so for wit, but it was my passport to the queue.

Ms High Heels continued to strut about with increasing displays of irritation. Then Suthersen uncoiled his lanky frame, rose and had a quiet word with her before saying:

"Ladies and gentlemen, I think we can get this show on the road."

The woman retreated into the shadows and a much younger one sat down beside Suthersen at his table. She had a badge which identified her as working for Suthersen's publishers and she began arranging small piles of his titles on the table.

Suthersen was dressed in a check shirt and jeans, which accentuated the impression of an outdoors man rather than a writer. He had an easy smile and pleasant words for everyone, even the guy with the bagful of books, all of which must have been at least twenty years old.

As we slowly shuffled forward, I felt a tap on my shoulder. I turned and saw a man with dark floppy hair and a lop-sided smile peering uncertainly at me.

"Nick Randall?" he said.

He was about thirty, dressed from neck to ankle in shades of khaki and fawn denim.

"Rhodri Davies?"

"Guilty, boss."

"How on earth did you know it was me?" I asked him. It had belatedly dawned on me that we hadn't exchanged descriptions.

"There's a photo of you on your company website. Not as dashing as in real life, of course."

From his shoulder bag he produced a single buttercup-yellow A4 sheet, offering it to me as if by way of introduction. It was the latest print version of his news bulletin, *Homeopape*, and he was pleased that I knew that the title had come from a Philip K. Dick novel. I mentioned *Babel Phishing* and the *Occam's Eraser* site with its spurious claim that Leo Parrish was just an in-house pen name. He looked slightly nervous when I mentioned Parrish's name, though he immediately dismissed the entry as something maliciously added by an unknown source to mislead.

There were people in close proximity all around us. Feeling a little theatrical, I murmured, "I assume you'd prefer not to talk about our particular interest here."

"Somewhere more comfortable might be better," he agreed. "There's a pub around the corner."

He said this with a hopeful expression. I grinned. "Perfect."

We edged forward while Davies told me a bit about himself. He was a Cambridge-educated physicist who now made his living as a freelance writer with a special interest in science fiction and pseudo-science, whose pretensions never ceased to amaze and delight him. He spoke in rapid-fire sentences and struck me as jolly and very clever but not in any way a smart arse. Refreshingly, I had no sense that he had a hidden agenda.

We were close to the front of the queue now. The older woman in the cream dress was still loitering in the background, watching everything with a sour expression.

"That's his wife, Barbara," Davies told me.

"You've met her?"

He shook his head. "Just seen her around from time to time at conventions."

We moved a step closer to the table.

"Do you buy your books here?" I asked.

"God forbid," he said. "Not that I've got anything against it. Well, not this floor, anyway. But I get more review copies than I can read. I do a fanzine with capsule reviews of the latest titles, and publishers are very obliging about feeding my addiction. Though they didn't contribute to the cost of the extension I had to get built."

"Just for books?"

"If Ruth would let me, I'd move us into the extension and use the house for the books."

I assumed that Ruth was his wife or girlfriend. "Have you met Suthersen before?"

"We were both up for Hugos at a convention a few years back." He caught my blank look. "They're science fiction awards named after an old-time editor. Our Oscars. Walt's were for professional writing and mine for fannish stuff. We were sitting at the same table and we had a few drinks afterwards. He's a friendly guy."

Suddenly we were at the head of the queue. We stepped forward. Suthersen reached for my copy of *Zeta Prime*, then did a double take.

"Rhodri Davies," he said familiarly. "Good to see you again."

He stood up and shook Davies's hand, and then mine also as Davies introduced me.

"Ah yes," he said. "Cyrus told me to expect you. Look, I can't really chat now but I'd be happy to meet afterwards if you guys can make it."

"We're going to The Eagle around the corner," Davies told him. "OK with you?"

"Believe me," Suthersen said in a low voice, "once this is over I'll be ready for a stiff drink."

We moved out of the way so that he could use his practised skills on his next customer.

*

The Eagle was pleasantly unreconstructed, all Edwardian mirrors, deeply varnished wood and brass fittings. Davies and I sat with pints in an alcove of the main bar. It wasn't especially crowded, but both of us had checked that no one was sitting within earshot.

I filled him in a bit more about why I had become interested in Parrish's work and what had happened as a result. When I told him about Noah Byrnes claiming the Parrish stories were being used as terrorist codes, he looked curious. Though familiar with Cyrus Hammond, he didn't know Claire Whitney.

"I don't get too involved in movies," he told me. "Only just enough brain cells to cope with all the books, to be honest. I can tell you as much as I know about Leo Parrish, but it's not exactly encyclopaedic. There's still a fair amount of mystery about him and his work."

"How long has all this cloak and dagger stuff with Parrish been going on?"

He thought about it. "Certainly ever since people like me discovered the internet was created for them. Though one or two older fans would claim there's been evidence of censorship for a lot longer because all their efforts to get his work back into print have come to nothing."

"But he didn't publish much, did he? And in pretty obscure magazines."

"That's true. Which makes it all the more puzzling that someone wants to censor any discussion of him."

"No idea who?"

"Maybe it's the Vatican."

I just waited.

"I could give you plenty of crackpot theories. The difficulty is that we don't really know enough about the man himself."

"Is he still alive?"

"That's anyone's guess. Nothing's been heard of him since he stopped publishing at the end of the 1950s."

"Could he really be someone who went on to be an important figure in the US administration?"

This wasn't a suggestion he had encountered before. "There's no evidence as far as I'm aware. But even if he's still alive and now guarding his anonymity, his stories are in the public domain. Well, in theory they are, though as you've discovered they're incredibly hard to come by. I think the main thing missing for your purpose is his one-and-only novel."

"*Exaltation*."

"The very same. I've got *Shock 1* with the first part and I'd have brought it along if I'd known your pages were missing."

"Why would anyone cut the serial out in the first place? I got the impression from Arthur that any desecration of those old magazines was like heresy."

Davies was fatalistic. "Not everyone who's handled magazines is a collector. I've seen copies with annotations, corrections, pages with all the letters O filled in with red ink, adverts torn out, you name it. I know someone who cut all the Henry Kuttner stories out of magazines and had them bound. Should have been bound himself and neutered into the bargain to stop him passing on his genes."

I decided not to ask who Henry Kuttner was in case I got out of my depth in some bottomless pool of enthusiasm.

"I can send you a copy of the first part," Davies said. "But I've never been able to track down issue two of the magazine. The circulation was low and few copies saw the light of day even at the time." He explained that both *Shocking Stories* and *Awesome Adventures* had folded immediately afterwards. "It happened a lot in those days."

"So would it have had a small print-run?"

"Almost certainly. It's likely the distribution was shambolic and a lot of copies were probably pulped rather than sold. But the first part is fascinating in its way, and legend has it that overall *Exaltation* is Parrish's best work. And highly influential in ways you might not expect."

This was intriguing, but I said, "Don't send anything original in the post. I'm not sure I can trust it, given what's been happening."

"Wasn't planning to. It would be a photocopy. But I could actually put it straight into your trembling hands. There's a monthly meeting of SF fans in London this Thursday evening, if you fancy coming along." He saw my reluctance. "Not that daunting, honest. It's in a pub!"

He scribbled an address on a notepad, tore it off and handed it to me. "Eight o'clockish? You don't have to wear fancy dress."

I smiled. "So what's so influential about the novel?"

He finished off his pint and sat back. "You've heard of the Church of the Ascendancy?"

I nodded, hiding my surprise. I hadn't told him about Claire Whitney being a cultist.

"Did you notice who the editor of *Shock* and *Awe* was?"

I thought back. "The Senate Committee report mentioned Ridge Publications."

"Indeed. The magazines were edited by Ed Ridge. Ring any bells?"

Now Davies had a mischievous look. I remembered the name from Arthur's magazines, but it didn't mean anything.

"A shortened version of his real name. Edgar Eldridge."

A little light went on. "The guy who founded the Ascendant Church?"

"The Howard Hughes of cultists. The Robert Maxwell of loopy religions."

"Is he Parrish?"

Davies laughed. "Well, that's a decent guess, but no. Eldridge has never made any secret of his origins, though the Church doesn't exactly want him publicizing it. And he wouldn't like it at all if you tried to suggest that he based his church's beliefs on the trappings of a science fiction story."

I knew the Ascendants were supposed to have some weird beliefs, but this was crankier than I had anticipated. "It's a multi-million dollar enterprise. Are you trying to tell me that it's based on rockets and bug-eyed monsters?"

"You're closer than you think. Eldridge co-opted some fictional concepts to do with increasing mental powers and accessing higher dimensions in a sort of afterlife prior to achieving immortality."

"That's in their credo?"

"The science-fictional bits are hidden away these days. But they're there."

He reached under the table and produced a well-thumbed paperback from his shoulder bag. The cover painting showed a Rock Hudson look-alike being bathed in a ray of light shining through the clouds. Above the figure, arranged like an enormous rainbow, was the book's title: *How Deep Cognizance Can Transform Your Life*. The author was Edgar Eldridge.

"It looks like a science fiction novel," I remarked.

"You might still think that when you've read it. It's a collection of Eldridge's early writings on Ascendant philosophy."

The book had been published in 1963. I started to flip through it, but Davies said, "I'd put it away, if I were you. Save it for later." He was glancing around, checking that no one else was watching. "It's long out of print, and you won't find it in any of the Church's bookshops. These days it's considered slightly, well, not exactly heretical, but a little too *bizarre* for general consumption. A few old-time science-fiction fans reckon that the ideas were actually taken from Parrish's novel."

"Really?"

"Not as daft as you might think. I can see plenty of echoes in the half I've read."

I slipped the book into my rucksack. "Go on."

"Very few people still alive today have read the whole of *Exaltation*. From what I can gather, Eldridge plundered it pretty freely for his religion. Especially the second part."

"Isn't that plagiarism?"

"Probably not technically. I don't think the law protects writers from having their work used as the basis for a fake religion."

"If this is true, how come it isn't more widely known?"

"Well, you could call it uncommon knowledge. You won't find it mentioned anywhere on the internet, or in any publications. The Ascendant Church has colossal resources and simply threatens anyone with libel if they even get a sniff that someone's going to write a critical piece, let alone an exposé. They've won so many cases over the years that it's warned people off. I've been threatened enough to be told off by Ruth for recklessness, so I keep everything low key and disguised now. Ruth's not even swayed by the prospect of my losing a court case and having to sell off all my science fiction."

I thought about all this. "So the Ascendants could be behind the problems I've been having with finding Parrish stories?"

"They have a programme of buying up copies furtively and, I imagine, destroying them. Rumour is, there's even an in-house reward system. That's the other reason there are so few around. And I wouldn't put it past them to use more devious means of preventing people from getting at the magazines either."

"Arthur's fire?" I said.

"Well, that was my first thought, but while they may be heavy handed I'd be surprised if they stooped to arson. More likely the fire was due to Arthur's tendency to run a small electrical factory off one dodgy socket."

I didn't think the idea could be so easily dismissed. "Arthur was definitely visited by people I'm pretty sure weren't who they pretended to be. I was there."

I told him about the window cleaners and my sense that it was just a pretext to get Arthur off guard and raid his collection.

"I'm not saying the Church isn't above a bit of bullying," he conceded, "or even bribery. It also wouldn't surprise me if they regularly turned a blind eye to anyone who gets their hands on Parrish's stuff and wants to claim the reward. But deliberately breaking in or starting a fire? That's extreme even by their standards."

"Maybe the stakes are now higher in some way we can't fathom. What about this Noah Byrnes, who says he's working for an American intelligence agency. Could he have been after the stories for the same reason?"

"For the Ascendants?"

"No. Well, not directly. But for some related reason, perhaps."

Now it was Davies who looked dubious. "You have to ask yourself why. It just doesn't make sense for the intelligence agencies to be interested in Parrish."

"It would if he was someone eminent whose identity they were tasked to protect."

Davies was still thinking along his own lines. "On the other hand, it's not beyond the bounds of possibility that some of the nuttier cultists are engaged in something subversive. The Church isn't exactly on good terms with the establishment over there. But that wouldn't explain why government agents were looking for Parrish stories. Unless they were using them as a passport into the Ascendancy, with agents trying to win the church over by feeding its own search for the stories."

Our speculations were in danger of descending into a fruitless circularity. I finished off my drink and got up to buy us a couple more.

Further along the bar someone vaguely familiar was being served. I could feel my skin prickle, then I realized it was the guy with the carrier bag of books from the signing. He wasn't paying me any attention whatsoever.

A hand came down heavily on my shoulder. I jolted and whirled around.

It was Walter Suthersen. His wife was standing beside him, buttoned-up in a smart raincoat as if she was expecting the worst of the weather.

"Let me get those," Suthersen said, his breath smelling of cigarette smoke. He had obviously had a few desperate drags on his way here.

He told me he liked English ale, but he only ordered a small brandy for himself. "Waterworks," he explained. "Try not to get old."

He introduced Barbara, who let me shake the tips of her fingers and formed her lips into a pleasureless smile. Scrupulously poised like a fragile ornament, she requested a low-calorie tonic water with ice. Both she and Suthersen spoke with what I took to be a Midwestern accent, though with New York City overtones. While Suthersen was properly weathered by age, she looked embalmed by it.

We took the drinks back to the table, Barbara perching herself on a padded stool, not unbuttoning her coat.

"So," Suthersen said to me, "Cyrus tells me you're in the film business."

"His company has done a couple of excellent animated features," Davies said before I could reply. "*DisOrg* and *Absolute Hero*. Have you seen them?"

"I've heard of them," said Suthersen, "but I don't spend much time watching movies or TV these days."

"He goes fishing," Barbara Suthersen remarked. "All the time."

Which perhaps explained the rugged look.

"We're small but we've done plenty of interesting stuff," I told him. "It generally gets well-received."

"Then it's a shame all my books are optioned." He said this without smugness or sarcasm. "Since Universal picked up *Zeta Prime* I've got very respectable money for options, but not always from people I feel comfortable with. I'd like to work with a smaller independent company for a change. But what can you do?"

"You take the money," Barbara Suthersen said pointedly.

Suthersen just smiled at her. "Helps keep you in the manner to which you're accustomed, doesn't it, dear?"

There was a definite edge between them. Had they had an argument earlier? "Universal doesn't have to worry about competition from us," I said. "I'm looking for something less familiar. And less expensive to option, if I'm honest with you. Cyrus may have mentioned my interest in Leo Parrish."

Suthersen took a sip of his brandy. "There's a name you don't hear every day."

"And we know some of the reasons why," said Davies.

Suthersen turned a fierce look on him, and the atmosphere cooled noticeably.

"The Ascendancy," Davies said hurriedly. "I was just telling Nick."

"Ah ... Yes." I could see him visibly relaxing. "If memory serves me correctly, you've been a bit of a thorn in their side, eh, Rhodri?"

He was back to being affable again. I thought I knew what had just happened and resolved to check with Davies later.

"What do you think about them suing people into silence?" I asked.

Suthersen shrugged. "All religions in their early days fear persecution."

"You think it's justified?"

"I think it's nonsense. I'm a rationalist, Mr Randall, and I've never been able to understand why people could be so credulous. Now Barbara here, she's a devout Christian, so I must be careful what I say. But the Ascendant Church, that's New Age Flying Saucer theology. A fast-food recipe for our times." He shrugged again. "People want to believe that the world is more numinous than their senses dictate. Who can blame them?"

"Numinous?" Barbara Suthersen said scornfully. "What does that mean?"

"Full of feelings of divinity, dearest."

"Then why couldn't you just say that?"

There was more than just an edge between them. But Suthersen kept his smile on and said to me: "I didn't get around to signing your book, did I? Shall we rectify that now?"

I rummaged in my bag and retrieved my copy of *Zeta Prime*. Barbara took herself off to the ladies' room.

Suthersen opened the book and wrote on the title page:

To Nick

Here's hoping excellent movies are in the ascendancy!
Best wishes
Walt Suthersen

"Good one," I said to him. "I certainly hope so."

"So how exactly can I help you?"

I thought about it and decided to launch straight in. "I'm after a copy of the second instalment of Parrish's serial *Exaltation*. Arthur Townsend—"

"A well known collector over here," said Davies when he saw Suthersen's immediate look of incomprehension.

Suthersen nodded. "I remember now. I signed enough books for him to fill a small library. There are so many fans and collectors, though."

"Well, he loaned me the first issue of *Shocking Stories*," I said, glossing over Molly's role, "but the Parrish serial had been cut out. Rhodri has a copy, so that's OK, but I'd really like to read the whole thing, and issue two is mythically rare. Cyrus Hammond thought there was a chance that you might be able to help."

Suthersen's face went slack with memory for a moment.

"I actually knew Leo," he said. "I wouldn't go so far as to say he was a close friend but I met him a few times when, well, when I was just starting out myself. I admired his work and it did give me the inspiration to pursue my own writing. Though not as much as some critics have implied ..."

His last words were defensive. I presumed he was referring to the suggestion that his writing actually owed more to Parrish than he might care to admit. Which would explain his prickly moment earlier.

"What was he like?" I asked. "It's impossible to find out anything about him."

Suthersen gave it some thought. "He wasn't much for small talk. With Leo, you always felt that his mind was somewhere else. I don't mean that he was unfriendly. But it was as if he had his own agenda. And didn't care to share it with anyone else."

"You didn't discuss his writing?"

"He had a 'take it or leave it' attitude about that. I think he probably knew his stuff was better than most of what was being published. Particularly in *Awesome Adventures*."

This was intriguing. "Is he still alive?"

I was fishing with this one, on the off-chance that Suthersen might have maintained some sort of secret contact over the years.

Suthersen sat back. "I don't know anyone who's heard from him in more than half a century."

I got the impression that this was a stock answer to a question he had been asked time and again.

"He disappeared?"

"Lives collide and ricochet. Think of all the people you've lost touch with. Happens all the time."

Barbara Suthersen reappeared. "I'm going to take some air," she announced, and promptly walked out, ramrod straight.

Suthersen just smiled again. "Don't mind her. She always gets tetchy when I reminisce."

There was more to it than this, I was sure, but I had no idea what.

"Where were we?" Suthersen asked. "Ah, yes. Leo."

"It's good to know someone who's actually met him," I said. "I was beginning to believe that he didn't exist."

He looked me over. "How about if I get you a photograph?"

"You've got a photograph of Leo Parrish?" Davies said excitedly. "I didn't think there were any."

"It was taken over half a century ago," Suthersen replied, looking wistful. "When we were new kids on the block. My secretary in New York can probably hunt it down."

Suthersen took out a small black book and made a note. He was happy to email the photo to both of us, so we gave him our business cards. For some reason I hadn't expected Davies to have one, but I wasn't surprised to see it had a cartoon of a four-armed alien using a typewriter.

"And the second part of *Exaltation*," I reminded him. "Do you actually have a copy?"

"It's certainly in my library." He tapped his pen against his lips. "But that would have to be a Xerox. Nothing personal, Nick. These old magazines are fragile and precious."

"Of course. It's the story I'm interested in."

I hoped that it wasn't just a gesture that he would forget about the moment he walked out of the door.

"This is really good of you," I said. Then, on the off chance: "Do you happen to know Claire Whitney?"

For an instant Suthersen looked startled, a little alarmed perhaps.

"Why do you ask?"

"She storyboarded something by Parrish for a TV dramatisation and I understood she'd sold the production company the rights in the first place. I just wondered if you'd heard of her. She might have access to other Parrish stories."

"Did Cyrus suggest you ask me about her?" he said with obvious irritation.

"No," I replied, staying quiet about the fact that Cyrus had put me onto her in the first place. "I met her at a film festival."

He relaxed again. "As it happens, I do know her. Professionally, though not well."

Did Suthersen know she was a cultist, hence his discomfort? How had she met him? And what exactly was Cyrus Hammond's connection with Suthersen? Through movies, perhaps? Did Hammond also know about her cult connections? Maybe it didn't bother him in the way it clearly did Suthersen. It was certainly interesting that Parrish was linked with all three of them, and that they knew each other. But I had no idea what the connections might be.

Suthersen had drained the last of his brandy and was looking at me speculatively.

"If Parrish did write anything that could be made into a movie," I said, "Claire could benefit as well as my company. She'd make money from selling the rights if she owns them and she'd probably be able to work on it, too. I wondered if you had any way of talking to her about this. Sort of persuading her that I'm on the level."

"Now how could I possibly know whether you are or not?"

He said this deadpan, but then his face creased into a smile. "I jest. It's a fair proposition. I can't promise anything, but I'll see what I can do."

He hauled himself up. "I'd better go and track down Barbara. Rhodri, we haven't had much chance for a chinwag this time around, but I guess I'll see you soon at the Worldcon?"

"Yes, indeed," Davies replied enthusiastically. "I'm looking forward to it."

After Suthersen was gone, Davies and I agreed that he was an approachable guy, friendly enough but with certain sharp edges.

"What was that thing about Parrish?" I asked him. "When Suthersen gave you the evil eye? Has he read the rumours on your website about him ripping Parrish off?"

"He obviously thought I was having a dig. But it's more than just the gossip about creative plagiarism. There's actually been a suggestion that he was involved in Parrish's disappearance, even killing him and then using unpublished manuscripts as the basis for his own success."

This was something I hadn't remotely considered. "Do you believe that?"

"Of course not. That's just people taking things to the extreme. Though I'm less confident that Walt didn't draw on Parish's work to some extent, whether consciously or not."

I hit my forehead theatrically.

"There's something I forgot to ask Suthersen," I told him, annoyed with myself. I explained about my research into the Senate committee and brought up the report on my phone. He had no idea what SFU represented—there had been no such thing as a Science Fiction Union, for example—but he agreed that WXS could only refer to Suthersen.

He was fascinated by the details on the hearings. "I've heard rumours about the committee, but nothing ever surfaced until now. It looks like the report was put on this site only recently and has probably never been anywhere else on the internet."

"I wanted to ask Suthersen if Leo Parrish had also appeared before them."

"Given that Parrish's works are cited in the report, he might have. In those days you had to stand up and show you were a good citizen."

"They specifically thanked Suthersen, so presumably he gave them his full cooperation. He hadn't actually started out on his own writing career at this point, is that right?"

"He'd just moved on to editing *Vantage*," Davies agreed. "Of course, if you like a good conspiracy theory, there are a number of possibilities at this point."

He paused with an air of schoolboy melodrama.

"Which are?" I said.

"Aside from murdering Parrish, you mean?"

"I'm happy to rule that one out."

"As long as you appreciate I'm only playing Devil's Advocate here."

Clearly Davies relished a certain amount of drama and intrigue. I urged him to continue.

"He might have been responsible for jealously ending Parrish's career by drawing the committee's attention to *Shock* and *Awe* and forcing Edgar Eldridge to stop publishing such provocative stuff. I'm not saying I believe it, by the way. Why be jealous of Parrish? He was just another obscure writer."

"Or?"

"Well, I don't believe this one, either. But another possibility is this: what if Walter Suthersen was actually Leo Parrish? Maybe Walt was writing stories for Edgar Eldridge as Leo Parrish, so Leo Parrish never actually existed. Not the sort of thing he might have wanted to admit to the committee, I don't think. But the scare of being under scrutiny could have made him decide to kill off Leo Parrish and re-invent himself as a more polished writer under his own name." He flourished his empty glass. "Another pint?"

TWELVE

The Church of the Ascendancy had steadily grown over the past twenty years. Its new London temple was just along the Embankment from Charing Cross station, circular tiers of dressed marble that made it look like an overgrown wedding cake. It was fronted by a paved garden sporting dry-weather plants that must have been planted with global warming in mind. When I met up with Claire Whitney, the sky was overcast and full of drizzle.

I had been surprised when she agreed to meet me for lunch, especially since I told her that I wanted to find out more about the Ascendancy. I was even more surprised by her suggestion that we rendezvous at this temple.

There was a gusty wind and she was huddling under a lilac umbrella outside a snack bar. We bought a couple of baguettes and wandered around the garden. She didn't initiate much in the way of conversation, but she seemed perfectly relaxed and ready to answer my questions.

"So," I said, "the founder of the religion, Edgar Eldridge. He's still alive, isn't he?"

"He's well into his eighties now, but by all accounts still pretty hale and hearty."

"Lives in Zona, Arizona."

"So we're told. You've obviously done your research."

"I looked a few things up," I confessed.

Zona was a desert community Eldridge had established with like-minded followers soon after starting his "religion". Reclusive in recent decades, he lived in a vast hacienda-style home surrounded by electrified fencing and staffed by several dozen dedicated volunteers.

"I gather he was a publisher before he started the Church."

"I believe so."

"Cheap fiction magazines. Westerns and thrillers as well as science fiction."

"Well, I don't think it was high literature."

Nothing in my tone was designed to provoke her, but I still found it hard to credit that she could take all this stuff at face value. I had speed-read Eldridge's *Deep Cognizance* book and spent half the morning on-line, finding out all I could about the Ascendants. Many of their beliefs were higher up the bonkers scale than I had imagined.

"Didn't he originally publish Leo Parrish?" I asked. "In *Awesome Stories*?"

"*Awesome Adventures*," she corrected me without hesitation. "But you knew that, didn't you?"

"Just checking," I replied with what I hoped was an endearing grin. "Are you some kind of expert on Parrish?"

"No," she said emphatically, this time distinctly irritated.

"But you had the rights to one of his stories?"

"No again."

I let my confusion show.

"It's delicate," she said to me, relenting a little. "If I tell you, I need you to promise you'll keep mum about it."

I nodded eagerly. "I promise."

"Well, I've always practised storyboarding using vintage magazines that I bought in job lots at house clearance auctions and the like. One of the batches happened to contain a few issues of *Awesome Adventures*. Not long afterwards I met a man working in television who was looking for stuff for a *Twilight Zone* type series. I sent him the storyboard for 'The Cosmic Controllers'." She paused, still looking hard at me. "I was broke at the time, a single parent with a young child. Perhaps you can guess what happened next."

I had an inkling, but I waited for her to tell me.

"When he got back to me with a good offer, I jumped at it."

"Was this Cyrus Hammond?"

"No. I met him later, after the *Nightscapes* series was broadcast. This was a commissioning editor."

"You sold him the story?"

"I forged Parrish's signature on the contract," she confessed, her cheeks flushing at the memory of it. "I pretended that I was acting on his behalf."

We had stopped between some raised beds holding yuccas and cacti.

"I've never told anyone that before," she said.

"Well, I feel suitably honoured," I responded with genuine sincerity. "And I promise I won't go running to the Fraud Office."

She smiled. "Pretty despicable, eh?"

I didn't quite know what to say.

"I really liked the story and thought it was a good opportunity to bring it to a wider audience. But I needed the money, too. So there you are. I'm a con-woman, a leech off a long-dead writer."

"You're hardly a leech. It was just one story."

"I still shouldn't have done it."

This might explain her earlier reticence about Parrish.

"Is that why you told me he was dead?" I asked.

"At the time I wrote to Ridge Publications on the off chance they still existed. I got an anonymous typed postcard back saying that both they and Leo Parrish were defunct."

If this was true, it was interesting if only because of its ambiguity.

"Didn't Edgar Eldridge or any of his associates make contact? After all, he was the publisher."

"I found that out later. No one ever came out of the woodwork to claim the money."

From what Rhodri had told me, Ridge Publications had ceased to exist soon after *Shocking* and *Awesome* folded. Perhaps Eldridge had relocated to the West Coast to found his religion.

We started walking again. Very carefully I said, "But now Eldridge has come into your life in a different way."

The rain had slackened but she was still huddling under her umbrella, hiding her face from me as though in embarrassment. "That's how I found out about the Ascendancy. I was drawn to it."

There had to be more to it than this, although I was aware of the danger of letting my curiosity stray too far. I didn't want her to think I was interrogating her, but I still wasn't quite done yet.

"I was talking to someone," I said casually, "who claims that a lot of the elements of Eldridge's church were actually based on ideas he stole from Leo Parrish."

This time she did lift her umbrella to glance at me. "Is that what you think?"

"I have no idea," I admitted. "But the Church is pretty sensitive about this particular suggestion, isn't it?"

She started to look wary. "Where is all this leading?"

"I gather it was the serial he wrote. *Exaltation*? Have you read it?"

I was obviously beginning to strain her patience. "Who have you been talking to?"

"Just someone I met. I also met Walter Suthersen. You know one another, don't you?"

Now she was frowning. "Who is this someone?"

"A fan of Leo Parrish's work. We were talking about him, and about the Ascendancy. He said he couldn't understand why intelligent people could swallow a religion based on ideas lifted from a cheap science fiction magazine."

I hadn't intended to be quite so blunt. I was surprised to see her cheeks reddening again.

"If you've come here to mock," she said with a trace of anger, "then I've got no intention of taking you inside."

"No," I assured her hastily. "I don't want to pre-judge it. But I don't pretend to understand it either."

Diligently she began to fold up her umbrella, perhaps now wishing she hadn't agreed to meet me. I didn't want to alienate her, and it wasn't just for business reasons.

"Look," I said softly, "I'm sorry for all the questions. It's just that I'm really curious about Parrish. He wasn't your average magazine writer, was he? I've heard rumours that the Church is trying to destroy all the existing copies of his stories. And maybe even posting spurious articles on the web suggesting that he never actually existed."

She just gave me a fierce stare. "Do you want to go through with this or not?"

I didn't flinch. "Yes. Of course."

"Then I need you to be respectful. And open-minded."

"OK," I replied. "But in return I'd really like it if you'd let me ask you reasonable questions without me feeling like a policeman interviewing a suspect."

After the merest instant, she laughed, her entire face relaxing, instantly reminding me of how much I liked the look of it.

"You're right," she said. "I apologize. It's complicated. I don't mind talking about the Church, but you can't expect me to bad-mouth it or do anything to jeopardize my position as an Initiate. For all I know, you might secretly be planning on making one of those warts-and-all documentaries."

I had to admit that the idea had occurred to me, but I was ready to shelve it to keep her on side.

"Search me, if you like," I said, holding out my arms. "No hidden microphones or cameras. Not even a notebook. But feel free to fondle. I think I'd rather enjoy it."

Now I had got her smiling again. She grabbed my arm and tucked it through hers, suddenly much more jaunty.

"So best behaviour, then," she warned me.

Above the arched Romanesque entranceway was a gold stylized representation of a rising sun with seven rays coming out of it. It was one of the church's official symbols, copyrighted so that its use could be controlled. The central ray rose higher than the others, pointing straight up.

"So the seven rays are the seven levels," I remarked.

"Uh huh," was all she said.

I liked the feel of her arm against mine. "And you're an Initiate. Does that mean you're not on the level ladder yet?"

"They need to be sure you're Pure In Intention and Ready To Commit."

I knew from Eldridge's book that both phrases were capitalized.

"Is there some doubt about it? Do you have to confess all your sins to begin?"

I asked this without a hint of sarcasm. She just smiled. "Something like that."

She didn't volunteer any more. I said, "So Level Seven is the ultimate?"

I'd been tempted to say "seventh heaven" but I didn't want her to think I was mocking.

"They've added Levels Eight to Ten in recent years," she replied. "They're for the really high achievers."

Was this a deliberate pun? I couldn't tell from her expression.

"Like Ryan Carmichael and the other celebrities?"

She didn't dispute this. "I think only Mr Eldridge has reached the highest level."

"Higher Plane Adept."

At that moment the mirror-glass entrance doors swished open and two men and a woman walked out, all looking very bright and shiny, well-heeled in executive suits. They passed us with radiant smiles and brisk hellos.

"Are you sure about this?" Claire said to me.

I'd told her I wanted to experience LEAP: Latent Evaluation Ascendancy Profiling. "Latent" was their jargon for any person who hadn't yet seen the light and been accepted as a fully-fledged member of the Church. Over ninety-nine per cent of the human race, in other words.

"I'm sure," I said firmly. "Shall we go in?"

She shook her head. "Not here. You have to be at least a Level One Adept to be allowed access to the temple unless you're going to a service. You won't get past the Welcomers."

These were general church functionaries. From witness accounts on the net, they acted like a cross between hotel reception staff and bouncers.

"How would they know?" I asked. Could they tell just by looking at you, I wondered, or would we trigger an alarm due to us being Impure?

"It's on the database."

Which was pretty extensive, according to what I had been able to find out. Details of church members were mostly obtained from lengthy "ministerings" during the LEAP and SOAR procedures. SOAR stood for Spiritual Optimum Advancement Routes. It went without saying that you had to LEAP before you could SOAR.

We walked down through the garden to a low-rise building flanked by squat lines of dripping palms. Its white walls with their arched windows supported a roof of plate glass panels bolted to aluminium girders. A big sign above the entrance said WHOLENESS CENTRE alongside the caduceus symbol with its coiled snakes rising out of the sunrise emblem. Posters beside the door were advertising FREE MENTAL HEALTH CHECKS.

Inside, a young black man and white woman were sitting at a desk. I suspected they hadn't had too many customers that day because they brightened considerably when Claire and I walked in.

"Good day!" they said in unison, making it less of a salutation than a revelatory fact. "Welcome!"

Both were late teens or early twenties, in lavender T-shirts and crisp blue jeans. They looked like anyone's well-groomed son and daughter.

"I'm *Sar*a," the girl informed us, stressing the first syllable. "Have you been here before?"

"I have," Claire told them. "I'm an Initiate. Claire Whitney."

Sara asked her to spell out both names before she typed them into her laptop. Meanwhile her companion, *Anth*ony, was already referring me to the literature on display at the desk, lots of full-colour pamphlets with inspiring slogans like TAKE CHARGE OF YOUR LIFE and SUCCESS THROUGH SELF-AWAKENING.

A broad central corridor divided the building, with rooms on both sides. At the far end it opened out into something that looked like a modernistic altar on a carpeted dais surrounded by a display that featured the sunrise emblem on a little plinth and vases of scarlet and sky-blue gladioli. Red and blue were big colours amongst the Ascendants: red represented human passions and earthly physicality; blue the higher mental attributes such as intellect, curiosity and the acquisition of wisdom.

I let Claire do most of the talking at the desk. When Sara asked her if she wanted to undergo a ministering herself, she replied that she would welcome the opportunity to "exchange" with Monica or Michael.

"Do you get any credit for bringing new people in?" I asked Claire while Anthony went off to fetch a Mentor.

"You get a Salutation," she told me. "It's put on your Church Profile. Like a gold star for good work."

She said this straight-faced. Then she added, "You're on your own now."

"What?"

A stout woman in a floral dress and tight blonde perm had appeared. She and Claire exchanged smiles and greetings. This was evidently Monica. They went off together.

Now Sara asked me for my full name.

"Nicholas Orlando Randall," I said, randomly making up a middle name.

"Thank you," she said as if I had just bequeathed my entire estate to the church. She briskly typed it in. "I just need a few more details. They are of course optional. Address?"

"1 Fuschia Mansions, Farringdon," I extemporized.

She typed it in. "EC1?"

I nodded.

"Full post code?"

"Ah. I'm not sure. I've only just moved in."

She did a little more keyboard tapping. "It's not on the A to Z."

"Well, it's a new development," I said hastily. "On Farringdon Road."

She typed this information in. "Telephone number?"

"Hasn't been connected yet."

"Email address?"

I shook my head.

"Mobile?"

"No." It would be my luck if it started making toilet flushing noises at that moment.

"Can we reach you through Claire for the time being?"

"Yes, I suppose so." It couldn't do any harm.

She managed to maintain a professional smile, and I returned it, no doubt with patent insincerity.

Anthony reappeared, accompanied by a thin man who looked swamped under baggy pleated cream trousers and a plum-coloured shirt. Close-set eyes stared out at me from a taut face with a pointed nose and a thin-lipped mouth. Had he had a face-lift? Or had he just been washed at too high a temperature?

"This is Ken," Anthony told me.

We shook hands and Ken switched on a smile. "Good to meet you!" he said with great emphasis, as if favourable reports had already reached him.

He held my hand between both of his for a second or two, as if this would help him get the measure of me. I guessed that he was in his forties, black hair slicked back from a widow's peak. Like Sara he had a tan. How did they manage it, I wondered, given the usual crap weather we had been having? Did the Church supply sun beds to its adherents? Or were their UK operatives sent to Arizona to perk them up after the interminable British winter?

Ken led me down the aisle to a room close to the floral altarpiece. Inside it was disappointingly normal, a wood-panelled chamber with modern armchairs and a desk with a laptop on a docking bay. There were no Church symbols or paraphernalia, just a blonde wood cupboard against one wall and a big blank screen on another.

Ken indicated that I should sit on a chair facing the screen.

"Before we begin," he said, "I'd like to show you a little presentation. It explains the ideals and aims of the Church. It's quite short, only a few minutes. All right with you?"

He was solicitousness itself. I could only nod.

"We think it's better if first-timers view it in complete privacy, so that they have time and space for reflection. So I'll just step outside until it's finished."

The computer was already running. He typed something in and the screen lit up. As he went out, he dimmed the lights.

A few seconds later the room filled with orchestral music that might have been composed for an as-yet-unmade episode of the *Star Wars* saga. Appropriately, the screen itself filled with images of planets, stars and galaxies whirling past.

"Do you believe that we have it in our power to take charge of our own destiny?" intoned an authoritative male voice. "Are you beset by doubts, insecurities and feelings of powerlessness? Do you feel that life is beyond your control?"

By now the galactic panorama on the screen was whirling, but suddenly it slowed and settled into a single blue dot floating serene in the blackness of space. The dot rapidly grew in size, while the narrator announced: "Almost half a century ago our founder had a revelation of some simple but important truths. We all have the capacity to remake our lives. We have the capacity to take control of them, to conquer fear and self-doubt and forge our own unique destinies. All it takes is the will to harness powers that lie dormant in every human mind!"

The Earth filled the screen now, its oceans speckled and spiralled in cloud, its pale landmasses insignificant at first but growing ever more noticeable under the rapid descent. "Just as a healthy diet promotes physical well-being, so good mental habits promote mind-body well-being and extinguish negative thought patterns. Through a program of Life Logic classes you can gain a clarity of vision and purpose that will allow you to command your own destiny by using abilities you never knew you possessed."

Now we were close to the ground, descending over spacious houses set in ample gardens and tree-lined streets. On the verdant sunlit lawns, multi-ethnic children tossed balls while dogs gambolled and parents watched indulgently from shaded porches.

"Transformative Deep Cognizance is an applied system of thought development that activates all areas of the brain," the narrator went on with movie-advertisement gravitas. "It engages the passions as much as the mind, giving you emotional as well as intellectual wisdom. You are trained to think *and feel* appropriately, to overcome negative nurturing patterns and replace them with positive can-dos. Take charge of your life! Release the ultra human within you!"

The picture cut to another multi-ethnic group, this time all smiling adults who were standing together, slim, handsome and full of the joys of living. One of the women piped up: "Your Life Logic classes will be run by experienced Mentors who will train you to use revelatory wisdoms. I was once an alcoholic and prescription drug addict. Now I'm a mother of three!" Three young children ran enthusiastically to her side and she embraced them. A black guy in a crisp suit and striped tie stepped forward: "I did time for armed robbery and domestic violence. Now I run one of the Church's drug rehabilitation programs!"

The camera panned back, showing more of the group. It was suburban America writ large, some fond Technicolor version of the glory days of yore when neighbours were neighbourly, criminals safely locked away and no one was depressed, addicted to alcohol, sleeping pills or designer pharmaceuticals.

"Join us today!" they cried as one, raising their arms and waving merrily, grinning like lottery winners. "You have nothing to lose but your insecurities!"

The introductory music came on stream again as the scene gradually faded to black, or rather to a sliver of lunar landscape across which the camera panned until it showed a gibbous Earth hanging in blackness above the ashen horizon.

"Earth," said a female voice. "It's our world. We can only care for it if we empower ourselves ..."

This time the voice-over had an English accent. She spoke in the breathless come-hither tones of the woman who advertised Marks and Spencer food on TV: as if the Earth was some desirable creature that you could only possess if you treated it right. Planet porn. You know you want it.

Again the fade, though this time the image of the Earth was replaced by the sunrise symbol as the stirring theme went diminuendo into the ether. This last bit of the presentation had a tacked-on feel, designed to show that the Church was responsive to the growing environmental concerns of its flock. But flaunting a green agenda was a risky business, given that senior church officials had a well-publicized fondness for private jets and luxury yachts.

Within seconds of the screen going blank, the door opened and Ken came in, switching on the lights, as if he had been hovering right outside the door.

"So," he said brightly, "what did you think?"

"I, uh ..." I had to get my thoughts in order and make sure I didn't blow my cover. "I'm amazed. Utterly amazed."

Ken slid behind the desk. "Intrigued?" he offered.

I nodded vigorously, resisting the temptation to say that some of the production values were a little amateurish. "It's what I hoped it might be. The chance to take charge of my life."

He gave me a penetrating look. "Do you feel that your life is out of control?"

"Well," I said, "not in a bull-in-a-china-shop way. More a where-the-heck-are-my-socks or why-am-I-eating-dinner-out-of-a-plastic-tray-in-front-of-the-TV-again." I swallowed. "If you know what I mean."

His expression didn't change. "You feel unfulfilled?" he asked.

"Very," I replied. "I'm definitely not fulfilling anything. Especially my potential."

"You'd like to achieve more?"

"Most certainly. Release my inner strength, you know?"

He was idly fingering the laptop mouse "The Church can certainly help you achieve that."

"I'm thrilled to hear it."

I was doing my best to come across as gung-ho, but he was still looking at me somewhat sceptically. Sincerity is very hard to fake.

"Would you describe yourself as a spiritual person, Nick?"

"Oh yes," I lied. "I do yoga, spend a lot of time thinking about things, you know."

"Well, that's good," Ken replied, patently unimpressed. "But communication is important, too. The Church lays great stress on being open, being able to express our thoughts and feelings."

I thought about this one. "That's a problem area for me," I told Ken. "Communication. Especially of the emotional variety."

Ken just waited, his intense, unwavering gaze clearly designed to prompt further admissions. It looked to me as if he dyed his hair and trimmed his eyebrows regularly. It was cheering to think that the unleashing of his latent powers hadn't dampened his vanity.

"Let me give you an example." I managed to say. "The woman I came here with—Claire Whitney. I find her incredibly attractive but I haven't been able to tell her so."

I think I said it just to get it off my chest, knowing that Claire herself couldn't hear me. Ken didn't even nod. He just kept looking at me as if I had told him something entirely unremarkable, even boring. Or perhaps he was waiting for more. I decided I had already said enough.

"We need to assess your current equilibrium," he said at last. "Carry out a few straightforward non-invasive tests. Are you happy to proceed with this?"

Yippee, I thought to myself: here comes the Ment-Cap. I'd seen a picture of someone wearing one on a scurrilous website. It looked less like a cap than a bulky silver crash helmet with a black hair net slung over the top of it.

But I was swiftly disappointed when Ken opened the cupboard and produced a fancy pair of headphones with the sunrise motif on the ear pieces.

"Oh," I said, unable to stop myself. "I thought it was a helmet."

Ken straightened. "Where did you hear that?" he asked suspiciously.

Oops. "I saw a photograph once," I said vaguely. "Years ago, when I was a boy."

"Is that so?"

"My mum was interested. She went to a drop-in and came back with some literature."

Why was I inventing this stuff? Why was I even here? Apart from giving me another pretext for meeting Clare Whitney, I suppose I had hoped that the Ascendancy would have a credo rational enough for me to understand what she saw in it. But while they had obviously made it more respectable on the surface, it was still a concoction of dodgy mysticism and cod-psychology with a spurious "scientific" gloss. And I hadn't even got to the more exotic bits and the links with Leo Parrish.

"We dispensed with those years ago," Ken was telling me sternly. "This is less cumbersome. It performs the same function."

"Revealing my Mindscape?"

"Well," he said briskly, "we don't claim that it indicates anything more than basic mental responses, but it can be a useful guide to our emotional condition at any given time."

You used to claim a lot more than that, I thought. In the early days of the Church the Ment-Caps were touted as being able to reveal "neurosensive knots" that were blocking up your energies and preventing the body-mind from working in harmony. I let him fit the earpieces around my head. From the crosspiece dangled two lengths of wire ending in crocodile clips. Ken opened a little packet of silver adhesive pads which he attached to the clips before sticking the pads to my temples. The wires trailed to a small box plugged into the back of the laptop. Ken did something to it and my ears filled with the distant hiss of static.

"What's that?" I asked.

"A data-logger," he told me. "It'll give us a display of your current equilibrium. Just relax and look at the images on the screen. You don't have to do or say anything, OK?"

Abruptly the screen filled with the leering image of a circus clown who looked like a demented version of Ronald McDonald. After several seconds it was replaced by a dappled woodland scene. Bizarrely this was followed by an enlarged image of an integrated circuit, a human sperm about to fertilize an egg, the United Nations flag, a bee, a spanner, a chocolate éclair and full-length colour portrait of Henry VIII.

Was this some kind of weird Odd One Out exercise? Ken was too busy studying his laptop screen and manipulating his mouse to say.

I concentrated on the images. A picture of Homer Simpson was followed by a line of angry demonstrators, then a pistol with a daisy sprouting from its barrel. I've got the gist of this sequence I thought, but was promptly confounded by a banana, the Eiffel Tower, Einstein with his tongue sticking out and a bottle of Jack Daniel's. Idly I wondered if they ran the same sequence for all Latents. Or did they have a shuffle function to keep the Mentor from being bored? The parade of images continued for some time and I lost concentration for a while. Ken cleared his throat, as if to remind me to pay attention.

I focused again. There was a chessboard. A Humvee. The crescent Moon. A dollar bill. Six eggs in a carton. A beautiful woman. A handsome man. By all accounts the Ascendants were liberal in their attitude towards sexuality, but their "Clean Streets" programme advocated getting drug-users and down-and-outs into rehabilitation centres, presumably so all their neurosensive knots could be untangled during lengthy ministrations.

Abruptly Ken froze the screen. "I think we've got enough."

I lifted the headphones away from my ears. "Are we done?"

Ken was studying the laptop screen, moving his mouse around the pad and clicking. The pad bore another of the Church's symbols, a capital letter C whose curve was outlined in thick bands of red, yellow, green and blue so that it resembled a child's rainbow sideways on. The Church was still disputing the copyright of this image with several secular organisations.

I peeled the contacts from my temples and laid the headphones on Ken's desk.

"So," I said to him. "What's the verdict?"

He drummed his fingers on the armrest. "We have to process the results before we give a full assessment. You'll need to come back in a few days so that we can elucidate what we found and consider the best way forward."

I knew the Church prided itself on what it called "evidence-based faith", but this was more like a business plan.

"Can't you give me a few hints?" I pleaded. "I'm really keen to know."

"Well," he said, looking straight at me. "You scored high for scepticism. That can often hinder acceptance of the spiritual." He paused. "There are also anti-authoritarian tendencies."

I made a shocked face. "I'm a very law-abiding citizen."

The nostrils of his prominent nose were flared, as though I was giving off a dodgy smell. I was pretty sure that you could infer almost anything from the images he had shown me, and his summary of my traits could easily have been a series of educated guesses. Or a standard ploy to draw out potential troublemakers. In recent years the Church had apparently grown more rigorous in screening candidates after pranksters had infiltrated their ranks.

"You also show imagination," he told me, "and a certain degree of mental flexibility."

"Is that bad or good?"

"It means that you're open to new experiences."

"Oh yes," I agreed. "I like a bit of novelty."

"You have your own personal morality."

What were you supposed to say to this? It was like being told you had a head on your shoulders.

"And there's a sincere yearning to get more from your life."

"I couldn't agree with you more about that," I told him. "So what does your screen actually show?"

Without hesitation Ken flipped it around so that I could see. He rolled his chair forward and used the mouse to show a sequence of what looked like bar charts, ECG and skin temperature traces.

"What can you tell from all those?" I asked.

"We do a holistic analysis. It has a spiritual and statistical dimension. At a glance, it shows you have plenty of potential for personal growth. Your main enemies are doubt and suspicion."

I mulled this over before saying, "I'm surprised to hear that. I've always thought I have a very trusting nature."

Ken clearly thought otherwise. His fingers were tapping again: it was obvious that he wanted to wind things up.

"Do you mind if I ask you a few questions before we finish?" I said to him.

"By all means," he replied without enthusiasm.

Against my usual instincts I had been pretty respectful up to now, but I didn't want to be fobbed off and sent out of there without having asked at least a few probing questions. I resisted the temptation to show him the dog-eared paperback of *How Deep Cognizance Can Transform Your Life* that I was carrying inside my jacket. Rhodri Davies had warned me not to show it to anyone associated with the Church.

"I wanted to ask you about the Ultrans," I said.

Ken went rigid, as did his smile.

"According to something I read, the Ultrans were an advanced race of energy beings who lived in a star but had to flee when it became unstable. They spent eons wandering through space, slowly withering away due to space dust and cosmic rays."

Ken didn't move. He didn't say anything.

"Then they stumbled on Earth about fifty thousand years ago, took an interest in primitive humans and *blended* with them."

I waited. Ken slowly nodded, though not in a particularly affirmative way.

"It was they who kick-started human evolution. They became the human soul—"

"That's not the word we use," Ken interrupted. "It's too misleading. It's the higher mental and emotional attributes—"

"The four Cs," I said, indicating the symbol on his mouse pad. "Curiosity, cogitation, consideration and compassion."

Ken was studiously unimpressed that I had cited them correctly. "They activated them," he said.

"And the Ultrans lost their identity, became part of us as a result of the merging."

"Well, that's one way of looking at it."

"They were like the sky blue that makes the red into mauve and got our intelligence up and running," I quoted. "They became an integral part of the mental core of humanity."

Ken obviously didn't want to be discussing this but he was doing his damnedest to look unconcerned.

"In their previous existence they had powers of telepathy, levitation and psycho-kinesis," I said. "And these powers are now dormant in all humans."

"Where did you source all this?" Ken asked as if I was quoting from a torture manual.

"In an old book a friend showed me," I lied blithely.

No visible reaction to this. "The book was lost?"

I nodded, praying he wouldn't summon a bevy of minders to strip-search me.

"I found it really intriguing," I ploughed on. "They could also access the higher dimensional plane. And at the Time of Enhancement these powers will re-emerge so that all Adepts will be able to go there and escape the ravages of the Final Days."

Ken steepled his hands and put them to his mouth. "In today's Church we prefer to concentrate on bettering ourselves in the here-and-now rather than concerning ourselves about future events that are beyond the individual's power to influence."

"And in that phase of existence we'll be physically immortal and permanently empowered," I persisted. "The old will be restored to the prime of life, all sickness and pain will be cured, and even the Passed will return in their original bodies."

The Passed were Ascendants who had suffered "corporeal shut-down"—died, in plain English. They were presently "dormant" in the Higher Plane, mentally hibernating until the big day. I was having trouble keeping a lid on all this nonsense.

"My question is—how long will we have to stay there in the fifth dimension before we go back to Earth and begin transforming it to a state of natural bliss? Mr Eldridge doesn't specify. Is it days or weeks or months?"

Ken was obviously struggling to muster a diplomatic response. I hadn't originally intended to push him so far: a sense of mischief had overtaken me.

"These are all matters we can discuss at a future session," he said at last.

He came around to my side of the desk and took my arm.

"Mr Eldridge says that by learning to empower the four Cs we can overcome the fifth malignant one."

"Absolutely," Ken agreed, helping me to my feet and gently propelling me towards the door.

"Which is Cruelty," I said. "But what about jealousy, lust and all the other deadly sins? Where do they fit in?"

"They all arise from self-absorption," Ken said by rote. "Which is in itself a form of cruelty to others." He pulled the door open. "These are very interesting matters, and I would be more than happy to discuss them in detail with you on some future occasion."

"Can I ask for you next time?" I asked devotedly as he manoeuvred me across the threshold.

"Goodbye, Mr Randall."

Before I knew it, he had closed the door on me.

I lingered outside for a few moments, wishing I had asked him if he had heard of Leo Parrish. Somehow, I suspected not. Ken was obviously a well-trusted member of the Church, given that he had known what I was talking about when I mentioned the Ultrans; but Parrish was probably a guilty secret known only to the uppermost echelons of the hierarchy.

Despite a certain juvenile pleasure at having got him rattled, I was conscious that perhaps it hadn't been all that clever of me to ask about the more ludicrous aspects of the Church's theology. I had promised Claire I would behave, but the absurdity of it all had strained my patience to breaking point. Ken would probably have me blacklisted. Maybe he was already on the phone, summoning a few burly "Welcomers" from the temple to escort me off the premises with maximum haste.

At this point Anthony sidled up. He amiably suggested we both go back to the desk.

"Was it a fruitful experience?" he asked me.

"Words can't express," I told him.

Sara was still sitting bright-eyed at the desk. Suddenly I had had my fill of the place, and when she began asking about a follow-up ministering I said, "I need to check my appointments schedule when I get home. Can I ring you later?"

She instantly produced a large business card. I plucked it from her hand with a "Thank you," and walked outside.

The drizzle was coming down again. Never had it felt more refreshing. I zipped up my jacket and just stood there, watching a pleasure boat going down the Thames, people waving from its packed balcony, sipping wine, talking. Ordinary pleasures. The meat and potatoes of life. It looked like a few of the revellers had already reached a higher mental plane by a more liquid route than the Ascendants.

Ten minutes later Claire emerged. She did not look at all happy.

"What did you say to them?" she demanded to know. "They told me you were disrespectful. Rude even."

Oh, hell.

"I invited you here in good faith. You promised me you weren't going to mock it. You've made things very difficult for me."

I couldn't really defend myself. "You want the honest truth?"

"That would be a start."

"I like you, Claire. It's more than just a professional interest, though of course I'm hoping you'll help me with Leo Parrish. But when I went through their LEAP thing I just, well, it was nonsense. What do you see in it? I'd really like to understand."

My phone started cackling.

Claire backed away, still looking angry.

I brandished the mobile. "Ashad's idea of a joke."

I had tried several times to restore the ringtone to its default settings, but with no lasting success.

"Well," she said, "aren't you going to answer it?"

The caller was Ashad himself. Claire looked as if she was ready to stalk off at any minute. I pressed the answer button and put the phone to my ear.

"Nick," came Ash's breathless voice. "I need your help. I'm in fucking custody. They've picked me up under the Prevention of Muslims in Public Act or whatever the hell it is. I need a lawyer. ASAP."

THIRTEEN

Ashad started to tell me that he had been interviewing Bennett Irwin when a gang of security men had bundled him into a hearse-like people carrier. Then his mobile cut off. I couldn't raise him when I tried to call back. The phone had either been switched off or—I tried to resist this idea—deliberately nobbled.

I phoned DI Merrick. Infuriatingly I got her answer service. I left a heated message telling her that Ashad had been arrested and saying that I didn't have any details of where he was being held. My voice was full of outrage. What the hell was going on? If Ashad had been taken into custody by the police, why hadn't they followed standard procedure and let him make the call on one of their land lines?

Claire stood watching me, her anger slowly defusing. I explained what had happened, mentioning the Muvart story and Bennett Irwin. She had the sense not to press me for details, to set aside her own annoyance in the face of my obvious agitation.

I called Valerie. Fortunately she was at her desk. When I told her the news she took it calmly, said she would get in touch with our legal people and advised me to do nothing further until I got back to the office.

I was already on my way, Claire walking with me. I tried to explain more about the Muvart documentary and our eagerness to interview Bennett Irwin, but for some reason I couldn't stop thinking about Leo Parrish. It seemed to me that all our troubles had kicked off the moment I started taking an interest in him. Not that Ashad's arrest had any connection whatsoever with Parrish. Unless it was all part of a package of someone trying to shut us down.

I let all this out in a stream-of-consciousness fashion as we jostled our way past crowds of tourists. I hadn't forgotten that she was a cultist, that she hadn't told me everything she knew about Parrish. I probably couldn't trust her at all. But I had to vent this stuff on someone, as irrational as it was. I expected her at best to tell me that I was being paranoid, but her only response was a contemplative silence.

At Leicester Square we were due to go in different directions. But to my surprise she lingered.

"Have you heard of Rhodri Davies?" I asked conversationally. I was due to meet Davies again that evening.

"I don't think so."

"He's a big fan of Leo Parrish's work. The first time we talked, he said something interesting. 'The curse of Parrish strikes again.'"

I was certain she reacted to this, but she swiftly hid it.

"Any idea what he meant by this?"

"No. Shouldn't you be more worried about your partner?"

"Oh, I am," I assured her. "But if there's the remotest chance that Ashad has been arrested because we've been asking about Parrish, then it would help to know, wouldn't it?"

"That's ridiculous."

"Is it? In what way?"

I was certain that something I had said was bothering her.

"I can't see any connection between them," she insisted.

"Maybe not. Though what if Leo Parrish is now some Big Cheese up on Capitol Hill who's scared we're going to publicize his murky past?"

"No. I don't think so."

I could tell she didn't want to be talking about this.

"Or maybe some bigwig in that church of yours?"

I was just fishing with this one, but she gave an incredulous laugh.

"Is that so unbelievable?" I said.

"I really have to go."

Without meaning to, I had started interrogating her again.

"All right," I said, "Look, I'm sorry I didn't keep my promise to behave earlier, but I hope you can see I haven't given up on Leo Parrish. I can't help being curious."

Her gaze was very candid and unwavering. All around us people were milling about, jostling us.

"He's dead," she said emphatically. "I promise you. I think you should concentrate on finding your business partner."

She hurried away and was swallowed by the crowd.

*

Valerie was upstairs with Jamilla when I got back. As was Milos, our sound man, who had been secreted in the viewing theatre and was watching an old episode of *Strictly Come Dancing* with the volume turned down and a pissed-off expression on his youthful face. No sign of Zoran, though.

He told me that Ashad had ambushed Irwin as he was getting out of a diplomatic car in the forecourt of the Savoy. With the camera running and the microphone on they had got as close as they could to Irwin's security cordon before Ashad had shouted his opening gambit: "Mr Secretary, is it true that the administration is performing germ warfare experiments on illegally detained Khanistani nationals?"

This less-than-subtle approach had had predictable consequences: Irwin's surprise had quickly given way to fury and a barked order to: "Take them down!" They had swiftly been surrounded by security men who wrestled their equipment from them before manhandling them into the back of a black dark-windowed SUV. Or at least Ashad and Zoran had been manhandled inside: Milos had managed to stamp on someone's foot and break free, dodging in and out of the path of a couple of incoming taxis before hotfooting it down The Strand. He had gone to ground inside a McDonald's for an hour before making his way to the office a few minutes before me.

I could tell he was angry about what had happened, but his choir-boy face gave little away beyond an expression that might have been read as: "Shit happens. Get used to it." The only thing he wasn't philosophical about was the prospect of being arrested by anyone connected with the intelligence services. I assured him we would keep him hidden until we found out what was going on.

"McDonald's," I remarked to him. "Nice one."

"Their toilets always work," he told me.

I left him in seclusion and rejoined the others while we waited to hear back from our lawyers. Normally they dealt with copyright and libel issues, but Valerie assured me they had people who specialized in international law. Privately I doubted that they had experts who could unravel this particular knot of intrigue.

Jamilla wanted to know if I should ring Ashad's uncle to tell him the news. I told her to wait until we had a clearer idea of where Ashad was. I was anticipating a call from DI Merrick, but when my mobile burst into applause, I saw that the caller was Gerry.

It wasn't a good time, so I didn't pick up. I put the phone on mute. As soon as he rang off, I tried Ashad's number again. The line was still dead. I phoned Merrick a second time, and when the answer service clicked on I said, "We think Ashad was arrested by Bennett Irwin's people while trying to interview him outside his hotel." I deliberately didn't provide further details in case she began to wonder how I knew so much. I particularly didn't want her to know that we were harbouring Milos.

On the office line Jamilla was busy telling any callers that we were all in an important meeting. When someone from our lawyers finally phoned I let Valerie speak to them. She explained that we now had a witness to what was clearly an illegal abduction by agents of an overseas power in a public space on British soil. But when she got off the phone she didn't look hopeful.

"When I mentioned Bennett Irwin," she told me, "I could almost feel their arses clenching in alarm."

*

I phoned DI Merrick for a third time but she still didn't pick up. I didn't bother leaving another message, though I urgently wanted her to call. She was probably our only hope, unless Ashad was belatedly given access to a phone.

I'm not very good at playing a waiting game, but there wasn't much else I could do. I retreated to my alcove, making sure I had my mobile beside me. Belatedly I realized I had been sent an email. It was from Gerry. With three attachments.

It turned out that both Gerry and Liz Martindale had read the Parrish stories and were highly taken by them, though not just for the sturdy excitement of their plots or the wacky stimulus of their invention. Gerry's message stressed that they had been most impressed by the *predictive* power of the stories, the way in which they appeared actually to have anticipated events to a degree which was uncanny.

Like the good scientists they were, Gerry and Dr Martindale had provided documentation to support their assertions. The first attachment was an abstract from a climate science journal entitled "Targeted Interventions and Transient Weather Modification". Despite the dry title, it described a sequence of derring-do exploits in which climate scientists had flown into the heart of developing hurricanes and were using pulses of microwave and infra-red radiation in an attempt to disrupt the circulation of the storms and so reduce their intensity. The details were cross-referenced with Parrish's "Weather Warriors" story. Though there was no actual talk of negentropy beams in the journal, there were distinct parallels between the two.

The second attachment provided a much flimsier link with Parrish's "Know Your Enemy". It was a *Daily Mail* article suggesting that immigrant members of "terrorist cells" had become so enamoured of life in the UK that they were now subsisting as "parasites on the Welfare State" and were so settled that some had even applied for citizenship. Gerry had highlighted the title: "Hostile Aliens Live the Good Life".

The third attachment was a news report from the *Wall Street Journal* on a psychological condition dubbed WIReD, for Web Induced Reality Disfunction, in which teenagers who had spent hours obsessively playing a new immersive computer game were experiencing symptoms akin to autism, primarily an inability to communicate and a severe detachment from their physical environment. The game, an illegal import whose origins were obscure, was called *Transmission*.

My initial urge was to dismiss all this as sheer coincidence. A few years ago I had co-scripted a documentary we produced for BBC4 called *The Nostradamus Effect*, and I knew about the obsessive way in which doom-mongers and conspiracy theorists operated, sucking significance from unrelated events by sheer bloody-mindedness, using selective or misleading or downright obscure quotations to bolster their particular obsessions.

The trouble was, I had a strong gut reaction to Gerry and Dr Martindale's revelations because they crystallized what had been bothering me about these and other Parrish stories. Weren't the "mini-numerators" in "Figure It Out" just palm-top computers by another name, conceived by Parrish decades before they were developed? Wasn't the news story about malevolent survivors of the Chernobyl disaster very similar to the scenario in "Atomic Avengers"? Granted, the connections were loose enough to be open to other interpretations *if they had been isolated cases*. But we were talking about at least five distinct stories, all written half a century ago, featuring inventions and storylines which had real-life counterparts here in the twenty-first century.

Clearly Gerry thought so too, his accompanying email jocularly asking me if I had any Parrish stories set on Bali since he intended to spend Christmas there and wanted to be sure he would avoid any natural or man-made disasters that might be in the offing. I did wonder, though, about his assurances that Liz Martindale had helped him track down the cross-references. She had struck me as the archetypal scientist who wouldn't have had the slightest truck with anything that smacked of irrationality. Maybe I had misjudged her. Or maybe she was another person with an agenda that was obscure to me.

I was in thrall to these deliberations when Jamilla walked in.

"Someone's here for you," she said rather breathlessly, and I knew who it was.

*

"Let's walk," Merrick said to me. "I could use some air."

Her unmarked blue BMW was parked right outside, a young male driver sitting behind the wheel.

"We're taking a stroll," she told him. "Back in ten."

We headed off through the crowds in a southerly direction.

"I didn't want to talk in the office," Merrick announced. "In front of Ms Ali."

"Is it bad news?" I asked urgently. "He's all right, isn't he?"

"As far as I can determine, he's in what they're calling protective custody."

"They?"

"The US intelligence services."

"Have you seen him? Where is he?"

She was shaking her head. "I haven't quite been able to establish that yet. All I know at present is that it's probably one of their secure locations in central London."

"Probably?"

"Almost certainly."

Passing Leicester Square tube station, we accepted leaflets from a young woman in a hijab.

"Can they do that?" I asked.

"According to them, he accosted the Secretary of State with threatening intent."

"He didn't do anything of the sort!"

She gave me a look that was both sympathetic and wry. "How do you know?"

"He was just trying to get an interview. We had a lead we were following."

"I know what he intended," she replied. "He told me."

"You've spoken to him?"

"Not today. He talked about it the last time we met."

"Then you must know he wasn't threatening Irwin."

"I know he thinks Irwin's a basket case and wanted to catch him napping. Irwin might not have seen it that way, though."

The leaflet was headed THE KHANISTANI WOMEN'S COOPERATIVE and its first bullet point said: END FOREIGN INTERVENTION IN KHANISTAN.

"But surely you can vouch for him?" I said. "Tell them he's a person of good character?"

"First I have to locate him. If they think he's a terrorist, he might be not easy to track down."

"What—they can just disappear someone in someone else's country?"

"In the short term, yes. He could be bureaucratically mislaid."

"Mislaid?" My tone combined scepticism with anger. "But you're in the trade. Didn't you say you liaised with other overseas services?"

She stopped and gave me her full attention. "It's not that simple. The security apparatus of any state is a many-headed Hydra. Some services are at odds with others. You don't always get the cooperation you expect."

"This is outrageous. He's a British citizen, doing a legitimate investigative feature in his own country."

"And Irwin's the Secretary of State for Defense."

I didn't like the way the conversation was heading. "So that allows them to kidnap him off the street and lock him away where no one can find him?"

"No," she said firmly. "Of course it doesn't. Don't you think I want to find him too?"

"I don't know," I said bluntly. "Do you?"

She arched a jet-black eyebrow. "Of course I do. But you can't just charge in yelling and screaming blue murder. You have to go through the right channels."

"Is he in danger?"

"Of what?"

"You tell me. Extreme rendition? Torture?"

She didn't dismiss the suggestion out of hand, as I had expected.

"Listen," she said, "I'm desperate for a coffee. Do you mind?"

We were outside Prêt A Manger.

Merrick insisted on buying. While she was at the counter I found a pair of stools by the window. The day was drab, but Trafalgar Square was full of tourists. At that moment I envied them, almost wished I was an innocent abroad, somewhere remote and exotic, far away from all mystery and intrigue.

On a nearby stool was a discarded copy of the *Evening Standard*. Like many other newspapers it was still carrying the necrotizing fasciitis story, this one supporting the government line that it had been entirely fabricated by "extremists" who wanted to spread psychological terror. Most newspapers had reached a similar consensus in recent days.

I took another look at the leaflet. Merrick returned with a couple of lattes and a chocolate croissant. For the first time I noticed the dark crescents under her eyes

"Late night?" I asked as she took a gulp of coffee.

"Something like that," she murmured, and proceeded to attack the croissant with gusto.

I wondered if I should tell her all I knew in the hope that this would help Ashad. No. I still didn't entirely trust her. But there were things I needed to find out.

"Did Ashad tell you what he wanted to interview Irwin about?" I asked.

She just shook her head. "We didn't get into that sort of pillow talk."

Did she mean this literally? And why was I shocked at the idea that they had already slept together?

I flourished the leaflet from the Khanistani Women's Cooperative. It was no one-sided anti-imperialist rant. Among the bullet points were: RESTORE FREE ELECTIONS and STOP ALL ARRESTS. I indicated the latter. "Are we detaining innocent Khanistani nationals here?"

She frowned. "I don't know. Are we?"

"You're the policewoman." I kept my tone polite but firm. "There are rumours of Khanistanis being held at a secret site in the UK." I wasn't going to tell her all the details, particularly since the press hadn't yet got wind of it. "Rumours that they've been deliberately infected with this new disease by the authorities."

I thrust the newspaper in front of her, with yet another lurid photograph of a disease sufferer on its cover. If Merrick already knew about my version of the story, she hid it well.

"Are you telling me he was going to ask Irwin about that?" she asked, puzzled.

"Well, this place, this illegal internment centre, if that's what it is. We wanted to find out if it's being run by the CIA."

"Unlikely," she said immediately. "Not on foreign territory."

"You talk as if it's never happened before."

"It couldn't happen without the knowledge of the British government."

"Without their active support and assistance?"

"I'd find that hard to credit. I suppose there's no point in me asking you where you got this information?"

"No," I replied. "None at all. Anyway, that's what Ashad wanted to ask Irwin about. It appears Irwin was greatly offended by the suggestion."

Merrick took a slow sip of her latte. "He had two others with him, didn't he?"

I couldn't see any point in denying it. "Zoran and Milos," I told her.

"One of them got away."

"Really?"

This came out too quickly. She gave the thinnest of smiles. "If you see him, advise him to keep his head down for a while."

I swallowed some of my own latte. "Don't you think it's extreme that they should whisk them off the street and then deny them access to a phone and legal counsel?"

"We don't know they are denying them that."

"Have you tried ringing Ashad on his mobile?"

She had to admit that she had.

"He's not answering, is he? It's not even switched on. Assuming it hasn't just been chucked in the Thames. As far as I'm aware, he hasn't made any other calls."

"It's standard procedure to take a mobile phone away from a suspect after arrest."

"There's the funny thing. I don't think they did. Not immediately. They must have yanked it off him in mid-conversation with me."

She gave every indication that she didn't like the sound of this. The blue BMW pulled up outside, its hazard lights flashing, her driver at the wheel.

She took a hefty swig of coffee. "I've got to go."

"How did you manage that?" I asked, indicating her car. "Was he tailing us?"

"I phoned while I was getting the coffees. I need you to do me a favour."

She was already standing. Her face was etched with fatigue.

"Which is?" I asked.

"Trust me on this. Give me a little time to find out what's going on. Don't do anything to muddy the waters."

"The waters look pretty muddy to me already."

"I'm looking into it," she assured me. "Believe me, it's a priority. It may be hours or days before I find out anything, but as soon as I do I'll let you know."

"Jamilla wants to let the rest of the family know he's in custody. I'm not going to stop her from doing that."

"Of course not. But give me some time to do my job."

Her tone was eminently reasonable. I stared back at her. "I'm not hearing anything about getting him released. He hasn't committed any crime."

"Trust me," she said again. And then she walked out.

*

I went back to the office and did my best to pretend that nothing unusual had happened, a ludicrous proposition, but I needed to keep busy. I suggested to Jamilla that I should phone Ashad's uncle with the news of his arrest, but she insisted she wanted to do it. Despite her usual doughty manner she was visibly upset afterwards, so I told her to go home and said I would ring her if there was any news. Valerie sent Ross Buchanan upstairs to man Jamilla's desk and route any calls down to her office. Which meant that I was totally free to brood for the rest of the afternoon.

Fortunately I found a swift distraction. Among my emails was one from Walter Suthersen, or rather, his US secretary. Attached to it was the photograph.

It was a grainy black-and-white print, showing three young men standing in what looked like a cramped cubby-hole filled to bursting point with piles of books and manuscripts. Suthersen's secretary, whose accompanying note merely said: *Walter asked me to send the attached to you*, had appended a caption that read:

WS, Edgar Eldridge and Leo Parrish in the offices of Ridge Publications, January 1959.

Suthersen was on the left of the photograph, a smiling tousle-haired version of his present-day self, dressed in jeans and a pale sweater with a snowflake motif. Next to him was a shorter, stockier young man in a two-tone open-necked shirt and slacks. He had slicked back dark hair, a big grin and his arms looped proprietarily around the shoulders of the other two men.

If Suthersen and Eldridge radiated youthful energy and confidence, Leo Parrish cut a rather different figure. Handsome but studious-looking in a Clark Kent lookalike way, he wore a white shirt and narrow tie under a buttoned V-neck cardigan. While Suthersen and Eldridge were staring at the camera, Parrish was gazing across it, his eyes narrowed as if he wasn't entirely comfortable with having his photograph taken and would have liked to get out from under Eldridge's embracing arm.

So this was the mystery man. I felt a mixture of excitement and anti-climax. It was good to know that he had actually existed, that he wasn't some made-up character or just a pseudonym for another writer. But, as Suthersen had suggested, there was something not quite there about him, as if his mind was otherwise occupied. As usual with writers, it was hard to equate the physical man with his work, to see any suggestion of his fertile imagination behind his guarded-looking face. And, oddly, I found it impossible to envisage how he might have aged. If indeed he ever had.

*

Rhodri Davies's shoulder bag was even more voluminous than my backpack, a trove of all sorts of goodies including magazines, books and single-sheet copies of the latest edition of *Homeopape*, this one on sage-green paper.

"Where's the Parrish photo?" I asked, scanning both sides of the close-printed sheet with its bullet-pointed items, thumbnail cartoons but no pictures. Like me, he had received an electronic copy of the photograph that afternoon.

"It's a newszine," he reminded me. "I don't run photos. But see the Stop Press."

It was right at the end and said:

Shock&Awe! Long-lost mystery writer Who Shall Be Nameless in revealing antique photo with Before They Were Famous Big Name Author and Religious Leader!

Next to it was a link where the photograph could be accessed.

"I hope you took Parrish's name off the caption," I remarked. "Otherwise someone out there is sure to close it down."

Davies winked at me. "It says: 'Ed Ridge brings impressionable young authors Walter Suthersen and Dai O'Seas into his fold.'"

We were seated at a table in a corner of *The Black Hole*, a pub off Farringdon Road where the UK Science Fiction Society held its monthly meetings, though "meeting" was actually a bit of a misnomer, as Davies had pointed out to me soon after I arrived, because the entire bar was packed with people who were doing a lot of drinking and socializing with a lack of any formal structure. Predominantly aged between thirty and sixty, most were male but there was a healthy sprinkling of women who seemed less inclined than the men to consume copious amounts of beer but were equally sociable, moving around the throng, handing out fanzines and generally engaging in a lot of good-humoured banter, an understanding of which was wholly dependent on an intimate knowledge of both science fiction and a social network in which everyone knew everyone else. According to Davies the landlord was an SF fan who had renamed the pub when he took it over, and the place had a suitably dark and hermetic atmosphere. In this world, I was the only Martian present.

"We got the photo pretty quickly," I remarked to Davies. "Walter Suthersen was eager to honour his promise."

"Spookily so," Davies agreed, "given all the other demands on his time. Maybe he's finally realized that Parrish deserves a bit more limelight. Or that he needs to prove he and Parrish aren't the same person."

"It's genuine. I got a mate of mine to check."

I had downloaded the photo to Ozzie Hogg, just to be certain that it was authentic. He had image-analysing software that was pretty reliable in spotting cut-and-paste jobs as well as airbrushing and fake "vintage" signatures sometimes used to make an image appear old. Though I had no reason to suspect Suthersen of any subterfuge—why pretend there was a photo in the first place?—the very promptness of its arrival made me wonder if he had a hidden agenda. I had grown suspicious that anything associated with Parrish wasn't as straightforward as it appeared. But Ozzie had responded within the hour to say that all the indications suggested it was a real unadulterated snapshot from the 1950s.

"It's definitely Walt Suthersen and Edgar Eldridge," Davies said.

"So we can be pretty confident it's also Leo Parrish."

"I'd like to think so. But we've only got Suthersen's word for it, don't forget." Davies had a mischievous look on his face again. "You can't always believe what you see."

"What do you mean?"

"The picture might actually be of Walt, Eldridge and *anyone*. Well, not Greta Garbo obviously. But I've been suspicious of photographs of SF writers since one edition of Phil Dick's *The Man in the High Castle* had a photo on the back which was later revealed to be Ted White, another SF writer."

"You're having me on."

Davies shook his head merrily. "Not that I don't think it's Parrish, mind you. The circumstances here are very different. There's no reason for Suthersen to shoot himself in the foot by sending a fake."

"It's a pity we can't ask Edgar Eldridge to confirm it."

"That would be the clincher," Davies agreed. "I've heard it said that Suthersen and Eldridge were the only two people in the SF world actually to have met Parrish in the flesh."

"So he was elusive even then."

"It wasn't particularly unusual. There were plenty of marginal writers around trying to earn a few pennies from the magazines. A lot of them remain completely anonymous to this day. We're fortunate to have a photograph of Parrish."

"What do you make of him? I thought he looked like a fish out of water."

Davies nodded emphatically. "His track record suggests he wasn't the type to court publicity. Maybe the other two had to drag him kicking and screaming in front of the camera."

He delved into his rucksack again and produced what looked like a pristine copy of *Shocking Stories* issue 1 in a transparent folder. It turned out to be a full-colour scan of the magazine's cover and black-and-white equivalents of the inside pages featuring *Exaltation*. Davies claimed that he kept the original safe in his own collection, hidden in a fire-proof strongbox in a black hole of his own devising. As usual, it was hard to tell whether he was joking, though I suspected not. Despite his sometimes facetious manner, he plainly had a sincere and abiding love for science fiction and its history.

He had also brought along photocopies of two more Parrish stories from *Awesome Adventures*. One of them was "The Cosmic Controllers".

I was eager to go home and read the first half of the serial, but it would have been churlish to take the folder and run. I slid it into my rucksack, which I kept close to me throughout. I didn't want to take any risk that it might be stolen.

As far as I could tell, no one else paid us any attention. All the people crammed into the bar were immersed in their own conversations and those standing around our table conveniently formed a barrier through which no outsiders could see us.

I told Davies about Ashad's arrest and the nagging feeling that it was somehow linked with Leo Parrish. He didn't look convinced, though he didn't actually laugh it off. I hadn't heard anything further from Merrick and had decided to meet Davies as planned because it was a far better option than brooding at home, hoping that the phone would ring.

"I'm grateful to Walter Suthersen for the photograph," I said, "but I can't help feeling he's holding something back. I thought he went a bit defensive every time Parrish's name was mentioned."

"Perhaps he *did* murder him!" Davies said, obviously not believing it in the slightest.

A middle-aged man in a suit and tie pushed through the crowd and asked Davies for a copy of *Homeopape*. He dutifully handed one over. They had a brief animated conversation, filled with arcane words like "fannish" and "skiffy". When he was gone, Davies told me that he was a senior editor for a publishing company with a strong science fiction list.

"Most of the people here are fans," he told me, "but there are a few authors and editors scattered about."

"Anyone who might have known Parrish?"

He laughed. "Even in this place, there's only a handful of us who've ever heard of him." He drained his pint. "I take it you haven't received the second part of the serial from Walt yet?"

I shook my head: I had promised to send him a copy when I did.

"I've got something else for you, though," I told him. I finished my drink before delving into my rucksack and producing a hard copy of the material Gerry had emailed me.

"Have a look at that," I told Davies, picking up both our glasses. And then I went off to the bar.

It was three deep all along the counter, and everyone else in the pub was better known to the people serving behind it than I was. Ten long minutes passed before I was served, time enough to notice two young men and a woman sitting apart from the throng at a table near the door, the woman with her back to me. Whereas most of *The Black Hole* crowd were hairy and clad in baggy casuals, this well-groomed trio sported crisp summer shorts and polo shirts. They might have been pub regulars patiently sitting out the monthly invasion of their domain. But I doubted it.

The moment I got back to the table, Davies started enthusing.

"This is great stuff, boss," he told me. Gerry's pages were spread out all over the table. "Leo Parrish really is a Master of the Universe!"

"It spooked me when I read it," I confessed. "Some of the parallels in the stories are close to the real thing."

"Maybe that's why Parrish is such a hot potato. The Bennett Irwin crowd want him to tell them whether they should invade Khanistan."

I smiled soberly. "It made me think, I have to tell you. Weather control technology, portable computers, a virtual reality game with the same name as the one Parrish wrote about."

"It's not beyond the bounds of possibility that the game was developed by someone who actually read the Parrish story."

"And the others?"

"They could be lucky strikes. Science fiction writers always have an eye on the future. That's what the genre is about. Possibilities. In 1944 a writer was investigated by the FBI because he'd written about a trigger device for an atomic bomb while secret work was going on at Los Alamos. He didn't know that. He'd based the story on information freely available about nuclear technology."

"And did he make at least four other successful predictions?"

"No," Davies conceded. "You're not the first to suggest that Parrish might be some kind of real visionary." He indicated the stories. "The artificial eyes in 'Cosmic Controllers' aren't dissimilar to work currently being done on retinal implants. Better still—" he selected the other story, which was entitled "Tracers" "—this one has China as a world superpower at a time when everyone was obsessed with Soviet power. They pursue what Parrish called Communocapitalistic policies and use an 'electrophoton field grid' to monitor the activities of their citizens." Rhodri was grinning. "It's a pretty good guess at the internet."

"Wow."

"It's easy to get carried away with this sort of thing," Rhodri cautioned. "Some writers have a better track record in the predictive stakes than others. H.G. Wells for one. And I'll grant you that Parrish had keener eyes than most. But it would be a big mistake to go overboard and start believing in him as some kind of clairvoyant."

"Perhaps he's a time traveller," I said.

"Maybe that's why he disappeared. He vanished back into the future."

We were joking; except that I wasn't, not entirely at least. The stories hadn't immediately leapt out at me for their prescience, I had to admit. Though I liked what I had read, Parrish's prose style was unremarkable, his stories steeped in the culture and concerns of the era. But the accuracy of his guesses was a real puzzle. The fanciful thought occurred to me that it was all one gigantic hoax, that the stories had actually been written in the present day and the whole thing retrofitted with a fake history to make it look as if they were half a century old.

When I mooted this to Davies he gave a hearty chuckle. "You should tell that idea to Walt. But make sure he cuts you in for a percentage of the royalties."

He began gathering up Gerry's papers.

"I have to tell you," he said quietly, "I make a living out of being sceptical. But all this—" he indicated the sheaf of papers "—almost makes me want to start believing in fairies. Can I hang on to these?"

"By all means."

A couple of people pushed through the crowd and began engaging him in conversation. Fanzines were exchanged, and there was a lot of in-group talking which meant nothing to me. I skim-read "Tracers". It was a futuristic police procedural set in Hong Kong, with a detective electronically tracking down a rebel who proves to be his beloved wife. Neat but a little old-hat for today's audience because the theme had been so well-worked. But the Chinese setting and the idea of the grid marked it out as highly unusual and intriguing for its time.

I deposited the stories in my rucksack and got up to go to the loo.

"Don't stray too close to the Dark Side," Davies said gleefully, indicating the table near the door.

"Ascendants?"

He nodded. "A few years back they set up this competition to discover new SF writers. Brave New Words, they called it. Showed up at conventions with lots of glossy publicity material, offering to fund publication for the winners. When we found out they were behind it, we got the heebie-jeebies."

"We?"

"The science fiction world. You know, all of us with that secret third eye in the middle of our foreheads."

I could see that there were a few glossy pamphlets on their table. “They were interested in science fiction?”

“They probably thought we were kindred spirits. Into UFOs and all that tosh. According to my researches, the competition was Edgar Eldridge’s idea. Recapture some of the magic of the old days.”

“Your researches?”

“They’re still active on the fringes of the scene. They’ve got one of their big annual *convocations* coming up soon at their UK headquarters.”

“What, at the new temple?”

Davies shook his head. “Their HQ is in my neck of the woods. Makes it easier for me to snoop on them.”

I knew that Davies lived in Maidenhead, to the west of London. He told me, with a degree of relish, that the Ascendants’ headquarters was a refurbished factory on the outskirts of nearby Slough. “Word has it, there’s going to be a few Big Name Celebrities turning up. Vincent Kubilius is almost certain to be there.”

Kubilius had long been the public face of the Ascendants, a dynamic individual who was as eager to promote both himself and his beliefs as Edgar Eldridge was to avoid publicity.

“Fancy coming along?” Davies asked me.

“You’re going to the meeting?”

He grinned. “I thought I might just loiter with intent and see if I can sneak in. Be interesting to see who shows up.”

I was about to recount my own visit to the London temple when someone else pushed through the throng and sat down to talk to him. Before the press of bodies closed around us again, the woman at the far table turned so that I saw her face for the first time. Just as quickly she turned away. Though she was dressed very differently and wore her hair down I was certain I recognized her.

Someone at our table started asking me questions about Xponential’s future output. I answered them as best I could while trying to locate the memory.

She was Pony Tail from Arthur’s flat.

Or was I just imagining it? There was only one way to find out.

I excused myself and stood up, taking my rucksack with me. By now the pub was packed and it wasn't easy to manoeuvre through the crowd. Already I was rehearsing the casual but committed way in which I would saunter up to the table and make sure I was facing her before I said, "Don't I know you from somewhere?" before asking her if she had been back to Arthur Townsend's place since the fire.

But by the time I had battled through into clear space, the only thing left at the table was an unfinished glass of orange juice. All three of them had gone.

New York City, October 1972

Seated on the wooden bench outside the Director's office, he studied the floor tile mosaic. The Director had asked to see him, and suddenly he was certain that within the tile pattern there resided a clue to his reasons. You only had to get the correct distance away and it would emerge from the interlocked shapes like a stained-glass picture in a cathedral window.

He was standing on the bench when Louise Pancucci appeared, looking a little alarmed. Not wanting to arouse suspicion, he swiftly clambered down, whereupon the door opened and the Director was ushering both of them in.

He took a seat to the right of the Director so that Louise would have to peer over the bulky chrome desk lamp to talk to him. He hadn't known Louise would be coming too. Were they finally going to give him some positive news on the Probability Bomb?

The Director was all fussy bonhomie to begin with, shuffling papers on his blotter and asking them if they wanted a drink. They both declined.

Now the Director put his hands together like a man about to pray.

"This is a delicate matter," he announced, his gaze focused on the door, as if he was expecting someone else to come in at any moment. "How long have you been with us now?"

The Director was asking him.

"Two years and two months," he replied, knowing that the Director would already be aware of this information.

The Director was studying some papers, or at least pretending to study them.

"You made a very promising start here," the Director said agreeably. "And you're still a young man, with plenty of future prospects. Wouldn't you agree, Dr Pancucci?"

Louise gave a startled nod as though she had been put on the spot and had no choice but to agree.

"The difficulty is," the Director said, "I'm wondering if you've been rather overdoing it lately."

Was this a question? Evidently it was.

"No," he said as calmly as he could. "I don't think so."

"Would it be fair to say that you've been working very long hours recently?"

The Director waited. He was tempted to confirm it, to stress the vital importance of his researches and how essential it was that he constantly applied himself to them: but something told him that silence was safer.

"Perhaps on occasions staying well after dark?"

"Sometimes," he admitted.

"Even over-nighting here?"

They must have found his sleeping roll and pillow.

Before he could even muster any defence of his actions, the Director changed tack. "Dr Pancucci is just one of several colleagues who has become rather concerned for your welfare, isn't that so, doctor?"

Louise nodded again, looking uncomfortable.

"She tells me you've visited her department a total of twelve times in the past month to ask for updates on their current projects."

He thought about it: thought about the most prudent way to frame his reply. "As a field agent I consider it vital that any intelligence I gather is fed back to the R&D people and that they in turn keep me abreast of their latest initiatives."

"Is that so?" the Director replied, not hiding a sceptical tone. "And would that include repeated requests to initiate work on something called a Probability Bomb?"

He couldn't hide an involuntary smile. The Bomb had been his very own idea, inspired, as it were, by the Shaper's tales, an actual means of wiping his influence from the world by a form of enhanced Butterfly Effect which could be deployed in any circumstances to alter the likely outcome wherever one of the Shaper's unwholesome predictions was in danger of coming true.

The Director was now holding up a fat tightly bound bundle of papers which he instantly recognized.

"These," the Director was saying, "are, I believe, your own specifications for the project?"

He nodded.

"Close on four hundred pages of closely typed text."

He had written them in a fury of inspired invention. Sometimes he had kept going through sunset and sunrise, driven by the fact that only this could save the world.

"Dr Pancucci tells me you've made repeated requests to her for a working prototype of the device."

He was beginning to feel uneasy, the Director's voice taking on a droning quality.

"I believe it's vital for our future security."

"Yes," the Director said flatly. "I can see that you do."

Dr Pancucci now launched into a defence of her own actions, explaining at length why the prototype had not been built and even claiming that her department had merely an evaluative function and was not equipped for advanced technical projects, even if such an invention had been possible, which it patently wasn't, given that the so-called specifications were quite incoherent.

Her voice was becoming a disagreeable whine. He had told no one about his slaying of the Shaper because he knew he would get no credit for it. No one appeared to appreciate the danger apart from him. The very people who were supposed to be helping him protect the world were now conspiring to thwart him.

He let them talk, bringing a laser-sharp scrutiny to bear. The Director had sprouted dark mutton-chop sideboards in recent months and a fondness for florid shirts, while Dr Pancucci's unusually heavy makeup was an obvious mask hiding her real self. She had always pretended to be his friend, but now he knew otherwise.

What if the both of them were imposters, not the original colleagues he remembered at all? What if they were replicas placed there by the Shaper's minions for the very purpose of confounding him?

The door behind him opened. He didn't dare look around, but saw a blurred white-coated image in the hemispherical desk-lamp shade.

"I think it would be helpful if you had a chat with Dr Rammel," the Director was saying.

Rammel was already behind him. He was the Unit's medical doctor, first name Thomas. On his door it said T. Rammel. Trammel. It meant to constrain, to strait-jacket even.

Wasn't the director a doctor of some sort too? Had all the doctors in the Unit been replaced by drones of the Shaper?

He was surrounded by them and knew it was only a matter of seconds before they pounced. He coughed, and then put his hand on his chest and slowly started to slide it inside his jacket. Field agents weren't allowed to carry their service pistols in the building, but for weeks he had had a growing sense of his own vulnerability. His only chance was to act first.

FOURTEEN

Briony Potts had the face of a prim schoolmistress but a soul full of mischief. She lived in St Albans, and it was easy to loop off the M1 and pick her up on my way to Dunstable. Fortunately she was also an early riser. By eight-thirty we were approaching the site of Paradys Biosciences on the outskirts of the town.

I had been awake half the night, thinking about Ashad, trying to imagine what he would want me to do while I was waiting for news of him. And the answer was this: he would expect me to be getting on with my job, and in particular pursuing any leads we had on our current projects. So I had decided to drive out of London soon after dawn and get up the motorway before the rush hour traffic started building up.

It was only while on a coffee stop that I had had the inspiration to phone Briony. She had voiced one of the characters in *Absolute Hero* and we had struck up a friendship, especially after she had revealed herself as a free-thinking radical very much in sympathy with Xponential's stir-'em-up philosophy. I phoned more in hope than expectation, but when she answered and I explained that I was hoping to dig up some dirt on a story we were following, she had immediately agreed to help.

I parked the Bravo on the side of the approach road and we walked up to the entrance. What was left of Paradys looked pretty threadbare behind saggy diamond-wire fencing, a few low buildings like army barracks surrounded by weed-lined roads, unmanned bulldozers and concrete foundations on which stood mounds of rubble. A young man in a crumpled security guard uniform was slumped at the window hatch in a spacious sentry box, dozing while The Kaiser Chiefs sang "I Predict a Riot" on the radio.

I tapped on the window and he stirred.

"Morning," I said cheerfully. "Ms Potts and I are here for our eight-thirty appointment."

Briony, tall and slim, showed her face at my shoulder. The guard half-gagged in surprise. He switched off the radio and hurriedly backhanded a streak of drool from the corner of his mouth.

"And what an extremely pleasant morning it is," Briony said elegantly, delivering a well-known line from her character in *Them and Us*, a Posh versus Slobs sitcom that was currently showing on ITV. She was a familiar face to television viewers, having also appeared in soap operas and costume dramas.

The security guard managed to look both bewildered and in awe. Which was just the reaction I had been hoping for.

"The location-check?" I said to him as if I assumed he would know all about it. "We arranged to take a look around the place with your site manager."

"Mr Wainwright?"

"Indeed. Eight-thirty for nine."

Tearing his awed gaze from Briony, he reached for a clipboard and scanned it.

"There's nothing here," he informed me.

I had already got out my mobile and was making a show of checking it. After a moment I put my hand to my mouth and said theatrically: "Ms Potts, I feel such an awful fool. I've made a mistake on the date. The appointment's for *next* month."

Briony did an even better job of looking thoroughly peeved.

"That's not going to be possible," she said. "I shall be in Africa."

"Africa?" I said.

"Doing a wildebeest special for children's BBC. I really can't make it any other time." She fixed her gaze on the guard. "Young man, I'd be terribly grateful for your assistance on this matter."

He was gawping at her again. "It's Phil."

"Well, Phil, can you help this damsel in distress? It's really rather imperative that I take a look around the site. It's stipulated in my contract. I want to be sure it's a civilized setting for filming."

Phil was clearly intrigued. "What's it for?"

"The new series of *Doctor Who*."

"*Doctor Who*?" he said enthusiastically. "You're in that?"

She winked at him. "I might be playing the evil warden of a prison camp on a hostile planet. Of course with plenty of latex appendages to cover up my natural beauty."

Phil laughed. But he still looked a little dubious. "I should probably check with the office."

"Is that really necessary? I can tell you what they'll say—we'll have to come back next month. Do you know how ghastly the M1 is at this time in the morning?"

He nodded heartily. "Absolute nightmare."

"We just need a quick look around," I added. "Twenty minutes, half an hour at most, to get the lie of the land. I'm sure Mr Wainwright wouldn't mind. He's a *Doctor Who* fan as well, isn't he?"

Phil plainly had no idea. He mulled it over.

"I'd have to accompany you," he told me.

"No problem," I replied, already wondering how we could get around that.

Phil unhooked a chunky bunch of keys and swung the door of his box open.

The main gate was secured by a hefty padlock, whereas those on the few buildings that remained on site were clearly of the swipe-card type. Phil told us as much as he walked us around while quizzing Briony about acting. She gave good value, telling him amusing anecdotes about well-known actors. I was more focused on trying to think of a way to get inside the Lister building. It lay at the end of a rank of four, the others also named after medical pioneers.

Fortunately Briony once again rose to the challenge. Knowing my intentions, she led Phil towards what was evidently the building housing the toilets and showers.

"Is it still connected to the mains?" she asked Phil.

He nodded. "We need it for the contractors."

"I really do hope they have no intention of shutting it off before we begin filming in the summer. I just can't abide unsanitary conditions. Do you know, when we were doing *The Faraway Tree* I spent days on end sitting in a muddy field with nothing but a portaloo. It was simply intolerable. Is it fit for human habitation? Would you show me inside?"

Phil was cheered to be receiving such insights into the world of film and programme making. He was only too happy to oblige.

The instant they went inside, I bounded up the short flight of steps to the Lister block and slashed Sam Oliphant's swipe card through the slot. I scarcely expected it to work, but the dot of light on the brushed metal face plate flashed from red to green. I turned the handle. It opened.

I moved with as much haste as I could muster. The interior of the building had been mostly cleared of equipment and what remained were a few desks in corners and alcoves. Everything was covered with a layer of gritty dust from the demolition work outside. Above the desks there were still personal effects like planners and calendars on the walls. One of the workstations had a cluster of photographs and postcards pinned to a cork board. Among the photos was one of Gerry playing pool. And another of Gerry and Sam Oliphant holding up drinks and grinning.

I dragged the desk out from the wall and immediately saw where screws were missing from one of the panels. I found an edge and pulled it free. In the narrow space inside was a slim cardboard document wallet that said "Gas Bags" in a peculiarly scribbled combination of upper and lower case as: GaS BAgS.

The capitals were picked out in bold. Removing the lower case letters gave: GSBAS.

Genotype Specific Biological Agents.

I plucked the file out and stuffed it down the back of my jeans, folding my shirt over the top so that it sat snug against my lower back. Outside I heard voices. Phil and Briony had emerged from the shower block and were walking back towards me. Hastily I replaced the panel before shoving the desk back into place.

"I do believe he's gone for a walk around the perimeter fence," I heard Briony saying loudly for my benefit. I crept to the window and saw her pointing towards a line of conifers at the far end of the perimeter. "Would we be able to use the land beyond for filming?"

"Unlikely," Phil told her, now plainly a little worried at my absence. "It's a golf course."

She led him away from the building, still talking so that I could gauge when they were a reasonable distance away. Then I crept out, closing the door as quietly as I could behind me.

I scampered around in the opposite direction, keeping myself hidden behind the other buildings. There was a big yellow earth-mover right in my path. Without hesitating I clambered up into the driver's seat and sat down before calling out, "I'm over here!"

Phil spun around and I could see relief suffusing his face to find me so innocently occupied.

"I've always wanted to drive one of these things," I told him.

"I'm afraid it's not allowed," he said nervously.

"Don't worry," I reassured him, "I wouldn't know how to start." And I descended with as much dignity as a document wallet stuffed down my pants would allow.

I made a point of thanking him effusively as we walked back to the gate, telling him that the site was perfect for our purposes and that we really appreciated his cooperation. He began to look a little mollified, though I suspect he was now wondering whether he had made the right decision in letting us in.

While he was padlocking the gate I whispered to Briony: "You're an absolute star. I owe you mightily."

"Nothing that a lunch at the Ivy wouldn't cover," she whispered back. "Did you get what you were after?"

I nodded.

"I haven't had as much fun since I last did Pinter," she said.

Phil walked us back to my car. I think he wanted to get us on our way as swiftly as possible, presumably before the day shift arrived.

"Will you be here when we start filming in the summer?" Briony asked him brightly, playing her part to the end. "It's absolutely hush-hush, by the way, so you mustn't blab to anyone."

"I'm here till the site is decommissioned," he told her. "I thought that wasn't until the autumn."

Briony winked at him again. "Perhaps we know something you don't."

*

After dropping Briony home, I called the office. I had been checking my emails and text messages regularly but had heard nothing from anyone. Now Jamilla informed me that our legal team had found a lawyer who was prepared to take up Ashad's cause, a man called Felix Nancarrow who specialized in cases with sensitive diplomatic overtones.

I rang DI Merrick's number first. She didn't pick up and I decided against leaving a message. I hadn't actually promised that I would sit back and do nothing while she was making her own enquiries, and I still wasn't convinced that we could entirely trust her. I phoned the number Jamilla had given me and got a secretary who put me straight through.

"Mr Randall," Felix Nancarrow greeted me. "I gather your friend Mr Husseyin has got himself into a bit of a bind."

"That's putting it mildly," I replied. "Have you been told the details?"

"I've had a précis. But I'd rather you went through it again so that I'm as certain as I can be about the facts in the matter."

I told him the story in as much detail as I could, giving him a character resumé of Ashad into the bargain. He hummed affirmatively and made lengthier interjections at various points, in particular asking me to clarify exactly what I understood that Ashad had said and done when he confronted Bennett Irwin.

"We need to be on as firm a ground as possible on that score," he told me. "Otherwise it could be a very sticky wicket."

Before I had phoned him I had been given the impression that he was something of a maverick who was particularly interested in challenging vested interests. Yet he spoke in the refined Establishment tones that suggested a public school education. You could have poured his voice into a decanter and served it after dinner.

"He asked Irwin if the US government was carrying out biological experiments on illegally detained Khanistanis," I told him. "Irwin took offence and had his security people arrest him and one of our employees."

"Zoran Vasic?"

"He was the cameraman. His brother, Milos, got away."

Nancarrow was silent for a moment. "The American Embassy admits they were apprehended. Their story is that Mr Husseyin and Mr Vasic tried to force their way into Mr Irwin's diplomatic car. Which is, in effect, American territory."

"That's rubbish! I'm as sure as I can be that Ashad waited until Irwin was out of the car before he approached him. Zoran was trying to film it. He wouldn't have got much through a tinted window."

Nancarrow made a vague rumbling noise which conveyed the impression that he agreed with this logic. "There's a barely plausible case to be made that the bodyguards acted legally in removing Mr Husseyin and Mr Vasic from the scene, but they have no powers to take British nationals on UK soil into custody. According to my information, both men were detained for several hours before being handed over to SO15."

It took a moment for me to remember the details of a feature we had once done on the security services. SO15, a branch of the Metropolitan police, was also known as CTC, the Counter Terrorism Command.

"Counter terrorism? You're joking."

"Most likely Irwin's people took the line that the incident was a security breach rather than common assault. That Mr Husseyin's foreknowledge of Bennett Irwin's exact movements merits further investigation."

"But it was common knowledge he was visiting London."

"They'll have a pretext of some description."

I didn't like the direction of this at all, especially since nothing in Nancarrow's measured tones suggested that it was of any more pressing concern to him than the latest Test Match cricket score.

"Irwin's people took the Pontius Pilate option," he told me. "Washing their hands of it by passing it on to the local law enforcement. Except that SO15 has specific responsibility for domestic terrorism and subversion. They might have done it to scare your friends, or it might simply be an overreaction by Bennett Irwin and his aides."

"But Ashad isn't involved in any subversion, for God's sake. We're film makers."

"You said Mr Husseyin wanted to interview Irwin in relation to a documentary you were making. Is it possible they had wind of it?"

"They?"

"Someone in the State Department, for example, who might have forewarned the Secretary of State for Defense?"

I thought about it. "We've played our cards pretty close to our chest up to now, and some of our leads are very recent ones. It's more likely Ashad caught Irwin unawares and he reacted so strongly because Ash had touched a nerve. Don't you think it's way over the top? All Ashad did was ask a question. That's not a criminal or diplomatic offence in this country."

Another silence at the other end of the line. I wondered if Nancarrow was writing any of this down. At length he said: "I understand you had a brief conversation with Milos Vasic before he went into hiding?"

He obviously didn't want me to suggest that I knew where Milos was.

"I did," I replied.

"And that, as an eye witness, he can corroborate your version of events?"

"Yes."

"Then we have a firm basis on which to proceed." He took my mobile number, promised me he would be in touch when he had further news, and rang off.

I felt less than encouraged by the tone of our conversation, which to me had been far too casual and gentlemanly, given the stark facts of Ashad's arrest. I had this vision of Nancarrow going into the legal bear pit not fighting for Ash but coughing politely and apologizing for the disturbance.

There was nothing I could do about it for the moment. I had parked on the hard shoulder to make the call, and, after checking that no suspicious-looking vehicles were lurking behind me, I pulled out the document wallet from under my seat and began to leaf through it.

There wasn't much, just a handful of internal emails and memos that Sam Oliphant had hard-copied, accompanied by a short toxicology abstract that hinted at plenty while carefully saying nothing definitive. But it was more than enough. The material clearly suggested that the company had developed GSBAs as part of a Home Office initiative and that covert clinical trials had been given the nod by someone high up in governmental circles. Coupled with the information on Walid's USB stick, this suggested more than one official programme of dirty tricks, or possibly two stages in the same operation. As yet, we had no direct proof that the incarcerations in Halstow Island and the GSBA trials were connected, but the circumstantial evidence was strong. The tricky bit would be incorporating Sam Oliphant's dossier into the documentary without revealing that we had stolen it.

*

Valerie wasn't in the downstairs office when I got back. Raised voices were filtering down the stairs from above, barely muffled by our spanking new carpet.

I hurried upstairs and found Val confronting about a dozen people, men and women, all of them of Middle Eastern or Asian appearance, none of whom I had ever seen before. Their voices were agitated rather than aggressive, though there was plenty of expressive arm waving.

"We have a situation," Val said to me, barely managing to restrain her natural impatience. "And it's all yours."

She turned and went out with a relieved look on her face, ignoring my protestations.

"What's going on here?" I said with a boldness I didn't feel.

There was a sudden silence. Everyone looked at me.

Jamilla, standing at her desk behind them, waved her hands at me in what I took to be furtive calming motions. The small crowd was mostly made up of men and women in early to late middle age. One of them, a stocky and fearsome-looking man in his fifties, said something to Jamilla in his native tongue. She replied in kind, her tone calm but respectful.

It dawned on me that this was a delegation from the extended Husseyin family. Maybe a domestic council of war.

Before I could speak again, Jamilla said something in which I recognized only the words "Ashad" and "Nicholas Randall". I was being introduced.

Now the entire group started talking and gesticulating again, but this time they were addressing me rather than Jamilla in a language that could have been anything from Arabic to Urdu. I worked my way over to Jamilla's side.

"It's my family," she told me apologetically. "I didn't exactly invite them, but they're really worried. Now I've told them who you are they want to know what you're doing for Uncle Ash."

Again there was silence. Everyone was waiting, including a couple of small children clinging to the hands of their mothers who were staring at me with naked wide-eyed curiosity.

"OK," I said to Jamilla. "Will you translate?"

"We understand English," the stocky man said to me. He had pushed forward to the front. "My name is Kalim. Tell us what is happening, if you would be so kind."

"This is my father," Jamilla informed me.

"I'm very pleased to meet you," I told him. "Your daughter has been an asset to this office. Is Ashad your brother?"

"Brother of my wife," he told me. "We know that Ashad has been arrested. What progress is being made in securing his release?"

Reluctantly I said, "Our lawyer has just established that he's been handed over to a branch of the Metropolitan Police that investigates possible terrorist links."

There was uproar at this news, which Kalim only gradually managed to quell.

"I understood there is a policewoman who is sympathetic to our cause," he said at length.

I didn't hide my surprise. "Yes," I agreed. "We have a Detective Inspector looking into the case."

"Detective Inspector Paula Merrick, is that not so?"

I glanced at Jamilla, who for once looked shame-faced. "I'm sorry," she murmured to me. "My father asked me, so I told him."

I guessed that it had been inveigled out of her during previous family discussions. I didn't really blame her since they had the right to know. But strategically it wasn't a smart move.

"It's very important that's she's allowed to conduct her inquiries without interference," I told Kalim, feeling like a complete hypocrite.

"Can she be trusted?" he asked me bluntly.

I drew a mental breath and said, "I firmly believe that she has Ashad's best interests at heart."

He stared back at me for long seconds. "I am told they had a friendship, Ashad and this policewoman."

Did Jamilla know they had seen one another socially? I didn't think so. Perhaps she had simply mentioned that they had got on well. Or perhaps Ashad himself had mentioned it prior to his arrest.

"Ashad has no friends in the police," Kalim stated before I could say anything. "Perhaps we should involve our family lawyer. He has wide experience of dealing with illegal searches and arrests within our community."

"I'd be grateful if you could wait until we have more concrete news before taking any action," I replied. "This is a very sensitive issue, as I'm sure you appreciate. Your daughter is here and can keep you informed of all developments on an hourly basis if necessary. I promise you we're doing all we can to locate him and obtain his release."

"And when can we expect to hear more?"

"I'm hoping for further news today."

He kept staring for a few more seconds before finally saying, "Very well. Ashad has spoken of you favourably, Mr Randall, and we are putting our trust in you. For now. I pray that you and this Inspector Merrick will prove to be our champions."

*

I was downstairs with Valerie discussing the contents of the Paradys folder when she was startled by my mobile yodelling.

DI Merrick had finally called back.

"Where are you?" she demanded to know.

"At work," I told her.

"Stay there. I'll be with you in a few minutes."

"You sound pissed off. What's happened?"

"I'm pissed off with *you*, Nick. You and Ashad. What part of 'leave it to me' didn't you understand?"

Before I could reply, she cut the connection.

Valerie was looking at me across the desk. The squawking ringtone on my mobile had startled her, and Merrick's voice had been sufficiently raised that she had caught our entire exchange.

"Stand your ground," she advised me.

"Like you did upstairs earlier?" I said peevishly.

"They were asking for you. They didn't want to talk to me. Remember, everything we've been doing has been to help Ashad."

"Yeah," I conceded. I gathered up the contents of the folder. "Lock everything in the secure cabinet, will you? I think I need to deal with this upstairs."

I told Jamilla that Merrick was on her way and settled myself at one of the desks in line of sight of the door.

Merrick stalked in a few minutes later.

"You've been a real idiot, Nick," she said without preamble. "And so's Ash. Remember what I said about muddying the waters? The pair of you have stirred them up mightily."

She threw herself into a chair but looked more worried than annoyed.

"Have you seen him?" I asked. "Is he all right?"

She glared at me. "He's worse off than when we spoke yesterday. Bloody hell, Nick!"

"I tried to ring you," I said firmly. "You didn't pick up."

"I was busy laying my neck on the line for you both."

"So what's happened?"

She let out a long slow sigh. "I spent a lot of yesterday putting out feelers through the security agencies and meeting with some sources. I called in a few favours and got to speak to someone. Apparently Irwin's people just wanted Ash off their backs while he was in London. I was as reassuring as possible about Ash and I could tell I was getting through. I got the impression they just wanted to hold him and your cameraman overnight until Irwin was gone before letting them go."

Behind her, Jamilla was loitering in the doorway, listening in. I didn't try to shoo her away. Ash was her uncle; she was entitled to know what was going on.

"I assumed they'd both be released this morning," Merrick went on, "and I was getting on with my day job, which doesn't happen to be nursing you and your partner, when I got a call about an hour ago. Apparently, some fancy lawyer had been in touch, one with enough connections to get through to senior people who were mightily pissed off. He's raised all sorts of hell. Human rights, race relations, illegal arrest and detention."

"Felix Nancarrow," I said. "Are you telling me he isn't entitled? I think we have a case."

"Maybe you do. But it's not endearing. The services don't like being told they've been naughty after they've agreed to a bit of give-and-take. It puts them on the back foot, makes them more inclined to be difficult. And you haven't heard the best bit yet."

There was a frustration that was close to anger in her voice. I waited.

"They decided to take another look at Ashad's case. At Ashad himself. He has an interesting portfolio, as you know."

"It's years since he was an activist," I pointed out.

"They can't be certain of that, can they? Especially when he's got form. So they decided to ask him a few more questions. And guess what?"

Merrick's voice was thick with sarcasm. I knew I wasn't going to like what was coming.

"He told them he was Khanistani. Insisted he was, by all accounts."

"You're having me on."

"I wish I was. I wish I didn't have to tell you how incredibly stupid that was. He virtually challenged them to do their worst."

"But they know he's not. They'll have a file a foot wide on him."

"A mole could easily have a file like that. They might see it as a ploy to have some merely irritating lefty things to hide behind."

Being Khanistani wasn't a crime but it might be unwise to end up in custody at the moment if you were a Khanistani who made anti-authoritarian documentaries and had a charge against you of physically attacking a senior member of the US administration.

"But that wasn't the end of it," Merrick said. "Apparently there was something else that suddenly made them take a hard line. They wouldn't tell me what."

The phone rang. Jamilla took it at her desk, then came through and said, "Mr Nancarrow for you. Shall I ask him to call back?"

I looked at Merrick. She gave a pissed-off shrug. "Go ahead."

She didn't get up from her chair but folded her arms in a perfect illustration of someone throwing a sulk.

"I'm afraid it's rather bad news," Nancarrow said as soon as I spoke my name. "They're insisting on detaining Mr Husseyin."

"What? On what charges?"

"Suspicion of affiliation with active terrorist groups."

"That's ridiculous!"

"He's being kept in one of their holding bins in Paddington. I'm going over to see him now."

"I'm coming too," I announced.

I anticipated that Nancarrow would try to fob me off, but he said, "Why not? I'm allowed to take another lawyer with me. I don't think we'll burn in hell if we pretend you're from my firm." He gave me the address and I scribbled it down on a Post-It note. "There is some good news," he told me, "they've released Mr Vasic without charge."

"Well, that's a result at least."

"It may give us leverage. How can one person be engaged in potential terrorist activity when another isn't? But frankly I don't like the drift of this one little bit."

On that cheery note, he rang off.

Merrick was sitting there waiting.

"He's in a detention facility in Paddington," I told her.

"North Wharf Road?"

"Do you know it?"

"What else did he say?"

"They're detaining him on suspicion of being a terrorist."

She just shook her head.

"I was on the verge of getting him released," she said with genuine regret.

"I'm sorry. His family are concerned. We had to try to help."

"What possessed him to tell them he's Khanistani?"

"Back Ash into a corner and you can expect some counter-provocation."

"I'd like to wring his neck, the stubborn fool."

"He might enjoy that."

She didn't smile.

*

Felix Nancarrow was younger than I had anticipated, a slim man in his forties rather than a portly buffer. He was dressed smartly but not slickly in a dark suit, which encouraged me a little since Ashad was definitely not the type to respond to Flash Harrys.

I had done my best to spruce myself up so that I vaguely looked like a lawyer, but it was clear that the plainclothes police at the detention centre weren't convinced. But Nancarrow schmoozed them effortlessly, explaining that my "unorthodox" attire was the price his firm was prepared to pay for my "intuitive" legal mind. He had warned me before we went in to say nothing unless I was directly addressed but to try to look interestingly inscrutable.

A cheery beer-bellied man in shirtsleeves who identified himself as Assistant Chief Officer Dyte took charge of us. At first he tried to fend off Nancarrow's questions with an air of blithe unconcern, but Nancarrow was persistent and finally Dyte took him aside and they went into a brief whispered huddle that left the lawyer looking less than thrilled.

Dyte led us into a smelly overheated room painted cheerless shades of institutional green. We sat down at a Formica table on grey plastic chairs designed to make your bum sweat if you occupied them for more than five minutes. A CCTV camera in one corner was pointed directly at us, its red light on.

Dyte positioned himself by the door and told us that "Mr Husseyin will be along shortly". The upper half of the wall directly opposite mirrored our reflections. I wondered how many people were standing behind it, watching us.

After a minute or so, the door opened and Ash was marched in by two burly men in shirtsleeves. He was handcuffed.

The two men set him down unceremoniously in the chair opposite ours and went out, Dyte remaining beside the door.

While Felix introduced himself to Ashad I reached across the table and grabbed Ash's handcuffed wrists. He looked more dishevelled than usual, unshaven, the expression on his face a mixture of outrage and sullen resentment. There was something else there, too. Was it fear?

"You plonker," I said gently to him. "Why did you tell them you were Khanistani?"

He scowled. "Seemed like a good idea at the time. Keep the sods guessing and maybe find out more about any other Khanistani internees. Besides, it's partly true. My grandmother on my mother's side was from Tyzkuk."

The Khanistani capital. I had no reason to disbelieve him, but it still wasn't a very clever admission.

"If I'd known you were coming," he said, "I'd have asked you to bring a kebab and a Fanta. The food's shite here."

Felix asked Ash whether he had had a shower that morning.

"We offered," Dyte interjected. "He refused."

"I'm afraid I must insist that the camera is switched off, if you would be so kind," Nancarrow said affably. "My colleague and I would also like to speak to Mr Husseyin in private.

After a significant hesitation, Dyte went out, closing the door emphatically behind him. Seconds later, the camera light winked off.

"So," Ashad said to Nancarrow, "when are you going to get me out?"

"I'm afraid I can't arrange that immediately," he said. "To begin with, you need to appoint me your lawyer. Here's my card."

Ashad took it and tucked it into his shirt pocket without looking at it. "OK, you're appointed."

"Even then, it will take some time. Are you aware that they're considering you a possible terrorist suspect?"

"They know that's bollocks."

"Under the Terrorism Act they can hold you for up to twenty-eight days."

Ash looked unrepentant. "Got them rattled, didn't I? Shows how close I was to the target when I challenged Irwin."

Nancarrow glanced at me.

"Ash," I said, "you can't mess around with this."

"No offence," he said to Nancarrow, "but why should I cooperate with an illegal arrest?"

"They must have reasons for detaining you," Nancarrow pointed out. "Reasons which go beyond simply accosting Bennett Irwin, whom I have to say is the kind of man I'm always happy to see accosted and made to answer difficult questions."

"He's a fanatic," Ashad agreed heartily. "But I was polite. I didn't accost him. I didn't lay a hand on him. We just stuck a microphone in front of his face."

"But they're not actually keeping you here because of that, are they?"

Nancarrow's tone remained, as always, civilized and gentle. I could tell that Ash was still weighing up whether he could be trusted.

"I told Mr Nancarrow about the documentary," I explained. "And about the accusations you put to Irwin."

"This has nothing to do with the documentary," Nancarrow interrupted. "Does it, Mr Husseyin?"

Ashad gave him a cagey look. "It's Ashad."

"I can't represent your interests effectively unless you're completely candid with me."

Ashad looked defiant at first, but it quickly melted away.

"Walid's flash drive," he said to me. "They took it from me."

I made him explain to Nancarrow what was on the drive. No doubt the CTC had experts who could access encrypted files. I guessed that this was what Dyte had told Nancarrow earlier.

Nancarrow didn't look in the slightest bit daunted by the news.

"It's not an act of terrorism to be in possession of a leaked document," he told Ash.

I couldn't hold back any longer. In a low voice I told both of them about the Paradys dossier and my suspicion that the GSBA trials were linked to the Halstow Island site.

Ashad looked as if I had slapped him across the face. He leaned across the table, now looking urgent. "My DNA's on file. If I'm compatible, what's to stop them from using it on me?"

Nancarrow looked astonished at the suggestion. "Even if it's true that such a weapon exists, no civilized government would countenance that."

Ashad gave him a look of naked disbelief. "I might just happen to fall ill while I'm in custody," he said sarcastically. "There's a lot of that haemorrhagic fever going around prisons at the moment, isn't there?"

Nancarrow had no answer.

"Did they tell you they're shipping me out of here tomorrow?" Ashad asked him. "Maybe they're going to find me a cell with an *estuary* view."

He plainly meant Halstow Island. It scarcely seemed credible. But Nancarrow, for once looking disturbed, stood up, went over to the door and banged on it.

Dyte opened it immediately, as if he had been lurking at the threshold. Nancarrow insisted they speak in the corridor outside.

Although Dyte closed the door behind them, we could clearly hear their raised voices, though not the precise words.

"Think they're having a domestic?" Ashad said cheerfully.

"This is no joke, you know."

"What do you want me to do? Curl up in a corner and start whimpering?"

"Of course not. But don't make matters worse by being deliberately bloody-minded." I eyed him. "Are you worried?"

"What do you think? This is high stakes stuff. They might do anything to keep a lid on it."

Outside, Dyte and Nancarrow were still arguing. I asked Ashad what his impressions of the lawyer were.

"There used to be a High Court judge called George Nancarrow. Venerable old cove of the Spartan persuasion. There's a distinct family resemblance."

Ashad had always been good at remembering stuff like this. "Do you want me to find someone else?"

He shook his head. "Just because he's a toff doesn't mean he's a hang-'em-high Tory. I'll take whatever help I can get."

"That's unusually generous-spirited of you. Merrick's on the case as well. She wasn't well pleased when she found out we'd appointed a lawyer. Said she was on the verge of getting you out. I told her where you are."

"Tell her what's going on, will you? The more people we can get rattling the cage, the better. How's everything else going? Work-wise, I mean."

I was surprised he had asked. "This has been something of a distraction, Ash."

He gripped my hand in his. "Promise me you'll keep everything afloat while I'm in here, keep pushing all our projects. We can't afford to let things slip."

"We've got to prioritize getting you out."

"Leave it to Mr Smooth Talker out there. Just keep me informed. No stinting, right?"

I shook my head at him. "You're incorrigible. I've been invited to an Ascendancy meeting tomorrow. I was going to cancel."

"Go," he insisted. "We're bound to get something useful out of it."

Nancarrow came in, pocketing his mobile. There was no sign of Dyte.

"We've got you a temporary reprieve," he said to Ashad. "Forty-eight hours, while I try to find out exactly what skulduggery is going on here."

"I appreciate that," Ashad said sincerely. And then, with a hint of mischief: "Did you phone a friend? Your father, perhaps?"

Nancarrow wasn't fazed. He smiled easily. "My uncle, actually."

*

After we left Ash, Nancarrow came back to the office with me. On the way I used a call-box to contact Zoran and Milos, and we made arrangements for the three of them to meet. I let Nancarrow inspect Sam Oliphant's folder, and then Valerie and I sat him down in the viewing theatre and showed him the footage and background materials we had gathered for the Muvart documentary.

I think he was pretty much persuaded that not only had research been carried out on developing a gene-specific infective agent but also that it might well have been done with the approval and possibly active encouragement of both the UK and US governments. He was particularly interested in the clip of Halstow Island and promised me he would use his contacts to investigate further. His uncle, The Honourable George Nancarrow, still had plenty of contacts with former ministers and senior civil servants, including a current Cabinet secretary. The old man, he told me, was a libertarian with a particular aversion to secretive state activity, especially when it hadn't been sanctioned by Parliament. He was confident that pressure could be applied to facilitate matters in our favour. He would keep me informed of any developments.

I sent Jamilla home early that evening and finally got Part One of Leo Parrish's *Exaltation* out of the secure cabinet.

The story had a large black-and-white interior illustration, with some smaller ones interspersed throughout the text. The main illustration showed a glowing naked man with a strategic shadow between his legs so that there wasn't even a suggestion of genitalia. A bright stylized star shone above his head and he was holding the Earth in his cupped hands with the other planets swirling in the background and an indistinct spaceship lurking in the background. Around this cluttered but vigorous composition were the words:

EXALTATION – a book-length story by Leo Parrish, author of THE COPYIST and THE WEATHER WARRIORS

Only THEY could save the best of mankind from destruction.

Set in the near-future in a time of political and economic instability, it began with a point of light appearing in the sky, rapidly growing brighter. Earth-based instruments were scrambled by its radiance so that its nature could not be discerned. Some believed that it was a luminous artificial world, or a psychic transmission from an advanced race. A few claimed that they could see a spaceship at the centre of the brightness, shaped like a cross or a crescent or a sunburst. The details varied depending on the observer.

Soon social order around the world decayed as people surrendered to fear and their basest instincts. Only a minority reacted differently, developing improved mental and physical powers that helped protect them from the growing chaos. They believed that the Radiance had emanated from higher-dimensional space and heralded the arrival of beings who would "exalt" the human race. It was stimulating mental changes, unlocking dormant capacities in those who came to call themselves the Exalted while the rest of the population descended into savagery.

The story, told from several different viewpoints, moved along at Parrish's usual brisk pace, with plenty of good set pieces and some vivid visual imagery. The main characters used their unleashed powers and their ingenuity to reach an island sanctuary over which the Radiance was now in geostationary orbit. It ended abruptly with a band of the Exalted completing the construction of a spaceship-ark which they named the "Exaltation" to carry them to the Radiance.

The tale had plenty of cinematic potential. The main characters were surprisingly well-drawn, the general breakdown in social order skilfully conveyed through their individual dilemmas. I was prepared to withhold my usual concerns about any narrative with overt religious overtones featuring chosen people of any description until I read the second half. Given Parrish's knack for avoiding the obvious, I had the feeling that the story wasn't going to pan out in quite the way that any of his cast or readers expected. If the second half of the serial delivered on the promise of the first half, we might well have the basis for a fast-paced movie with plenty of spectacle and perhaps even some depth.

Still, I didn't want to get too carried away: the entire narrative might go off the rails in the second instalment. I did, though, allow myself a certain malicious glee because I could see how freely Edgar Eldridge had plundered the novel when developing the Ascendancy. The parallels between the Exalted, with their growing insights, and the Church's Adepts, were too stark to be coincidental. If Parrish was still alive and now someone eminent, then no wonder he didn't want his writing days publicized; especially if he shared the view of the Ascendancy as a pernicious cult, which he had inadvertently inspired. As for the Ascendancy themselves, their credibility might not survive a public airing of their less than elevated origins in a blatant act of imaginative theft from a cheap magazine serial.

FIFTEEN

The next day passed without any further word about Ash. DI Merrick didn't answer any of my calls or messages. Nancarrow rang to tell me that although Ash remained in custody in Paddington, Zoran and Milos's testimonies gave him a strong case that Ash had merely been carrying out a piece of investigative journalism and that Bennett Irwin's aides had had no basis for involving the Met. He was doing all he could to block any attempts to move him elsewhere.

Jamilla remained her usual unflappable self, fending off all but the most important calls and microwaving us baked potatoes and melted cheese for lunch. I felt a bit unworthy as I scoffed it down that I had no positive news for the family, but she assured me they were relieved to hear that he was in good spirits and had not been tortured. When a business call to my mobile was announced by car-alarm noises, Jamilla spent a fruitless half an hour trying to restore its factory settings. I decided that I was going to live with it, embrace it even. Sometimes you had to take the line of least resistance. And at least it served as a continuing reminder of Ash's presence.

I tried to apply myself to our bread-and-butter work for the rest of the day, but even the arrival of the rushes for *Seconds Out*, a panel game in which celebrity contestants had to create linking scenes between unrelated excerpts from famous movies, failed to stir me, despite the general enthusiasm of everyone else in the office. I spent a distracted afternoon posting clips of the show to the agents of potential panellists, who needed to be inventive and prepared to act out their ideas. We got a couple of quick-fire email responses back, both very encouraging. Even so, I was relieved when it was finally time to leave.

*

Rhodri Davies didn't drive, so I picked him up at his rambling house near the centre of Maidenhead. Though I had left the office early, the drive out of London had taken me longer than I had anticipated, so we didn't hang around. I did briefly meet his wife, Ruth, a droll forthright woman who asked me if I was a new recruit to her husband's League of Extraordinarily Troublesome Gentlemen. Draped in a long silver cardigan despite the balminess of the evening, she stood in the doorway as we walked down the tree-tangled driveway to my car.

"Don't stay out too late," she called after Rhodri. "And try to behave yourself!"

We took the A4 towards Slough. It was thick with commuter traffic. Rhodri told me an anecdote about Isaac Asimov, who, despite being renowned for his galaxy-spanning visions of the future, disliked travelling by air. I think he was making the point that while science-fiction people like himself might enjoy contemplating all the clever technological fixes awaiting us, they weren't necessarily very handy with existing aids like motor vehicles and hedge trimmers.

The Ascendants' headquarters occupied the shell of an old brick factory on the edge of an industrial estate. An extensive area around it had been landscaped into undulating swathes of grass interspersed with rock pools, shrubs and weeping willows. The building itself, a squarish red-brick tower, had been made to look more grand by the addition of cloister-like wings and a white conical spire. No doubt it was meant to suggest the Ascendants' spiritual aspirations, though in reality it made the building look as if it was wearing a dunce's hat.

Apart from a few minibuses for group travel, the spacious car park at the front was full of upmarket vehicles, all gleaming emphatically in the evening sunlight. The police were also present: a Land Rover was prominently parked on one of the verges, and a patrol car had been positioned beside the car park entrance, two young officers lounging against the bonnet. Rhodri told me that the Ascendants went out of their way to cultivate good relationships with local law enforcement agencies. The police were here to check that no undesirables gained admittance.

Before we drove up to the entrance Rhodri gave me a badge that identified me as a Delegate to the convocation. A friend of his who specialized in mischievous forgeries had made them, in my case using a photo downloaded from the Xponential website. Mine was in the name of Randall Nicholas, while Rhodri was using R.L.M. Davies, which he assured me was short for Rhodri Llewellyn Mostyn Davies. So technically neither of us was using a fake name.

We showed them to one of the policemen on sentry duty. Middle-aged and disgruntled-looking, he gave the passes only a cursory examination but had a good look at both of us. I was wearing a typical work outfit of blue jeans and baseball shoes, though for once I had a white shirt on. Rhodri, in a mouse-brown corduroy jacket and an olive-green shirt, looked as if he was in camouflage. He evidently favoured earth colours, and at one point his wife had referred to him as "Rhodri of Sherwood".

"You're official delegates?" the policeman said, his tone implying that he doubted it. "If I didn't know better, I'd have guessed you were journalists."

We were already half an hour late, so there were no other delegates lingering outside that might have given us some clue of the dress code. Were they all in suits, dinner jackets, or fancy dress inside?

We assured him we weren't journalists, but he didn't look convinced. Yet neither was he hostile.

"Would we be barred if we were?" I asked, looking candidly at him. "Or am I right in thinking that you would rather be doing more useful police work at this very moment?"

He made to say something, and then thought better of it.

"Just make sure you behave yourselves," he warned, returning our passes. "And be careful when you're parking."

I had to admit that my beat-up Bravo looked dowdier than ever as we pulled in alongside the pristine Mercs and BMWs. We climbed the entrance steps like a couple of Cinderellas who had missed their Good Fairy makeovers before the ball.

Two young men in dove-grey suits and lavender ties greeted us politely enough at the lobby-cum-cloakroom. Both were fragrant with spicy aftershave. The Staff tags pinned to their lapels identified them as Kyle and Brett. Both looked like male models from an upmarket catalogue.

They gave our passes only a brief scrutiny before slotting them into clip-on holders. Then Kyle asked if we were carrying any cameras or mobile phones.

"We ask you to surrender them," he told us. "You can collect them afterwards."

Brett held out a dark felt bag for the guilty objects. Behind him was an array of lockers, most of them already closed up. Rhodri had previously warned me that the Ascendants were particularly touchy about people taking unauthorized photographs of their meetings.

"We left them in the car," Rhodri told him, and then stuck his arms out straight. "You can pat us down if you like."

Both men maintained their smiles while at the same time managing to make it clear from their expressions that such zealousness would not be necessary. We were now in shirtsleeves, Rhodri having also left his jacket in the car, so it was pretty obvious just from the look of us that we weren't carrying any equipment.

We clipped our badges on, and Kyle led us into the hall, explaining in a reverent whisper that mobiles and cameras going off in the middle of meetings were an unwelcome distraction from what was meant to be above all a time of "focused attention and contemplation".

*

Vincent Kubilius was short, dark and relentlessly energetic, strutting about the stage like a man who had overdosed on espresso. Before our arrival he had evidently cast off his suit jacket, loosened his tie and rolled up his sleeves, conveying a brisk and businesslike informality as he addressed his audience without a microphone, projecting his voice effortlessly to the rear of the hall where Rhodri and I were sitting on a latecomers' row of hard chairs, talking without notes about the value of *community*, the importance of *commitment*, the necessity of making a genuine *contribution* to improving the lives of others.

We had missed the opening part of his spiel, so I wasn't entirely sure exactly where he was going with it. There was no direct mention of the Ascendancy, just a lot of motivational rhetoric that made him seem more like some socially conscious politician than a religious leader. Yet he was drawing approving nods from an audience that must have numbered a couple of hundred and was largely composed of financially comfortable professionals in early to late middle-age.

The usual symbols of the Ascendancy—the sunrise, the flowers, the rainbow—were absent, Kubilius striding around an empty stage with a curtained backdrop that accentuated the impression that he was speaking directly and plainly to them, giving them the unvarnished truth with no other aids than his own dynamic charisma. I wondered about his origins: he had Levantine looks, a Lithuanian surname and a middle-of-the-road American accent. I knew that in his early twenties he had been a Californian beach bum but had rapidly progressed through the Ascendants' hierarchy after "seeing the clear light". Rumour had it that the Church's finances had improved spectacularly since he had taken over its day-to-day running from Edgar Eldridge.

Rhodri had discreetly got out a slim notebook and was scribbling notes in it from time to time, hiding it away whenever any staff went past on their intermittent patrols of the rear aisle. Positioned at intervals around the hall were smart-suited young men with fixed smiles and active eyes that scanned the audience for any signs of misbehaviour. All the exits to the place were manned.

Presently Kubilius called up on to the stage a senior policeman in full brass-buttoned uniform regalia. This turned out to be Chief Superintendent Rowbotham, whom Rhodri informed me had proved very sympathetic to the presence of the Ascendants in his parish. Rowbotham, a moustachioed middle-aged man who looked as ill-at-ease in the limelight as Kubilius had been confident, muttered some words about how important public-spirited individuals with clear moral principles were to helping maintain social order, and how much he and other community leaders appreciated the help the Church had given in providing volunteers to assist in local schemes, particularly drink and drug rehabilitation programmes.

"He'll get a few free church-sponsored lunches out of that," Rhodri murmured to me. "And a sizeable donation to a charity of his choice."

A woman in a Burberry coat immediately in front of us turned and gave Rhodri a stern look. He bowed his head in mock shame. Now a local female councillor came on stage and espoused similar sentiments about the Church's volunteer work. She was followed by someone from the Parks Department, who explained how a nearby civic amenity had been transformed by the unpaid work of "principled young people who give lie to the myth that today's youth are only interested in themselves".

"I don't know how much more of this I can take," I whispered to Rhodri. "It's one big PR exercise."

He pointed to a side door near the stage. Being ushered in by a posse of minders was Ryan Carmichael.

Kubilius was back at centre stage.

"We are a broad church," he told the audience. "Our philosophy and teachings can improve the lives of everyone, regardless of their educational and social status, regardless of their colour, nationality or political leanings. There are countless examples of how our programmes of self-knowledge and directed insight have benefited those who know that to change world for the better they must first change themselves. Some have harnessed their latent energies to rise to the highest peak of their chosen professions and have gained widespread acclaim." A broad grin broke across Kubilius's face as Carmichael was led forward. "Ladies and gentlemen, a man who needs no introduction from me. Ryan Carmichael!"

Carmichael did a single-bound leap onto the stage, replicating a move from his recent pirate blockbuster, *Corsair!* I was almost disappointed he wasn't wearing a blouson shirt and buckled boots, but the black jeans and lilac shirt were perfect for the occasion, accentuating his bronzed skin and cornflower eyes.

There was applause and a smattering of cheers. Carmichael stretched out his arms and gave a palms-first wave. Then he launched into an intense burst of thanking everyone for coming, saying how delighted he was to be here, informing us that he felt a genuine sense of belonging, being just one among a crowd of like-minded folk, people just like himself who had received the same revelation of the power of the human mind, who saw the importance of *acting* to make their lives meaningful, and by *acting* he meant *enacting* rather than the kind of fakery he indulged in for a living.

The audience laughed. Carmichael started talking about the *cognitive outreach* of the mind, how it was actually far more *extensive* than the confines of our individual brains, was an invisible halo that surrounded us, fluctuating in size and power, depending on the use we made of it.

The curtains behind the stage had drawn back and now a series of images began shuffling on a big screen, stills of Carmichael in a dark cloak-like trench coat, in a variety of dramatic poses. In one he was running across a blighted landscape, pursued by a giant floating eyeball with dangling tendrils. In another he and a small band of leather-clad guerrillas were perched on the art deco ramparts of a skyscraper, gazing down on a mob of zombified humans who were rampaging through the city streets. Then he was pictured with a beam of electric violet light radiating from the centre of his forehead, levitating the body of a fallen female comrade. And finally tangled in the tendrils of the eyeball but protected by a shining violet aura as he prepared to hurl an amethyst jewel sling-shot at the creature.

The last two of these images were CGI-generated rather than actual movie frames. I knew from my own researches that they were taken from an as-yet unfinished movie currently and somewhat mystifyingly called *Epocrypha*, which Carmichael had been filming sporadically for the past few years when not working for the mainstream studios. It had been conceived and was funded by the Ascendancy.

Carmichael was still going on about how we weren't *confined* mentally, how the *enactive embodiment* of our will permeated beyond both the physical and mental space where it was commonly believed to be limited. Thanks to modern technology our psyches now radiated even beyond our local environments into the *global space*, and way beyond that even, TV and radio signals having been leaking out into the universe for decades, so that there might even as he spoke be aliens on their home planets sitting around their TVs, trying to puzzle out just what it was that made humans tick.

By now Carmichael's enthusiasm and loquaciousness were in inverse proportion to his lucidity. He had the manic air of the celebrity actor who had been intensively researching a topic and was certain that others would share his current obsession. But his audience was looking increasingly unsure of his drift.

While Rhodri scribbled furiously on his pad, Vincent Kubilius rose from a table at the side of the stage. Thanking Carmichael "for his splendid words which validate our teachings", he then explained to the audience that they were now about to treated to an exclusive preview of "our movie-in-the-making". There would be a short questions-and-answers session immediately after the screening.

He and Carmichael sat down at the table. The lights dimmed.

We were shown less than fifteen minutes of *Epocrypha*, a few unrelated scenes which involved a lot of rushing through deserted buildings and blasting various nasties with chunky pistols that spouted pretty blobs of violet light. The bad guys themselves ranged from the demonic Savagers, feral humans whose higher mental functions had been erased, to the chrome-armoured Mechumans, whose brains had been replaced with "electro-cortexes" so that they could act as enforcers for the chief villain, the one-eyed floating jellyfish called Psiclops, an alien entity intent on subjugating the human race.

Carmichael played Xero Summers, the leader of the resistance, who had discovered how to harness the power of the human mind so that it could actually power the E-weapons that the freedom fighters used. A brief scene showed him visiting his Mentor in the early stages of the uprising, a man who espoused meditative and thought control techniques very similar to those of the Ascendants.

The audience was enthusiastic. They clapped and whistled at the end of each scene. Rhodri and I shared a few dumbfounded looks. Ryan Carmichael had worked with some of the best action-adventure directors in the business, but whoever was putting this one together wasn't one of them. Both the acting and the dialogue veered between the melodramatic and the stilted, while the story itself could have easily been lifted from some routine futuristic shoot-'em-up computer game.

Kubilius called for quiet and asked if anyone had any questions. A young man got up and asked Carmichael where the location filming was being done. Carmichael made a joke about using empty Woolworth stores, diplomatically adding that the chain had lasted longer in England than in the USA. He loved England, and was here to research a new role as a maximum-security prisoner. He wanted to take a look inside a few jails, hopefully without having to commit any crimes.

A woman asked who the unknown actress playing his co-star was. Carmichael pointed to the first row of the audience, and she stood up, a glacial blonde, and did a little curtsey while Kubilius pointed out that she was a Church member just starting out on what was certain to be a glittering career.

Another man rose and made complimentary comments about the production values while asking why it was taking so long for the movie to be completed.

"Funding," Carmichael replied bluntly. "We want this to be an independent movie, made without any interference from the major studios or other vested interests. But that's where the money is, and that's why we can only work when we've rustled up the cash ourselves." He gave his best white smile. "Of course, if any of you guys out there would like to invest in a good cause, we'd be delighted to talk to you!"

And there, I realized, we finally had it. The pitch. Every question had previously been rehearsed and delivered by stooges whose purpose was to lead the audience gently to the heart of the matter. Money. The Church was trawling its membership for funding.

Soon afterwards Kubilius wound up the Q&A session before inviting anyone who wished to make a financial donation up on to the stage, where he and Carmichael remained seated. A respectable queue swiftly formed, mostly older men with decorative younger wives whom I suspected were most eager to have a one-on-one conversation with Ryan Carmichael.

Then two things happened simultaneously. A woman got up on stage and strode across to the table. And the spicily deodorized Brett from the lobby was at our shoulders and asking Rhodri why he was taking notes.

"I'm writing a news report for my local branch," he replied.

"May I see it?" Brett asked pleasantly.

"It's in shorthand," Rhodri said. "You won't be able to fathom a word of it."

"Unfortunately we must insist, Mr Davies," said Kyle, who had now appeared at Brett's side. "This is a private service. Everyone here is an invited guest. For confidentiality purposes you're not permitted to make any recording."

"I thought it was just cameras and mobiles," Rhodri protested.

Kyle shook his head patiently. "*Any* recording, Mr Davies. Including hard copy."

He reached down and plucked the notebook out of Rhodri's hand.

"Do you want my pencil stub as well?" Rhodri asked.

"I'm afraid we must ask you to leave now," Brett told him.

I had been only half-following this exchange, and didn't look in their direction, hoping that they wouldn't remember that we had arrived together. On stage the woman was having a conversation with Kubilius that had grown into a remonstration while a rather baffled Ryan Carmichael looked on.

The woman was Claire Whitney.

"You, too, Mr Nicholas," Kyle said.

I stood up. "That's my wife up there on stage. She appears to be causing a fuss. Do you mind if I collect her so that we can leave together?"

Kyle and Brett looked at the stage before exchanging glances.

"Perhaps you could escort Mr Davies outside," Kyle said to Brett. "I'll accompany Mr Nicholas."

I scarcely waited for him, or gave Rhodri more than a fleeting glance, before striding down the aisle, Kyle in pursuit.

Kubilius was now on his feet and Claire Whitney was jabbing a finger at him while a clutch of minders converged on her. I managed to do an ungainly Carmichael-style leap onto the stage and shoulder my way through the press of bodies.

"All we want is to be left in peace!" I could hear Claire shouting at Kubilius. "Is that too much to ask?"

Kubilius was masking his fury with a condescending smile.

"I think it's time we left now, dear," I said loudly, reaching out and gently taking hold of her arm.

She turned and started at the sight of me.

"I think we've overstayed our welcome. I've got the car waiting outside. Come on, let's go."

The minders were already forming a barrier between her and Kubilius. When a couple of the more zealous ones started trying to shift her I moved between them.

"Please take your hands off her. We're going home now."

It was Kyle who brought some order to the proceedings, getting everyone to move back so that we had a space to descend the steps at the side of the stage. He accompanied us down the aisle. Everyone was staring. Claire went relatively meekly, not looking at me; but I was still holding her by the arm and I could feel her trembling, feel the tension and anger in her.

"Have you any belongings to collect?" Kyle asked her as he led us out through the lobby.

She just shook her head, staring at the floor as if her entire attention was concentrated on getting out of there without boiling over with rage.

Kyle had the grace to look embarrassed. Escorting us through the door, he wished us a safe trip home.

There was no sign of Rhodri. We started walking across the car park.

"Did you bring your own car?" I asked.

She shook her head. "I came in a minibus. Have you been following me?"

"I didn't even know you were here until you stormed on stage."

She didn't reply. I spotted Rhodri, lounging on the bonnet of my Bravo.

"That's a friend of mine," I told her as we approached the car. "Why don't you let me give you a lift home?"

*

It turned out that she lived in Twickenham, not very far from my own place. We did the first stage of the journey to Rhodri's house in subdued silence, me not wanting to ask too many questions too precipitately, Rhodri quite cheerful that he had actually managed to infiltrate the convocation but mindful of not saying anything tactless after I had made a point of mentioning that Claire had been ferried to it in one of the Church's minibuses.

I had originally intended to drop Rhodri off and head straight on. But when he asked if we fancied a cup of tea or a stiff drink, Claire said, "I'd like that very much."

Soon we were nestled in cosy armchairs in Rhodri's front room, where every spare wall was shelved with books. There was also a glass-fronted cabinet containing various volumes that carried Rhodri's own name. He wasn't at all bothered that his notebook had been confiscated, tapping his temple and telling me that most of it was already stored there. He had long come to the conclusion that the Ascendancy was actually a slick business enterprise rather than a bona fide religion, especially since Kubilius had taken charge.

We had this exchange while Claire Whitney was in the bathroom. When she returned, Rhodri's wife came in with mugs of tea and a plate of homemade flapjacks. She doled out the teas and sat next to Claire on the sofa. Earlier Rhodri had had a brief conversation with her in the kitchen, and he must have filled her in about Claire's background because she came straight out with: "So tell me, is it true that the Ascendants sacrifice babies and flay the skins off their enemies?"

Claire was holding her mug of tea in both hands. She had been very subdued over the past half hour, but now she laughed.

"Rhodri reckons you're all being taken for a ride," Ruth went on. "He thinks you're being fleeced by smooth-talking operators and should know better. Flapjack?"

Claire took one, still smiling.

"Feel free to dunk," Ruth told her. "I've read their literature. Surely you can see it's a load of codswallop? What's in it for you?"

Claire took a mouthful of tea and sat back, visibly relaxing for the first time. She glanced briefly in my direction, and I tried to mime a "This is nothing to do with me" expression, but she didn't appear to mind being put on the spot.

"I couldn't agree more," she told Ruth. "Actually I joined the Church under false pretences. I think they're dangerous. Their ideas, and the way they act."

"What?" I interjected. "Are you telling us you're not really an Ascendant at all?"

She let out a slow breath, as though coming to a decision.

"I'm Leo Parrish's niece."

*

"I don't remember anything about it," she told me as we drove back towards London in the dying light of the day. "I wasn't much more than a year old."

"But you were with her when it happened?"

She nodded. "According to my mother, I started crying at the noise of the gunshot, then I got excited because I had red spots all over me. I didn't see the gun and thought my uncle was just playing when he fell down."

"He was shot right in front of you?"

"Yes. He died instantly. They never found who did it." She twisted around in the passenger seat to look behind her. "You realize they're probably following us."

"They?"

"The Church. Or their stooges."

She was still angry. It had all come out over the tea and flapjacks, how strange things had been happening at the house where she lived with her mother and son: people seen lurking in the garden, attempted break-ins, threatening notes shoved through the letterbox in the middle of the night, warning them to liquidate their stock of Leo Parrish stories. It was all too familiar. She was certain the Ascendants were responsible because her mother had told her how Leo Parrish's stories had been the inspiration for the Ascendancy. Her mother was elderly and frail and couldn't cope with the continued stress. So she had joined the Church in London with the express purpose of getting close to someone important so that she could tell them to lay off. She had kept up the pretence with me because she didn't want to risk her cover being blown.

"What did Kubilius say when you confronted him?" I asked.

"He pretended he didn't know what I was talking about. But when I told him my mother was Leo Parrish's sister, he couldn't hide his surprise. They don't want any reminders of where the Church got its ideas from."

I had started keeping an eye on my rear-view mirror. A dark grey saloon had been sitting some distance behind us for the past few minutes.

"Mind if we take a detour?" I said, lurching left down the nearest turn-off before she could reply, accelerating and making a few more rapid turns at random before pulling over in a narrow suburban side street and switching off the lights. I felt absurdly theatrical.

We waited in silence for a few minutes. Dusk had fallen, the streetlights already on. A scruffy dog came by and started to pee against one of the wheels before I shooed it off.

I was about to drive away when the grey saloon pulled into the street about fifty yards behind us. It came to a halt in the middle of the road, engine still running, only its side lights on.

In the twilight it was impossible to see who was driving it, though I was pretty sure that there were two men inside. Claire had gone rigid, resolutely not looking in the mirror, staring straight ahead as if by refusing to acknowledge them she could somehow make them vanish.

I wondered what to do next.

"Can you drive?" I asked her, a vague plan formulating in my mind that I would just get out of the car and stand there in the middle of the road, blocking the passage of the car while she drove away. Not the cleverest idea I ever had, and fortunately I didn't have to carry it out. At that moment another vehicle pulled into the road behind the saloon, a big dark four-by-four with its headlights blazing.

It just sat there right behind the saloon, not honking its horn but revving its engine angrily. Its headlights were full on, blazing through the car, illuminating the entire road with its harsh light.

For long moments nothing happened. It was as obvious to me as it evidently was to the men in the saloon that the four-by-four driver wasn't trying to get by them. Suddenly they accelerated forward, driving straight past us. There were indeed two young men inside, but the light was too poor to see them in any detail.

The saloon turned a corner at the end of the road and vanished from sight. Abruptly the four-by-four driver also accelerated forward, going in the same direction, though not in obvious pursuit.

The man at the wheel had his right hand against his face in a salute-like gesture under a military-style cap pulled low on his forehead. He might have been acknowledging us, or he might have simply wanted to hide his face.

Neither Claire nor I moved or spoke for several minutes. Neither vehicle came back. Finally we got tired of waiting. Cautiously I pulled out and did a U-turn before driving off in the direction we had come.

We both kept watching for some time afterwards, while I wondered what to say next. Finally, when it was clear that no one was tailing us any longer, I pulled over again and settled for: "I've got absolutely no idea where we are."

She laughed. It was partly in relief but also, I sensed, because she was at last beginning to feel comfortable in my presence, having confessed her secret and shared the motorized equivalent of a stalking.

"So that story you told me at the temple. About buying the stories in an auction—"

"It was a lie," she confessed without hesitation. "To throw you off the trail."

"But why?"

She shrugged. "For my family. Their safety. It's hard to know who to trust."

"And do you trust me now?"

She looked straight at me. "What choice do I have?"

It would do for now. "Are they really threatening you because of what Leo Parrish wrote?"

"Can you think of any other reason?"

"Have you tried getting the police on the case?"

"Without concrete evidence, there's not much they can do."

I made a mental note to ask Merrick about it. If I ever heard from her again.

"Who do you think scared them off?" Claire asked.

To all appearances she was asking the question innocently, with genuine curiosity, but I wondered if she was still keeping something back from me.

"I was about to ask you the same thing."

"I really don't know," she assured me. "It's spooky. Can you imagine what it feels like to have people watching you, bothering you all the time?"

I squeezed her hand. "Your uncle is a bit of a man of mystery all round."

"Tell me about it."

"Did you get the *Nightscapes* story out of his archives?"

After a fractional hesitation, which I guessed was born of habit, she said, "My mother kept what she could of his published work when we moved to the UK."

"So when was that?"

"About a year after he was murdered. She wanted to get away. She didn't feel safe."

"That's hardly surprising."

"I don't remember anything much of New York City. Eventually we got citizenship here."

"What about your father?" I asked tentatively.

"I never knew him. I was an out-of-wedlock baby. My mother refused to talk about it, except to say that he was a friend."

"So Whitney is your married name?"

She shook her head. "It was *her* mother's maiden name. She adopted it after Leo was killed, and I reverted to it after my divorce. Keeping it in the family."

I turned my phone on for the first time since putting it in the glove compartment hours earlier. It made its little warbling text noise.

There were a couple of messages, but it was just routine work stuff from Valerie and Jamilla. Nothing about Ashad and no word from Merrick. No missed calls.

We drove on. I asked her whether she had a complete collection of Leo Parrish's work.

"I doubt it," she responded. "But it's probably more than anyone else has."

I had the urge to quiz her in more detail but knew that the timing was bad. She might assume I had only offered to drive her home so that I could interrogate her about Leo Parrish. And I didn't want her to think that.

Eventually I found a road signposted to London.

"How's your friend?" she asked.

"Ashad? Still in custody. He's worried they're going to try to bump him off."

"What, the CIA?"

"Someone like that."

"Why?"

"I'd rather not go into it, if it's all right with you."

I didn't want to tell her everything because I was still reserving judgement on whether she was telling me the whole truth. For purely selfish reasons I was hoping that the story about Leo Parrish having been shot dead was false, if only because I was still entertaining the romantic notion that I would find him alive and well in due course and that he would open up his entire archives to me, showing me loads of brilliant hitherto-unpublished material that would prove to be a cinematic gold-mine.

"Do you think they'll lay off now that you've had words with Kubilius?" I asked.

"Who knows? I wanted to make as big a public scene as possible, and the Chief Constable being there was a bonus."

"Even though he's pretty tame about them?"

"I told Kubilius I was going to contact friends in the media and publicize everything if he didn't. Not that I actually know anyone."

"You know me. I'm in the media, in a sense. And I'm your friend, aren't I?"

She laughed again. "Today you've been my knight in shining armour."

We reached her house, a detached Victorian property close to the river. I caught a glimpse of an extensive garden behind it as I walked her to the front door.

"This was very kind of you," she said to me.

"Believe me, it's my pleasure."

"I'd invite you in, but it's a little late and my mother gets agitated when I'm not home before dark."

"No problem," I assured her. "I'm done in and I need to get an early start tomorrow. Besides, someone's waiting for you."

A boy in his late teens was standing at one of the windows, waving. It was the same spiky-haired lad who had been with her in the play room.

"Daniel," I remembered.

She returned the wave. "He keeps an eye on things while I'm out."

"He's got his mother's good looks."

She gave me another of her sceptical glances.

"Can I see you again?"

She jingled her keys. "Maybe."

"Of course I only want a date so that you can tell me everything about Leo Parrish."

"Of course."

I took out my phone. "Give me your number and I'll call you."

She smiled. "That's what they've been saying since I was sixteen."

But she extracted her own mobile, called it up on screen. I added it to my address book.

"Stay safe," I told her, giving her a quick kiss on the cheek before walking back to my car.

I waited until I was certain she had also gone inside before getting into the car. I brought up the number and compared it with the one used to send me the original email message about meeting Arthur Townsend.

They were completely different.

I was still sitting there when a vehicle pulled out of a side road behind me and drove away. It was a dark four-by-four, and this time I made an extra effort to scrutinize the man in the military cap at the wheel.

It looked like Cyrus Hammond.

SIXTEEN

Arriving at work next morning, I was greeted rather too cheerily by Valerie. I had the feeling that she had been waiting for me.

"Any news on Ash?" she asked.

"Nothing yet. I'll let you know as soon as I hear anything."

She was genuinely concerned, even though they always argued. It wasn't just the blatant injustice: Ash was an endearing character despite his stroppiness.

She waited a beat before thrusting a green folder at me.

"What's this?"

"Employee appraisal reviews. We agreed we'd get them done this week."

I groaned. We had a dozen regular staff in the downstairs office. I knew them all well but didn't relish having to go through any sort of formal procedure. My management philosophy was pretty simple: In the absence of evidence to the contrary, assume that everyone is doing a good job and let them get on with it.

"We have to go through with this," Valerie said. "It's not just about us evaluating them. It's a chance for them to tell us how they think things are going and how we can help them get the best out of their job."

"I know. That's what bothers me most."

"I'll do most of them, but you've got to show willing. Starting with me."

"What?"

"That's how it works. You cascade down."

I hadn't anticipated having to do an appraisal of Valerie. She was far more efficient at her job than I was.

"So who does me and Ash?"

"You're the bosses. You decide."

Outside my office, Jamilla had the blankly innocent look of the truly guilty. She had allowed Valerie to ambush me into a management day rather than real work.

"Shall we get straight on with it?" Val said.

"I need the loo," I told her. "Give me five minutes. Jamilla, would you be a star and rustle us up a couple of coffees?"

She just smiled agreeably at me, which was further evidence that she had colluded with Valerie.

I sat on the toilet seat in the shower room and phoned Claire Whitney's home number. I was keen to check that she was OK and wanted to do so in private. Halfway through Claire's cheery recorded message the phone was picked up.

"Yes?"

A slightly croaky female voice, a little hesitant, swamped by Claire's briskly efficient tone.

I waited until the recording had finished.

"Who is it?" said a querulous voice at the end of the phone.

"Hi," I said. "My name's Nick. I'm a friend of Claire's. Is she around by any chance?"

No immediate reply. I could hear her breathing at the other end of the line. She had sounded elderly, with a distinct American accent. It had to be Claire's mother.

"Nick who?" she said. "What is it you want?"

There was definitely an edge to her tone. I wanted to put her at ease, though mentioning Leo Parrish was probably not advisable.

"Nick Randall, Mrs Whitney. I—"

"It's *Ms,*" she corrected me with emphasis. "Ms Nora Whitney, for your information. I'm not married. Never was."

"I beg your pardon," I said, wondering if she was a prickly customer or was merely concerned I had the facts right. "I work for a company called Xponential Productions. I've been talking to Claire about the possibility of her doing some work."

"She's never mentioned your name before."

This was turning into outright hostility. I gambled: "Well, I promise you it's not a ploy to sell you life insurance."

"Then what are you selling? Wait a minute. A film company, did you say?"

"Yes."

"I do recall her saying that she'd been seeing someone who made films."

Phrased in that way, it suggested that Claire and I had been dating, not an impression I was inclined to dispel.

"Would it be possible to speak to her?"

"She's at work. I can take a message if you want, though I can't promise I'll write it down legibly. Or remember to pass it on."

Was she mocking me or herself?

"Thanks for the offer, but I'd like to speak to her direct. I've got her work number."

"You know she's got a teenage son, don't you?" she said, and hung up before I could reply.

This closing remark threw me. Was she warning me off? Or trying to make it clear that my intentions had better not be frivolous? Or was it that she simply didn't trust men? I didn't know anything about Claire's father, but perhaps he had walked out, leaving Nora to raise Claire on her own.

I was no more successful at Claire's office but left my name and number with the receptionist, a different one from the snide character I had encountered there.

Still huddling in the cubicle, I phoned Cyrus Hammond. I was sure that I hadn't simply fixed his face onto someone who merely looked like him and that it was he who had been driving the four-by-four last night.

"Filmscope Foundation," said a voice I recognized as his rather precious and protective secretary.

"Nick Randall, Xponential," I said. "Is Cyrus around?"

I actually heard him sniff at this point, as if I was transmitting a bad smell over the airwaves.

"I'm afraid he's not available at the moment," he said.

"I see. And can you give me any idea when he might be?"

A slight pause, as if to suggest that he was checking an appointments diary. I was pretty sure he was doing no such thing.

"I rather think it might be easier if he phones you when he has a moment. We have your number. I'll let him know you called."

"I'd appreciate that," I said, biting back the urge to inform him that he was a supercilious prick. "I'm here all day. I'd really like to talk to him."

"I'm sure he'll contact you as soon as he's able," he said with a palpable lack of conviction.

I hung up, feeling more than a little frustrated, wondering if Hammond had actually been sitting nearby, silently indicating that he had no desire to speak to me.

"Nick?" came Val's voice from outside. "Are you hiding in there?"

"I'll be out in a minute," I called back, hastily pulling the stuff out of the folder and leafing through it.

Valerie had downloaded a set of generic *pro formas* from a website. They began with the usual set of tick-box questions such as: *How do you rate your job satisfaction?* but soon progressed to more management-speak offerings involving "developing person-friendly solutions" and guff about "vertical and lateral zones of responsibility". Stuck on the front of the folder was a list of people Valerie had delegated me to appraise. Apart from her own, there were four other names. Alison and Patrick were both production assistants whom I suspected would be unlikely to be overly concerned about career progression or Xponential's corporate structure. The other two were Ross Buchanan and Jamilla.

I let out a big groan. Ross was cheerful and willing but had precious little initiative or understanding of how the company worked. Jamilla was so new it would be hard to know where to begin.

"Can we get on with it?" Val called.

An hour later I emerged from our session more encouraged that Ashad and I weren't such bad bosses because Valerie was essentially happy with our hands-off philosophy of letting her run the downstairs office in the way she saw fit. She had, however, reminded me of the danger looming for the company if we didn't find extra financing or work that was less speculative than a lot of what we currently had on the go. We would have to lay off staff, in which case the appraisal interviews would become a means of determining who was most expendable.

I hated the idea of being a hatchet man, of having to sack anyone who wasn't outright incompetent or crooked. It occurred to me that Jamilla, our most recent appointment, might actually be the first to face the chop. How did you sack somebody you liked and who had great potential?

"How come you want to be interviewed?" I asked her; Valerie had told me that she'd expressly requested it. "You've only been here five minutes."

My tone was jolly, but Jamilla kept it businesslike.

"I'm entitled," she said. "I think I deserve a hearing."

"That's ominous. Are you going to tell us we're rubbish? Or do you just want a raise?"

"Felix Nancarrow called," she announced, deftly avoiding the question.

"Oh. Any news on Ash?"

She shook her head solemnly. "But he'd like you to call him back."

Felix wanted to talk to Zoran and Milos and I gave him the numbers of the pay-as-you-go mobiles that Jamilla had got for them. They had been dubious about continuing to use their old phones, Zoran's having been confiscated after his arrest and his address book doubtless checked and catalogued by the secret service.

"I'll be in the vicinity of your office this afternoon," Felix said. "Do you think I could have another look at your documentary on Mr Muvart. There's one or two things I'd like to check on, if it's convenient."

I hadn't yet pencilled in any times beside the appraisal list on the front of the folder. I could do Alison, Patrick and possibly Ross this morning, leaving Jamilla for later that afternoon, preferably as late as possible so that she would be keen to go home and hence cut short any stinging critique she might be planning.

"Two o'clock OK with you?" I said to Felix.

"Splendid."

I swallowed my coffee, and then went downstairs to fetch Alison. There was no putting it off any longer.

Fortunately her appraisal went smoothly. This was her first full-time job, and she intended to go travelling overseas with her boyfriend in the near future so she was pretty content with her current lot. It occurred to me that we might not be able to afford to replace her when she went. Patrick's took longer. He had ambitions to work for a major movie studio and felt that we at Xponential weren't giving him enough opportunities to show his mettle. I gently pointed out that we weren't yet in the same league as Universal and Paramount, though Ashad and I were working on a secret project that would have everyone from Amy Adams to Rene Zellweger hammering on our doors. Patrick didn't even crack a smile when I said this. He had no sense of the absurd, a big drawback if he wanted to get anywhere in Hollywood.

I asked Ross Buchanan to give me half an hour. Then I called Rhodri Davies on my mobile.

Ruth answered. She was taking a sick day off her work as a primary school teacher.

"Nothing serious, I hope."

"I'm pregnant," she announced. "I only told him this morning."

By "him" she plainly meant Rhodri. She was just suffering a healthy dose of morning sickness.

"Are you excited?" I asked.

"Ecstatic," she said, both deadpan and sincere.

"How did Rhodri react?"

"You can ask him yourself. Hang on, I'll send a transmission to Galactic Central."

This entailed her shouting Rhodri's name up the stairs. Seconds later I heard heavy descending footfalls, and then Rhodri came to the phone.

"Hello, proto-dad," I said, feeling a pinch of envy. "Congratulations. Been on the champagne yet?"

"Bloody hell," he replied breathlessly, "it's great news but also scary. Not sure I'm ready to be a parent. You know what Ruth said? 'Soon I'll have two children in the house.'"

I laughed.

"What do you *do* with babies?" he asked me rhetorically. "I'd rather face a bunch of Ascendants any day."

"Now there's a thing," I replied, and told him about me and Claire being tailed after we left his place, then our pursuers being scared off by someone I was pretty sure was Cyrus Hammond.

"Blimey," he replied with a hint of scepticism. "I thought he was just a film financier, not Jason Bourne."

"I promise you it wasn't funny at the time."

"No," he said. "I don't suppose it was. I'm just finding this all a bit hard to take in. He wasn't at the convocation, was he?"

"Not as far as I'm aware," I admitted. "But he might have been keeping an eye out for us, waiting in the wings, as it were. Claire's certain it was the Ascendants who were following us."

"You think Kubilius put them up to it?"

"He's slick, but I'm not convinced he's responsible. Apparently he looked genuinely surprised when Claire revealed that she was Parrish's niece. I don't think he'd have had time to release the attack dogs."

"Who then?"

"Kubilius might not have known, but I wouldn't put it past some obsessed individuals lower down the hierarchy to be acting on their own initiative."

"That's more possible," Rhodri agreed. "Did you report the incident?"

"You must be joking. From what we saw last night, the police are a bit too cosy with them."

"Precisely what I've been suggesting on my e-zine. Studiously naming no names, of course. The Worldcon committee want to post selected extracts on their final progress report, given that the Ascendants are going to have a presence there. They especially liked the movie synopsis and the Famous Actor talking bollocks."

"Mind your language," Ruth shouted from the background. "I've got a foetus in here!"

"I didn't mention Claire's starring role with VK," Rhodri told me, "but there's enough there to stir up the pot. It should be an interesting convention."

"Are you still going?"

"Of course," he said, puzzled. "Why wouldn't I?"

"Ruth, too?"

"Ah, I see what you mean. No, she's staying put. Be glad to put her feet up for the best part of a week without me cluttering up the place." He was quiet for a moment. "So how did Claire Whitney react when you were being followed? She's a pretty plucky character, judging by the way she took on Kubilius."

"She wasn't well pleased," I told him. "It's not the first time something like this has happened to her." I described the harassment the family had been subjected to and how they had been forced to move home. "She's convinced it's all to do with the Ascendancy. Someone there is pretty ruthless, if you ask me. Remember what happened with Arthur?"

"Well," he said slowly, "we don't know it wasn't just an ordinary house fire, do we?"

"No way."

"I'd like to believe the worst of them, but we're a bit short of actual evidence."

"Don't forget I saw one of the people who pretended to be cleaning Arthur's windows when we were in *The Black Hole*. A bit more than circumstantial."

"No, *precisely* circumstantial."

I was surprised that he was being so scrupulously fair, but I had to concede that we had no proof.

Still, I felt sure the Ascendants were behind much of what had been going on with Parrish's stories. Some of it might be down to Byrnes, but the people I had seen at Arthur's surely weren't American secret service agents. Byrnes might be aggressive and bull-headed, but I couldn't believe that even he would descend to setting fire to people's homes. At least I was confident the office wasn't bugged because I had tasked Jamilla with sweeping the place first thing every morning with Ozzie's device. She called it snoop dusting.

"Does Claire Whitney think her uncle was killed by a cultist?" Rhodri asked.

Not a notion I had considered. Rhodri had been fascinated by her familial connection with Parrish and her insistence that he was dead, though he had steadfastly promised her he wouldn't publish anything about it. Like me, he was probably hoping to find out more about Parrish in due course.

"She didn't say so. Her mother told her that the shooter came out of nowhere and was jabbering nonsense when it happened. Claire was actually there, you know."

"What, when he was shot?"

"She was just a toddler, in the park with both of them."

"Good God."

"Fortunately she doesn't remember much about it. It's only now she's having to deal with what may be the consequences of the murder."

Rhodri didn't reply to this. Perhaps I was overstating things, but there was something about Leo Parrish that attracted trouble, alive or dead.

"As it happens," I told him, "I had a brief phone conversation with her mother this morning. Understandably she's a bit cautious with strangers."

"Do you think she'd be interested in reminiscing about LP? Doing an interview, perhaps?"

"Ah, I can almost see your reporter's nostrils flaring at the prospect of a scoop."

"Well, he's not exactly a household name, is he? But there are a few fans out there who would be interested in finding out more about him."

"If I get the chance, I'll ask her."

"What's happening with your business partner?"

"He's still locked up. I can't believe that all this isn't connected somehow. I just wish I knew how. Listen, I've got to go. Congratulations again, and thanks for taking me to such a fascinating evening in Slough."

"Those are words I never thought I'd hear."

*

Ross Buchanan's appraisal took up the rest of the morning. He was cheerful and garrulous, telling me how much he enjoyed the job and how much he liked everyone here and how he wanted to be a movie star one day. He saw his "work experience" with Xponential as a valuable way in to the acting world. When I pointed out that the usual route was through amateur dramatics and drama school, he just gave me a look of vacant wonder. When I asked him if he had any actual acting experience, he thought for a moment before telling me that making tea for Valerie was just a step removed for making tea for Jennifer Lawrence or Ryan Gosling on a movie set and that because he got on well with people he was confident they'd find a bit part for him in one of their movies, and that would be his way in.

There was much more in this surrealistic vein. At the end of it, my pen hovered over the blank summary box at the end of the *pro forma* before I finally scribbled: "Ambitious and starry-eyed". So starry-eyed he was light-years removed from planet Earth.

Jamilla fetched in a Moroccan salad for our lunch, and we scheduled a four o'clock slot for her appraisal, earlier than I would have liked and giving her ample time to detail my shortcomings as a boss. When I attempted advance mollification by telling her, quite sincerely, that she was doing an excellent job, she fixed me with her lilac-shadowed eyes and unnervingly said nothing.

When Felix Nancarrow arrived Valerie and I sat him in the viewing theatre so that he could have another look at the Muvart footage. His uncle had met with furious denials about a secret internment site, so furious that the old man was now convinced there was something in it but wanted to be sure that he had his facts right. Nancarrow took copious notes, assuring us that he would keep them confidential. He had also recorded both Milos and Zoran's accounts of the confrontation with Bennett Irwin and was confident they would bolster the case for Ashad's immediate release.

After he left I found Jamilla in her work area, standing with her back to me at the photocopier, looking almost furtive while it spewed paper. Normally she let it run on long jobs and got on with something else.

"Your first script?" I asked, startling her.

"Have you checked your emails?" she wanted to know.

I hadn't even got around to turning on my computer that morning. Jamilla kept an eye on my mail and I sometimes got through a whole day using it only as an expensive clock.

"Walter Suthersen's secretary has sent you something," she told me.

There was an email from someone called Lorraine at *SuthersenEnterprises.com*. It said, "Walt asked me to let you have this story by Leo Parrish. He sends his best wishes."

I clicked on the attachment and got a flashing pop-up message saying PRINT NOW!

I didn't like the look of this, so I closed the dialogue box. A second one came up in its place. It said:

MESSAGE DELETED

I went back to my inbox. The email wasn't listed. I checked the recycle bin. No sign of it there either. For a second I wondered if I'd imagined it.

"Jamilla!" I shouted. "That message from Walter Suthersen. It's disappeared."

She came in to look at the screen. Then she checked the Inbox and Trash folders.

"Interesting," she said. "Half a tick."

She went out again. A couple of days previously, I had suggested that she tweak our office system so that any incoming messages would automatically be copied to her desktop. But she returned shaking her head.

"I've got a MESSAGE DELETED window, too. Never mind."

"Never mind!" Suddenly I was frantic, furious at the loss of the serial.

The phone on her desk started ringing.

"Get that," I told her hastily, snatching up my mobile and walking away, punching out Rhodri's mobile number.

When he answered I explained what had just happened. He checked his email while I wandered back to my desk, hoping that somehow mine would have miraculously reappeared. It hadn't.

"Nothing here, boss," he said.

"But that could either mean Suthersen's secretary didn't copy it to you or it's disappeared from yours as well."

"Why don't you ask her—wait, did she write a covering email? What did it say?"

I frowned. "She said that Walt had asked her to send the story he promised—"

"Did she mention the author's name?"

I saw what he was getting at. "Ah, you think ... "

"It's a possibility," said Rhodri. "I think some pretty nifty electronic censorship may have just gone on."

"Can I recover it from the hidden depths of the computer?"

"It's a pretty safe bet that they'll have thought of that."

Jamilla walked in and put a red laminated folder on my desk. She opened it to reveal a wodge of paper. The top page was a colour-print picture of a vast spaceship blasting away from the Earth. Above it were the words: "The astonishing conclusion of Leo Parrish's acclaimed new serial, *Exaltation*."

Rhodri's voice came from the phone: "Nick, are you still there?"

"Hang on," I said and pressed the mute button.

"Hard copy," said Jamilla. "You're always telling me how important it is. Did you notice the print message?"

"I didn't like the look of it."

"It said PRINT NOW! With an exclamation mark at the end. So I thought I'd better get on with it."

A grin spread across my face. "Jamilla, if I wasn't your manager I'd be inclined to kiss you."

"Gross," she said without malice and swiftly retreated.

I explained to Rhodri how Jamilla had rescued the situation and told him I would post him a copy. When Rhodri mentioned that he was going to get his computer virus-checked, I decided it would be prudent to contact Ozzie.

One of his shop assistants answered, but Ozzie came to the phone when they told him who was calling. He said he would come over immediately.

I locked the printed copy of *Exaltation* in my secure cabinet and instructed Jamilla not to open any more office emails until Ozzie had checked our systems. She went downstairs to pass the warning on to Valerie. I still had one more call I wanted to make: Gerry. I asked Jamilla if she could contact him for me before I went down to the kitchen to brew myself the coffee I had been craving ever since Ross Buchanan sat down at my desk. I took my time over it, mulling over the business with the attachment. I was pretty sure I knew who was behind it.

When I got back, Jamilla announced that she had Gerry on the line.

I picked up the phone and put it to my ear. Jamilla leaned over my keyboard and suddenly Gerry's face appeared on the PC monitor. Another few clicks and the screen split in two with Liz Martindale on the left.

Jamilla pointed to a tiny indentation in the top rim of the screen and mouthed: "Webcam."

I heard Gerry say, "So there you are."

Jamilla indicated a small, dotted indentation in the bottom edge of the screen and mouthed, "Mike".

Valerie had set up videoconferencing a while ago, generally for when we were out and about, but somewhat irrationally I had felt it would be taking me all too close to the time-sucking world of twitters, blogs and message groups. Obviously she and Jamilla had got fed up with my unfulfilled promises to try it out. To my relief, Gerry's image was clear and his words weren't lip-synched like a bad foreign-language sex film. I gave Jamilla a thumbs-up before she disappeared back to her desk.

"I hope you don't mind me bringing Liz in on this," Gerry was saying

"No, of course not." I said hello to her, and got a smile back.

Because time was short, I began to tell them about my trip to Paradys with Briony Potts. Gerry started making throat-cutting signals with his hand. Clearly he didn't want me identifying the place on camera. Liz looked aside, away from Gerry as if snubbing him, and said, "Miss Ali told us this conversation was encrypted."

It took me a moment to realize that the set up had got the images reversed from how they were really sitting.

I had no idea what encryption actually involved, but I tried to look wise. Valerie must have anticipated the confidentiality issues when she had the system installed.

I told the story. They were suitably impressed with Briony's part in getting us into the site, and Gerry was especially pleased that I had retrieved Sam Oliphant's secret file.

"So what are you going to do with it?" asked Liz.

"Well, it's explosive stuff so we'll have to think carefully about that. And there's something else."

I told them about the flash drive that had been confiscated from Ash and the information it contained.

"Let me get this straight," Gerry said. "The government funded research into a genetically-specific virus just before an infection begins killing people of Khanistani origin in prison."

"Quite a coincidence," said Liz. "I'm assuming you're concerned not to stir things up while your friend is in custody."

She was much more relaxed and communicative than previously. Was it just the protective nature of the interface? Or had the photocopying episode been a bonding experience?

"I imagined we'd get him out pretty quickly," I told her, "until he started claiming he was Khanistani as well. Now I'm worried that he's going to end up in one of their prisons."

"But surely they can't hold him indefinitely without charge?" Gerry said.

"If he catches a dose of haemorrhagic fever, he won't be going anywhere."

Liz and Gerry looked in opposite directions on the split screen, as though they'd had a tiff. It was quite disorientating.

"Something I should know?" I asked.

"It's an odd thing," Liz said, "but quite out of the blue I met up yesterday with someone I used to work with and he's actually involved in all this."

"What, infecting Khanistanis?"

"No, no. The research. I have to say that he's one of the good guys and wouldn't have anything to do with illicit practices. From what he was telling me it's possible, but only *possible*, that he might be able to help."

"How?"

"We may have something in the pipeline," Gerry said in a manner suggesting that it was better not discuss it further here, even with encryption.

"One more thing," he said. "Have you got any more Parrish stories knocking around?"

"Why? Have you become a fan?"

"You betcha. I'd be interested to see them."

"I'll see what I can do," I told him.

The screen flashed a window saying: DISCONNECTED.

I had meant to mention *Exaltation*, but Gerry had cut us off too abruptly. I was sure he would be interested, especially with the Ascendancy connection, though I needed to see whether the second half lived up to the promise of the first. Perhaps Leo Parrish would turn out to be a prophet in more than one sense of the word.

I heard a familiar voice in Jamilla's work space. Ozzie was sitting at her desk, looking like a Hollywood pirate in a hooped T-shirt, pounding the keyboard into submission as if it had been involved in a mutiny.

He stopped.

"Like I thought," he said to me, "a virus. But I reckon I've sorted it."

I was almost disappointed. I'd really wanted it to be some on-the-spot intrusion by a government agency or a branch of the Ascendancy.

"You sure?"

"It was in your system already. Triggered when the attachment was opened. It was set up to destroy files containing key words."

I hadn't anticipated this. "Like Parrish?"

He shrugged. "I need to run a check. I've got a copy of the beastie now—" he held up a dinky flash drive "—and I'm wiping it off your system."

"How come our virus-checker didn't spot it?"

He was fatalistic. "New ones popping up all the time. It's a fucking arms race out there."

"Any chance of recovering the original email?"

He just shook his head. "Want to know how it got there?"

He reached across to the printer and picked off the top sheet.

"Embedded in this email. It was in your trash folder. You've been spammed, man."

Apparently an email had automatically been sent back to the spammer. Ozzie had taken a copy of that and promised to let me know if he got anything useful from it. He had already begun updating our firewall and anti-virus definitions.

I studied the printer copy of the email from the trash folder.

It was dated a couple of days previously. The subject line was: "Big." And the message read: "Take a look at these," followed by a web address.

"It'll be a phishing site," said Ozzie. "I'll check when I'm back in the pit."

He left, and Jamilla pointedly checked the wall clock. We were already three-quarters of an hour past her appraisal time-slot.

"We'll do it tomorrow," I promised. "I really have to deal with this. Feel free to go home early."

She didn't look mollified.

"Listen," I said, "I think you're doing an excellent job and I really don't have the time or the energy for this right now. What do you want? A pay rise?"

She brightened. "That would be good."

"OK. Let's say an extra hundred a month. I'll need to OK it with Ash. Can't see that it'll be a problem."

She looked genuinely delighted, as if that was all she had really wanted. Just eighteen, I reminded myself; despite her impressive competence, she was only eighteen.

"But you've got to agree that I can just fill out the appraisal form saying how wonderful you are, let you look it over, and then we're done with it. OK?"

"Deal," she said without hesitation.

I wandered back to my desk. The sender's email address was *Lauren36D@gmail.com*. A typical come-hither offering suggestive of sex spams. But it was quite familiar to me.

The virus had been sent by Theresa.

SEVENTEEN

Theresa's mobile was switched off, so I phoned her work number. A colleague eventually answered and told me she had left early to meet a client.

I wasn't sure who I was most furious with: Theresa for sending the email, or Byrnes, who was surely behind it all. Theresa had already been threatened with deportation and it was easy to imagine how Byrnes might have pressurized her. Even so, I hadn't expected that she would cave in to him. I assumed he had acted to prevent me from getting my hands on a copy of the second part of *Exaltation*. But why? That was still the big unanswered question. Along with a host of other ones, all of them connected to Leo Parrish.

I needed to talk to her, face to face. Which wasn't going to be possible at the moment. We were lucky that Jamilla had managed to save the attachment from electronic oblivion, though suddenly the hard copies of both parts of the serial seemed more than ever an endangered species whose continued existence I couldn't take for granted.

It was getting late. I waited until everyone else had gone home. Then I locked the office door from the inside and opened up the secure cabinet to check that Part 1 was still there.

I almost expected to find it gone. But it sat safe in its transparent sleeve with its weirdly compelling cover of the beatific naked man clasping the Earth and Leo Parrish's name to the fore. He might have gone on to a more prominent and successful career had he kept writing and found better-paid markets. Was he really dead? Or was Claire Whitney lying to me?

I flicked through the pages, the story still vivid in my mind. Then I turned to my computer and did a search for Draco Nova.

There were plenty of references. The most recent indicated that the nova was still growing in luminosity at all wavelengths. Some astronomers were suggesting that it might be a hitherto-unknown white or brown dwarf in an unstable phase. Others were dubious that such a stellar close neighbour—its distance from Earth was thought to be under twenty light-years—could remain unknown until now. A suggestion that the object might be a just-born proto-star was also dismissed on the grounds that there was no observable gas and dust in the vicinity. More speculative notions invoked dark energy and dark matter to postulate a variety of possible objects, but it was obvious that there was no consensus. Which inevitably made me think of *Exaltation* and the same lack of consensus on what the Radiance was.

This was more than a little spooky; and something else struck me. If Parrish's work *was* truly predictive, then perhaps the serial had predicted the establishment of the Church of the Ascendancy. Though I knew this was a dangerous line of thought, it was also seductive. One of the main characters in the story was an eccentric newspaper magnate whom I had initially assumed to have been inspired by Orson Welles's *Citizen Kane*. But this particular character had long believed that all human progress was as a result of "superior disembodied intelligences" acting as secret mentors to the human race. He had even formed a movement to espouse his ideas and became convinced that the Radiance had mind-boosting properties that would "exalt" the human race. It was perfectly possible to see him as a not-so-exaggerated version of Edgar Eldridge. Had Parrish known that Eldridge would steal the story's ideas to set up a religion but deliberately disguised this foreknowledge when portraying his fictional counterpart in *Exaltation*?

This might become clearer in the second part. But I knew I was in danger of letting myself believe that every word Parrish had written was a coded oracle. I needed to get out of the building and go home.

I locked the first part of the serial back in the cabinet and slipped Jamilla's red folder containing Part Two into my rucksack. Hesitating only slightly as I opened the door to assure myself that no one was lurking on the landing, I went down the carpeted stairs more gingerly than normal. And double-checked that no one was loitering outside before I ventured out.

Rain was lashing down. I wrapped the red folder in an orange carrier bag for extra waterproofing. Zipping it in my backpack, I made a dash for Charing Cross station.

The train was packed. By the time I got off I had decided to have dinner at an Italian restaurant just off the high street where the owner had been serving bumper portions of Italian staples for over thirty years.

While I waited for my meatballs I phoned Theresa again on her mobile. I wasn't actually expecting her to answer, but she abruptly picked up.

"Nick," she said immediately. "I know what this is about. It's not a good time. I'll call you back later."

I got the impression she was more than a little harassed.

"Is everything all right?"

I had intended to be angry with her but I immediately began to wonder whether she was still under threat from Byrnes.

"It's fine," she said hastily. "I really can't talk now."

"Where are you?"

"I'll call you back in half an hour."

"Is Byrnes there?"

A humourless laugh. "That bastard better stay the hell away from me. Later. I promise."

And she hung up.

My meal arrived in short order and I helped it down with a couple of beers before walking home through the rain. Theresa hadn't rung back but when I tried her mobile again she didn't pick up. I left a message reminding her that we needed to talk. I knew her well enough not to expect an apology for having sent me the virus; it wasn't her style. But she owed me an explanation and I was determined to get one.

The rain started coming down with even more determination. I scampered under the shelter of my front door porch, unhooking my backpack, finding my front door key and turning the lock. As I pushed open the door and stepped inside someone came rushing at me and jabbed something under my ribs.

An electric pain exploded through me, and I went down quivering. I may have blacked out for a second or two. As I rolled over I glimpsed a figure in a grey hoodie and jeans fleeing down the pathway.

It was several seconds before the shock of the attack subsided. The pain had been intense but it lasted only a split second. Long enough, though, to poleaxe me.

I clambered to my feet, feeling for a wound, any sensation of damage under my ribs. There was none. No pain when I breathed in and out.

Cautiously I edged into the doorway and peered out.

The gate hung open and my rucksack was lying in the middle of the pathway.

I went out and gathered it up. It was empty. Jamilla's folder was gone.

It's amazing how long you can make a four-letter expletive yell last when your sense of outrage is strong enough. Of course it helps if you repeat it several times.

"Carry on like that," said a voice from the gate, "and the Neighbourhood Watch will be sending in the attack dogs."

It was Cyrus Hammond, swamped under one of those overcoats with buttons and flaps everywhere. He was a little breathless.

He came up the path looking bulky, the shoulders of his coat freckled by the rain.

"I think I've been tasered," I told him.

He helped me up the stairs and into my living room, letting me flop on to the sofa. I was still in shock and slow to get my brain working again.

Hammond sat down in an armchair and unbuttoned his overcoat to reveal a package in an orange carrier bag.

"I'm guessing he was after this," he said.

I took it from him. The bag was soggy but the red folder inside was undamaged.

"Bloody hell," I said, clutching it to me. "You got it from him?"

He nodded but his expressionless face didn't change.

"I don't know what to say. Thank you."

"You're more than welcome."

Everything felt a little surreal, my reactions slow-witted.

"Who was it?" I asked, though I was pretty sure I knew.

"Probably a local yob," he answered. "He came haring down the pathway wrenching the package out of your carryall. It was pretty obvious what had happened. So I got in his way. Grabbed the package as he came out through the gate. He just turned and ran for it."

I didn't believe this for a moment. If it was Byrnes, I doubted he would have surrendered the package so easily.

"What did he look like?" I asked.

"I didn't see his face. He was hunched up under his hood."

I couldn't see any point in being cagey.

"I know him," I said. "I'm pretty certain it was a man called Noah Byrnes. We've crossed swords recently. He's an American intelligence operative."

Hammond looked intrigued, but he showed no sign that he knew the name.

"I assumed it was just some random mugging by a kid."

"He was wearing black brogues."

I had spotted this from my quivering vantage point on the floor just before he ran for it. The jeans and the hoodie were just a convenient disguise, I was sure.

Hammond took a small silver flask from the inside pocket of his overcoat.

"Mind if I find some glasses?" he asked.

"Go ahead."

He heaved himself up and went into the kitchen. Byrnes was in his forties, Hammond fifteen to twenty years older. Though I was grateful that he had rescued the folder, I couldn't see how he could have won out in a confrontation between them.

Hammond returned with two glasses which he filled from the flask.

I took a glass and swallowed a mouthful. I rarely drank spirits, but its warming strength radiated through me like a balm. I murmured my appreciation.

"Eighteen-year-old Macallan," he announced as though he had personally distilled it.

"You're not just a film financier, are you?"

I wanted him to explain without being asked how he had conveniently been on hand to rescue the folder. He gave a dismissive shrug. "It's my day job. Occasionally I multi-task. Strictly on the side of the angels."

"Are you an agent yourself?"

"Good lord, no. I'm too old for that."

I had noticed him panting at the gate, which possibly suggested a pursuit or at least a tussle.

"This man Byrnes works for an agency called DEFCOS. Ever heard of them?"

He shook his head a bit too readily. I wasn't convinced.

"Why is he so interested in Leo Parrish? In preventing any of his work from being circulated?"

"Is that what he's been doing?"

"This isn't the first time he was here. He tried to warn me off before."

Hammond mulled this over. "Are you certain it was him this time?"

"He tasered me! A random mugger wouldn't do that."

More contemplation. He wiggled the flask at me. I shook my head and he slipped it back into his overcoat.

I held up the red folder. "Do you know what this is?"

"Enlighten me."

I had a feeling he knew but there was no harm in playing along with it.

"Part Two of Leo Parrish's *Exaltation*."

He actually smiled. "I'm pleased for you. Never read it myself. Always wanted to."

I wondered whether this was true: he wasn't an easy man to read. I explained how I had come by it, how the electronic version had been wiped.

"For all I know, you and Byrnes could be working together."

He didn't flinch. "According to you, this man Byrnes just tried to steal that. I've just delivered it back to you."

"Very convenient you happened to be on hand." His silver hair was glistening with the rain but he wasn't soaked, which didn't suggest he had been lurking outside for any length of time. "Am I the dummy in a good cop, bad cop routine?"

"I'm not working with Byrnes," he insisted with an air of distaste. "Can I remind you that I was the one who put you on to Leo Parrish."

"And I've had nothing but grief and aggravation since. Is this some kind of set up?"

"No."

"You followed me and Claire last night, didn't you?"

"Hell, yes," he said to my surprise. "I wondered if you'd seen me. In fact, I came here this evening to fess up to you and explain why. I was outside in my car so it's not exactly a surprise that your assailant and I both saw you arrive home if he'd been waiting too. I'm only sorry I didn't spot him sooner."

It was plausible but it could just as easily have been a cover story that he and Byrnes had worked out beforehand.

"If I tell you why I was following you last night I hope you'll appreciate that I want it to stay between us."

Was he expecting me to promise? He was virtually a stranger who had been less than candid with me.

"I wasn't actually watching both of you," he said. "I was only watching Claire."

I hadn't quite expected this. "Why?"

"I guess you've struck up some sort of relationship with her."

"That's between the two of us."

"I'm pleased. For her, and for you. She's a fine young woman."

He gave the impression that he was edging around a sensitive subject. I waited.

"I keep an eye on her and her family," he told me. "It's personal. Something I've done for a long time. They have, well, enemies that they don't know about. Last night was an example of why they need someone to watch over them. Obviously I can't always be there but being able to intervene yesterday was fortuitous."

"I think Claire's more than aware that there are people who wish her family ill. This is all to do with Leo Parrish, isn't it?"

He didn't deny it. "In ways that I haven't completely fathomed myself."

"Was it the cultists who were following us?"

"Most likely. They took off when I showed up."

"Were you at the convocation?"

He shook his head. "I steer clear of that sort of thing."

But presumably he had followed her there, been waiting when we all came out.

"I've read part one of Parrish's novel," I told him. "I think it was quite an inspiration to the Ascendants. Though not something they might ever want to acknowledge."

He didn't follow this up. "Did you tell Claire that you'd recognized me?"

This was unexpected. "Why?"

"I need to know. It's important."

"As it happens, I didn't."

"I'd rather you kept it that way. And not mention me being here tonight. I don't want her to think I'm tailing her. She doesn't need anything else to be worrying about at the moment. It might be easier on her if you didn't mention anything about what happened tonight."

"That's a big ask. Especially since you haven't explained *why* you're so protective of her family."

Even as I was talking I had a moment of clarity. "You're Claire's father."

It all fitted. His interest in her welfare, his knowledge of Parrish.

But Hammond was shaking his head.

"No. That's way off beam."

There was a note of what seemed to be genuine regret in his voice. Could he then have been a former lover of Nora's? He was at least a decade younger than her, but the age difference wasn't prohibitive. That would explain his attachment to the family.

"What, then?" I asked. "Did you and Nora have something going?"

I thought I saw a flash of anger, or even disgust. Then he caught himself and spoke in his usual measured way: "This is no soap opera, Mr Hammond. It's complicated. The important thing is that you believe I have their best interests at heart. And that they wouldn't benefit from knowing that I'm looking out for them."

I had touched something very sensitive, though I had no idea what. There was plainly still a limit on what he was prepared to tell me.

I tried another tack: "Claire told me she's Leo Parrish's niece."

If he was surprised, he hid it well. "You've obviously made a favourable impression on her. It's not information she gives out freely."

"So if I asked you whether you were actually Leo Parrish, what would you say?"

I knew he was too young and I expected him to laugh. He didn't show a trace of amusement.

"He's dead. Didn't Claire tell you that?"

So Hammond was taking the same line. I didn't want to believe it was true.

"Yes, she told me. She said she was there when he was shot. But nothing's quite what it seems when it comes to Leo Parrish."

"Some facts are indisputable." Abruptly he rose. "I should be getting along. I only came to clear the air about last night."

"Wait a minute," I said. "I'm grateful to you for saving the folder, but I think you owe me more than this. Why is the secret service interested in Leo Parrish?"

He was buttoning up his overcoat. "'Secret service' covers a lot of sins, particularly since 9/11. Sometimes I think we have more organisations dealing with terrorism than there are actual terrorists."

"We?"

Hammond turned up his collar: rain was still gusting against the window. "I do have some contacts among the intelligence community. Like most countries, the United States has a number of agencies which ask concerned US citizens working abroad to share sensitive information that might be of interest."

"You're talking about spying?"

"That's too self-important a word for it. And it suggests we might be trying to steal state secrets, which isn't the case. We just keep an eye out for extremist groups or individuals who might be acting in ways that could be considered potentially threatening to both the US and the UK."

I thought about this. "Noah Byrnes told me that terrorists were using Leo Parrish's stories as codes to coordinate their activities."

"That's baloney."

So he had obviously looked into it. Or been in touch with someone who had.

"Or there's the possibility that Parrish is now someone eminent in Washington who doesn't want his past coming back to haunt him."

"Leo Parrish is dead."

He was just as insistent as Claire Whitney.

"Well, someone with plenty of clout doesn't like what we're doing."

I told him the bare bones of our work on the Muvart documentary and Ash's arrest. If Hammond was in league with Byrnes he would know this already, but he didn't let anything slip.

"I don't see what this has to do with Leo Parrish," he said.

"Neither do I. But don't you find it more than merely coincidental that all this has kicked off only since I started showing an interest in Parrish and Byrnes got on my case? And why is Byrnes after the Parrish stories if it's not for the reason he gave me?"

Hammond thought it over. "It could be a cover for something else. Such as getting at this stuff involving Muvart. It's a huge issue for the US government and they won't want anyone stirring the pot. Maybe he's trying to misdirect you with all the Parrish shenanigans."

Was this a genuine suggestion or was Hammond misdirecting me, like so many others were?

"That doesn't seem very likely to me. Ashad's in custody, yet Byrnes turns up here and tries to get away with the Parrish serial."

He mulled it over.

"I think you're right," he said at length. "It needs looking into. I'll see what I can find out."

He started heading for the door. I grabbed my jacket and the red folder and followed him.

"Going out again?" he asked.

"Byrnes might still be loitering," I said, following him down the stairs. "I wouldn't put it past him to try again, and I'm not taking that risk. Besides, there's someone I need to see."

"Claire?"

"Not tonight. Don't worry, I'll keep mum about what you told me when I do see her next. For now. But I also know you're still not telling me everything."

"Listen," he said as I locked the outer door, "believe this if you don't believe anything else. I set up Filmscope to fund movies and I've been doing so for over thirty years. If you find a worthwhile Leo Parrish project I'll give you what help I can. That's a promise."

He was offering his hand.

We shook. His grip was like iron.

*

A muted light shone artfully through the Japanese blinds of Theresa's top-floor apartment window. The warehouse still had its loading platform and pulley hook, now painted a pristine matt-black and never again to be sullied by grubby commerce.

I buzzed her intercom. I had tried phoning to let her know I was on my way but she still wasn't picking up. All the more reason to make a personal visit.

"Who is it?" came her voice, a little bleary.

"It's Nick."

There was a momentary silence. Then: "I'm not dressed."

"Throw something on. I'll wait outside until you're decent."

There was a further longer pause while I wondered if she was still suffering the after-effects of her flu. Then she buzzed me in.

I climbed the spiral staircase with stately decorum, giving her time to make herself presentable. When I reached her doorway I just loitered outside without knocking. I had had plenty of time to think about her email, and by now it had dawned on me that was no way that Theresa would have used an address that I might have remembered unless she wanted me to recognize it. She had set it up to hide her identity on the more off-the-wall chat rooms she liked to visit. She had used her middle name and her age at the time, and wasn't amused when I joked that she had deliberately chosen a tag that suggested a porn star.

So if she had known I would recognize it, then perhaps she had been trying to warn me.

The door opened and she was standing there in a black silk kimono and pyjama bottoms, bare-footed and her hair still damp from the shower.

"Everything all right?" I asked.

"Hunky dory."

I recognized the tone: one of self-satisfaction.

"You said you'd ring back," I reminded her.

"Oh, God. Sorry. I got caught up with something."

Inside the lighting was subdued, the main living space at body heat. As she ushered me in, I saw that she had left the bedroom door ajar. The bed looked as if it had been the venue for a wrestling match.

"Can I get you something?" she asked, clocking that I had seen the evidence, which was plainly what she had intended. So that was why she hadn't phoned back: she had been in the middle of a marathon bout of sex.

"Coffee would be good," I said, my spirits unexpectedly lifted.

There was a cupful still in the percolator alongside two empty wine bottles. We stood in the kitchen, Theresa sipping sparkling water. She had obviously spent most of the evening on her backside, and I had no desire to give her the impression that I intended to linger. Was I jealous? I genuinely thought not.

"I owe you an explanation about the virus," she said.

"You do."

"I didn't really have any choice. That guy threatened to have me shipped out on the next transatlantic flight."

"The same one that threatened you before?"

"Well, he sounded the same, only this time he turned up here in person."

She gave an easily recognisable description of Byrnes, at least a Byrnes wearing his usual jacket and tie rather than a grey hoodie. He had flashed his ID card but so quickly she hadn't spotted his name.

"This time he went straight for the jugular. If I didn't cooperate, Homeland Security would be writing to my boss asking the kind of questions that would ensure I'd never get a job anywhere ever again. Or ever be allowed to leave the United States once I'd been shipped back there. Then he told me he'd been instrumental in securing Ashad's imprisonment."

"Ah."

"The English message boards in Ash's community are buzzing with it."

She was more pissed off than rattled, and I didn't bother offering words of comfort, knowing that she would tell me she was a big girl who could look after herself. Especially now, when she was so obviously replete with someone else's more than soothing company. But it was useful to have confirmation of Byrnes's involvement in Ashad's arrest.

I told her briefly what had happened to Ash and how we now had a lawyer on the case. "So what exactly did this guy ask you to do?"

The memory clearly angered her. "He claimed he was expecting you to receive an email with an attachment containing highly sensitive information that would compromise you and put you in danger of arrest. And that I had to come up with something that would take it out. Those were the words he used—*take it out*—before it did any damage."

"Did you believe him?"

"Of course not. You don't threaten someone unless you're engaged in something shady, do you? But my livelihood, my freedom, was at stake."

"So you had to come up with a piece of electronic trickery to wipe it as soon as it was opened."

"That's more or less it."

"Triggered, I assume, by a keyword."

"By anything sent to you from the offices of Suthersen Enterprises."

I thought of Rhodri. "And to anyone else who might be copied in?"

"Uh huh. He wanted all bases covered. I also had to set up a temporary email address to copy the email so that he could check what was in it."

All of which was perfectly within her capabilities.

"You got past Ozzie's firewall."

"I took a gamble he'd still be using the same architecture," she said, unable to resist a fleeting grin: it was a matter of professional pride. On the few occasions they had met they had talked of nothing but computer software and she probably had a better insight into how his mind worked than anyone else I knew.

So Byrnes had been aware that Walter Suthersen was sending me something by Leo Parrish. Maybe he had been tailing us when Rhodri Davies and I talked with Suthersen in the pub and had a remote listening device. Anything was possible. What if Suthersen had decided to send a hard copy rather than an email? Had Byrnes also recruited a mole in the Royal Mail's central sorting office to cover that eventuality?

"I did my best to warn you with my call-girl tag," Theresa said. "And I made sure it wouldn't delete until it was opened and closed again. You got my pop-up print message?"

"My Girl Friday did. It saved the day."

"I'm glad."

"I appreciate it. And I'm really sorry you got snarled up in all this."

"Luck of the draw. One thing about life with you, Nick, it was never dull."

Her tone was almost affectionate. Good sex always made her more generous-spirited.

"He's famous, isn't he?" she said. "Walter Suthersen. Didn't he do that new movie?"

"He wrote the book. Weren't you curious? About why Byrnes would want to censor me?"

"Of course I was. Still am. But I don't want to know anything. It's too risky for me."

I understood. It suited me, too, not having to explain. Especially when I could no longer be confident that someone wouldn't be listening in.

"There is one thing, though," she said.

"Yes?"

"If this guy was on official business, then why come to me? Why blackmail me into doing it? Surely he could have got the job done by some backroom spook."

Something I should have thought of myself. It suggested that Byrnes might be working semi-officially, perhaps alone, or at least with very limited resources. This was interesting and might give me leverage, especially if it turned out he was acting illegitimately. His activities still didn't make any sense to me.

When driving over to Theresa's I had contemplated asking her if I could spend the night on her sofa, strictly platonically, rather than risk Byrnes coming back to my place. This idea now seemed wholly inappropriate: I had no desire to rain on her emotional parade.

"I should be going."

"You're brooding on something. Spit it out."

"You told me you didn't want to know."

"Well, I think you're allowed one for the road."

So I related how I had been attacked, how I felt certain it was Byrnes and that he had tried to steal my copy of the second part of Parrish's serial. I didn't mention Cyrus Hammond's intervention, just said that he hadn't got away with it.

"That's terrible," she commiserated. "Did you call the police?"

"I don't want to risk doing anything that might take attention away from Ash's predicament."

She put a hand on my arm. Very platonically. "That's noble of you. I'm pleased you're still in one piece."

"What I don't get is why he would bother to steal it if you'd already sent him the attachment."

"To stop you being exposed to all the dangerous stuff it contains?"

"It's just a science-fiction story. Walter Suthersen's had a copy of it for years. And how did Byrnes know that I'd managed to take a hard copy of it?"

"He might have simply been covering himself, wanting to check whether you had or not."

This was plausible but somehow insufficient.

"If you ask me," Theresa said, "it suggests he doesn't want you or anyone else reading it. Is it really that incendiary?"

"I'll let you know when I've read it."

Theresa accompanied me to the door. As I went out I kissed her chastely on the cheek and said, "Have a nice evening, did you?"

"Terrific."

"Anyone I know?"

She shook her head, a big smile spreading across her face.

"Well good for you," I told her, and meant it. Now we could both move on.

As I drove home I kept turning over the day's events, trying to work out all the possible permutations. Something else occurred to me.

Could Leo Parrish have been Cyrus Hammond's father?

EIGHTEEN

I slept late and only woke because my mobile started up like a barrel-organ. It was Valerie calling to find out where I was. I waited until I got into work before explaining what had happened the night before. Val couldn't understand why I hadn't contacted the police about the assault. Because, I told her, for all I knew it might have been sanctioned or at least given the nod by them.

There was no news on Ashad, but Ozzie Hogg had left a message about updating our internet security systems. I phoned and let one of his assistants know that I was coming in to see him. It was always easier to make a personal visit since Ozzie tended not to answer the phone, especially his mobile, it being an article of faith of his that all telecommunications signals in the UK were monitored by GCHQ.

"Ask him what he can find out about Cyrus Hammond of the Filmscope Foundation," I told the assistant, and made him write down the details and promise he would pass them on. Ozzie loved any whiff of intrigue, and I suspected he would take on the task with relish.

When I turned up there just before lunch I wasn't really expecting anything revelatory, but he greeted me with a big black-bearded grin and led me downstairs to his basement laptop.

This time he didn't let me anywhere near the keyboard but sat down himself and began typing, giving me a stop-start commentary as he went along which mostly entailed explaining how he had "back-threaded" through a series of links, starting with organisations know to have funded Filmscope over the years, then moving through affiliate corporations, the links expanding and branching, most of them ending with perfectly innocuous companies or individuals.

"Not this one, though," he said, indicating a company called Optimia Office Solutions.

Ozzie quickly flashed through some of the company's catalogue pages: they sold everything from pencils through to filing cabinets and high-spec photocopiers. He returned to the welcome page.

"What do you notice?" he asked me.

I couldn't see anything of particular interest, apart from the fact that the company was American and had what looked like spanking new offices with a colonnaded frontage and lots of mirror glass.

"Address?" Ozzie prompted. "Town, I mean."

"Potomac Hills, Virginia?" I read out, stressing the second syllable of "Potomac" as Theresa had once imperiously instructed me.

"Not far from Washington DC," Ozzie pointed out.

I couldn't see any especial relevance to this. Ozzie was smirking.

"Go on," I said.

"It's just down the road from Langley, Virginia."

Headquarters of the CIA.

"Probably a coincidence," Ozzie said as if he didn't believe it for a moment. "They're a federally-run company disguised as a private one."

I looked at him. "How do you know this?"

He tapped the side of his nose. "Keeps everything in-house. Envelopes to computers. They know exactly where they've come from."

I thought about it. "OK, so they may be an associate company. How many links did you have to follow to hunt them down? Surely if you go back far enough, everything turns into something significant."

"Not this one," Ozzie replied. "Your friend Hammond got an email from a director of the company—"

"You hacked into his emails?"

Ozzie shrugged. "Just dipped my toe in the water. Took a quick glance at recent traffic. The point is, ask yourself why. Why would a movie man in London be in touch with an office supplier in Virginia? Chasing a gross of paperclips, are they?"

I couldn't fault this logic. There was also the fact that Cyrus Hammond himself had more than hinted he had government contacts.

"So what did the email say?" I asked.

"Thanks for the latest delivery. No details. Which is shifty in itself. And why bother if it's just a business arrangement?" Ozzie was emphatic: "He's a CIA man."

I asked him about the random ring-tones on my mobile and whether anything could be done about them. He actually smirked just like Ashad before denying he knew anything about it.

*

I said nothing to Jamilla or Valerie when I got back to the office. Both of them treated me as if I was a convalescent and left me largely in peace. This suited me. I was mulling over Ozzie's speculation about Filmscope's CIA links, speculation resulting from an illegal act of electronic intrusion. Hammond had told me he was keeping a paternal eye on Claire. How innocent was this? Were the intelligence services interested in Claire, perhaps because of her association with the Ascendancy?

I wondered if I should warn her. Not a very clever idea, I decided, particularly since I only had a tenuous link and no hard evidence. Given Ozzie's own paranoid view of the world, it was possible that he was simply seeing threads of intrigue where none actually existed.

I took a call from Felix Nancarrow. He had arranged for us to visit Ashad at three o'clock. His uncle was putting pressure on his contacts in government as a result of the more detailed intelligence we had provided and had also raised the subject of Ashad's incarceration. He was optimistic that Ashad would soon be released.

Gerry had phoned earlier that morning. I called him back.

"We've got it," he began. "Liz has—"

"Tell me later," I interrupted, still feeling a little twitchy. "I'm not sure I can vouch for the confidentiality of this call. Can we meet up?"

"That's just what I had in mind. How about dinner tonight somewhere central? Six, six-thirty-ish?"

"Fine with me."

"Liz knows a place. She's coming too. I'll text you the details later. I think we've got what you need."

He rang off. I contemplated my mobile. It was supposed to be easy to track one, monitor calls without the user suspecting a thing. Other people claimed that this was rubbish. What did I know? The ring-tone shuffle might be only half of it. There was a lot to be said for sticky notes.

I put a package of Leo Parrish stories together for Gerry. An hour or so later, Felix Nancarrow turned up outside the office in a sporty blue Bentley Continental with tinted windows.

"My brother's," he told me as I opened the passenger door to take a look inside. "Mine's in having the brakes looked at."

We had previously driven to see Ashad in his more environmentally friendly Honda Civic Hybrid.

"It's a bit posh for a prison run," I said, noting that there was even a small TV screen under the wood-panelled dashboard.

"He works for De Beers," Felix replied, as if that explained everything.

Before I could get in there was a sudden beeping and a white Transit van pulled in behind us. Nigel got out and made a beeline for me. A woman in a white fur outfit climbed out languorously after him.

"Nicholas!" he said heartily, his gaze roving over the car with what I can only describe as greedy admiration. "Nice motor."

"It's on loan," I told him as he leaned down and stuck his head through the open door beside me.

"Good morning," he said to Felix, ducking his head back up again before he could reply.

"That's Mr Nancarrow," I told him. "He's one of our lawyers."

The woman came up, her ample figure wrapped in what was actually a lightweight sheepskin coat that matched her pale complexion and accentuated her crimson lips and plum-coloured eyeliner.

"This is Irina," Nigel told me. "She is a school teacher."

"Pleased to meet your acquaintance," Irina said in heavily accented English.

With her short cream leather skirt and low-cut top that amply advertised a different set of credentials, never had anyone looked less like a school teacher.

Nigel was staring at me in his intense way, obviously waiting for me to tell him something. I suddenly wondered if he was going to ask me whether I had made use of the pistol.

"Ashad's been arrested," I said to distract him. "The Met have got him in a lock-up in Paddington."

"You're having me on."

He said this without any tone whatsoever. Almost as if he already knew.

"They're accusing him of being a terrorist," I said, my mouth on automatic. "We're going to visit him."

Nigel shook his head slowly, in the manner of someone all too familiar with the stupidity of policemen and perhaps people in general.

"Have they come here again?" he asked with a slightly shifty air. "The Old Bill?"

"They picked him up outside the Ritz," I told him, deciding that it was better he didn't know that Merrick had called by on more than one occasion. "He was trying to talk to Bennett Irwin."

Nigel looked surprised. "That moron? He would nuclear Moscow if they let him near the red button."

"Well, he certainly didn't want to talk to Ash."

"That man is a zealot. No imagination. They are the worst."

This was the first time that Nigel and I had actually broached the subject of politics—indeed, had anything approaching a meaningful conversation at all. Then he abruptly reverted to type.

"Politicians and police," he said scornfully. "The scum of our earth. Do not trust any of them Nicholas. They will fuck you around mightily if you show weakness."

Unsure of how to reply to this, I pointed towards the van. One of his henchmen had unloaded a big cardboard box brimming with a tangle of wires and was carrying it into the sushi outlet just up the street. It was another of Nigel's properties.

"Got a job on?" I asked, determined to keep him away from the subject of the gun.

"Electrical," he said, for once sounding exasperated. "They claim one of their workers was short-circuited by the oven." He made an incredulous noise. "Explain to me why they need one when all they are serving is fish in the raw!"

Unexpectedly Jamilla appeared, and Nigel instantly brightened. She ignored his salutation and said hello to Irina before giving the Bentley the once-over.

"Do you know how many miles these do to the gallon?" she said scathingly.

"It's borrowed," I told her. "I'll jog to work tomorrow if it'll make you feel better."

She was holding my phone. "You left it on your desk," she told me with a long-suffering air.

The driver's window slid smoothly down. Felix greeted Jamilla, and then said, "We ought to be on our way."

Nigel was still loitering, looking as if he already had the car earmarked as his next acquisition and envisaged Irina displaying her ample charms on the sumptuous back seat. I led Jamilla around to the passenger side and climbed in.

"Don't tell him anything you don't think he should know," I whispered with reference to Nigel.

"What does that mean?"

"Nothing." I hadn't told her about the gun. "Whatever he says, just pretend ignorance."

"Who says I'll have to pretend? I only know a fraction of what's going on around here." She indicated the dashboard. "You might want to put the radio on. President Muvart's in the news again." Her hand tightened around my wrist. "You will make sure he's OK, won't you?"

She plainly meant Ashad. I nodded.

As soon as we drove away, I asked Felix to turn on the TV. He told me to rummage in the glove compartment, where I found a dinky remote.

Muvart was on practically all of the news channels. He was intending to occupy a disputed stretch of territory bordering the Caspian Sea that was currently being policed by an international force. Neighbouring states were protesting to the United Nations, and Bennett Irwin had issued a statement on behalf of the US President saying that no "territorial violations" would be tolerated. In response, Muvart had called a press conference and, speaking in broken English, had scorned the idea of violating a territory that was historically Khanistani but was currently being used by US forces to launch covert attacks on his country. When this was quoted back to Irwin as he was leaving a dinner in Washington, he angrily retorted that "unless the Khanistani president wants a very overt attack he'd better restrain himself". The White House press office had promptly issued a "clarification" to the effect that the Secretary of State's words had been intended to imply an international response to any aggression, not unilateral action by the United States.

I wondered if Ashad would know about this latest escalation. Or would his detention entail no access to news sources?

"Unlikely," Felix told me. "He hasn't been formally charged and he should be allowed a newspaper at least."

"Do you think you'll be able to get him out today?"

"That might be asking a bit much. But I don't believe they'll be able to come up with any evidence to charge him. I'm confident that if we keep the pressure on we'll have him out in no time."

Despite road works, diversions and double-parked delivery lorries, we made good time to Paddington. Felix parked the Bentley in a side street and we walked the short distance to the detention facility. It was a shabby anonymous building, squatting in the shadows of the Westway as though hiding in disgrace.

We were kept waiting for several minutes before Dyte appeared. He looked as if he was still wearing the same shirt as the last time. Whereas on our previous visit he had been relaxed to the point of flippancy, today he had a defensive air.

"He's gone," he told us without any preamble. "They took him away last night."

"What?" Felix said with disbelief. "What do you mean, they took him away?"

Dyte looked uncomfortable. “Someone from the service. It’s out of my jurisdiction now.”

“Where?” Felix demanded to know.

“All I know is that he’s been taken for further questioning.”

“Halstow Island?” I blurted.

Dyte glanced briefly at me, showing no hint of recognition of the name. He addressed Felix: “They’re not happy with his story. They want to know how he got hold of the files on the memory stick they took from him.”

“Who?” Felix asked with soft emphasis.

“You’d have to ask the duty officer on the night shift.”

“Let me guess. He’s not here at the moment.”

Dyte smothered a fleeting smug smile.

“And does he have a telephone?”

“He’ll be sleeping. I’m not going to wake him.”

Felix gave a gentle sigh. “Am I dealing with gross incompetence here? Or are you merely being obstructive?”

“What do you mean?”

“Here’s how it looks to me: I’m being denied lawful access to my client and also information that would allow me lawful access to him into the bargain. You’re the man in charge. How does that appear to you?”

“I wasn’t here.”

“Please don’t insult me,” Felix said with silky venom. “I suggest you fetch the duty log. We’d be happy to inspect it ourselves. Or you can read it out to us if you like. To refresh your memory.”

Dyte made to bluster, but Felix raised a hand. “Don’t even begin to tell me that you can’t provide the information. What service did they say they were working for?”

Dyte gave a surly shrug."I told you, I wasn’t here.” There was something in his tone that suggested he wasn’t happy that Ashad had been taken without his knowledge or permission. “The lead man was someone attached to the NCA. An American. He had the paperwork, and the badge.”

The National Crime Agency was a relatively new organisation that some of the tabloids had already dubbed “the British FBI”.

“DEFCOS?” I asked. “Defence Coordination Service?”

Dyte looked surprised that I had heard of them. I wondered if this was the first time he had encountered them himself.

"I'm interested," I said innocently. "Who are they exactly? We're a little hazy on their role in this."

Dyte's surprise turned wooden. "It's not my job to be discussing the operational reach of other agencies."

Felix insisted he fetch the papers, while I resisted the urge to blab the name of the only DEFCOS agent I knew.

Dyte returned in short order, brandishing the signed custody transfer forms as if they were an alibi.

I looked over Felix's shoulder at the DEFCOS logo and the scrawled signature at the bottom.

It was practically illegible unless you knew the name already. Unfortunately I did.

Noah Byrnes.

*

I rendezvoused with Gerry and Liz Martindale at a Lebanese restaurant in Covent Garden. Liz Martindale looked less formidable shorn of her lab coat and severe expression. She and Gerry already had a bottle of rosé on the table, with an extra glass for me. Gerry poured a healthy glassful. I swallowed most of it in one.

"Tough day?" Gerry asked.

"You could say that." I decided to defer telling them about my tasering and Ashad's disappearance. "I really appreciate this."

"Liz," Gerry said, "do you want to show him what we've got?"

From her shoulder-bag she produced what looked like a blue asthma inhaler.

"They've been working on a preventative for the fever," she told me. "One puff does the trick. It delivers enough anti-viral to protect you for about a week."

I took it from her and turned it in my hands, trying to not contemplate the prospect that Ashad might be banged up for more than a few days.

"Neat," I said. "But what if you're already infected?"

She shook her head. "It's a prophylactic, not an antidote. Disables the virus in the respiratory tract. Once it's inside your body cells and busily multiplying it's already too late."

I realized that I couldn't hold out on them any longer. "This is great. Or it would be, if I knew where Ashad was."

I explained what had happened. Felix had made various phone calls immediately after our meeting with Dyte, but none of his usual contacts had heard about the transfer. I had phoned Merrick, got no answer, left a message telling her that Ash was gone and urging her to do something about it. After that, it was a waiting game until Felix got some hard news. He had driven me back to the office and told me to do my best to be patient. Then he had departed to expedite matters.

I was now more worried than ever and more frustrated at my inability to do anything useful. Not wanting to tell Jamilla or Valerie what had happened, I had fobbed them off by saying that Ashad would have to be released within forty-eight hours because he hadn't been formally charged. This factoid cheered Jamilla and made me feel angrier than ever at the injustice of things when I heard her phoning her family to tell them the good tidings. Valerie, older and shrewder, obviously sensed that I was hiding bad news but had the grace not to press me.

I shut myself in the viewing theatre for the rest of the afternoon on the pretext of giving the *Seconds Out* rushes another viewing. I continued trying to get through to Merrick, leaving increasingly fraught messages but without result. What exactly did Byrnes want with Ashad? To put pressure on him to drop our interest in Leo Parrish? Or was there more to it? And how far would he go to extract information or warn him off? My mind raced over lurid possibilities. Although the US government had banned the use of water-boarding and other coercive techniques, it was perfectly possible that Byrnes might act unilaterally if he was desperate or mad enough. An even worse possibility was that Ashad had already been bundled aboard a motorboat and ferried down the Thames to Halstow, where he was sitting in a cell with other Khanistani inmates, his own genetic profile making him a prime candidate for succumbing to whatever infection might be raging there.

I poured all this out to Gerry and Liz Martindale, aware that I was also pouring cold water on all their efforts, that the inhaler had come a day too late for Ashad if he was already incarcerated on Halstow. When I also told them about the tasering, they looked incredulous.

Despite his own demons, Gerry was a good man in an emotional crisis. He ordered another bottle of wine so that we could get pleasantly merry and consider the possibilities. Liz Martindale also proved encouraging, pointing out that Ashad wasn't an anonymous illegal immigrant with no representation but a moderately well-known film-maker with a lawyer who seemed efficient and well-connected. I couldn't deny any of this, but I was the only one who had first-hand experience of Byrnes's manic intensity and his capacity for violence in the pursuit of his goals. I had to trust that Merrick would also be active in tracking Ashad down and that Felix's high-placed contacts meant that there was no way his case would be allowed to sink into bureaucratic oblivion.

We lingered long over our dinner and the restaurant staff didn't seem at all bothered. The place was crowded and I kept checking to see if anyone nearby was watching me, had been planted there by Byrnes or Hammond or even Vincent Kubilius to keep track of my movements. Everyone looked innocent, which somehow wasn't comforting.

When Liz Martindale excused herself, I commented on her warmth and animation, both absent on our first meeting.

"She had good reasons to be suspicious of you at first," Gerry told me, "She thought you were one of my exes." He was grinning. "She doesn't approve of them because I told her how unlucky I'd been in love."

When he had joined Biope she had been drawn to him and was at first disappointed to discover he was gay.

"But when I told her what had happened to Sam, she became very protective of me. I think she saw you as one of the big bad ghosts from my past."

"In that case I can safely give you these," I said, handing him the package of Parrish stories.

He looked delighted. I asked him if he wanted Sam Oliphant's key card back. He shook his head. Just then my phone warbled.

I pulled it out of my pocket and opened the text. All it said was:

51.505778, 0.149453

There was nothing else. Whoever had sent the message didn't want to be identified: the number had been withheld.

"Good news?" Gerry asked tentatively.

Liz Martindale had returned to the table and was looking curiously at me.

I showed her and Gerry the text. I expected them to go into a flurry of speculation, but almost immediately Gerry indicated my mobile and said: "Look it up on Google Earth."

"What?"

"It's a location. Latitude and longitude."

NINETEEN

Next morning Felix picked me up at my place in the early hours. He was still driving the Bentley and I sank gratefully into the leather seat, putting a small holdall into the back. I was thick-headed from too much wine the night before, when I had phoned him from the restaurant with news of the grid reference message. According to Google Earth it was on the south bank of the Thames opposite the Dagenham motor works, the satellite image showing a long low hut with a pitched roof close to a small jetty and accessed by what looked little more than a track way.

I had been keen to go there immediately, but Felix urged me to wait until he had a chance to look into it. Later he had called back, saying that according to his sources there was no listed governmental building in the vicinity.

Up to that point I had limited my discussions with him to Ashad's involvement with Bennett Irwin and the Muvart documentary. But Byrnes was now involved, so I told him about the break-in at my place, including Byrnes's claim that he worked for an agency called DEFCOS and his particular fixation with Leo Parrish. Felix was merely amused by the idea that the intelligence agencies might be interested in an obscure science-fiction writer—until I told him about my tasering. Then I recounted Claire Whitney's story about Parrish being shot dead in a Brooklyn park in the early 1970s. There was a lengthy pause before he asked for the date. I remembered Claire telling me it was the summer of 1972. After receiving this information, Felix suggested that I go home and get some rest while he made further inquiries.

He had phoned me while already en route to my place the following morning, telling me that although he still had no actual evidence that Ashad had been taken there, the very remoteness and isolation of the location was suggestive enough of a hiding place that it was worth looking into, particularly since Ashad had vanished from the radar so abruptly.

"So what have you been able to establish?" I asked him as we headed eastwards, the traffic not too troublesome at this hour.

"No one appears to know very much at all. According to my friends in the Met, the transfer shouldn't have been sanctioned, particularly since no details of the intended destination were given. They really don't like it when the paperwork's not up to scratch. The duty officer's in very hot water."

"Unless they're just covering themselves. Fobbing us off."

"It's possible," Felix conceded. "The man Byrnes is known to them. He's been on secondment to the UK for a month or so. Special operations. No one was quite able to tell me what that means."

That at least fitted with Byrnes's own claims. "What about DEFCOS?" I asked, and told him what I had already gleaned myself.

"Not easy to find out anything about them," he agreed. "They were set up three years ago as a kind of globetrotting emergency-response unit. We're not clear what their brief is, only that they're answerable directly to the Secretary of State for Defense."

"What?" This was very bad news indeed. "Bennett Irwin?"

"He's the titular head."

"Why would Irwin be interested in Leo Parrish and Xponential Productions?"

"We have no evidence that he is."

"What if he set Byrnes on Ashad because he wants to interrogate him?"

Felix laughed. "Irwin's notoriously irascible, but I don't think even he would go that far. Besides, he's back in Washington and I think he has more important matters on his mind."

I wasn't so sanguine. "What about Byrnes's claim that he wanted our Parrish stories because terrorist groups were using a code based on them?"

"Someone from the NCA confirmed that one of their active lines of enquiry involved what they called 'pre-emptive retaliation'. But they wouldn't discuss codes and they denied all knowledge of Leo Parrish."

"So no one's admitting anything."

"You can't expect security people to tell you anything more than they absolutely have to. Still, we do know that Byrnes is interested in Leo Parrish. If he thinks you're making a programme about him or intending to bring him to the public's attention in any way, it could be why he wants to keep Ashad in custody. To make you stay your hand."

"What do you mean?"

"They might have an operation planned that they don't want jeopardized by premature disclosure."

An operation like the raids earlier in the year that had led to the arrests of Khanistanis living in the Midlands and the North, perhaps. Most of them no doubt now banged up on Halstow Island.

"Or Byrnes could just be lying," I said.

Felix conceded this. "Well," he said, "we do know that Parrish is dead."

He pulled a folded sheet of paper from the inside pocket of his jacket and passed it across.

It was a faxed page that had obviously come from a newspaper archive file. The newspaper was the *Brooklyn Daily Bulletin* dated Tuesday July 25th 1972, the story just a stub on a page that had given greater space to other news:

HOSPITAL WORKER GUNNED DOWN

PROSPECT PARK – Three days ago an unknown assailant walked up to Brooklyn health visitor Leonard Parrish, 37, and shot him dead. The killer was described by witnesses as a young Caucasian male who had been behaving strangely beforehand. After firing a .38 cartridge at point-blank range, he walked calmly away and was not apprehended. Police sources say they are mystified by what they describe as a "motiveless attack".

"How did you find this?" I asked, a little agog. Until now I hadn't actually known that Leo's full name was Leonard.

"My assistant Ellie's a wonder," Felix told me. "Apparently she has an aunt who has a friend who works in the local newspaper archives. There's nothing online for that period, but card files work just as well if you know what you're looking for."

I had this unlikely notion of them beavering away through the night, then remembered that it would have been daytime in New York.

There was no photograph, and Felix told me that they had been unable to locate any further reference to the shooting in subsequent editions of the newspaper. This was scarcely surprising, given that such incidents were commonplace in the city at the time. It appeared that Claire Whitney's version of events corresponded with what had actually happened.

Halfway to our destination, Felix insisted we pull over and have breakfast at a roadside café off the A206. He looked incongruous in his smart suit and polished brogues, tucking into a plate of bacon and eggs, surrounded by hairy lorry drivers and meat market traders in bloody white overalls, cheerfully assuring them that he wasn't really a nob and worked for a living just like them. And, no, he couldn't give them a spin around the car park in the Bentley, even though he appreciated their offer to strip down to their vests and Y-fronts not to soil the seats. I worked my way through a plate of baked beans and scrambled eggs while this cheery banter was going on, swallowing two cups of tea served with working-class irony in ornate willow-patterned cups.

As we were walking back to the car, my mobile alerted me to a text. It was from DI Merrick and said: *On the trail. Will be in touch as soon as I have news.*

I thought about calling back or sending a return text, but decided against both. She might try to warn me off, and that was the last thing I wanted. Instead I muted the phone and stuffed it back in my jacket.

Twenty minutes later we were driving down a dirt road towards the shoreline, scrubby untended land all around us, hemmed in to the east by low-rise industrial parks, to the west by lines of sewage tanks. We skirted a fence, and suddenly I saw the sinuous bulk of silver metal-clad building with a curving roof and a slender spinnaker-style chimney that sat close to the river like some gleaming art deco vision of the future.

"Wow," I said to Felix. "Look at that."

"It's a sewage sludge incinerator," he told me brightly.

Despite the general grimness of the surroundings, Felix was positively cheerful.

"This is way beyond the call of duty for a lawyer," I pointed out to him.

He didn't disagree. "This whole business is rather exciting in a murky sort of way. It's refreshing to get out of the office and do something active for a change."

He started extolling the virtues of the Crossness Pumping Station, which lay just further west, and of Joseph Bazalgette, the engineer who had brought clean water and effective sewage disposal to much of London. We agreed on the general merits of Victorian engineering, its robustness and attention to detail, and the particular charms of Crossness, with its brass-pistoned beam engines and ornate iron work. Theresa had dragged me along there one open-day afternoon in the final years of our marriage. It was one of the few occasions when we hadn't argued, when the industrial elegance of the place, its pillars and arches, all being painstakingly restored and repainted by volunteers, had made our marital squabbles seem petty.

"Just think," Felix remarked, "it started with MPs in Parliament being inconvenienced by the stench from the Thames and ended with vastly improved sanitation for everyone."

"I sense a moral winging my way."

"A pretty straightforward one," he admitted. "When things start to smell bad, you have to do something."

The track became bumpier, roughed up by bulldozers. We passed through a gap in the coastal fence and came in sight of the building, which looked entirely unprepossessing, its low-rise corrugated roof peppered with lichen and bird droppings, its windows sporting broken panes that had been patched with plywood and covered with grilles. A white van with the logo Isis Maritime Logistics was parked next to a wooden jetty, and two cars stood on the crumbling concrete forecourt. A light was shining through the grille-covered window above the entrance.

Felix reversed the Bentley back up the track, and we parked just beyond the fence. I heaved the holdall off the back seat. We approached the shore again to the squawking of seagulls and the drainy whiff of the river.

There was no sign of any security around the building. We skirted the jetty, which lay in a little bay, the Thames lapping its greenish boards, a scummy froth of urban litter coating the shoreline. No one came out to intercept us. A short flight of steps led up to the entrance. Felix and I had formulated no plan other than to walk brazenly in and see what happened.

Immediately inside a moon-faced young man was sitting at a desk, doing a newspaper Sudoku puzzle. He was sallow-skinned, with a fat black moustache that didn't suit him.

"Felix Nancarrow," Felix said confidently, thrusting out his hand. "Mr Ashad Husseyin's lawyer. I'm here to see my client."

The man lurched to his feet. Down the long central corridor I could hear raised voices from a nearby room. A man and a woman having an argument. The place looked decrepit, paint flaking from the partition walls, the strip-lighting speckled with dead flies.

The man at the desk didn't take Felix's hand.

"How did you get here?" he demanded to know. He had an American accent.

"I'm Ashad Husseyin's lawyer," Felix repeated. "This is my colleague. And you are?"

The man didn't reply. He started nibbling on his moustache, looking both irritated and perplexed. He indicated the holdall. "What's in the bag?"

"Clothes," I said, giving it a thorough kneading for his benefit.

"Stay right where you are," he ordered us, and then scuttled off down the corridor to the room where the voices were coming from. He knocked on the door and opened it. For the first time I could hear the voices clearly. I recognized both of them.

He went inside, closing the door behind him. Immediately I darted down the corridor. The door had a wired glass window. Carefully I peered through it.

Byrnes and DI Merrick were standing there, side by side, listening to the man.

My first immediate thought was that she had come to rescue Ashad, arriving just before we did. That was why she and Byrnes had been arguing, and if I burst in I could add weight to her cause. But something made me hesitate. She was glancing at Byrnes in a manner that was thoughtful rather than antagonistic. They exchanged a few brief muttered words, looking more anxious than hostile. The dismaying realization dawned that they knew one another.

Hastily I withdrew and retreated back to Felix. He was sifting through the scattering of paperwork on the desk while holding his mobile to his ear.

"It's Byrnes," I told him in a whisper. Prudence bordering on paranoia made me averse to declaring that Merrick was also there. I think I wanted to see what might happen next. I swallowed. "Ashad must be here."

"I don't doubt it," Felix replied. He was still inspecting the papers, shuffling them around on the desk. "Isis Maritime Logistics," he said into the phone. And then to me: "There's nothing here that identifies this location as an official holding facility. And no record of it anywhere else, either." He pointed to a calendar hanging on the wall. It was for the year 2001. "I'd hazard a guess that was the last time this place was in regular use."

I heard footsteps in the corridor, but going in the opposite direction to us, brisk, fleet-footed, diminishing into silence. A woman's tread.

"Abbey Wood or Belvedere, SE2," Felix said into the phone. "A little east of the Crossness Incinerator."

Was Merrick going to see Ashad? The guy with the moustache emerged and came striding back to us.

"I can't help you," he said. "We have no knowledge of this person. And you're not allowed to use cell phones inside the facility."

Felix, still holding the phone to his ear, ignored him and said, "Yes, I've got that. Good work."

He cut the call and addressed the guy with the moustache: "What exactly is this place?"

The guy bristled. "I'm not at liberty to discuss it."

"Really? According to my information, these premises belong to Thames Water."

No response to this.

"Isis Maritime Logistics?" Felix said to him.

Still he stayed silent.

"They don't exist, do they? Would you kindly ask Mr Byrnes to come out and explain why he's acting in breach of UK law by detaining my client."

"Who?"

Felix smiled. "Please don't be coy. We know he's here."

The door opened and Byrnes emerged. There was no sign of Merrick.

"You have no business being here," he said angrily, addressing me rather than Felix. He looked drawn, a little unkempt, short of sleep perhaps.

"Tasered anyone lately?" I said angrily, suppressing the urge to hit him.

He squinted hard at me. "What the hell are you talking about?"

"I know it was you," I said, though I wasn't one hundred per cent certain. "Make a point of assaulting citizens in your line of work, do you?"

I stepped towards him. He didn't flinch. The only expression on his face was one of contemptuous anger.

Felix put a hand on my arm, and I understood it probably wasn't a good idea to antagonize him any further if we wanted to help Ashad. Both my fists were balled. I took a step back, wondering where Merrick was, if she had heard anything of this.

Felix handed Byrnes a sheaf of papers and explained that, among other things, they contained notification that Ashad was to be released within twenty-four hours unless formal charges were to be made against him.

Byrnes didn't even bother to look at them. He was still glaring at me.

I had a feeling that Merrick wasn't going to show. She didn't want us to know she was there.

"Ashad needs his inhaler," I said, pulling it from my pocket and showing it to him. To all appearances it looked like an ordinary asthma pump.

"No chance," Byrnes said.

"It's just an inhaler."

"He didn't say anything about being an asthmatic."

"He's a proud man. He's not going to admit to any weakness."

"Forget it."

"Are you denying us lawful access?" Felix asked. "And the provision of essential medication?"

"There could be anything in that gadget," Byrnes said. "Maybe something to fake a heart attack so that you can get him out by ambulance."

I put the inhaler to my mouth, pressed it and took a deep gulp. It was like swallowing an icy fog.

"See?" I said to Byrnes, stifling a cough. "It's just a medicine."

He tossed Felix's papers on to the desk as if they were of no concern to him.

Felix was unruffled. "Among those documents is a restraining order preventing my client from being moved over the next twenty-four hours. I'll need your signature to confirm that you received it."

"No way." Byrnes was furious. "You're in deep over your head here."

"Really? How, precisely?"

"I don't have to explain myself to you. We're dealing with issues of national and international security that go way beyond local legal niceties."

"Is that so? Then I regret to throw a bureaucratic spanner into the works, but what alternative do I have? I work for Mr Husseyin, not the British or American governments. I'm charged with protecting his interests and I intend to carry out that duty. Which is why I've instructed my office to take immediate action and contact the CPS in the event of non-compliance with our legitimate requests. That's the Crown Prosecution Service, in case you're not familiar with it. As it happens, the Director of Public Prosecutions is an old friend of mine."

Byrnes was growing increasingly rankled by Felix's suave brand of sarcasm. "Do you think you can voodoo me with those upper-crust tactics? I'm not signing anything."

"I'm afraid you have no choice in the matter, especially since you haven't explained to us why you're holding him here. This isn't an official detention facility, is it? I gather the premises were formerly occupied by the local water board. I've asked one of my assistants at the office to establish whether they're absentee landlords who are aware that you're using it."

Felix was holding out a fountain pen. Byrnes, looking as if he might explode at any second, snatched it from him and began leafing hurriedly through the documents.

"Do be careful with the nib," Felix said in a tone that was both agreeable and patronizing. "It's a Montblanc. Leather and sterling silver. A twenty-first birthday gift from my grandmother. I'm rather attached to it."

Byrnes scrawled his name at the bottom of one of them and thrust the pen back at him. To me he said, "Open up that bag."

I set it down on the desk and unzipped it. It contained socks, a change of underwear, and the floppiest sweatshirt and jogging pants that I could find in my wardrobe. Both were grey fleece. Ashad would hate them, but they were the only clothing of mine that had the remotest chance of fitting him.

Byrnes went through every item, pulling out each one and shaking it down before discarding it, checking all the nooks and crannies of the bag. Either Merrick or the guy with the moustache had been with him when he had burgled my place. It had looked like a man, but maybe Merrick had dressed for the occasion. She had kept herself hidden, sneaked out of there when Byrnes and I were on the street. She had been betraying us from the start.

Byrnes rammed everything back in the bag but still didn't look satisfied.

"And now I really must insist on seeing my client," Felix said.

"You're sticking your nose in a beehive."

"How unfortunate for me," Felix replied heedlessly. "Still, I see no reason for you to obstruct us further."

Byrnes turned his glare back on me. "Not him," he said. "He's not legal counsel. He stays here with Alvarez."

This was evidently the name of the moustachioed man, who had retreated into a corner of the room and was actually smirking, as if he had enjoyed watching Felix get the better of Byrnes.

I couldn't see any point in arguing because I wanted to be sure that Ashad saw at least one of us. I was about to hand the bag and the inhaler to Felix when a car started up outside. Abruptly Byrnes turned solicitous, saying, "No, forget it, it'll be easier if it's both of you," and actually putting a hand on the middle of my back to propel me gently towards the corridor.

I knew at once that this sudden change of heart was just a manoeuvre, and I thought I knew why.

"Is it all right for me to let him have the inhaler?" I asked as a delaying tactic.

"I'm giving you five minutes max," he said angrily. "Are you going in or not?"

I shuffled forward obediently. But as we passed a window I glimpsed a car reversing quietly out of one of the parking spaces, a silver Vauxhall Vectra.

Byrnes clearly hadn't wanted me to see it and I let him hustle me forward, keeping my expression resolutely blank. Was it Merrick making her escape to avoid having to explain to Felix what she was doing here? Did she know that it was me accompanying him rather than a nameless associate? I was pretty sure she hadn't actually seen me, but she might have overheard me talking and recognized my voice.

Ashad was locked up in a windowless room towards the far end of the building opposite the toilet facilities. Still wearing the tie-dyed top and combat fatigues in which he had been arrested, he sat slouched at a table littered with KFC wrappers and empty drinks cartons. What bothered me most was that his defeated-looking expression didn't alter when Byrnes ushered us into the room. When I grabbed his hand he barely responded beyond nodding dolefully. Did he know that Merrick had betrayed him?

Byrnes lingered until Felix insisted on privacy. He withdrew without great protest but loitered just outside the door, pacing up and down on the squeaky floor as if to leave us in no doubt that if we could hear him, he could hear us too.

An electric wall heater filled the room with a sickly heat, a bare neon strip providing a stark light. A portable TV without a plug sat in one corner and in the other was a tubular metal bed that wouldn't have been out of place in a prison cell. Motoring and golf magazines were scattered on the floor, two things in which Ashad had no interest whatsoever. He looked bleary, his hair more tousled than ever, a two-day growth of black stubble on his chin.

"Have they done anything to you?" I asked him.

"Like what?"

"I don't know. Roughed you up in any way?"

He just shook his head. "What the hell's going on? No one's telling me anything."

"Who have you seen?" I asked gently.

"Just the two tossers who drove the van."

So Merrick hadn't made herself known to him. I couldn't see what purpose it would serve tell Ashad about her treachery other than to confirm all his worst suspicions about authority figures and probably depress him even further. But I was disappointed that she had proved even more devious than I had imagined.

"They still haven't brought any charges against you," Felix told him. "We'll have you out in twenty-four hours."

I said nothing to contradict this, but I had good reasons for not sharing Felix's confidence.

"Did the guy in charge here say who he was?" I asked Ash.

He shook his head. "They came for me in the middle of the night. I was fast asleep. They handcuffed me, bundled me into the back of a van and drove me here. I was yelling all the way, but the pair of them just sat in the front with Classic FM turned right up."

I let Felix explain the situation before telling Ashad that Byrnes was the man who had burgled my flat. Ashad received this news solemnly, without his usual vocal indignation. He really was subdued.

"I've brought you a change of clothes," I told him, dumping the holdall on the table and pulling out the items.

Ashad looked at them and removed the socks, jockey shorts and T-shirt only. He shook his head at the rest.

I stuffed the sweatshirt and jogging pants back in the bag and said, "I brought the inhaler for your asthma, too."

I widened my eyes theatrically as I told him this while scribbling on a Post-It note pad which I held up for him:

Immunisation against the prison plague. Say thank you.

"Thank you."

I tore the sheet off and scribbled again:

One puff gives a week's protection. Do it now.

Ashad put the inhaler to his mouth, pressed it and gulped. The vapour caught in his throat and he began coughing.

"What's going on in there?" Byrnes demanded through the door.

"Ashad's just taking his medication," I called back while scribbling:

Keep it safe!

Ashad promptly stowed the inhaler in his fatigues.

"You've got two minutes," Byrnes announced.

I let Felix take over, explaining all the legal pressures he was bringing to bear to secure Ashad's release. There was no time to fill him in on anything else because Byrnes flung the door open and stalked in, saying, "It's time."

Ashad didn't raise a murmur of protest; he just looked at Byrnes with a kind of vacant fury. I wondered if they were drugging his food, or had put some other pressure to bear on him which he hadn't been able to discuss with me. More likely he was simply exhausted from being cooped up in various cells.

"I'll be back," I told him as we stood in the doorway.

He just looked at me as if he wasn't sure he believed it.

While Felix had a further discussion with Byrnes about the legality of Ashad's incarceration, Alvarez escorted me back to the Bentley.

As we passed the jetty I said, "You planning on shipping him out to Halstow Island from here?"

He squinted at me. "I don't know what you mean."

"Of course you do. It's all wrong, you know."

"He's a terrorist suspect," he said with a confidence that I thought was brittle.

"Is that what Byrnes told you?"

He didn't reply to this.

"We make films. That's what we do. Ashad's no more a terrorist than I'm the Sugar Plum Fairy." I let him digest this. "Why is Byrnes so interested in Leo Parrish?"

Alvarez kicked a discarded Pepsi can out of his path. "We don't discuss our operations with outsiders."

"He hasn't explained it to you, has he?"

"I work on a need to know basis. And a lot of what I know, you don't."

"So enlighten me. Do I look like someone in league with the guys who want to destroy Western civilisation?"

He smiled. He was young, and beneath his service training, perhaps still retained a trace of idealism.

"None of this is remotely funny, you know."

He shrugged. "I'm just doing my job. It's a good cause. Trying to keep the world safe from threats."

"Well, I wouldn't disagree with you that it's an important task. As long as you know who the enemy really is."

We walked up to the gap in the boundary fence, the Bentley sitting just beyond it. Felix was still standing on the forecourt, talking to Byrnes, but he must have been watching us because he pipped the car locks.

Alvarez started inspecting it with some relish. I guessed that the motoring magazines in Ashad's room had come from him.

"I want to be clear about this," I said to him. "Ashad's arrest has nothing to do with Leo Parrish."

"He was in possession of sensitive documentation," he replied.

"Nothing to do with Leo Parrish," I repeated.

"Not directly, no. Is this an automatic?"

"Take a look for yourself," I told him, opening the driver's door. "I've heard rumours that Parrish is a big fish up on Capitol Hill."

"News to me."

"You were told something different? He's still alive, I take it?"

Once again I was fishing. Though I didn't doubt that the newspaper report was genuine, I had begun to wonder if there was perhaps *another* Leo Parrish, or if the entire story had been fabricated for mysterious reasons.

Alvarez just shrugged. "No idea." He stuck his head inside the car. "It's not Parrish they're worried about. It's the stories."

"Terrorists using them for their plots?"

He was peering around the car like Aladdin in the cave of the forty thieves. "Who told you that?"

"Your boss. Mr Byrnes."

He withdrew his head from the Bentley and looked at me. "OK."

This too glib. Was it what he hoped I'd think?

"But that's just the cover story, isn't it?"

"What do you mean?"

"You're only pretending the stories are being used by terrorists."

"No." He shook his head emphatically. "That's not true."

He didn't have a face that was capable of guile, and it was clear that he did believe in the codes story.

"There's got to be more to it than that," I insisted.

"Why?"

I shook my head. "It's just doesn't feel ... " I searched for a suitable word. "*Sufficient*."

I couldn't explain it any better than that. Alvarez just looked blank. He struck me as a decent guy, put in a situation where he hadn't been given all the information he was entitled to.

"Help me out here," I pleaded. "My friend's in trouble, and you've got it all wrong about him."

Alvarez gnawed on his moustache. Felix was walking up the track.

"Byrnes is a true believer, you know."

"What?"

"Evangelical. Thinks the world is heading for damnation." Suddenly he looked awkward, as if he felt he had said too much.

"You take care now," he said, and promptly jogged off down the track.

Felix was talking on his mobile as he approached. He cut the connection and climbed straight into the car. I got in beside him.

"I think we'll have him out of there by this time tomorrow," he said to me.

"Really?"

He started up the car. "Byrnes wouldn't or couldn't supply me with any official paperwork to show that Mr Husseyin's transfer to his custody has been properly authorized. They have no basis for holding him."

"There was someone else there with Byrnes," I told him. "DI Merrick. I thought she was helping us. Now it looks like she's working with Byrnes."

"Ah."

"If Special Branch are also involved in this, then what are our chances?"

Felix considered this without any hint of defeatism.

"The more we know," he said, "the more room it gives us for manoeuvre."

It was the best gloss he could put on things under the circumstances, but it wasn't much. I decided against voicing my suspicion that Byrnes might now move Ashad somewhere else. There was no telling what his next step might be. Especially with Merrick's collusion.

A little distance along I saw the silver Vectra, parked way off the track behind a line of straggly hawthorn. I would never have spotted it if I hadn't been looking.

We turned a corner at a fence and I asked Felix to pull over. Leaving the engine running, we got out and crept to the corner.

A few minutes later the Vectra pulled out of cover. It drove towards us, and I could clearly see Merrick at the wheel. We were about to scamper back to the Bentley and drive off when the Vectra turned down the track, heading through the gap in the fence back towards the shore.

One way or another Merrick would soon know from Byrnes that I had been there with Felix. The question was, did she know that I had also seen her too?

TWENTY

Felix took me for lunch to his gentleman's club off Piccadilly. It wasn't the stuffy, cigar-smelling enclave I had envisaged but a bright airy place of stripped floorboards with a wrought-iron conservatory full of ferns and palms at its rear. We sat on the balcony above a leafy courtyard, Felix sipping a Pimm's, me trying to behave myself with a lime and soda. You could barely hear the traffic.

"So this is how the other half live," I said to him, looking around at the scattering of members, who mostly comprised Bright Young Things in chinos and boat shoes rather than venerable old buffers ensconced in armchairs.

"Family membership," Felix told me. "It's convenient. A bit of an oasis."

"The Nancarrows are estimable, are they?"

"Oh yes," he said without a trace of pretension. "Cornish, originally. Porthleven. My grandfather traced us back to the sixteen hundreds, but then it all gets a bit murky. Family rumour is that we had a windfall after a Spanish galleon was wrecked off Lizard Point."

"Very exotic."

"Yourself?"

"My grandfather ran a market stall in Deptford. That's about as far back as we go. My dad had ambitions to be an architect. He worked in the Housing Department for Lambeth Council."

Felix smiled. "Where would we be without merchants and home builders?"

"So how come you're helping out proles like me and Ash rather than keeping the peace for errant aristocrats or highly-strung celebrities who like to slap their maids around?"

"Black sheep of the family. I've been known to vote Monster Raving Looney. Just mentioning the words 'redistribution of wealth' was enough to cause a family scandal. I was threatened with excommunication."

"You believe in it? The redistribution of wealth?"

"It's worth a try, done with proper British moderation."

"It would probably mean an end to this sort of exclusivity."

He raised his glass as if in a toast. "All the more reason to make the most of it while I can."

Ashad was never far from my mind as we talked, but we had discussed all we could about his current situation and there was no point in raking over it again. I had set my mobile on the table, wondering if Merrick would call or text, and what she would say. So far there had been nothing.

A young waiter brought a couple of club sandwiches to our table. We ordered more drinks. The truth was, I was relieved to have the opportunity for some respite in a haven like this. Visiting Ash and seeing him so deflated had left me feeling more concerned for his immediate future than ever. Felix hadn't actually seen Byrnes at his most threatening. Who knew what he might do next?

Halfway through my sandwich my phone started throbbing. I had left it on mute not to disturb the patrons.

It was Rhodri Davies.

"Breaking news," he said excitedly to me. "Word is out that a new story by You-Know-Who is going to be posted on a website Real Soon Now."

"What?"

"First one in half a century."

"You're kidding me. I thought he gave it up years ago." This was all very unexpected, and confusing. "I thought he was supposed to be dead."

"When has that ever stopped anyone? Think Robert Ludlum and Virginia Andrews. The books kept coming long after they were corpses. Of course this is a bit more modest. The site's called *A Disturbance in the Ether*."

Rhodri was cheerful. He loved any whiff of intrigue.

"When you say 'new', do you mean 'new' as in 'newly discovered' or 'new' as in 'newly written'?"

"The second one. At least that's how it's being advertised. By the Man Himself, allegedly. It even has a message from him."

"Saying what?"

"Hello. It's good to be back."

"You're having me on."

"I promise you," Rhodri insisted.

"Is that it? It sounds like Gary bloody Glitter."

He was keen to let me see the site for myself and suggested I follow the link he had sent. Then he rang off.

I brought it up on my screen. Felix dragged his chair around so that he could see what was coming up.

The welcome page had a starry night sky with *A DISTURBANCE IN THE ETHER* billowing out in wispy white lettering like glowing gas from an exploded star. A subtitle at the bottom said: *A blast from the past*.

I tapped on the ENTER icon and got the Gary Glitter message on the same background in the same vaporous lettering. Then the words slowly dissolved, were replaced by: *Remember me?*

The screen faded to white before images began to emerge out of it. Gradually they resolved themselves into three black-and-white photographs.

One showed a young boy in denim dungarees holding a toy metal rocket of 1950s vintage. A second was a blurry distance shot of a young man flying a kite in a field. The third was a slightly more formal head-and-shoulders portrait of a man who was probably in his early thirties, staring slightly dreamily off-camera. He wore longish hair, mutton-chop sideburns and a print-shirt with a rounded collar that looked early 1970s. Underneath was a stippled effect legend like a colour-blindness card. You had to squint to decipher it. It said:

Three faces of Leo Parrish

The first two pictures could have been of anyone, but there was no doubt that the face on the third matched the one in Walter Suthersen's photograph. It was slightly fleshier, the hair worn longer in concession to the prevailing fashion, but definitely the same man a dozen or so years on.

I tapped CONTINUE and the pictures faded and were replaced by a chattering teleprinter-style message in red sans serif:

To celebrate the half-centenary of my last published work, a brand new story will appear here soon. To all my loyal fans, thanks for waiting! Look to the heavens!

This last line was a recurring phrase in *Exaltation*. There was nothing further. I backtracked to take another look at the photos. The young boy could possibly have been Parrish as a child but you couldn't have said with certainty. The kite-flier was just too far off to be discerned in any detail. But there was no mistaking Leo Parrish in the third.

I worked through the whole thing again before closing it down and calling Rhodri back.

"It's an American site," he told me.

"*A Disturbance in the Ether*. Kind of suggests he wants to make waves."

"It's not one I've ever encountered before."

"It's a bit flashy and melodramatic, don't you think? Not exactly the man's style, I wouldn't have thought. If he's still alive he must be in his seventies. I'd have expected something more ... well, sedate."

"He could have got some zippy young web designer to do it for him."

"I suppose so. Do you think it's pukka?"

"I very much doubt it. At least, I don't believe it's being written by the man himself, though it's obviously been done by someone who has some knowledge of him."

"Because of the photos?"

"No one I know has ever seen any of them before."

"One of them is definitely him."

Rhodri made an affirmative noise. "It might have come from a personnel file. Maybe from the records of the hospital where he worked. But putting photos like that on your site is a bit like protesting too much, don't you think?"

My thoughts were running along a slightly different track.

"This isn't a wind-up, is it?"

"Not by me," Rhodri insisted. "And not, I think, by whoever's doing it. More in the way of a provocation."

"A nice distinction. Any idea who it might be?"

"Not a clue. The possibilities are more numerous than you might imagine. Our man has a small but vocal core of fans who might be wanting to stir things up just for the hell of it. Especially since I've been dropping hints in my bulletins about all the trouble lying in wait for anyone who shows an interest in him."

"Like me, you mean?"

"Don't worry, I didn't name names. The other possibility is that it's someone else entirely who wants to raise a smokescreen."

"Like who?"

"One of the Bad Guys."

I considered this. "Everyone I've encountered seems to want to keep Parrish under wraps, not announce him with a big fanfare."

"Don't mention the war," he said hastily, and I realized he was cautioning me against using Parrish's actual name. "Maybe we'll find out sooner rather than later. I think it's been deliberately timed to coincide with the Worldcon."

The Miami convention was due to start at the weekend and would run for the best part of a week.

"I'm flying out in a couple of days," Rhodri told me. "Maybe I'll even get to meet the Man Himself, risen from the grave. Keep watching your phone for a photo of us shaking hands."

"I'm almost tempted to come myself."

"It could be more than usually interesting. Rumour is, Edgar Eldridge is going to be there."

"Now I know you're having me on."

"I swear. Well, I swear it's a real rumour. No one believes it's going to happen, though his lot will be out in force. They've got their story competition to publicize, and they'll probably be trying to rustle up more finance for their wondrous movie."

"Does this sub-culture of yours operate entirely on speculation and hearsay?"

"Meat and drink. Your friend out of jail yet?"

"Don't ask." I really didn't want to discuss it. "I'll let you know if there are any developments."

"Likewise." He rang off.

Felix was looking at me calmly.

"This man Parrish is something of an enigma," he observed.

"Like a poltergeist," I suggested. "Making things go bump in the night."

*

I decided to walk back to the office and phone Claire on the way to find out if she knew about the website. I rang her work number, but a female receptionist I hadn't spoken to before told me she was on a day off.

I tried her mobile, wanting to avoid having to speak to her mother at home in case she decided to interrogate me about my intentions toward Claire.

"Yes?"

It was Claire's voice, but extremely guarded.

"It's Nick," I told her.

"Hi."

She couldn't have put less greeting into the word.

"Are you all right?"

There was a pause before she said, "We've been getting calls. On the landline. I'm jumpy about answering any phone."

"Calls? What sort of calls?"

"Malicious ones, Nick. Whispery voices, warning us, threatening to do us harm. Threatening to burn us alive in the house."

"Bloody hell." A blaze of outrage ignited in me. "Are Daniel and your mother with you?"

"Yes. I've been fending the calls. I haven't told them."

"Did you phone the police?"

"I've tried before, when it happened the last time. We moved here to escape it, but they've found us again." She paused; I could almost hear her trying to gather her composure. "It's been going on since the early hours of this morning. I can't have them being exposed to it. My mother's frail."

"Of course not. Did they say who they were?"

"They're not going to identify themselves, are they? They're cowards. Robotic, as if they're reading from a prepared script."

"Saying what exactly?"

"That we should stop meddling, go into permanent seclusion, live in a cave where we can't bother anyone."

"What do they mean by that?"

"That's what I kept asking them! I was yelling down the phone. They wouldn't give me an answer, just kept telling me that we'd be safer if we just vanished off the face of the earth."

Her anger was a good sign, an indication that she wasn't capitulating to the threats. I wondered if the calls had anything to do with the new website, and whether she knew about its existence. These were questions I needed to ask her face to face.

"I'm coming over," I told her.

I expected her to try to fob me off, but she didn't.

"Give me half an hour," I said, going to the kerbside and hailing my second taxi in as many days.

I phoned Jamilla en route to let her know I wouldn't be back that afternoon.

"What's happening with Uncle Ash?" she asked.

"Felix thinks we'll have him out in the next few days," I said, with a dispiriting sense of not telling her the whole truth.

"Is he all right?"

"Well, he's pretty fed up and frustrated, as you might imagine. But I'm sure he'll be released soon."

Technically I wasn't lying to her but I knew I was accentuating the positive against my worst suspicions. When she rang off I felt shabby.

The cabbie dropped me off right outside Claire's house. I walked down the gravel path to her front door.

She came out on to the steps before I even got there. She had the cordless home phone tucked into her jeans pocket, presumably so that no one else in the house could answer it.

I put my arms around her and gave her a hug.

She tensed for an instant, and then relaxed, her hands creeping up to grasp the back of my jacket, balling it in her fists. It was a nice moment.

"You must be exhausted," I said after I had milked it for as long as I could.

"I'm too rattled to feel tired."

We went inside, straight along the rug-lined hallway, past good-sized rooms full of smart modern furniture and tasteful prints, to the bright, spacious kitchen at the rear. An extensive patio overlooked a large garden, lawns and flowerbeds extending to a round-topped hedge with an arch screening the lower reaches, a substantial greenhouse off to the side of the house.

She put the kettle on before taking me outside to meet her son and grandmother. The sun had burnt away the earlier cloud, and I could smell the odour of the box hedge as we walked through the archway.

Nora and Daniel were beyond the arch in one of the vegetable patches that extended to the bottom of the garden. Nora was sitting next to a potting shed in a canvas director's chair, supervising Daniel, who was crouched amongst a row of brassicas.

"I think they've gone to seed, nan," I heard him say to her.

"They're purple-sprouting broccoli," she retorted somewhat tetchily. "They're supposed to look like that. Check under the leaves."

Claire introduced me. Nora stood up carefully as if she was meeting royalty, using a knobbled polished walking stick to support her, giving my hand a surprisingly firm shake. She was a handsome woman who wore her age well, and there was something familiar about her. Then it came to me: she was the same person who had been asleep in the playroom at the film festival when I had first met Claire.

"Did you know that President Bush hated broccoli?" she said to me.

Not a question I had been expecting.

"Would that be junior or senior?" I asked.

"The father. That son of his was a disgrace to the Constitution."

Though her accent was muted by years of living in England, she spoke in the brisk no-nonsense style of a New Yorker and seemed much more alert than when I had spoken to her on the phone.

"They can lurk anywhere, you know," she told me.

"Really?" was all I could think of to say in reply.

"You don't know what I'm talking about, do you?"

"Terrorists?" I hazarded.

"Caterpillars."

Daniel, looking slightly abashed, offered me a soil-smeared hand.

"My mum's been saying nice things about you," he told me with a self-conscious smile.

"Is that so? Well, I think she's pretty great, too. And she reckons you're the bee's knees."

He laughed and blushed. There was a certain gawkiness about him that was quite endearing.

"Is he your new man?" Nora blurted.

"Mother!" Claire was mortified. "He's the film maker I told you about."

Nora abruptly sat back down again. "Are you going to offer him something to drink?"

"I'm making tea. Do you want one?"

"Not that Earl Grey," she said, flapping at a passing cabbage white. "It's like drinking deodorant."

Claire and I wandered back into the house.

"She's quite a character," I observed.

"Sometimes she is," Claire replied. "It comes and goes. I think it's partly to do with her medication."

"She's sick?"

"She had a minor stroke a few years back. It can take her a while to remember things."

She clicked the electric kettle on again, putting the phone down on the worktop as if it was an unexploded bomb which she preferred not to carry unless it was absolutely vital.

"Do you think it's the Ascendants ringing?" I asked.

"I'd lay odds on it."

"You pissed off Kubilius mightily at the convocation. They're probably just trying to get their own back with a bit of mindless aggravation."

I could tell it was something she had already considered. "They don't like it when they're challenged. But whoever's doing it is very careful not to say anything specific."

"Is it just one person?"

"I can't be sure. They go for a spooky hoarse-voiced effect."

"Male voices?"

She nodded. "I'd make sure their throats were *really* sore if I could get my hands on them."

"Did you try 1471?"

"The number was withheld."

She put a couple of teabags into a white china teapot.

"It might be to do with this new website," I said.

She just frowned. "What website?"

"The one promising a new Leo Parrish story?"

The look of surprise on her face was unrehearsed. I described the site to her. It was plain she didn't have any idea of its existence.

She fetched a laptop from one of the front rooms and set it up on the kitchen table. While it churned through its start-up routines Claire made the tea and got a can of Coke out of the fridge for Daniel. I copied the website address from my mobile into the computer's browser and hit Return.

Scant seconds later we got a stark message on a plain white field that said: *ADDRESS NOT FOUND*

There was no explanation, no indication of who had posted the message.

I tried again, with the same result. The same thing happened when I attempted to access the site on my phone.

"It was there an hour ago," I assured her. "Rhodri Davies put me onto it."

"It's impossible," Claire said, but not as though she disbelieved me. "There can't be a new story. He's dead."

So she wasn't changing her position on that. I had no reason to think she was lying about it: she was adamant.

"It could have been someone pretending to be him," I pointed out.

"Who?"

"I was hoping you might have some idea."

"How would I know?" she said with renewed anger. "Why won't they leave us alone? Why is my uncle so important to them?"

"You've no idea?"

"I can't even remember him. He's just a face in a photograph album. It's as if he's haunting us."

Something occurred to me.

"Have you had any calls in the past hour or so? Anonymous ones, I mean."

She considered for a second, shook her head.

"Maybe they've gone quiet because the site's been shut down."

*

Claire insisted I stay for dinner. There had been no more calls that afternoon and I wondered if she had begun to see my presence as a kind of talisman that would ward them off. Which was fine by me. Daniel was ostensibly keeping an eye on Nora in the garden, and while in reality it was probably the reverse, the arrangement suited me perfectly since it gave me more time alone with Claire.

We sat out on the patio in the sunshine. I told her about Ashad's continuing predicament, about our visit to the Crossness site, my tasering and Cyrus Hammond coming to my rescue. I didn't mention Cyrus's claim that he was keeping a protective eye on her, but I wanted to see what her reaction would be.

"What was he doing at your place?" she asked.

To hear her asking this question with apparent innocence gave me confidence that she and Hammond weren't secretly in league with one another.

"He must have been following me," I said. "Or following the madman who attacked me."

Her hand found mine. "Aren't you scared he might try it again?"

"Of course I am. But I'm not ready to give up yet. Especially on you and your elusive uncle. Is Cyrus a close friend of the family?"

She looked at me. "Why would you say that?"

"Well, the connection with the *Nightscapes* story. The fact that he introduced me to you and told me about your uncle's work."

She took this on board. "I just think he feels Leo was unfairly neglected as a writer. I see him occasionally at film events or art shows. He's always friendly, but not in a creepy way."

There was no point in revealing that it was Cyrus who had followed us home from Slough: it wasn't something she needed to hear at this particular moment.

"I thought it was odd that he should be on hand when I needed him," I said. "I'm grateful he was, of course. Has he ever said anything to you about what his job entails?"

She thought about it. "I always assumed he was just someone involved in the film and television business. But it can't be just that, can it?"

I shook my head.

"Then what?"

"I wish I knew." There really was no point in spooking her further by saying that Cyrus might be some kind of government agent.

"It wasn't him ringing," she announced. "I think I would have recognized his voice. But it might have been an American. I thought I heard a trace of an accent."

Byrnes, I thought. But then again, it might have been someone from the Ascendancy hierarchy. Or Alvarez. Or Walter Suthersen. Or someone I had never even heard of or met in the flesh.

"Some people believe that your uncle's stories predict the future," I remarked.

This was perhaps overstating it a little but I wanted to see how she reacted. I could tell from her look that it wasn't the first time she had heard this.

"Judging by the ones I've read," I went on, "I'd have to say that he was pretty prescient about a few things."

"Like what?"

"Hand-held electronic devices," I said, thinking back to the stories. "Climate change. Maybe even the creation of the Church of the Ascendancy."

"What?"

"I read the first part of *Exaltation*. It's all in there."

She looked angry at the mention of the Church. "If they think my uncle was some kind of prophet, then why do they keep harassing us?"

It was a fair point. "So you don't give any credence to the idea?"

"To what idea?"

"That your uncle had some kind of window on the future. That his stories are actually visions of what was to come."

It sounded ridiculous even as I was saying it.

"He wasn't like that," she replied. "According to my mother, he was just an ordinary man, Brooklyn born and bred. He hardly ever left the borough. I think he was probably just a very lucky guesser."

"You've read all his work?"

"Pretty much all the published stories, but not the novel. Though you can never be sure how many he wrote. There were a lot of small fly-by-night magazines out there."

Daniel appeared from the vegetable garden, telling us that Nora was asleep in the shade. He would sit with her until she woke.

"He's a very decent lad," I remarked to Claire. "Does he know about any of this?"

"Not this latest stuff. I try to keep him out of it as much as possible, but we've had this sort of harassment before and I'm sure he knows something's going on."

"You mentioned an album, family photographs. Any chance I could see them?"

She just gave me a curious look.

"There were three photos on the website," I told her. "I wanted to see if any of them matched."

She looked half-amused, half-incredulous. "You think it was me?"

"No, that wasn't what I was implying. It could be anyone. But it might be useful to know if they match any that you have here."

She thought this over. "My mother keeps the albums locked in a bureau in her bedroom. I'll ask her when she wakes."

She stiffened. Inside the house the phone had started ringing.

It turned out to be a friend of Daniel's called Toby who was calling to invite him out later that evening to a party in Richmond, to which Claire gave her assent. I phoned Felix to check for news on Ashad but he was in a meeting with another client. Claire gave me a brief tour of the downstairs of the house excepting one room, which was locked because the house's owner used it for storage.

Above the mantelpiece in the dining-room hung a triptych of pictures: a shingle beach with offshore forts at sunset, empty chairlifts hanging on a moonlit alpine landscape, a waterfall glimpsed through a web of power lines. They looked like digitally-edited photographs, their off-kilter colours giving them a mysterious, otherworldly air.

"I like them," I remarked, eyeing her. "Are they yours?"

"Guilty," she admitted.

"They're good. Have you sold any?"

"Not exactly. It's the 'rent' we pay our landlord."

"Oh? I hope he's not as weird as our landlord."

The place wasn't the usual furnished rental accommodation: it was someone's well-heeled home. But Claire didn't volunteer any more. I wondered anew why she was so guarded about certain aspects of her life. I didn't press it for fear of stiffening her defences.

"So are your uncle's archives upstairs?"

"In the attic," she told me. "Guarded by a three-headed, demonic dog."

"I'd be interested to have a look."

I had left the second part of *Exaltation* in the secure cabinet at the office. Because of the tasering I hadn't got around to reading it, but it was possible Claire might have a copy here.

At this point Daniel hurried in from the garden.

"Nan's just woken," he announced. "She says her legs aren't working."

It turned out to be a false alarm, Nora having temporarily forgotten the extra effort needed to get out of a canvas chair. We shepherded her into the living room and Claire settled her in an armchair with a book while we readied dinner. She was reading a paperback called *The Lunar Men*.

We ate roasted vegetables and cous cous on the patio in the warmth of the evening. Nora had awoken somewhat disorientated, and her first question on seeing me was to ask if I was the new gardener. During dinner she resolutely refused to join in the conversation beyond complaining about being bothered by midges, though occasionally I caught her peering at me as if she was trying to remember who I was. Daniel was more animated, especially at the prospect of going out that evening. Claire reluctantly conceded that he could stay overnight at Toby's on the condition that Toby's father not merely picked him up as already arranged but delivered him back safely in the morning.

We had just finished spooning down a stick-to-your-ribs summer pudding when the house phone rang again. Claire went inside to take it, and when she reappeared soon afterwards I could tell from her face that she was unnerved again.

I ushered her into the kitchen on the pretext of helping to wash up.

"Another malicious call?" I asked.

"I don't know." She pushed her hair back from her face, suddenly looking exhausted. "No one said anything. It was silent, and then they just put the phone down." She looked at me. "It could easily have been a wrong number. I'm so strung out I just froze."

I pulled her to me. She was trembling. I just held her and she went limp against me, her breaths so deep they were like sighs.

"If it rings again," I said, "I'll pick it up."

"Will you stay here tonight?" she asked. "I can make up a bed in the spare room."

I drew back so that I could look her in the face. "Are you sure?"

"You can read yourself to sleep with the second part of *Exaltation*. If we can find it."

"We?"

"I'm not going up in the attic on my own. That three-headed dog bites."

"I'll chuck him a biscuit."

"I'm assuming it's there, but I don't know for sure. Until recently I didn't even know it existed."

"Didn't your mother tell you about it?"

"Why would she? It's a part of her life she'd rather forget. Believe me, it's hard to get her to reminisce about my uncle at the best of times. She's convinced he was killed because of something he wrote."

A little chill went through me. "She told you that?"

"Only once. She said, 'It's the words that did the killing'. I've never forgotten that."

TWENTY-ONE

"So," I said to Nora as we sat over coffee in the living room, "*The Lunar Men*—is it about space flight? Astronauts?"

She looked at me as if I was an idiot, putting the paperback down on her lap.

"The Enlightenment," she said brusquely, unhooking her reading glasses and letting them hang from the strap at her neck. "Erasmus Darwin, James Watt, Josiah Wedgwood. You've heard of them?"

I nodded with a mixed degree of confidence.

"They were insatiably curious about the world. What is it you're doing here?"

Her conversation had a habit of veering off in an unexpected direction. Which was to my advantage at this moment since I had been trying to find a way to broach the subject of her brother. Claire was in the kitchen, Daniel upstairs getting ready for his evening out.

"Well, I'm rather fond of your daughter," I began in as civilized a tone as I could muster. "We've met a few times, and I enjoy her company."

She was now staring hard at me, a strong-featured woman who at that particular moment looked extremely alert and focused.

"There's more to it than that," she said adamantly. "It's Leo, isn't it?"

I didn't mind admitting it with a nod.

"They always want to know about him," she said, looking from me to the big flat-screen TV in the corner, which she had insisted Claire put on with the volume off. A group of young people were haphazardly slouched on sofas in a large room, apparently having an argument with one another.

"In the future," she remarked, "historians won't be leafing through court rolls and dusty manuscripts. They'll be watching this."

I had a feeling it was an episode of *Big Brother*.

"Assuming there is a future," I said, just to be provocative.

Her gaze turned back to me, but it was clear she wasn't interested in having a debate about the matter.

"There's nothing much I can tell you," she remarked. "It's all in the stories. Are you the one who wants to make a film of them?"

"Possibly," I said. "I think his work is really interesting. Cinematic."

"I can't allow that."

I had the sense of a door abruptly slamming in my face. This wasn't what I had been expecting.

Claire came in just at that moment with a box of after-dinner mints. She put them down on the table, giving me a quick glance but saying nothing.

"It was a long time ago," Nora said, gazing at the screen again. "They won't let him rest in peace. Has my daughter told you that?"

She was looking at me again. "Yes," I said. "It must have been terrible, seeing him shot in front of you."

Her eyes went glassy, but her expression didn't change. "We were always close. He would do anything for me. I'd like to say there's not a day that passes when I don't think of him, but when you get old you forget to remember." She fondled the handle of her walking stick. "Have you ever seen anyone killed, Mr Randall?"

So she had remembered my name. Or had she known it all along?

"No," I said softly.

"That young man was deranged. I often wonder what became of him. It's such a stupid thing. Such a waste. No one deserves to have their life ended like that."

Claire was looking startled, and I had the feeling that she hadn't heard her mother talk so frankly about the killing before, at least not to a relative stranger.

"Perhaps he deserves some sort of memorial," I suggested. "A movie might bring his work to a wider audience. If we could find the right story."

She had the intense stare going again and was squinting at me, as though my face was a picture she couldn't quite get in focus.

"I used to sit next to him at the kitchen table, watching him type. He had an old Imperial from the 1940s. A Good Companion. He always liked to get each page just right."

She fell silent. I waited, resisting the many questions I might have asked. This had to be on her terms.

"Nothing good ever came of them," she said. "And still they won't leave us alone." She glanced sharply at Claire. "Don't think I don't know why you've been hogging that telephone."

Claire didn't respond. Carefully I asked, "Who exactly are this 'they'?"

"Fanatics," she said bluntly. "They're all the same, whatever their gospel is." She was silent for a moment, as if deep in thought. "Do you know what Thoreau said? 'Beware of all enterprises that require new clothes.'"

I was going to have to think about that one, but I couldn't afford to let myself be sidetracked.

"My impression is that they want to hush you up, pretend that Leo Parrish never existed. I think you would be better off publicizing him rather than trying to hide his light."

She kept looking at me, and for a long time she didn't speak. Claire was sitting very still, deliberately not saying anything. Then Nora put her spectacles back on again, picked up her book and resumed reading.

"Is that it?" I said, trying to not betray my frustration. "Is that all you have to say on the subject?"

She didn't reply.

"I read part one of *Exaltation*. I'd really like to read the other half of it."

Her hands were now in constant motion, clasping and unclasping the edges of the book. She was frowning, her head beginning to nod like a slow-witted student struggling with a piece of mental arithmetic.

"I gather you've got a copy of the second part here," I persisted. "Could I read it?"

She started shaking her head, and closed her eyes as if that would blot out my voice. "I have nothing more to say," she told me angrily. "If you don't stop pestering me I'll have to insist you leave."

There was no mistaking her agitation. Claire went to her side, taking hold of her hands, stroking them and telling her that everything was all right.

"I'm sorry," I said to Claire, a little bewildered. "I didn't mean to upset her."

She looked sympathetic and shook her head as if to suggest that it wasn't my fault. On the tray was a little white plastic box containing her mother's various tablets. She proceeded to dole them out one by one. Nora took each with a sip of coffee, complaining not about the medication but her coffee, which was decaffeinated.

"You shouldn't be drinking coffee at all," Claire told her.

At this point the house phone started ringing from the kitchen. Claire froze. For long seconds no one moved or spoke. Nora was frowning resolutely at the television as if she couldn't hear anything.

"Do you mind if I get it?" I said, having conjured up a pretext. "I'm expecting a call from work. I told them I'd be here."

"Go ahead," Claire said with audible relief.

I went into the kitchen, picked up the phone and gingerly pressed the answer button, wondering what I might get. More whispered threats? Heavy breathing? A sinister unbroken silence?

"Dan?" said a youthful male voice. "That you?"

It was Toby, calling to let Daniel know that he and his father were on their way and would be arriving shortly. Daniel himself appeared in skinny jeans and a white shirt. I passed the phone over and headed back to the living room.

Pausing in the corridor outside the door, I heard Claire say, "He's just trying to help. He's not our enemy, you know."

"Was I rude?" Nora asked.

"No. Not exactly. But you were, well, a bit *abrupt*."

The temptation to loiter, to snoop on their conversation, was strong, but so was the knowledge that it would have been an abuse of their trust and hospitality. Instead I went up to the bathroom and spent a few minutes splashing water on my face and trying to make myself look spruce, a pretty futile task that would have required more dedication than I was capable of.

When I returned, Nora was dozing again; or at least her eyes were closed.

"She likes you," Claire mouthed at me without actually speaking

"Really?" I whispered back. "You could have fooled me."

I took an after-dinner mint from the box before perching myself on the arm of her chair. Leaning close to her, I whispered, "Is she worried I'm going to whisk you away? It's very tempting, you know."

"Stop flirting."

"Flirting implies a lack of seriousness. I'm in earnest."

A horn parped outside. I accompanied Claire to the front door with Daniel. I had expected to see Toby arrive in a flash car or four-by-four, but he and his dad were hanging out of the windows of a venerable white Mondeo, Toby plump and curly-haired, his father a burly man in rolled-up shirtsleeves that revealed muscular forearms.

Claire had a brief murmured conversation with him while Daniel climbed in the back. I suspected she was telling him about the threatening calls and asking him to keep Daniel safe. He nodded emphatically, telling her that the party was in their back garden, looking every inch the sort of guy under whose guardianship Daniel would be amply protected.

The car drove off. Claire turned to me and said, "She's agreed to let you have a look through Leo's archives."

I just stared at her. "Really?"

"I surprised myself by agreeing with what you said to her," she admitted. "I'm tired of us having to skulk around, of having to keep my uncle's work under wraps. Not that that's been very difficult. You're the first person in years to show an interest in doing something with it."

My sense of anticipation was tempered by the awareness that I shouldn't get carried away.

"I'm really keen," I assured her. "Of course, I can't guarantee anything. It depends on what we find."

"Understood. But allow me a little hope. Apart from anything else, we could use the money. What I earn doesn't go very far in supporting the three of us."

"Does Nora get a pension?"

Claire shook her head. "She's still a US citizen, and proud of it. She gets a monthly income of a few hundred pounds from some bonds, but money's always been tight."

More than ever I hoped that Parrish's novel would live up to the promise of its first part.

In the living room Nora was still sitting upright in her chair with her reading glasses on, but her head had fallen back and she was snoring softly.

Claire put a cushion under her neck, and then we crept up the stairs to the top of the house. She used an angled pole to unlock the hatch and pull down the loft ladder. I followed her up the squeaky steps.

The loft was fully boarded and a light switch had been mounted on one of the eaves, a single bulb providing a decent enough illumination that didn't quite penetrate the very corners of the roof space. Cardboard storage boxes were stacked along one wall, there were a couple of portable clothes rails with winter wear in zip-up protective bags, and some rolls of carpet on the floor. Near the overflow tank stood a three-drawer filing cabinet.

The drawers were unlocked, and the moment we opened them the characteristic fusty odour of ancient paper and print assailed my nostrils, the very essence of past time and the promise of long-forgotten treasures.

One drawer was full of paperwork: correspondence, postcards, fliers and pamphlets from Leo's youth. The second held the stories. They were stacked in hanging files, individually sealed in zipped plastic wallets. Claire confirmed that she had done this after their last move, to protect them from mildew. Each one was a carbon-copy of the original, painstakingly typed on yellowed American quarto, double-spaced, with the author's name and address on the first page. They had lived on Clarkson Avenue, in an apartment, Claire told me, with leaky plumbing and a temperamental air conditioner, though she had no memory of it herself.

From a dark corner Claire dragged out a collapsible camping table and a couple of fold-up stools. We heaved out the stories and began inspecting them. Some, like "Weather Warriors" I recognized, but there were others I had never heard of. Perhaps they had been published in issues of *Awesome Adventures* that I hadn't yet seen; perhaps they were ones that had never found a home: Claire didn't know since her mother's only concession to discussing them had been to allow her to store them in the wallets for preservation.

The temptation to unzip the wallets and read at least the first few paragraphs of each one was strong, but I knew I had to stay focused. We returned them to the drawer, still searching for *Exaltation*, me beginning to wonder if our quest was about to end in anticlimax.

I needn't have worried. In the bottom drawer there were more files. Here the wallets enfolded bulging brown manila envelopes, which Claire confessed she had bagged up in haste without paying much attention to the contents.

The very first wallet we removed turned out to contain the first part of *Exaltation*. The second held the other half. My face must have shown my delight because Claire said, "Who's a happy boy, then?"

I cupped my hands around her face and kissed her full on the lips. There was an instant's hesitation, or it might just have been surprise; then she just gave in to it.

When I broke the clinch, she gazed at me, smacked her lips and said, "That wasn't bad."

"I think I can improve. What I need is more practice."

She gave a crooked smile. This time she came forward and initiated the kiss. And then: "I have to confess you've got a certain dishevelled charm."

"You've got finger marks all over your cheeks," I told her. My hands were covered with dust from our rooting around.

"Where are you?" came a voice from downstairs. "What is this place?"

It was Nora, bewildered and alarmed.

Claire hurried down the ladder while I tidied everything away apart from the two halves of *Exaltation*. These I tucked under my arm before switching off the light and descending the steps. As I closed up the hatch I had a sense of returning Leo Parrish to the shadows where he had languished for half a century.

Nora was visibly distressed by the time I got downstairs. She looked at me without recognition, clutching Claire's hand while Claire gently manoeuvred her towards the stairs.

"She's woken up in a muddle," Claire whispered to me. "I'm going to get her bathed and ready for bed. Help yourself to a drink if you fancy one. They're in the cabinet in the dining room. Just make yourself at home."

There was a selection of spirits in the cabinet, including a bottle of Southern Comfort. I poured myself a generous glass and chucked in a few ice cubes. I was intending to settle down in an armchair with part two of *Exaltation*, but first I decided to check my phone. I had left it on mute in my jacket pocket on the hallway coat stand.

As I went down the passage I thought I saw a movement outside through the stained-glass panel of the front door. I wrenched the door open. A bird burst out of the tangle of ivy that overhung the doorway, chirruping in alarm as it fled into the dusk.

I wandered out a short distance, looking around the driveway, checking the pavement beyond. There was no one about. It was a tranquil evening, the last shreds of daylight lighting the horizon. I made sure the door was latched when I closed it behind me.

There was a text message from Felix, sent when I was up in the loft:

Call me when you get this.

I retrieved my drink from the kitchen table, already punching out his number. He picked up within a few rings.

"It's Nick," I said. "What's up?"

"Nick!" Felix was positively jolly. "Good news. He's out."

I put the drink back down on the table. "Out? Do you mean Ashad?"

"The very same."

I made him repeat the news, just to be sure. Ashad had indeed been released from custody.

"How?" I asked. "Can I speak to him?"

"He's not here at the moment. Our man Dyte phoned earlier to say that he had been delivered back to Westbourne Terrace and that they had no further basis for holding him. I didn't call you in case it turned out to be a false alarm, but they had him ready and waiting for me." Felix took a sip of something. "It was all sweetness and light. They even apologized for the inconvenience suffered to both of us."

I needed a few moments to process this. "Is he all right?"

"Buzzing like an angry bee. But no scars to show."

"Where is he?"

A pause; then: "Not something I particularly want to discuss over the phone, given everything you've told me. We're going to keep him somewhere safe overnight, until we're sure the dust has settled."

I knew better than to ask for details. "Who delivered him back to Dyte?"

"An American, they said. They didn't give a name."

"Byrnes?"

"I don't think so. I rather think it was his colleague. He didn't linger."

Alvarez. Byrnes had doubtless sent him rather than suffer the indignity of surrendering Ashad himself. Did Merrick know? Had she and Byrnes decided that the game was up because we had found out where they were holding him?

"I think we have a strong case for unlawful arrest," Felix remarked, sipping something again.

"Are you in the boozer?"

"We have dinner guests. I mustn't be long."

I picked up my own drink and took a mouthful. "What does Ashad say about pressing charges?"

"I have the strong impression he doesn't want anything to do with the law, even when it's on his side."

This was typical; Ashad preferred to fight his own battles. To him, the judiciary was just another enveloping arm of the octopus-like Establishment.

"When can I see him?"

"I'll be in touch first thing in the morning."

He rang off. Relief flooded through me. I finished my drink, made myself another. Upstairs the bath water was still running. Suddenly my mood was considerably lighter; suddenly it seemed as if all the things I wanted were starting to fall into place.

I picked up the manila envelope and carried it through into the front room with my drink.

*

By the time Claire eventually came back downstairs I had skim-read the second part of Parrish's novel. The story had positively rattled along, with plenty of twists and a rousing climax.

Claire was carrying a photograph album. Before she had fallen asleep, Nora had given Claire permission to show me the album.

There were family snaps of Leo and Nora covering their early years, some showing them together, others taken separately, right up to their teens. After this, the photos became sparser, showing Leo and Nora standing in front of a funfair ride, in tennis whites, in Sunday-best outfits at what might have been a wedding.

"I assume he had a full-time job when he was writing," I said. "And later."

Claire made an affirmative noise. "According to my mum, he was some kind of psychiatric case counsellor, working out of one of the local hospitals."

The *Brooklyn Daily Bulletin* had described him as a "health visitor", which was more or less a match. "Did he do house calls?"

"I think so."

"So he was out and about quite a bit?"

"He worked all sorts of hours."

"And fitted his writing around them?"

"I suppose so. It was years before I was born."

There was nothing especially noteworthy about any of the photographs. Although the young boy in the album bore a close resemblance to the one on the website, none showed him holding a toy rocket or as a young man flying a kite. I asked Claire if she remembered seeing either of the pictures. She shrugged, shook her head, told me that her mother had only ever taken the album out on rare occasions and it was perhaps ten years since she had last seen it.

Some of the mounts in the album had missing photographs.

"Do you think Nora might have removed them?" I asked.

She looked dubious. "I can't see why she would."

"Don't go mad at this suggestion," I said, "but is it humanly possible that Nora put the photos on the website?"

She laughed incredulously. "Why on earth would she do that?"

"I've no idea. I was just wondering—is she capable?"

Claire shook her head. "She can use a computer but she's never really got to grips with the technology. The only thing she ever does on ours is play solitaire."

She turned more pages. The adult photographs were mostly of Leo and Nora together, with relatively few of Leo alone. In one he was a young man standing outside a store front, holding a bulky acoustic guitar, identical to the man in the photograph that Walter Suthersen had sent. In another, taken some years later, he had fleshed out a little and was wearing bell-bottomed jeans under a white hospital tunic. It was the same man as in the third photograph on the website. By now I was pretty certain that, even if the website photographs hadn't come from the family album, they were nevertheless actual pictures of Leonard Parrish. In many of the close-ups he looked preoccupied or even shifty, uneasy at having his image captured on camera. In the shots that included Nora he tended to stand at her shoulder, a little behind her, or would choose a shady position that slightly obscured his image. All of which conveyed a sense that he preferred to stay in the shadows, craving an anonymity he subsequently attained.

"He never married?" I asked.

Claire shook her head, flipping to the last page. Here Leo and Nora were walking towards the camera, holding between them the tiny hands of a grinning toddler who could only have been Claire. Underneath Nora had scrawled: THE LAST PICTURE. Claire told me it was the only one to feature all three of them.

I felt a little sombre as she closed the album and set it aside. Was this, in the end, all that most of our lives would ultimately amount to? A sequence of stills leaving the onlooker groping to imagine how all the hours and days and years between them had been filled?

"It was him," I said to Claire. "The photos on the site were definitely of him. Any idea where they could have come from?"

She hadn't. "According to my mother, my uncle didn't have many friends. He kept himself to himself and didn't get out much. But, you know, there are always photographs, even when you don't remember them being taken by others."

"More so than ever these days," I said. "Mini-movies of us all on CCTV."

She went back upstairs to check that her mother was sleeping peacefully. I flipped through the album one more time. None of the photographs here featured Leo with Walter Suthersen or Edgar Eldridge or anyone else who might have been associated with his writing career. It was as if it had never existed.

And yet it had. In the shadows, perhaps, but indisputably so. No wonder the Ascendants didn't want Parrish's work to be more widely known: they might have based their theology on *Exaltation*, but the novel itself was no thinly fictionalized religious text but something rather more subversive. And more unsettling too.

Claire returned and indicated the typescript. "So how was it?"

"I think we have a runner," I told her.

"You do?"

"It ends a little abruptly, but that should be something we could fix. What it's also going to need is someone to bring out all its visual appeal. Fancy having a crack at the storyboards?"

She smiled at me. "Aren't you getting a bit carried away?

"I'm assuming your mother now owns the copyright."

Claire picked up my empty glass and sniffed it. "We'd have to get her permission."

"Do you think she'll give it?"

"She's asleep. We'll ask her in the morning, assuming she's not in a wayward phase. I think I'll join you in one of these."

She took the glass through into the kitchen. When she came back in, I had the typescript on my lap and I must have been looking thoughtful because she said, "What is it?"

I looked up at her. "You haven't read this?"

I wanted to be sure. She shook her head.

I gave her a précis of the first part of the novel, followed by a slightly more detailed synopsis of the second half. Part two began with an unnamed dictator attempting to cure the derangement of his own people by the use of a "synthetic antimicrobial" delivered as an aerosol from the country's stockpile of missiles. Launching errors caused other nations to believe that an attack was being made on their territory and this triggered retaliatory action which escalated into global nuclear war. Our heroes barely escaped from Earth before the entire planet was desolated.

The ark-ship *Exaltation* made it to the Radiance, where they received the revelation they that were to become the inheritors of the Earth. The disembodied intelligences inhabiting the Radiance now completed their exaltation by filling them with their essence. They were able to manipulate time, and promptly reversed the effects of the war, though those who died were to be reborn as docile innocents, with no memory of their past, to be guided and mentored by the Exalted on a new enlightened path for mankind.

Claire began to stare at me with increasing concern. Finally she couldn't restrain herself.

"It pains me to say this," she announced, "but it's a bit *fascist*, isn't it? The triumph of the Homo Superior and all that."

"On the surface, yes," I agreed. "But one of the characters is a sceptic who secretly avoids being Exalted and remains suspicious of what has happened. When they return to Earth the rest of the Exalted marvel at the beauty of the planet but he just stands there, watching them while they pluck apples from a tree because they're hungry. He's got this feeling something isn't quite right."

I read the last line to her:

The apples were golden, like no others he had ever seen before. They shone in the dusk light with their own inner radiance, like tiny suns, throwing into sharp and eerie relief the avid faces of the inheritors of the Earth.

She kept looking at me. "And then what?"

"That's it. The story ends."

She was silent for several moments, pondering. Then she said, "What do you think it means?"

"Maybe it's a trick and it isn't Earth at all."

She looked dubious. "There's the obvious parallel with Adam and Eve and the Garden of Eden, isn't there? Except that they're eating strange apples. I think it's Earth, but it's been changed."

"Could be. It's one of a number of possible interpretations."

She mulled it over a bit more. "I rather like the ambiguity."

"Assuming it was intended. It does end in a bit of a rush, like having the narrative rug yanked out from under you. Almost as if he'd run out of space."

"Is that possible?"

"I got the impression from Rhodri Davies that those magazines were voracious in consuming writers' copy. Perhaps he had to get it done to a fixed word length or a tight deadline."

The ending as written wouldn't work in a movie, but there was still enough in it to make an action-packed feature that would have a deeper message about the dangers of uncritically accepting promises of salvation or paradise from whatever source. Parrish had portrayed the disembodied aliens as rather supercilious intellects and I was certain he had intended that readers shouldn't sympathize with them.

Claire set the typescript aside and perched on my lap. "You really think it could work as a movie?"

"If we could get the funding, it could be a cracker."

We clinked our glasses together and drank a Southern Comfort toast in anticipation. What happened after that is going to stay between us.

TWENTY-TWO

The *Our Man Flint* ring-tone catapulted me from sleep early the following morning. It was Felix, offering to drive me to see Ashad, whom he had secreted safely "beyond the M25". We arranged for him to pick me up at Xponential by nine. I phoned Jamilla at home to let her know I that I was going into the office early but wouldn't be around for the rest of the day. Valerie and I were due to meet with potential financiers but she would have to go it alone. Jamilla, delighted with the news of Ashad's release, assured me that Val would understand.

I got into the office just after eight-thirty to find that Jamilla was already there, for once looking as if she had got out of bed an hour too early.

"This was delivered by courier yesterday evening," she told me, holding out a small Jiffy bag with *For the attention of Mr Ashad Husseyin* on it. "The man said it was urgent. I thought it might be better if I didn't mention it over the phone."

I tore the package open and found a silver memory stick inside. There was nothing else, no note, and no postal strip on the bag, just a printed label with the inscription.

Jamilla had gone down to the kitchen to brew us coffee.

"Did you see him?" I asked her. "The courier?"

"Of course. I took the delivery."

"Description, please."

"He was about my age. Had a big motorbike helmet on and was in a hurry. He just handed me the package and told me to make sure it was passed on urgently. Then he drove off. Do you want any breakfast with this?"

She had a shopping bag of rolls and various fruits on the worktop.

"I'll have a banana. Anything else?"

"Like what?"

"Like—did he look suspicious, have you ever seen him before?"

"He was just a delivery boy."

"There's no company name on the package. What did he look like?"

"He reminded me a bit of my younger brother."

"He was Muslim?"

She gave me a freeze-ray stare. "So it must be a bomb, then."

"That's not what I meant. It might be relevant."

The memory stick was similar the one Walid had sent to Ashad. He had probably posted this one, as anonymously as possible. But Jamilla didn't need to know that.

Soon afterwards Felix arrived in the Bentley. We didn't linger. I switched off my phone for the duration of the journey, just in case. As we were threading our way out of London Felix told me he had put Ashad in a "safe house" near Chichester. "It's my brother's place. All the family are away, but Morwenna's housekeeping."

"Morwenna?"

"My younger sister. She's not someone to trifle with."

He wouldn't elaborate apart from saying that she was a very single-minded person. His brother Rufus was the eldest of the family, a trader in both diamonds and high-end antiques who was constantly on the move around the world, doing deals everywhere from California to the Far East.

"They won't think of looking for him there."

"Do you think he's still in danger?"

"We don't know whether Byrnes sanctioned it. So we need to be prudent until we're clearer about how the land lies."

"Does Byrnes know he's been released?"

"That I couldn't say. He appears to have gone to ground."

There was no news from Merrick either. Even if she hadn't seen me, Merrick would have been told by Byrnes that I was with Felix at the Thames Water site. She must have realized I had also seen her there: her continuing silence spoke volumes.

We took the scenic route out of London via A roads. Felix was returning the Bentley and planned to get the train back to London once he was satisfied that Ashad was being comfortably looked after. Again the sun was shining and all around us the rolling countryside was going about its usual unfussy business of looking beautiful, fields and woodland cloaked in late summer greens and golds, enfolding quiet villages where the stately rhythms of normal life just carried on regardless.

Predictably Rufus Nancarrow's house was suitably ancient, a redbrick Jacobean mansion enveloped in rural tranquillity, not large but pleasingly ornate with mullioned windows, a pilastered entrance and square top-heavy chimneys that stood like sentries at its corners, one of them sporting a satellite dish that you could only spot when you came up close.

A Range Rover was parked on the gravel driveway, but no one answered the doorbell, so Felix let himself in. We walked through a wood-panelled hall into another wood-panelled living room, which didn't have any of the period furnishings you might have expected. Instead, twisty abstract sculptures in black and white Perspex stood like Gaudi chess pieces in the corners, while two big leather sofas faced the empty vaulted fireplace, above which hung the graphite slab of a massive flat screen TV. Heavy-duty blinds were scrolled above the windows should daylight need shutting out.

Next door was a study with blond wood furniture and a computer on a big modern table. Another held nothing but a full-size billiards table and a dartboard fixed to the back of the door. There were no books or family photographs anywhere. According to Felix, Rufus and his wife had two adolescent sons and a younger daughter. He told me, slightly wistfully I thought, that the family spent little time in the house, Rufus and his wife constantly globetrotting, the children tucked away in boarding schools.

He led me into a kitchen that had so much brushed chrome and LED displays you had the feeling it might start a launch countdown at any second. He rummaged in the capacious fridge for soft drinks while I looked out at the garden. Off to one side was a neglected-looking swimming pool flanked by tall Leylandii.

In the centre was a big trampoline in a high nylon mesh cylinder surrounded by a verdant ring of what I was certain was Astroturf. A couple of low-slung rusting go-karts were parked in a cage, a tarmac track winding away into the distance, passing what looked like a crazy golf course. There were two figures on the course: a squat woman in leggings and a man wearing a baggy corduroy shirt tucked into dungarees.

Felix had poured out a couple of iced lemonades from a jug. We took them out into the garden.

Morwenna was a sturdy-looking young woman in her late twenties with a ruddy outdoors complexion and a very direct stare. Over a red polo-shirt she wore a khaki gilet replete with bulging pockets. She shook my hand very robustly when Felix introduced us.

"And this must be the gardener," I said, trying not to laugh at the sight of Ashad, who had had his hair shortened and been kitted out in spare clothing that was several sizes too big for him. Ashad wasn't a small man himself, so either Rufus was a giant or perhaps Morwenna was married or attached to a man three times her size, a minor mystery later clarified when I learnt that she was engaged to a six-foot-four prop forward from the England Saxons rugby team.

"Ho ho," Ashad said morosely, swishing a little putter as if he would have liked to decapitate someone with it.

I gave him a hug, told him I was really pleased to see him. From his grunt I could tell that he reciprocated but he looked harassed and irritable.

"What's up?" I asked him the moment Felix and Morwenna had retired to the house so that we could have some time alone.

He shook his head and blew out air in an explosive sigh. "That woman," he said, obviously referring to Morwenna. "She's absolutely relentless. I was up at six, helping her feed the horses. Then I had to ride with her. For a whole bloody hour. Can you believe that?"

"Now you come to mention it, you do look a bit bandy-legged."

"My thighs are giving me tremendous gyp. She's on the go all the time. After that, it was walking her dogs—or rather, being dragged by them through the woods." He squinted at me. "What do people see in the countryside? It's all bloody brambles and nettles and drooling animals."

"And the haircut? Did Byrnes insist on a convict's crop?"

I was teasing him out of relief and pleasure at seeing him free; but he was positively morose.

"She runs a hairdressing salon in Arundel and insisted on doing me in the kitchen—" he glared at me "—meaning cutting my hair, before you say anything smutty."

"And then a round of novelty golf for afters?"

"I never realized freedom could be so exhausting."

I offered him my lemonade, and he drank it down in one.

We strolled around the extensive garden just to give us a chance to catch up. There was a paddock at the bottom overlooking a stream and a bridleway leading off into the woods, accessed by tall padlocked gates. The grounds were surrounded by what looked like electrified fencing, which seemed to me rather futile, given that it was open at its front to the road.

We recapitulated the details of his release, with me telling him that I thought Alvarez might be a more decent human being than Byrnes and that he may have acted of his own accord. Perhaps he had checked with his bosses in the US and decided that Byrnes was overstepping his remit. Or perhaps Felix's efforts had proved crucial: during our drive south, he had told me that his uncle had "gone for the jugular" with someone in the Home Office and was threatening to arrange an interview with a close friend who was the editor of one of the heavyweight broadsheets. He would have no compunction about raising his concerns about Halstow Island and illegal detentions unless a full and frank statement was given to Parliament at the earliest opportunity.

"This was delivered to the office this morning," I said, producing the package containing the memory stick. "Jamilla's keen for us to have a look at it."

I told him I thought it might have been sent by Walid, and at last he started to brighten.

He didn't have much to say about his time in captivity. Mostly he had been left alone, and when Byrnes did interrogate him he said nothing about the documents on the confiscated memory stick but instead had wanted to know why Xponential were so interested in both Leo Parrish and Zhuyldz Muvart.

"It was like he'd decided the two were linked," Ashad told me. "And that we knew too."

"So what did you tell him?"

"I didn't give him anything. I told him that our interests in Parrish and Muvart were separate things, that they were commercial media projects that were none of his damn business. Or words to that effect."

"And what did he say?"

"That thing about codes. He claimed we were using codes based on Parrish stories to communicate with the Khanistani dictatorship, encouraging terrorist threats and destabilizing the international situation."

"He mentioned Muvart?"

"Not by name. But Muvart's the only dictator in Khanistan, isn't he?"

Ashad was obviously intrigued by the implied connection, as was I. Until now Byrnes had only talked vaguely about "terrorists" and hadn't mentioned specific nationalities. Was our dual interest in Parrish and Muvart the reason why we were of such malevolent interest to him?

"Did he say anything else about this?"

Ashad shook his head. "I wasn't exactly in the mood for small talk. I didn't like his belligerent attitude and his mad missionary zeal. Do you know what he asked me? Did I believe my God was going to save me from damnation at the final accounting? I almost laughed in his face. I thought he'd said 'the final countdown' and started humming the song. He wasn't amused. When I told him I was an atheist he looked at me as if I'd spat in his face. He's a complete nutter, if you ask me."

Maybe an edginess bordering on instability was par for the course in his profession. Someone with a lot of clout must have been involved for him to be working with Special Branch.

I told Ash about the tasering, how I was pretty sure it was Byrnes. "He's obsessed with getting the Parrish stories out of circulation." I explained about staying at Claire's and meeting Leo Parrish's sister. I was especially positive about *Exaltation*, telling him I was confident we could make a commercial movie out of it if we could rustle up a few backers.

Ashad wanted to know more about the bread-and-butter stuff at the office, how our various on-going projects were panning out. There was precious little to tell and I fobbed him off as we walked back towards the house by talking about the employee appraisal interviews, something for which he had even less enthusiasm than I did. But then he asked me if I had heard anything from Merrick.

I instinctively shook my head, conscious that I had been putting off telling him the one thing he really was entitled to know. And it wasn't fair to do so.

"When Byrnes had you locked up in that place," I remarked, "did you see anyone else apart from him and Alvarez?"

He thought about it. "Once I heard an ice-cream van in the distance. But that's about it. The place was pretty isolated."

His mood had lightened, which only made it harder.

"Someone else was there," I said. "When Felix and I arrived. I'm not sure she saw us."

"She?"

"It was DI Merrick," I said gently. "She was in one of the rooms, talking to Byrnes. I think they know one another. Then she left quickly without showing herself to us. She drove off in her car just before Byrnes let us in to see you."

Ashad went very still. His face lost all its animation and all trace of expression. I tried to imagine what he might be thinking. He had overcome so many of his own prejudices in deciding to ask her out, and from what I had seen there had been a real rapport between them.

At last he said, "You saw her yourself?"

I nodded. "I got the impression she was pretty keen for us *not* to see her."

Another long silence. Then: "How come you didn't mention it at the time?"

I considered my reply. "I couldn't see how it would help your situation. Also, I wasn't sure what to think about it. I needed time to process the whole thing. It was a pretty massive surprise."

He nodded in the fashion of someone barely holding back an overwhelming sense of impatience.

"And now you have. What did you conclude?"

There was no sugaring the pill. "She promised me she was working on finding out where you were, but I think she already knew. I think it's likely she and Byrnes are colleagues. It's possible they've been working with one another from the start. She might even have been with him on the day Byrnes broke into my flat. And I can only think that she was involved when our office was burgled, unless Byrnes compromised her afterwards."

A further brooding silence was abruptly broken by dogs barking. Morwenna appeared from the kennels at the side of the building, pulling a pair of black-and-tan Airedales while telling us that she was about to take Felix to Chichester so that he could get the train back to London.

We followed her around to the front of the house. The terriers were reluctant to get into the back of the Range Rover, but Morwenna shoved them in.

Felix appeared, apologizing for his swift departure but telling Ashad that he was hoping to get the equivalent of a restraining order issued for Byrnes and needed to get back to London to oversee matters. Ashad just nodded, his face blank. Morwenna asked if we would like to accompany them and take the dogs "for a yomp". They were already agitated at the prospect in the rear of the vehicle. I mustered a smile but shook my head.

"Ash and I have urgent business to attend to. Can we use the computer here?"

"Go ahead," she said. "Never use the damned things if I can help it myself."

We waited until she and Felix had driven away before going inside, booting up the computer and slotting in the USB stick. Ashad hadn't said anything for several minutes and his expression was still unreadable.

"I'm sorry," I said to him. "I know you really liked her. I think she liked you."

"Forget it," he told me brusquely. "Let's get on with what we have to do here."

Ten minutes later we were still scrolling through the documents on the memory stick. Ash had already told me that they resembled the ones on the original stick, except that these had largely been turned into gibberish, with swathes of cod-Latin and random bursts of symbols. Had Walid inadvertently sent us a corrupted version of his original? Or were they in a code whose key we hadn't yet found?

The house phone started ringing. I was inclined to let it ring but Ashad snatched it up and said, "House of the Baskervilles."

Then his expression hardened. He put the phone down without saying anything to the caller.

"It was Nancarrow," he told me. "He's just seen Byrnes. He's on his way here."

We hurried to the window. At first we could see nothing. Then I spotted a car twisting its way along the hedged lane that was the house's access road.

A silver Astra.

"It's too late," I said to Ash. "They're almost here."

He had already shut down the programme. Though I had no idea what to do, I couldn't just stand there and wait for them to show. I tugged the memory stick from its slot and followed Ash into the main room. Merrick and Byrnes must have been tailing the Bentley.

Ashad was all for confronting them; but when the car pulled into the driveway, Byrnes, sitting beside Merrick, had a fierce and unforgiving look on his face.

There was no sign of Alvarez. But someone was huddling in the back, a pink baseball cap pulled down over her eyes.

"Bloody hell," Ash said in deepest Birmingham, "is that Jamilla?"

It was. Ash's surprise quickly turned to fury. Again he wanted to storm out and take them on.

"We have to hide," I insisted. I reminded him of how violent Byrnes could be and that we couldn't let him take us both into his custody by gunpoint.

Some instinct made me drop the memory stick into a lotus-flower bowl on the mantelpiece. Ash dragged me to the side of the chimney breast. He did something to the panelling there. It was hinged and opened. Beyond was a narrow space about two feet wide and three times as deep which I realized stretched behind the fireplace.

"A priest hole," he told me with an air of grim triumph. "What you Christians used when you were persecuting one another."

We climbed inside, both of us having to crouch to fit into the space. Ashad pulled the panelling back into place so that only the thinnest crack of light penetrated. It was enough to illuminate the bare walls with their ancient bricks and rough mortar. Morwenna must have shown him the hidey-hole earlier.

Seconds later there was a hammering on the door knocker and the ding-donging of the bell. Then Byrnes shouting: "Open up! We know you're in there!"

And after that, a period of suspenseful silence.

Ashad and I could just about edge past one another in the gloom. It would have been an uncomfortable and dangerous place for fugitive Catholic priests to spend any length of time, particularly if the fire was lit. Not switching on my mobile hadn't preventing them from finding us. Perhaps Felix had been bugged.

Ashad let himself slide to the floor and pulled his knees up to his chest. He looked fatalistic, as if he had decided he could no longer trust anyone and couldn't care less. We had no means of seeing outside, but I remained standing right next to the panel, listening, waiting.

For several minutes there was nothing but silence. Then I heard Merrick's voice say from the hallway: "It's open."

"Anyone at home?" came Byrnes's voice, echoing in the empty hallway, not quite so strident now but curious, teasing. And then, presumably to Merrick: "They're either gone or hiding."

"There's no car here," Merrick pointed out. "They must have guessed the memory key was tagged and got out."

So that was how they had done it. And somehow persuaded Jamilla to pass it on to us.

I thought I detected a measure of relief in Merrick's voice. It occurred to me that she must have been steeling herself for a face-to-face confrontation with Ash, who would finally know that she had lied to him. This, I had to concede, indicated a degree of professional bravery, though perhaps she just saw it as doing her duty and felt no guilt whatsoever.

There were further muted exchanges between her and Byrnes, still coming from the hall. Merrick clearly wasn't keen on entering, whereas Byrnes was adamant. Not surprisingly, he prevailed.

After a minute or so they entered the room where we were hiding. I could feel my heart rate multiplying. I heard them rummaging around, Byrnes checking the kitchen and then the study and saying something about the computer being on. I heard him telling Merrick he was going upstairs to check the bedrooms.

Merrick was moving quietly around downstairs. There was no indication that Jamilla had accompanied them inside. Most likely they had left her in the car. They must have forced her into cooperating with them: she'd been hunched up in the seat like a prisoner.

It wasn't long before Byrnes came back downstairs. "There's no one around, but one of the beds has been slept in. Husseyin was here. They must have rendezvoused."

I heard a chink of porcelain. Merrick said, "Here it is."

I guessed that she had found the USB stick. Presumably they had loaded corrupted versions of Walid's original files onto it and arranged for it to be passed on to me, knowing that I would be likely to be seeing Ash.

Byrnes had gone back into the study. I could hear him thumping around in there, a chair being overturned, something being dumped on the floor.

"Hey," Merrick said to him from the doorway. "Take it easy. Technically, we're breaking and entering."

"Do you think I care about that?" Byrnes said angrily. "If they went in a hurry they may have left some Parrish material behind. We've got to eliminate Muvart once and for all."

A silence, and then Merrick said, "What do you mean *eliminate*?"

"He's dangerously unpredictable. It has to end."

"What—like have him assassinated?"

"If they'd done that with Hitler, millions of lives would have been saved. The world will be a better place without him and his ilk."

Merrick gave an uneasy laugh. "Who exactly do you mean when you say *we*?"

Byrnes, still rummaging, didn't reply.

"I thought you were looking into the Ascendants and then this thing with the Dmitri connection. What's Parrish got to do with Muvart? That was just a cover—"

"Forget it. It's no big deal."

"Hold on," Merrick persisted. "That's not good enough. Is there something else I should know?"

"Only that we have to take all copies out of circulation. We know from the secretary that Randall was with the family overnight. I can guarantee he'll have left there with some Parrish literature."

Byrnes was now overheated, almost manic. Little did he know that I had left there empty-handed, though the serial was still safe in my secure cabinet at the office: I'd checked that morning. But why was it so important to him?

Before Merrick could say anything a horn blared outside, followed by the noise of a vehicle coming swiftly to a halt.

"Shit," said Merrick.

There was a flurry of activity in the study, which I suspected entailed Merrick tidying up the mess Byrnes had made.

The front door opened and I heard Felix call: "Who's in there?"

I sensed Byrnes and Merrick hastily evacuating the study.

"Who the devil are you?" came Morwenna's stentorian voice. "What are you doing in this house?"

I heard Byrnes say: "Security services."

The panel behind which we were hiding was on a little latch. I took the opportunity of releasing it and inching it open a fraction.

It was just possible to see that Byrnes was showing Morwenna and Felix his ID card. Morwenna scarcely gave it a glance.

"We apologize for the intrusion," Merrick began. "We did knock. The door was open."

"And you are?"

"Detective Inspector Merrick."

"Do you have a warrant to search this place?" Felix asked with his usual gracefulness. "This is a family home, and Mr Byrnes in particular is far from welcome."

"Where are Husseyin and Randall?" Byrnes asked angrily.

"If you think I'm going to answer that, you're very much mistaken. Especially since we are currently pursuing legal redress on my client's behalf for unwarranted abduction and incarceration in non-judicial premises without the knowledge of the leaseholders."

"Where are they?" Byrnes repeated.

"Get out of here right now," Morwenna said, her ruddy complexion deepening by several degrees.

Merrick was plainly ready to make a brisk exit, but Byrnes didn't budge.

Morwenna stalked out.

"I really would advise you to leave immediately," Felix said, addressing Merrick. "You must realize that neither I nor my sister will be browbeaten."

"Oh yes," Byrnes said sarcastically. "She really stood her ground, didn't she?"

Merrick tried to usher him towards the doorway, but he stayed put, looking furious. I wondered if he was about to draw his handgun and take charge by force.

I heard the padding of animal feet in the hallway. Morwenna appeared with the Airedales. They started growling on sight of Byrnes, straining on their leashes.

"You've got five seconds," she told him. "Then I intend to let them loose. One ... Two ..."

Merrick slipped out the door. Byrnes hesitated, and scampered after her. Morwenna followed them out.

I restrained Ashad for a short time before we shouldered our way out of the priest hole, silently greeting the startled Felix and creeping over to the window.

Merrick was already at the wheel, turning the engine while Byrnes bundled himself into the seat beside her as Morwenna kept the dogs in close proximity. Jamilla was still sitting hunched in the back under her baseball cap, her face set so hard she looked like a different person. I had the urge to rush out there and try to rescue her but I knew I couldn't reveal myself.

Merrick reversed hurriedly down the driveway, swung the car around and drove off. By this time Ash and I had followed Felix outside. We watched until the Vectra had disappeared into the far distance.

"I spotted the car passing us on the way to the station," Felix told me. "It was a stroke of luck. We decided it would be prudent to turn around and play the Seventh Cavalry. I was rather surprised to see Ms Ali sitting in the back. Do you think she's all right? They forced her to come here, didn't they?"

"It's us they're interested in," I assured him. "They probably brought her along for extra bargaining power if they'd managed to corner us. I'm sure they won't harm her. Merrick won't let Byrnes do anything stupid."

Ashad bristled at the mention of her name.

"What the hell is the Dmitri connection?" he said to me.

None of us had any idea, but Felix was intrigued and said he would look into it when he got back to London. Ashad used the landline to call Jamilla's father. There was no answer on his mobile, and no one picked up when Ashad tried their home phone.

"Right," he said, "I'm on the next train back to London. I want to make sure that Jamilla's all right and find out what's been happening while I was banged up."

There was more than a hint of reproach in his voice, directed at me, as if he felt that I had let things slip while he had been under arrest.

And perhaps he was right.

Morwenna drove all three of us to the station and we got the first Victoria train, Felix generously stumping up the fares.

En route Ashad used my phone to call Jamilla's family again. He still couldn't get a reply. He rang Walid's mobile and got straight through. Walid didn't know anything about a second memory stick and insisted he hadn't sent us anything. So Byrnes must have copied and corrupted the original before fitting it with a tracking device, a ploy designed to allow him to locate both of us and get his hands on more Parrish stories. And somehow this was connected with Muvart and possibly the Ascendants. But how? None of us could make any sense of it.

When Ashad tried the office, Valerie answered. She was only just back from her meeting. Ross Buchanan was manning the office phone, having come upstairs when calls weren't being answered and found the place deserted. Merrick and Byrnes had probably abducted Jamilla from the office after Felix and I left for Chichester.

I tried ringing Claire again, but her mobile was still off. No answer on the landline.

In central London we parted company with Felix, who had advised Ashad to make sure he stayed in public places and was surrounded by other people at all times. I could tell that Ashad had no intention whatsoever of following this advice.

On the way to the office my phone launched into *The Ride of the Valkyries*. It was Ashad's brother. The entire family had just arrived in Camber Sands, Jamilla included. She came on the line to say that she was all right, having been despatched by train to the campsite by DI Merrick, who had advised the family to take an immediate vacation and keep Jamilla "out of the firing line" for a few days. Earlier that morning Byrnes had turned up and threatened to arrest her parents unless she cooperated and passed the doctored memory stick on to me. After it was done, he had practically frogmarched her out of the office to Merrick's car.

Jamilla, pleased that we had escaped Byrnes's clutches, promised that she would be back at work as soon as possible, but it was obvious that the threat to her family had rattled her more than her own temporary arrest.

Valerie was upstairs at the office, for once looking a little harassed. She and Ross Buchanan had been fending calls from BBC producers and freelancers who wanted to know where the hell Ashad and I were. She also had something to report from her meeting with our financiers.

"They're prepared to extend our overdraft facility for a further three months."

"And then what?" I asked.

Valerie had taken plenty of notes but she didn't bother to refer to them. "If our balance sheet still looks dodgy they're going to send in auditors to conduct a full review with a view to declaring Xponential bankrupt."

It was what we had most feared, though Ashad greeted the news with steely aplomb. He changed into a spare set of clothes and left me to follow up our most pressing calls while he accompanied Val downstairs to update himself. He was obviously determined to absorb himself in work matters, though there was also a not-so subtle subtext: You can't trust anyone except yourself.

I spent the rest of the afternoon on the office line making the calls, which mostly entailed reassuring people that our various projects were still steaming ahead. Drum rolls alerted me to a mobile call. It was Claire.

"Hey," I greeted her. "I tried calling earlier, but you were switched off."

"Yes. It was deliberate." She left a pause.

"Everything all right?" I asked.

"We're going away for a while."

"Away?" I hadn't remotely anticipated this. "Where?"

"I don't think it would be wise to discuss it on the phone."

I knew I couldn't guarantee the confidentiality of the connection, but I was eager to know more.

"When are you going?"

"Soon. Very soon. We need to get away from here."

"Can I see you before you go?"

A pause, and then: "It would have to be this evening."

*

Ashad was in the editing suite working on the latest Muvart documentary footage when I left the office at six o'clock. He was scarcely speaking to me, but Valerie had volunteered to keep him company until he was done. I had the feeling she was in for a long evening.

There were two packed suitcases in Claire's hallway, zipped and ready to go.

"Our landlord's here," Claire informed me as she led me through to the kitchen.

Two people were sitting at the table: Nora and Walter Suthersen.

"Mr Randall," Suthersen said amiably, rising and offering me his hand. "Good to see you again."

We shook. Somehow it all made sense, so that my surprise was muted by a sense that I should have guessed. Nora was watching me from a wheelchair with an expression resembling mischief.

"How are you?" I asked her.

"Tip-top," she replied, though she looked frail. "You do realize you've brought nothing but trouble? I hope Claire knows what she's doing."

It was hard to be sure, but I think she was teasing.

"Will you be polite for once?" Claire told her sternly.

"If he's got any mettle he can take it."

"I couldn't wait to get here," I told her. "The thought of more delightful repartee really spurred me on."

"See?" Nora said to Claire. "He's perfectly capable of holding his own."

Suthersen was a benign spectator to this little bit of banter; he'd clearly witnessed Nora in action before.

"Nora and I have known one another for years," he told me, sipping an after-dinner coffee while I worked my way through the plate of risotto that Claire had put in front of me. "We met through Leo, way back in the old days when he was producing stories for Ed Eldridge and I was just a fledgling writer."

The house was Suthersen's UK home, where he often spent the summer months. When he had heard from Claire about the family's distress he had arranged for it to be made available as a temporary sanctuary. He was only just back from the last leg of his book-signing tour. Claire and Nora had a free run of the place, with the exception of the study, which he used when staying in England and which was kept locked because it contained works-in-progress.

"Your interest in Leo has brought all sorts of creatures out of the woodwork," he remarked. "I gather someone tasered you. I'm surprised you're still in the game."

"Is that what it is? A game?"

He raised a placatory hand. "I'm not suggesting it's anything frivolous. Far from it. Heaven knows why Leo's work is attracting such malevolence. I admire your persistence. And bravery."

"It's a cause worth fighting for," I said. "For both Xponential and the family. Though I still don't understand why there's so much secrecy surrounding him. Can you enlighten me?"

"I wish I knew," he said, a little too quickly. "Especially this business with the secret service. That, I believe, is something new."

I wanted to ask him about the evidence he had given to the Senate committee half a century before, which might well have brought him into contact with intelligence operatives; but the timing wasn't right, especially with Claire and Nora present.

Still, there was one subject I couldn't resist raising.

"When did you last read *Exaltation*?"

"Years ago," he said airily. "I have to confess I don't remember too much about it."

"Do you?" I asked Nora.

She gave me a disapproving stare.

"They've been in storage for donkey's years till you blew the dust off them." She fidgeted in the chair. "I need the bathroom."

Claire, used to this, wheeled her away to the one downstairs.

"You might want to take another look," I told Suthersen. "Some of the events in the story have a scarily prescient ring."

This was putting it mildly. Suthersen squinted at me. "In what way?"

"Well, for one thing it features a dictator with a rather close resemblance to Zhuyldz Muvart. And another 'executive officer' to the US president who's not unlike Bennett Irwin."

Suthersen topped up his coffee. He was smiling.

"For another," I went on, "there's a deadly new disease in the story that goes global. And a crisis involving the dictator that escalates into the destruction of the world."

He just shrugged. "Pestilence, dictators, apocalypse—they're the staples of SF writers."

"Some of his short stories also read like a bit more than just intelligent guesswork. I know it sounds insane, as if I'm being some kind of obsessive loony. I promise you I didn't go looking for these connections. They just jump out at you."

The bathroom toilet flushed and we heard the door opening.

"I don't think we should talk about this in front of Nora," Suthersen said firmly. "She still gets het up about Leo, even after all these years. And who can blame her?"

He needn't have worried. Upsetting Nora would have been counterproductive, though I was surprised that neither she nor Suthersen appeared to be interested in Leo Parrish's gift for writing stories with elements that the real world obligingly echoed some years later. Perhaps it was simply because neither of them had actually read Leo's stories in many years. It was a reminder that he was a writer whose underground reputation had always exceeded his actual readership.

"So what happens now?" I asked.

"I rather think it's time we brought all this out into the open," he said. "That's why I'm taking Nora and Claire to Miami for the World Convention. Maybe we can drag the ghost of Leo Parrish out of the shadows and see who starts yelling blue murder. They're flying out with me in the morning."

"Walt arranged it in a hurry," Claire told me, wheeling Nora in. "We're flying first class. My mother's really keen. It's years since she last flew."

They were leaving in the early hours for Heathrow. Daniel was going on holiday in the south of France with Toby's family. It would be just Claire and Nora with Suthersen.

Though I was pleased for them, I also felt a frustrating suspicion that all my work on the Parrish project would come to a halt while they were away. Just when things were getting really interesting.

There was only one thing for it. I got out my mobile and called Rhodri Davies.

TWENTY-THREE

Rhodri was waiting for me with his spare ticket when I arrived at Heathrow next morning. On bidding Claire farewell I had gone home and packed a suitcase after finally locating my passport at the back of a drawer.

Rhodri was his usual jolly self, and he was accompanied by several other science-fiction fans, some of them preoccupied not with the actual programme of events at the convention but with plans for ensuring that they got their hands on a supply of proper ale. The word "Budweiser" was an anathema to them. The women were just as hearty as the men, and I had the feeling that any of them could have easily drunk me under the table.

We checked in our bags and all went well until we arrived at passport control. Rhodri and his friends were allowed through without any trouble, but the guy in the booth kept scrutinizing my details before calling over a beefy colleague in dark trousers and rolled-up shirtsleeves. With his thick neck and pug nose, he looked more like a wrestler than a Customs official. I knew that I still had ESTA approval for entry into the US, having travelled to Boston eighteen months before with Theresa in the dying days of our marriage. So what was the problem?

After answering a few questions to confirm my identity and my flight destination I was allowed through, but then the beefy one walked me over to an unused conveyer belt which he promptly started up and used to scan my hand luggage. Another Customs man had appeared, as little as he was large. I was frisked and then the small guy said, "Please come with us, sir," handing me my flight bag.

Both men marched me down a partitioned corridor. They hadn't actually opened up my flight bag.

"Is there something wrong?" I asked. "The ticket was a friend's wife's, but she's pregnant, so I took it over. Short notice, but we've paid the surcharge."

The smaller man unlocked a side door. Rhodri had phoned me in the early hours to confirm he had had the ticket transferred to my name. I was pretty sure it wasn't that—or that if it was, it was just a pretext to detain me.

"Please wait here, sir," the short man said, as the giant ushered me inside.

I fully expected to find Byrnes waiting for me. But the room was empty apart from a table and a couple of chairs facing a small wall-mounted TV. The burly guy stood with his back to the door, his eyes on the screen.

The TV was turned mutely to a news channel, which was showing footage of one of the space shuttles being trundled out of its hangar. I sat down, putting the bag on my lap. It held the office copy of part 2 of *Exaltation*, which I had planned to show to Rhodri during the flight. Now it looked as if I wasn't going to make it. Byrnes had probably pulled strings to stop me from boarding the plane. He would be thrilled to discover that I was carrying the manuscript.

"Do you know what this is about?" I asked the big guy. "I'm just taking a holiday."

He looked at me without expression. "Someone will be along shortly, Mr Randall."

"I'm a film-maker," I told him. "That's what I do."

Some people can shrug without moving a muscle. He was one of them.

The room was windowless, made up entirely of wall panels that could probably be reconfigured and reassembled in a matter of hours. It was the kind of anonymous transitory space that has no personality apart from a stripped functionality. No one lived here, no one really owned it, no one was going to put a plant in a corner or a picture on the wall. Airports were modern monuments to impermanence, decked out with aspirational retail stores and fast food outlets liable to morph into something else overnight. A couple of years ago we had produced an animated short called *Now Boarding* which in a speeded-up style portrayed an airport as a glorified sausage machine, a mass of travellers being funnelled and squeezed through all sorts of channels before they were finally extruded into the skins of the aeroplanes that blasted off like pneumatic frankfurters. I was beginning to feel like a bit of bony gristle clogging up the works.

The TV was tuned to CNN News, and suddenly I saw the banner headline: KHANISTAN CRISIS ESCALATES. The screen flashed a still picture of President Muvart.

"Any chance you could have turn up the volume?" I asked.

The big guy obliged without demur. The photograph had been replaced by mobile phone footage of a motorized unit raising dust as it raced across a rocky desert. There were trucks and troop carriers and a couple of vintage-looking Chieftain tanks with green Khanistani scimitars stencilled on their flanks.

"... forces crossed into the buffer zone in the early hours of the morning," the voice over was saying. "UN garrisons in the zone are reported to have been encircled, and small arms fire has been exchanged."

There was more. The gist of it was that Muvart had finally sent his forces into the disputed territory, the spearhead of which was rapidly converging on the main US base and demanding its immediate withdrawal or unconditional surrender.

The US president came on screen, condemning the actions as "totally unwarranted and in complete violation of United Nations' accords". Then Bennett Irwin was shown outside his local church with a woman described as his eldest daughter. Irwin was a widower and I knew he regularly attended services with his extended family. I scarcely listened to his stern denunciations and strident assertions that force would be met with force. I was looking at his daughter, a slim fair-haired woman in her late thirties who had one of her children standing in front of her, an adolescent boy with a hostile-looking stare who reminded me of someone.

The reporter had mentioned her name: Mrs Rebecca Byrnes.

Of course I might have misheard it and couldn't be certain of the spelling. It might have been Burns or even possibly Berg. But I didn't think so. The square-jawed boy, squinting suspiciously at the camera, was a miniature version of Noah Byrnes.

Now here was a neat arrangement. Noah Byrnes worked for DEFCOS, whose director or head of operations had to be ultimately answerable to Bennett Irwin.

So Byrnes had married his boss's daughter. Was it possible that Irwin was ultimately setting Byrnes's agenda?

The door opened and the little guy walked in. Behind him was DI Merrick.

The big man killed the TV. Merrick was in her work attire of white blouse and dark trouser suit. I felt a pang of sadness for Ashad because she really would have been quite a catch for him and I had hoped, despite my worst suspicions, that she and Ashad might have actually formed a lasting bond against all the odds.

"Good morning, Mr Randall," she said to me. She was carrying two takeaway coffees and she slid one across the table to me.

I didn't move or speak. A whole parade of angry denunciations were marching through my mind.

She sat down opposite me.

"Where's Byrnes?" I asked, not hiding my bitterness.

"I don't know," she replied.

"Yeah," I said. "Right."

"I came to talk to you about him."

She took the lid off her coffee and blew on it, looking at me all the while. Looking at me without guilt but also without hostility or suspicion.

"I can't believe you led Ashad on like that," I said. "He trusted you."

She took this as if she felt the criticism was justified. But then she said, "It's not what you think."

"No? Then what is it?"

"Shall we walk?" she said unexpectedly. "You can take your coffee with you."

Clearly Little and Large hadn't anticipated this, but Merrick was determined. She had them unlock another door. I left the coffee but made sure I was carrying my flight bag as I followed her outside. The two Customs men trailed in our wake.

We walked down a long corridor with views of the runway. It wasn't a public space: there were no passenger direction signs.

"Byrnes has gone AWOL," Merrick said. "We don't know where he is."

"Really? What is this—another good cop, bad cop routine?"

"It's true," Merrick insisted. "It turns out he was acting on his own agenda from the start. I didn't know. None of us knew."

I studied her face, looking for signs of guile.

"I admit I came to you after the burglary under false pretences," she confessed. "We sold you a line. Byrnes's line."

She waited for me to say something. I was still too angry with her to oblige. But I knew from the overheard conversation in Rufus Nancarrow's house that she had been alarmed when Byrnes talked about getting rid of Muvart.

"When Byrnes and Alvarez came over to the UK I was instructed to work with him," she told me. "I was ordered to follow his lead. According to my brief he was operating under a direct mandate from senior US officials, tasked with investigating the growing influence of the Church of the Ascendancy on public and private bodies. It was a maximum security, high level priority operation."

We crossed a deserted area stacked with wall panels and stanchions. What next? Were they going to shove me down an unused baggage chute where burly officers would bundle me straight into the back of a police van?

"So you and Byrnes first smashed up our office, then burgled my place."

"No," Merrick insisted. "The burglary was in all likelihood carried out by Ascendants. You probably know by now why they're keen to destroy any works by Leo Parrish."

She wanted me to tell her. I stayed mum.

"Because their founder stole his ideas for their religion from Parrish's sci-fi stories," she said.

I wasn't inclined to tell her what I knew; but she might have information for me.

"Is Parrish still alive?"

"He died years ago in a random shooting in New York."

"You told us he was now someone eminent."

"We made that up. I did warn you that I wasn't telling you the whole truth. Parrish himself is almost incidental, alive or dead. It's what he wrote that counts. Because of the connection between his work and the Ascendants we have his name flagged up on our search protocols and intercepts. That's how your name cropped up. When it was quickly followed by the break-in at your office, we had to investigate."

"So all that stuff about terrorists using his stories as codes was just guff."

"It was the cover story Byrnes suggested we give you. Though I'm beginning to wonder whether he started believing in at least a version of it himself. When he found out about Ashad's ethnic origins he insisted we investigate further."

I couldn't resist it: "So that's why you got into bed with him."

She had obviously been expecting this.

"It was at first. If by 'got into bed with him' you mean pursue my interest in him." Her gaze challenged me to elaborate the innuendo. "I didn't take the initiative. He did. But I really liked him. I know you probably don't believe that. We had more in common than you might think. But I had a professional duty that predated any personal interest, and I had to follow it through."

She let a silence fall. I wasn't going to fill it.

"For what's it's worth, we didn't sleep together. Though under other circumstances, it might have happened."

"I'm sure that'll be a great consolation to him."

"It wasn't clear to me at the time how obsessed Byrnes also was with Zhuyldz Muvart. Alvarez didn't know either. That's why, when Ashad got himself arrested, Byrnes was determined to interrogate him. When he was transferred from Special Branch detention, Alvarez and I assumed the authorisation had come right from the top."

"From who?"

"We assumed it was Byrnes's agency chief. Byrnes told us he was convinced that Ashad had more than a documentary interest in Khanistan."

I made a sceptical noise. "You're asking me to believe that? He locks Ashad away in a disused Thames Water site and neither you nor Alvarez thinks there's something dodgy about it?"

"I didn't know about it at first. And Alvarez had been told to follow Byrnes's orders without question. We all had."

"Orders that stemmed from Bennett Irwin?"

Merrick didn't hide her surprise. "We assumed he was following agency directives, which in turn came straight from somewhere on Capitol Hill."

"Did you know that Byrnes is married to Irwin's daughter?"

It was immediately plain that she didn't. Under any other circumstances I might have felt smug. I could see her furiously recalculating her actions in the light of this knowledge.

"So when Felix Nancarrow and I turned up there you'd only just found out?"

"It's true," Merrick insisted, ignoring my incredulity. "If the authorisation came direct from Bennett Irwin, then it's no wonder we were told to follow Byrnes's lead and not ask awkward questions."

"Why should I believe you?"

"Because I'm here. Because I want any opinion that you and Ashad might have about me to be based on the facts, not on lies and evasions."

We had now arrived in a shuttered-up snack area that overlooked various service buildings. Outside the grey sky was full of rain and the prospect of me going to Florida appeared to have receded to vanishing point. Merrick led me into a deserted transit lounge while the two Customs men loitered outside, having obviously decided that I wasn't going to try to take her hostage and mount an escape bid. We perched on a couple of seats so that she could finish her coffee.

"Were you with Byrnes when he burgled my flat?" I asked her.

"No," she said emphatically. "That was Alvarez. I was furious when I found out."

I still didn't trust her, but it did seem that Byrnes had systematically misled not only her but also Alvarez.

"So why was Byrnes so desperate to get his hands on any Parrish stories I might have?"

"He came over here with enough evidence to persuade my bosses that there's been a wave of criminality in the US and the UK associated with the Ascendants' obsession with Parrish. Theft, harassment, cyber-crime, even actual bodily harm. Not to mention their intimidation of anyone who's publically critical of them, or former believers who've got out. But they cover their tracks well, he told us, and amassing evidence to bring criminal charges had proved difficult, especially since there are celebrities and politicians and even people in the media who are sympathizers—"

"Not to mention the police."

This stopped her.

"I was at their recent gathering in Slough," I told her. "I saw it in action."

"We knew about that. That's another reason Byrnes was suspicious. You were interested in Parrish, you had links with his niece, who was known to regularly attend their meetings."

"She's not a believer."

Merrick gave a considerate smile. "We know what happened there. We had a couple of our own people in the audience, keeping an eye on things. But for Byrnes it was a rather worrying series of connections. The last thing he wanted was someone to be looking to make a film of Parrish's work."

"Why not? Wouldn't that just expose how much their faith is based on a science-fiction story? Isn't that a better way of subverting their credibility than anything else?"

"He told us he had orders to do the opposite. Shut it down. He claimed he was tasked with vacuuming up anything by Parrish because his agency was planning on mounting a Big Sting operation to really bring them down."

I still didn't get it. "But surely us wanting to do a Parrish movie is like serving up a honey pot for the Ascendants. Byrnes could have got us onside and been ready to pounce when the Ascendants made their moves against us."

"There is no Big Sting operation. Alvarez checked with his agency boss yesterday. There never was."

"Bennett Irwin wasn't mentioned?"

She shook her head. "Maybe no one imagined he would involve himself with actual operational details. Assuming that he actually did."

Merrick looked genuinely chastened. If she was at last telling me the whole truth, where did that leave us?

"Someone must have authorized all the paperwork to persuade CTC to go along with it," I pointed out.

"Oh, yes," she agreed, "the paperwork was pukka, though it turned out to be rather grey around the edges when we came to look at it more closely. It gave Byrnes plenty of room for manoeuvre. But of course everyone in DEFCOS is now denying all knowledge of it. They might just be trying to cover their embarrassment."

"Which makes it even more likely that Byrnes got authorisation direct from Irwin. The question is, what's Irwin's motive?"

Her look was speculative. "I assume you have a theory."

"Maybe your cover story about protecting someone prominent was true. Someone who used to be Leo Parrish."

She gave this a moment's contemplation. "I can't see how. Because of the Ascendancy connection the FBI kept Parrish's file on record. I've seen an electronic copy. He's Ms Whitney's uncle. And he died over forty years ago."

Which fitted with what Felix had unearthed. I suppose that I had still been clinging to the faint hope that somehow the elusive Leo Parrish was masterminding all this and would finally appear like a trickster from a magician's cabinet.

"Do you think that Alvarez knows that Byrnes is Irwin's son-in-law?"

"It's possible. Thinking Irwin might be involved could explain why he was so ready to follow Byrnes's orders without question."

"Cooperating with you now, is he? If not confiding everything."

I could tell she was angry at the thought that Alvarez might have deliberately kept her in the dark. But she didn't proceed to condemn him.

"He's mortified about the whole affair, misleading us and all the other unauthorized activities. The agency director is adamant he knew nothing about it."

According to Merrick, Alvarez was currently trying to locate Byrnes, both of them having been summoned back to Washington to explain their actions.

"I wanted to thank you for appealing to Alvarez's conscience," Merrick said. "Otherwise we'd still be chasing shadows and Byrnes would be doing as he pleased."

I knew that although Irwin had spent his youth and early manhood in New York, he was about twenty years too young to have been Leo Parrish. Still, there were other possibilities. Just to see what reaction it might generate I said, "Is Bennett Irwin in any way related to Parrish?"

Merrick looked surprised. "I'm not aware of any connection between them."

"He couldn't have been a cousin or nephew or something?"

"I don't think there were any relatives outside the immediate family. Parrish's mother and father both died young. There was only Leo and his sister."

I had the feeling that Merrick was now telling me as much of the truth as she knew, or was inclined to admit, but it still left plenty of unanswered questions.

"So what's the Dmitri connection?"

This time her look of surprise was genuine. "How did you know about that?"

"Ashad and I were in a hidey-hole behind the fireplace when you came looking for us."

She was silent for an instant, and then she laughed.

"I knew it! I had this feeling the pair of you were lurking somewhere close."

"You seem almost pleased we outwitted you."

"By that stage I was beginning to have my doubts about Byrnes. I didn't particularly want Ashad in his clutches again. Or you, for that matter. But I'd been ordered to give full cooperation."

"Dmitri?" I prompted.

"Another red herring. Only this time I was the one who ended up chasing it. Once we'd looked into your company and couldn't find anything that gave us any cause for concern from a security standpoint, Byrnes then mentioned you'd pulled a pistol on him when he was in your flat. A Russian pistol. He started dropping hints about your landlord."

This was unexpected. "Nigel?"

"Not his real name, as I'm sure you're aware. Byrnes claimed that he was actually called Dmitri and was from one of the former Soviet republics bordering Khanistan and still had connections there. He said intelligence had come from Washington suggesting that he might be using his cover as a London landlord to supply either arms or information to the Muvart regime. He asked me to look into it."

At the time, using the gun to scare Byrnes had felt like a good idea; but it had only given him more ammunition against us. Either Nigel was under constant surveillance or Byrnes had intuited that the pistol must have come from him.

"I spent days chasing it up and found nothing," Merrick said. "Well, nothing suggesting that he's involved in terrorist or intelligence activities. But he's more than a petty criminal. We're pretty sure he's involved in shipping things into the UK from Eastern Europe. At first we thought it was just merchandise like pirated DVDs and fake branded clothing. But he may also be trafficking in women. If we find evidence for this, his days here are numbered."

That Nigel was indeed shady wasn't a surprise, but I couldn't help wondering what affect his arrest or deportation would have on our ongoing occupation of his premises. Assuming Xponential survived, that is. Apart from our financial problems, there was also the strain on the partnership I had with Ashad. He had been less than pleased when I had called to say I was going to Miami. And with good reason. I hadn't been giving enough attention to our existing projects since I set off on the trail of Leo Parrish.

"Obviously," Merrick said, "the information I've just given you is not be shared with anyone. I could lose my job if it got out."

Was this her way of telling me she was finally on the level? I mentioned the women I had seen in Nigel's van. Merrick knew about them but stressed that she wasn't at liberty to discuss the scope of this particular investigation.

"The other night," I told her, "someone tasered me and tried to make off with my rucksack."

"What?"

I took her reaction to mean that I wasn't under permanent police surveillance. I told her what had happened, though I didn't mention Cyrus Hammond. "I don't have any proof but I'm pretty positive it was Byrnes. He tried to get away with something that was very valuable to me. Something connected with Leo Parrish."

Merrick actually looked angry. I mentioned the scuffle on the Craven Cottage terraces, Byrnes's verbal threats, the general sense I had that he was on the edge of rationality and quite dangerous.

"Alvarez thinks so, too," she admitted. "I'm inclined to trust his judgement. He's spent more time with Byrnes than me. But neither of us had any idea of the full extent of his *extracurricular* activities."

I was still thinking through things.

"You said you had people at the Ascendancy meeting in Slough. Were any of them detailed to follow me and Claire Whitney home afterwards?"

"Not that I'm aware of," she said. "They were there to see what links the Ascendants might have with the local constabulary and how Vincent Kubilius might be going about fostering them."

I had a sense that for once she was trying to play things strictly straight. Unless, of course, it was an even more devious double bluff.

"Byrnes and Alvarez weren't there?"

"This was a Home Office operation. They would have been aware of it, but they weren't actively involved."

I deliberated, and then said, "Do you know Cyrus Hammond?"

There was no hint of recognition on her face. "Should I?"

"I wondered if he was one of the people you'd planted. He's an American, but he's lived in this country for years—or at least he spends most of his time here. He's probably around sixty. Runs a media-funding foundation called Filmscope but also has links with the American intelligence agencies."

Merrick frowned. "It's not a name I'm familiar with."

I explained how he had followed us and claimed to be keeping a watchful eye on Claire. And how he had conveniently been on hand to foil Byrnes's attempt to steal my rucksack.

Merrick was intrigued. She indicated the flight bag. "So was he trying to steal what you have in there?"

She put the coffee cup to her mouth. Was this the moment when she hoped to coerce me into admitting that it was an original Leo Parrish manuscript? Presumably the scanner would have registered something that looked like papers, but they hadn't confiscated anything.

"It's nothing that's a threat to domestic or international security."

"I'm pleased to hear it."

She gave no sign that she wanted me to show her what I had. Not, at least, without my consent.

"Why are you here?" I asked.

"I've told you why. I wanted to explain some things you wouldn't have been aware of."

"There's more to it than that. Am I under arrest?"

"Of course not."

"Then I can get on my plane and fly out of here?"

This was said in hope rather than expectation: the plane was due to depart in fifteen minutes.

"Of course you can."

I stood up, hefting the flight bag.

"I understand why you're still reluctant to trust me," Merrick said. "But this isn't some remote place on the bank of the Thames, is it? It's a big, busy airport, and HM Revenue and Customs have given us full assistance. When your name appeared on the flight manifest, they contacted me. I was in the vicinity."

"Following me?"

"Making sure Parrish's sister and niece got their flight without interruption."

"You escorted them on?"

"They don't know me. We're just keeping an eye on certain international flights. It could have been one that Byrnes might have wanted to board."

"But he didn't?"

"No sign of him. It'll be better for everyone when he's finally out of circulation."

This might have been heartfelt, but she had still betrayed us. Ashad in particular.

"So then you decided to come here and set your conscience straight?"

Merrick looked solemn. "If you like. I'm sorry for most of the things you and Ashad went through. Particularly his extended unauthorized detention. But I'm also here to ask you if you think this is a good idea."

"What exactly? Talking to you?"

"Flying to Florida. Pursuing this Leo Parrish thing."

"Why? Am I still in danger?"

Merrick ignored my sarcastic tone. "Of course you are."

"From who exactly? I know about the Ascendants. Anyone else I should be worrying about?"

"If I knew that, I could tell you precisely what to look out for. But whatever Byrnes's agenda was, he was ruthless in pursuit of it. And he must have had some help or at least sanction from someone in the United States. I understand that the Ascendants are going to have a presence at this conference of yours."

"Convention. Know all about that, do you?"

"We wouldn't have been doing our job properly if we hadn't followed up all the links with due diligence."

"By tapping our phones."

She stared me out. "These were questions of national security. We had to act on the information we were given."

"So is Rhodri Davies also being shadowed?"

"No," she said a little sharply, as if she was wearying of my suspicion and hostility. "From what little I know about him I rather admire his keen sense of the absurd. But you shouldn't underestimate the lengths to which some elements in the Ascendancy will go to preserve the sanctity of their beliefs."

"Like burglary and arson?" I talked about the fire at Arthur's Townsend's but she shook her head and said she had no information about that.

"And the break-in at our office?"

"That was Byrnes. I didn't know about it until it was done."

She said it with a plain matter-of-factness that inclined me to believe her.

"Sent you in to pour snake-oil on troubled waters afterwards, did he?"

"Something like that. I had to sell you a line. Don't forget I was acting under orders. I thought it was in a good cause."

I changed tack. "What about illegal experiments on Khanistanis?"

She made me explain. I had the impression that these accusations were news to her, but I was taking nothing for granted. Again she promised me she would look into them.

"Have you ever read any of Parrish's work?"

She shook her head.

"Byrnes never talked to you about it?"

"Not beyond saying it was subversive, that too many people were using it for their own ends."

"What did he mean by that?"

"I assumed he was talking about the Ascendancy."

"He didn't mention its *predictive* qualities?"

I had hesitated to broach this but I wanted to see what her reaction might be. She just looked puzzled.

"What do you mean?"

"Nothing. It doesn't matter."

I didn't want to go into it now: I just wanted to get my flight. I could tell that she would have liked to quiz me but she too was aware that time was running short.

"If you've got what Byrnes was after in your hand luggage you'd better guard it carefully, stay close to friends."

"You're letting me go?"

"You've done nothing illegal, and your documents are in order. What basis would I have for holding you?"

She led me out of the lounge and down another corridor. The big guy was gone but the small one was now leading the way.

"I take it you haven't phoned him," I said to Merrick as we followed him down another corridor.

She knew who I meant.

"I think it's a bit late for that, don't you?"

I had no intention of making it easy for her and didn't say anything.

"How is he? He must be livid."

"Of course he is. But you owe him the explanation more than me."

There was no artifice now: she looked genuinely sad.

"I doubt that he'd listen."

"He'd listen. Though I can't guarantee that he'd believe you."

"Do you?"

Somehow we had emerged at the boarding gate. It was deserted. The Customs guy went to the mouth of the gangway, ready to escort me on to the aeroplane.

"I think," I said to Merrick, "you've told me the truth but maybe not the whole truth."

"I don't know the whole truth myself. But I do know this: you're not necessarily out of danger."

"Does that apply to Ashad, too?"

"Him I can try to keep an eye on, whether he likes it or not. But you can never guarantee someone's safety. He's an adult and we aren't babysitters. You might be taking an even bigger risk."

I thought about it. "Are Claire and her family in danger?"

Their plane had taken off two hours earlier and they would already be a good way across the Atlantic.

"They might be protected by Walter Suthersen's celebrity. Assuming they stay close to him. Whereas you're not exactly a household name. And word will have got around about your interest in Leo Parrish."

Maybe her concern was genuine, but there was no going back.

"Sorry, but I've got to see this through."

She gave a slow nod. I think she had been expecting it.

I walked towards the Customs guy, who had been joined by an airline employee.

"Escaped with a caution, did you?" he said to me, and gave a silly little sniggering laugh.

The steward checked my ticket. Merrick was still lingering.

"Phone Ashad," I reminded her.

"Watch your back," she told me softly.

I took my ticket and headed down the gangway, hugging the flight bag as if it was a parachute.

TWENTY-FOUR

If I had entertained visions of basking on Miami Beach or hobnobbing with celebrities in Ocean Drive nightclubs, they were banished on our arrival. The convention was being held in a big hotel close to the airport, a gaudy ziggurat sitting in its own marina with creeper-strewn balconies like a kitsch version of the Hanging Gardens of Babylon.

Rhodri and his friends had booked into a more modest hotel nearby where the room rates were more favourable, though the place turned out to be modest only in the sense of being small in scale. Inside it was a surreal blend of Art Deco, Hawaiian rustic and tropical rainforest bucolic in a colour scheme of mango, bamboo green and cedar reds. Your eyes were assailed with texture, pattern and ornamentation from the moment you walked into the stringently air-conditioned lobby where sherbet-lemon fish spiralled in bubbly Plexiglas cylinders and the barstools looked like a design collaboration between Rennie Mackintosh and Liberace.

The Latino staff proved urbane and efficient, and in no time at all Rhodri and I were inside our room. Rhodri had booked a twin rather than a double because, he cheerfully told me, he had a habit of flailing around in his sleep, a practice which Ruth had long deemed intolerable. The beds had leopard-print satin covers, and the massive red velvet headboards looked as if they had been designed to cushion the impact from a stray 747.

I phoned Ashad on his mobile. He was still at work and he informed me that Jamilla had also been in, having returned early from Camber Sands, determined not to let Byrnes's intimidation prevent her from getting on with her job.

"Byrnes has vanished," I said. "Did you hear?"

"I heard."

"He might be still lurking in the vicinity."

"So I gather."

I was trying to broach the subject tactfully, but from Ashad's tone I knew that Merrick must have been in touch.

There was a rather ominous silence at the other end of the line: he was waiting for me to say something.

"Did she phone?" I asked.

"She turned up here this afternoon."

After she had spoken to me at Heathrow. "And?"

"I listened to what she had to say. Then I asked her to leave."

His tone was as cold as a fillet of wet fish.

"I think she's genuinely sorry," I said.

"I bet she is."

I took a breath. "Did you believe her?"

"Does it matter?"

"I think it does," I replied, rather surprised to find myself in the position of actually defending Merrick. "It explains a lot."

"It doesn't justify any of it."

"No," I conceded, more to avoid an argument than because Merrick hadn't convinced me of her remorse. "Perhaps not. But I got the impression she actually liked you and was really sorry about how things turned out."

He made no reply to this.

"Did she talk to you about Nigel?"

"We always thought he was a bit of a villain, didn't we?"

"It looks like he might be more than that. Just be careful if he comes around, OK?"

"I think you're the one who needs to be careful."

Now it was my turn not to answer.

"Is this worth it?" he asked.

I knew he meant the whole thing with Leo Parrish, not just my abrupt departure.

"I think it is. I need you to trust me to see it through."

"OK," he said brusquely. "I have to go. It's late."

"Let me know if you hear anything useful from Merrick."

He made a contemptuous noise and cut the connection.

I wasn't entirely surprised that he had given me pretty short shrift, though I hoped he hadn't lost sight of the fact that I was ultimately doing this for what I hoped would be the good of our company.

I hid my flight bag with the *Exaltation* copy behind a large tiger-stripe baroque-style dresser. Rhodri had been at first intrigued and then glum when he had read the second part on the plane, telling me that it was like a prototype tract for the Ascendancy and expressing disappointment that Parrish, whom he had always considered a genuine subversive, had promulgated the intellectually sloppy idea that superior beings could somehow save humanity from its sins.

This wasn't how I remembered the second part at all. When we discussed it further it quickly emerged that the published Part Two was substantially different from the original manuscript version. Skim-reading the pages, I could see what Rhodri meant: all mention of the Unenlightened and their horrific fate had been excised, everything ending neatly with the Exalted inheriting a beautified Earth and having "stewardship" over lesser mortals. I assured Rhodri that the original was far more cautionary in its message, and that if we ever managed to make a movie of the novel it would be based on what Parrish had originally written.

We showered and dressed and sauntered over to the main hotel, just five minutes' walk away, though all of us were swampy again by the time we got there. The convention was occupying three entire floors, and while we queued for our membership packs a small parade of costumed people passed by. There were *Star Wars* storm troopers in full white armour, barbarian warriors and queens, aliens and robots and other characters whose provenance was unknown to me. Then a blue-skinned young woman in a figure-hugging costume walked by, ochre hair slicked back, yellow contact lenses in her eyes.

"Mystique from *X-Men*," I said, impressed not only by the fidelity of the costume but also the rather stimulating way in which it emphasized every sinuous female contour.

Rhodri just blinked noncommittally, telling me that Ruth had issued dire warnings about him ogling other women and that in any case he wasn't really a superhero or comics buff.

I quickly learned that the convention was a welter of sometimes fractious subcultures. In addition to old-time *Star Trek* and *Star Wars* fans, there were devotees of more recent SF movies as well as long-running TV shows like *Doctor Who* and *X-Files*. Alongside these were computer gamers, spaceflight enthusiasts, exotic cat lovers, vampire fetishists, intense men in horn-rimmed glasses who could talk at length about the superlative nature of the original radio series of *The Hitchhiker's Guide to the Galaxy* over all other versions.

I stayed close to Rhodri for most of the evening. Like me, he was on a tight budget and we gravitated towards economy locations where food and drink could be purchased most cost-effectively. At some point, as a floaty sensation of weariness began to kick in, I realized that I was in some sort of party in a room packed with a bunch of articulate and effervescent people who were complete strangers. I had intended to attempt to contact Claire, whom I assumed was staying in the main hotel, presumably in Walter Suthersen's suite, which Rhodri had assured me would be capacious. But it was late and I was tired and people had started asking me to sit on programme discussion panels about cartoon superheroes and Leo Parrish's novel. I couldn't recall having mentioned this, but Rhodri and his friends might have enthusiastically blabbed it abroad. I murmured my excuses and slipped away.

Outside a group of fans had set up a small reflecting telescope in a corner of the hotel forecourt. With the glare from the airport and the cream and lavender hotel up lighters, viewing conditions weren't ideal, but the night was dark and cloudless and a scattering of stars could be seen through the palm-fringed haze. Unsurprisingly they had focused the reflector on the Draco Nova, which latest reports suggested had now reached naked eye magnitude. I was allowed a quick glimpse of a twinkling dot of white light that at one point gave the impression of moving slowly but remorselessly towards me. I jerked my head away in alarm, though I knew that it was just the effects of mild inebriation and jet-lag.

I headed back to the hotel, got my clothes off and had barely slithered under the mahogany sheet before I fell asleep. In the depths of the night I woke and saw a snoring Rhodri splayed on the other bed as if he had been dropped there from a great height. I managed to get the French windows open and went out on to the balcony. It was a still night and the air carried the sultry whiff of nocturnal flowers and gasoline. Nova Draco was visible overhead, a new bright point in the night sky.

*

I woke the following morning to find Rhodri tapping away on his laptop, writing a contribution for the convention bulletin, which was produced in single-sheet hard-copy twice-daily, with a censored digital version not mentioning Parrish by name for those with laptops and smart phones. It was free to anyone who was interested in up-to-date news and gossip. Rhodri wanted to post something about Leo Parrish but reluctantly agreed to defer it until I had spoken to Claire. Instead he skirted around it by mentioning reputed sightings of Edgar Eldridge and Vincent Kubilius at the hotel and mischievously asking whether they were looking for Parrish. Neither of us had actually seen either man, but it made for entertaining copy.

Once he was finished we joined the others in the breakfast room. I kept trying to contact Claire but her mobile didn't ring. Rhodri and I decided track her down through the convention information desk at the main hotel.

When we got over there, Rhodri was soon whisked off to participate in a panel discussion which he assured me would be of interest only to the initiated. He was clearly a respected and well-known figure in the field, fans of all shapes and varieties greeting him with great goodwill wherever he went. Most of the convention attendees were Americans but there was a healthy UK contingent as well as groups from continental Europe, Australasia and a particularly exuberant quartet from Brazil done up in grass skirts, *Buffy the Vampire* T-shirts and silver deeleeboppers.

The information desk was able to confirm that Suthersen and his wife had "two other guests" in their suite, but they had a policy of not volunteering names or putting unofficial phone calls through to guests' rooms. Since his arrival Suthersen himself had made only a fleeting appearance at an author reading and was currently believed to be "off-site". I was made to understand that he would be a busy man, much in demand and difficult for individuals to contact direct. His Guest-of-Honour speech had a peak-time slot that afternoon.

I picked up a copy of the convention newsletter and swiftly discovered that I too was appearing on a panel discussion later that afternoon with Rhodri. It was entitled "Raiders of the Lost Archives", and would focus on the unearthing or rediscovery of science fiction works by forgotten writers. Leo Parrish was prominently mentioned in the blurb, along with the fact that I, "an independent producer whose credits include *DisOrg* and *Absolute Hero*" had acquired a "never-before-seen full version of Leo Parrish's legendary lost novel, *Exceleration*, which is certain to generate a buzz of controversy".

"It wasn't me, boss," Rhodri said sheepishly after I had texted him and we had met up shortly afterwards at one of the balcony bars. "It's not even in my bit, is it?"

"You must have mentioned it to someone."

He didn't attempt to dispute this, but pointed out that I had also been heard talking about it, a possibility that I had to concede on the grounds that I may have been drunker and more jet-lagged than I'd imagined at the time.

I pointed at the sheet. "*Exceleration*," I said scornfully

"They must have misheard it."

"Does everyone get to read this?"

"It's not compulsory, but people do give it a glance to see what programme updates there are."

I gave him a stern look. "This *is* your doing, isn't it?"

Again he pleaded innocence, though there was mischief in his eyes. I could imagine him pitching the idea to the programming committee, persuading them that an item on Leo Parrish would be a good wheeze with the Ascendants also in attendance. Not that anyone had yet seen any concrete evidence of their presence. They were reputed to be keeping a low profile prior to the launch party for their writing contest later that evening.

"So what will I have to do?"

"Just show up and answer the moderator's questions," he told me. "Personally I'd avoid any mention of your brushes with the police and secret service and only talk about the Ascendancy if you're directly asked. Even then you'll need to be careful. They're a pretty litigious lot if they think you're slandering them."

"Great," I said without enthusiasm. "Who else is going to be on the panel?"

"It's still being finalized. It might be just me and you."

I didn't believe this for a moment. "So what are you intending to say?"

He gave a shrug as if to suggest he hadn't thought about it in depth. "I'll probably just burble on about forgotten treasures in the field. There are lots of neglected writers out there."

"I meant about Leo Parrish."

"I thought I'd ask you those questions."

I did a double take. "You're the moderator?"

"Guilty, boss," he admitted, grinning.

"So it *was* your idea."

"Someone came and asked me about it last night. It was late and I was feeling, uh, *empathetic*. I said I thought you'd be up for it."

"Thanks a pile. I'm no expert on Parrish."

"Who is? Anyway, they'll probably want to know about the movie angle."

I wasn't keen. "What if I say I won't do it?"

"You'd disappoint a small but worthy bunch of people. And the chance to give Leo Parrish a little bit of limelight."

I was still dubious. "Any mention of Parrish has a habit of attracting all sorts of dodgy characters."

"You'll be in a room, seated at the front in full view."

"*That's* supposed to inspire confidence?"

Rhodri chuckled. "Only a handful of people are likely to show. It could be interesting. You could bring the typescript along to prove that you've got it."

"No chance," I said firmly, entertaining a vision of Bennett Irwin materializing from some dark space and personally wrenching it out of my hands.

"Will you do it?" Rhodri asked with what I'm certain was a fake air of desperation.

"Sod it," I said. "Yes."

We went our separate ways again for a few hours. I found a quiet room where a handful of people were watching the international news. Muvart's motorized units had now encircled an American base in the border territory and there were reports of small arms fire. The Secretary-General of the United Nations had issued a statement calling for the unconditional withdrawal of Khanistani troops. According to a statement from the Khanistani government President Muvart was at an "undisclosed location" outside the capital where he could continue to direct operations without fear of "Western retaliation".

I was wandering around the art show, looking at paintings of what one of Rhodri's friends had described as "cyber-sleaze"—lots of busty young women in chrome-fetish gear and pouting "plug-in-here" mouths—when my phone burst into the *Mission Impossible* theme.

It was Claire.

"Sorry I haven't been in touch," she said a little breathlessly. "Walter took us sightseeing in the Everglades. My mum's never been before."

"Spot any swamp crocs?"

"Alligators. We went on an airboat."

"How was it?"

"Exhilarating. Where are you?"

"At the convention hotel. You?"

"On our way. We should be back within a couple of hours."

I told her about my impromptu panel, stressing that I hadn't been instrumental in organizing it. Rather than being bothered she was, to my surprise, intrigued.

"I think Walter's planning on saying something about Leo in his speech," she told me in a low voice. "He wouldn't say what. Keep mum about it, will you?"

"Of course. Did you tell him we found the original manuscript of the novel?"

"I did."

"What did he say?"

"Nothing much. He'd like to read it some time, I think."

"Did you know it's different from the published version? Very different."

"In what way?"

I explained the gist of my conversation with Rhodri, speculating that perhaps her uncle had revised it before it was submitted and wondering why. The published text was proto-Ascendancy and Claire herself had later "joined" the Church. I was hoping that the connection between these two facts wasn't something sinister.

But she gave me no impression she knew anything about it and reminded me that she had never read either version.

I considered telling her about my conversation with DI Merrick but decided it could wait since she was obviously in transit.

"Everything else all right?" I asked. "No one stalking you?"

"Fine. So far, so good."

"I'm on at three o'clock," I told her. "Be good to see you afterwards."

"I'll be there," she promised.

I wondered what Suthersen planned to say about Leo Parrish. Aside from Nora and Edgar Eldridge, Suthersen was the only other living person I was aware of who had actually known him. I assumed his comments would be benign, especially with Nora and Claire likely to be in the audience, but on the flight over Rhodri had reminded me that Parrish was a slightly touchy subject for Suthersen. It wasn't inconceivable that he was keeping Claire and particularly Nora close to minimize the risk of any revelations that might damage his status as one of the Grand Old Men of Science Fiction.

I had lunch at a Cuban bar on one of the mezzanine balconies, sitting with a group of movie fans over *empanadas* and alcohol-free daiquiris, watching the flights come and go at the airport, me mostly listening to fairly animated discussions about French noir, the career of Robin Williams and the respective merits of the various *Red Dwarf* series. What struck me most about the varied groups of people at the convention was a common thread of deep engagement with both high and popular culture. They enjoyed the kind of intellectual discourse that flipped effortlessly between the sacred and the profane.

Half an hour before the panel was due to start Rhodri found me and introduced another panellist, a black American woman in her early thirties called Rheanna Finch. I had a dim recollection of briefly meeting her at the previous night's party. A science-fiction fan, she was interesting in several respects, not least because she was carrying her three-month-old daughter in a papoose. She was also, I now remembered, a lapsed Ascendant, which was notable because the Church membership was overwhelmingly white. As, it occurred to me, was the convention audience.

Though the Ascendancy connection bothered me in case Rhodri intended it as a provocation, I found Rheanna herself to be articulate about the cult, which she had joined as a young woman, spending thousands of dollars on its courses before discovering that the community of fans existing around her other interest was far less expensive to service and much more fun. When she learned that the Church had been founded by a go-getting former editor of ephemeral magazines who was reputed to have said, "There's big bucks in belief", her disillusionment was complete.

But the Church wasn't finished with her, and she had continued to suffer bouts of mostly legal harassment, being threatened with court orders if she made any "unauthorized disclosures" about its inner workings and in particular revealed any details about the rituals and financial demands of progressing up the seven levels.

"You're not going to raise this on the panel, are you?" I said to Rhodri.

"I'm not here to talk about my past," Rheanna assured me, one arm cupped around her sleeping infant.

She told me she had never read Leo Parrish or even heard of him before last night and had agreed to go on the panel to talk about some feminist SF writers of the 1960s and '70s whom she felt had been unjustly marginalized.

"Has Rhodri told you that Leo Parrish's novel was a direct stimulus for Edgar Eldridge's religious notions?" I asked.

"He mentioned it. I can't say I'm surprised. The Ascendancy belief system is a real mishmash when you look at it with a proper perspective. But I'm happy for you to talk about that. I'd rather keep out of it."

I gave Rhodri a stern look. "I hope you're paying attention. She has her baby to think of as well. Imagine it was Ruth."

He looked alarmed at the idea. "You have my word," he said solemnly.

I had assumed that the panel would be held in one of the small subsidiary rooms, but I found myself walking into a place the size of a ballroom, with chairs arranged in rows on both sides of a central aisle. Thankfully, fewer than a dozen people were present, six of them Rhodri's pals, another two an elderly couple who had the perplexed look of tourists at the wrong location. And in the front row was a black man in his thirties with two pre-teen children whom Rheanna introduced as the rest of her family.

It was a shrewd move to have her baby in her arms and her family sitting close just in case there was trouble. A woman from the convention committee appeared and effusively apologized to Rhodri for not having been able to come up with a fourth panellist. Good, I thought to myself, imagining that we might be able to get it over with sooner rather than later.

There were still five minutes to go. We were given bottles of water and there was a brief microphone check. More people had started to drift into the room, as though our arrival had finally persuaded an incipient audience that the panel was actually going to happen. I saw Arthur Townsend in Bermudas and black T-shirt with a star map showing a prancing golden lion on his chest. I gave him a diffident wave but he blanked me completely, sitting down at the far end of one row close to the front, his face already a mask of intense concentration and perhaps latent disapproval.

"He's brought Leo with him," Rhodri remarked, deadpan.

Others were coming in, most middle-aged and elderly, taking up seats towards the rear of the room, probably so that they could make a quick exit if the panel proved dull. As yet, there was no sign of Claire.

The convention committee woman hastily introduced us, doing Rhodri at some length, then quoting my CV direct from the flyer since she obviously didn't know anything about me. She was even more clueless about Rheanna, whom she asked to introduce herself.

At this point a small retinue swept into the room and strode straight down the aisle, taking up seats in the front row opposite Rheanna's family. There were six of them, two pairs of smartly-dressed men and women in their thirties who were obviously minders, flanking Vincent Kubilius and an elderly but sprightly-looking guy, a little stooped perhaps, his tanned head naked apart from threads of grey hair that were all that remained of a once-dark and prominent widow's peak.

"Bloody hell," Rhodri murmured gleefully. "It's Edgar Eldridge."

And there really was no mistaking him. Both Rhodri and I had seen the photograph of Eldridge in his youth, and images of him had been published intermittently over the years, though none in the past decade. It was the first time he had been out in public for many years as far as I knew, but he didn't have that haunted, twitchy air of the recluse. Sitting there in a cerise polo shirt and putty-coloured slacks he looked, if anything, as if he was already enjoying himself before the panel had even got underway.

I don't suppose that anyone in the room really clocked what Rheanna was saying about herself apart from her loyal family. A buzz had gone around the room and most of the attention was directed at the front row. Here was, in effect, the Prophet and Pope of the Church of Ascendancy and we only had a Parrish to challenge their authority.

Everyone was now ready for proceedings to begin. The doors at the rear were still open and even more people were now slipping in: word was getting around.

Rhodri pulled his mike closer.

"Thank you all for coming," he began with slow deliberation. He looked straight down at the front row. "I'd particularly like to welcome our distinguished guests, Mr Vincent Kubilius and in particular Mr Edgar Eldridge, whom it's intriguing to see renewing his associations with science fiction after many years."

There was a little flurry of rather uncertain applause. Beyond giving a curt nod, Kubilius sat rigid, whereas Edgar Eldridge immediately got to his feet and executed a good-natured bow which caused the applause to redouble as though the audience was now sensing that there might be some fun or fireworks to come.

"Perhaps," Rhodri said provocatively, "since we're short of one panellist, Mr Eldridge might like to join us on stage and give us the benefit of his reflections on his time as a magazine editor and in particular his memories of Leo Parrish."

Rhodri later told me that he never expected Eldridge to take up his offer, and certainly Vincent Kubilius made it clear from his body language and a whispered exchange that he didn't think it was a good idea.

Eldridge, still on his feet, ignored him completely. Giving a little wave like a five-star general about to depart on a conquering mission, he said, "Why the hell not?" and promptly clambered up on to the stage.

I have to admit that a really peculiar feeling went through me when we shook hands. Eldridge, though stooped and wizened, came across as a convivial figure, grinning and patting our arms as he shook, planting a kiss on the back of Rheanna's hand while she looked on in astonishment. Then he plonked himself down next to her at the end of the row, dragging his chair up close.

"Let's get rolling," he told Rhodri. "You guys pitch in first and say whatever's on your mind and I'll just sit back until I can get up to speed."

A clever move, I thought, forcing the onus back on us so that he could wait and listen and see what cropped up. Rhodri did the most sensible thing at that point, which was to start with Rheanna, asking her to come up with a short list of feminist writers whom she considered important and to explain why she did so.

With Eldridge sitting right next to her and making a show of being enchanted by her baby, she proved more confident and lucid than anyone had the right to expect, talking for several minutes about writers whose names were completely unknown to me but who had obviously inspired her as both a woman and a black woman. I think that under any other circumstances her comments would have generated plenty of discussion and feedback from the audience, but there was a sense on this occasion that they were just a prelude to the main show.

Rhodri asked her a few probing questions which kept her going a little longer before things petered out. He looked at me, obviously striving to think of a link; and, realizing that I was useless in this particular context, instead turned to Eldridge.

"The sixties and seventies were times when there was a great deal of interest in the counterculture and gender relations," Rhodri said. "How does that compare with the late fifties, when you were editing *Awesome Adventures*?"

Eldridge gave him a steady look out of narrowed eyes. For a moment I thought he wasn't going to answer.

"In my day there were no black writers around that I knew of," he said. "And precious few women. All my contributors were young men who'd write practically anything for a few bucks. Most of them had names like Rosenberg and Liechtenstein." He paused to acknowledge a little flurry of laughter. "Science fiction was just a small part of it. We did everything. Westerns, thrillers, crime, you name it. Ridge Publications was a fiction factory."

Rhodri was nodding earnestly, playing the attentive and accommodating host.

"I gather, though, that science fiction was your particular favourite," he said, framing it as half-question, half-statement.

"Couldn't get enough of it," Eldridge agreed. "Particularly when it came to stories that explored the untapped powers of the human mind." He leaned forward, rubbing his hands together. "You're going to want to ask me if they had any influence on how I developed my own systems of belief, and I'll tell you, it was big time. Big time. I used to talk things through with my contributors, get them into the office and do some brainstorming. We'd go at it until we were on to something good, then I'd send them off to make a story out of it. Almost never failed."

This was new, to Rhodri as much as to me. Eldridge appeared to be suggesting that he was as much responsible for the creative input of the stories he published as were the writers themselves.

"Was Leo Parrish an important part of this process?" Rhodri asked.

"Ha!" Eldridge said, midway between a laugh and an exclamation. "Leo Parrish was a different kettle of fish. Worked to his own rhythms, brought a story in whenever he had one and then disappeared again till payday."

"He delivered them by hand?"

"Well, he didn't live too far away. He'd phone first to ask if it was convenient to drop by. It always was. We could never get enough good copy."

"You rated his work?"

"Sure as hell did."

He didn't elaborate but murmured something to Rheanna off-microphone. He was smiling, but she looked slightly unsettled and didn't reply.

Rhodri now turned in my direction, obviously wanting to include me in the discussion.

"Carry on," I urged him. "We're all really interested."

The audience was quiet and expectant. People were still filtering in at the back.

Rhodri turned back to Eldridge, who gave every impression of enjoying being in the spotlight. "Can you remember how many Parrish stories you published altogether?"

Eldridge pouted, shook his head. "It was over half a century ago. Some of the people here in this hall weren't even born." He was looking at Rheanna's family. "Some of their *parents* weren't even born."

This time the laughter was more restrained.

"Between fifteen and twenty, perhaps?" Rhodri prompted.

"Maybe. In that ballpark."

"All in *Awesome*?"

"It was the only science fiction magazine in our stable."

"But later you started up a sister magazine."

He just nodded.

"Would you like to tell us something about it?"

"It was called *Shocking Stories*. Hell of a name to give a magazine but we thought—why not? *Shock* and *Awe*." He chuckled to himself. "I'm sure they stole that from us."

A few more people had joined the front row on the Ascendants' side, all youngish, one of them wearing big black sunglasses and an over-large fedora. It was Ryan Carmichael, ostentatious even in disguise. No one else in the audience was paying him any particular attention.

"You serialized Leo Parrish's novel, *Exaltation*," Rhodri said to Eldridge.

Eldridge nodded, showing no sign that he was uneasy about the direction in which Rhodri was going.

"Nick Randall," Rhodri said to me, "you've recently become interested in Leo Parrish's work with a view to possibly filming it. I gather you managed to get your hands on typescript copies of the original novel."

"That's true," I said.

"Anything you'd like to tell us about that?"

"Well," I said, making a last-minute decision not to hold back, "one interesting thing is that the published version in the magazine is completely different from the original. Part two of the serial at least."

"That's because I rewrote it," Eldridge said bluntly.

There was a brief pause while Rhodri took stock.

"You did?" he said slowly as if he was still absorbing it. "A complete rewrite?"

"Pretty much," Eldridge confirmed.

"Was that common practice?"

"Not at all. There usually wasn't time, even if I'd wanted. And Leo was always pretty reliable."

"But you did in this case."

"It was essential. What he'd written didn't fit."

People were shifting around in their seats, though not with impatience. Even if they had never heard of Leo Parrish before, they were listening to the founder of the Church of the Ascendancy openly talking in a public forum about his former role as an editor of a word-hungry publish-or-perish science-fiction magazine. They were eager to hear more.

"I had my own ideas by then," Eldridge said. "They were developing fast, taking me by storm. They were the prototype of a full belief system, if you like, and I had to get them down in my own way."

In his seat, Kubilius had actually put a thumb and forefinger across his eyebrows in what was a blatant signal of discomfort. He had neither expected nor wanted Eldridge to be so forthcoming.

"So your later interest which became the Ascendant Church grew out of this?" Rhodri asked carefully.

"I don't deny it," Eldridge said heartily. "It was the prototype, the seed. But as far as I was concerned, I had to do the planting and watering so that the whole thing would bear fruit."

There was a silence. Even Rhodri didn't seem to know quite what to ask next. I knew there was no point in being cagey now.

"The second part of the author's original ends quite suddenly," I remarked.

Eldridge gave another pouting shrug, as if to say: So?

"I was wondering—did you originally plan to publish it as a three-parter?"

He looked as if he was thinking about it. Or thinking about precisely how to frame his answer.

"The way it was," he said, reaching up to stroke the naked foot of Rheanna's baby, "I never had the whole thing to start with. The arrangement was that Leo would deliver each part as it was finished. We had a pretty quick turnaround, so the first issue was already out there on the newsstands before he came in with part two." He was still stroking the baby's foot, as though it was helping him dredge up the memories. "Times were tough. By then we already knew we would have to fold the magazine. There wasn't going to be a third issue."

The baby woke and started to snuffle. Rheanna, who had been looking increasingly uncomfortable, pushed her chair back so that her daughter was free of Eldridge's attentions.

"So how did Leo Parrish take the news?" Rhodri asked

"I didn't have the heart to tell him," Eldridge replied. "Leo was never much of a conversationalist. He was always eager to get in and out of the office as quick as possible."

Rheanna's baby started to cry. There was no quietening her. Rheanna blurted her apologies into the microphone, got up and left the stage. Her husband led her and their other two children out of the hall, the baby now squalling freely.

Eldridge kept smiling throughout all this, radiating benevolence and bonhomie. From Rhodri I knew that he had two grown-up children himself, a son who was a lawyer working for the Church and a daughter who had rejected it entirely, marrying a French Buddhist and emigrating to Peru, where she ran a second-hand CD store in Arequipa.

During this little interregnum there was a flurry of movement in the audience, people coming and going, most taking the opportunity to get closer to the action. Ryan Carmichael had slipped out as stealthily as he had come, but Kubilius was still sitting there with his minders as if he had been carved from wax, determined to keep an eye on things.

As the hubbub began to die down Rhodri tapped on the microphone and then gave a brief resumé of Leo Parrish's career for the benefit of the majority of the audience who would never have heard of him until now. Eldridge sat listening to this with a genial expression, as though it was conjuring fond memories of his youth. Rhodri didn't go into detail about Parrish's work, merely saying that his stories were notable for their invention and that Parrish had died tragically much later in a shooting that was never explained.

"Maybe it was the FBI," Eldridge said.

"What?" said an astonished Rhodri.

"It might have been a case of mistaken identity, which is why they covered it up."

"They?" said Rhodri. "Who?"

Eldridge shrugged. "You tell me. But it happens."

His tone had a hint of the paranoid whose deepest fears had proven well grounded on other occasions. The Ascendants had always had an ambivalent relationship towards various law enforcement agencies, complaining in their early years of excessive snooping by the intelligence services in a variety of countries while at the same time seeking to cultivate closer ties with local police forces, especially since Kubilius had taken over the reins. Had Eldridge been the one who had instilled their earlier paranoia?

"Why would they want to do that?" Rhodri asked gingerly.

Eldridge just shrugged. "Who can say? But it's always worth asking the question when you have a killing that's never been solved."

The comments made me wonder for the first time whether the Ascendants had been behind Parish's murder while simultaneously finding it hard to believe that Eldridge would publicly float the suggestion if he wanted to avoid any discussion of it.

"Hadn't Parrish stopped writing years before?" I chipped in.

"As far as I'm aware," Eldridge agreed. "I never saw him again after *Shocking* folded. Maybe you ought to ask someone who kept in touch with him, like Walter there. Hello, Walt!"

He was indicating the audience. Sitting in the front in the spaces formerly occupied by Rheanna Finch's family were Suthersen, Nora and Claire.

I hadn't spotted them coming in. Or had they been there from the start, seated further back, only moving forward when the seats became vacant?

For the benefit of the rest of the audience who might not have been able to see, Rhodri announced that Walter Suthersen was in the front row. It occurred to me that at last Leo Parrish was getting a bit of full-frontal publicity. The entire room, perhaps a hundred people, had now heard of him, and his name had attracted the attendance of at least two internationally-known people. Three if you counted the mercurial Ryan Carmichael. Whatever else happened, it was unlikely that Leo Parrish's genie would ever go back in the lamp now.

Suthersen acknowledged the greeting with a self-effacing smile. Claire waved at me, looking relaxed. Nora sat with Suthersen's arm tucked through hers, a remote expression on her face. Was she having one of her wayward episodes? Or was she just absorbed in old memories and emotions? There was no sign of Barbara Suthersen.

"Walt was one of my office boys in those days," Eldridge said jocularly. "He was just starting out, looking to make his own way in the field. That right, Walt?"

Suthersen nodded in acknowledgement. It was interesting that Eldridge had claimed that Suthersen had kept in touch with

Parrish after he had stopped writing. Suthersen hadn't denied it either.

"He did a lot of the copy-editing, some of the typesetting too, as I recall. Like me he was always pleased when Parrish showed up with one of those stories of his. We all pulled together. Worked eighteen-hour days, weekends too when it mattered."

Eldridge seemed ready to drift off into a series of generalized musings about the old days, but Rhodri cut across him: "Perhaps Mr Suthersen would also like to join us up here to share a few reminiscences?"

Suthersen rose but said, "I've got my own place in the spotlight tomorrow, and I'm happy for Edgar to have his now. I'll let you know if I think any of his recollections are faulty."

This was said lightly, and Eldridge acknowledged it with a chuckle. Suthersen sat down again. I wondered how many years had passed since he and Eldridge had last exchanged words.

Rhodri again addressed Eldridge: "After the second issue of *Shocking* appeared, Leo Parrish never published any other stories, did he?"

Eldridge gave the question a second or two's consideration. "Not to my knowledge."

"Was he unhappy about the fact that you'd rewritten the second part?"

"I've never met a writer who's happy about being edited," Eldridge said bullishly. He paused. "Hell's bells, this is like being on the witness stand!"

The laughter he had expected didn't come.

"I was just interested," Rhodri said affably. "Since Leo Parrish is one of the subjects of this discussion, I wondered if you could throw any light on why he suddenly stopped writing."

For the first time Eldridge showed just a hint of irritation. But he quickly recovered.

"What can I say? I'm sure he was pissed but, hey, we're not talking about Shakespeare or *Esquire* magazine here, are we?"

This again failed to raise any laughter. Eldridge, perhaps sensing that the audience's interest in the issue was respectful, changed tack.

"It wasn't done out of malice," he assured everyone. "It was a straightforward practical matter, a simple question of economics. We paid on publication but we were haemorrhaging money. I had to make the serial fit into two issues. I saw a way of doing it, a way that tied in with my own ideas. As the editor, I had to make a tough decision to salvage what I could."

There was a lone cheer from somewhere in the audience that swiftly died away to silence.

"If it's any consolation," Eldridge said. "I still paid him the half cent a word for both parts. Came out of my own pocket. I felt I owed him."

"How did he take it?" I asked.

"Like a gentleman," Eldridge replied.

I indicated by my silence that I was hoping for more.

"He thanked me politely for the money and then walked out of there. I never saw or heard from him again."

TWENTY-FIVE

Perhaps because the audience were growing restive with the minutiae of Parrish's writing career, we drifted away from the subject. Rhodri let Eldridge tell anecdotes about the difficulties in running a shoestring magazine stable with a bunch of mostly eccentric contributors, and he gave good copy, coming across as a pragmatic editor who wasn't deluded about the nature of his publishing operation. Despite being the founder of the Ascendant Church and presumably at the highest spiritual level within it, Eldridge didn't reveal any advanced mental powers and his language was quite earthy, laced with slang and mild expletives. If this was part of a charm offensive to persuade the convention audience that he was an ordinary Joe, it didn't appear to have been sanctioned by Kubilius, who continued to look as if he was sitting on a bed of nails.

But Eldridge knew his audience, or did in the sense that he was shrewd enough not to attempt to proselytize or even mention the Ascendancy by name. He stayed focused on his time in the science-fiction world, on his humble yet worthy role in trying to publish the best "mind-blowing fiction" his meagre budget would allow. As he talked about his magazine days, I imagined that Walter Suthersen might interject to elaborate an anecdote or even engage in a little banter when Eldridge was obviously exaggerating or teasingly referring to him as "my office boy". But Suthersen appeared content to listen. Beside him, Nora looked as if she was dozing, her shoulder resting against Claire's

But then Eldridge said something that made both Rhodri and me sit up mentally. Referring to the fact that the small team who produced the magazines was like a family, he then added, "When

Walt joined us as a young man, he even brought his wife along." Eldridge described a young blonde "straight out of the boondocks" who was the most upright person he knew and a damned efficient secretary. He obviously meant Barbara. She and Suthersen must have got married when they were in their teens.

If this was conversational bait, Suthersen still didn't rise to it. Rhodri didn't pursue the matter but now opened the floor to questions from the audience. I had said relatively little but I didn't mind a bit: to have Edgar Eldridge on stage was far more of a coup for the convention than the discovery of an original Leo Parrish manuscript.

The first question from the audience came from an American pal of Rhodri's.

"I'd like to know if Mr Eldridge thinks there's any connection between science fiction and the Church of the Ascendancy," he said.

You could immediately sense an expectant hush falling over the room.

"Depends," Eldridge said, slouched in his chair and giving no indication that he considered the question improper. "I suppose you could say I'm the connection."

This again was meant to induce a laugh which did not materialize.

"I mean," Rhodri's pal went on, "do you think your experience as a science-fiction magazine editor influenced your religious thought?"

"Absolutely," said Eldridge. "Our Church is about harnessing the power of the human mind, and a lot of the science fiction I was interested in dealt with that."

"So your religion is derived from science fiction."

This was the nub of it, and I could see that Kubilius was ready to leap up from his seat at any moment and drag Eldridge out of there if necessary. But Eldridge was the founder; Kubilius was just his major domo.

Eldridge himself stayed relaxed. "Everything grows out of everything else, you know? My revelation was my own—"

"A religious one?" Rhodri interjected. "A flash of blinding light, like Saul on the road to Damascus?"

Rhodri had been very diplomatic up to now, but this was dangerously close to outright mockery.

Eldridge just smiled. "If you like. It certainly had the quality of a newly emergent truth. Though it was more slow-burning, a coming together of insights and undercurrents that became so pressing they just had to be released into the world—" He caught himself. "But, hey, I'm not here to talk about that, right? This is a science-fiction convention. People's personal faiths are a matter for them and them alone. If you want to find out more about mine, then our information desk is now open in the third-floor lobby. Come along and ask. Or not—it's up to you. But I hope we get a healthy turn-out at our "Future Voices" launch this evening. We want to foster some incredible new talent in the field. There'll be a free drink in it, but we're not going to ask you to give blood or anything."

I knew from earlier conversations that the science-fiction community was deeply suspicious of any association between themselves and the Church. There was considerable controversy over the committee having accepted a sizable donation from the Ascendancy in exchange for a presence at the convention. Science fiction fans already saw themselves as unfairly stigmatized by the outside world as nerdish obsessives who believed in aliens and flying saucers. The last thing they wanted was to be thought of as sympathetic to a cult they considered ludicrously irrational.

And yet Eldridge had done a clever job in presenting himself as a man who hadn't lost touch with the ordinary world and had a relaxed view of his own belief system. His homely style was far better suited to his audience than some slick presentation from the likes of Kubilius. What I couldn't decide was whether Eldridge actually believed in his own religion in the accepted sense of implicit faith arising from sublime revelation or whether it was just an eccentric personal philosophy that he had glorified to make a few bucks.

"Are you aware that some people feel they've been harassed by members of your Church?"

This was Claire, who had got to her feet the moment the opportunity presented itself.

Eldridge gave her a long squinty look while Kubilius went very still.

"I'm assuming you're speaking from personal experience," Eldridge said.

"I am," she replied boldly.

"That's unfortunate. And unacceptable if it's true. But I can't really comment without knowing all the facts. Sometimes people get overzealous, you know?"

She held his gaze. "That's what people at the top always say. It sounds like you're fobbing me off."

"Then I apologize," he replied immediately. "I'd be happy to have it looked into if you give the details to one of my aides afterwards." He kept eyeing her. "Do I know you?"

"No," she replied. "But I met Mr Kubilius recently—well, it wasn't so much a meeting as a confrontation."

This time it was Eldridge who waited.

"I'm Leo Parrish's niece," she told him. "My mother here was his sister."

Nora now had her eyes open and looked alert; but she wasn't saying anything or giving anything away.

"Well, well," Eldridge said, his face creasing in a broad smile. "I'm very pleased to meet you both. I promise you—I will look into your complaint."

"Is that an *official* promise?" Claire asked.

Eldridge made a motion of licking his forefinger and then crossing his heart.

He was still smiling, giving no sign that it was forced or that he felt cornered. I could tell that Claire would have liked to have said more but that this wasn't the time or place. She sat back down again. Without looking at her, Nora reached across and squeezed her hand.

As if to lighten the mood, another questioner rose and asked me if I was serious about making a movie out of Leo Parrish's work

"We're seriously looking into it," I told him.

"Do you have a particular story in mind?"

The guy was elderly, obviously someone who had read Parrish. While I didn't want to disappoint him, I knew it might be dangerous to give too much away.

"I can't tell you that," I said, "in case someone from Universal or Sony is sitting in the audience, ready to steal it from us."

He didn't crack a smile. I'm not sure he liked the idea of Parrish being filmed.

"Do you think they'll let you get away with it?" came another voice.

It was Arthur, who had got to his feet, the Leo constellation emblazoned across his chest. He struck an upright and defiant pose, as if he expected a posse of Ascendants to come surging out of the shadows at any moment to trample him down. Presumably he had made the trip to Florida alone: there was no sign of Molly.

"Well, Arthur," I said, "I hope I have better luck than you." I looked around the audience and went on: "Arthur had a house fire recently back in the UK. Fortunately no one was injured, but he lost a lot of valuable books and magazines. The police haven't found out who was responsible."

"That's tragic," Eldridge said. "Taming fire was the main thing that set humans on the path from primitive to modern."

No one quite knew what to say to this *non sequitur*. I was worried that Arthur might blurt out his suspicions and get himself into legal hot water.

"You know what I mean, don't you?" Arthur persisted to me.

He had evidently got word of the difficulties I had encountered since our meeting. I was rather relieved he wasn't publicly asking for his magazines back.

"I do, Arthur," I assured him. "I do. But this probably isn't the appropriate place to be discussing it."

As I spoke I was looking at Kubilius and his cronies to gauge their reaction. Eldridge had seemed innocent of any knowledge of what might be behind the fire, which didn't surprise me in the slightest given that he had been thousands of miles away and apparently wasn't sensitive about people making connections between the Ascendancy and Leo Parrish. But Kubilius, with his emphasis on PR and surface respectability, was a different matter.

Kubilius was staring straight at me. He looked as if his face had been sprayed with novocaine. I was guessing he couldn't wait to get Eldridge out of there.

One of the convention committee appeared and started making winding-up motions. Phone cameras began flashing, their owners doubtless eager to get a personal snap of the elusive Eldridge, who duly smiled and gave his audience another military wave, perfectly comfortable to have his photograph taken despite pre-convention rumours to the contrary. Then he got gingerly down from the stage and exchanged a brief word with Suthersen before he was surrounded by Kubilius and his aides, who swept him away through a side-door like a covey of magicians jealously guarding their prize party trick.

"That was interesting," Rhodri said to me and Claire as we stood around in the aftermath. "Not what I'd expected at all."

People were still milling about, though Walter Suthersen had taken Nora back to his suite for a siesta as soon as Eldridge left.

"Good for you for speaking up," I commented to Claire

"It was essential," she replied. "I wasn't going to pass up the opportunity of letting him know who we were."

"I think he's pretty clear about that now. What did he say to Walter afterwards?"

"'Those were the good old days'. I think he really meant it."

"Were you there for the whole item?"

"Most. We got back shortly after it started. My mum was really nervous."

"How did she take it?"

"She's good at putting her mind into neutral when she has to. I think it's a way of dampening down the stimulus."

"She didn't say anything?"

Claire shook her head.

"Where's Barbara?" I asked. "Didn't she come to the Everglades with you?"

"According to Walter, she hates these conventions. I think she's gone off to play golf and go shopping in Palm Beach."

I had Eldridge pegged as a golfer, despite his age. Provided you stayed supple enough, it was one of those sports you could keep on playing until your heart gave out.

"No wonder the published serial reads like the Ascendant's vision of the future," I said to Rhodri, "given that Eldridge was the author."

"Not a bone of contention for him either."

Plenty of other people wanted to talk to Rhodri in the aftermath, and there were a couple of individuals keen to discuss the film angle with me. Neither them of looked like a secret agent or Ascendant in disguise and I was happy to chat to them, mostly about the difficulties of a small production company raising the funding to make such a project possible. At the same time I was looking around for Arthur, wanting to apologize for the trouble I had unwittingly caused after showing up at his door. He was nowhere in sight. But I did spot someone else I recognized: Cyrus Hammond in his pale linen suit. He gave me a distant wave before slipping out at the back. By the time I had pointed it out to Claire, he was gone.

"Did he tell you he was coming?" I asked.

She shook her head. "I haven't heard from him."

I didn't know whether I was reassured or disturbed by Hammond's presence. Given his official business interests, it made sense that he would attend the convention. But he claimed to have links with the US intelligences services, and it seemed to me at that moment that too many people associated with all the intrigue around Leo Parrish were in attendance.

Claire and I eventually managed to thread our way out of the room. We were both eager for some time alone together.

"I'd like to get away from here," she told me. "Do you fancy a drive?"

"Did you have somewhere in mind?"

"As a matter of fact, I do."

*

Suthersen had a virtuous white Fusion hybrid on hire for the convention, and Claire had a spare set of keys. We drove north through Fort Lauderdale, eventually reaching a low-rise coastal town with the quaintly British-sounding name of Lauderdale-By-The-Sea, though with its palms and long sun-drenched beach it looked nothing like a British seaside resort. Claire took a road west out of the town and soon we found ourselves in front of a big arching sign of flashing comets and starbursts that said:

WELCOME TO FAR FRONTIERS
HOME OF FUTURES PAST

Rhodri had already mentioned the place. Conceived as a theme-park based on science-fiction visions of the future and intended to complement similar visitor attractions in the state, it had been a doomed enterprise from the start, running out of money when the credit crunch hit with many of its rides and exhibits unfinished. This, Claire told me, was part of its appeal to her.

"I'm drawn to white elephants," she had told me. "I like places that never quite got off the ground or have just been allowed to slide into neglect."

She mentioned a series of photographs she had taken of the dilapidated Battersea power station, said that modern images of dereliction influenced her own art, that rust was more intriguing than chrome. It was an aspect of herself she hadn't revealed before. She was jaunty, pleased to be spending time with me, and I had no wish to ruin the mood at that moment by telling her about Merrick and Byrnes. We hadn't spoken at any length about the panel either, both of us just wanting some normal time together and perhaps sensing that the full story of her uncle might still be unfolding.

Far Frontiers was ringed with electric fencing and KEEP OUT signs, the drive-through entranceway sealed with heavy-duty security gates. To one side stood a check-in booth styled after the monolith in Kubrick's *2001: A Space Odyssey*. Claire produced a Far Frontiers Stellar key card, courtesy of Walter Suthersen, who had been one of the original backers of the project and had allowed the place to be named after his best-known book series. She swiped it through a slot next to a large recessed oval. After a second or two the oval began to iris open, the curved segments squeaking as they ground over one another, little showers of dust cascading from them. Even the future wasn't immune to the ravages of time.

The road that spiralled through the park was bordered with spore-like streetlights beyond which a welter of unlikely architectures jostled for visual attention. There was a flying saucer spin-ride, Martian war machine rocking tripods, bucking broncos based on the beach-ball aliens from *Silent Running*, a *Terminator* shoot-'em-up game in a half-finished maze. We passed a tunnel ride from *Moon Stalker* in which Ryan Carmichael had played a bounty hunter tracking mutant serial killers on the satellites of Jupiter.

As you went further in, the attractions became sparser, bordered by the concrete skeletons of incomplete installations, or bare foundations that had lain untended long enough for native grasses and weeds to start re-colonizing them. It was as if we were nearing the edges of this particular universe, boldly going where few had gone before, into a zone where the place's own sense of integrity began to break down. Only now did Claire get out her Nikon and start taking photographs.

I let her wander off while I looked around, wishing the souvenir store had been open so that I could have purchased a futuristic space cap to wear against the low evening sun. In the solitude of the site, that familiar unnerving sense that we were being followed arose in me. On the journey out I had occasionally checked to see if any vehicle was tailing us. There was none as far as I could judge, and no sign of any life here apart from us. Yet still I felt as if someone might have crept up one of the pre-cast stairways or scuttled along the unfinished maglev track and was watching us from hiding.

My phone began pulsating on mute. It was Rhodri, calling from our hotel.

"You'd better get back here, boss," he said. "I think we might have been robbed."

It took us less than half an hour to make the return trip, Claire driving with all the urgency I would have expected after I told her my hotel room had been turned over. Though I was disgusted with myself for even entertaining the notion, I couldn't help but reflect that she had actually taken me away while the burglary had probably been happening.

Nothing else had been taken from the room apart from my flight bag. Rhodri had only guessed that someone had searched it because the furniture was out of place. The hotel manager was hugely apologetic. None of the staff had any idea how the intruder or intruders had got in, he told me. The keys were electronic cards and the cleaner insisted she had closed the door behind her that morning. No one had seen anything. He wanted me to make a list of everything that had gone missing before he contacted the police.

"It was just some photocopied pages from an old magazine," I told him. "Nothing else."

Rhodri looked bewildered, Claire merely anxious—which were just the reactions I would have expected from innocent parties.

It took a while to persuade the manager that I didn't want to follow up the incident and wasn't even going to make a claim on my travel insurance. By the time I had finally got him to leave, both Rhodri and Claire were giving me very curious glances.

"It's fine," I said, and then I showed them where I had actually hidden the package rather than the bunch of hotel and convention literature I had used to bulk out the flight bag.

Delving under my pillow, I lifted the loose lower section of the padded headboard. I had spotted it the previous night when it moved after I had got into bed and decided that this would be a safer place for storing the pages. The space wasn't big enough for the bag as well, and in any case I had wanted something that would act as a decoy. So I had secreted the manuscripts there while Rhodri slept on undisturbed by my rummaging.

"Clever," he conceded. "I'd have stuffed it in my underwear drawer."

"Who do you think it was?" Claire wanted to know. She looked rattled again.

"Most likely the Ascendants," I told her. "Maybe Kubilius sent someone over after the panel."

I hadn't mentioned my sighting of Cyrus Hammond, and it seemed unlikely he would want to steal something he had already rescued for me.

Her mobile started ringing.

It was Walter Suthersen, calling with breaking news. The space shuttle Endeavour was being launched that night.

*

Suthersen had pals at NASA, many of whose scientists were fans of his work, and he had wangled a ringside seat at the launch for himself and Barbara. Rhodri and I accompanied Claire back to the convention hotel, where big screens were already being made available in several of the conference rooms for TV coverage of the event, which was attracting greater than usual public interest because of the abruptness of the announcement and the uncertain international situation.

The stealing of my flight bag had left me fatalistically calm. I had almost expected it and was relieved that no one had actually been scared or hurt in the process. It might have been anyone from the Ascendants to an Arthur Townsend madly determined to pay me back for the fire—not a possibility I gave any credence to. I couldn't see the point of involving the police, since I didn't want to be distracted from further opportunities to speak with some of the principals in the Leo Parrish story. Even so, it seemed prudent to stay in public and among company, so when Claire went off to check on her mother, I decided to accompany Rhodri and his pals to the "Future Voices" event.

Already under way by the time we arrived, the launch was being held in one of the larger conference rooms and had been arranged as an informal panel where half a dozen bemused-looking fresh-faced authors were sitting under a big full-colour banner that proclaimed their names and the fact that they were "exciting new talents of speculative literature". Piled on side-tables were mounds of the fat hardback anthologizing their stories, funded and published by the Church, available at a special-offer price to convention attendees.

Evidently there hadn't been many takers. The hall itself was thinly occupied, mostly with younger people, and noisy with the over-demonstrative voice of an M.C. who kept stressing that the writers' panel were ready to answer any questions they wished to ask. There was no sign of Eldridge, Kubilius or anyone from the upper echelons of the Church. It didn't look any fun whatsoever, so we turned around and walked straight out of there.

Still fatigued from the flight, Nora had her dinner in Suthersen's suite with Claire keeping her company. I joined Rhodri in a room with a good-sized screen and a north-facing balcony. Cape Canaveral was nearly two hundred miles away, but the launch was taking place close to midnight and it was a clear evening. We might have a glimpse of it.

Rhodri and his pals were all great advocates of the space programme and if anything disappointed that they hadn't had sufficient notice to get themselves to the vicinity of the Kennedy Space Center. Jokey speculations for the precipitate launch ranged from making a rendezvous with aliens fleeing from the Draco Nova system to dumping tons of municipal garbage from high orbit on Muvart's capital city.

In the meantime Rhodri had been using a laptop to do some background research on Barbara Suthersen.

"She came to New York City with Suthersen in 1955," he told me. "Suthersen was nineteen and she was a year younger. They were already married. When Suthersen got a job with Ridge Publications, Eldridge agreed to take Barbara on board as well. She stayed there until Suthersen left to start editing *Vantage SF* and writing his own stuff. That was in 1960."

"Immediately after Parrish stopped writing."

Rhodri nodded, looking mischievous. "Perhaps the rumours are true that Suthersen got his hands on Parrish's notebooks after he retired."

"Did she work with Suthersen at *Vantage*?"

Rhodri shook his head. "She'd signed up for a campaign team in the presidential election that year. Guess whose?"

I had no idea.

"Nixon's," he told me impishly. "Sample slogan: NO APOLOGIES! NO GIVE AWAYS! NO PIE IN THE SKY!"

There was nothing to suggest that Barbara Suthersen had had any involvement in her husband's career over the intervening years. She had trained as a kindergarten teacher and spent many years teaching classes at smart schools in Westchester County.

"What do you think?" I asked Rhodri.

"Hard to say. There's something pent-up about her, isn't there? Maybe you need to ask Suthersen a few more searching questions."

I wondered whether I would get the opportunity. And whether Suthersen would be amenable to giving answers. Clearly he had been closer to Leo Parrish than Eldridge, and had maintained links with the family; but it was quite possible he would not want to divulge anything about his personal life in those days, especially if it might throw a shadow over his subsequent career.

The launch time was growing closer, though the ongoing background features were interrupted from time to time by news bulletins about the Khanistan crisis. Fighting was still continuing in the disputed territory, where the surrounded US garrison had apparently been relieved with no loss of life, at least on the American side. It was early morning in Khanistan and Muvart had delivered a nationwide TV broadcast stating that in the event of US or international forces crossing his border, he would use "every means at our disposal to protect our sacred territory".

There were scathing responses to this, but they hid a certain unease. Everyone knew that Muvart was capable of rash acts. The limited nuclear arsenal he had acquired from neighbouring states after the break-up of the USSR was aged, but even the experts were divided about its current potency.

As the evening wore on Claire brought Nora downstairs in what looked like an executive version of a wheelchair, with soft padded leather upholstery and a lightweight frame whose silver metal had a faint golden lustre.

"Titanium," Nora told me proudly. And in advertising-speak: "Because I'm worth it."

Apparently Suthersen had rented the chair so that Nora wouldn't be restricted in getting about if she had one of her turns. She, however, was in good fettle, content to watch the television proceedings with a crotchety disregard for small talk.

Suthersen's generosity in catering to her needs was interesting in itself. Claire had previously told me that he had always felt a debt to Nora because of what had happened to her brother, but it still wasn't clear to me why, unless it really was true that he had stolen all Leo's ideas. All my attempts to discuss Leo with Nora were stonewalled with silence. When Claire tried to intervene on my behalf she was also met with resistance in the form of an irritable: "Leave him in peace!" from her mother.

The TV company was now doing a profile of William Robert "Bill Bob" Valentine, the shuttle commander, a resolute-looking father of four who had flown on two previous missions.

"He's one of Irwin's people," Nora remarked.

"What's that?" I asked her.

"A high-flier. In more than one sense."

I wasn't about to let this pass. "I don't get you," I said.

She squinted at me. "Don't you ever read the newspapers? Born in Des Moines. That's Iowa, in case you didn't know."

"Is that relevant?"

"Presbyterian stock. Father was a sinners-to-hell minister. Same flavour as Irwin—come the final days, only they are going to escape the fires." She turned to Claire. "If I'm going to sit through this whole production I could use a stiff espresso."

"Forget it, mum," Claire said firmly.

Rhodri, who had overheard this exchange, began working his laptop, and in no time at all had tracked down an interview with Valentine for a church magazine in which he clearly stated his belief that in the final days the righteous would be "manifestly" raised up as a prelude to being restored to a cleansed Earth. By "manifestly" it was clear he meant in a physical, bodily, sense.

In other words, like Irwin, Valentine believed in the Rapture.

The sky had grown a little hazy as the night wore on. The countdown was proceeding without hitch but much of the footage on the screen was frankly dull. Plainly being an astronaut was a bit like being a front-line soldier: a hell of a lot of waiting around before an eruption of life-threatening force.

When the shuttle did finally launch, we watched the billowing clouds around the blazing white exhaust columns as it crawled up into the night, a bulky vintage aeroplane forced painstakingly aloft, pinioned to its boosters and huge fuel tank, passive and vulnerable. There was something grand and comical about it. Would space-travel historians in a future of antimatter drives and economy interplanetary travel look back on our era and laugh at the antiquated way in which we launched our spaceships, the profligate energy wastage, the sloughing-off of the boosters and tanks like a pair of old shoes, left to go plummeting downward to the earth?

We all piled out on to the balcony. After a few minutes someone spotted a smear of light to the north. It looked small and almost insignificant compared to the weight of human ambition and expertise that was behind it. People had brought binoculars and hand-held telescopes along. Looking down one of these I could just about make out the shuttle's form, but it was swamped by the brightness of its rocket streams, which lit up the clouds all around as it bored through them on its way into orbit.

Later I helped Claire wheel Nora into an elevator. As we rode upwards to Suthersen's suite, Nora said, "My brother always believed there would be a colony on the Moon by the year 2000."

I sensed she was addressing me. It was the first time she had volunteered information about Leo without being prompted.

"What did you think?" I asked.

"This was just after the first landings. Nineteen sixty-nine."

"Really?" I said, having no idea if this was significant beyond the fact that Leo only had three more years left.

"Do you know what else was going on in the world at the time? Vietnam. Biafra. Charles Manson. I told him he was deluded."

If it was true, then this was one prediction that Leo Parrish had got spectacularly wrong. But the opportunity to ask her more about Leo was swiftly dashed when the elevator lurched to a halt and the lights went out.

We waited long seconds in the darkness, me feeling a growing sense of foreboding.

"Looks like they're coming for us at last," Nora said with a chuckle that was both heedless and evil.

There was a clunking noise like a bad gear shift. The elevator plummeted.

TWENTY-SIX

We dropped with that stomach-churning rush. I know I yelled, and I think Claire did too. I grabbed the rail with one hand and Nora's wheelchair with the other. It almost jolted away out of my grip as the elevator abruptly banged to a halt. Claire, clinging onto the other handle, came hurtling into me.

Nora was still secure in her chair, and I heard her give a gasp of relief. We must have dropped several floors, but it was all over in a few seconds.

A gap at the top of the brushed steel doors allowed a sliver of light to penetrate the gloom. Claire crouched in front of her mother and asked if she was all right.

"Hunky dory," Nora told her sharply. "Don't start fussing."

We waited in silence for long seconds. The elevator itself was now quiet and apparently stable. Claire and I exchanged concerned looks but didn't actually say anything.

"Emergency brake's on," Nora remarked. "We're not going anywhere."

What would happen now? Would some movie-style assailant start cutting through the elevator walls with a laser? Or pump in poison gas through the ventilation duct?

Claire pressed the emergency button and spoke into the little wall grille; but the panel lights weren't on and no comforting words issued from the speaker.

I started banging on the doors and shouting, "Hey! We're stuck in here!"

Further minutes went by when nothing happened. Periodically Claire and I banged on the door and yelled that we were trapped inside. Nora looked surprisingly resolute, though she was saying nothing. I don't think any of us believed that the elevator had suffered a routine malfunction: it had been done deliberately. A scare tactic, or an actual attempt to kill us? Had Kubilius finally decided to send his heavies against us? Or was it someone else?

Finally we heard voices outside, and then a male voice talking through the top of the elevator doors, solicitously asking how many of us were inside and whether anyone had been injured. It was one of the hotel's assistant managers. Evidently the elevator had lurched to a halt between floors.

Within minutes, it began to rise and slowly came to a halt. The doors whispered open to reveal a quartet of blue-blazered staff. Once they had established that none of us had suffered any harm, they were fulsomely apologetic but unable to offer any immediate explanation of what had actually caused the fault.

It was Nora who finally cut through all the hand-wringing by announcing that she needed to get to bed and wanted her and her daughter to be "chaperoned" to the suite to ensure that "everything is as it should be". She intended to walk up the final flight of stairs to the suite and would need assistance. No, she didn't need me to accompany her and Claire: it was time I returned to my own hotel. I could tell that Claire didn't want to risk distressing her by arguing. She murmured, "I'll call later," before she and her mother were shepherded away. If the elevator had been tampered with to distress Nora, it hadn't had anything like that effect. She might be frail and prone to confusion but in this particular crisis she had proved pretty robust.

I went downstairs and found Rhodri and his friends, all of whom had been sampling beers from various North American micro-breweries. They were far too merry to listen sensibly to my account of what had happened in the elevator, or to take much notice when my phone burst out with the shower-scene screeching from *Psycho*.

It was Claire, calling to say that her mother had gone straight to bed without discussing the incident and was now fast asleep.

"Do you think she suspects it was sabotage?" I asked.

"Do you?"

I didn't answer directly. "What did you say to the manager?"

"At the moment we've got no evidence that the elevator was deliberately interfered with, have we? But I stressed that I didn't want my mother disturbed tonight by anyone wanting Walter Suthersen. He assured me that the night staff would be alerted about the need to respect our privacy and keep all visitors out. You need to take care, too."

"I'm sticking with Rhodri and his mates," I told her. "Safety in numbers."

It was the small hours of the morning before we finally headed back to our hotel, Rhodri's crowd having somehow managed to avoid getting completely plastered despite the impressive array of empty bottles left behind in the hotel bar.

I woke several hours later, amazed that I had slept without incident through that night and that Rhodri was already at work on his laptop. He had been researching the elusive Cyrus Hammond, who wasn't scheduled to appear on any programme items and wasn't staying at the convention hotel or any of the obvious overflows. But Rhodri had made a discovery that he couldn't wait to impart.

"Hammond," he told me gleefully, "is Ryan Carmichael's uncle."

He had all the evidence ready for display on his laptop. Carmichael's film career had begun a decade before with a cheap remake of *Dr Jekyll and Mr Hyde* that had gone straight to DVD. It had been funded by Filmscope under a production company called Arte de Xerxes, an obvious nod to Hammond's Persian first name. Carmichael's parents were dental hygienists who ran a practice in Tampa. His mother was Cyrus Hammond's younger sister and his only sibling.

There was no evidence that Hammond had connections with the Ascendancy beyond this familial link with Carmichael. He had no affiliation with any church and to all appearances wasn't at all religious. As for Filmscope, the company's backers were a medley of small international companies in a variety of business sectors, most based around north-western Europe and the Pacific Rim. Some of them might easily have had federal connections, yet all of Rhodri's attempts to establish associations with US intelligence agencies had drawn a blank. But Hammond plainly sat at the centre of a web of connections involving Leo Parrish, the Ascendancy and the secret service. The nature of those connections remained to our frustration elusive.

I phoned Claire. She had spent a restful night and was keeping her mother under wraps in the suite that morning while awaiting the Suthersens' return from Cape Canaveral prior to Walter's Guest-of-Honour speech.

"The assistant manager came by first thing this morning," she told me. "They think there was a malfunction in the elevator system that caused it to shut down."

"What sort of malfunction?"

"A short circuit, maybe. They're not sure."

"Could it have been tampered with?"

"They can't rule that out, he said. It might have been a prank."

"A prank?" I said sceptically. "Did you enlighten him?"

"No," she said firmly, "What would be the point? We have no idea who's behind it and I don't want my mother involved in some long-winded internal investigation. She's pretty resilient, but there are limits. At least we all got out safely."

The family had had so much hassle in recent months that I could see her point. We arranged to meet up later and she rang off. I had a feeling she wasn't telling me everything and I still hadn't broached with her the fact that Walter Suthersen had kept in touch with Leo Parrish after he stopped writing. Had Suthersen or even Nora told her something she wasn't ready to reveal to me?

In the crowded breakfast bar we saw that the Khanistani crisis was still all over the TV news, with the US President warning that the space shuttle had expressly been put into orbit to forestall any attempts by the Khanistani government to launch weapons of mass destruction on neighbouring territories. He steadfastly refused to elucidate what exactly he meant by "forestall" but said that he intended to issue a deadline for the withdrawal of Khanistani forces from the border zone. Zhuyldz Muvart was shown launching of all things not a fleet of missiles but an American baseball at an important domestic game whose popularity in the country exceeded that of all other sports. Muvart boldly asserted that the Khanistani people would not be deterred by imperialist aggressors and would "strike at the sky itself" should their nation come under threat.

The rhetoric was both theatrical and scary in its escalation. Rhodri and I agreed that it was good to have the distraction of the convention, trivial though it was in global terms: the fate of the world was out of our hands and we might as well carry on partying.

Rhodri and his friends weren't outdoors types, but I was determined to take a swim in our hotel pool before joining them at the convention. After flailing around for a half an hour in the bracingly sterilized water, I crawled on to a sun bed in a bower screened by gardenia and hibiscus. A waiter arrived with a giant vodka martini, gratis from the management in recompense for the distress of the room break-in. I took a hefty swig and let myself float away on a reverie that I was a secret agent, basking under cloudless skies in the Sunshine State, awaiting the arrival of some mysterious femme fatale in a sleek sports car on whom I would naturally have to use all my powers of persuasion to make her surrender her secrets ...

I pulled myself together and decided not to drink the rest of the cocktail. Living like this, it was no wonder most movie stars went a little loopy.

I had just got out of the shower in my room when my phone started howling. It was Gerry.

"I hear you're in Florida," he said.

"I made a furtive escape," I admitted.

"How is it?"

"Glorious," I replied, deciding not to go into the episode with the elevator.

He had phoned the office and had spoken to Jamilla. "She sends her regards and asked if you'd bring her back a souvenir."

This cheered me up, particularly since Ashad was still chilly.

"I thought I'd update you on Gas Bags," Gerry said. "They're closing the chicken farm down."

My sluggish brain ponderously computed that he was talking about the Halstow Island detention centre.

"Really?" I said. "When?"

"A.s.a.p. A pal of Liz's forwarded some internal correspondence. The one who helped with the asthma pump, you know?"

Gerry was obviously intent on not spelling anything out directly.

"I'm sending something on," he told me. "They're quite worried, and I'm not surprised. It could have serious ramifications."

Without knowing what he was talking about, it was difficult to comment.

"Did you find what you were after on the movie material front?" he asked.

"I may be on to something," I replied. "In more ways than one."

Gerry promptly launched into a renewed burst of enthusiasm about Parrish's farsightedness based on the last batch of stories I had given him. As well as the considerable prescience of "Tracers", with its proto-internet and Chinese-dominated future, he claimed to have found an early take on the notion of life-logging—the exhaustive electronic storage of an individual's personal records—in the background of "The Cosmic Controllers", which I had to confess to him I hadn't actually got around to reading.

"The guy's amazing," he assured me. "His prose may be meat-and-potatoes but his ideas are pure caviar."

It wasn't the moment for extended cogitations on Parrish's predictive powers, uncanny though they appeared to be. I computed that it must be about two o'clock in the afternoon at home. "Are you calling from work?"

"I'm on my lunch break. In a pub just down the road. Don't want to disturb the locals, if you know what I mean."

He was obviously worried about possible surveillance.

"This isn't going to jeopardize your job, is it?"

"Sod it if it does. Worthy cause. I ought to go. Check your messages."

I left the phone on the bed while I got dressed, but nothing came through. Had someone listening out there in cyberspace blocked or diverted it into a security black hole? Or had Gerry been dragged out of the pub immediately after talking to me by a couple of burly spooks who had confiscated his phone and bundled him into a car? I thought about calling him back to check that he was all right, but I forced myself to wait a while. It didn't always pay to let your imagination run wild.

I went over to the convention hotel. Rhodri was in the book room and already had a carrier bag of purchases. I had just caught up with him when Gerry's email came through.

Liz Martindale's friend must have been someone who either had personal access to the Halstow Island facility or was in its communications loop. In the email attachment Gerry had selected quotes from what must have been internal memos. They described "a potentially hazardous scenario" resulting from "the possibility of non-gen-spec infective pathways on immune systems compromised by common viral infections." Fortunately Gerry had provided a layman's translation, though some of it was still obscure to me.

"Bad news?" Rhodri asked, seeing that I looked worried.

I told him about Halstow Island. Rhodri listened with fascinated incredulity. I gave him the gist of Gerry's attachment, which was that there had been a case of a medical worker at the facility becoming infected with the Stealth Virus. The woman in question had been suffering from a cold at the time and had apparently been rendered vulnerable as a result.

Rhodri took a moment to absorb this. "Did she get the full-blown disease?"

"It seems so."

I let him look at Gerry's email himself.

"It doesn't say whether the woman concerned was of Asian origin. If I understand this correctly, that could be important. She might have been carrying the necessary genetic markers for infection."

"You don't think that's likely?"

"It might not make any difference either way. They're implying that the genetic material from the manufactured virus has actually piggybacked on one of the common cold rhinoviruses."

"Just what I thought," I said with patent lack of conviction. "It's bad news, isn't it?"

"It could be if it gets out into the general population. Anyone might catch it from a sneeze."

This was an extremely sobering thought, and I hoped that the facility had rigorous quarantine procedures in place. The difficulty was that we knew so little about the site's exact nature. Was it a secret but properly maintained germ warfare research establishment or just a glorified prison camp where an amoral medical team was allowed free rein?

There was something else that bothered me too—something I was reluctant to broach with Rhodri but knew I couldn't avoid.

"Quite a bit of the stuff in Parrish's version of *Exaltation* reads rather like what's going on now."

To my surprise, Rhodri didn't make a joke out of it. "Whichever way you look at it, things are certainly starting to take on an apocalyptic air."

"*Could* Parrish have had a hotline to the future?"

Rhodri laughed, but I could tell his heart wasn't in it. It occurred to me that Ruth's pregnancy and the prospect of having a child of his own might have given him a different perspective on the issue, at least to the extent that he couldn't be cavalier about the possibility of both a life-threatening pandemic and a nuclear conflagration. Pestilence and War: two of the four horsemen of the apocalypse, with Famine and Death no doubt riding hard on their heels.

"Maybe Muvart's the Great Satan or something," I said.

It was years since I had looked at the Bible, but my grandmother had been a jaunty Spiritualist and had a big illustrated version that she liked to show me whenever I visited. When I think back on it, the book scared me more than any other in my childhood. Morbid curiosity always drew me to the dramatic pictures from the book of Revelation—fireballs and frightful angels, terrified populations succumbing to war and disease. But I couldn't remember the details well enough to be sure that Leo Parrish had made direct biblical borrowings when he wrote the original version of *Exaltation*.

"Can't help you on that one," Rhodri said. "My parents were devoted Rationalists. For them, religion wasn't so much the opium of the masses as the candyfloss."

"Maybe I should take a look at a Gideon bible and check it out myself."

"Let's see if we can do better than that," Rhodri said. He took out his mobile and made a call.

"Stan?" he said when it was answered. "It's Rhodri. Are you in the vicinity? ... Could we meet up? ... A friend of mine needs to talk eschatology with you."

Stan Berenbaum was a Harvard linguistics professor who was attending the convention to indulge his passion for science fiction, which extended to giving humorous talks on invented languages such as Klingon and the possibilities for human-alien communication should we ever actually make contact with them. His professional expertise was in the Semitic languages, an area that had required much scholarly delving into biblical texts.

Rhodri and I met up with him at one of the poolside bars, where he was reading the sports section of *The Miami Herald*. He wasn't the tweedy academic I had expected but a lean long-limbed guy of middle years in a scarlet palm-print shirt and ragged-edged denim shorts. His rigorously shaven head was as brown as the rest of his well-toned body. He looked more like an ageing surfer than a porer over ancient parchments.

"Revelation's the trickiest book of the Bible," he told me. "Show me six experts and I'll show you as many ideas about what it means."

I explained briefly about *Exaltation* and my feeling that some of the details had not only biblical resonances but also very close parallels with current international events.

Stan was relaxed about it. "Well, you could make practically anything fit," he insisted. "It's almost impossible to take literally for a start, and a lot of it could be read as allegory or rhetoric or even poetry making free use of metaphors."

"But not everyone believes that, do they?"

"True," he conceded. "What's important to remember is that all writers are bounded by their times—even the ones claiming divine inspiration. John was more than a little peeved about the Roman Empire. There was a lot of persecution of Christians going on, so Rome was the Great Satan from his perspective. I don't see a specific latter-day version of that in the offing. Unless we

Americans are the New Romans." He grinned. "Which is a point of view I've heard expressed on more than one occasion."

"There's plenty of stuff about war and pestilence, isn't there?"

He gave me a long studied look, and then said to Rhodri, "Are you going along with this?"

"We're interested, that's all. Leo Parrish has a bit of form in the predictive stakes."

It was the first time I had heard Rhodri concede that some of Parrish's other stories had shown real foresight. But Stan obviously thought I was an obsessive. So I told him about my work as a documentary filmmaker and what Ashad and I had unearthed about the secret GSBA programme and Halstow Island. There really seemed to be no point in keeping it secret any longer.

He didn't make light of this, but in the end he just shrugged. "Maybe the end of the world is coming, maybe it isn't. Your guy isn't the first to predict it."

"It wasn't exactly a prediction. It was a story. My point is that some of the things in his other stories have come to pass in some shape or another. I'm not particularly thrilled about the idea that this one might."

This time Stan did look as if he was giving it some consideration.

"It's interesting," he said, leafing back through his newspaper and finally showing us a short news item on one of the inside pages. The Israeli government was conducting ongoing negotiations with representatives of the Muvart regime with a view to signing non-aggression accords between the two countries.

"Some Christians believe that Israel will unthinkingly make peace with the Antichrist and precipitate a great Tribulation lasting seven years."

"Bloody hell."

"A very bloody hell indeed if you take it literally." He was grinning. "If we truly are living at the End of Days, then there's not much we can do about it, is there? Maybe we should all be making hay while the sun shines."

He saw that I didn't find the idea amusing.

"A lot of people, including plenty of Christians, take the view that John was a complete flake. Apocalypse or not, you've got to keep a sense of proportion."

Stan called the waiter over and ordered us a round of Ginger Blazes, which turned out to be an invigorating cocktail of lime juice and ginger ale with a dash of chilli sauce.

"What about the Rapture?" I asked him. "Bennett Irwin's a believer, isn't he? And a big mover and shaker behind current events. Then you've got the Ascendants."

"Wow," he said, "you really have been mixing it up, haven't you?"

"Is there a connection between the two?"

He frowned. "What do you mean exactly? There's more than one interpretation of what the Rapture means."

"Well, Irwin's lot and the Ascendants both believe that they're some kind of chosen few who are going to be physically removed from all the death and destruction in the final days. Lifted up, either by God or aliens."

"That's broadly true," he agreed.

Rhodri and I told him about the two versions of *Exaltation* and Eldridge's admission that he had deliberately rewritten the serial to reflect his own theological ideas.

"The Ascendancy is a truly modern church," he remarked. "It's magpie, a bit of this, a bit of that, a bit of the other. It's run like a business organisation to which the theology is almost subservient."

"Unless you're a true believer," Rhodri remarked.

Stan didn't dispute this. "I'm no expert on the Ascendants," he admitted. "Perhaps Eldridge incorporated Rapturist notions, made them his own."

"How long have these Rapturist ideas been around?"

"Well, they really got up and running with the Puritans in the seventeenth century, if memory serves me. Cotton Mather and others. But they've always stayed pretty much out on the edge of mainstream Christian belief. In the 1950s and '60s they weren't anything like as well known as theological ideas as they are now."

"But Eldridge could have been aware of them?"

"Sure. Every new religion is like a form of philosophical evolution in action—it grows right out of what has gone before. And transcendence is usually at the heart of it. What Rapture Christians and Ascendancy cultists have in common is the belief that the transcendence is going to be physical, that it will involve the preservation of their earthly forms."

Cheerfully he raised his glass.

"A toast," he said, "to whatever Armageddon suits your palate."

We drank, and I couldn't resist asking, "So what's your particular poison?"

"My belief, you mean? What do you think? I'm a devout atheist, God forgive me."

*

After we left Stan, I phoned Ashad to give him a paraphrase of our conversation and also to pass on Gerry's news. He and Valerie had not long got out of an early-morning screening with BBC executives of the Muvart documentary material.

"The emphasis has shifted," he told me. "We're calling it *Ethnic Cleansing: Britain's Secret Shame.*"

"You've finished it?" I said, incredulous.

"It's been dragging on for too long. Me and Valerie have been working twenty-four-seven to give it a coherent framework." He explained that Muvart and his regime were now just the starting point. The main focus was on the detention centre and the covert programme to inflict biological warfare on Khanistan.

"You might need to add something in," I said. "According to Gerry, a guard at Halstow's been infected."

"We know," he said. "They're shit-scared there's going to be an outbreak."

"Did you speak to Gerry?"

"No."

Ashad's manner was still terse, as if he was too busy or preoccupied to want a lengthy conversation.

"I'll send you the attachment in any case," I told him. "How did you find out?"

"Merrick confirmed it."

"Merrick? How did she know about it?"

This time he hesitated. "I might have mentioned Halstow Island in passing in one of our conversations—back when I trusted her."

His tone was still bitter.

"She was there? At the screening?"

"She'd been doing some digging and insisted on showing her face. Which worked in our favour, as it happens. When they saw it, the BBC guys were terrified we might be making unfounded accusations. Or accusations that weren't 'cross-referenced from at least two independent sources', as they put it. Merrick was able to confirm the story. She's being credited as 'an anonymous Special Branch source'."

"They're going to show it?"

"Sooner than you think. They realized that this was breaking news, and I warned them that Alec Furneaux was still sniffing around the same story and might steal our thunder."

Furneaux had almost been our nemesis on the necrotizing fasciitis story, his *Talking Points* show reaching a far wider audience than we could hope to get. But it had more breadth than depth.

"When?" I asked.

"They'll run it as a news item within the next day or so. And make space in the schedules to show the full version as a *Panorama* special."

"Bloody hell, Ash, that's brilliant!"

"You'll get full credit. Your mate Gerry was a big help."

"That wasn't what I meant. I'm pleased for us. For the company. But most importantly because the story needs to be out there. The sooner that place is shut down, the better."

"Yeah," he drawled in a way that made it impossible to know exactly what he meant.

"Do you think Merrick's trying to make it up to you?"

He didn't answer.

"Maybe she's keen to show she really is on our side this time."

He made a dismissive noise. "She'll have her own agenda. They always do."

He wasn't going to relent on her. And why was I so eager to see the good side of her actions? Because I wanted Ash to have some sort of life outside his work that mirrored my hopes for my own.

"Any word on Byrnes?" I asked. "You haven't seen him creeping around the place or trying to bug our phones?"

"No sign of him, if you believe Merrick."

"Interesting collection of noises you've stuck on my mobile."

"Yeah, it was me," he admitted. "Seemed a good wheeze at the time."

"How do I fix it?"

"I haven't finished punishing you yet."

Another silence. I tried again: "Jamilla OK?"

I heard him sigh at the other end of the phone. "We're all fine."

"I'm due a holiday, Ash," I blurted, exasperated with his wilful petulance. "And it's a working one. I'm not just sitting on my backside having fun."

It was a moment before he said, "Yeah. I know that. It's just that I'm going to be happier when you're back here and we're all pulling together."

"At last! A ray of light penetrates the fog of disapproval. You really do miss me!"

"Just stay safe," he said, and abruptly cut the connection.

I rendezvoused with Claire and Nora about half an hour before Walter Suthersen was due to give his speech. They had been allocated priority seats at the front of the hall and I was included as an extra member of the party. I left a space beside me for Barbara, who was apparently in the green-room with her husband.

The place was already quite full, and half the audience were in costume, the fancy dress parade being due to start immediately after Suthersen's speech. Nora had arrived not in her wheelchair but walking, her arm tucked through Claire's. She appeared to be in a good humour, actually smiling at me and saying, "Good day to you, Mr Randall. And have you been enjoying yourself?"

This was a parody of solicitousness. Claire gave me one of her long-suffering looks.

"My daughter keeps telling me to mind my manners," Nora said as I helped her sit down. "Though I don't see why I should. In old age you have few privileges."

"Well," I said, "I think I can live with it if it's a general policy of yours and not a case of specific dislike."

Her hand was on my arm. I could feel it tightening, the bony fingers surprisingly strong. "Depends on whether you're just using her as a means to an end. That husband of hers was a completely feckless piece of work. I don't want her making the same mistake again."

I held her gaze, wondering if she had perhaps experienced a similar fecklessness from Claire's father. "Surely you can see there's more to it than that?"

For an instant I got the impression that she was prepared to give me the benefit of the doubt, but she wasn't going to admit as much.

"Time will tell," she said, releasing me from her grip.

I saw Arthur Townsend wander in, wearing a movie tie-in T-shirt of *Zeta Prime*. He took a seat towards the rear of the hall. Cyrus Hammond was also in attendance, standing at the back near the doors.

I slipped out of my seat and went straight up the aisle.

"I've been looking for you," I told him. "Have you been in hiding?"

"I've been around," he replied. "Here and there."

He was standing in the shadows under the tech ops bay and gave no indication that he was about to take a seat.

"I didn't realize you have a movie-star nephew," I remarked.

His smile was slow in coming. "Ah, yes. Ryan. My sister's son."

"Is she an Ascendant, too?"

The smile didn't relent. "Episcopalian, if memory serves me correctly."

"What about yourself?"

He took his time before answering. "I'm hoping that if there is a God he'll be forgiving to the sceptics when the Day of Judgement comes."

Which was pretty much my own philosophy. "Can we talk later?"

"Sure."

"You're not going to take a seat?"

"The view's more panoramic from here."

Claire was looking around, though she hadn't spotted either of us. I scurried back just as the lights began to dim, deciding not to mention Hammond's presence to her for now.

The hall was one of the few conference rooms without external windows, a decent-sized stage fronting a screen, a little podium at its centre. Soon there was only a spotlight over the podium, giving a suitably intimate and atmospheric feel to the occasion. With minutes to go, it was mostly full and Cyrus Hammond was now lost from sight in the growing crowd at the back. Only the front row on the other side of the aisle was empty: the same equivalents as those used by Eldridge, Kubilius and their minions for the panel discussion.

And indeed they entered on cue, Eldridge in a polo shirt and slacks as before, Kubilius's only concession to informality being an open-necked shirt under his suit. He looked as stiff and watchful as ever. Ryan Carmichael was with them. Though resplendent in a white silk top and designer jeans Carmichael looked hung-over and out-of-sorts, as if he had stayed up too late and over-indulged himself at some celebrity party. He sat down at the far end of the row as though positioning himself to make another early exit. According to the convention's programme booklet, he was scheduled to be interviewed in tomorrow's Media Guest-of-Honour slot about his latest projects, which I suspected would involve more publicity for the Ascendancy movie and which I knew a sense of professional duty would compel me to attend.

Carmichael's appearance sent a buzz through the audience, though no one jumped up to mob him. The entire convention was full of writers, artists, publishers, agents as well as minor movie actors who, when they weren't appearing on programme items, spent a lot of it just sitting having drinks or wandering around like any other punter. Occasionally they might be surrounded by admirers, though mostly the approaches were polite but not overly deferential, as if their attendance and interaction with their audience was an accepted part of proceedings. True,

Carmichael was much more famous, a global heart-throb, and under other circumstances there might have been a bit of hoopla. But it was Walter Suthersen's slot, and he was no less well known within this world.

Barbara emerged from the wings, looking as if she had been shrink-wrapped into a gold lamé dress more suited to a formal ball. Shuffling along geisha-like, she lowered herself on to a seat next to mine like a gaudy stick-insect, not actually greeting anyone but saying to no one in particular, "Isn't it rather stuffy in here?"

It was a statement rather than a subject for discussion. She produced a black lacework fan from her handbag and began fluttering it in front of her face, though the air-con was keeping the room at a perfectly comfortable temperature. Her hair was artfully piled up, an expensive-looking necklace at her throat with matching pendant earrings. Were she and Walter meeting royalty later?

Suthersen's American editor came on stage to introduce him, a rotund bald man in a penguin suit. In a jovial manner he told the audience that Walt had always been a delight to work with, his growing renown never getting in the way of his urge to make his books as good as they could be—which I assumed was code for Walter not objecting to being edited. After a potted overview of his career, he reminded the audience about all the awards Suthersen had won and made a joke about Walter needing a live-in carpenter who was good at building shelves. Then he invited Suthersen on to the stage.

There was plenty of applause as Suthersen appeared from the wings, wearing a dark suit over a white shirt with a red knitted tie loosely knotted at his neck. I had the impression that he didn't like to dress formally—an impression confirmed when Suthersen joked that he was going to an embalming immediately afterwards.

He took out some folded sheets of paper, then immediately put them back in his jacket pocket, saying that he'd only refer to them if he lost his thread, though at his age he might need the audience to let him know if he became too digressive or incoherent.

"And if I suddenly dash off the stage in a middle of a sentence," he told everyone, "just hang in there—I'll be back once I've answered the call of nature."

All this was said in a good humour which the audience reciprocated.

He continued in this cosy vein, beginning by referring to Edgar Eldridge's presence at the convention and talking about his early days in the science-fiction world and in particular his work for Ridge Publications. He portrayed a cramped and cluttered office that was always a maelstrom of feverish activity, no fewer than five magazines being produced each month—detective, romance, suspense fiction, war stories, and of course science fiction.

"If we didn't have enough copy," he told his audience, "then we had to write it ourselves, not just editorials, but stories, non-fiction articles and even on occasions letters-of-comment so that it looked as though we had plenty of reader interest. One of the fun parts was making up the names. I was especially fond of Brook Linbridge while Edgar, as I recall, produced a couple of corset-rippers for *Flights of Passion* as Gladys Finitch."

Laughter. Eldridge was grinning and nodding enthusiastically.

"We've both come a long way since then," Suthersen said pointedly.

Behind him, the screen had lit up, and he used a remote to begin a slide show of stills from the *Zeta Prime* movie. Suthersen had served as a consultant, and he described the frustrations and even humiliations he had suffered while attempting to explain to the producers the difference between a planet and a galaxy and why you couldn't fly to distant stars in a matter of hours unless you had a handy wormhole or some other means of travelling faster than the speed of light.

Like Eldridge, Suthersen knew his audience and in particular the irritation that these scientifically-literate and technically-minded people felt when movie producers played fast and loose with the laws of physics or were sloppy about the details of their invented universes. "Internal consistency" was the mantra here: be as wacky as you like in your world-making but then play fair with its rules.

The tales Suthersen told were mildly self-deprecating—he might be an award-winning author but the producers regarded his repeated pleading for scientific accuracy as a nuisance. He claimed that his experience of big-budget movie-making was like being caught in "a windstorm of hurricane-force egos".

To my surprise Ryan Carmichael didn't appear to be paying much attention to this. He was fidgeting in his seat, his head slightly bowed, looking distracted and uncomfortable.

Before the slide show finished I was dimly aware of someone in a Wookie bear suit squeezing cumbersomely into a vacant seat a few rows behind. Suthersen actually waited until he was settled.

"From digest magazines to movie spectaculars," he continued. "It's been an interesting journey and most of it has been a hell of a lot of fun. I'm particularly grateful to the science-fiction community for all the awards and other forms of recognition that you've bestowed on me over the years. I'm even grateful to the people who don't think I deserved them—you, as much as anyone else, have kept me on my toes."

He paused, allowing this to sink in. I knew it was unusual in such circumstances for an author to publicly acknowledge any dissent about his achievements.

"Apart from Edgar down there," Suthersen went on, nodding in Eldridge's direction, "there's one other name I would like to bring to your attention—a name that's already been mentioned at this convention, though it's one that few of you will have heard of."

Now he made a show of gathering his thoughts while looking straight ahead into the shadowy recesses of the hall.

"Writers always claim they don't pay any heed to their critics," he said. "Don't believe it for a minute—bad reviews have the power to wound, no matter how old or well-established you are. I've long been aware that there's a small but not insignificant body of opinion that my entire career was based on the work of another writer, a man who died many years ago but whose influence is still being felt. A writer called Leo Parrish."

There was nothing from the audience on hearing the name. Which wasn't at all surprising, given Parrish's obscurity.

"Edgar published Leo Parrish's stories in the days before he discovered religion," Suthersen said without being snide. "Leo's stories were inventive and thought-provoking—qualities not much in evidence in most of the submissions we received."

"We were only paying half a cent a word!" Eldridge shouted cheerily.

More laughter.

"Up to half a cent, anyway," said Suthersen, but he wasn't about to be deflected.

"No more fiction by Leo Parrish appeared after 1960, even though he lived until 1972. This was the exact same period in which my own career got up and running in earnest. All of which led one or two shrewder commentators in the field to suggest that I had somehow stolen his career, based my own success on mining Parrish's mother lode, if you like."

Now the hall was silent. Even Kubilius looked rapt.

"What if I told you that it's all true?" Suthersen said with a wry smile "And that it's true because *I* am Leo Parrish." He waited a second for this to sink in. "Or at least—"

There was a flurry of movement behind me and a firecracker bang. As I instinctively ducked I saw Suthersen fall.

Barbara Suthersen started shrieking. I spun around. A few rows back Cyrus Hammond was grappling with the Wookie and had torn his headpiece off. It was Noah Byrnes. Hammond was trying to wrestle something out of his hand. A pistol.

I acted without thinking, practically diving over the seats that separated us, flinging myself at him.

Chairs went crashing, people started yelling, and Byrnes, Hammond and I were enveloped in a tangle of flailing limbs. I felt a naked hand grab my ear, a furry knee come up feebly into my groin, an elbow ram itself against my jaw. I swung and parried and struggled for domination.

And then, as quickly as it had started, everything went quiet, and I found myself looking down on Byrnes's pinioned form. I was lying sideways across his furry chest, my hands clamped around one wrist, while Hammond crouched at his shoulders, his brawny arm locked around Byrnes's neck. All three of us were panting heavily, Byrnes completely dishevelled with a mad look in his eyes.

"And the angel thrust his sickle into the earth!" he yelled at no one in particular, "and gathered the vine of the earth, and cast it into the great winepress of the wrath of God!"

The main lights came on. People were standing all around us, stunned and fearful. Byrnes was still raving: "There fell a great star from Heaven, and the name of that star was Wormwood! The kingdoms of this Earth are become the kingdoms of our Lord--"

Cyrus Hammond tightened his grip on his neck, and to my surprise he subsided.

Someone had managed to get Byrnes's gun and was holding it by the tip of the barrel. A posse of hotel security staff burst through, taking hold of Byrnes and hauling him to his feet. I struggled upright. I appeared to have survived the mêlée without injury. Everyone was staring at me and Cyrus as if we were maniacs.

There was no sign of Eldridge, Kubilius or any of their retinue. On stage Walter Suthersen was being helped to his feet by a man in a sausage-balloon headpiece. Barbara hovered like a praying mantis, checking him for wounds. Suthersen was looking down towards the front row in alarm.

Beyond the capsized seats, Claire crouched over Nora, who lay like a corpse on the floor.

TWENTY-SEVEN

"She's stable," Claire told me when I met her at the hospital's Urgent Care Center. "They're not sure whether it was another stroke or just shock."

"Is she conscious?"

She shook her head. "She hasn't woken. They're keeping her under observation."

"My first thought was that she'd been shot."

"Me, too." Her voice was wobbly. "Who was it?"

"Noah Byrnes. He's the secret service agent who's been stalking me."

She looked alarmed. "He followed you from London?"

"I'm not sure he was following me precisely. I think he was on the trail of Leo Parrish. That's why he tried to shoot Walter."

I was guessing about this but pretty sure it was the reason. The shot had only narrowly missed Suthersen, possibly because Hammond had intervened before Byrnes could fire.

"Where is he now?" Claire asked.

"In custody, I would imagine. They got him out of there as fast as possible."

Byrnes had become very calm and blank-faced soon after the attack. He had refused to say a further word and had been bundled away.

"Why?" Claire said. "Why would he want to shoot Walt?"

We had reached the visitor area, which was being refurbished. I spotted a vending machine. "I could use a drink," I said, leading her towards it. "I think he was trying to shoot Leo Parrish."

She half-leant, half-slumped against the wall.

"Walter isn't Leo Parrish," she said after a moment. "Leo was my uncle. They killed him forty years ago, and now they're trying to kill him all over again."

"They?" I said gently. "Who exactly?"

"I don't know. You said this Byrnes was a government agent."

"He is. But Byrnes must have been desperate to attempt an assassination in public. I'd be amazed if it was an officially sanctioned secret service operation."

She didn't say anything. I contemplated the Bennett Irwin connection but didn't mention it. She was barely holding herself together.

"I didn't know Walt was going to pretend he was Leo," she told me. "He'd hinted that he wanted to stir things up, find out once and for all who was making all this trouble for us. He'd talked to my mother about it. I never imagined it would lead to this."

"He certainly had the audience believing him. Me being one of them. Do you want a drink?"

She shook her head. I think she realized I was still wondering whether the story might be true.

"It was a bluff that backfired horribly," she insisted. "I don't really understand why Walt would want to put his reputation on the line like that."

I selected an iced lemon tea. The can thumped into the maw of the vending machine like a lobbed grenade.

"Why?" Claire said again. "Why are they so interested in him?"

I didn't have any clear answer for this. I could tell she wasn't quite ready to take me in to see her mother, so I led her over to a corner of the seating area that wasn't cluttered with decorators' equipment.

The hospital was close to the convention hotel, and Nora had been rushed there immediately after her collapse. I had wanted to accompany Claire, but Cyrus Hammond and I had been detained by the security staff and put in separate rooms. Half an hour later, two detectives had arrived to interview me. I stuck to the facts and didn't go into any past history. I simply told them that I had been sitting immediately in front of Byrnes and had reacted to disarm him after the shot went off. There were plenty of witnesses to corroborate my story. Neither cop asked me if I knew

Byrnes, and when I said that I urgently needed to find out what had happened to Nora Parrish the older of the two gave me a long hard look and told me that I had been brave but incredibly stupid and was lucky to be sitting there rather than going cold in a morgue. He took down my details and agreed to release me on condition that I kept my cell phone on and was prepared to be called back for further questioning if needed.

The moment I walked out of there I knew it had been a foolish decision not to tell them of my previous encounters with Byrnes. Cyrus Hammond only had to mention that both he and I knew Byrnes from London, and the Miami-Dade Police would haul me back in for a full interrogation before I knew it. But I was eager to check on Nora's condition and gambling that Hammond might not want to say anything about his own murky background. The grateful hotel staff had found me a taxi in short order.

Just along from us a young Hispanic woman was desolately weeping into the shoulder of a grave-faced older man who looked like her father. Someone close to them had obviously died, probably the wife and mother of the two. At least Nora was still alive. For now. But Claire was restless with worry.

"We'll get to the bottom of this," I assured her. "The police are bound to interrogate Byrnes. It's attempted murder, after all."

"Is Walter all right?"

"Just bruised, I think." He and Barbara had been escorted away immediately afterwards.

"He phoned the hospital earlier but I didn't get to speak to him. They told me he was mortified about my mum's collapse."

"Well, neither of you could have known there was a maniac in the audience."

I peeled open the can and offered it to her. She took a mouthful and handed it back to me.

"My first thought was that the Ascendants were behind it," she said. "But now I'm not so sure. Vincent Kubilius and Edgar Eldridge were in the audience, weren't they?"

I nodded, having come to a similar conclusion—though at first I had fleetingly entertained the notion that Byrnes might have been employed by the Ascendants as a hit man in the event of Suthersen saying something disrespectful or outrageous, the very presence of the Church's Big Two as innocent witnesses in the hall giving them a perfect alibi. But the idea didn't bear close examination. Byrnes certainly wasn't an Ascendant, and if he was a Christian Rapturist his beliefs would be antagonistic to theirs.

"But it doesn't necessarily rule them out of other hassles you've suffered," I said. "And at least the debt their religion owes to your uncle is now public knowledge."

"That's a dubious honour."

"True, but it means that Leo Parrish is finally getting some of the attention he deserves."

"Not exactly for the right reasons. And years too late."

I finished off the drink, and then Claire took my hand and led me along the corridor to the ward.

I could hear people groaning and someone swearing before we even got there. Claire was saying something about the ward being full of gunshot-wound victims and road-accident casualties, though Nora was still in one of the critical care bays in a windowed-off section.

Except that she wasn't. Another patient was being wheeled into the bay, and Claire's legs almost buckled. I supported her as a woman with a ward supervisor's badge came hurrying up.

"We were about to come and find you," she said quickly, seeing Claire's shocked expression. "She's just been moved to another facility. You signed for it, didn't you?"

The supervisor was defensive. Claire nodded numbly.

"Another facility" turned out to be a spacious private room further along the corridor. Nora lay under a single white bed sheet, wired to a life-systems monitor that looked pretty state-of-the-art to my untutored eye. Her face was perfectly tranquil, though she was pale and quite motionless.

"She's out of immediate danger," the supervisor was telling Claire. "We're moderately confident there's no physical trauma but at present she's not responding to stimuli."

She reassured Claire that this didn't necessarily mean the worst. The monitor was linked to an observation post where a medical team could keep an eye on her vital signs indicators. Both her pulse and heart rate were steady, though slow.

It transpired that Walter Suthersen was paying for the room. He had phoned through funds to cover the costs, wanting to be sure that Nora was as comfortable and well-looked after as possible.

"That's very generous of him," I remarked.

"He shouldn't feel guilty," Claire said. "He wouldn't have made that announcement without my mother's consent."

I didn't say anything but I wondered if Suthersen did indeed have more than this one immediate reason for feeling indebted to Leo Parrish's family.

We sat at Nora's bedside for a while, watching the traces on the monitors, knowing only that their constant movement, the wavering lines and shifting numbers, meant continued life, though the motionless body in the bed was like a cipher of the feisty, cantankerous person it contained.

"Does Daniel know?" I asked.

"I called him earlier," Claire said. "Told him to stay where he was until there was further news. If he got on a plane to come here, she might be dead before he arrived."

"Or sitting up, giving the nurses a hard time."

She managed a smile. My phone made popping noises. Anticipating a summons from the police, I slipped outside. The number was unfamiliar to me.

"Hello?" I said with a degree of trepidation.

"Mr Randall."

It was Cyrus Hammond's voice.

"Where are you?" he asked.

I hesitated before saying, "At the hospital."

"The Jackson Memorial?"

I stayed silent, neither confirming nor denying it. I wanted him to make the conversational running this time.

"How is she?" he asked.

"Nora? Do you know her?"

"No, just Claire."

"Peaceful," I replied, "but she hasn't regained consciousness. At the moment we don't know what the outcome might be."

"It's an insane business," he said with feeling. "We've just got to hope for the best. Let Claire know I phoned and asked after her mother, will you?"

"Of course," I told him, keeping it formal and cool. "I'm sure she'll be appreciative of your concern. It's fortunate you were on hand."

"I had a feeling something might be brewing. You did a good job helping me get Byrnes to ground."

"The second time in a few days you've had to grapple with him."

I was referring to Byrnes's attempt to steal the serial from my rucksack.

"He's a dangerous man," he replied. "His type always are."

He hadn't actually confirmed that my assailant had been Byrnes. And I still didn't know why he was quite so solicitous of Claire's wellbeing.

"Why do I always feel you're playing cat and mouse with me?" I said, not bothering to hide my impatience. "If you want me to trust you, it would help if you let me know what the hell's going on."

"It's complicated."

"I'd worked that out."

"I hadn't anticipated the stakes would get so high. I apologize."

"Apologies are futile unless I know what you're apologizing *for*."

He didn't reply.

"We need to talk," I insisted. "Face to face. No flim flam."

"You're right."

"When?"

"Well, not tonight—I'm nursing a few bruises, and at my age you have to be gentle on yourself. It's a hot bath and a chilled scotch, then shuteye."

"When?" I said again. "You owe me."

"Tomorrow morning, ten am, the hotel's Matanzas bar, OK?"

I didn't know it but was confident someone would be able to point me in the right direction.

"All right," I said. "Did you tell the police you were a federal agent?"

He made a gruff noise. "I'm not about to start telling them lies. I said I'd spotted Byrnes behaving suspiciously when he showed up for Suthersen's speech. That there was something furtive about him."

"So when exactly did Byrnes turn up?"

"He might have been skulking around the hotel for days for all we know."

"But how did he get out of London?"

"He could have skipped as soon as the heat was turned on him."

"How is this possible if his own agency is looking for him? They were watching the airports."

"Borders are porous these days, especially if you're an old hand at duck and run. He could have taken a Eurostar and got a flight from Paris or anywhere else in Europe. You can't cover all the avenues of escape."

"Did you know he's Bennett Irwin's son-in-law?"

"It's not exactly a secret."

"So it's not impossible that Irwin could have pulled strings and arranged for a rapid extraction."

Hammond allowed a meaningful pause before saying, "That would be a very serious accusation to lay against a senior figure in the administration."

Was he worried that the line might be bugged? Or just hedging his bets as usual? It scarcely mattered to me now.

"Not as serious as flouting criminal law," I said. "Correct me if I'm wrong, but wasn't the president elected on a platform of transparent government and an end to state-sanctioned dirty tricks?"

"Irwin was forced on him by the hawks in the administration. I think it's highly unlikely that the president knows anything about this."

"Then shouldn't someone be telling him?"

"He's probably heard that Irwin's son-in-law tried to shoot Walter Suthersen. You can bet your bottom dollar that Irwin will be busily assuring him that he had no prior knowledge of it."

Hammond clearly wasn't ruling out the possibility of Irwin's involvement. The chain of connections between Irwin and the attempted killing of Walter Suthersen was far from implausible. Byrnes would no doubt have known that the Suthersens and the Whitneys were on their way to Miami: he would have headed straight there.

"So what did the police say?" I asked.

"Well, not surprisingly they wanted to know who I was. So I showed them some accreditation—"

"Accreditation? What does that mean?"

"I also gave them a couple of numbers to call," he said, avoiding the question. "When they'd done that, they weren't exactly happy but they were satisfied that I wasn't making it up."

He was beginning to weary of the conversation. I wasn't quite ready to let him go.

"As usual," I said, "this is all as clear as fog to me. Did you tell them I know Byrnes?"

"I didn't tell them anything they didn't need to know for the purpose at hand. You smell sweet at the moment, though I can't guarantee they won't want to pull you in for another chat."

"Is Byrnes talking?"

"As far as I know, he's gone Trappist."

This didn't surprise me. "I assume they're holding him."

"Hell, yes. Even in America they take a dim view of people taking pot-shots in auditoriums."

"His wasn't an official operation, was it?"

"You've got to be kidding!" he responded. "Tomorrow at ten."

The line went dead.

I thought over what he had told me. Not actually a great deal that I couldn't have inferred myself. Even so, I had a sense of inching ever closer towards the truth. Maybe Byrnes's interrogators would extract something from him as well. And at least he was now out of circulation.

I went back into the room. Claire was still sitting at Nora's bedside.

"That was Cyrus Hammond calling," I told her. "He was asking after Nora. I'm meeting him tomorrow. Is there anything I need to know about him that you haven't told me?"

She thought about it, shook her head. "Is he really an agent of some sort?"

"I'd bet on it."

There were footsteps outside, a woman's high heels doing brisk click-clacks on the vinyl. The door opened. Walter and Barbara Suthersen walked in.

Walter had dispensed with his tie but Barbara was still wearing her gold lamé dress under a cream raincoat which she had obviously thrown on for decorum's sake. She did not look at all happy.

"I'm sorry I couldn't get here sooner," Suthersen said to Claire, giving her a big hug. "The detectives were keen to question me. They wanted to know why anyone might want to shoot me. I told them that I've had some severe critics in my time but that this takes the biscuit."

Claire didn't crack a smile. "Are you all right?"

"I'm fine," he told her, already moving towards the bed. "What about Nora?"

Barbara stayed put at the doorway, though I saw her stiffen. Walter was poised over Nora's pillow, looking down at her with undisguised affection while Claire gave him a brief update. Almost involuntarily he began to stroke Nora's head. He and Claire shared the same jaw line, the same leanness of frame, the same long-fingered hands.

Barbara turned and walked out.

Claire and Suthersen didn't notice her go: they were standing beside one another next to Nora, Claire holding her mother's hand, Suthersen squinting at the vital signs monitors. They reminded me of the Hispanic father and daughter we had seen in the waiting area.

Suddenly feeling that I was intruding on something private, I slipped outside and saw Barbara disappearing through the swing doors at the end of the corridor. I followed her, hearing her heels clacking down the stairway, then across the lobby and outside.

By the time I caught up, she was standing by a low wall, looking as statuesque as the terracotta pots of succulents that flanked the approach road.

I approached cautiously, not sure what I was going to say; but as it turned out, Barbara initiated the conversation.

"I know I should be charitable," she said, still looking straight ahead at nothing in particular. "I know the woman may be at death's door. I sometimes think I could have forgiven her if I had known it was finally over. But it never has been."

This was a minefield of allusions, and I knew I had to tread carefully.

"Is Walter Claire's father?" I asked tentatively.

She gave me a sharp-eyed look. "What do you think?"

Given her bitter tone, it was obvious the question was rhetorical. I waited until she looked away, and then said, "Does Claire know?"

"Why don't you ask her? You're her new man, aren't you?"

"I'm just trying to understand," I said, ignoring the implication that I was some kind of affliction Claire had picked up. "I'm new to all this. There's a lot of undercurrents."

"It's a sin, you know." She wasn't looking at me. "It's against the Lord's teachings. I forgave him once, but I'm not going to stay here and be humiliated. If he asks, you can tell him I've gone back to the hotel."

Then she stalked off toward the car park with as much decorum as her restricted hemline would allow.

I lingered after she had gone, deciding that Walter and Claire needed some time alone together with Nora. The sun was slowly dipping into the west, lengthening the shadows of the hospital blocks and the multi-storey car parks. Vehicles kept coming and going on the slipways and exit ramps, cars and ambulances circulating visitors and patients like corpuscles in a network of arteries, the occasional jogger and cyclist darting nervously between them, foreign bodies in the system. From time to time ambulance sirens dopplered, and a hospital helicopter took off from one of the roofs, banking as it headed inland, scattering pale birds from their perches.

"So there you are."

It was Walter Suthersen, squinting against the sun as he approached.

He sat down on the wall beside me, got out a pack of Marlboros, then thought better of it and put them away.

"Is she gone?" he asked. "Barbara?"

"Back to the hotel," I replied. "She asked me to let you know." I hesitated, and then added: "She wasn't very happy."

"No," Suthersen replied. "I'm afraid I'm the cross she has to bear."

He didn't elaborate and I decided not to enquire directly. There were other things I was determined to air.

"Does Claire know you're her father?" I asked him.

He was still staring at the sun. "We never formally announced it to her," he said. "Nora wouldn't allow it."

"She's never asked you?"

"Sometimes a question is left unsaid because you already know the answer."

"Get that from a fortune cookie, did you?"

He sighed, turning to face me. "You're angry. I understand that."

"Do you? I don't think you do. Why should I be angry? She's not my daughter."

"I've had to keep my distance over the years," Suthersen said with real regret. "It was what Nora wanted. But Claire had begun to suspect. She finally asked me a few minutes ago."

I hadn't been expecting this. "What did you say?"

"I told her the truth. That, yes, I was her father."

He looked more sad than elated. Or perhaps it was just the sheer exhausted relief of someone finally confessing a long-held secret.

"How did she take it?" I asked.

"We hugged. She cried. Then she asked me to leave her alone with Nora for a while so that she could take it all in."

My instinct was to rush up there to be with Claire, but Suthersen assured me she had insisted she wanted some time to herself.

"She's quite taken with you, you know."

"Well, at least that's one thing I can rely on. Are you Leo Parrish?"

"Of course not."

"He's dead?"

Suthersen nodded. "Nora never really got over it."

"Were you two having an affair at the time?"

"It started long before that. We fell in love."

I was tempted to make some sarcastic comment, but I knew I was only angry for Claire's sake. I had to give him time to tell me in his own words. In the event, he launched straight into it.

"When Leo started hand-delivering his stories, Edgar and I were intrigued by him," he told me. "We both realized that he was a cut above the ordinary. He was pretty businesslike when he came in, as if he had more important things he wanted to be getting on with, but one day we collared him into letting Barbara photograph the three of us."

"This was in—what, 1958?"

"Or '59. I remember it was winter. Eventually he let me walk home with him. He never said much, but people always warm to enthusiasm and praise, and it helped that he lived not too far from our offices." He produced a toothpick and started gnawing on it.

"That was where I met Nora," he went on, "and it was more or less love at first sight." A dry laugh. "Can you believe it? We just hit it off straight away. Instant attraction."

I could see from his unguarded smile that he was telling the truth.

"She was a terrific-looking woman in those days, with a personality to match. And I was in my prime, too."

"But you were already married."

He nodded solemnly. "I'd got Barbara pregnant while we were still living in Minnesota. She couldn't bear the thought of the shame it would bring on her. Her parents were devout Christians, you see."

"Rapturists?"

"Most definitely not. Lutheran, but of the evangelical persuasion. So we upped sticks and ran with our tails between our legs to New York City."

He fell silent again. I waited.

"Barbara already saw herself as a fallen woman, lured into sin by me. That's why she insisted we got married straightaway. To make us respectable."

He spat out bits of toothpick, looked me full in the face. "She lost the baby five months into her pregnancy. I don't think she's ever forgiven me, especially since she was never able to conceive again. It truly was adding insult to injury."

He got to his feet. "Do you mind if we walk awhile?"

I had no objections. We took one of the many paths that coiled between the hospital's various buildings.

"We weren't in love," he continued. "I seduced her because I was a young man who couldn't keep his pecker in his pocket. We married out of necessity, out of respectability, out of guilt. Barbara might tell you differently. She would see it as duty, as a sacred covenant. For me it became a trap, especially after I met Nora. It was only then I realized what it truly felt like to be alive in the presence of someone who electrifies you."

"Did Nora know you were married?"

"I never told her," he confessed. "When she eventually found out she was furious. She broke it off. We didn't see one another for the best part of ten years."

I got the impression he was prepared to tell me whatever I needed to know. Perhaps he wanted my approval or at least understanding if I was of interest to his daughter.

"So how did you two get back together again?"

"I used to phone her every month. Sometimes she'd refuse to speak to me. Sometimes we'd have a stilted conversation. She knew that Barbara and I were unhappy, but she also knew that Barbara would never agree to a divorce."

"You discussed that?"

"With Barbara and with Nora. For the first few years I couldn't bring myself to broach it. I suppose I still felt guilty about the child we'd lost. But we were leading lives of not-so-quiet misery together and eventually I thought it would be better for both of us if we parted. Barbara refused outright. I'd compromised her morals, but I wasn't going to make her break her marriage vows."

He was peering at me, trying to gauge my reaction. I remembered the picture of him as a young man, handsome, confident, brimming with energy and ambition. It must have been a time of great conflicting passions for him. Perhaps it still was.

"I told Nora all about it," he said. "I was determined to be as honest as I could with her from then on."

"How did she take it?"

Suthersen gave a derisory laugh. "She was blunt. Nora always was. She told me I couldn't expect the world to arrange itself to my convenience. There were strong words about sowing wild oats and not expecting there to be weeds as well. You know what Nora's like."

He was trying to make light of it, but I wasn't going to pretend to be amused. Suthersen was gradually picking up his walking pace, staying in the shadows of buildings, giving them the once-over as we passed. Was he worried we were being watched or followed? I couldn't see anyone lurking in our vicinity.

"So how did Claire come about?" I asked.

"Nora had reached her thirties," he told me. "She wanted a child. She hadn't met anyone else. I like to think she was still carrying a torch for me. No, damn it, I know she was. We were unrequited lovers—it's corny but true. She was the one who suggested it."

He didn't have to spell it out, but I was determined to have absolute clarity. "So she let you father her child?"

Suthersen had stopped at the rear of a building stacked with big trash cans and pallets crammed with flattened cardboard boxes.

"She made her terms crystal clear," he said, removing his pack of Marlboros and lighting one up. "If she had a child I could see it once a year for a few hours, but there would be no paternal rights beyond this. And the child wasn't to know."

"And you agreed?"

He exhaled smoke through his nostrils. "Of course I did. I loved the woman. Still do."

He had chosen a spot where there were no windows overlooking us so that he could smoke without being seen by either staff or patients.

"So what happened after Claire was born?" I asked. "Did you reach a settlement on maintenance?"

"It was never discussed. But my career was flourishing and I was determined to provide for Claire. Monthly credit transfers, straight into Nora's account, even after she moved to England. It wasn't much—just enough to keep them ticking over. Nora wouldn't accept any more, even when I started making good money."

Presumably he had acquired the house in Twickenham so that he could visit her there: it was a question I didn't need to ask him.

"Did Barbara know?"

"After Claire was born, I told her everything. By then, Nora had relocated to England."

"How did she take it?"

He took a deep drag of his cigarette. "I think I was secretly hoping it would compel her to agree to a divorce. But she's made of flint, that woman."

"You could have just walked out."

"It wasn't that easy. Flint's brittle, and she'd nearly gone to pieces when she miscarried. I always felt that that was my fault somehow." He looked at his cigarette with disgust and flicked it away into the grass. "Besides, walking out wouldn't have solved anything. Nora always insisted she would never share her life with me unless Barbara freely agreed to a divorce."

We began heading back the way we had come.

"So where was Leo when all this was going on?" I asked.

"Working a lot of the time. The neighbourhood hospital had a mental health clinic and he was one of the case workers. He'd gotten himself qualified through night school and he did all the hours that were available."

Which fitted with the information from the newspaper report on his death. "He was still living with Nora?"

"He was always there for her. He never got involved, never offered an opinion, but I think he was the rock that kept her grounded and made the whole thing an effective family unit, even though they were brother and sister."

"He never met anyone himself?"

Suthersen shook his head. "Not that I'm aware of."

"And he never wrote anything else?"

"Ridge Publications had folded by then, and everyone had moved on to other things. The '60s came in, and suddenly it was a different ball-game. I think he'd had enough of that world."

I was trying to remember the chronology I had gleaned from Rhodri and others.

"But you were editing *Vantage* by then, weren't you?"

"And doing an increasing amount of my own writing."

"You didn't think of asking Leo if he'd like to contribute something to your magazine?"

He didn't immediately answer. Then: "There wasn't much in the way of regular communication between me and the family for quite a few years after Nora found out about Barbara."

He wasn't looking directly at me. I said, "Why do I still get the feeling you aren't telling me everything? Especially about Leo."

He laughed again, but this time it was forced. "Leo just led his life as a loyal brother to Nora and an uncle to Claire for that short time before he was killed. It was cruel."

"Did you and Nora ever speculate about who might have done it?"

"Well, it's hard to accept that someone you think of as a friend has been the victim of a random shooting by a lunatic. But that's the way it seems to have happened."

Which corroborated Nora's story.

"When I began researching Leo Parrish," I said carefully, "I started to wonder if perhaps he hadn't secretly gone on to a more eminent life, under another name perhaps."

Suthersen looked perplexed. "How could he have? He was dead."

"Then how come Noah Byrnes tried to shoot you when you claimed you were Leo?"

Suthersen gave it a moment's thought. "Maybe Byrnes is the same kind of lunatic as the one who shot Leo."

Which was a creepy idea indeed; but Suthersen had suggested it too quickly, too glibly.

"Maybe it's because some people believe his stories predict the future," I said.

Suthersen checked his stride for a moment, and then carried on walking. "I've heard it said," he remarked.

"And what's your opinion?"

"Some people are better prognosticators than others. If you attribute that to mystical powers, you're missing the point."

I still had the feeling he was evading something.

"I'm assuming the Ascendants don't want *Exaltation* resurfacing because it would just ruin their credibility."

"Well, it's far too late for that now, isn't it?"

"Edgar Eldridge doesn't seem particularly bothered."

Suthersen gave a mirthless laugh. "Edgar always was a bit of a benevolent rogue. Most people who know him have a suspicion that he saw establishing a church as a quick way of making money and I don't think it's something that he's ever bothered to deny. The Church hierarchy, though, they're a different matter."

"Noah Byrnes was working for an agency affiliated with the Department for Homeland Security."

This time Suthersen did stop. "Really?" he said. "That's interesting."

"Is it? In what way exactly?"

"In the 'Why the hell would they be interested in an old-time science fiction writer' sort of way."

He was bullish.

"You have no ideas?"

"None whatsoever."

I didn't believe him. At the same time, he wasn't exactly objecting to me interrogating him.

"Can I ask you something else?" I said.

We were back at the hospital building. Suthersen settled himself on the same stretch of wall and said, "Shoot." He winced. "Or rather, don't."

"You testified before a Senate committee back in those days, didn't you?"

He eyed me. "How did you know about that?"

"The archives were put online in the UK."

"That was Barbara's doing."

"What?"

Suthersen took out his Marlboros and lit one in full view of the reception area.

"I gather from Claire that you've read Leo's original version of *Exaltation*," he said to me. "You know it's not very flattering about blind religious faith. Particularly the second part."

"True," I agreed.

"Barbara did all the secretarial work for Edgar. When he'd decided to write his own version of the second part, he passed the original on to her. He probably told her to file it, but Barbara was more than usually interested. By then I'd confessed to my affair with Nora."

Someone came out of the building and Suthersen discreetly hid his cigarette.

"So Barbara read it," he continued when the coast was clear. "And was suitably appalled by its theme, which to her was a travesty of the scriptures. So she sent it off to a Congressman, along with other stories of Leo's that we'd published."

"Did you know about this?"

"Not at the time. The Congressman promptly passed the material on a group of people who were already taking an interest in science fiction."

"What group of people exactly?"

"I only found out later," Suthersen said. "After I'd been summoned to the hearing. Certain members of the committee were more than a little bothered by intelligence they'd received from what they kept calling 'a State Department think tank'. Eventually I discovered that this think tank called themselves the SFU." He studied the tip of his cigarette. "Not the Science Fiction Union, in case you were wondering. It was an acronym for the Strategic Foresight Unit."

A little light went on in my head. This was the trio of initials I hadn't identified from the Senate committee hearings.

"As far as I can gather," Suthersen said, "the SFU was either a covert part of the CIA or an independent agency answerable to the Department of Defense. I never did enquire too closely. It emerged in the post-war years, its brief being to look into the very latest scientific and technological trends—ideas as much as actual gadgets—to see whether any of them might prove useful to the USA. These days we might call it looking for examples of blue-sky thinking."

"Which explains the 'strategic foresight' bit."

"Precisely. By the late fifties the Advanced Research Projects Agency had also been established in response to the Soviets launching Sputnik. It was the public version of the SFU, if you like, initiating projects designed to establish and maintain US technological superiority. Later it became DARPA."

"Which developed the Stealth Fighter," I said, just to show I knew something.

"Among other things," Suthersen replied. "The SFU weren't afraid to look into the wildest kinds of notions. In fact, it was actively encouraged. I think quite a few of them must have been science fiction fans. They'd obviously read plenty of it."

"So what exactly did they want from you?"

"Well, I didn't actually talk to them direct. But the senators were interested in two things. Firstly, were science-fiction stories that postulated different societies in danger of destabilizing American family values and patriotism." He chuckled. "I gave that one pretty short shrift, telling them that they were cautionary tales whose precise point was to flag up the dangers."

"And secondly?"

"They wanted to know whether I believed science-fiction could accurately predict the future. And whether some people were better at it than others."

"People like Leo Parrish?"

"Well, there were plenty of other better known names, though I did give Leo credit as someone I thought was particularly good at near-future speculation."

"Wasn't that a bit naïve?" I said, thinking about the very negative story summaries I had read online. "You must have known it was an investigative committee and that their agenda wasn't exactly the promotion of science fiction."

"I did it innocently, I assure you. Remember I was young and full of zeal. I believed that science fiction could solve most of the world's problems if only enough people started reading it." He smiled at such naiveté. "I thought Leo deserved a wider readership. What surprised me was how familiar these respectable-looking gentlemen already were with his work. Given that I couldn't imagine any of them scouring the newsstands for the latest issue of *Awesome Adventures*, I began to think that someone in our office must have sent someone in federal circles the texts. And since that there was only me, Edgar and Barbara, it wasn't difficult to figure out who."

"You didn't suspect Eldridge?"

"Edgar's never been a fan of big government or any of its agencies. It wasn't his style. Besides, the committee had specifically requested me. Which was odd, since I was relatively unknown at the time."

"So why go?" I asked. "Hadn't McCarthy been discredited by then? Public opinion had turned against all the hysteria he'd whipped up."

"Well, it wasn't that sort of summons, more a polite request. They weren't asking if we were harbouring Communists or anything. I was curious to find out what they wanted."

It was easy to imagine Suthersen as an ambitious young man, eager to forge his own career and perhaps flattered to have the attention.

"So what did they ask you about Leo Parrish?"

He made a show of thinking about it. "They were interested in some of his notions about miniature gadgets and weather control. Were they possible? Was he advocating the use of them if they were? In particular I remember them being bothered by the anti-religious tone of *Exaltation*. Was he an *atheist*, they wanted to know? Did he see himself as some sort of secular prophet? Were his ideas being taken up by anyone else?"

"Which version of the serial had they read?"

"The unpublished one. That's when I knew it had to be Barbara. She denied it afterwards but we had a stand-up row about it. It was only years later she owned up. After Claire was born."

I remembered him telling me that he couldn't recall much about Leo's stories. Either he had been lying or had boned up in the interim. I decided to let it pass.

"So what did you tell them?"

"I stonewalled, said it was just a story in a cheap magazine. They wanted to know if Leo would be amenable to coming to speak before the committee and I told them no. I said he'd retired from writing and that we had no further contact with him, not even an address."

"They believed you?"

"Of course they didn't, even though the first part of it was in effect true. But by then I'd figured it was Barbara's meddling. It was obvious she was trying to hurt me and Nora through her brother, and I was determined to protect Leo." He raised his hand to stop me from interrupting again. "Here's the interesting thing. One of the committee members was a senator from Maryland called Bradley Irwin. He had his nine year-old son with him. I remember the boy playing with a toy robot but also listening to what the grown-ups were talking about. He's come a long way since then. Like to take a guess who?"

TWENTY-EIGHT

I spent the rest of the evening with Claire, Walter insisting that he would watch over Nora while we went out for dinner. He wasn't concerned about leaving Barbara to her own devices, telling us that she would probably take a couple of sleeping pills and go to bed early, which she always did when she was in a huff. I think he was eager to display his sense of duty to Nora and particularly to Claire, who finally knew for certain that he was her father. He took me aside and handed me a hundred dollars to cover the meal, being adamant that I take it and admitting that it was blood money in the sense that he had long wanted to spoil his daughter and that I could act as his proxy that evening. I felt a little sorry for him at that moment; despite all his success he had spent half a century unable to share his life with the woman and then later the daughter who meant most to him.

Neither Claire nor I was especially hungry, but we took his recommendation of a seafood bar close to the beach within walking distance of the hospital. It served monster prawns in a chilli and ginger sauce. We ate them with potato wedges and a bottle of over-fragrant Californian rosé on a balcony overlooking the waterfront, watching the moon rise over the palms and listening to the drum-and-bass rhythms leaking out of a nightclub in the Egyptian-themed hotel next door.

I was hoping for a romantic after-dinner stroll on the beach, but Claire was eager to get back to her mother. She told me that she had suspected that Walter was her father in the weeks leading up to the convention, given his active involvement in the welfare of her mother and herself; but the actual confirmation had left her a little stunned, particularly since Nora was showing no signs of regaining consciousness. What if she died with this particular bit of emotional business unfinished?

We returned to the hospital to find that Nora's condition was unchanged. The atmosphere between Claire and Walter Suthersen was charged without being tense and I knew I had to step aside for both their sakes. I took a taxi back to my hotel and found Rhodri blissfully snoring in his usual splayed position on his bed.

*

I woke before anyone else next morning. The air was humid, the sky pebbled with cloud. I was nursing a coffee at a poolside table when a refreshingly gentle bleeping alerted me to a call. It was Walter Suthersen. He wanted to know what Barbara had said to me before she left the hospital.

"If he asks, you can tell him I've gone back to the hotel," I recited.

There was a pause at the other end. "Was that all?"

"Yes," I assured him. "What's up?"

"She didn't say she was stopping off anywhere on the way?"

"That was it. Has something happened?"

"She wasn't here when I got back from the hospital this morning. Her bed hadn't been slept in. It looks like she never came home. And her cell phone's off."

I couldn't see any point in being diplomatic. "She was pretty annoyed with you. Maybe she's deliberately taken herself off somewhere."

"That's not her style. She'd rather stay put and wait so she can go at me with all moral guns blazing."

I thought about it. "She was a bit deflated. As much sad as angry."

"Believe me, I know how she'd be. Wounded and full of righteous indignation. It's not like her. It's not like her at all."

He told me Claire was napping, having been awake half the night. There was still no change in Nora's condition. Now he had two women to worry about. He said he had some other calls to make and rang off.

I decided to go straight over to the convention hotel. It was quiet after the drama of the day before. The Matanzas bar was on the lobby floor across from the reception area, a place of potted plants and suede armchairs in dusty shades of sage and salmon. I had half an hour to kill before my meeting with Cyrus Hammond so I slipped into one of the games rooms where they were running beta versions of the latest releases. Never having been a games buff, I just sat and watched a few young few die-hards play *HexCalibre*, a bewildering adventure in which you were a sorcerer's apprentice having to master various spells and magical implements to avoid being eaten by the wizard's loathsome familiar. Then I got a text message from Cyrus Hammond saying: *I'm here. Where are you*?

As I was crossing the reception area I saw Walter Suthersen surrounded by a cluster of hotel staff. He was comforting a distraught Barbara. She was still in her pale raincoat and gold lamé dress, but her coat was smudged and she was barefoot.

It quickly became clear from the exchange of conversation that she had been abducted overnight.

The hotel security staff ushered them over to a quiet corner of the foyer while they waited for the police to arrive.

"She was offered a lift as she was leaving the hospital," Suthersen told me. "By that lunatic of an actor."

"It was fine at first," Barbara said, her eyes blackened with tears, her voice almost at breaking point. "He took me to a bar and we had cocktails. I didn't think anything was wrong, even though he was fidgety. He offered to drive me back to the hotel, but instead he parked off-road and started demanding to know if Walter really was that man Parrish."

"Are we talking about Ryan Carmichael?" I said, disbelieving.

"It was him," Suthersen said. "Apparently he kept asking about the missing part of *Exaltation*—"

"He was obsessed with it," Barbara interrupted, almost shrieking. "I kept telling him that Walter wasn't Leo Parrish and that we didn't know anything about it. But I couldn't get through to him. I think he was high on cocaine or something. He said he wasn't going to let me out of there until I told him the truth. It was terrifying."

Suthersen cupped his arm around her and pressed her to his chest. The hotel staff now wanted to get them both into a private room post haste, but Suthersen wasn't quite done.

"He ended up driving her around for most of the night," he told me. "Asking the same questions over and over again. He finally threw her out of the car not far from here. She's only just walked in."

There were spots of blood on her dress, though she was insistent that Carmichael hadn't actually touched her.

"Does Claire know?" I asked Walter.

"I'd rather she didn't at the moment. She's got enough on her plate."

Suthersen agreed to let the staff escort him and Barbara away. I wasn't allowed to follow.

I just stood there on my own for several minutes, thinking furiously, still not quite able to take in the fact that Ryan Carmichael had actually kidnapped Barbara Suthersen. Was he working with Byrnes? Or on some bizarre mission for the Ascendants? Then I realized that it probably wasn't a good idea to be standing in the lobby when the cops arrived, so I walked into the Matanzas bar. Cyrus Hammond was ensconced in an armchair, sipping a tall glass of what looked like tomato juice.

Sitting opposite him was the diminutive Vincent Kubilius.

Neither man had noticed me entering. I retreated behind a luxuriant fern on a chest-high plinth.

Kubilius was agitated, leaning forward and remonstrating, though keeping his voice low. Hammond was listening to him with narrowed eyes, not saying anything, holding his glass close to his face as if to mask his expression. A waiter went over to their table, but Kubilius waved him away, still talking. Then abruptly he got up and walked towards the exit.

He spotted me and walked directly over.

"I want to make it perfectly plain," he said without preamble, "that our Church is a law-abiding institution and will distance itself from anyone who takes unilateral illegal action, whether or not they believe they are acting on our behalf. And however eminent they are."

He stalked off before I could muster any sort of reply.

Hammond was watching from his armchair. I stood over him, determined not to initiate the conversation.

"Take a seat," he said.

"Having a meeting, were you?" I said. "Are you two friends?"

"Not in the slightest," he replied. "One of his cronies found me and said he urgently needed a word."

And yet Kubilius had come alone, probably to ensure privacy. It occurred to me that if Hammond wanted to keep a connection between them secret he was hardly likely to agree to meet him in the bar when he was already expecting me. Even so, Hammond wasn't his usual relaxed self, which was hardly surprising.

"So is there something else I should know about?" I asked.

"That depends on what you've already heard."

"Stop playing cat and mouse. What did he want?"

Hammond looked dishevelled and sweaty, even though the bar was air-conditioned. His cell phone was tucked in his palm.

"I take it you've heard about Barbara Suthersen?" he said.

"I've just spoken to her and Walter."

"It seems my nephew has lost his mind. My sister's beside herself."

It transpired that Hammond had been staying with his sister in Palm Beach, but they had received a call in the early hours of the morning saying that Ryan Carmichael had left his entourage behind and gone AWOL. Hammond had got to the convention hotel just in time to discover that Carmichael had kidnapped Barbara Suthersen overnight and was still at large.

"The boy's an egotistical fool, but he is family and I've done my best to keep him on the straight and narrow. But this is beyond the pale."

I still hadn't sat down. "Did Kubilius ask you cover up for him again?"

"For Ryan?"

"Well, you're a fixer, aren't you?"

He looked at me as if the suggestion wasn't worth a response.

"To cover up for the Ascendants then?"

Hammond was scornful. "I think they're a bunch of money-grubbing phonies. Ryan never had any common sense. That's why he got mixed up with them in the first place."

He took out a handkerchief and swabbed his temples. The tomato juice at the corners of his lips made it look as if blood was leaking from his mouth.

"According to Kubilius," he told me, "Ryan phoned him in the small hours to say that he was on the hunt for the final part of Parrish's serial. The original version. And had taken Walter Suthersen's wife to find out where it was."

"She wouldn't know," I was keen to insist. "Walter Suthersen isn't Leo Parrish. That was just a ploy."

Hammond didn't say anything but I could tell that he wasn't doubting it.

I lowered myself into the armchair opposite him. "Kubilius is claiming he has nothing to do with it?"

"Of course he is. He was eager to assure me he ordered Ryan to set Mrs Suthersen free. He thinks he may be suffering some sort of breakdown."

"He's not working with Noah Byrnes?"

Hammond actually laughed. "Ryan? Of course not."

"Do you think Kubilius is telling the truth?"

"I do," Hammond said emphatically. "He's scared witless it'll reflect badly on the Church."

I wasn't convinced that Kubilius was entirely blameless in initiating some of the Church's more aggressive activities but I doubted that he would stoop to having high-profile people kidnapped and held hostage.

"Does Kubilius know you're a federal agent?" I asked, hoping to provoke him into an admission.

"If he thought that, he'd be wrong. He knows I'm Ryan's uncle, and I think he's hoping I'll be able to reason with him. He got him to agree to release Mrs Suthersen but Ryan's still out there and Kubilius is worried he might be planning more mischief. Even by Ryan's usual standards this is way up the fruitcake scale."

"Have you tried contacting him?"

Hammond waved his phone at me. "He's not answering his cell."

A waiter came up. I told him I didn't want anything and he went away.

"Kubilius is only interested in protecting himself and his Church," Hammond said. "Whatever happens, this story is going to get out and there'll be plenty of adverse publicity. I would imagine he's already got a team of lawyers working on a variety of *mea culpas*."

"Why are they so interested in the final part of the serial?"

"I doubt that they knew about the unpublished version until you and Suthersen spilled the beans. The loopier fringes of the cult have always wanted to destroy Parrish's work once and for all to exterminate any links between him and the origins of their religion."

"That much I'd worked out myself," I told him. "But I still don't understand why Ryan Carmichael would risk his entire reputation on such an insane stunt."

Sweat was trickling down Hammond's temples again. "He's been a Walter Mitty character since he was a kid, prone to wild fantasies and exaggerated ideas of his own importance. I don't think Hollywood fame and fortune has dampened that. If anything it's made it worse." He looked at me candidly. "I have a feeling that Ryan sees it as his duty to rid the world of the serial so that he can gain more clout with his co-religionists. As if being their best-known follower wasn't enough."

"Presumably it's the Ascendants who've been doing most of the harassing of the Whitneys?"

He made an affirmative noise. "The Whitneys and anyone else who might have copies of his work."

"Like Arthur Townsend."

"The police can't prove anything, but I'd place bets on it."

"And Noah Byrnes?"

Hammond sat back in his seat.

"Byrnes is different," he said. "He's a Rapturist."

He started pressing buttons on his phone. I assumed he was trying to get through to Ryan Carmichael again, but someone answered and Hammond said, "We're ready."

"Who was that?" I asked.

"You'll find out in a minute," he told me.

He was looking over my shoulder. As if he had been waiting for his cue, Alvarez walked into the bar. He was wearing chinos and a polo shirt, but his expression was anything but casual.

"Good day, Mr Randall," he said before plonking himself down on the sofa between us.

"Agent Alvarez has obligingly agreed to put us in the picture about Noah Byrnes," Hammond informed me.

A few fans had drifted into the bar and were watching the advertisements on the TV mounted high in one corner. The sound was off, and scurrilous commentaries were being improvised.

"How come you two know one another?" I asked.

"We didn't," Hammond said, "until I contacted the agency about Noah Byrnes."

Alvarez showed no indication that Hammond was lying about this.

"Byrnes isn't saying anything," he told us. "He appears to have gone from mania to catatonia. But I think we've pretty much pieced it together."

He didn't disguise the fact that he was rattled, as if he still couldn't quite believe that his former superior officer had attempted to assassinate an eminent writer in a public place. He had been summoned back to the US as soon as Byrnes absconded, but no one in the agency had realized that Byrnes had made it back to the United States until now.

"Did he mention Bennett Irwin?" I asked.

"Nope. But it's a racing certainty that he was acting on orders from Irwin to shut down anything to do with Leo Parrish."

"Including shooting the man he believed to be Parrish?"

"Unlikely that Irwin would have sanctioned attempted murder," Alvarez said doubtfully, "but we do believe he's the one behind the program. Our difficulty is that there's absolutely no evidence at this stage. Irwin will have been shrewd enough not to leave a paper trail."

"Program?" I said, finding it hard to take in despite my prior suspicions. "What program? Why is Irwin so obsessed with Parrish?"

"It's mostly about *Exaltation*," Hammond said. "Irwin and his co-religionists have a big problem with the final part."

"We think that's why Byrnes ultimately flipped," Alvarez added. "As far as we can establish the Future Fellowship group around Irwin—"

"Future Fellowship?"

"Rapturist evangelicals who actively promote the coming of the End of Days. They want the original version of the serial kept out of circulation because they view it as a divine message."

"They think it's prophetic?"

"Not the published one but the original version. We found a copy in the archives of a branch of the intelligence services."

"The Strategic Foresight Unit?" I guessed.

Alvarez looked impressed. "Irwin worked for the unit when he was a young man in the late sixties and early seventies. He must have had access to the Parrish file. Someone in the organisation set up surveillance protocols to remove material about Leo Parrish from public view."

There was that word again: *protocols*. "When did this start?"

"That's the interesting thing. Shortly *before* Parrish was killed."

Assuming that Leo Parrish had actually been shot dead in 1972, the chronology fitted.

"You say 'someone'. Was it Irwin?"

"He was working there," Alvarez admitted, "but there's nothing on record. The program continued after he'd moved on, maybe under its own momentum, maybe because as his influence grew he made sure it did from outside."

"It seems like a lot of trouble for an agency to go to for an obscure writer who published in small-press magazines. Didn't anyone else think to question it?"

"It isn't uncommon in covert agencies," Hammond said. "You inherit a set of duties and procedures and you just get on with them, assuming that their rationale is national security issues beyond your pay grade."

"Irwin was a Rapturist in those days?"

"He's always been a devout believer."

And more recently Byrnes had picked up the torch with a vengeance. But it was still puzzling. "I still don't see why they'd put so much effort into keeping all of his work out of circulation. If it was a Rapturist agenda, then surely they'd just be interested in the novel."

Alvarez responded: "We think they took the view that all of it was the divine word of the Lord in some disguised form. But they were mostly concerned to prevent any copies of the original novel from getting out."

I thought about this. "But if they see it as the truth, why wouldn't they want as many people to know about it as possible?"

Alvarez nibbled his fat moustache. "The Future Fellowship is pretty exclusive. Maybe they like to restrict access to what they believe is the truth."

I was still puzzled. "The original version of the second part of *Exaltation* is pretty anti-religious if you read it carefully."

"It was the road map and the destination that they were interested in," said Hammond. "Not the author's views on what Paradise would be like."

"But how would they square that with their belief that Parrish was an oracle?"

"You don't give up cherished beliefs in the light of inconvenient evidence. They might have rationalized the sceptical tone of the second part as God's vessel becoming corrupted and trying to deny the truth. It probably doesn't matter to Irwin and his ilk whether or not Leo was a believer himself. He was just the divine conduit."

It was quite clear that Hammond had spent plenty of time thinking about the Future Fellowship and their relationship with *Exaltation*. He knew more than Alvarez.

"I thought we owed it to you to put you in the picture," Alvarez said. He got up. "We're shipping Byrnes back to DC for further questioning. And after that I guess he's going to be facing a long prison sentence. Either that, or a psychiatric institution."

"What about Bennett Irwin?"

Alvarez stopped looking so bullish. "We have to tread much more carefully there. Beyond the family connection and the shared fundamentalist beliefs, we have nothing to link Irwin directly with Byrnes's actions. And he is the Secretary of State."

"That shouldn't make him immune to the law."

"Of course not. But you have to swim carefully when you're dealing with a Big Fish."

"You zig-zag," Hammond remarked. "Close in on your objective by degrees."

"I assume you're speaking from experience," I said. And to Alvarez: "Is Cyrus on your team?"

"Mr Hammond retired years ago," he replied without hesitation. "He's simply filled us in on some of the background details, that's all."

It was obvious that they had rehearsed this answer. All three of us were now standing.

"I've had a word with the local police about your innocent involvement in the Parrish affair," Alvarez said to me. "I've put them in the picture as much as I was able, asked them not to give you unnecessary hassle."

There was the ghost of a smile on his big round face.

"Thanks," I said. "I appreciate it."

"It was the least I could do. Sometimes you don't see the rot at the heart of things until someone points it out to you."

He was offering his hand. I took it, and we shook. He produced a card with a cell phone number scribbled on the back.

"I'll be in Washington," he told me, "but feel free to call me any time you need to."

After he was gone, Hammond and I sat down again.

"So," I said to him, "you were a federal agent."

"Long time ago," he replied.

"But you've maintained your connections with the service."

"Once you've been an agent, you never drop off their radar entirely. And I was happy to help out whenever I got the call."

"Filmscope isn't just a front?"

He looked offended by the suggestion. "It's been half my life's work."

"It was you who set me on the trail of Leo Parrish in the first place," I reminded him. "You sent the text about meeting Arthur, didn't you?"

"Guilty," he admitted. "I wanted to whet your appetite. I think Leo Parrish is a worthy cause."

"Then why haven't you funded a movie based on his work yourself?"

He gave a crusty laugh. "We're a foundation, not Sony Pictures. We don't have that sort of financial clout. But I was aware that the Ascendants and the Fellowship were trying to airbrush Parrish from history. He deserves better than that."

"Done a lot of research on both of them, have you?"

Hammond didn't answer. He was trying Ryan Carmichael's number again.

The fans in the corner were now watching what appeared to be the news. I had deliberately refrained from checking it so far that morning but it was dominated by the successful shuttle launch, with real-time shots of the crew drifting around the cabin and signalling to the on-board camera.

Carmichael still wasn't answering. Hammond wrapped his phone in his fist as if he could squeeze a response from it.

"I'm still not clear why Irwin and Byrnes want Parrish's work out of circulation," I said. "If they think his writing was divinely inspired, then wouldn't they want everyone to know about it? Especially if they believe it validates their faith."

"That puzzled me for a long while," Hammond admitted. He leaned forward conspiratorially. "Want to know what I think? The Fellowship has some unsettling ideas about the End of Days. If you read their literature carefully you find that they're not passive about waiting for the Rapture. They believe it's their divine mission actively to bring it about." He mopped his brow again. "What if Irwin and Byrnes see the serial as a *blueprint* for what has to happen to bring about the Rapture?"

I just gaped at him. "A plan of action, do you mean?"

"Nothing more, nothing less. Something they have to facilitate themselves to bring on their desired end. And who would be in a better position to jerk the strings in the direction they want than the Secretary of State for Defense?"

I wanted to laugh at the idea but I knew I couldn't.

"Have you mentioned this to Alvarez?"

"And risk losing any credibility? He might start thinking I'm just another wacko. Not exactly *mainstream*, is it?"

Given Byrnes's actions, it didn't seem at all far-fetched to me.

"The shuttle commander is a Rapturist," I pointed out, indicating the screen shot of Valentine sitting at the controls playfully twiddling his thumbs.

Hammond looked grave: this wasn't news to him.

"Part of the mission is to do reconnaissance," he said. "Ostensibly they're looking for evidence of Khanistani missile emplacements. They'll be a few miles up but making regular passes directly over Khanistani air space."

"What are you suggesting?"

"If they wanted to provoke something, they have the perfect opportunity. All they need is the means. Valentine probably couldn't sneak anything explosive or radioactive onto the shuttle. But he might have better luck with a vial of something biological. Like that virus they've been secretly developing."

I pretended ignorance.

"The one you were so concerned your business partner might be exposed to."

It no longer surprised me that Hammond knew far more than I had even imagined.

"A vial of it might be enough," he said. "Especially if it could be dispersed as an aerosol over the capital."

I looked at him sceptically. "Do you know something?"

"I assure you I'm just speculating."

"A vial launched from orbit?" I said. "Wouldn't it burn up long before it reached the ground?"

Hammond contemplated this; but not for long.

"Valentine's a true believer. He might be prepared to make the ultimate sacrifice for the cause, secure in the conviction that total physical resurrection awaits him when it's all over." He paused, gazing at me with grim relish. "In which case, he might not baulk at taking the shuttle itself straight down there so that he's sure of hitting his target."

*

Claire's mobile was switched off, so I decided to go straight over to the hospital to make sure that everything was OK. Hammond offered to drive me. He had a venerable red Charade in the hotel's basement car park, on loan from his sister. Fortunately the car's air-con was working perfectly.

"How is Nora?" he asked as we drove.

"No change, as far as I'm aware." It occurred to me that even a positive outcome for Nora might be rendered irrelevant if Hammond's doomsday scenario came to pass.

"What exactly does that mean?" Hammond asked. "I thought she'd just fainted."

For once I knew more than he did. I shook my head. "It was a collapse. They don't think it was a stroke, but she hasn't regained consciousness."

This was clearly news he hadn't been expecting.

"I'm getting the impression you *do* know her," I remarked

He shook his head. "No. Just Claire. That family could use a break."

This was said with some feeling.

"I'm still detecting a sense of obligation," I remarked. "Particularly towards Claire. Like to elaborate?"

He shrugged. "I admired her pluck in getting a Leo Parrish story televised. That was a tall order."

"So you're not a secret uncle or some other relative of hers?"

"I told you before—there's no family connection between us. We know one another because I introduced myself to her in my professional capacity after watching the *Nightscapes* episode. What else can I say?" He appeared to think about it. "We all need worthy causes, and I guess Parrish is mine."

He swiped his forehead with his sleeve and turned down the road into the hospital.

We found a parking space in short order and climbed out into the sticky air. Again I tried phoning Claire to let her know I was on my way, but her mobile was still off. I quickened my pace, leaving Hammond struggling to keep up.

I hurried up the stairway and along the corridor, turning the corner that led to Nora's room. Fortunately I encountered the ward supervisor, who recognized me.

"Nora Whitney," I reminded her, just to be on the safe side. "Is everything all right?"

"She woke about twenty minutes ago," she informed me.

I felt my spirits lift. "That's great news!"

"She's still a little disoriented, but we are encouraged."

"Can I see her?"

"I'm afraid we can't let anyone in without family permission."

I was probably coming across as a little breathless and overheated. "If you could let her daughter know I'm here I'd be very grateful."

"She's not available at present."

"What do you mean?"

"She left about half an hour ago."

This bothered me. Claire wouldn't have left her mother alone before she had woken.

"Did she say where she was going?"

"Wait here," the supervisor said. "I'll go check."

She disappeared into one of the monitoring stations.

The door to Nora's room opened, and Nora herself came shuffling out.

Draped in a white hospital gown, she looked a little bewildered, her hair awry, as if she had only just got her bearings and had decided to go exploring.

I called her name. On seeing me, her eyes widened and shock suffused her face. She grabbed the door jamb before feverishly retreating back into the room.

The supervisor had reappeared with another nurse and both of them spotted her.

"Just wait a minute," the supervisor told me, and she hurried inside with the nurse, closing the door.

I began to wonder if Nora had woken in one of her confused states and whether my sudden appearance had terrified her. I must have looked pretty agitated which probably wouldn't have helped.

There was heavy breathing behind me. Hammond was leaning against the wall, looking completely done in.

"Well," I said, a little shaken, "she's awake."

"Can't say I've ever cared for hospitals," he informed me. "In my experience, you live longer if you stay out of them."

I led him a little way back along the corridor and sat him down on a chair. He used his handkerchief like a hand towel to mop his entire face before popping a white tablet from a blister strip and asking me for some water.

I found a dispenser and filled a cup. Hammond had already put the tablet into his mouth. He rinsed it down with the water.

"Are you all right?" I asked.

"I'll survive."

"Regular medication?"

He just nodded but didn't elaborate.

"I'm going to wait downstairs," he told me, heaving himself up. "The air con's more efficient there."

I got the impression he wanted a little time to recover himself so I didn't offer to accompany him. Besides, I needed to find out what had happened to Claire.

Ten minutes passed before the supervisor finally emerged from Nora's room.

"We've got her settled," she told me. "But she's a little confused."

"Can I see her? Speak to her for a few minutes?"

"She doesn't know where her daughter is. At first she thought she was still in England."

"Would you mind if I asked? You can supervise."

"It's out of the question. You'll have to wait until her daughter returns."

I did my best to persuade her but she wouldn't budge.

I headed downstairs, yet again trying Claire's number. Still the phone wasn't on. I thought about calling Walter Suthersen but decided against it. He had to prioritize Barbara's well-being at the moment.

Hammond was sitting under the air con unit in the lobby, looking a little less florid.

"They wouldn't let me talk to her," I said. "We have to wait until Claire gets back."

He hardly appeared to hear me. He was holding his phone, a strange expression on his face.

"I've just received this," he said, holding it up so that I could see the screen.

Claire's face appeared on what was obviously a video clip from a cell phone. She was distraught.

"I can't talk for long," she said hastily. "This is a message for Cyrus Hammond to transmit to anyone who knows me. I'm being held to ransom. My captor is Ryan Carmichael." She paused, as though trying to remember the exact wording of a message. "He demands that you contact Mr Nicholas Randall and instruct him to make available the Leo Parrish manuscripts that he has in his possession. Further instructions will follow in exactly one hour."

She stepped abruptly to one side, forcing Carmichael, who must have been holding the phone, to track her. There was a brief swirl of background landscape and he yelled, "Stand still, you bitch!" Then his fingers closed over the screen, smearing it before it went blank.

The smears were blood-red.

TWENTY-NINE

"Are you sure about this?" Hammond asked.

I studied the swirling images of Claire on his phone screen one more time, giving the background particular scrutiny. There was a flash of the truncated monorail, a glimpse of a rocket-shaped booth.

"I'm sure," I told him. "It's Far Frontiers. He's taken her there."

We were already at his car. Hammond took his phone from me and punched out a number as he walked over to the ticket machine. I heard him say, "Miami-Dade Police" before everything flashed like a faulty fluorescent strip. It was lightning. I couldn't see any signs of rain.

Hammond came back from the machine. "They're sending a couple of patrol cars to the location. I'm heading out there as well."

"I'm coming too," I said automatically.

He didn't try to dissuade me. We got into the car and he started the engine. He still didn't look too great, but he was determined to drive. I was hoping he knew the local roads well enough to get us there as quickly as possible.

I couldn't stop myself from thinking about the video footage on his phone. I hadn't been able to make out any obvious wounds on Claire, but the video clip was low-resolution, shot in jerky haste.

"If there's blood," I said as we drove out of the hospital grounds, "he must have a weapon of some sort. Does he own a gun?"

Hammond was already reversing out. "It's not something I've ever discussed with him. Knowing Ryan, he might have a laser cannon."

This was not reassuring. "What about Parrish's manuscript?"

"Where is it?"

"In my hotel room."

"No time," he said firmly.

Hammond took us out of the hospital as quickly as any emergency ambulance. Soon we were on the expressway and then the interstate, heading north. He tried to call Alvarez, but after a few moments he cut the call with frustration.

"Number unobtainable," he said. "He's probably already on a plane back to Washington with Byrnes."

Then, muttering to himself as if making a mental note, "I'll have to ring Harry Lindemann."

He glanced at me, twiddling through his addresses and then making the call.

"Guy at NASA," he explained. "I need to tell him about Valentine." He held the phone to his ear for long seconds. "Crap, he's not answering." He flung the phone into the car's drinks holder.

I used my own phone to call Rhodri, praying that he was still at our hotel. When he answered, his voice was furry with sleep: he was only just surfacing from the night before. I explained the situation with as much calmness as I could muster, omitting any mention of blood.

"I need the Parrish manuscript," I told him. "It's still behind the headboard. Get a taxi. We'll be at Far Frontiers. Make sure you've got your mobile with you and call me when you're close. I don't want to put you at any risk."

"Will do," he said earnestly. "How on earth is Carmichael connected with this business?"

"I'll explain it later," I said, and cut the call.

Hammond didn't make any comment on my involvement of Rhodri, though I suspect he felt that it would make no difference to the outcome. Which was something I couldn't allow myself to contemplate; or to consider the many ways in which Claire might have been hurt.

At least the police were on their way. Carmichael was unlikely to do anything extreme before his deadline was up. And as Carmichael's uncle, Hammond was in a good position to negotiate with him. Failing that, I knew he was carrying his handgun: I could see the edge of his shoulder holster under his jacket.

He caught me looking at him and smiled grimly. Then he snatched at his phone again and tried the man at NASA once more, with no more luck.

Under brooding skies backlit by lightning flashes we worked our way north through a sprawling landscape of low-rise housing and business parks intersected by roads and waterways. The Charade's air con was finally up to speed, and Hammond looked less bleary and sweat-soaked than earlier, more focused and intent. His presence reassured me, the silence between us attaining an air of resolute determination. I didn't want to say anything to break the spell.

Soon we were close to the coast, passing ranks of white houseboats anchored in squared-off inlets and marinas. The gunmetal water was dead calm, everything spick-and-span, human order imposed on nature's unruly contours. Overhead, though, the sky was like one vast bruise fluoresced by sheet lightning that was now directly overhead.

Hammond swung the car inland, and I knew that we were close.

The smart suburban housing became sparser, interspersed with patches of untended land. And then we were turning down the approach road to Far Frontiers.

Close to the entrance, a scarlet Ferrari had been driven into the scrub just off the road. It was Carmichael's car, Hammond confirmed, though there was no one inside it. Carmichael had phoned about half an hour ago, which meant that we still had time.

Hammond parked under a stand of laurel oaks close by. There were no police cars outside the gates, no sign of any activity whatsoever. I tried calling Rhodri but couldn't get an answer on his number.

Halogen-bright lightning burst overhead, followed by a barrage of thunder, and then it started teeming down.

It was exactly like a Hollywood thunderstorm with full special effects. Rain cascaded off the overhanging trees, pummelled the car roof and ran in waves down the windshield. It fell so hard that when the lightning flashed it turned everything into a grey blur as if the very colours of the world were water-soluble and had been leached away.

Hammond pulled something out of the glove compartment. It was a woman's pocket umbrella in a pink flower-pattern sleeve. He levered open his door and clambered out.

"Wait here," he said to me. "I'm going to take a look."

He slammed the door before I could reply and waded across the road, unfolding the pink umbrella over his head.

I was contemplating going after him when my mobile started making Tarzan noises.

It was Claire's number.

"Are you all right?" I asked urgently.

"Is that Mr Randall?"

An elderly woman's voice, which for a moment I didn't recognize.

"Yes," I said.

"Where's my daughter?" she demanded to know.

It was Nora Parrish. I did a swift mental recalculation.

"Are you still in the hospital?"

"Of course I am. Where is she?"

Claire must have left her mobile in the room. Presumably Nora had found it and was now sufficiently recovered to want to know what was going on.

"We're looking for her," I said, anxious not to alarm her but unsure what to say. "Do you have an idea when she left you?"

"Something's wrong, isn't it? Are you with that man?"

"What man?"

"The man in the corridor."

"Cyrus Hammond?"

"I don't know his name. Is he a friend of yours?"

This was a slightly bizarre turn for the conversation to be taking.

"Not exactly," I said. "He—"

"I recognized him. Even after all these years, I'll never forget his face."

"What?"

"He's the man who killed Leo."

The thunder and lightning kept up their show overhead, but it didn't stop me thinking. Hammond must have been standing behind me in the corridor when I called out to Nora. It was him she had reacted to.

"Well?" I heard her say

I was still trying to process it all. I had no idea what to say.

"Is he with you?" she was asking.

I swallowed. "Not at the moment."

"What's that noise?"

"A storm. It's probably heading your way."

"Did you know? Are you working with him?"

"Are you sure he was the man?"

"Even after forty years," she insisted. "Tell me the truth. Did you know about it?"

"I swear to you I didn't. My only concern is Claire's welfare."

There was a silence at the other end of the line. My skin was crawling with apprehension. Abruptly the noise of the rain on the Charade's roof diminished. The rain was petering out almost as quickly as it had started.

"Has he got a gun?" Nora was asking.

"No," I lied. There was no point in distressing her further. "I got the impression he genuinely wants to help."

"What's happened to her?"

I hesitated before deciding that it would be futile to try to fob her off. She might be elderly and very fragile, but she was Claire's mother: she had a right to know.

"She appears to have been kidnapped," I said. "By a man who's demanding we hand over the final part of *Exaltation*."

There was an even longer silence which extended so much I said, "Are you still there?"

"Give it him. Give him whatever he wants."

She was resolute, in full command of her senses. I decided against mentioning that Claire's abductor was Hammond's nephew. She had more than enough to worry about.

"I think I know where she's being held," I told her. "The police are on their way, and I'll do whatever I can to ensure her safety. I just hope it's as simple as handing over the manuscript."

"Those stories have been nothing but trouble. I should have burnt the whole lot when I had the chance."

"I doubt that would have solved anything. I know this is shocking news, especially since you're still recovering—"

"I'm tougher than I look. Where is that man now?"

"Hammond?" I decided to keep it vague. "He's reconnoitring."

"He's extremely dangerous. Be very careful."

"I promise," I assured her, though I had no idea how I could possibly outwit him. "I really need to go."

"He mustn't know you're on to him," she insisted. "Tell the police. Let them handle it."

"I will."

"Don't let anything happen to my daughter, do you hear me?"

And it was she who rang off.

The moment I pressed the end call button the driver's door opened and Hammond said, "Who was that?"

Somehow he had completely outflanked me. I had lost him in the rain and hadn't seen him approach from the rear. He had asked the question amiably enough, with a smile on his face. This only made it more sinister.

"Claire's mother," I told him. "She wanted to know where Claire was."

He shook off the umbrella, got into the driver's seat and mopped his face with his handkerchief. His hair was wet, his suit stained dark at the shoulders and thighs. Despite Nora's advice, I debated telling him that she had recognized him, wanting to get it all out in the open and end the suspense. But it wouldn't have been a clever move. We were completely alone and there was nothing to stop him from taking out his pistol and shooting me. I was also clinging to the vague possibility that Nora had been mistaken in her identification of him.

"What did you tell her?" he asked, reaching behind and pulling a bulky leather briefcase from the back seat.

"I tried not to say too much. I didn't want to alarm her." I was eager to change the subject. "Shouldn't the police be here by now?"

"Maybe they've come and gone. From the outside there's no sign of anyone being in there."

"Wouldn't they have spotted the Ferrari?"

Hammond eyed me. "Not if they'd just driven by. It's easy to miss if you aren't looking for it."

I didn't believe this for a moment, but it would have been foolish to challenge it.

"Heard back from Rhodri Davies?" he asked.

I shook my head.

"I don't think he's going to get here in time," he said, extracting a clear plastic document wallet from the briefcase and thrusting it at me. It had a typescript inside.

"What's this?" I asked.

"A film script. But for Ryan's benefit we're going to pretend that it's Parrish's manuscript for as long as it takes to get close and disarm him."

I stared at him. "Will it work?"

"You have any better ideas?"

I was scared, and Hammond's proximity only made it worse. I wrenched open my door and climbed out.

The skies were clearing, and already the sun had broken through, jewelling the raindrops falling from the trees. I was shaking. I began walking quickly towards the entrance.

I heard Hammond pip the lock on the car and follow, calling to me to slow down. My skin was crawling and I had no idea what to do. Except that I had to try to rescue Claire.

Hammond caught up with me at the entrance. "Take it easy," he told me. "If we rush in there, we're likely to make a mess of things."

"I just need to find out if she's all right."

The place was utterly deserted apart from the two of us. Not even a hint of approaching police car sirens. It would have been easy for him to pretend that he was making the call. If the police weren't coming then I had no choice.

"I don't think we can wait," I said. "We need to go in and try to save her."

"I agree," he replied, looking at me curiously.

"Now," I said. "We have to do it now."

He bit back what he was going to say and instead led me along to the side of the main gate. There, a lower section of galvanized fencing had been detached by a previous intruder and shoved back into place in a fashion that was easy to miss unless you had a keen eye.

Hammond squeezed himself through and wedged the panel open with a broken tree branch. If I made a run for it now he would almost certainly shoot me down, and in any case I would be abandoning Claire. Of course going in might mean that he could shoot me and then rendezvous with his nephew.

I squatted like a soldier under fire and crawled in.

Puddles of water lay in hollows on the access road, already steaming in the sun. The theme park had a spruce rain-washed appearance but the intensity of the downpour had splattered the bases of the structures with sandy mud so that they looked like things that had suddenly thrust themselves out of the damp earth like monstrous fungi. Everything seemed crystal sharp, the rides and booths garishly bright, their intricate contours stark against the sky. I think my senses must have been heightened by sheer terror.

Hammond took the lead as we began checking out the attractions for signs of life. We did our best to stay in the shadows, skirting the road that snaked in towards the lumpy bulk of the *Moon Stalker* ride, where we both agreed that Carmichael was most likely to be hiding out. I put my mobile on mute but tucked it close to my chest.

Hammond hadn't taken out his pistol, for which I was grateful while at the same time wondering if he actually intended to do anything to detain his fugitive nephew. True he had improvised a fake manuscript, but what if it was all yet another piece of duplicity to lure me in and allow him to corner and possibly kill both me and Claire before he and Carmichael made a getaway? In which case I ought to try to lose him and find Claire on my own. But Hammond was on high alert and very watchful, constantly checking to see where I was.

The *Moon Stalker* ride looked as if it had been finished before the foreclosure of the park, its chrome-egg cars sitting on rails under a Jupiter-striped awning. The rails ran towards a cratered entrance tunnel that bore the legend: *The Caves of Callisto*.

Hammond and I crept into the space platform ticket booth to prepare ourselves for going in. He was panting and dripping with sweat again. He tried to call Carmichael on his cell phone, but his nephew wasn't answering. Only now did he pull out his gun.

"Service pistol?" I asked to hide the dread I suddenly felt.

He just looked at me, and there was a new expression on his face: suspicion. Before I knew it, I was saying, "You didn't phone the police, did you?"

His face hardened. "What makes you say that?"

I was amazed and horrified at my own boldness, but I couldn't carry on with Nora's revelation unspoken between us.

"She recognized you," I said softly.

Inwardly I was telling myself that I couldn't have picked a worse time to confront him with this fact, but logic goes flying out the window when stalked by mortal fear. If anything, Hammond appeared to relax.

"Ah," he said in a knowing way. "I guessed as much."

I waited, feeling perfectly powerless, wondering what was going to happen next.

"No, I didn't actually call them," he admitted. "The police might have complicated matters. I'm rather hoping I can sort this out myself with a minimum of drama."

"So it's true?" I blurted. "You killed Leo Parrish?"

He gave a drawn-out sigh. "My younger self did."

He was now giving his handgun plenty of scrutiny. As if considering to what immediate use he might put it.

"What does that mean?" I demanded, knowing I had nothing to lose now.

"I was nineteen at the time. Nineteen and out of my mind."

He could have thrown me out of the car on the way here if he wanted to be rid of me. Or marched me into the scrub and put the gun to my head. Shooting me now, when we were so close to his nephew, would be foolish. Or so I frantically rationalized.

"You got away with it," I said.

"Is that a statement or a question?"

"I'd like to know."

"Yes," he said finally. "I was never found out."

"Why?" My voice was half-way between hysteria and rage. "Why did you do it?"

"You really want to discuss this now?"

"I have to know whether Claire is going to be safe in your hands if we find her. Not to mention my own safety, too."

Without taking his eyes off me, he reached into his jacket pocket and produced a carton. Inside it was the blister pack of tablets I had seen earlier. It was labelled ZYPREXA.

"What are they?"

"Maintenance," he replied.

"For what?"

"Schizophrenia. I've been on medication most of my adult life."

I turned the carton. There was prescription label on the back, made out in his name. Two ten milligram tablets, three times a day.

I handed them back. "Did you know him?"

He shook his head, sighed again.

"Then why?" I persisted.

Suddenly all his previous resolution had given way to what looked like deep-rooted weariness.

"When I was a young man," he told me, "I didn't know I was suffering from it. I'd been recruited to the Strategic Foresight Unit. It had been set up to—"

"I know why it was set up," I interrupted, my curiosity greater than any sense of self-preservation in that moment. "Why did you kill him?"

He looked dolefully at me. "I came across Leo Parrish's stories as part of my work. They impressed me. They impressed me more and more. There was one about a woman called Minna, who was the opposite of a mind-reader—a mind-*seeder*, Parrish called her, who could project her thoughts into other people's heads. It screwed up all her relationships until she was saved by a young man who trained her to focus her talent and use it to help cure patients suffering from psychiatric disorders by blotting out their skewed thoughts with saner, more positive ones."

Hammond shook his head at his own foolishness. While he talked he was also checking out the tunnel entrance, perhaps looking for any sign of movement and possible danger. There was none.

"Then the illness must have really kicked in," he went on. "I got obsessed with the idea that the young woman who lived above me in my apartment block was Minna. And that she was going to save me. By now I'd become convinced that Parrish wrote visions of the future, that all his stories were going to come true sooner or later."

He must have seen my expression because he said, "I know. I'm not the first or last person to think that."

"You still believe it?"

"I'm telling you what I thought at the time. When I was clinically insane. One day I got home and found that the girl I called Minna wasn't there anymore. She'd probably moved out, but I began to believe that I'd read a second story in which she'd killed herself by jumping under a subway train. To this day I've never been able to find that story, so I probably just hallucinated it. But the upshot was that I became convinced that Parrish was a murderer, an evil genius who deliberately wrote stories designed to inflict torment on the persons he brought into being."

"You believed he actually created them?"

"You think my nephew's wacko? I was hurricane force twelve by then."

He spoke calmly, almost as if he was talking about someone else.

"So you decided you had to kill him?"

"It was very premeditated," he replied matter-of-factly. "When you're in that obsessive state of mind, you're meticulous to the extreme in your planning. His address was in the SFU files, so I stalked him, established his routines, bided my time. I thought I was doing the whole world a service, ridding it of an evil power."

He fell silent, though all the ghosts were still behind his eyes.

"And after?" I said.

"I carried on working at my day job. Until my illness got so bad my colleagues began to notice. In the end I was hospitalized for six months. Eventually I met a girl. She wasn't Minna but she turned out to be my salvation. We got married. I was reinstated, though not with the SFU. By then they'd finally gotten me on a suitable drug regime. It took a couple of years. And it was only then I fully appreciated the enormity of what I'd done."

"You never told anyone?"

He shook his head. "Not even my wife. Many times I was tempted to go visit his sister and confess. Beg her forgiveness. But what good would it have done? I was another person. Not responsible for my own actions." He looked directly at me. "Maybe it was cowardly. Maybe I should have just turned myself over to the police. But I couldn't. I was finally happy. And that kind of illness doesn't just disappear overnight. A small part of me still believed that I had done the right thing."

Was a madman always mad in some respect? Was Hammond now preparing to enact what was just a different form of lunacy? I had to believe otherwise if there was to be any hope for Claire.

"It was me who originally set up the Unit's censorship program on Parrish," he told me. "I believed the world would be a better place if all his stories were taken out of circulation."

"So Bennett Irwin hijacked it later?"

"I guess so. For his own purposes."

"Is that why you've been trying to get someone to make a movie out of Parrish's work?"

"Of course it is," he said bluntly. "I needed to do something good for the family. I knew Nora didn't have that much money and I wanted to see them on a secure financial footing. It wasn't just guilt or charity. I genuinely believe Leo Parrish was an original."

I thought about all this. Very carefully I said, "Did you follow Nora and Claire to London?"

He shook his head ardently. "I kept my distance for many years. I was in New York, though I knew she'd emigrated. Then my wife died and I relocated to England to get Filmscope up and running. That was when I picked up contact with the family through Claire. I was always careful to stay out of Nora's way."

"In case she recognized you?"

"I don't think you're likely to forget the face of someone who shot your brother at point blank range right in front of you, are you?"

I thought back to my very first encounter with Hammond. "You took a risk at the film festival then, didn't you? Appearing on a panel in full view of everyone with Nora there?"

"I didn't know Claire was bringing her. That's why I skedaddled."

And hence the conspicuous dark glasses he had worn while on the panel, I supposed, in case Nora had decided to attend it.

"Want to know how my wife died?" Hammond asked.

For a horrible moment, I thought I knew: she had thrown herself under a subway train.

He saw my unsettled look and shook his head. "She was mugged on the street one day. Knocked over, her purse stolen. She was bruised and shaken but we thought she was all right. What we didn't know was that she had a bleed to the brain. When I got up the next morning, she was cold in bed."

I was watching him all the while, but even the thought that he might be spinning me a lie was disrespectful, even scandalous.

"That must have been horrible," was all I could say.

"Divine judgement," he replied in a flat tone. "A life for a life."

Now he was watching me, wanting to gauge my reaction.

"I know it doesn't really work that way," he said finally. "It's just blind bad happenstance. But that's how I chose to interpret it. It was my punishment. So I decided to atone by trying to resurrect Leo Parrish. Over the years I've done what I could to use my contacts and call in favours. But nobody was interested, even with the vogue for science fiction movies. Brief outlines don't do Parrish justice, and film companies generally can't be bothered to read even a short story. Especially when it's by a writer they've never heard of. You're the first person to recognize Parrish's vision and his cinematic potential."

"And look where it's got me," I said pointedly. "Searching for the niece of the man you killed who's being held by your nephew. Can you see why I might be just a little uneasy about that?"

"I swear to you I mean her no harm," he said. "Or you, for that matter. You can go if you want to. Leave it to me."

Would he shoot me if I tried to walk out of there? It wasn't an option. Apart from anything else, he didn't actually look in peak physical condition and could probably use my help. The corners of his mouth were still caked with what I had taken to be tomato juice. But it had blackened: it was blood. I could see it in his nostrils, too. Something wasn't right with him. But I had to stay focused on Claire.

"I need to find her," I told him. "She could be badly injured."

"Then we have to go in."

The ride had no power supply, and there was nothing for it but to enter on foot. We skirted the chrome cars and I saw a used condom under the seat of the leading one. The car might never have moved but it had certainly been ridden.

I expected it to be dark inside the tunnel, but the craters set into the dome were actually windows that admitted enough light for us to wind our way sure-footedly between the narrow gauge rail tracks.

We passed through cave-like hollows full of ornate stalagmites and stalactites in lurid earth colours. There were overhanging ledges sporting pulleys and zip wires for what presumably would have been mutant figures ready to fly out and threaten the joy riders. The place was still dripping after the rain, adding to the cavernous atmosphere; but it was also deserted.

We moved through another narrow tunnel into *The Gorges of Ganymede*, a more vertiginous terrain of raised rock bridges and precipitous descents. Though we kept to the relatively level rail track, Hammond was panting again by the time we had threaded our way through it, still without any signs of life. *The Ice Wastes of Europa* proved equally deserted, a grey-white landscape of jagged angular blocks and big stylized snowflake crystals hanging like overgrown Christmas tree decorations. We proceeded carefully, looking into the many nooks and crannies designed to hide mutant assailants, me checking every raindrop that fell from above to ensure it wasn't blood. The sense of emptiness persisted, as though we truly were exploring uncharted territory.

Finally we entered *The Inferno of Io*, a pizza-coloured place where fibre-glass volcanoes and geysers were represented in abundance, where it looked as if the designers had gone mad in lolloping shades of mustard and ketchup wherever the fancy took them. The contours were plastic and amorphous, with bubbling mozzarella inclines and blotchy tomato-coloured sinkholes so dark at their centres you felt that if you slipped down them you would vanish forever. It was at this point that I heard a muffled yell. Claire.

The noise had come from a drooping ledge close to the exit. The ledge was in deep shadow but I could just make out two figures there.

Hammond and I moved towards the access incline as one, without exchanging a word. He had his handgun at the ready, whereas I was holding nothing except the folder. Neither Claire nor Carmichael had seen us, and as we crept upwards we were protected from sight by the ripples and folds of the terrain.

We halted less than twenty yards away, crouching behind an orange fibre-glass boulder. Claire had been gagged with what looked like surgical tape and Carmichael had kitted himself out in the movie's black-and-silver jumpsuit. He had Claire's hands bound in the bulky matt-black cuffs his character had used, linked by a chain to his black-gloved hand. I assumed he had ransacked the souvenir shop for the props, but he looked nothing like his on-screen character because his face was wild and the lower half of it bearded with blood.

Claire, in a white T-shirt and denim shorts, was blood-covered too, though this didn't stop her from vigorously kicking out at him every time the opportunity presented itself. I couldn't see any cuts on her face or limbs and she looked full of fire. Carmichael was dodging the blows while brandishing a very terrestrial-looking pistol and yelling that he would shoot her if she persisted.

I made to surge forward, but Hammond pushed me back, snatched the folder and stood up in my stead.

"Ryan!" he called, without threat or anger. "Ryan! It's Uncle Cyrus."

Hammond stepped forward. He wasn't holding his gun. Carmichael stopped moving, looking at him with a bemused expression. There was blood all down his black-zippered front and I couldn't imagine how Claire could still be so active in resisting him if it was hers.

Hammond brandished the folder.

"I've got it, Ryan," he called. "What you asked for. It's here. It's yours."

Carmichael jerked the chain, forcing Claire to her hands and knees. He stepped behind her and tightened it, pushing his foot into the middle of her back as she straightened, holding her there in front of him like some human guard dog. A surge of fury went through me and I started forward until Hammond yelled at me, "Stay back! Leave this to me!"

"Claire!" I yelled. "Are you hurt?"

All she could do was give a muffled grunt before Carmichael screamed "Shut up!" at me. His blue eyes were glassy and unfocused, his hair also matted with blood. He was shifting restlessly to keep Claire in place.

"Ryan," Hammond said, taking another step forward. "There's no need for this. Let her go. I've got what you wanted."

Again he flourished the folder. But Carmichael was now pointing his gun at us, oscillating between me and his uncle.

He looked like some kind of frantic vampire that had just finished feeding. But the blood was his own, seeping from his nostrils, mouth and ears.

"I'm alive," he said in a joyous tone to Hammond. "Brimming with the life beyond life."

"Let me help," Hammond said, moving forward. "You know I can help, Ryan—"

There was a bang. Hammond halted and then keeled over, the folder skittering across the ochre floor and falling over the edge. Carmichael pushed Claire to the ground and hastily began fiddling with something above his head.

I ran forward as Claire scrambled away from him. She sprang upright and came racing towards me, practically hurling herself into my arms while Carmichael launched himself downwards on a zip wire, whooping like a kid playing Tarzan as he went.

Carefully I peeled the surgical tape from Claire's mouth and got the plastic cuffs off her. They were toy things, easily broken, but underneath her wrists were tightly bound with more layers of tape. She was trembling with fear and anger as I laboriously freed her. I still couldn't see where her wounds were.

"Are you all right?" I asked. "What did he do to you?"

"I'm OK," she told me with a determined look. "The blood's his. He's leaking everywhere. We've got to help Cyrus."

Hammond lay on his side, blinking slowly but otherwise not moving. He was oozing blood from his mouth and there was a dark hole centred on his collar bone.

"Tell Nora I'm sorry," he whispered to me. "I did my best."

His body deflated and his head drooped.

Claire took his wrist and checked for a pulse before shaking her head at me.

Another shot went off, the bullet thunking into the fibre-glass rock face above our heads. Carmichael had detached himself from the zip wire and snatched up the fallen folder. Giving another whoop, he scurried down one of the sinkholes and disappeared from sight.

Claire and I just stared open-mouthed at one another. She told me that Carmichael had phoned her from the hospital grounds and persuaded her to go downstairs to meet him. He had then forced her into his car at gunpoint and expertly taped her wrists and mouth before driving away. As with Barbara Suthersen's abduction, Carmichael had babbled about Leo Parrish without being very lucid about what he actually wanted. And without actually injuring her in any way.

"Let's call the police and get out of here," I said.

She shook her head. "Call the police, yes of course. But we need to help him."

"Carmichael? You're kidding, yes?"

"He's a danger to himself."

"He's an even bigger danger to us."

"He's sick. He wouldn't have shot his own uncle if he was in his right mind. We can't just leave him."

I could tell she was determined. She had already suffered under Carmichael's hands, and yet she was prepared to show him this charity.

"All right," I said. "You stay here and contact the police. I'll go and see where he might have got to."

I hoped she couldn't tell that I doubted the sanity of pursuing Carmichael. I gave her my phone and she quickly tapped in 911.

"Don't forget to let your mother know you're OK," I reminded her.

There wasn't any ammunition in Hammond's gun: he had only been carrying it for show. I took it anyway and headed down the incline. My footsteps were muffled on the fake terrain and I could clearly hear my phone's dial tone, diminishing rapidly.

I approached the sinkhole down which Carmichael had vanished. Unlike the others, its centre hadn't been painted dark for effect but was actually an access chute with a ladder down its side.

Claire's voice was now carrying across the fibre glass landscape, talking urgently to the police. I fixed her image in my mind and scrambled down the ladder.

The chute provided both maintenance access and an emergency exit. Light was leaking along a corridor from an open door which led outside. A partial red footprint told me that Carmichael had come this way.

Hammond's gun was like a stage-prop in my hand, a bluff even if it had been loaded. I crept to the end of the corridor and cautiously peered out. The door exited on the rear of the egg-car awning with the road just beyond. The door bar was smeared with red but there were no signs of blood outside. No sooner had I registered this when a voice behind said, "Move a micrometre and I'll shoot you through both your hearts".

It was a line from the *Moon Stalker* movie. Ryan Carmichael came out the corridor shadows, the folder stuffed into his zip top, his pistol at the ready. He grabbed me, pulling the gun out of my hand, his blood-drenched face so close to mine I could feel the heat of his raw-meat breath.

He pushed me outside, grinning like his fictional counterpart, though he was a horror-movie parody of his screen self, blood even leaking from his eye sockets so that he had to keep blinking it away. He looked like he had the haemorrhagic fever, must have caught it in the UK. Had he had contact with someone from

Halstow Island? That could well explain his extent of his delusionary behaviour, bizarre even for him. But did this mean that the disease had already escaped into the general population?

Carmichael tossed his uncle's gun to the ground a body's length away from me.

"Are you fast enough?" he taunted. "Can you get to it before I blow your twisted brains out?"

Again he was quoting lines from *Moon Stalker*, themselves a blatant steal from *Dirty Harry* the first time around and now with the air of amateur but macabre theatrics. He wanted me to dive for the gun so that he could shoot me in the head.

"I'm the only law enforcement this side of the asteroid belt," he told me with such a pantomime intensity that I actually wanted to laugh, possibly out of mortal fright.

A cock started crowing. Carmichael, at first startled, managed to keep his focus on me until it fell silent.

"Last chance," he said, indicating the gun again. "I don't think you have the guts for it."

Now there was a burst of operatic "Ave Maria". Carmichael looked around. The singing was coming from ground level just outside the escape doorway. There was no one in sight.

Carmichael was torn by this distraction and his desire to finish me off.

There was a crashing noise. This time it was from the direction of the park's main entrance.

"The police are here," I said. "It's all over."

"Go for you gun!" Carmichael shrieked at me.

Popping-corn noises came from behind him. I spotted my mobile, lying on the ground where Claire must have tossed it. In that same instant I launched myself forward.

I managed to knock him backwards but he stayed on his feet. Then Claire darted out of the tunnel and whacked him across the shoulders with a metal pole. The gun spilled from his hand.

Carmichael staggered away and decided to make a run for it. He reached the road as the vehicle came around its curve at labouring speed. It wasn't a patrol car but a vintage black-and-white Volkswagen camper van with the spare wheel dangling from its nose and THE ASTRAL LEAGUE hand-painted in red along its flank.

There is a scene in *Moon Stalker* where Carmichael's character saves a child from danger by realizing that the bullet train racing towards both of them is just an illusion projected by one of his enemies. He stands his ground and the ghost train passes harmlessly through them. I think Carmichael must have been convinced that he was reliving a variation on the scene as he stepped without hesitation into the middle of the road. I sometimes wonder whether in the final instant he had the time to register surprise as the camper van flattened him like a skittle. The sound of his skull hitting the tarmac is one I hope I never hear again.

The van expired to a halt just a little way along the road, the now detached spare wobbling away before collapsing in a ditch. Rhodri and a few of his friends were looking out, horrified. They must have rammed the gates in order to get inside. I started yelling to them to stay inside the van and keep the windows closed. If Carmichael was infectious, it was important they weren't exposed to him, alive or dead.

Carmichael's mashed body lay face up in the van's wake. We knew he was dead before Claire and I got to him, though there was a smile on his mangled face as if in some weird way he felt he had been vindicated.

THIRTY

We spent a chaotic and restless night in the Jackson Memorial's isolation unit, Claire and I being put into in separate rooms as hospital protocol demanded. Barbara Suthersen was also somewhere in the unit, though I never saw her.

Our phones had been quarantined but Walter Suthersen sent in a couple of new ones for me and Claire so that we were at least able to talk to one another. It had been a neat idea of hers to put my phone on ring-tone play to confuse Carmichael, but had this only deferred the inevitable? There was a distinct possibility that we might both have contracted the haemorrhagic fever from Ryan Carmichael.

At length two medical staff in blue biohazard suits turned up. They wore thick rubber gloves and capacious headgear with domed tops like floppy cardinals' hats. Behind the clear plastic face panels they were masked for extra protection, moving with crinkly plastic bag noises as they extracted blood, saliva and snot samples. There was little in the way of small talk and I was glad when they finally rustled out of there and left me in peace.

I spent the rest of the morning watching TV. This entailed sitting through regular news updates about the Khanistani crisis (Muvart was claiming to have signed a missile deal with the Israelis), the Endeavour mission (there were uncorroborated rumours that one of the crew was sick) and the latest theories about Nova Draco (it was about to go supernova and sterilize the planet). Not exactly cheery fare. Better news was that Rhodri and his friends had only been kept in quarantine for a few hours before being released because they hadn't got out of the van.

Neither the potential outbreak nor Carmichael's final mad escapade had yet been picked up by the media, though Fox News showed Vincent Kubilius grinning like his life depended on it while making a pre-emptive donation to a disabled children's charity outside Florida's version of Hogwarts. The attempted assassination of Walter Suthersen was already yesterday's news.

In the afternoon one of the bio-suited pair returned and informed me that an FBI agent called Alice Underwood wanted to take a statement from me. He handed me a laptop and said that it had a wi-fi connection to the hospital broadband. All I had to do was click on the Skype button on the desktop.

Alice Underwood was a studious-looking black woman of middle years who had even less facility with the webcam zoom than me. Her face kept drifting off the screen. When we eventually managed to sustain visual contact, she informed me that it was standard procedure to record the interview and if I had any objections I needed to say so now. I just shook my head. She then asked me to give "a full account" of everything I thought was pertinent leading up to my ultimate confrontation with Ryan Carmichael.

This was a tall order, but I had plenty of time. I gave her an edited version of my interest in Leo Parrish, my acquaintance with both Noah Byrnes and Cyrus Hammond before moving swiftly on to our pursuit and final showdown in the ersatz worlds of the theme park.

As I unfolded my tale her face became a slideshow of incredulous tics that seemed to say: "Are you making this crap up?" She showed especial interest in Hammond's speculations on the Rapturists' agenda and Bennett Irwin's possible orchestrating of events.

When we were finally finished, she checked her notebook. "The ward supervisor asked me to tell you that a relative of Ms Whitney's has been calling, wanting to speak to both of you." She squinted at her own scrawl. "Leonora Parrish?"

It took me a moment to realize who she meant.

After Claire had been interviewed we spoke via our laptops. She tried ringing Nora on the phone she had left at her mother's bedside, but it wasn't switched on. Walter Suthersen's phone was only taking messages.

Claire still looked comparatively well, though the merest hint of a nosebleed could suddenly change everything. But she was as calm and resolute as the situation allowed. For once, everything was entirely out of our hands.

That afternoon I managed to spend half an hour talking to Ashad in London, where the screening of the documentary had generated plenty of publicity and provoked the Home Secretary into issuing a public denial that there was a state-sponsored programme of biological warfare while at the same time promising a full investigation into any misuse of government facilities. It was a typical piece of political having-your-cake-but-pretending-you-hadn't-eaten-it, Ashad told me, and he went off on a lusty tirade about self-serving politicians and their pathological inability ever to admit to doing anything wrong.

"Things are starting to look up," he told me. "Assuming we still have a place to work."

"What do you mean?"

"Nigel's been arrested."

This wasn't exactly a surprise. "When?"

"Yesterday. They've got him on suspicion of human trafficking."

"How did you find out?"

"Merrick phoned it in."

"You spoke to her?"

"Jamilla took the message. I told you, we have nothing to say to one another."

"She might have some further intelligence about Byrnes or Halstow Island that we could use. Is there anything more on the outbreak?"

"It's all gone very quiet. Either they've contained it or slapped a DA-notice on it. I'm making enquiries."

Ashad then suggested that I write some notes about my experiences with a view to perhaps doing a dramatic reconstruction of events in the near future.

"You're kidding me," I said. "Has it occurred to you that I might not necessarily have much time left?"

He wasn't going to countenance this. "You'll pull through. We can't run this place without you."

This was the closest he was going to get to showing any sentiment. I said would consider it and asked about Jamilla and her relatives. He told me that the entire family was gathering that evening to celebrate the resolution of their difficulties. Though Xponential wasn't yet out of the financial woods, he was hopeful that our strong showing with the documentary would bring in plenty of new commissions. The sooner I got home the better so that we could get cracking on things.

I phoned Rhodri and discovered that he and his friends had also been interrogated, this time by the Miami-Dade police, who viewed their status as science-fiction fans as both suspicious and risible.

"One of them was an old-time *Mork and Mindy* fan," he told me wearily. "There was a lot of *Na-Nuing* and *Shazboting*. At the same time they obviously weren't taking it for granted that we hadn't actually intended to knock Ryan Carmichael down."

"Did you manage to persuade them?"

"Eventually. All our stories matched because they were the truth. They were also very interested in the Astral League. It took a long time to convince them that it wasn't a sinister secret organisation but just a daft fannish thing."

"They're not charging you with killing Carmichael, are they?"

"Well, at first they started threatening us with something like negligent homicide. Or was it culpable manslaughter? But I don't think their hearts were really in it. Carmichael was obviously delusional, not least from the fever, and he had been holding your friend Claire captive. By the way, we think we've found out how he might have contracted the virus."

It turned out that Carmichael was due to play a convict in his next movie. He had done a celebrity slot for prison staff in exchange for some interviews with guards.

"At Halstow Island?" I said with disbelief. "I doubt that he could have charmed his way in there, even if he knew about it."

"He might have had an inkling. He did his slot at the nearest privately-run mainland prison to the island. What if one or more prison officers from Halstow had either been transferred there beforehand or had got themselves overnight passes for the event. They might have carried the virus with them."

Was this likely? "I can't see Halstow Island staff being allowed leave for any reason under the current emergency."

"It might have been someone really senior at the prison who could do their own authorisation. Carmichael had plenty of friends in high places."

Given that the Ascendants were pretty cosy with local police forces in the UK, it was possible. Would Carmichael prove to be one of the main vectors in the escape of the virus into the general population? If so, his notoriety was assured.

"How are you both doing?" Rhodri asked.

"Living in a bubble," I replied. "Physically and mentally. Everything's on hold until we know what the prognosis is."

"We're all rooting for you," He said in a weary voice. "Today's convention bulletin is going to be a humdinger."

He admitted that he had been shaken by the whole affair and was looking forward to going home. The convention, although still continuing, had abandoned what remained of its formal programme, given that its guests of honour were either dead or unavoidably absent. The Ascendants had already packed their bags and departed the night before. Everyone was sitting around chewing over all that had happened. Everyone wanted to know more about Leo Parrish.

"I have to go," I announced, not wanting to get into that particular discussion now. "Send my regards to Ruth."

"When you get home you must come around for dinner. She does a cracking vegetarian moussaka."

That evening Walter Suthersen contacted Claire. Not wanting Nora to be disturbed, he had switched off her bedside phone just when Claire was trying to contact her. And he had initially failed to pick up her message on his own phone because he had been busy trying to arrange authorisation to visit us. In this endeavour he had been completely thwarted. So he and Nora had simply turned up at the hospital and were waiting downstairs.

In the interim Claire had discovered that the hospital was trialling a version of Skype that allowed video conferencing. Her father was determined to commandeer a computer terminal somewhere in the building where it was enabled.

Given Suthersen's eminence, I wasn't surprised when within the hour a three-way video link was all set up. I fiddled with the sizing on the windows and got a view of Walter and Nora that was pretty crisp, given that this was in a publicly funded hospital. Walter was seated in what looked like an executive office, while Nora, in a neat cream trouser suit, walked slowly towards the leather armchair beside him using only a stick. She looked, if not exactly spritely, then at least much more in command of her own body than before.

I let the rest of them do most of the talking, watching Nora and feeling that she was also keeping an eye on me, though it was hard to tell on the reduced video window. At one point I resized Claire's image and just watched her talking, feeling a soup of warm emotions laced with a tart terror that I might actually lose her if the worst came to pass. She ended up recounting most of our story and at Nora's insistence did not spare any of the very gory details.

"Pretty good job," Nora said when she was done "I think you'll do."

I realized she was addressing me. "If that's the best you can manage, then forget it."

This amused her. "Did you tell her?" she asked.

I assumed she meant Claire. "About what?"

"That man." She glanced at Suthersen. "What was his name?"

"Cyrus Hammond," he said.

I shook my head, having scrupulously avoided mentioning it. "I think that's your job, don't you?"

"What?" Claire asked. "What is it?"

"He was the man who shot Leo dead in Prospect Park," Nora said bluntly.

Claire's eyes moved fractionally as she obviously focused on me.

"He only confessed minutes before we tracked you down," I told her. "I wanted you to hear it from your mother."

She was still taking it in. "Why? Why did he do it?"

"He was psychotic at the time," I said. "He thought Leo Parrish could see the future, manipulate it." I was looking at Nora as I spoke but I doubted she could tell. "Did you know that, Nora?"

"Yes," Nora replied, holding herself rigid. "The FBI woman told me."

Evidently Agent Underwood had been quite thorough in interviewing all the principals in the case.

"They're autopsying his body," Suthersen said. "Apparently they suspect that he was also infected."

He spoke with a haste that made me wonder whether he was also in on whatever last secrets Nora was surely hiding.

Hammond had probably contracted the disease from his nephew. Maybe there was still a genetic element in the disease's mutated form even if it was no longer ethnically specific. Its ease and speed of spread didn't bode well. I was especially fearful for Claire who, like Barbara Suthersen, had spent hours in Carmichael's malignant company.

I think Nora knew it too, because there was a moment in which I thought I could see her looking at the screen with naked love and concern. And it wasn't because she had suddenly developed a deep regard for me. Though their chairs were close together, Nora and Suthersen were still not able to touch one another in a simple affectionate way that would have been appropriate in the circumstances. It was sad, but not half as sad as the possibility that they might lose their only daughter as well. I hadn't told Claire that I had taken a puff of Ashad's inhaler and might have some protection, though I wasn't confident about my prospects, given that I had inhaled bloody aerosols direct from Carmichael's diseased lungs. I started thinking about Ashad and Gerry, about Theresa and Jamilla and all the other people in my life that I might never see again.

It was so easy to go slip-sliding down this maudlin slope that I knew I had to keep it together.

"I'm tired," Claire announced. "We didn't get much sleep last night. I'm ready for bed."

All three of us assured her that this was fine with us. There was no indication that she was showing any symptoms of the fever.

"I'm going to I hang on here for a few minutes," I told her. "There's one or two things I need to discuss with your mother and father."

Suthersen involuntarily swelled at what was perhaps the first public acknowledgement of his status in relation to Claire. Nora looked more guarded. I think she knew what was coming from me.

Claire blew kisses to all of us and signed off. I looked at Nora.

Over the past twenty-four hours I had done a lot of thinking. *Leonora Parrish*, Alice Underwood had said. Was it possible? Did my notion make any sense at all?

"Well," Nora said to me. "Spit it out."

"I want to talk about Leo Parrish," I told her.

Nora sat back like someone steeling themselves for an interrogation.

"There's a few things I don't get," I began.

"Really," she said sharply.

"I'm not denying that your brother existed—I've seen the photographs—or that he was shot dead by Cyrus Hammond all those years ago. What bothers me is that I still can't get a handle on him. He wrote all those inventive, provocative stories, and yet the man himself is somehow forever in the background. Why is that?"

Nora just shrugged. "He never made a big deal of things."

"Is that so? Even in his photographs he looks as if he'd rather be somewhere else. As if he had other things on his mind."

"So? What's your point?"

"Was he a dreamy, self-effacing type?"

"He was a practical man," she told me. "He just got on with his life."

"Leonard and Leonora," I remarked.

She just waited, her lips drawn tight.

"You weren't twins, were you? But your parents must have liked those names. Anyone ever call you Leo for short?"

"Never," she replied emphatically. "That was my brother."

Walter Suthersen was holding back what I'm certain was a smile. This encouraged me. But I didn't want to come right out and ask her. I think I was interested to see how far she would continue to go in trying to avoid telling me the truth.

"Was it unfair that Leo was shot?"

"What a ridiculous question," Nora retorted. "Of course it was unfair. No one deserves to die like that."

"I mean, did Cyrus Hammond get the right person?"

"What are you trying to say?"

"I've been thinking about it," I told her. "In all our conversations you've never directly acknowledged that your brother wrote those stories."

Nora sat even more upright than before. She was giving nothing away.

"I'm not suggesting you lied to me, just gave me partial truths. You kept all the original manuscripts but at the same time you hated the trouble they had caused. Excuse the amateur psychology, but that seems to me like someone who's deeply conflicted. Who feels a responsibility way beyond the normal tokens of remembrance for a dead loved one."

She frowned. "I kept them all because I'd sat there and watched him type them out." Her voice was breaking slightly. "He was an excellent typist. Quick and accurate. You won't believe the palaver it was making corrections in those days. All those carbon copies as well."

She was looking at Suthersen, who was nodding agreeably, relishing the memory of those pre-electronic days.

"So he composed straight onto the typewriter?" I said, not believing it for a moment.

"No, they'd already been drafted in long hand."

I smiled at her. "You see? That's just the sort of thing I was talking about. Why not say: 'He'd already drafted them in longhand'?"

She just pouted at me, a schoolmarm to a bothersome pupil. If she had been able, I'm sure she would have whacked me with her walking stick.

"For heaven's sake, Nora!" Suthersen said. "Does it matter anymore? This man probably saved our daughter's life!"

"I'm grateful," she said.

"Then show it. Tell him what he wants to know."

"I've been answering his questions," she insisted.

"Then let me finally ask a direct one," I said. "Was it you who composed them first in longhand?"

She gave a brisk impatient sigh.

"All right," she said at last. "Yes. I wrote them. I wrote them and Leo typed them up and took them in."

Now she looked petulant, like a child forced to reveal a long-cherished secret.

"Satisfied?" she said to Suthersen.

"They were your ideas?" I asked.

"I didn't have a day job like Leo. I had plenty of time on my hands."

"And the imagination to go with it," Suthersen added.

Though I had considered this possibility beforehand, I still couldn't quite believe that I was actually hearing it confirmed, was actually talking to the author Leo Parrish.

"I never suspected," Suthersen told me. "I never knew until after I'd met Nora. And she only confessed to save Leo the embarrassment of having to keep pretending he was the writer. I've been sworn to secrecy ever since."

"But why?" I asked. "Why the charade?"

"It started as a joke," Nora told me. "Eldridge's magazines weren't publishing any stories by women."

"Fifty years ago they were thin on the ground in general," Suthersen remarked.

"We mailed the first one in," Nora said. "When it was accepted, I decided that Leo could walk in the next one. Deliver it direct and save us the postage. That was fine the first few times. What we didn't expect was that Leo would get himself photographed with Eldridge, or bring Walt home one day."

"So why didn't you just own up to the real authorship?"

"It was more fun to keep pretending," she said mischievously. "Leo wasn't very happy, but I persuaded him to go along with it. It wasn't as if we were fooling *Time* magazine, was it?"

"Leo was putty in her hands," Suthersen said fondly. "He could never refuse her anything."

I could well imagine it. "So why did you stop?"

"They never paid anything more than nickels and dimes," Nora said. "When Eldridge rewrote me it was the final straw."

"You never thought of trying better-paid markets?"

"I was having a fling with Walt by then. Did he tell you he never said he was already married?"

I nodded. "So you stopped writing altogether?"

"I had other things on my mind."

"After she dumped me, Leo got ill," Suthersen elaborated. "Nora was doing all kinds of jobs to keep them afloat and spending her spare hours nursing him back to health."

"He was the only family I had," she said. "Walt was always writing me, urging me to take it up again, but I'd lost the spark by then. When Leo was killed, I knew it was something to do with what I'd written."

She pretended to shrug it off, but I could tell that the idea still pained her.

"Besides," she said, "I'd given my bright ideas book to Walt when we first got together."

"I've still got it," Suthersen said, pulling a small but bulging scarlet notebook from a breast pocket of his denim shirt and holding it closer to the camera than he really needed to. It was dark with age, its fabric spine frayed, the whole assemblage held together with a length of grimy silver ribbon.

"You carry it with you?" Nora was saying, astounded.

"Always," he told her. "And do you know what? To this day, I've never opened it."

I found this hard to believe. But not Nora, who took it from him and smiled at the sight of the neat bow in the ribbon. She didn't untie it.

"Don't let anyone tell you Walt stole his ideas from me," she said. "I've been reading him closely for years. They're his own. And he can stitch a better sentence together than I ever could."

"That's just practice," Suthersen responded. "Anyway, you were my inspiration."

"You never told Claire?" I asked Nora.

"Easier to keep it all under wraps. It was the past. Dead and gone. Or so I thought until it all started coming back to haunt us."

I began to wish that Claire had stayed. "Isn't she due the truth now?"

"Given that you and Walt have made me spill my guts, of course she is. I'll tell her in the morning. You have my word on it."

For once Nora had set aside her defensive crankiness, and her relaxed features gave a better clue to the beauty she must have been in her youth.

"I'm amazed at your tenacity," I told her. "Over all these years it's hard to imagine that you never felt the urge to own up to anyone else apart from Walter."

"Who would have cared?" she responded. "Leo Parrish the writer was less than a footnote, and I've never kidded myself that my stories were great literature. Or more important than life itself."

"But isn't that exactly what happened to them? They leaked out into the world? How did you feel about Eldridge stealing your ideas for the Ascendancy?"

"One thing you learn as a writer," she said, "is that once a story's out there, it takes on a life of its own and you can't do anything about it. From what I've seen, Eldridge is a blithe, conscience-free rogue. I doubt that he's an Ascendant himself. What can you do? The world is full of noise."

It was obvious she had absolutely no vanity about her brief writing career.

"You might have made a bit of money if you'd sued him," I pointed out.

"That's a vulgar suggestion," she said with something of her old tartness.

"Or exposed the Church for the shoddy confection it is."

"Do you really think it would have made any difference? People can't resist a shiny new package of spiritual glitz."

She passed the notebook back to Suthersen without having opened it. He tucked it back in his pocket and said, "We should be going. I need to look in on Barbara."

"Is she all right?" I asked.

"No symptoms, if that's what you're asking," Suthersen said.

Nora grabbed her stick.

"There's just one more thing," I said. "Where did the ideas come from for your stories?"

Her laugh was scathing. "You're asking me that one? There's an old chestnut store on Fifth Avenue that sells 'em cheap."

"What I'm getting at," I said, "is that some people think your stories have foretold actual events. In greater detail than mere speculation. They suspect you have genuine foreknowledge of the future."

Nora exchanged a look with Suthersen.

"Who are these people?" she said. "Believe in fairies too, do they?"

I could tell that this answer was rehearsed, that Nora had encountered the suggestion before and had a standard response to it, a response that was flippant and dismissive without necessarily being honest.

I think she could tell that I was thinking just that.

"An alien intelligence that can travel in time spoke to me through my dreams," she said.

"I'm serious."

"About believing it?"

"About the spooky concordance of some of the stuff you wrote with what actually came to pass. Do you want me to list the instances?"

"No," she said with an emphasis that tended to confirm my suspicion. "What do you want me to say? That I'm a seer? That I have secret knowledge. Would it help if I confessed it?"

"If it was true, it would be scary."

"Pattern recognition," she said. "Humans are designed to find signals in noise. Maybe I just have better antennae than most."

"Is that it?"

"That's the best explanation you're going to get."

I found it interesting that she had used the present rather than past tense when referring to her "antennae". But I knew I had reached the limits of what she was going to tell me.

They said their farewells. Then Nora surprised me by saying, "Make the movie if you want to. You have my blessing."

It took me a moment to register this. "Really?"

"Just make it true to what I actually wrote, deal?"

I nodded madly. "Deal."

"And don't forget to look to the heavens."

Suthersen rose and helped Nora up. They walked off camera.

I recognized Nora's parting line as a recurring quote from *Exaltation*, spoken by several of the Exalted group in the story. In most cases it had referred to the Star, but on one occasion it concerned a threat from a hostile Earth-launched ship that had been intent on destroying their island sanctuary before an alert Exalted used his mental powers to neutralize it.

Had Nora been giving me a clue? Was this a coded reference to the *Endeavour*?

It was an insane idea, but I knew I had to follow it through. Cyrus Hammond had been concerned that Valentine might be a threat and I simply couldn't risk letting it pass. Hammond had said he was going to contact—who was it? Harry something. Lind or Lindman. Was he at NASA or the FBI? He'd said NASA.

Hammond was dead, his phone probably in deepest quarantine. I cursed myself for not asking Agent Underwood if she had a contact number. The only other agent I knew was Alvarez, but unfortunately the helpful number he had given me was also in quarantine along with all my clothes. Life was never as neat as in the movies.

I used my new phone to find the page for NASA. There was a phone number for the public communications office. I tried it, and after making a few choices I managed to get through to an operator who actually recognized the name Lindemann from the versions I offered.

Soon afterwards a jaunty voice said, "This is Harry Lindemann. To whom am I speaking?"

This was said in a slightly jocular tone, which encouraged me.

"Nick Randall," I replied. "I'm a friend of Cyrus Hammond's."

"Cyrus!" he exclaimed. "What's that old dog up to these days?"

So news of Hammond's death was not yet widespread. I made an immediate decision to be candid with him on the basis that it was vital he felt me to be trustworthy.

"I'm afraid I have bad news. Cyrus was killed yesterday in pursuit of someone who was carrying a dangerous new virus."

There was a long silence at the other end. Finally Lindemann said, "He always told me he'd never make it to retirement."

"I don't have time to go into all the details," I went on, "but I'm in quarantine at a hospital in Miami as a result of the encounter. Cyrus probably saved my life by risking his."

This time there was a longer pause.

"What did you say your name was?"

"Nick Randall." I spelled out my surname. "I'm a civilian, but I was with Cyrus at the end. He tried to contact you yesterday, which is how I know your name. Earlier today I was interviewed by an FBI agent called Alice Underwood, who can vouch for the fact if you need to check it. The main reason I'm calling is that Cyrus was very concerned that the *Endeavour* mission might be compromised. I'm talking here about the pilot, Valentine. Cyrus believed he's a religious obsessive who might be inclined to take an extreme form of unilateral action against Khanistan that could have catastrophic consequences."

Keeping it brief, I explained about Valentine's Rapturist persuasions, Noah Byrnes's activities and ultimate aims of the Future Fellowship with which both men were probably associated.

Lindemann was silent for a while.

"I've heard about Byrnes," he said finally. "Our message boards have been full of it. But this is a hell of a rich brew you're asking me to swallow. You'll appreciate that I'll need to get some independent verification."

"Of course," I replied. His voice remained good-natured but it was now cautious. "But I wouldn't hang about, if I were you. This could happen sooner than any of us think. Talk to Alice Underwood. She'll vouch for me."

I had a sense that he was scribbling the name down. "Are you contactable on this number?"

"At the moment it's almost the only way anyone outside can get in touch with me."

Lindemann rang off. Only then did I notice on the laptop screen that Nora was sitting down again, with Walter fussing solicitously beside her.

I put myself in view. "Is everything all right?"

Suthersen started, having forgotten the link was still running.

"She had a dizzy turn," he told me. "We're waiting for her wheelchair."

Nora was sitting with her eyes closed, a glass of water in her hand. She didn't react to my presence. It was is if she was sending the message: This can be managed by me and Walter.

"If there's anything I can do ..." I said, and left the sentence hanging, unsure of what the odd etiquette of the situation demanded.

Suthersen didn't reply. Feeling increasingly intrusive, I stepped away from the webcam but didn't close down the link.

Sooner than I had anticipated, Harry Lindemann called back.

"OK," he said, "I'm buying it."

"You think the threat's real?"

Again there was a hesitation before he said, "I hope I can trust you to keep this to yourself, Mr Randall, but I've just learned that Valentine has sought permission to take the shuttle into a lower orbit by the time it next passes over Khanistan. He asked to be given manual control for better manoeuvring."

"Bloody hell. Cyrus had the idea that he might be planning some sort of germ warfare attack."

"Well, I don't think he wants to wave to the locals from one of the windows. I've got a few things to check and not too much time to do it in. I really appreciate the heads-up and I hope we can speak on another occasion."

He cut me off.

I didn't exactly feel relieved, but at least they were now aware of the threat.

On screen I saw that both Walter and Nora were getting up. Nora gently pushed Suthersen away as though determined to walk only with the aid of her stick. They moved off camera before I had the chance to get to the microphone and wish them well.

Seconds later I heard a thud and then a stick clattering on the floor.

EPILOGUE

We held the post-premiere party for the UK opening of *Exaltation* in the members club at the top of Centre Point in the heart of London. Jamilla had arranged it through a friend of hers who was one of the events' organizers there. Valerie had got the tech ops team to rig up a holographic projector that was beaming three-dimensional movie tag-lines like THE EXALTED ARE COMING! and WILL YOU BE ONE OF THE CHOSEN? into the rainy London night. The low cloud-base provided a better backdrop for the messages than if the skies had been clear.

We had invited about two hundred people and it looked as if most of them had shown up. The buffet tables were laden with exotic-looking fare—canapés, crudités, cakes and confectionaries in unusual shapes and colours that suggested otherworldly foodstuffs, sparkling drinks dyed in rainbow hues to stimulate the eye and remind everyone of the movie, in which a full palette of spectral colours had been used when the Exalted were closing in on the Star. Not that anyone needed reminding: they were all talking about it. Too excited to eat, I was clutching a glass of lavender fizz while looking around for Claire.

Exaltation had opened in New York City a month previously to positive reviews and excellent audience figures. I hadn't been able to attend the US opening, but the rest of the gang at Xponential had returned to London cock-a-hoop afterwards. I was still amazed that we had actually managed to pull it off. From conception to launch in little over two years. Already people were asking us whether we were going to do a sequel.

The buffet area was slowly emptying as people headed upstairs to the observation gallery. Theresa was nibbling sweetbreads with her new man, a rangy Australian musician in his thirties. Arthur Townsend and Molly were talking to two of the relatively unknown actors we had cast in the lead parts. Arthur was wearing a double-breasted pinstripe jacket over a black T-shirt that said X+ALT. He had accosted me as we were leaving the premiere in Leicester Square and announced himself satisfied with the general standard of the movie, which Molly translated as: "He liked it". She had her arm tightly through his and had been keeping him on a tight leash ever since. But she had told me that Arthur was thrilled to have been invited and had sat through the entire movie without ever once complaining about logical inconsistencies or unconvincing SFX, which she assured me was praise indeed.

I spotted Rhodri drinking purple beer and chatting with Felix Nancarrow and his brother. We had used Rhodri as a consultant for the movie to ensure the science-fictional elements were plausible. Felix had persuaded Rufus to invest some of the family fortune into the movie. Rufus, who wasn't entirely a philistine, had agreed to stump up useful extra finance during post-production after seeing the rushes. He was a big fan of blockbuster sci-fi, he had told us.

Rhodri's wife Ruth was nearby, chatting with Jamilla and Briony Potts, who had relished her casting in the movie as a Machiavellian Exalted whose character was loosely based on that of Nora Parrish.

"Seen Claire?" I asked them, and they shook their heads.

Ruth was looking at me doubtfully.

"What?" I said jovially, and, eyeing Jamilla: "Don't believe anything she tells you about me not paying her enough."

Jamilla protested, and Ruth flourished something convoluted on a barbeque stick. It was the culinary equivalent of a strand of lurid DNA made from coils of rainbow-coloured streaky bacon and wedges of tinted cheese.

"Is this movie being funded by E-numbers?" she asked. "I think we should be told in case Rhodri goes hyperactive. He's worse than Bryn."

Bryn was their eighteen-month-old son, whose christening Claire and I had recently attended, Ruth being adamant that she wanted a proper ceremony despite being as much an unbeliever as Rhodri. I had realized too late that *Exaltation* was opening in the US over the same weekend, so Claire and I had gone to the service instead. Without Rhodri, the movie would never have been made.

"Mine's rather divine," Briony remarked, holding up another stick whose mother-of-pearl pasta shells made it look like a jewelled butterfly. "Far too pretty to eat. I'm thinking of donating it to the Natural History Museum."

I spotted Claire, wheeling Nora through one of the exits. I made to pursue her but was waylaid by Alec Furneaux, who had wangled an invitation to the party and now stood before me in a shiny slim-line suit which looked a size too small for him.

"Impressive bash," he remarked, swirling his drinks glass, which held something the colour of absinthe.

"Be careful with that stuff," I responded. "They dyed it with more than one variety of grass."

He cocked his head quizzically like an avid bird searching for titbits but temporarily encountering something perplexing. He was still fronting *Talking Points* and ever on the look-out for juicy stories or new angles to old ones.

"Interesting movie," he said without enthusiasm. "Rather surprised you didn't cast any big names."

"Ryan Carmichael was unavailable," I said.

"That's in rather poor taste, isn't it?"

Furneaux wanted to know more about our funding, and I went over what was already public knowledge. A lot of the money had come from Filmscope, Cyrus Hammond having left a will allowing the transfer of all its assets to the Whitney family on the proviso that it be used to finance "a feature-length cinematic production" based on Leo Parrish's work. Walter Suthersen had also been able to use his contacts in the movie industry to get major studio support, assisted by the fact that he had agreed to script the movie on a no-fee percentage profits basis.

"Wasn't there also a sizeable contribution from S&A Enterprises?" Furneaux said.

"That's right." I knew where he was heading with this.

"A 'philanthropic foundation' based in Palo Alto, aren't they?"

"So the mission statement on their website maintains."

Furneaux obviously didn't believe it. "S&A," he repeated with false jocularity. "Not taking money from some offshoot of the porn industry, are you?"

"That's a good one. Did you ask Ashad the same question?"

"He told me to fuck off," Furneaux said without rancour. "Isn't Palo Alto close to the headquarters of the COA?"

"The Church of the Ascendancy?" I said with patently fake incredulity. "Why would they want to fund our movie? It's a pretty direct attack on their kind of religion, don't you think?"

"That's what puzzled me. Were there any strings attached?"

Furneaux was obviously trying to sniff out a story.

"None whatsoever," I told him. "We've had no direct talks with them, but we did get a covering lettering saying that the only condition was that the money be used to assist the completion of the movie. I'll email you a copy of the letter, if you like. We have it on file."

Furneaux looked thwarted, which pleased me no end. I wasn't about to admit that Walter Suthersen and I had been convinced from the start that S&A stood for Shock & Awe and that the donation had been bankrolled by Edgar Eldridge's considerable personal fortune. This was interesting, given that the Church-funded *Epochrypa*, cobbled together from existing footage and released the year before, had bombed, despite all the publicity surrounding Ryan Carmichael's notorious demise. Maybe Eldridge had decided to pay his dues to the person who had been his real source of divine inspiration—Leonora Parrish.

Partly to deflect him but also because I was actually interested, I asked Furneaux about the necrotizing fasciitis story, which he was still pursuing in the face of official denials that there had ever been a state-sanctioned biological warfare programme utilizing gene-specific infective agents. The US and UK governments had taken the line that what had happened at Halstow Island was a tragic blunder resulting from a high-security biological research centre being unfortunately sited next to a detention centre, the inmates having been accidentally contaminated due to a lapse in safety procedures. Hardly anyone was buying this.

"Even if it was true," Furneaux said, "they still can't explain why they were looking into these gene-specific agents in the first place."

"Aren't they claiming it was a programme to investigate possible treatments for illnesses endemic in certain ethnic groups?"

"On a muddy island in the middle of the Thames estuary? Give me a break! You were lucky it didn't go really potent."

The illness had lost some of its virulence once it got out into the general population. Claire and Barbara Suthersen had suffered only mild fevers, while I hadn't got ill at all. But it had been a horrible few days before I knew that Claire was going to recover, and the disease was now firmly established throughout the world, where it typically afflicted poor and overcrowded populations and caused deaths among those already weakened by poverty or disease.

Ashad, too, was still maintaining an interest in the story, though over the past two years he had also shown more enthusiasm than I had expected for the *Exaltation* movie project, whose subversive themes appealed to his anti-Establishment side.

Furneaux sidled closer, looking sidewise at me. "Sure I can't persuade you to do an interview about your experiences? We could run it as a peak-time special, tie it in with the movie launch."

"Nah," I said. "It'd be like playing for the opposition, wouldn't it?"

I had done a few general press interviews in the immediate aftermath of Florida but nothing since. Ashad and I had been too busy with the movie to follow up Ash's idea of a drama documentary of events and I hadn't yet told him that I had decided against it in any case on the grounds of not wanting to put Claire and her family through it all again. But that didn't mean I was going to give Furneaux the in-depth story.

"I can't even bribe you with the fee," he said dolefully. "You must be rolling it in now."

"I wish," I said, thinking of the costs we had accrued, though it was true that the medium-term future of Xponential Productions was at last secure and our general visibility in the industry transformed. We had already promoted Jamilla and she had actually managed to train Ross Buchanan into some semblance of an efficient receptionist.

I swallowed the last of my lavender plonk. "I should circulate."

"It's not over yet, you know," Furneaux said portentously.

"What isn't?"

"Any of it. Do a search on gutty."

"What?"

"Spelled G-O-O-T-Y."

And with this, he was the one who slipped away through the throng.

I still couldn't see Claire, so I decided to check the viewing gallery upstairs. Climbing the stairs, I keyed GOOTY into my phone, and quickly found that it was a railway town in Andhra Pradesh that was suffering an outbreak of what might be a resurgent form of the English Bleeding Disease. This was what the rest of the world had christened the virus.

No, it wasn't over: it was far from that. The press release had been issued the day before, since when the entire town had been quarantined and units of the Indian Army moved in to enforce its isolation. The subsequent news blackout suggested a real emergency.

Somehow I wasn't surprised. Though I hadn't actually anticipated this, I had continued to be nagged by a sense of foreboding ever since Florida. The world wasn't exactly in great shape. Though the immediate heat had gone out of the Muvart crisis, Muvart himself remained belligerent and had announced that Khanistan had its own biological weapons programme and would not hesitate to use such weapons on any enemies of the state who sought to destroy their people by whatever means.

Khanistan had suffered no greater ravages from the attenuated virus than any other nation, though it might have been far worse had Valentine not been thwarted. The shuttle flight had been curtailed even before I left Florida. Harry Lindemann had phoned to tell me that a box of personal items that Valentine had been allowed to take on board had contained "a bit more than a family Bible and a few keepsakes." He couldn't give me the details, but the rest of the crew had been ordered to confiscate the box and detain Valentine for the duration of the flight. Apparently Valentine hadn't put up a fight. Maybe the notion of martyrdom wasn't that appealing in the end. The shuttle was hurriedly returned to Earth, ostensibly because Valentine had been suffering from influenza. Rumours persisted that he had in fact smuggled at least one canister of the virus aboard the craft and had accidentally infected himself. The US government was admitting nothing of the sort.

Meanwhile, the world continued to suffer its usual afflictions of famines, wars, genocide, terrorism, earthquakes, volcanic eruptions and extreme weather events. People continued to fret about global warming, pollution, the exhaustion of natural resources and the number of sunspots. Many remained preoccupied with whether Draco Nova was a celestial time bomb, an unstable near neighbour relentlessly building to a crescendo of nuclear frenzy and soon to explode without warning or mercy. The zeitgeist that the planet was on the brink of something awful refused to go away.

Were these the years of Tribulation, as foretold? Neither the Ascendants nor the Rapturists were saying as much. Eldridge had returned to the seclusion of his desert ranch after the convention, leaving Kubilius to do the PR repair work, which he appeared to be managing quite efficiently. He claimed that Church membership had actually increased in the months following the Ryan Carmichael scandal and that alleged Ascendancy borrowings from science fiction were in fact the reverse, Eldridge having instructed his writers to produce fictional versions of his earliest visions and prophesies in those magazine years. This was a neat reversal, and Church followers had rallied to the cause, as Nora herself had anticipated. It was a shame she wasn't in a position to rebut his claims.

By contrast, the Future Fellowship Rapturist sect had gone entirely silent, especially since the US President had accepted Bennett Irwin's resignation a matter of hours after the Endeavour returned to Earth. The jailing of his son-in-law had given Irwin a suitable pretext for resignation on family grounds. He had then disappeared completely from public life while a Senate committee began investigating allegations that significant sectors of the

Federal government had been compromised "by persons pursuing religious and ideological programmes contrary and inimical to the Constitutional separation of church and state".

It was likely to be several more years before the committee actually produced its report and in the interim there had been numerous exposés of the links between Irwin, Byrnes and Valentine and the sinister underside of the Future Fellowship's activities. But not a mention of any links with Leo Parrish, who hadn't so much been airbrushed from history as not even noticed in the frame in the first place. At first we took this merely to be reflecting popular prejudice that anything to do with science fiction was just frippery and that a lowly writer couldn't possibly be a significant factor in matters of international security and radical religious belief. But then I, and everyone else from Suthersen to Rhodri, received visits from various representatives of Special Branch or the FBI, warning us not to broadcast "any intelligence relating to this writer" while the current investigation was underway. The threat of having our movie spiked had been enough to gag me and Ashad, though none of us could understand why the security services were so keen to preserve Parrish's anonymity in the affair. Could it be that they were giving Leonora's fictional predictions some credence?

It was small consolation that even the spooks hadn't got wind of Leo Parrish's real identity. I certainly had no intention of enlightening them. Apart from Claire, I had told no one else, not even Rhodri, who would have been thrilled to hear the truth; but it was simply too risky for the moment. Claire had greeted the revelation with the surprised calm of someone to whom a lot of other mildly perplexing things now made perfect sense. She had done her share of storyboarding for the movie but was more preoccupied with the actual care of her mother, though it must have been frustrating not to be able to discuss it with her.

And now the immediate future looked distinctly uncertain again. But what could you do? Sit and brood and surrender to your forebodings? It wasn't an option. I fixed a smile back on my face, assumed an air of bonhomie and continued circulating. You had to keep going, even if you were soon going to exsanguinate or fry.

Upstairs, the viewing corridors were packed with people, most watching the teaser messages still being flashed on the sky or gazing down at the gleaming night-time panorama of rain-wet London with its ribbons of streetlights and endless streams of shining red-and-white traffic coming and going from all four quarters. Gerry and Liz Martindale had been cornered by Nigel in one of the alcoves. Nigel was dressed from head-to-toe in shades of brown leather and had another blonde on his arm, a very tall and large-boned young woman whom he introduced to me as "Svetlana from Velikiye Luki, a fully qualified physiotherapist".

I didn't doubt it. Though Barbie beautiful and made up to the nines, Svetlana had big hands and broad shoulders that I could easily imagine being effortlessly brought to bear in bending limbs and pummelling muscles. I was pretty sure that Velikiye Luki was in the heart of Russia rather than in the regional warzone where Nigel had apparently been extracting refugees to safe havens in Western Europe rather than selling them to the sex trade. Ashad and I had enlisted Felix to represent him when he was threatened with repatriation. Recognizing the genuinely humanitarian side to his activities, the Foreign Office had decided against immediate deportation, though he was still under caution. Not entirely a villain then, but definitely someone who enjoyed operating in the shadowlands of legality.

"Fantastic fucking movie," he said to me. He gestured towards the window, almost slopping his bubblegum pink drink. "Here you are, Nicholas, at the top of the fucking world."

He had a point, and I knew I needed to relish these moments, that they were possibly going to be the peak experiences of my professional life. More so now than ever.

"Richly deserved," Gerry remarked generously. "I'm only hoping that none of what's in the movie is in the real world pipeline."

He was only half joking, being far from persuaded that Leo Parrish's stories weren't simply better-than-average guesswork about the future. I had given him copies of other Parrish tales and he had managed to find correlations with real-world events in most of them, though some were tenuous or ambiguous. Liz was more sceptical, claiming that the pursuit of secret connections was a male obsession that probably reflected something deep and twisted in the masculine brain. Both were still working for Biope Industries, and they had recently set up home together in a platonic relationship that increasingly resembled an actual marriage without the sex.

I finally spotted Claire, Daniel and Walter Suthersen, standing at one corner, with Nora in her wheelchair in front of them. Walter was pointing something out to Nora, who sat immobile, giving no indication that she was actually registering anything. Her collapse had been the result of another stroke, and since then she could only communicate through a limited series of movements which did at least suggest that her mental functions weren't impaired. Suthersen had bought her an electronic wheelchair with a keypad in one arm to facilitate the vaguely coordinated forefinger movements she could occasionally make. In practice, she had never been able to do more than jerk the chair forward a few inches. She looked completely beached in it, her head askew against a little white pillow on one side, her face slack and expressionless, slippered feet poking out uselessly from under the scarlet shawl draped over her lap.

"I've been looking for you," I said to Claire. "Everything all right?"

"It's good," she replied. "We were just showing mum the sights."

"I'm surprised you aren't surrounded by a gaggle of admirers," I said to Walter.

"Shooed them all away," he told me, crouching down beside Nora. "This is family time."

His devotion to her was plainly undiminished and he was now free to express it since Barbara had agreed to a divorce after her recovery from the virus, a generous settlement allowing her to take up residence in Hawaii. Out of courtesy and at Walter's request we had sent her an invitation to the premiere, malicious though her original involvement with Leo Parrish's work had been. I think it was a relief to everyone when she hadn't shown.

Nora was fully alert inside, I was convinced, and I couldn't imagine the frustration she must have constantly felt at being unable to communicate the full force of her presence with her characteristic acerbity. She had focused on something outside the window. The rain had stopped and skies were clearing. On one of the clouds was emblazoned the message:

LOOK TO THE HEAVENS!

It was impossible to judge whether she was pleased because her expression was unchanging. During the screening of the movie we had sat her right at the front of the theatre, and I took it as a positive sign that her eyes hadn't wavered throughout. Often they seemed to be either full of amusement or fury.

Now she began make little agitated moaning noises. Claire and Walter decreed that she needed to be taken to the bathroom. Daniel helped them wheel her away.

I stood at the window, momentarily alone for the first time that day. High above, the clouds had parted and Draco Nova shone down, brighter than Venus now, emitting increasing amounts of hard radiation, we were told, everything from high-energy X-rays to cosmic rays which were giving the magnetic field around the planet a pasting and improving the bank balances of tour operators who did Aurora Borealis sightseeing trips. The nova wasn't visible in the Southern Hemisphere and I wondered whether the residents there were more relaxed about their future and perhaps considered that they might even survive the full-scale disintegration of the star, as some commentators had suggested, since they would be in the radiation shadow-zone. Proper astrophysicists were contemptuous of the notion, claiming that a close-range supernova blast would sear the entire atmosphere in no time at all. Dragon's breath indeed.

If, of course, it really was a star and not some artefact made to look like one by an advanced extraterrestrial race with an unimaginably developed technology who were en route to our planet for unknowable purposes, maybe to exterminate us, maybe to offer us membership of some pan-galactic astral league. Or elevate us to god-like status as Leonora had foretold. I had been looking at plenty of speculative websites, and I definitely preferred the notion that the aliens were coming on the basis that we would then at least have a fifty-fifty chance of survival.

"If you want to jump you'll need to go outside," said a familiar voice behind me.

I turned, and there was Ashad. He was holding hands with Paula Merrick.

"Well, well," I said. "Now there's a sight for sore eyes."

Merrick was wearing a figure-hugging dress and a slinky cropped cardigan that gleamed like graphite. Ashad had opted for a dapper grey suit and white shirt.

"I thought you should know," Ashad said with Brummie dourness. "We're back on."

"Oh dear," I said, mimicking his tone. "Was it painful?"

Merrick just laughed.

They told me the story. I already knew that Ashad had spent the past couple of years trying to pretend that Merrick had never existed. He had done this so blatantly it was obvious that he missed her. I had made a few half-hearted attempts to get them together, mostly by suggesting she be invited to various work-related functions, which Ashad naturally rejected out of hand. So, as the premiere approached, I had insisted that he phone her and invite her to the party himself. In my view she had proved suitably contrite about her underhand work with Byrnes as soon as he was exposed as a dangerous obsessive, and she had subsequently continued to pass on useful information in the aftermath, particularly on the Halstow Island affair. Ashad had used much of this intelligence in a follow-up documentary, without crediting her or thanking her personally. Finally she had come up trumps for Nigel, composing an official statement to the effect that while his activities were not always letter-of-the-law legal, his work in evacuating genuine refugees without profiteering was certainly worthy of favourable consideration. How much longer, I wanted to know, was he going to continue to punish her, and himself?

Ashad had slouched off grumpily, and I had heard nothing more. But he had disappeared immediately after the premiere, to rendezvous with Merrick in a nearby pub, I now learned, where they had finally put the unfortunate past behind them.

I gave them both a hug and congratulated them.

"If I were you," I said, "I'd make the most of one another, if you haven't already started. The world might be coming to an end."

Now Claire appeared, asking whether I had seen her mother or Walter Suthersen.

She had left them outside the bathroom while she used the facilities herself. When she emerged both were gone. She and Daniel had scouted the downstairs party room without success. They weren't in the elevator which they had used to ferry Nora up to the viewing gallery and Walter wasn't answering his phone.

"Maybe they've gone on a tour of the building," I suggested.

Claire looked doubtful. "He usually tells me in advance if he's taking her somewhere."

At this point we were plunged into darkness.

Below us, without any fuss, the lights were going out.

CODA

London, present day

There was a collective murmur of unease. Oxford Street and Tottenham Court Road were already extinguished, and swathes of Soho and Covent Garden were also going dark. Everyone around the viewing gallery pressed closer to the windows. The West End and Bloomsbury turned black, now Mayfair and St James's and Marylebone.

Something flashed above, filling the gallery with red light. It was a sprawling message in crimson capitals back-dropped by scraps of cloud:

DIDN'T PREDICT THAT, DID YOU?